THE DELTA DIAMOND LIBRARY

Gems from the Past with
Enduring Appeal

The Foxes of Harrow

The
Foxes of Harrow

Frank Yerby

A DELTA DIAMOND

A DELTA DIAMOND BOOK

Published by
Dell Publishing Co., Inc.
1 Dag Hammarskjold Plaza
New York, New York 10017

Printed in the United States of America

September 1986

10 9 8 7 6 5 4 3 2 1

To Muriel Fuller who made this book possible

The Foxes of Harrow

Aʙᴏᴜᴛ fifteen miles above New Orleans the river goes very slowly. It has broadened out there until it is almost a sea and the water is yellow with the mud of half a continent. Where the sun strikes it, it is golden.

At night the water talks with dark voices. It goes whispering down past the Natchez Trace, past Ormand until it reaches the old D'Estrehan place, and flows by that singing. But when it passes Harrow, it is silent. Men say that it is because the river is so broad here that you cannot hear the sound of the waters. Scientists say it is the shape of the channel. But it is as broad by Ormand and D'Estrehan. Yet before Harrow in the night it is silent.

It is better to see Harrow at night. The moonlight is kinder. The North Wing has no roof and through the eyeless sockets of the windows the stars shine. Yet at night when the moon is at the full, Harrow is still magnificent. By day you can see that the white paint has peeled off and that all the doors are gone, and through them and the windows you can see the mud and the dust over everything. But at night the moon brings back the white again and the shadows hide the weeds between the flagstones. The Corinthian columns stand up slim and silver and the great veranda sweeps on endlessly across the front, and the red flagstone swings in perfect curves through the weed-choked garden where once the cape jasmine grew, past the mud-filled birdbath and the broken crystal ball on the column to the smoke-house and the kitchen house and the sugar mill and the slave quarters.

You walk very fast over the flagstones and resist the impulse to whirl suddenly in your tracks and look back at Harrow. The lights are *not* on. The crystal chandeliers are *not* ablaze. There are no dancers in the great hall. And in the garden the smell of the pinks and the lavenders and the white crepe myrtle and red oleanders and the mimosas and the feathery green and gold acacia and the magnolia fuscatas and the cape jasmines and the roses and lilies and the honeysuckle are ghosts too and figments of the imagination, but so real that at last you turn and scratch the flesh of your palms and your fingers with the harsh and rank reality of the weeds.

In the brick kitchen house it is dark. The great open fireplace, fourteen feet across, is silent and dust-covered and cold. But the small pots still stand on the trivets after eighty years and the pot-hooks and the game spits are rust-covered but otherwise un-changed. And the ovens with the hollowed-out tops where the live coals were put still stand on the hearth waiting for old Caleen to push them into the fire to bake her master's bread and hum softly under her breath.

It is no good to stay. So you come out of the brick kitchen house and walk very fast down the old wagon trail from the sugar mill where the machinery for crushing the cane rusts away in the swampdamp; stumbling in the eighty-year-old stone hard ruts made by the wagons that hauled the bagasse away to be dumped into the river, until you come to the landing and untie the boat and yank the cord that starts the outboard to coughing and barking and roar away downstream in the still water that is silent before Harrow. And you don't look back.

The Foxes of Harrow

I

THE *Prairie Belle* came nuzzling up to the bar. The big side wheels slowed and the white boiling of the water stopped. Still the boat slipped rapidly toward the bar so that at the last moment the captain ordered the wheels reversed and the water boiled briefly in the opposite direction. The port wheel turned forward again and the *Belle* came to a stop alongside the bar.

The captain took the cigar out of his mouth and spat into the yellow water.

"Run out the plank," he said quietly.

The two gigantic Negroes bent down and the black coils of muscle glistened. They came up with short, deepthroated grunts and the oaken plank wavered and came to rest on the bar. This was not the canopied, ropestrung plank they laid down for passengers to leave the vessel, but a single plank down which the Negroes used to roll the hogsheads of sorghum and molasses ashore and walk with marvelous surefootedness, bending under the weight of the cotton bales.

"All right," the captain said shortly. "You may go ashore, Mr. Fox."

Stephen Fox fingered the single rich ruffle that stood out from

1

his shirt front. Then his fingers caressed the pearl that gleamed like a bird's egg against the dark silk stock wound about his throat. He put his hand into his pocket and came out with the golden snuff box. Then he put it back again. To take snuff then, and under those circumstances, would have been a gesture and Stephen despised gestures. For the same reason he kept his tall gray hat firmly on his head, although convention demanded that he at least salute the ladies.

"All right, Mr. Fox," the captain said. "Up with ye."

Stephen stepped up on the plank. His weight was insufficient to make it springy. He strode along it very solidly, like a man treading firm ground, taking care to keep every trace of jauntiness out of his step. That would have shown something—defiance, perhaps; some indication that this that they were doing mattered. What he wanted was to give evidence of exactly nothing. It wasn't easy, but he did it. Going down the plank to a muddy bar one hundred yards from the left bank of the Mississippi, there was not the slightest indication in his bearing that the *Prairie Belle* existed or that the men and women lining her decks were alive. His disregard was Olympian.

A little murmur started among the passengers and grew and ran from man to man until all the people were muttering. Then someone said it aloud and another and another until they were all saying it, shouting it at the tall, slim man with the burnished copper hair who was standing on the muddy finger that lay in the water pointing downstream toward New Orleans:

"Cheat!"

"Sharper!"

"Card shark!"

The captain sighed a little and nodded to the second officer. "All right, Mr. Anthony," he said.

The second officer pulled twice on the bell cord. The bells jangled. Two great white clouds billowed up from the high twin stacks and the great side wheels turned over once, twice, then took up their steady beat, the water boiling white beneath them. The plank was lifted from the bar and slid inward to the lower

2

deck of the *Belle*. She stood out for midchannel, heading south-ward toward the river's mouth.

The captain took the cigar out of his mouth again and spat into the yellow water.

"A scoundrel, Mr. Anthony," he said. "A black-hearted scoun-drel—but still . . ."

The second officer nodded.

"But still a man," he said, "very much a man—eh, captain?"

The captain's bushy black brows came together over his nose.

"We're behind schedule," he growled. "Up steam, man. Let us be on our way."

The sun came down very low over the Mississippi and the muddy water gleamed golden. The *Prairie Belle* ploughed into the suntrack and blazed white there, then dropped downstream, growing smaller and smaller until she burned black in the sun-washed water, like a water beetle, and was gone at last, leaving only the white trails of wood smoke hanging over the river.

Stephen Fox turned his back toward the *Belle* and gazed up-stream. He had only two choices and one of them he rejected at once. That was to swim ashore and make his way southward through the bayou country afoot. The second was more reason-able: He could stay where he was and take the chance of hailing some passing river craft and making his way to New Orleans in comparative comfort. So he remained standing, from time to time taking off the tall gray hat and wiping the sweat from his face with a silken handkerchief. His brows gathered into a frown as he gazed over the surface of the water.

In that year, 1825, there were still only a few steamboats ply-ing the Mississippi, but there were hundreds of ungainly flat-boats drifting south, and even a lonely keelboat or two, stealing silently downstream with its sixteen poles shipped. Stephen shifted his weight from one foot to the other. He was going to have a long wait. There was no chance of sitting down; the bar was muddy, and Stephen had no desire to ruin the loose fawn-

3

colored trousers he wore or his rich green cutaway coat. Besides, his tall figure could be seen more easily if he were standing.

He took out the golden snuff box and poured out a pinch on the back of his hand. The brown dust caught in the bright hairs that gleamed like foxfire. He sniffed briefly up each nostril and straightened. The blue eyes, pale almost to colorlessness, burned in the freckled face.

He bent forward. Yes, there was a black dot moving on the waters to the north. Stephen stared at it without moving for almost ten minutes. There was no change in its size and shape. He looked away, counted one hundred, and looked again. This time the dot was definitely larger. Stephen kept up the little game, looking away and counting, then looking back again. Each time it was larger. But when he looked at it he couldn't see it move.

Then at last it was taking size and shape. It was a steamboat and now it was coming on fast. Stephen's heart sank. It was in midchannel and making all steam, the white smoke standing straight up in stiff, hard pants, the water breaking white around the prow. As it came abreast of the bar the whistle cried out twice, in long, belly deep tones, then she was boiling past, the paddle wheels cascading the yellowish white water down in a torrent, and the v-shaped waves moving out, out, and out until at last they broke over the bar and wet Stephen's feet.

"Damn!" he said without heat and turned his back on her, staring upstream. But nothing more came. The haze came down over the river and the warmth went out of the air. The sun went down quite suddenly behind the pines on the western side of the river and a star began to glimmer palely. Stephen put up the handkerchief and fixed the tall gray hat firmly on his head. The sky purpled, blackened. The stars strung a necklace over the river. There was no hope for it, he would have to wait until morning.

He started walking back and forth from one point of the bar to another, rubbing his long-fingered hands to keep the blood circulating. The water talked darkly in the night, but Stephen didn't listen. He walked along thinking—remembering London, Paris, Vienna, New York.

4

"A long trail," he thought. "A long trail to end thus." He stretched out the long, nimble fingers and stared at them in the darkness.

"Aye, ye've carried me far—and will again, no doubt; but it is a sorry thing—no certainty in it. A flip of the pasteboards and it comes and it goes. No more of that. This time the trail ends— for good. No more the river. It's the broad lands for me." He threw back his head and laughed aloud, the clear baritone carry-ing out over the water. "Fine chance of that. A Dublin gutter-snipe don't become one of the landed gentry—not even in this mad, new land . . ." He stiffened suddenly, listening. The sound came again, far off and faint, floating over the river.

"Hullo! Hullo, therrre!"

Stephen lifted up his head and cupped his hand.

"Hulloo!" he called, "Hullo!"

"Where are ye?"

"Here to your right—on the bar! For God's sake, man, make haste."

He could hear the splash of the great sweep now, and a lantern glowed faintly from the river. Then the black bulk of the flat-boat was looming up through the darkness and the smell came rolling in over the water and struck him in the face.

"A pig boat! By Our Lady!" Still he couldn't afford to be choosey.

A man was standing in the great curving bow holding the lantern at arm's length. By the Saints, Stephen thought, a face like that would chase all the devils out of hell.

The flatboat touched the bar now and hung there, grinding.

"Well, I'll be a pizen wolf from Bitter Creek," the lantern-bearer said, "if this don't beat all. A gentleman, no less—all got up in tophat and fancy waistcoat and cutaway standing up on a bar in the middle of the Mississippi and laughin fit to kill his-self! Who mought yez be, me foine lad?"

"I'm Stephen Fox and I'm plagued cold and hungrier than a grizzly. May I come aboard?"

"Now that depends. Furst I think yez had better explain what yez be a doin' thar in the middle of the river."

5

"Well," Stephen said, "as one Irishman to another, I am a gambler. But aboard the *Prairie Belle* there were tinhorn sports who bore their losses badly. They complained to the captain and here I am. Now may I come aboard?"

"Here's me hand. Up with yez, me lad!"

Stephen scrambled aboard. The smell from the hogs was formidable, but no worse than that from the various members of the crew, who came crowding around to examine Stephen.

Seeing them, Stephen frowned. He turned to the one-eyed giant who wore the red turkey feather in his hat which indicated that he had knocked down, gouged, bitten, and spiked into unconsciousness half a hundred fierce flatboatmen. It was to this one he had been talking.

"A word with ye, Captain?"

"Yes, me lad?"

"Might we not walk aft?"

The captain grunted, then nodded his massive head. He was a huge man, Irish and all muscle. The two of them walked back toward the stern of the craft, past the big pen where the hogs were, past the great oaken keg of Monongahela rye whiskey with the tin cup chained to it, back for nearly a hundred feet until they came to the place where the huge broadhorn sweeps were.

Stephen hesitated. His hand swept up to his throat with a lightning like movement. When it came away, the golden setting at the top of the stickpin gleamed empty; the big pearl was gone.

"Now, captain," he said, "when they put me off the *Belle*, they forced me to disgorge. In my money belt there are only thirty gold dollars—a twenty-dollar goldpiece and a ten. They are yours." He unbuttoned the wine-colored waistcoat and undid his white ruffled shirt. He unbuckled the money belt and handed it unopened to the captain.

The captain only grunted.

"Beside that, I have only this golden snuff box. I will count it a favor if ye will accept it."

Again the captain grunted.

"And now," Stephen said evenly, "ye have all my worldly

6

goods beside my clothes. I hope ye will not take it ill, but this crew of yours . . ."

The big mouth split into a grin.

"Right yez are, my lad. There's no one of them as wouldn't murder his own mither for a copper."

"I thought as much. Deliver me safely in New Orleans and ye get my coat and waistcoat and this hat. My trousers would not fit ye, I'm afraid. Is it a deal?"

The captain threw back his great head and laughed.

"Keep your duds," he said. "The box I will take, but I offer yez this pewter one of mine in its stead. A man should not be without his snuff, specially so foine a lad as yez."

Stephen put out his hand. The captain took it, and for a moment Stephen thought that the bones were crushed.

"Now if ye have something that a man might eat . . ."

"Right yez are. Louie!"

There was a shuffling of feet in the darkness and a hulk of a man whose spine curved over into a bow came into the glow of the lantern.

"Fetch some grub for Mister Fox, Louie," the captain said. Louie said nothing. He shuffled off into the darkness and came back after a moment or two with a moldy cheese, a jug of whiskey, and a loaf of stonelike hardness.

"Here," he grunted, and moved forward again.

The captain drew out a huge case knife and flipped it to the deck where it stood and quivered in the thick oaken planking.

"Eat," he said, and sank down beside Stephen.

Stephen scraped away as much of the mold as he could see by the flickering light of the lantern, and cut off a slice.

"So, it's finicky yez are," the captain laughed. "It's best that yez fortify your belly, for that's all we have aboard."

Stephen ate grimly. The smell of the swine was not calculated to add to a man's appetite, he thought.

"Me name's Mike Farrel," the captain said. Stephen waited. The man seemed in a mood for talk. The captain brought out a battered cob pipe and lit it with flint and steel. The smoke was even worse than the hogs.

7

"For forty year I've worked the river. The sights I've seen, lad, yez wouldn't believe them. But all that is going now."

"Why?" Stephen asked.

"The steamboat. When it came, the river died. Afore then . . . the river was the place for men. Why the ears I've seen chawed off and the eyes gouged out . . ." He sighed deeply. "Why I 'member one time when Annie Christmas . . ."

"Don't sell me that one," Stephen laughed, picking up the jug of whiskey. "She was just a legend. She never really lived."

"What!" Captain Mike roared. "And who were it that put out me eye? Why Annie were as real as you or I! She had a little mustache just like a man and a red necklace thirty foot long. Ever time she bit off a nose or gouged out a eye she added a red bead. That necklace coulda been over fifty foot, but she didn't count Nigras. Why I tell yez . . ."

"All right," Stephen said. "I believe ye."

Mike looked at him keenly, then turned his gaze out over the river which was lighted almost to daylight clarity by the newly risen moon.

" 'Tis a good life," he said; "I don't regret it. But now it grows wearisome, yez ken. It could be that I'm aheading for the salvage docks. A man don't last forever."

"Ye're not old," Stephen told him. "I see ye still wear the red feather."

"Yez know what it means?"

"Of course. It means ye're the champion of the river."

"Yes. Times I feel like throwing it away. It don't seem worth the trouble to defend it. Then ag'in it does—there's a glory in it, Mister Fox. I've held it nigh onto eight year." He sighed. "My river, it's mine, ever inch of it! Me fader brung me over from Ireland afore I could walk and the two of us come crosst the land to the river. Me mither wuz dead, yez ken. And we licked it, the two of us—we licked the river. Only it don't stay licked. It got the old man finally. It'll git me, too, someday."

Stephen looked at the huge man. But there was no sadness in the tone. Acceptance, yes—a kind of calm fatalism.

8

"I took me furst flat down the river at sixteen. Even then I had me growth. Yez know how it goes?"

Stephen did know, but he sensed also that the big man wanted an audience. Talking to this crew of his would be no better than addressing the hogs. Mike Farrel was intelligent, that he could tell. Intelligent and strong as a bull, and all man. A friend well worth the making.

"No," Stephen said kindly. "Tell me."

"Yez gets a consignment. Then yez picks up a flatboat and ships on a crew. First yez must knock their thick skulls together to let them know as who's boss. After yez have whipped them all, ye have their respect—not before. Then yez come driftin' down the river with the current, avoiding the shoals and the sand bars. When yez have done it enough yez knows where they be. Come night, be it fair, yez keeps on. Foul, yez ties up at some town and seeks out the bullies from the other flats and keels. Then yez thrashes them one at a time."

"Always?" Stephen demanded.

"Always. 'Tain't safe for yez or the crew 'til yez prove your mettle. After yez have licked the fear of God into their hides they stands yez a drink and yez stands them another and after a while the wenches come. Yez split up then and tumbles a foine wench. In the morning yez come back to the flat with a head like a melon and pray God yez did not git the French disease. Then yez slip hawsers and drift out and down until finally yez git where yez are going. Yez sells the consignment, stays roaring drunk for two weeks. After the money is almost gone yez rents a nag, yez and two others—we sell the boats too, yez ken, they're broken up for timber, and anyhow yez can't take a flatboat upstream.

"Then yez starts out up the King's Highway 'til yez gets to the Natchez Trace, going north. When yez have gone twenty or thirty miles through the Trace, yez ties up the nag and start walking. Yez pass up the other two who be agoing afoot while yez are ariding. Then when the next man come to where yez left the nag, he mounts, rides his stint and leaves him for the next— and so on all through the Trace. A foine life, if Wilson's cut-throats don't git yez while yez are passing through."

9

He fell silent, looking out over the river.

"At least ye're never bored," Stephen laughed. He stretched out his hand and picked up the jug of Monongahela rye whiskey that the flatboatman called Nongela. He put it to his mouth and drank deeply. Then he opened his mouth and the whiskey exploded out through his mouth and his nose and even it seemed to him through his eyes in a great whooosh, scalding and blinding him at the same time, as though he were being drowned in liquid fire.

Mike Farrel put back his head and roared.

"Good old Nongela!" he bellowed. "Ain't made for greenhorns. Got to have a caulked-oak throat and a copper-lined belly, that yez have, to drink it. Here give me!"

Stephen passed it over and Mike drank deeply. Afterwards, he was silent for a time. The moon rode high above the river and the water blazed silver. Mike raised his hand and pointed.

"See that oak afore the church?" he demanded. "That's where they hung the furst one."

"The first one of what?"

"Them twenty-three Nigras. That was in 'ninety-five—in me fader's time. The year after the big fire it were. Most of Nawleans burnt down. I tell yez that were sumpin'."

"But the twenty-three blacks?" Stephen asked.

"They tried to mutiny, the murderin' black devils. When they caught them the Frenchies took them up to Pointe Coupee and loaded them on a flatboat. Then they set it a-floatin down the river. And ever time they come to a Parish church, they took off a Bumbo and hung him. That were where they hung the first one. Only thing them Frenchies ever showed any sense about— handling Nigras. Ever read their Black Code?"

"No."

"Me neither. But a young Frenchie read it to me oncet—in English. Sure kept the Nigras laced up straight."

He stood up.

"Well, I'll see after me bullies now. See you later, Mr. Fox."

Stephen stretched out on the rough oaken planks and put his gray hat over his eyes. He swore that he wouldn't sleep, but that

10

is a resolution not easily kept when one has not closed an eye in more than forty-eight hours. The motion of the current was gentle. The little waves slapped against the sides of the flatboat and up ahead the hogs grunted peacefully. And Stephen Fox slipped down the river toward New Orleans wrapped in a bright dream of broad acres and a huge white house set down among the oaks not far from the river.

When he awoke the sun was high in the heavens and the current was laughing downstream. The crew was lounging about the flatboat, feeding the pigs and taking turns drinking the throat-searing rye whiskey. They wore no clothing but their spiked brogans and the trousers of linsey-woolsey. Their gigantically muscled chests were burnt brown as teak and most of them were as hairy as apes. Seeing Stephen, they laughed:

"Have some Nongela," they called. "Hit's good fer a fine gent like you!"

"Pipe the red wescut! Ain't he the swell, I ax you?"

"Maybe I should git heem a little dirty, no? Maybe then he won't feel so gar blame fine!"

Mike Farrel raised a paw like a grizzly's.

"Hish, me lads!" he said. "Mr. Fox is my guest and a paying one at that. If one of yez touches so much as one red hair on his foine young head, I will cut out your liver and make yez eat it!"

"Aw, Mike," the big Canadian half-breed growled. "Just a leetle I should tumble heem! Just a leetle, no?"

"No," Mike said. "Gawddamit, no!"

Stephen gazed at them for a half minute, then turned his back.

"I think," he said clearly, "I'll go aft among the pigs. I find them better company."

"I theenk," the half-breed said, "I theenk I keel heem now."

Stephen turned slowly. He put his hand inside his coat as though he were searching for his snuff box, taking his time about it, moving very slowly. When his hand came out again, the little double-barrelled derringer lay loosely in his palm. The sun picked up the rich silver mounting. The half-breed halted suddenly.

The rest of the crew broke into a roar of laughter.

11

"Go on, Frenchie," they said. "That little thing can't shoot!"

"Whatcha stoppin fer, Frenchie? Ascairt of flea bite?"

"Sometime I do it," the half-breed said. "Sometime I do it sure!"

Stephen put the pistol back in his pocket and looked out over the river. Here the trees came down to the water's edge and the current ran very fast and smoothly. The river was broadening out, so that the far bank was almost a mile away. And in the shoal water inside the sandbars the waterfowl circled and dived. Stephen turned back to the captain.

"How far?" he asked.

"Be there tomorrow," Mike said. "Afore noon, if all goes well."

That day they had more of the stone bread and the rotten cheese, but as an extra treat Mike ordered Louie to prepare some rancid bacon. Stephen threw his overboard when the others were not looking.

The hours went by like the river, so slowly that almost the sun seemed to be standing still. Stephen paced up and down the rough planking of the flatboat, gazing south toward New Orleans. And now, as the creaking, clumsy ark drew nearer to the city, something very like a fever ran from man to man. The card games on the deck stopped and one by one the men stood up and began to look down river. They stood there a long time, looking down the river, not saying anything until at last one of them said it in something like a deep breath or a half-audible prayer:

"Nawleans!"

"Yes, by Gawd!"

"Know what I'm agonna do?"

"Git stinkin drunk like you always do when you git money."

"Sure I'm gonna git drunk, but furst I'm gonna git me a young yaller Nigra wench with long legs like a half-year colt an' . . ."

"And then you gonna stand her up in a corner and look at her. That's all you good fer now, old man!"

"Who's a old man? Why I betcha I break you half in two, you little polecat puppy!"

"Polecat puppy! Why I wuz raised with the swamp 'gators and

weaned on panther's milk! And jist fer that I'm gonna walk you down and chaw off both your ears!"

"Me, I'm the chile of the snapping turtle! And when I starts to chawin I don't never let go! Why, you . . ."

Mike Farrel stood up slowly. He crossed the wide prow to where the two boatmen were circling and hopping around each other looking for an opening. When he was close enough, he struck out once with both arms. The two men crumpled to the deck and lay there without moving.

"Sorry, Mister Fox," he said ceremoniously. "But they mought a hurt each other. When I take on a crew I deliver them safe just like they started."

Stephen smiled.

"They're impatient," he said. "For that matter, so am I."

"I kin understan that," Mike said. "Nawleans. They ain't another town like it. It's the wickedest city in the whole blame country and I seen em all. But it sorta gits under your skin somehow. Once yez have tied up along Tchoupitoulas Road yez will always come back. That yez will."

"I don't aim to leave," Stephen said. "I'm through with the river. A place of my own, that's what I want."

"A hotel? A good saloon and café? That's the stuff, young fellow!"

"No," Stephen said slowly. "A country place—a plantation. A big one."

"Yez aim high, don't yez? Still, it is in my mind that yez will get whatever yez go after. And when yez do . . ."

"Yes?" Stephen said smiling.

"A glass and a bed fer old Mike Farrel when he comes ashore and wants to git away from the noise and the fighting. Your promise, lad?"

"My hand on it," Stephen said.

"Good. It grows dark in a little now. The haze is coming down yez notice."

"Yes," Stephen said. "And tomorrow . . ."

"Tomorrow we dock. A good night to yez, Mister Fox."

The night dropped down suddenly like a curtain. The great

13

Southern stars blazed low and close. The river was alive with craft: steamboats snorting and puffing upstream and down, rafts, flatboats, little fishing yawls up from the Gulf, all of them carrying lights so that it seemed that the stars moved over the face of the Mississippi.

Nobody slept that night. The voices of the crew rose up, quarrelsome, boasting. God help the women of New Orleans, Stephen thought, when these goats and monkeys come ashore. Then the dawn was coming up out of the Gulf in streaks of watery gray-yellow, behind them the sky lightening. Then the sun was up all at once without warning. One moment Stephen looked back in the direction he had come, staring up the muddy channel to where the river had broadened until the far bank was a mere haze and a shadow; and when he looked again the sun was up, so quickly did it come.

Five slow hours crept by and the city grew from a smudge on the bank to a cluster of tumble-down buildings. The crew was working the great oars now, the wide-bladed broadhorns, angling the clumsy flatboat in toward the landing at Tchoupitoulas Road.

Stephen looked, but he could not see the shore. There were miles upon miles of flatboats and shantyboats tied up in rows so that they hid the banks and already from them were coming the drunken roars of the boatmen. Then, miraculously, there was a hole, and the steersmen were sliding the flatboat in, the whole crew laughing and shouting at the top of their voices.

The men lined up, and Mike stood up in the prow, a canvas sack, heavy with silver dollars, in his hand. As they passed him, he paid them off, throwing in a small jug of whiskey for each man. With a whoop they seized their pay and swarmed over the sides.

Next to them was an ancient, dilapidated flatboat. Just before the last of the men had gone over the sides the sound of shouting and shrill feminine laughter came from the cargo box. Then there was the pounding of bare feet on the board decks and a skinny wreck of a woman, as naked as the day she was born, dashed across the craft screaming with laughter. Behind her,

14

roaring like an amorous bull, thundered a blackhaired giant of a man, a jug of Nongela cradled under one huge arm.

Instantly, the remaining boatman set up a howl and joined the chase. They bounded from deck to deck until at last they all disappeared into the hold of a shantyboat a few yards downstream.

"Nawleans," Mike Farrel breathed. "Good old Nawleans!"

Stephen grinned.

"Is it always like this?" he asked.

"Aye and worse. Yez'll be goin ashore, Mister Fox?"

"Yes. But the pigs—and the cargo?"

"I go to notify the owners. They'll come with roustabouts. Mought I have the pleasure of your company for a little, Mister Fox?"

"Yes—certainly. You might well steer me on my way. There's a place that a man can get lodging hereabouts?"

"Aye—fer a picayune yez kin get a bed, not too clean, all the whiskey yez kin drink and a wench to keep your back warm."

"A picayune?"

"I fergit—yez don't know the Frenchies' money. That's six cents American."

"Six cents!"

"Aye! But yez had better not close an eye; for sich boots and sich a wescut, they'd murder Our Lady herself."

Stephen looked at Mike.

"Then what on earth?"

"I dunno. The really good places cost a mint. If I were yez, I'd go first to the gaming places and repair my fortunes."

"Not today," Stephen said. "I think I'll chance one of your waterfront hostels for tonight. Tomorrow, I'll start the long climb."

"Well—come along with yez now. First yez should try the Swamp. At least yez will be closer to help if they try to murder yez. On Tchoupitoulas Road yez would have to run for miles until yez reached the *garde de ville*."

The two of them walked along among the flatboats until they came ashore. The urchins looked with openmouthed wonder at

15

Stephen's fine dress and the prostitutes sauntered out and clutched him boldly by the arm.

"This way, my fine gentleman," they said. "Nothing is too good for sich a fine gentleman. For you the best—all day with me and tonight too—one dollar."

Stephen shrugged them off as though they were not there. The two of them walked between the filthy, tumbledown buildings until they came to the Protestant Cemetery at Cypress and South Liberty Streets.

"It is here that I take leave of yez," Mike said. "If yez have need of me, leave word at the Rest For Weary Boatmen. And, for the love of God, be careful!"

Stephen put out his hand.

"It has been a pleasure," he said. "Don't worry about me, Mike. I can take care of myself."

"Aye—that I believe. But keep your pistol handy—and drink nothing! For yez it would surely be drugged."

Watching the big man rolling away, Stephen felt suddenly very lonely. He turned and walked back in the direction of the Swamp. There was the first ghost of a plan shaping itself in his mind.

He went first to a dive called the Sure Enuff. He took a table, ordered wine, and watched the play. The games were faro and roulette. In two minutes Stephen saw that the player had no chance at all. The wheels were fixed and the dealers' boxes in faro appeared to have some sort of mechanism which could change the order that the cards appeared. He paid the few cents that the watered wine cost and moved on. It was the same everywhere he went. There was not a square game in the whole length of the Swamp.

The Poker and Twenty-one games, Stephen could have beat, matching his skill against that of the dealers. But at the Rest For Weary Boatmen he decided abruptly that he would not risk even that.

While he was watching, another stranger, a riverman by his dress, entered a poker game. He won steadily, until the stack of silver dollars which they were using for chips were gathered

16

before him in irregular piles. Then, boldly, he risked his entire winnings against a single hand. He sat very quietly at the gaming table, a big black cigar angling upward from his mouth. Three of the men quit outright, but the dealer stuck doggedly until at last with a slow smile the riverman turned over his last card. Like three of his others, it was a Queen.

"Four of a kind!" Stephen breathed.

"He cheated," one of the other players declared. "He took that lady frum his sleeve!"

"You're a ring-tail polecat and a dirty liar!" the stranger declared flatly.

Without a word, the dealer raised the pistol high in the air and brought the barrel crashing down upon the stranger's head. The stranger buckled at the joints, loosening all over like a thing of India rubber, bending downward to the floor. Almost before he was down, the others were upon him, walking him down with their heavy boots. One of the ruffians set a heel upon the stranger's face, and turned it, bearing down with all his weight. When it came away, the stranger's face was a bloody mass, scarcely recognizable as human.

No one paid the slightest attention to Stephen. He left his bill unpaid and went out into the street. No, Stephen, he told himself, ye must not play in the Swamp. 'Tis a beginning ye wish to make —not an end.

Then at last it was night. Stephen entered the cleanest-looking of the hostels in the Swamp.

"A room," he said to the bedraggled harridan who sat behind the bar. "How much?"

"A room he sez!" she cackled. "This fine gentleman would have a room! A bed ye kin have—the best in the house for a bit. Aye, and a plump young thing to share it with ye. But a room— think ye this is the Hotel D'Orleans?"

"I want privacy," Stephen said. "If I can't get it, I'll go elsewhere."

"I kin give ye the grand bed with curtains," the hag declared. "King Louie of France hisself slept in it, so it should be good enough for ye."

"All right," Stephen said, feeling the weariness down in the marrow of his bones. "Let's see it."

"Not so fast, young gentleman. A bottle first—'tis a house rule."

"All right," Stephen said wearily. "How much?"

"What do ye care—so fine a gentleman as ye?"

"Fine clothes don't fatten a purse," Stephen said.

"A bit. None here is more."

"Bring it on."

The ancient harridan signaled a waiter. Stephen thought he had never seen so dirty a man, nor, when the man came closer, one with a viler odor.

"A bottle of the finest for the gentleman," the old woman said.

The waiter shuffled away. It seemed to Stephen that he had been gone an uncommonly long time when he finally reappeared with the bottle.

"Ye'll join me, my lady?" he said to the hag.

"Why, no thank ye, lad. Wine I cannot drink. Me liver, ye unnerstand. But if you care to stand me a draught of ale . . ."

"Bring the lady some ale," Stephen said.

He sipped the wine. Strange that it should be so bitter. Even the sourest wines of France had not this bite. He stiffened suddenly.

"Waiter!" he called. The man came over.

"Here," Stephen said. "Have a glass."

Beneath the grime, Stephen saw his face pale.

"No—I mean, no, sir—I dasn't!"

"Why dasn't ye?" Stephen demanded.

"House rule!" the old harridan snapped.

"I didn't ask ye," Stephen told her. "Here, man, have a glass!"

The waiter started to edge away. Stephen's hand went inside his coat and rested there. Just the smallest glint of the silver on the butt of the derringer caught the light.

"I insist," Stephen said softly.

The waiter took the glass. His hands trembled so that the wine slopped over on the floor. A little glint came into his eyes; the trembling increased. The glass crashed to the floor. The waiter

18

bent and began to pick up the pieces. Stephen watched him a moment, then kicked him with cold deliberation, so that he went down on his face and skidded across the floor.

He came up roaring, but Stephen's hand was fixed firmly inside his coat. The waiter's mouth hung open like a cavern. With his free hand Stephen extended the bottle.

"Drink it," he said. "Every drop!"

The waiter clutched the bottle with both hands, looking sidewise at the woman. Slowly she nodded. He put the bottle to his lips and the hairy adam's apple bobbed in his skinny neck.

"Thankee," he said. "Thankee, sir! Now I got to go!"

"No," Stephen said pleasantly. "I like you. Stay and have another."

"No, sir! Please, sir, I—I—I—" His eyes glazed. He blinked them open and gaped his mouth to say something; but then with his jaw still open he slid silently to the floor.

"Strange," Stephen said to the woman. "Is he always such a sleepy head?"

The old hag clapped her hands. Almost instantly two villainous brutes burst into the room.

"Any trouble, maw?" they growled.

"Naw," she said. "Throw that stupid bastid out. If he's got anything on him you kin keep it." She turned to Stephen and smiled a wide, toothless smile.

"Now," she said, "I'll show ye your bed. And I'll send ye a girl too—the best. My own daughter in fact!"

"No, thank ye," Stephen said, gazing over his shoulder to where the waiter swung down between the two male animals. "I'm too weary to have need of a woman."

He got up and walked behind the old woman through the doorway. Next to it was a large hall with twenty-five or thirty beds rowed off, so that every available inch of space was taken. About half of them were filled, the occupants snoring lustily. In the center was a huge, canopied bed of carved mahogany. Curtains hung down from the sides of it, drawn aside with cords. Stephen saw that when they were dropped his privacy would be complete.

19

"Wait," the old hag said. "For ye, I will send fresh bedding!"

Stephen gave her two bit pieces, the last coins in his pockets except a few coppers, and she scurried off. When she was gone he sat down on the bedside and drew off his boots and one of his stockings. His great toe was an angry red. He bent down and removed the big pearl from between it and his second toe.

"Ye're my last hope," he said gently.

But someone was coming, so he put it back and stretched out on the bed. When he looked up, he saw a young girl of perhaps seventeen, her arms full of fresh linen.

She was pretty. There was no denying that—for all that her hair hung like wisps of lank straw about her head. She giggled a little when she saw him, a high wild sound, completely senseless. Stephen looked at the watery blue eyes, set far apart in her broad face. They were as blank as the eyes of an animal.

"Mad, poor thing," he decided.

"Please, me lord," she said. "Kin I make your bed now?"

Stephen rose.

"Certainly," he said.

The girl giggled again. When she raised her arm, Stephen saw the brownish-yellow stain of old sweat, and in the hollows of her neck were thin lines of dirt.

"Water's free," Stephen thought; "and soap's not too dear . . . still . . ."

In a moment or two the girl had finished making the bed, smoothing the covers with an expertness born of long practice. Then she stood back, simpering at Stephen.

"It's ready now, me lord," she said.

Stephen pulled off his boots but left his stockings on. Then he removed his coat and waistcoat. He unwound the dark silk stock from his throat and loosened his collar. Sighing, he stretched out full length on the bed.

"Ye may close the curtains, now—what is your name?"

"Jenny."

"Jenny. Not a bad name, all things considered. Now, Jenny, be a good girl and be off with ye."

There was the sound of her hands tugging at the cords and

20

the rustle of the dropping fabric. Stephen closed his eyes blissfully. The tiniest ghost of a sound caused him to open them again. He turned his head. The girl had her arms swept up behind her head and bent at the elbows down her back. Her fingers were working away at her buttons. As he watched, the last button gave, and the girl's hands swung downward to the hem of her skirt. Before Stephen could get out more than a startled gurgle, the skirt and petticoats swirled upward around her waist over slim flanks utterly innocent of undergarments.

"No!" Stephen managed at last.

The girl stood there, staring at him, her skirts still clutched around her waist, the watery blue eyes widening.

"Why?" she said pitifully. "Don'tcha like me?" And the great tears started spilling over her lashes and down her cheeks. Where they went they left white channels of clean skin showing through the grime.

Stephen smiled.

"Of course I like ye, Jenny," he said gently. "Ye're a very pretty girl. But 'tis a finished man I am this night, by all the saints. Tomorrow, when I am not so tired perhaps . . ."

"Thankee, sir! Tomorrow then . . ." Then she was gone, her bare feet scurrying over the rough boarded floor.

Stephen sighed and turned over. A moment later he was asleep.

Twice during the long night, Jenny tiptoed to the heavily canopied bed. Twice she stretched out her hand to draw aside the curtains, but always at the last instant she would drop her arm and hasten away, weaving soundlessly between the snoring occupants of the other beds.

Toward morning she came again. When she reached the bedside, she stopped and put out her hand. The curtains were stiff and heavy with dust. She could feel them stir under her fingers. Then suddenly she had swept them aside and was standing there looking down at him, trembling like a small woods creature.

She straightened a moment, listening. Then she leaned forward and drew the curtains shut quickly.

Her mother had come into the room and with her were four

men, flatboatmen by their dress, and two women. The women were swaying on their feet, leaning their heads against the shoulders of the men, and giggling senselessly.

" 'Tis a bit from each of ye," the old woman said, "an a picayune for the girls."

"Lissen to her!" one of the rivermen bellowed. "Why, you old grandma of all the strolling wenches 'twixt here and Natchez! You'll take a bit for the whole likes of us and like it!"

"That I will not!" the old harridan snapped. "Pay up or git out!"

"Well I'll be hauled ashore and broken up for timber!" the riverman said. "You splayed shanked daughter of a dogfox vixen birthed in a ditch at the dark of the moon! You . . ."

Stephen groaned and propped his head up on one elbow, looking through a slit in the curtains at the little group. As he watched, Jenny scurried away from the bedside and darted toward the door. Instantly the waving of arms and the shouting died—just long enough for a lank Kentuckian to stretch out one lean arm and catch the girl as she tried to steal past.

"So," he said, yanking Jenny in against his chest, "you hide the best ones, you old witch!"

"Maw!" Jenny squealed. "Mama!"

"For her," the old woman said flatly, "it'll be two dollars extra —in advance!"

"I'll be a ring-tailed doodlebug! I'll wrastle down a grizzly and spit in a 'gator's eye 'fore I'll . . ."

"Take it easy, Hank," one of the womanless flatboatmen said. "Heah's yore money, maw." He dug deep into his pockets and came out with a bill. "Heah's a dixie," he said, extending the New Orleans printed ten-dollar note which was lettered in French with the word *dix* inscribed in the corners instead of the figure ten. "You kin bring us our change in drinks." Then he turned to the Kentuckian. "Now, Hank," he said. "Just pass me over thet little gal."

"I'll be double damned and pickled in brine 'fore I will," Hank declared. "Try and git her, you egg-suckin' blacksnake!"

"I'll git her, all right," the riverman said. "And no little polecat puppy like you is gonna stop me." He started toward the Kentuckian, taking out a wicked clasp knife as he came roaring at him.

Stephen sat on the edge of the bed and drew on his boots. Then he stood up, putting the gray hat on his head, and hanging his coat, waistcoat and the dark silk stock over one arm. He walked across the room toward the place where the Kentuckian was hammering at his rival's head with a post broken from one corner of a four-poster bed, while the other made blue lightning with his slashing blade. Then he was past them and out of the door, the crash of breaking furniture and the screams of the women echoing in his ears.

Outside, in the street, he moved off slowly until the sounds were left behind him in the darkness. He smiled wryly.

"A trifle strenuous, this town," he said. Then he was walking rapidly in the direction of the cemetery.

After he was out of the Swamp, Stephen stopped and arranged his clothing. It was still hours until morning, and he stood on the street corner looking in all directions. Irresolutely, his fingers touched the handle of the derringer.

"By all the saints," he thought, "just one thing more, just one and I'll know I'm mad—I'll know it!"

"Help!" a voice answered him like an echo, speaking rapidly in French. "Help me!"

Stephen opened his mouth and let the laughter rocket skyward.

"I asked for it," he roared. "By God, I asked for it!"

"If you please," the voice went on.

Stephen chuckled. "Where are ye?"

"Here, behind this wall. I've been robbed!"

Stephen put his hands on the wall and raised himself to the top. A young man was crouched on the other side, shivering in a shirt and silken underwear.

"By our Lady!" Stephen declared. "Now I've seen everything!"

"Do not speak such of the Virgin," the other rebuked him. "It is bad luck! Besides, you speak French, do you not?"

"Not if I can help it," Stephen said. " 'Tis a bastard tongue, not fit for the lips of a man!"

"Why, you! I demand—"

23

"Easy, lad, ye are hardly in shape to demand anything. And I mean no offense. French sits uncommonly hard on an Irishman's tongue. *Mais, si vous désirez . . .*"

"But you sound like a Parisian!"

"That's where I learned it," Stephen said. "But I think we'd better do something about your trousers."

"Yes, but what?"

Stephen's slim fingers caressed his chin.

"Is there near here a place where gentlemen drink heartily?"

"But of a certainty! Still, I don't see—"

"Listen, lad, ye aren't supposed to see. Just lead me to it. There'll hardly be any ladies around at this hour."

"All right, but I still don't see—"

"Listen, Mister whatever ye're called—"

"Le Blanc—Andre Le Blanc."

"Mister Le Blanc, I don't have a sou. Neither, it appears, do ye. I intend, therefore, to bow to circumstances and—borrow a pair of trousers for ye."

"Monsieur, you don't mean . . ."

"The name is Fox—Stephen Fox. And it seems to me that turn about is fair play. Besides, we're only borrowing the trousers. Come along with ye now!"

The mist was up from the river and rolling across the Swamp toward the center of the city. Already the gray had got into it, and in the trees the brown sparrows were beginning a soft, sleepy twittering.

Stephen lifted up his head and sniffed the fog, the nostrils of his thin nose flaring briefly.

"We must be quick about it," he said. "It will be light before long."

Andre moved along behind him, crouching in an odd half-cringing position.

"Straighten up, man!" Stephen told him. "Who are ye hiding from? The lady birds?"

They turned a corner. Across the street, yellow light was rolling out of the low windows of a two-story frame building richly ornamented with iron scroll work.

"*La*," Andre said. "There!"

Even as they watched, several shadowy figures came out of the door. Stephen could see that they were walking unsteadily, swaying a bit on their feet.

Andre looked up at Stephen.

"Not yet. There are too many. One man alone, and much, much drunker."

They waited. The slategray fog began to pale into morning. Andre shifted his weight nervously from one foot to the other.

"Now!" Stephen said suddenly. "Now!"

The man was weaving all over the wooden *banquette* and singing to himself:

"Roxane, mon ange, ma douce,
Je t'aime 'vec tout mon coeur!"

"Name of a name!" Andre said. "But he is too big!"

"Never for me could ye buy a horse," Stephen declared. "Ye are no judge of lines or build. Can't you see he is all belly? I'll wager he has legs like a ballet dancer and such slim shanks that ye'll find the going tight. Up with ye now. Ye take the inner track. When ye are close, a hand over his mouth—and don't let go, even if he bites."

The two of them moved through the rapidly lightening mist behind the fat man. When they were close, Andre's hand shot out and the song about the fair, sweet Roxane gurgled downward into their victim's throat. Stephen put his knee into the small of the singer's back and swept both his hands backward, twisting them cruelly.

"Quick," he said to Andre. "His stock!"

Andre whipped it over with his free hand, half-strangling their victim as he did so. He looked up at Stephen with a grin.

"Shall we hang him with it?" he asked.

Stephen laughed aloud.

"I thought ye had the makings of a man about ye—for all your girlish looks. No—just gag him. It might be more fun to slit his gullet slowly, don't ye think?"

The fat man's face was ashy pale and his struggles ceased. Stephen bound his wrists with his own stock, then they laid him gently upon the ground and removed his trousers. They both laughed.

"Can't say I admire your taste, my friend," Stephen said.

"Probably made by that scoundrel Clovis," Andre told the helpless man. "You should patronize Lagoaster. He's by far the best tailor in New Orleans."

Stephen ran his hands expertly through the fat man's pockets. He came up with a purse and several letters.

"This gentleman's name is Metoyer," he said, after glancing at the letters, "and he lives in Poydras Street. Remember that when we go to abduct his wife and daughter."

"Give him back the letters," Andre said. "Now how do I look?"

"Like a prince of the blood. But off with ye, we still have to bludgeon that old widow near the Ramparts."

"Shall I untie him?" Andre whispered, his voice shaken with laughter.

"No. Let the police find him. He'll probably describe us as two of the most fiendish footpads that ever desecrated the city. A good day to ye, sir!" he added loudly. "I trust ye will sleep most comfortably!"

The two of them moved off, arm in arm, leaving their clear laughter floating on the fog.

"We'll go to my home," Andre said. "First we'll breakfast, then we'll sleep an hour or two. Afterwards I'll show you the town. I'm not anxious to take my leave of you. Before this morning I was dying of ennui."

"Ye'll get your fill of me," Stephen said, smiling. "I'm here to stay."

They turned down a number of twisted, ill-paved streets. In the gutters the stagnant water still stood, although it had been a fortnight since it had rained. A smell rose up from the walk and struck Stephen in the face. When he looked, he saw the bloated carcass of a dog, dead three days at the least, floating in the cypress-lined gutter. He turned away quickly.

"By our Lady!" he swore. "This is the filthiest hole! Don't the authorities ever—"

Andre shrugged.

"No," he said, "and when it is hot, the people die like flies."

"And nothing is done?"

"Nothing."

They walked along in silence. The sun was up and the morning mist had melted away into the ground. The streets were narrow, mere lanes, innocent for the most part of any sort of pavement. Here and there were stretches of cobblestone, broken and irregular, which started, ran for a stretch and stopped all with the same apparent disregard for reason.

The houses, Stephen saw, came down to the very edge of the sidewalks, and lacked walks, verandas, or even a façade of any sort. Most of them, however, had overhanging balconies called *galleries*, richly ornamented with wrought iron. One instant, one could be within the privacy of his own dwelling, and the next, in the hurry and bustle of the streets.

Andre's house was the same way, though larger and finer than any of the others that Stephen had seen. The ironwork of the huge overhanging gallery was like delicate lace. They went through a massive oaken door which opened directly into the street without the intervention of so much as a half step. Inside, it was cool and dark, but even before his eyes had grown fully accustomed to the gloom, Stephen knew that it was magnificently furnished. The finest cabinet makers of old France had worked this oak and teak and mahogany, shaping it with loving care, and polishing it until it shone.

Andre's manservant took their hats and cloaks.

"Good morning, Monsieur Andre," he said. "Your father—"

"Is displeased. Papa is nearly always displeased," Andre said to Stephen. "I sleep in the daytime and prowl at night; that displeases him. I loathe planting. I go out to La Place des Rivières—that's our plantation—only when I cannot help it, and die of boredom all the time I'm there. That displeases Papa. I won't get married. Papa has the affair already arranged. He has even picked the girl. But me, I like variety in my bedfellows. And as for Marie de Pontabla—I'd sooner sleep with a hatrack. That doesn't displease Papa—it infuriates him. Ti Demon! What are you laughing at?"

27

"Nothing, Monsieur Andre!" and the white teeth disappeared into the black face with startling abruptness.

"We'll have our coffee in the courtyard. Black coffee, Ti Demon, no milk. And brandy. Chateau Elisee, '69, none of that *urine de cheval* that Papa keeps about the house. Come, Stephen —you don't mind if I call you that? It seems I've known you so long."

"Not at all," Stephen said. Andre walked through the cool rooms with the immensely high ceilings. The front of the house, Stephen saw, was in reality the back; the rooms were arranged so that the whole house seemed to be disregarding the outside world with true Creole hauteur. Crystal chimes, suspended from the magnificent cut-glass chandeliers, tinkled softly as they passed through the rooms to the courtyard.

The courtyard was paved with blue-gray flagstones. Flowering oleanders grew in large jars. There were ferns suspended from the windows overlooking the yard, and potted palms and a banana tree. In the center of the yard was a birdbath in which the little sparrows were already splashing. As he sank into a chair, Stephen's eyes wandered over a row of huge urn-like vessels, glazed a rich blue.

"Water," Andre answered his unspoken question. "Wait, I'll get you some." He went into the house and came back with a crystal pitcher and goblets of the finest glass. Standing on a low stone bench, he dipped the pitcher into one of the urns and came out with a clear, almost sparkling liquid.

Stephen raised the goblet to his mouth and drank deeply. Then his face reddened, and his ears stood out from his head.

"Spit it out," Andre laughed. "You see now why we always drink wine?"

"By all the saints!" Stephen spluttered. "What do ye put in it? It binds up a man's jaw like steel!"

"Alum and powdered charcoal. It would kill you, if we didn't. All the water here is deadly. That from the well is impossible, so we buy the nectar you've just tasted from wagons which bring it from the river. It kills you a little less quickly than well water. So we don't drink any of it. But this you can drink," he added,

28

indicating the coffee and brandy that Ti Demon was bringing through the archway. "In fact, I think you'll like it."

Andre laced his coffee liberally, but Stephen drank his brandy first. Then as the warm feeling began to swim up from his middle and swing in slow circles around the inside of his head, he gulped the coffee quickly.

"Now we will sleep," Andre said. "All day if you like. That's what I usually do."

"Excuse me, Monsieur Andre," Ti Demon said. "But today is the celebration for the gran' general, the Marquis de Lafayette."

"That's true. We mustn't miss that."

"De Lafayette is coming here?" Stephen asked.

"Yes. He'll arrive on the *Natchez* from Mobile this morning. The Mayor has appropriated fifteen thousand dollars—with the consent of the city council, of course—to entertain him. Everybody will turn out. You'll see more of the gentry of New Orleans today than ordinarily you could meet in a year." He stifled a yawn with the back of his hand.

"Ti Demon, show Monsieur Fox to the guest chamber. After you have seen to his wants, come to my room. I have an errand for you to run."

"Ye're sending back the trousers?"

"But certainly. And with them a little snuff box of gold inlaid with lapis lazuli that the skinny Mademoiselle de Pontabla brought me from Mexico. A horribly barbaric thing. I've been wondering what to do with it."

Stephen laughed aloud.

"'Tis very clear," he chuckled, "that your devotion to your father's choice is a little short of overwhelming."

"A little," Andre admitted. "I've always been a dutiful son, but this time dear papa is asking too much."

He put out his hand.

"Sleep well, my friend. Ti Demon will awaken us before the parades start."

Stephen followed the lean figure of the black man through a maze of rooms and up sweeping flights of stairs. Then Ti Demon

29

opened a door and stood aside. Stephen went in. The room was richly decorated. In the center stood a massive, canopied bed.

Already, Ti Demon had crossed the room and was adjusting the covers.

"Monsieur wants something?"

"Nothing now, thank you. When you wake me—some hot water for a bath, and a razor. That's all for now."

Ti Demon bowed silently out of the room.

That was it, Stephen thought. To live like this—graciously, with leisure to cultivate the tastes and to indulge every pleasure— a man must be free of labor. Leave the work for the blacks. Breed a new generation of aristocrats. Yes, there was no doubt about it. New Orleans had it all over Philadelphia, which he had called home since he had come to America. Four years ago, that had been, when he had just turned twenty-one. A mere stripling, perhaps, but a more accomplished rake and sharper than many a man twice his age. In the four years, he had filled out, broadened. He had lost that look of youth. Now, at twenty-five, he might be taken for twenty-eight or even thirty. The reflection pleased him.

It was the food that did it, he mused; the food and the good living, and something about the air of this land. It did something to you, that air. It was the height of the sky perhaps and the sweep of it. The clarity too—no muggy, cowed sky of shifting fog and whimpering rains. It was a sky that thundered and splashed sunlight like gold over everything, and rained and stormed like an angry Titan and whipped the land below with winds and washed it with light until everything took on a jewel-like clarity. Even the state of a man's mind. He knew what he wanted now: freedom for himself and his sons; mastery over this earth; a dynasty of men who could stride this American soil unafraid, never needing to cheat and lie and steal.

He pillowed his head upon his arms and slept.

II

ANDRE and Stephen moved through the crowds slowly. As they passed, heads were turned in their direction. There were not, in that day, many men so tall as Stephen, and his coppery red hair was like a beacon among the dark Creoles. It was surprising, too, to see a *'Mericain coquin,* a despised Kaintock on so friendly terms with an aristocratic young Creole. The older Frenchmen shook their heads sadly, and spoke of it as one more evidence of the degeneration of modern youth. The American city was growing like a rank weed, crowding the lordly Creoles back into the old square, the original boundaries of the city. And the Frenchmen had had many sad experiences with the fierce flatboatmen who fought with knives, bottles and their fists but never with a rapier or a colchemarde. The American business men, too, had many methods which to a Creole smacked of pure thievery. Certainly, no American had ever heard of honor.

"We had might as well rest," Andre said. "The *Natchez* won't be here for hours."

"All right," Stephen agreed. "I could do with a glass. What about that café yonder?"

31

"Heavens no! That's the Café des Améliorations."

"So?" Stephen said, still marching firmly toward it. "They have wine, don't they? Or even whiskey perhaps? Or is that too much to expect?"

"But you don't understand, Stephen. They—the men that go there are old, terribly old. And they have old-fashioned ways. . . ."

"Speak your piece, lad. Don't beat around the bush."

"All right. Those are men from the very oldest families. They see no reason why Louisiana should not still be a part of France. And perhaps they hate the devil himself worse than they do an American, but, frankly, I doubt it."

"I could say I was not an American," Stephen said slowly. "After all, I've only been here four years; but, when I think about it, I'm afraid I am. We'll go elsewhere then. I'm in no mood for quarreling."

"Good. May I suggest La Bourse de Maspero?"

"Ye may suggest what ye like. Maspero's it is then. Carry on, lad."

They started through the crowd, using their elbows to make a way. But the mass of people in the Square was so dense that they made little progress.

"It's not worth it," Stephen declared. "I vote we take our refreshments from the roadside like the others."

"Now really, Stephen . . ."

"Don't be such a damned aristocrat! That's what cost your nobility their heads. A man can be a gentleman without playing the rôle every minute."

Andre shrugged and the two of them moved through the crowd to the place where the dark little Greek in the enormous crimson fez was selling oysters in the half shell and ginger beer and sherbet. When they came away they felt full and vastly pleased with themselves. An old Negro woman called out as they passed:

"*Estomac mulâtre!* Belly of mulatto! *Estomac mulâtre! Achetez!* Buy! *Venez vous et mangez!* Come and eat! *Estomac mulâtre!*"

"Are ye cannibals too, in this country?" Stephen asked. "And what do ye do with the rest of the Nigra, if ye eat only his belly?"

"One moment," Andre said, turning to the old woman. "Tante! Give me eight pieces of mulatto's belly!" He gave her a coin. The old woman put her hand inside the basket and came out with eight small round cakes, smelling of spices, still hot from the oven.

"Here," Andre said. "Four for me and four for you. Our mulattoes have delicious bellies, do they not?"

"What a name to give gingercake! Now I know ye French are crazy!"

"Perhaps—but there is another of our products—look!"

Stephen's nimble fingers lifted a banana from a fruit vendor's stand. As he stripped it, he turned in the direction that Andre had indicated. A group of young girls, afoot, and dressed in bright colors was slipping through the throngs like gayly chattering songbirds. They carried no parasols, and their lovely young faces were bared to the sun. But strangest of all they wore on their heads instead of the bonnets of the Creole ladies, the bright tignons of the slaves.

"My God," Stephen said. "They're dressed like blacks. Better stuff, but the cut's the same."

"They're quadroons. Their fathers and grandfathers—"

"Were white. While their mothers were like the one who sold us mulatto's belly. I don't see how ye Frenchmen do it, Andre. To me there is nothing on earth so repulsive as a black. To sleep with that old monkey—ugh!"

"You haven't been here long. Your ideas will change. Besides, their mothers were almost as fair as they. We started bleaching them generations ago! You'll acquire your own pretty little *placée*, before you've been here many moons, I'll wager."

"Never," Stephen said flatly. "Never."

The crowd jostled them along the street. There was the sound of a cannon booming, and all the people surged forward at once.

"That's it!" Andre said. "The *Natchez* has docked!"

All the people were tense, waiting. Stephen let his eye wander over the throng. The people were dressed in their best clothes, and were waving the tricolor; but Stephen's glance passed on to where the coaches, barouches, landaus, phaetons and cabriolets waited. There the women were dressed in watered silk, and India muslin; there the little midnight bunches of curls bobbed over each shell-like ear as they smiled and talked, while the beribboned parasols nodded deliciously.

"They're coming," Andre said. "See—you can see them now. There's de Lafayette! That's Mayor de Roffenac with him, and Joseph Duplantier . . ."

But Stephen wasn't looking. A saucy little green and gold landaulette had come flashing up to the square, drawn by two spanking bays. Stephen, who was an excellent judge of horseflesh, thought he had never seen finer carriage horses. Their appointments were of the best and the Negro who drove them had on spotless green and gold livery.

Stephen's eyes swept past the horses and the coachman.

"And that," Andre was saying, "is Vincent Nolte, the banker, and that's General Villere . . ."

But Stephen's fingers were biting into the flesh of his arm.

"Who," he demanded, "is *that*?"

Andre turned.

"You have an eye for beauty, have you not?" he said. "Those are the Arceneaux sisters—in my opinion, the two loveliest girls in New Orleans."

"I didn't ask ye about both of them. That one—with hair like night cascading out of God's own heaven, unlighted by a star— that one!"

"And you're a poet, too! I hadn't suspected it."

"Holy Mother of God! I ask him to tell me the name of the girl I'm going to marry, and he talks about poetry!"

"Not so fast, my friend. Her name is Odalie. And she is directly related by blood to the late, lamented royal house. Also, every man of wealth and distinction in New Orleans has already asked her hand, either for himself, or in behalf of his son. I would suggest that you try someone a trifle less difficult—say the Crown Princess of England. I should also suggest that it is very, very rude to stare!"

"Hang your suggestions! Ye're going to present me—now!"

"I'm sorry, my dear friend, but that is quite impossible."

"Why?" Stephen demanded.

"Here, in this public square, it would be the height of impoliteness. I'm not at all sure Odalie wouldn't cut me dead for even associating with a *mauvais* Kaintock."

"I'm not from Kentucky!" Stephen snapped.

"To a Creole," Andre said gently, "all Americans are from Kentucky—and they're all bad."

"I see," Stephen said quietly. "An opinion in which ye doubtless concur?"

"Softly, my good Stephen. I have no desire to kill you in a senseless duel. Let's be frank about this affair. You're penniless and something of an adventurer. At the present moment, your chances with Mademoiselle Odalie Arceneaux are exactly nil." He stopped, looking at Stephen. From the center of the Place D'Armes, Mayor Louis Phillippe de Roffenac was making a speech to the city's most distinguished guest. Neither of them heard a word of his swift, sibilant French.

"Go on," Stephen said.

"Later, they might be better. The good God knows you're a hard and reckless man. If you'll accept my counsel, I'd say wait. Fatten your purse. Distinguish yourself in political matters, preferably in the interest of the Creoles—that, in an American, would win you many friends. Then with your lightning changes from youthful impetuosity to icy calculation—who knows? Truly many have failed; but they were none of them like you."

"I doubt that ye could kill me, Andre. I studied the small swords under Raoul Robert in Paris." He smiled suddenly and put out his hand. "Ye're right, lad," he said. "I'll go slowly." One of the fair eyebrows, fine as spun gold against the white skin, arched impishly. "But I'll wager ye a thousand dollars that I'll marry the girl!"

"Done!" Andre said. "Then we're friends again? I had a feeling a moment ago that my life was in danger!"

"It was. But it never shall be again from me, no matter what ye say."

They shook hands, and Andre turned back to the Square where the eloquent Bernard de Marigny was describing the valiant aid that the great soldier of France had brought to the infant republic of which Louisiana was now a part.

Stephen turned his back to the crowd and studied Odalie with half-closed eyes. She seemed to be completely captured by the most eloquent spokesman of New France. But the pink of her clear, shell-like ear lobes deepened. The color mounted to her face. Still Stephen stared.

Andre turned to him.

"Please, Stephen," he said. Stephen turned away to the Square, where the old soldier who had brought the gift of Liberty across the sea was rising to acknowledge his welcome.

"For my part," Andre whispered, "you've chosen the poorer one. The younger sister, Aurore, is more beautiful. You don't see it at first, nobody does. She is so much softer and sweeter that you don't notice it. Odalie with her imperious ways overshadows poor, gentle little Aurore; but the beauty is there—and it's from the heart."

The speaking was done now, and the welcoming party had borne Lafayette away to the booming of cannon and the cheers of the crowd. Stephen and Andre made their way back through the multicolored throngs, whites and octoroons, quadroons and mulattoes, ragged blacks, and sober merchants, and the sombre-gowned priests and nuns moving quietly off like dark strands in the patterns of bright colors. As they passed the landaulette, Andre lifted his hat. Stephen bowed. Odalie nodded stiffly, but Aurore both inclined her head and smiled so that the soft brown cluster of curls waved about her ears.

"What on earth are you looking at?" Odalie demanded, as the younger girl half turned in her seat, looking in the direction that Stephen and Andre had taken.

"Oh, nothing," Aurore said.

"Tell the truth, Aurore!"

"That—that man with Andre. He was so fair—like the sungod that Marie told us the Indians worship in Mexico . . . and he kept watching you so."

36

"That Kentuckian! Home, Roget! Quickly!"

"There is one other thing I want you to see," Andre said to Stephen as they left the Square.

"Why? Now I've seen everything."

"I disagree. Mademoiselle Arceneaux is indeed something, but everything—no. We turn here."

They came around the corner into another square, as crowded as the one they had left. But this time the people were Negroes —a solid mass of black humanity, laughing, chattering, jostling one another. On the edges of the crowd, the hawkers of refreshments cried out their wares, moving around with great trays suspended from their necks with leather straps. Other vendors, women, sat under cotton awnings and displayed their pies, lemonades, ginger beer, and mulatto's belly to the public—and the flies.

Stephen could see the huge Negro crouched over a cask, which had been fashioned into a sort of a drum by stretching a skin over the open head. There were several white persons present, standing aloof from the blacks and watching them with amused smiles.

Suddenly, a policeman stepped forward and raised his hand. The slaves moved forward, forming a solid square. The big Negro came down on the drum with two great beef bones and a shout went up from the crowd.

"*Bamboula! Danse Bamboula! Badoum!*"

The bones were moving against the dog skin so fast that almost they were a solid blur. The drum gave out a steady beat, never changing, never louder, never softer, a sound out of Africa, with centuries of dark magic in it. Stephen could feel the beat crawling along his body. It awoke a response in him— made him uneasy. Now the men were leaping into the air, the shells and bits of tin tied to their ankles matching the beat of the bamboula with their thin clatter.

Their movements were curiously stiff and angular: a strutting, stiff-kneed walk, shoulders thrown well back, necks arched, faces turned skyward. This was formula; this was a pattern full of ancient, hidden meaning that talked to sleeping senses, not to

37

the conscious mind. Even when they leaped into the air and shouted: "Badoum! Badoum!" Stephen could see that they were doing something that had been done thousands of times before in exactly the same way. The words had changed: Creole patois had replaced the guttural dialects of Africa; but everything else was the same, even the fluttering, gaudy rags of their masters' castoff garments became, to the half-closed eye, the ostrich plumes and cowie shells of the dark, half-slumbering land.

Now the women had joined the dance. Standing with their feet flat against the ground, they moved their bodies from the hips up, swaying from side to side, writhing their loins in broad, erotic movements. And as they danced, they chanted a dirge-like song, so slow and deep and sad that, to Stephen, the warm April air became suddenly laden with chill.

" 'Tis fay," he muttered to himself. " 'Tis the scream of the banshees."

"They're enjoying themselves," Andre laughed. "Look at that old black with the big nose. . . ."

"Let's go," Stephen said suddenly.

"Why?"

" 'Tis evil," Stephen said. "Apes and demons! Come."

They turned away from the square, walking toward Andre's house. Ahead, the street narrowed, the overhanging galleries almost meeting, so that the light was dim. Andre and Stephen walked without speaking, now and again falling back to let some tradesman, or old woman, or even an occasional nun, pass on the narrow *banquette*.

Suddenly, Stephen halted. Before him, a diminutive show window was jutting out halfway across the *banquette*. It was enclosed by window glass on three sides, and was only slightly wider than a man. In it were displayed rings, pins, pendants, ornamented duelling pistols, a rapier with a silver hilt, and snuff boxes galore. Stephen's eye wandered upward to the sign "Mont-de-piété," which swung on a green shingle in letters of tarnished gold.

"Why do you stop?" Andre asked.

38

"No reason," Stephen said. "I remembered something. Would ye mind proceeding without me? I'll join ye in half an hour."

"Yes," Andre said. "I mind very much. You're a stranger. You do not know New Orleans. And most of all, you're my guest."

Stephen laughed suddenly.

"Think ye I'd come to harm without ye here to guide me?"

"No. It's not that. Only it seems inhospitable of me to . . ."

"Forget it, lad. I have things to do and plans to make—some of them not fit for your young eyes." He grinned wickedly, looking at Andre. "Ye see, I value your good opinion. I'll join ye within the hour—truly."

"If it's money you want," Andre began, "I'd be glad . . ."

"Ye wish to quarrel with me again? From ye, not a picayune! I only fleece my enemies. Now be off with ye like a good lad."

Andre bowed a little, very stiffly.

"If Monsieur wishes," he said.

"Monsieur wishes," Stephen said flatly. "And now must I 'make a leg' to complete this little comedy?"

"No. I'll leave you. Pawn your back teeth if you like!"

Stephen stood looking after his new friend's retreating back.

"A very funny people, these Frenchies," he mused and he turned into the pawnbroker's.

Inside, it was close and the air had a musty smell. The pawnbroker was a fat little man, swart and oily of skin, wearing the huge powdered wig of the last century.

"I see by your sign," Stephen said, "that ye are a loan banker.

"Well," the broker began, "one has the necessity to live, Mont-de-piété—pawnshop. The difference is slight anyway. M'sieur wants something?"

"Still there is a difference," Stephen persisted. "And this is . . ."

"A pawnshop. The sign, she is for the effect. M'sieur understands . . ."

"Very well. For this pearl—how much?"

He loosened the spring-catch setting of the stick pin. The huge, milky pearl caught the light, and spun it into a rainbow. Glancing at it, Stephen remembered how it looked the night he had won it, gleaming against the green plush surface of the gaming table.

"One hundred dollar," the pawnbroker was saying.

"Ye're a thief," Stephen said calmly. "'Tis worth all of twenty thousand and ye know it."

"Five hundred? *Cinq cent dollar?*" the broker said hopefully.

"One thousand," Stephen said. "And ye're not to sell it for thirty days. Agreed?"

"'Tis my life's blood," the pawnbroker wailed; "perhaps M'sieur would take eight hundred . . ."

"One thousand."

"Name of the name of God!"

"One thousand."

The broker waved one hand weakly in assent. He waddled to the back of the shop and unlocked a heavy brass-bound chest. When he came back, his hands were filled with banknotes.

"Gold," Stephen said quietly. "I have no use for your skin-plasters. Gold, or I go elsewhere."

"Name of a consumptive horse! M'sieur asks too much!"

Stephen held the pearl higher. Now it was milky, now like snow; now it was seafoam breaking white on the crest of a long green wave; now it was moonmist riding the face of the river.

"M'sieur is right," the broker mumbled. "A thousand dollars . . . in gold!"

Stephen took the little canvas sack, heavy with gold pieces, and strode from the shop, his fair brows knitting into a frown.

"I'll have ye back," he muttered, "and soon!"

Andre was waiting when Stephen returned, his dark face still and unsmiling. Stephen looked at him and grinned.

"Ye're as finicky as a wench!" he laughed. Then soberly: "I meant no offense, Andre. What I had to do was painful, even to me. Ye'll forgive an old boor?"

"It's nothing," Andre said, taking the offered hand. "*Ma foi,* but you're a trying one!"

40

"And now ye really can help me," Stephen said. "I'll need rooms . . ."

Already Andre was picking up his hat and cane.

"I know a charming place," he said, "in Royal Street. You'll come now?"

"Right," Stephen said. "And send me your tailor. And a man-servant, if ye can purchase a good one."

"*Dieu!* Your ship from the Indies has arrived, no doubt?"

"No," Stephen said slowly, "No, Andre, the voyage has just begun."

Andre pushed open the door and the two of them went out through a shaft of falling sunlight into the street.

III

THE street sounds drifted up through Stephen's window and awakened him. He opened one eye lazily, blinking at the brilliant autumn sunlight that was glistening through the morning haze. Outside, the iron scrollwork of the gallery cast curious, lacy shadows against the window. Stephen stretched out his legs luxuriously and yawned. In a few moments now, Georges, his newly acquired manservant, would be tiptoeing into the room with a whispered "Good morning, maître," bearing the early prebreakfast cup of black coffee. Stephen didn't like black Creole coffee at first, but he was fast learning to. Georges was quietly, gently insistent. That any gentleman should do without his wakeup cup was clearly unthinkable.

Stephen smiled, remembering how he had discovered Georges' tremendous pride in his handsome young master. Georges and Ti Demon, Andre's valet, had almost come to blows in a quarrel over the merits of their respective masters. Only the timely intervention of the subjects of the quarrel had prevented fisticuffs. Stephen's discipline, never very rigorous, had slackened ever since. It was Georges who preserved the formalities that custom demanded.

From the street below, far away in the next block, the cries of the women street vendors drifted up to him faintly. *"Belle des figues! Figues clestes!"* Idly his mind translated the soft gumbo French: "Beautiful figs! Clesto figs!" *"Bons petit calas—tout chauds!* Good little rice cakes all hot! *Boules des Tic Tac!* Pop corn balls!

Listening, Stephen felt the first faint pangs of hunger. Where the deuce was Georges?

As if in answer, a soft knocking came from the door.

"Come in," Stephen called; and Georges was crossing the room, his black face lit with a pleased smile.

"Good morning, maître," he said, putting the black coffee down on the little bedside table. "The cheese woman she come this morning, so I go down and git you some, me." Then he exhibited his prize, a tiny heart-shaped cheese, covered with thick, fragrant cream, smelling faintly of claret.

"Thank you, Georges," Stephen said, taking the delicacy; "but for the love of Saint Peter hurry my breakfast. I'm starving!"

"Yes, maître, I go bring heem right now."

Stephen ate the cheese and looked out of the window. The sunlight was growing stronger. From outside came the cackle of geese, and Stephen knew, without even looking, that they were being driven to market afoot by a man and a boy, armed with long poles to keep them in line. Sipping the scalding coffee, he tried to define the quality of this, his city, but even now, although it was six months to the day since he had stepped ashore from Mike Farrel's flatboat, it eluded him. French to the core, it reminded him of Paris. Reminded him—that was all. The buildings with their overhanging galleries and their wrought and cast iron ornamentation were more Spanish than French; yet New Orleans had nothing of the quality of Seville or Madrid or Valencia. It was French in many subtle and definite ways: the housewives haggling over bargains, the swift play of gesticulation, the rapid, sibilant speech, for all its Creole softening. Those geese now—that was Normandy pure and simple. But the *bouillabaisse* in the cafés was Marseilles.

Georges was back with his breakfast in a surprisingly short

43

time. As usual there were several kinds of meats, cooked *à la grillades*, also as usual. That is to say, they were cooked in a deep skillet with a lid, and covered with a sauce of flour browned in lard, the whole thing being seasoned with onion, pepper, and garlic, and simmered with tomatoes at the last. These meats, Stephen felt, were enough to feed an army; but Georges had also brought biscuits, and steaming piles of *pain perdu*—slices of bread dipped in beaten eggs and milk and fried in deep fat.

Stephen looked at Georges.

"My God, man," he growled. "Is it that ye're fattening me for the slaughter?"

"The good maître should eat well," Georges said stiffly. "Ti Demon says that Monsieur Andre . . ."

"So," Stephen said, "I am yet a pawn in your quarrel with Little Devil! By our Lady, Georges, if ye bring me this much food again for my breakfast, I'll send ye up to the calaboose and have ye whipped! I'm not a Frenchman; I have not an elastic belly!"

"I will take it away, maître," Georges said sorrowfully. "It is only to me a shame that the good maître should not be well-fed. So now I cannot lift the head amongst the black boys, me."

"Damn!" Stephen groaned.

Georges was approaching the little serving table, his head bent, his steps slow.

"Leave it," Stephen snapped, "and get out of here before I murder ye!"

Georges fairly flew from the room, his white teeth gleaming in a pleased smile.

While Stephen ate the huge breakfast, his mind was busy with a thousand schemes. So far, everything had gone well. Slowly, cautiously, he had begun to make his pile, utilizing the one skill he possessed. Certainly he had come to the right place: New Orleans was a gambler's paradise. Everyone played: callow youths, striplings, men in their midyears, grandsires. And they played every known game, the Creoles being particularly fond of *vingt-et-un* and *écarté*, while the Americans played poker, faro, roulette, and the new game which Baron de Marigny was credited, erroneously perhaps, with having introduced. It was played with dice, and the Americans called it craps, a name shortened from the contemptuous appellation, Johnny Crapaud, which they gave to all Frenchmen.

Stephen, however, did not often play with the Creoles. When he did, the stakes were small, and he lost more often than he won. He pursued this same odd behavior with the more prominent Americans also, and succeeded to some extent in creating the very impression which he wished to implant—that of a gentleman sportsman who played for the love of the game.

There were others in the city, however, who had cause to know better. They were generally transients: steam boat captains, commercial travelers, merchants and the raw German immigrants from the section known as the German coast. With them, Stephen could afford to be merciless. They were people of no import in the city, their fates not likely to be noised abroad. So, always the stacks of silver dollars grew behind the lean fingers holding the fanned cards. The crisp green banknotes fluttered across the table, bright under the oil lamps, for all the blue haze of tobacco smoke. And Stephen pocketed them smiling, saying apologetically, " 'Tis the run of the cards. Better luck next time!"

He had redeemed his giant pearl from the pawnbroker, and Lagoaster, the celebrated quadroon tailor, had turned out for him several outfits: coats, waistcoats, trousers, richly ruffled white silk shirts, and stocks to be wound about his throat, all of a quiet elegance that commanded respect. Yes, he had done well. From now on, his moves could become bolder.

He rang for Georges, after having eaten the huge breakfast with surprisingly good appetite, and dressed with the aid of the manservant. Then he went down the stairs and out into the street. He walked slowly, his mind weighted with conflict. John Davis, one of the many refugees who had escaped the murderous uprising of the blacks of Saint Domingue, was planning to build two palatial gaming houses, the first of their kind in the city. Already a friend of the brilliant gallicized Englishman, Stephen had a chance to invest in the venture. Or should he rather buy an interest in the new railroad to Lake Pontchartrain, whose construction was also under discussion? Of the two, the railroad was by far the more respectable, but it was also much more risky. The gambling houses, due consideration being given to Creole temperament, were a sure investment. Still while the Creoles laughed and jested with gamblers and cheerfully lost fortunes to them, they did not invite them to their houses. And the Mademoiselles Arceneaux were Creoles in the best sense of that much abused term. . . .

More immediately, the problem of what to do with today was before him. The morning was hopeless, but in the evening he could go to the theatre. He would have preferred going to the American Theater with its marvelous gas jet illumination, the first of its kind in the city, but Odalie would almost certainly attend the Théâtre D'Orleans if she went at all.

He walked aimlessly, moving generally in the direction of the river. He turned northward and approached the Market. There were dozens of Negro women haggling with the vendors over the prices of foodstuffs they were buying for their mistresses. One of them in particular caught Stephen's eye. She was light yellow in complexion and decidedly pretty. Stephen recognized her suddenly. This was Zerline, the maid servant of the Arceneaux; Andre had pointed her out to him. One corner of Stephen's mouth curved upward in a smile. He moved very quietly until he was standing close behind her.

"Name of a name of a peeg!" she was saying to the merchant. "*Un escalin* for so small a bit of meat? I will not pay it, me. A picayune I will give—no more!"

"All right," the merchant said wearily, picking up the soup bone in his hairy hands. "Always an argument," he muttered, "with these Nigra wenches. *Ma foi*, they try to drive hard bargains!"

Stephen stood there laughing to himself as the girl continued her thrifty buying. A bit of cabbage, a leek, a sprig of parsley, a tiny carrot, an even tinier turnip—all tied in the same package, and all costing only a picayune. Then a cornet of *file*, a bunch of horse radish roots, and a little sage.

46

"I got nice grasshoppers," the merchant said, "all on the string, and well dried. Fine for your mistress's mocking bird."

Zerline spread out her fine, expressive hands.

"That one, he dead," she said. "Two, t'ree days agone he ups and dies, him. Mamzelle Aurore is very sad. Maybe we git nother bird—someday."

Stephen stretched out his hand and touched her on the shoulder. She whirled angrily. Seeing his white face, she stifled the flood of words that were trembling indignantly upon her lips.

"Your pardon, Zerline," Stephen said politely. "If you will step across the street with me to Gitano's shop, I should like to present your mistress with two fine mockers to replace the one that met with so unfortunate a death."

Zerline drew herself up stiffly.

"You knows well, monsieur, we can't accept the presents from the strange gentleman. We're Arceneaux, us!" She flounced away, her *tignon* held very high.

"Them Nigra gals is spoilt," the merchant said to Stephen. "And them yellow ones—they is the worst!"

Stephen laughed.

"She *was* insulted, too," he said, "so much she is become an Arceneaux! Give me two pralines, friend."

Walking away, eating the sugary confection, Stephen was busy with his thoughts. Zerline had only clarified the difficulties along that line. There was so much to be done.

He edged carefully around a fat Negro woman, on her hands and knees, busily scrubbing the cypress *banquette* and the steps of her master's house with latanier, the root of the palmetto. The steps were already spotless, but Stephen knew that this zeal was occasioned not so much by the lure of sanitation as by a fear that some evil *Mamaloi*, queen of Voudou, had sprinkled there a *gris-gris* to do the inhabitants harm.

Tonight, he must play again. Poker or *vingt-et-un*, he decided. No roulette or faro, which depended little upon the skill of the player, and which, in New Orleans, were usually fixed to favor the house. But the hand of a man, no matter how skilled, had its limitations, and few men in New Orleans were sufficiently fast to

47

cheat him. Cold nerve, and consummate skill had made him all but invulnerable. The increasingly popular American game of poker was bringing him a comfortable fortune. This he played only in the Faubourg St. Marie, the new American city which had grown up alongside the Faubourg Orleans and was already threatening its supremacy. Daily, too, he was becoming more skilled at *écarté*, the national game of the Creoles.

At the Théâtre D'Orleans, the French players were offering *Marie Stuart* as the evening's bill. Stephen arrived late in the second act and spent the entire time vainly scanning the boxes, the gallery and the main floor for a glimpse of Odalie. He even peered suspiciously at the *Loges Grilles*, the enclosed boxes which encircled the elevated parquet, although he knew full well that they were reserved for people in mourning, and pregnant women.

At the end of the act he left, having made certain that neither of the Arceneaux sisters was present. *Marie Stuart* might as well not have existed for all the attention he paid it. Outside in the street, he took out his massive gold watch that wound with a key and looked at the time. He groaned aloud. Now there was barely time to reach the Café des Emigrés, where Hugo Waguespack awaited him.

God, what a terrible player the huge German planter was! There was no pleasure in playing him—no sense of conflict— and absolutely no risk. Stephen sighed. What must be, must be. He turned his steps toward the café.

The German was waiting. Stephen knew him well enough by now not to waste time with courtesies. He simply sat down, rang for the waiter, and the play began. It went on for two hours, with Stephen winning constantly. He looked across the gaming table at Hugo Waguespack with a grimace that was very like revulsion. Six months of this now—six months of gazing across the tables of little smoky back rooms into stupid faces—fat stupid faces, sly stupid faces, lean, blue-jawed stupid faces—for, whatever else they were, always they were stupid. For a brief moment he allowed his attention to wander; then he sighed and picked up the cards. However great the pleasure of testing his skill against an opponent of intelligence, discernment and taste might have been, the risks were too great. He had to win. His whole future was at stake. This shooting of tame and tethered ducks must go on for a little while yet. He glanced at Hugo again. The German's face was florid, flushing to crimson below his flaxen hair.

"Enough for tonight?" Stephen asked, taking a pinch of snuff from the pewter snuff box and applying it to his left nostril.

"No!" Hugo growled. "Seven thousand you have already from me. And from Otto, ten. If I thought . . ."

Stephen looked at him, his eyes cold and blue as Hugo's own.

"Ye've won from me," he said, "and ye bring your own deck. I've told ye I never cheat at cards, but if ye persist in disbelieving me . . ."

Hugo's little pig eyes wavered, half lost in his enormous face.

"All right," he said. "One more round of seven up." He half turned away from Stephen. "Waiter!" he called. After a moment's wait, the fat mulatto appeared, bowing. "A pen and paper, and damned quick about it!" The waiter scurried off. Hugo turned again to Stephen.

"You'll take my note," he said, "for my lands upriver, against all I've lost to you. A single hand and I'm done with you. Either way I'm done—win or lose."

Stephen shrugged. "Agreed," he said. "I'll take your note, but ye may have a month to raise the money. After that I'll take the land. I want to be fair."

"You seem damned sure of winning," the German growled.

"I am," Stephen said. "Ye play badly."

The fat mulatto was back with an inkhorn and quill, and a small box of white sand.

Hugo took the pen and wrote laboriously, then sprinkled the document liberally with the sand. After he had poured it off, turning the stiff paper sideways, letting the inkstained grains run back into the little box, he passed the document to Stephen. It was in order, though full of misspellings and bad French twisted into the pedantic German arrangement of words.

Stephen put it upon the table, and beside it twenty bank-

49

notes. The mulatto whistled suddenly. The notes were all one-thousand-dollar bills. Stephen looked up at him.

"Ye've never seen such stakes?" he asked.

"Only once, maître. That was when Colonel Deveraux bet an Englishman thirty thousand dollars on a single poker hand. He lost the money and killed the Englishman the next day in a duel."

"Be still!" Hugo snapped, lapsing into German. "Hold thy mouth!"

Stephen extended the pewter snuff box, but Hugo waved it aside.

" 'Tis a hideous thing," he said. "I wonder that you keep it."

"It's lucky," Stephen declared, his slim fingers caressing the pearl that once more gleamed softly at his throat. "I exchanged a gold one for it—and I've never regretted the swap. Cut for the deal?"

"No. You deal. I trust you that far."

Stephen dealt the cards, six to Hugo, six to himself, passing them very rapidly, his fingers moving with certainty. The next card he turned face up upon the table. It was the trey of spades.

"I beg," Hugo grunted.

"Give ye one to let it stand," Stephen said.

"Agreed. Seven or ten points to the game this round?"

"Ten. I don't want to beat ye too quickly."

The play went on, first one player turning a trick then the other. Then, when they had exhausted their hands, Hugo said:

"All right, score it up."

"For me, the Ace—that's four," Stephen said, "and being high card, it gives me one more, making five."

"I have the Queen," Hugo said, "two points."

"The King," Stephen smiled, "three points, making eight."

"The deuce," Hugo grunted, "two points, and one for low, making five. And the next is my trick—the Jack, one point, and one more because it is Jack of trumps, making seven. And your Jack of Hearts taken by my five of Spades makes eight, and the point you gave me makes nine."

"So," Stephen chuckled. "Two for me on the last trick, your

50

Queen of Clubs taken by my trey of Spades—which, my good Hugo, were trumps."

Hugo stood up, slamming the cards across the table.

"You're clairvoyant," he said, "or else a rogue. I haven't decided which."

"And when ye do," Stephen said softly, "I shall have to decide whether to kill ye or let ye live. *Adieu,* Monsieur Waguespack."

"You weren't quarreling?"

The two of them turned. Andre was standing in the doorway of the little backroom of the café.

"No, monsieur," Hugo said. "We weren't quarreling. I don't quarrel, 'tis a sport for children. Goodday, Monsieur Le Blanc and Monsieur Reynard. Your servant!"

"The name," Stephen said, "is Fox."

Hugo shrugged his massive shoulders and walked past them out the small room.

"I don't like that man," Andre said.

"Nor I," Stephen agreed. " 'Tis the last time. Tomorrow I'm quitting this for good. Some business, perhaps. A few transactions at Maspero's and then . . ."

"Mademoiselle Arceneaux? You haven't changed your mind about that, Stephen?"

"No. I saw her again yesterday in Chartres Street with that sister of hers. Ye know, Andre, she almost nodded. Another quarter of an inch and it would have been a full-fledged nod. The sister, however, returned my salutation like an old friend. Too bad it isn't the other way around."

"If you'll condescend to leave this hole," Andre said, "I have a surprise for you, perhaps."

"Odalie? Ye're going to present me?"

"Not so fast, Stephen. It's not that. I'm afraid you'll have to content yourself with a substitute. A trifle older and not nearly so attractive, but still an Arceneaux. He's waiting for us now, at La Bourse de Maspero."

"He?" Stephen demanded.

"Vicomte Henri Marie Louis Pierre d'Arceneaux," Andre declaimed mischievously. "You're being honored, Stephen!"

"The father?" Stephen's eye was suddenly cold, intent on far distances. "Yes—that would be the way. A friendship with the old one. An introduction warmed by paternal sanction. Yes—ye're a wise one, Andre—and a very good friend."

"Then why do I not see more of you? Last evening I had two charming and agreeable—very agreeable—demoiselles on my hands. They quarrelled and quarrelled—neither of them desiring to leave the other in my rooms. So we sat up most of the night until I hailed a cabriolet and sent them both home."

Stephen rocked with laughter.

"Would ye have given me my choice?" he chuckled.

"Assuredly. There was little difference between them anyway. They were both agreeable and pretty and good bedfellows. But the company you've been keeping for the past six months— Germans from Law's German Coast, English travelers, merchants, ship captains . . ."

"Ye've put spies upon me," Stephen said.

"No. You're becoming quite a figure in New Orleans. Lagoaster raves over your taste in attire. He says you're the best turned out gentleman in the city."

"He's remarkably intelligent," Stephen said, "for a quadroon. Certainly he is the best tailor I've ever seen—even in London."

"I shall tell him. He's quite a good fellow. But people are noticing you, Stephen. Many ladies of high birth have dropped discreet hints in my presence for information about your background, your ancestry, and the source of your obviously large income . . ."

"Including Odalie Arceneaux?"

"No. Odalie would never condescend to admit whatever curiosity she might have. But tonight we're making the first step."

They passed down the narrow streets under the oil lanterns swinging on heavy chains set diagonally across the streets from the corner of one house to the corner of the next. Just as they reached Maspero's, a cannon boomed, far away and faint in the distance.

"Nine o'clock," Andre said. "All soldiers, sailors and blacks must now run like mad for home. But since we are neither—enter my friend."

"The old man," Stephen said as they entered, "I understand he does not fancy Americans."

"But you, my good Stephen, were educated in Paris. You studied the small sword under Raoul Robert. You're a gentleman. All of which you must sustain tonight by exhibiting your most polished Parisian, spoken as fast and as carelessly as you can, well larded with the idioms of Paris, which our friend won't understand, not having left Louisiana in the past forty years. But no English, I beg of you. You're a financier—lately of an old Philadelphia banking and brokerage establishment, now operating independently on your own."

Stephen bowed.

"As a liar," he said gravely, "I thought I had no peers; but tonight I salute ye!"

They went through the door into the café. The floor was sanded and a number of Creole and American gentlemen sat at the small tables talking and laughing in the friendliest possible manner.

"Yes," Andre said, seeing Stephen's raised eyebrow. "The barriers are going. We are both learning it is better to get along. Only the very old still persist in their ways. Why, only last week one of the Prudhomme girls married a Mister Wilson!"

"Good," Stephen said. "But where is my esteemed father-in-law-to-be?"

Andre inclined his head.

The old man sat alone at a table, pulling at a long-stemmed pipe of white clay. His tall beaver sat firmly on his head. His face was as brown as an Indian's, and his hair gleamed silver. Heavy white brows jutted imperiously over a nose like the blade of an ax. He wore a stock of the purest white silk, gleaming even above the snowy ruffle of his shirtfront, and his coat was of maroon, richly brocaded. The waistcoat, Stephen saw, was pearl-gray, and its studs were all diamonds. Andre stopped before him and bowed a little.

53

"Monsieur le Vicomte," he said in French, "have I your permission to present my good friend, Etienne Reynard?"

The old man nodded a bit, his black eyes boring into Stephen's.

"I am called Fox, monsieur," Stephen said deliberately, "not Reynard, and my first name is Stephen. Your servant, Monsieur le Vicomte!"

The thin lips twisted into a grim smile.

"You have right," he said in old French. "Make no apologies for your name. It is a good one. Andre thinks I'm an old ogre. That is why he translated it."

"And are ye an old ogre?" Stephen asked smiling.

"Upon occasion. You speak French well, young man. Andre tells me you learned it in Paris. What were you doing there?"

"What does one usually do in Paris, monsieur? Gambling, wenching, anything to amuse oneself . . ."

Pierre Arceneaux threw back his head and laughed aloud.

"*Moi*," he chuckled, "I have done the same thing when I was young. My father gave me the Grand Tour. For my education, you understand. I educated myself with every well-turned ankle on the continent. I've heard it said that you're a gambler, Monsieur Fox."

"Ye heard rightly," Stephen said, and Andre's eyes opened wide. " 'Tis a profession not without honor. But I am leaving it for good."

"Why?" the old man demanded. "I couldn't think of a more fascinating life."

"One grows older," Stephen said quietly. "And the blood cools. There are things a man wants: a home, a wife, children. Perhaps I aim much too high, but the sort of girl I'd take to wife would not ordinarily marry a gambler. Ye're a horseman, sir? Then ye demand good blood in a filly, do ye not?"

"I see," Pierre Arceneaux said slowly. "Then what are your plans?"

"I am going into business with a Mister Warren, a sort of brokerage, sir."

"I see," the old man said again. The black eyes regarded Stephen steadily. Then the wrinkles about their corners deep-

54

ened and something very like a smile played about the corners of the thin old mouth. "You don't mind advice, my son?"

"Not at all."

"Then look to the land. This of business—stocks, bonds, mortgages, holdings, is but little better than the cards. Get your roots in the earth and grow with it. When you've done that— with your looks and manners—there's not a house in Louisiana that will not welcome you. Now Monsieur Gambler, what say you to a little game? You play *écarté*, do you not?"

"Yes," Stephen said; "but make it *pool écarté*, so that Andre may be *retrant*."

Andre was conscious almost at once that Stephen was playing badly. M. Arceneaux won the deal, thus making Stephen the pone. Stephen's clear "I play" rang out at the exact times when he should have proposed. And he accepted, when dealing, all M. Arceneaux's proposals, no matter how disastrous the results. When the game was over, Stephen had lost a cool thousand to M. Arceneaux, who was beaming, and boasting of his skill.

"We must play again soon," he said to Stephen. "I must give you a chance to recoup your losses."

"Very well," Stephen smiled. "Wednesday night, perhaps? M. Maspero will hold the little room for us."

"Wednesday night it is. It was a pleasure, Monsieur Fox."

"The pleasure was mine, sir," Stephen said.

The old man touched his cane to the brim of his hat and strode through the doorway.

"Couldn't you have been a little less obvious?" Andre said. 'Even old Arceneaux will comprehend after a time. *Ma foi*, an imbecile could play better *écarté*! And Arceneaux is far from a fool."

"Next time I'll win a bit, but always allowing him to remain about three hundred ahead. I think my father-in-law is an agreeable old fellow, don't you?"

"But you shouldn't have admitted being a gambler. After all my careful groundwork too. What an ass you made of me! Old Arceneaux will never sanction a connection now."

"Softly, Andre. Who knows? I'm off to bed—alone," he added,

seeing Andre's mischievous grin. "I have much to do tomorrow. I want ye to come with me. Ye can help me, and I need help badly. I'm seeing Mister Warren in Chartres Street at seven o'clock. Ye'll meet us there?"

"Seven o'clock—*Mon Dieu!*"

"Nevertheless, I shall expect you. *Au 'voir*, Andre."

"*Au 'voir*. Seven o'clock, upon my word!" He wandered off, shaking his head.

The sun slanted low through Chartres Street as Andre stumbled along at half past seven in the morning. The mist had come in from the river and the light was caught in it, making a feathery silver gold blaze which took the edges off everything. Under the galleries, where Stephen and Thomas Warren waited, the shadows were a cool blue except on the edges, where the sunlight had passed through the wrought-iron scrollwork; there it had traced lacy patterns of infinite grace.

"Ye're late," Stephen said sternly. "I said seven o'clock, didn't I?"

"Late? Impossible! How can one be late before eleven? Before then time does not exist. My God, what a head I have! It is as big as a camel."

"If you'll come in," Thomas Warren said, "you'll find coffee waiting. It might help."

"A thousand thanks!" Andre said. "You are Monsieur Warren, no doubt?"

"Forgive me, Andre," Stephen smiled; "but I am almost as forgetful about introductions as ye are. This is my friend and associate, Tom Warren, who is broker, factor, entrepreneur— in fact, all things to all men."

Andre took Warren's big hand and looked up at him. Tom Warren was a huge man, all of two hundred pounds and more than six feet tall. His hair was very black and his eyebrows grew straight across his nose with no break in the middle, so that his small, rapidly shifting green-gray eyes were almost hidden by them. His voice had a certain resonance to it, a bluff hearty quality which, oddly, struck Andre as being carefully controlled.

He's practiced it many times before his mirror, that tone, the young Creole decided; strange . . .

They went in a doorway shaded by an overhead gallery. Inside, the room was furnished as an office, complete with desk, chairs, pens, and paper.

"My living quarters are above," Tom Warren said. "We can have our coffee there if you like. You'll pardon me, sir," this to Andre, "but my French is very bad. Mister Fox is endeavoring to improve it, but with scant success, I'm afraid."

"Then you'll have to endure my English," Andre said. "But that coffee, monsieur . . ."

"Immediately. If you will follow me." He went ahead of them up a stairway into rooms that were neatly, if plainly, furnished.

"Delphine!" he called. "Is the coffee ready?"

Without answering, a pretty mulatto girl came into the room, bearing a tray with cups, saucers, twin silver pitchers, one with coffee and the other with scalding milk, and a large *brioche*, or coffee cake. There were also small plates of *calas*, the small rice cakes which the Creoles enjoyed.

Seeing the girl, Andre straightened in his chair, taking his hand away from his brows.

"Black coffee, Delphine," he said. "*Ma foi*, but you are a very pretty girl!"

"Monsieur makes a pleasantry," the girl murmured, turning to Stephen.

"*Café au lait*," Stephen said, "and a piece of coffee cake."

"And now, Mister Fox," Warren said. "Perhaps you'll explain the reason for so early a visit. When your man brought your message, I thought I had interpreted it wrongly. Seven o'clock in New Orleans—not that I mind . . ."

Andre was watching Delphine pour the *café au lait*. The dark and light streams arched out of the graceful necks of the pitchers at the same time, combining in the cups in just the right proportions. He liked the way her hands moved, pouring. And that house dress was of such thin stuff—delightful, utterly delightful, he decided.

"Your attention, Andre," Stephen said. "I didn't ask ye here to decide upon the merits of a yellow filly. This is a thing of the utmost seriousness."

"A thousand pardons, my friend."

"That land along the river next to the Waguespack place, Tom. I want it."

"I've already purchased it for you, Mister Fox. Fifteen hundred acres at twenty dollars an acre. That's a song, even for uncleared land."

"Ye paid cash?"

"No. You could not spare that much cash, sir. I gave a note against the crop."

"I see. Now you must purchase blacks for me. Good ones, well-trained. None of these African brutes. I'm going to become a planter, Tom. And I want to make my first crop this fall."

"Hmmmm. The land has to be cleared, remember. And it's not far from planting time now, is it? You'll plant cotton, of course?"

"No. Cane. Cotton exhausts the land. I want something left for my sons."

"Then you'll need the Nigras at once. I think I can get them for you—and cheaply, too."

"How?" Andre put in. "Good blacks are scarce and dear."

"Your friend Herr Waguespack is going to put the bulk of his slaves up to auction in order to raise money to prevent a foreclosure on his place. I think we would do well to buy those Nigras. And I think we'll be able to name our own price. By the way, you hold that note against Herr Waguespack, don't you, Mister Fox?"

Stephen looked at him, his blue eyes very clear.

"Ye're a fast man, Tom," he said slowly. "I've only held that note since last night."

"It's my business to know things fast," Tom Warren said heavily, and for once the gray eyes held. "I'll buy that note from you at any reasonable price."

"No," Stephen said. "No."

"Then foreclose! That Waguespack is a swine, but he is a good planter. With his already cultivated lands you could make that crop with ease."

"I gave him thirty days," Stephen said.

"In writing?"

"My word." Stephen's voice was very low, but the tone was unmistakable. Warren's face flushed a darker red.

"I see. Then we'd better proceed with the other things. You'll need machinery: crushers, vats, kettles, ploughs, scythes, wagons, mules . . ."

"Get them. Give a note against the crop. But by all means get axes, spades and saws. We'll need them first." He stood up.

"And our business?"

"I'm staying in it. I never desert a friend, Tom. Ye know that."

"Good. Perhaps after a year I can buy you out. The plantation will be trouble enough, you'll find."

"As ye will, Tom. But now let us be off. I want Andre to see how our business works."

They went down the stairs and out into the street. As they turned west on Dumaine, walking toward the river, Andre said: "This is good news, Stephen—tremendous news! I'll see that it reaches the right ears."

"No. When it is done, it will speak for itself. Until that time I pledge ye to silence. When Mademoiselle Arceneaux sees Harrow, even her blood will thaw. Old man Arceneaux called me a gambler—well, this is it, the biggest game of all for the highest of stakes."

They were approaching the river now, seeing it black with shipping moored to the heavy timbers embedded in the batture. There were blunt-bowed trading brigs from Europe, coasting craft from the New England states, heavy Indiamen, and smaller craft from the Antilles. A dozen or more steamboats puffed busily up to the quays, white smoke pluming from their high twin stacks. The waters close to the shore were covered with flatboats, lying side by side so close that they rubbed against one another, their heavy timbers groaning in the swell.

"Which one is it, Tom?" Stephen asked.

"That one yonder. See the jug of Nongela tied to the pole in the center? That means they're open to business." He turned away and walked rapidly in the direction he had indicated.

Andre and Stephen looked along the row of flatboats until they saw the tall mastlike pole erected in the center of one, with the brown whiskey jug dangling from the top. As they watched, several men, richly if not tastefully dressed, began to converge toward the clumsy vessel.

"Brokers," Stephen said. "They go to bid for the contents and the boats. But we always outbid them—if it is worth our while."

"You bid for flatboats?"

"Yes. Or rather Tom does. The captains sell the whole thing, boats and cargo. The scoundrels would sell the crew if they could. We break the boat itself up for lumber which we sell to the carpenters and contractors, and we market the cargo at public auctions, getting much more than we paid for it."

"But suppose the public doesn't bid," Andre put in.

"They do—always. In the first place, ye must remember that we are 'Mericain coquins as the old song puts it. We don't buy everything. I have that old pirate, Mike Farrel, holing up in Natchez. He sends me word by the fastest packet what the boats passing there are bearing. So when they arrive, we are ready. Lately we have been buying all the wheat we could get our hands on."

"Why wheat?"

"One must have bread, mustn't one? Right now, the warehouse is bulging to the seams. I dare say, my good Andre, that every ounce of wheat that the steamboats don't bring in will soon be in our hands."

"And then?"

"When the millers start in to make the new batch of flour they'll buy from us, at our price."

"And the price of bread will go up," Andre said half to himself. "And the hungry children will go hungrier in the houses of the poor. You know, Stephen, you have the makings of a scoundrel about you."

60

Stephen shrugged.

"A man can't grow wealthy on a squeamish stomach, Andre. 'Tis regrettable, of course. But here comes Tom back again."

"I closed it," Warren said, as he came close, "for three thousand. It will be worth eight or ten when it hits the market. Shall I proceed with the stuff for the plantation?"

"Yes. When is the sale of Waguespack's blacks to take place?"

"One week from tomorrow. Now, if you don't mind, I'll take my leave of you gentlemen. I have a few errands to run in relation to that sale. Good day, sirs."

He lifted his hat politely and was gone, striding down the levee.

"A strange man, your Tom Warren," Andre said. "Yet he seems very devoted to your service."

"Tom is as good as gold," Stephen declared. "What say ye to a long ride?"

"Good. Where shall we ride?"

"To Harrow—my new place. 'Tis all of fifteen miles. It sits on the river between D'Estrehan's and Waguespack's and it's the most beautiful spot this side of Paradise. By the way, did I tell ye I've bought a horse?"

"No. But then you never tell me anything. Where is this steed of yours?"

"Being groomed at present. He is a palamino. I got him from Texas. He has a coat of buff satin and a mane and tail of silver. But we had better fortify ourselves for so long a ride. What say ye to breakfast at the Café des Réfugiés? I hear 'tis quite a place."

"It is. You've never been there? Good. I have much to show you."

A short block from the river front on St. Phillip's Street, they turned southward toward Dumaine. There, in sight of the market, they turned off into a doorway, shaded as nearly all the doorways were by the overhanging gallery. Nothing was different. From the street, the Café des Réfugiés was the same as any of a dozen others in New Orleans.

Inside, however, was another world. The men were smaller and darker than even the brunet Louisiana Creoles. The air was

61

alive with a richer, racier French. Laughter was readier, tempers more explosive.

"They've lost everything," Andre observed, "but their verve. I'll wager that more duels are arranged here than any other place in town. And what a way they have with women! Never let a Saint Dominican kiss your sweetheart—not if you want to keep her. And wine! Have you ever had *le petit Gouave?*"

"No," Stephen said. "What is it?"

"The good God and the Saint Dominicans alone know; but it is delicious." He turned to the waiter who was bowing over their table.

"Two *petit Gouaves,*" he ordered. "And two Saint Dominican breakfasts."

While they were sipping the long, cool drink of the Islands, Andre had a Negro sent to his house to order his horse saddled. Then they sat back and awaited their breakfast in the Saint Dominican style.

When it arrived, Stephen stared at it in amazement. There were oranges and bananas arranged in a pyramid, a clear, jewel-like liqueur, drip coffee as thick and black as molasses, and steaming piles of tamales, tortillas, sausages, and blood pudding.

"Does one eat it," he demanded, "or carry it away on a pack mule?"

"One tastes a little of each dish. Refuse anything, and you're no gourmand; eat it all, and you're both sick and a glutton. Go on, try it. It is really quite good."

Stephen tried the food gingerly, then after a taste or two, proceeded to eat with gusto.

"I shall come again," he declared, "often."

Andre was looking around the café.

"Poor devils," he murmured. "Have you ever thought, Stephen, how readily the same thing could happen here? We're outnumbered by our blacks almost as much as they were. A few firebrands, eloquent of tongue, a few bold blacks, and the whole mass of African brutes could sweep over us like a tide. My God! What a thought!"

Stephen laughed.

"Calm yourself, my old one," he said. "From all I've heard, your Caribbean black is a different breed of dog from ours. They are very cold and long of head, capable of thought. I've even heard them called intelligent. What American black can entertain a thought for half an hour without falling asleep?"

"You may be right," Andre said doubtfully, "but we get many of our Nigras from the islands . . ."

Stephen rose.

"Let us postpone your slave insurrection to some later date," he said. "I still want to try Prince Michael over a distance. Are ye with me on the ride?"

Andre got up and paid the check. Then they went outside and hailed a cabriolet which took them to Stephen's rooms, where Andre had ordered his horse brought.

"And this," Stephen said, as they climbed down from the two-wheeled vehicle, "is Prince Michael."

Andre looked the palomino over critically, before turning to Stephen with a smile.

"Now I know you're a liar," he said. "You've sworn by all the saints in heaven that you dislike show. You despise florid speech and eloquent gesticulation, yet you buy the showiest horse that ever these eyes have seen! Truly, Stephen, he is something out of the fairy stories. A steed, you might call him, or a charger, but never a horse."

"Perhaps the time has come for show," Stephen said. "Besides, he is a good horse, sound in wind and limb. Ye find him to your liking?"

"He is beautiful, Stephen. Such a coloring has never been seen in Louisiana. White—yes; but a pale golden buff with silver mane and tail, no, never to my knowledge."

Prince Michael whinnied a bit and stretched out his long, graceful neck toward Stephen.

"See? Already he knows me. Up with ye, lad, it grows late."

They were off, trotting briskly along the river front headed northward away from New Orleans. It was late in the winter, almost the spring of 1826, and the air was beginning to grow

63

warm. As they left the city they saw the first Negroes in the fields already busy with planting.

"They're too early," Andre complained. "One good hard frost and the whole crop would rot in the ground."

Stephen smiled.

"I shall value your advice, my fine son of a planter! Or should I say 'absentee son of a planter'?"

"You're right," Andre laughed. "But henceforth I shall take more of an interest."

They rode on in silence. On both sides of the river the land was springing into life. They remarked a full dozen houses in various stages of construction. Everywhere Negroes shivered unhappily in the still cold fields. Yet so great was the expanse of land that miles separated every house that they saw from the next, and thousands of acres of virgin river land lay in almost unbelievable fertility, as yet untouched by ax or plough.

Then Stephen was reining Prince Michael to a stop.

"This," he said, "is Harrow."

Andre looked out over the tangled woodland. Here were wild cane and palmetto stretching out for endless miles. In the center of the uncleared land was a grove of stately oaks, trailing streamers of Spanish moss. Off to the south was a cypress grove. Andre's reaction was simple.

"My God!" he said.

"Lovely, isn't it?"

"Lovely?" Andre groaned. "It's impossible! It will take you three years at the least to clear enough of it for even a small crop— five or six to clear it all. I assume it extends all the way to Waguespack's?"

"Yes—and to D'Estrehan's in the other direction. A huge place, Andre. A man needs room to breathe."

"But how on earth . . . ?"

"Will I clear it? Easily, Andre. Ye forget I'm not a Frenchman. I have no real aversion to hard work. God, but I'm tired! 'Tis a long time since I've ridden a nag."

"I'm hungry," Andre said. "And fools that we are, we brought no lunch."

"Ye're right there," Stephen said. "And 'tis a long ride back to the city. The horses need water and rest, and in that they're better off than we, because here they can have both."

He swung down from the saddle, and knelt, digging his fingers in the black, rich earth.

"Harrow," he said, his voice curiously soft. "The new Harrow, and such a place as the old one never was!"

"There was another Harrow?" Andre asked.

"Yes. 'Tis in Ireland not very far from Dublin." Stephen's blue eyes looked past Andre out over the face of the river. "Different from this—a place of mist and cloud and a gypsy sun, never all there, ye ken. Rains whispering to ye in the night, and the greenest sod ever granted to the hands of mortals . . ."

"You lived there?"

"Yes."

"And you loved it. Why did you leave?"

Stephen looked at his friend, a slow, crooked grin twisting his face.

"Ye're not prying, me lad," he said, "for the sake of some of those curiosity-stricken ladies ye told me about?"

"Heaven forbid! I'm curious about you myself, Stephen. You're such a strange combination of gentility and rascality that I cannot help wondering . . ."

"How and who and what I am? 'Tis a long tale, Andre, and perhaps a dull one."

"Why not let me be the judge of that?"

Stephen stood up, and looked straight at Andre.

"In the first place," he said, grinning wickedly, "I'm a bastard."

"I've often thought so," Andre laughed. "But go on."

"No, I mean truly. I was born out of wedlock. My mother never told me who my father was. How do ye like having a friend whose bar sinister blots out his whole damned escutcheon?"

"That's nothing," Andre chuckled, leaning forward. "Old Arceneaux swears that my family and his and nearly every other of any account in Louisiana are descended from a band of

65

female petty thieves and prostitutes who were brought from La Salpêtrière, a house of correction in Paris!"

"Correction girls? I've heard of them. But, according to the histories, they had no children."

Andre rocked with laughter.

"Who wrote the histories, my friend? Old Arceneaux has a diary reputed to have been written by the midwife, Madame Doville—Madame Sans Regret, they called her. Says he is going to publish it one day when he feels energetic enough to fight twenty duels a day everyday for three months. But I'm interrupting you—and you were going to tell me why you left."

"Had to," Stephen said. "I got possession of a certain article of value." His fingers strayed upward to the great pearl gleaming softly at his throat."

"You—you stole it?"

"No. I won it gaming. But my opponent was the son of a man highly placed in life. The pearl was his father's. I merely wouldn't give it back."

"Why not, Stephen? That would have been the simplest way."

Stephen looked out over the river.

"Ye give me a task," he said. "I don't know why I wouldn't. At the time it seems I couldn't return it. There's an alchemy about the thing, Andre. Perhaps it was some heritage of roguery in the blood." He was silent for a long time, watching the river.

" 'Twas not its value that I wanted. I've lain in gutters with my belly caved in with hunger, holding the pearl in my fist when it would have brought me food. I've fought like all the devils in hell to keep it. I've never owned it, Andre; always it owned me."

"You talk riddles, Stephen."

"No—truly. It was not to be sold. It must be worn. I think I always knew that. And it could not be worn by a ragged urchin; it could only be worn by a gentleman. I went up to Dublin, 'twas the best place to hide. I slept in the streets, and lived by begging food and stealing from the green grocers. All the time, Andre, this was with me, driving the restlessness in so deep that it can never come out. This seems mad?"

"Of course not. Please go on."

66

"It is, none the less. After a half year, I apprenticed myself as a printer's devil, because I alone of the dozen scrawny, dirty, starved-out applicants could read and write a fair hand. He was a perverse old scoundrel, this printer, Andre; but above all else he had a mind. I slept in a loft up over the presses, and he allowed me to take up books to read by a stub inch or two of candle, after my fourteen hours of work. I prayed over that candle, and I pinched it and cursed it that it should not burn out before I'd turned a page."

"My God!" Andre said. "When did you sleep?"

"I didn't. Ye have no idea what a starved young mind can make a body do. The old scoundrel beat me and paid me not at all, but I was happy. I read all the classics, setting them up in fine type, and inking the presses. Before I left, I could read the principal modern tongues and falter through the ancients. I mended my speech and my pants and freed my body from vermin. I kept myself washed and my hair combed. Every Sunday, religiously, I blacked my worn boots and donned my third- or fourth-hand clothes. Thin I was like a rail and stooped, and with a squint from so much reading."

"You've changed," Andre observed.

"That I have. Ye see, the printer had a daughter off in England at school. She came back, Andre." One corner of Stephen's mouth crawled upward in a half smile.

"And that was the finish," Andre laughed.

"I would have given her anything—except the pearl. I read Horace to her. The Odes, ye ken. But one day the old man found in her things a free translation from Sappho—inscribed in my own fine hand. 'Twas one of the more passionate fragments, and the printer concluded from some rare allusion that perhaps his daughter knew the way to my dingy loft."

"And did she?"

Stephen looked at his friend, one eyebrow lifting mockingly.

"The virtue of a woman, Andre—and her age—are never topics for discussion."

"You were discharged, of course?" Andre asked.

"I was impelled onto the wet cobblestones by a hobnailed

67

boot against my rear. So I stowed away on the London boat and went to England. My first and only connection there was with a wine merchant in London. He neglected his trade to follow the cards. When he lacked other partners he taught me to play and won back all my miserable wages. Under the circumstances, I had to learn to win. He used to journey to Italy, and the south of France to obtain his wines. I went with him. He'd grown quite fond of me then. But in France the need for fine raiment grew upon me. The girls, ye see, were most affectionate—your Frenchwomen, Andre, are designed by nature for love. So I began to beat him too regularly and he discharged me. 'Twas then I started my wanderings with nothing but the cards, and my fingers' skill to sustain me. I wore the pearl in France for the first time, feeling all the time as though I'd committed a sacrilege. But I brazened it out." He paused, frowning a little. "I'm still brazening it out," he added softly.

"But when you have held your land," Andre asked, "will you then be able to wear your pearl in comfort?"

Instead of answering, Stephen scooped up a handful of earth, letting it run like water between his outstretched fingers.

"In one year," he said, "I shall clear this land of debt. In the next, I shall build me such a house as was never matched in the Old World or the New. Ye believe me, Andre?"

Andre looked at him long and searchingly before answering.

"Yes," he said at last. "Yes, I believe you. You cannot be stopped. You must drive forward, because you can't help it. 'Tis a terrible thing, Stephen. Sometimes I pity you."

"Save your pity," Stephen said, rising. "I have an idea. We are not far from the lands of the gigantic Hugo. Let us presume upon his hospitality. He'll probably offer to cut our throats, but he'll end by feeding us. And for some good German cooking right now I'd endure even Hugo."

Andre laughed, and they turned their horses' heads again northward.

The tangled woodland dropped away abruptly and before them stretched cleared and cultivated fields. The work that had been

68

done here was masterly, every tillable inch of ground laid out in precise, orderly rows.

"*Ma foi!*" Andre said. "But that Waguespack is a planter."

The road that led to the house was as precise and orderly as the fields; but as they approached the house all order disappeared. It was built of cypress, with soft brick between the walls, *briquete entre poteaux,* and had fallen into an advanced state of decay. Débris littered the yard, and four flaxen-haired children, dressed in rags, played in the dirt with the swine. They started up at the approach of the horsemen, looking like players in a minstrel show, their blue eyes widening strangely in their dirt-blackened face.

"Your father," Andre began in French. "Is it that he is at home?"

The children stared blankly, their small mouths dropping open.

"Is your father at home?" Stephen asked.

Still the blank stares continued.

"Name of a camel!" Andre said. "Can't they talk?"

"Yes," Stephen said. "Watch this. Then he repeated the question in German, speaking very rapidly, rolling out the thick-throated gutturals.

At once all the mouths closed as one mouth and the children huddled into a little group like sheep.

"No," one of the children said in Low German. "He has to the fields gone."

"And your mother?"

"Yes, mama is to house."

"Go thou," Stephen said, "and tell her that two gentlemen wish with her to speak."

"Ugh," Andre said. "What a language! One clears one's throat, and gargles, and showers every visage within twenty yards with spittle. That is from your Vienna days, isn't it?"

" 'Tis the only thing I brought away," Stephen laughed.

The door of the house swung open, teetering perilously on its one remaining hinge, and a young woman came out. She was blond and pretty in a buxom sort of way. Andre was sure he had never seen such large breasts. It was her eyes, however,

69

that stopped them; large and blue as the children's, they kept shifting, glancing every half minute in the direction of the fields.

"Good morning, Madame," Andre said.

"I speak only German," she said softly.

"Goodday, gracious lady," Stephen said in German.

"Greet God," the woman answered softly.

"We are friends of your husband's," Stephen said. "And we want to see him. But we have ridden many miles and are very hungry . . ."

At the sound of the *sehr hungrig*, the woman nodded rapidly.

"Come in," she said. "There is not in the house much to eat. But I can the *Pfannkuchen* and coffee make. If the gentlemen wish?"

"*Pfannkuchen?*" Andre said blankly. "What on earth?"

"Pancakes. They're good," Stephen declared. "Thank you very much, gracious lady."

Inside the house, the furniture was falling to pieces, but the rooms were fairly clean. Frau Waguespack seated them at the big table and busied herself before the huge grate.

"In the house!" Andre said. "She cooks inside! *Ma foi!*"

"And what's wrong with that?"

"In the city, nothing. But on a plantation where there are no fire brigades—a kitchen house of brick at least one hundred yards away from the house, remember that, Stephen, when you build."

Frau Waguespack turned the pancakes over in the huge iron skillet, and the coffee gurgled softly on the hearth. Then she was approaching the table, huge stacks of pancakes piled in steaming, golden mounds on the thick china plates.

She brought the coffee and butter and a tall pitcher of syrup. Andre watched Stephen.

"Not bad," he said, after his first bite, then: "Good—very good, indeed!"

"What are you called?" Stephen asked Frau Waguespack

"Minna—Minna Wagonsbeck."

"Wagonsbeck?" Andre echoed.

"That is Hugo's name. Waguespack is Frenchified."

He turned to Minna.

"Thanks for your kindness," he said. "And now if you will tell us where we may find your husband . . ."

Minna's blue eyes wavered.

"Out there," she said. "In the southwest fields, but—"

"Yes?" Stephen said.

"Do not to my husband say that you to this house have been. Please!"

Andre turned to her, his eyebrows raised, but Stephen lifted his hand warningly.

"Do not worry—Minna," he said to the girl, for she was scarcely more. "I'll say nothing!"

"Why?" Andre demanded as they mounted their horses.

"Ye'll see," Stephen said grimly.

To the southwest fields was a short ride. As they rounded a cypress wood, a group of Negroes came in sight, digging furiously in the earth, laying the long stalks of cane end to end in the furrows.

"Never," Andre declared, "have I seen blacks move that fast! I wonder . . ."

As if in answer they could hear Hugo's bull-like voice roaring: "Faster, you black swine!" and between each word came the singing whine of the lash, ending in a crack like a pistol shot.

"My God!" Andre said. "What bestiality!"

Another half turn and they were suddenly upon him. Hugo pulled up his nag so savagely that the ancient animal actually tried to rear. But the German's great weight was too much. The old horse settled back on his feet, his thin neck hanging.

"Good day, gentlemen," Hugo grinned. "This is an unexpected honor!"

"Your blacks," Stephen said without ceremony. "I hear ye intend to sell them. I'll buy the lot—now."

"No, Monsieur Fox," Hugo said smiling. "I must make sure that they are in good hands. I fear your sentimentality. You'd spoil them to the man."

"My God!" Andre said in a hoarse whisper. "He's beaten them all!"

71

"Only ten lashes apiece," Hugo said. "I'm humane, Monsieur Le Blanc. Besides, your friend should be pleased that I take such excellent care of lands so soon to become his."

"Have you asked for an extension?" Stephen demanded.

"From you," Hugo said slowly, "nothing. I shall pay you the debt. I know you're short of cash. With thirty thousand in the land, and twenty thousand more in that warehouse with that thieving Tom Warren, you're plagued short."

"Ye're right," Stephen said evenly. "But it's entirely too much that ye know about my affairs."

"It's my business to know things," Hugo said. "And fast!"

I've heard that phrase before, Andre thought. Somebody said it, somebody else—in almost the same words—but who? Where?

"You've got to have this land to make a crop. Yours can never be cleared in time. And you've got to have Nigras. And you've got to sell whatever it is you have in that warehouse. It seems to me, Monsieur Fox, that you're in as bad a spot as I."

"That," said Stephen, "is my affair. All I ask of ye is that ye sell me some of your blacks."

"No," Hugo said quietly. "No."

Andre had got down from his horse and was bathing the face of an old Negro, who lay prostrate on the ground, with water another slave had brought from the spring.

Hugo climbed heavily from his horse.

"One moment, monsieur," he said politely. Then with slow deliberation, he kicked the old Negro in the ribs, not quite hard enough to break them.

"Get up," he said, "you old jackass!"

"You're a swine!" Andre said; "You're a dirty, German swine!"

"Softly, monsieur," Hugo said calmly. "'Twould be very convenient if you provoked me into a duel, wouldn't it? You know I have no skill with the rapier or the *clochemarde*. And people would never know that you were killing me so that Monsieur Fox could get my land and my Nigras."

Andre struck him then, hard across the face.

"Andre!" Stephen said.

72

"Don't worry," Hugo said calmly. "I shan't give him the pleasure of killing me."

"You may have pistols," Andre cried. "Or rifles, or shot guns! You're a good shot!"

"I don't want to kill you either, monsieur. You're a nice boy —although a little unwise in your choice of friends. Now may I suggest that you gentlemen cease delaying my planting? I'd like to be more hospitable; but time grows short."

"Come, Andre," Stephen said. "There is nothing we can do here."

"Swine," Andre half wept. "German swine!"

"The best breed there is. Such swine as will ultimately root up the whole world. *Adieu*, gentlemen!"

"Come, Andre," Stephen said. "Come."

IV

STEPHEN's knees felt uncommonly stiff kneeling in the pew at the St. Louis Cathedral. The mass that Père Antoine was reciting seemed unusually long, and Stephen was having difficulty following it. Half a dozen times he rose late, after most of the parishioners were already on their feet; several other times only the rustle of feminine garments warned him in time to kneel. At his side, Andre, wearing the serious expression that came to his handsome young face only in church of a Sunday, could not entirely repress a smile at his friend's flounderings.

Part of the trouble, Andre knew, was due to the fact that Stephen had not been to confession or mass in six or eight years; but the overwhelming cause of his inattention was kneeling devoutly just across the aisle, her slim fingers busy with her rosary. Truly, Andre was forced to admit, that Odalie, as he always thought of her, was a beautiful creature. Now as he stole a glance from time to time, he was conscious that her color was deepening. Yet she seemed quite unconscious of Stephen's increasingly long looks. I'll watch her eyes, Andre decided.

It was time now for the sermon. Père Antoine was mounting into the pulpit. Glad to ease knees aching from so much kneel-

74

ing, the worshippers sank gratefully into their seats. The old Spanish priest started his sermon in a powerful voice that captured Andre's wandering attention. Strange, how time changed a man. Strange to think that the dreaded Padre Antonio de Sedella—who had very nearly succeeded in bringing the Inquisition, with rack and wheel and brand and whip, into Louisiana— and this kindly, mellow old priest were one and the same man. . . .

He turned his head slightly to the left. Stephen was sitting tall and erect in his seat, his blue eyes caressing Odalie. Andre stared recklessly. Yes! This time he'd caught her! The black eyes had shifted for the tiniest part of a second. The glances had crossed in midair like épées! Now again, thrust and parry. She couldn't stop it now, Andre decided; she must look to see if Stephen was still watching, must be angered if he were, angered and pleased and strangely stirred, and more angered, disappointed and relieved, all at the same time, if he weren't.

Beyond her, Aurore too was watching this visual fencing, and her young face, angelic almost in its sweetness, was shadowed by an indefinable expression.

Beside Aurore, Pierre Arceneaux was snoring gently, his jutting chin resting on his bosom. In the pulpit, Père Antoine was justly condemning the follies and vanities of mankind. Pierre Arceneaux snored on. Odalie's and Stephen's glances clashed almost audibly in the incense-laden air. And Aurore's hazel eyes were clouded and troubled.

Then it was over. Père Antoine had descended the pulpit and knelt at the foot of the altar. The last Ave Maria had been said, and the parishioners blessed. They were filing out now, past the niches where the holy water was kept, having genuflected reverently toward the altar. Crossing themselves, they came out into the brilliant sunlight sweeping across the Place d'Armes into Chartres, where the Cathedral stood.

"I'm afraid that the blessings of Mother Church are not for me," Stephen said. "Never could my knees stand the kneeling."

"I'll wager that they're supple enough for the dance floor," Andre said.

"Ye're right," Stephen smiled. "The truth is there's still a sight too much of the devil in me yet. Praying won't get him out. I'll have to wear him out with deviltry."

"Then his case is hopeless. You even bring him into the church and set him up as one of your two patron saints."

"And the other?"

"Aphrodite. You're a thoroughgoing pagan, Stephen."

Stephen laughed aloud.

"Ye were watching me, then?"

"And the Arceneaux. The glacier begins to melt. I'm afraid I'm going to lose that thousand."

"Pay me in advance then; I could use the money to advantage."

"I'm sorry, Stephen," Andre said; "but I haven't got it. Dear papa . . ."

"Is in one of his disapproving moods?"

"Constantly and chronically of late. But if there is any other way, I'd be glad to help."

"Forget it. Look. Here come the two Graces now."

The green-and-gold carriage came abreast slowly, moving in a swarming tangle of vehicles. Andre and Stephen both removed their hats and bowed. Pierre Arceneaux saluted them gravely in return.

"You know that man, father?" Odalie demanded.

"Who doesn't? Monsieur Fox is one of the best known gentlemen of the city. I play *écarté* with him every Wednesday night."

"You gamble with an American?"

"Don't be old-fashioned, child. Stephen is quite a good fellow. Besides, I always win. Roget, stop the coach!"

"You're going to introduce him, father?" Aurore asked, and her voice was curiously soft.

"Yes, certainly. Do you both good to meet someone different. Monsieur Fox!"

"Father!" Odalie said sharply. "I don't wish . . ."

"Nonsense. Come here, gentlemen."

"Holy Mother of God!" Stephen said under his breath. The two of them walked over to the coach.

"I want you to meet my daughters," Pierre growled. "Odalie, Aurore—Monsieur Fox. You know Andre already."

"Too well," Andre murmured.

Stephen bowed.

"The hope of this honor," he said in perfect French, "has been the one thing sustaining my drab existence."

"Do you customarily go around staring at girls, sir?" Odalie asked boldly.

"Only when they're as beautiful as Mademoiselle," Stephen said. "Therefore I can truthfully say that I've never before stared at a woman."

"Odalie!" Aurore gasped.

"My daughters have no manners," Pierre chuckled. "They're just like me!"

Andre laughed.

"Your second, monsieur?" Odalie nodded toward Andre.

"In all things. And my very good friend."

"Oh, we know Andre very well—although of late we've wondered at his associations."

"Odalie!" Aurore said sharply. "Now you're being positively rude! Please forgive her, Monsieur Fox. She's had her way for so long that she forgets to be ladylike. Everybody spoils her—even I."

"Naturally," Stephen murmured. "How could they help it? But you, mademoiselle, does no one spoil you?"

"No one," Aurore said, and her voice was genuinely sad.

"An oversight which I shall attempt to remedy at my earliest opportunity," Andre declared. "Your permission, sir?"

"Permission? For what?" Arceneaux grunted.

"To call upon Aurore."

"Ask her. My girls have been reared very independently."

"May I, Aurore?"

"Of course, Andre. You've always been like a brother to me."

"I had imagined as much," Andre said sadly.

"And I, mademoiselle," Stephen asked Odalie. "Might I?"

"No. Later, perhaps. I shall have to know you much better. I should like to know what other accomplishment you have besides

77

staring at women and speaking French like a gilded youth of Paris." Odalie surveyed him calmly.

"Mademoiselle may have time for reconsideration," Stephen said; "but not too long." He bowed.

"You're both welcome at my house any time you choose to call," Arceneaux declared flatly.

"Thank you, sir," Stephen said quietly. "But ye'll forgive me if I don't avail myself of your courtesy until such time as I feel my welcome is both unanimous—and warm. Goodday, monsieur. Goodday, ladies. Your servant!"

"Now you've hurt his feelings!" Aurore complained as the coach moved off. "He'll never call now."

"Aurore," Odalie said. "I do believe you *like* the man!"

"I do. And so do you—so there!"

"Girls," Arceneaux said wearily. "No quarreling—please!"

"You were right, Stephen," Andre declared as the coach rolled away. "Never give in to that lovely witch or your life will be miserable. Well, what shall we do now?"

"I haven't the slightest idea. Have ye no suggestions?"

"Yes. Dinner at my house, then the animal fights at the Rotunda. Agreed?"

"I need diversion. Very well. But first I must have sleep. This early mass goes against the grain. 'Til three then?"

"Right. *Au'voir*, Stephen."

" *'Voir*," Stephen said, and strode away with his back very stiff and proud.

As soon as he and Andre reached the auction block the next afternoon, Stephen knew the bidding was lagging. The auctioneer wore a harassed look. He kept mopping his forehead with a large cotton handkerchief and looking out with disgust at the tiny crowd.

"Gentlemen, gentlemen, please!" he shouted. "I have here a

prime field hand, sound of wind and limb, capable of the hardest kind of labor! I ask you, gentlemen, what am I bid?"

"One hundred dollars," Tom Warren said calmly.

"Do I hear another bid? Gentlemen, do you realize what you're doing? Why this Nigra would bring twelve hundred in the poorest market in the state! Look at the muscles of his arms! Look at these teeth. Sound and unmarked. Why this Nigra could do anything, gentlemen, anything!"

"Right," a voice behind Stephen declared. "Even murder!"

Stephen and Andre both turned. The man hadn't taken any particular trouble to lower his voice, and several other bystanders laughed grimly.

"I say," Stephen demanded. "What did ye mean by that?"

"Don't you know, stranger? Everybody else does."

"No. What is wrong with the black? He looks all right to me."

"He is all right. There ain't nothing wrong with him 'ceptin' his mind."

"Is the black crazy?"

"Naw—not exactly. The truth is, stranger, the whole shootin' match of them was brung in from Santo Domingo. They've seen other Nigras kill white men and maybe they've kilt some theyself."

"I thought the importation of Saint Domingue blacks was forbidden," Andre declared.

"It is. But they was smuggled in. That Waguespack were a smart one."

The Kentuckian looked at Andre. "You parley frog, don't you, mister? Well, say sumpin to one of them Nigras."

"But all Louisiana blacks speak French."

"Not like them Bumboes. They speak *good* French—I l'arned hit a little when I furst come here and I know."

Andre strode boldly up to an old woman who was standing very quietly awaiting her turn on the block.

"Tante," he asked, "are you from Saint Domingue?"

"But yes, young master, it is that you want to buy me?"

Without answering, Andre turned and strode back to Stephen

"He's right!" he snapped. "They are Saint Domingue Negroes You'd better stop Tom from buying them!"

79

"No," Stephen said quietly. "No."

Tom Warren was walking forward now, approaching the auctioneer.

"Mister," he said, "you can see that you aren't going to make no sale here. Tell you what I'll do. I'll buy the entire lot off of you for five thousand."

"Five thousand! Are you crazy? Any three of them field hands there are worth that much!"

"Take it or leave it," Tom Warren said.

The auctioneer was looking rapidly, imploringly, from face to face. Every face stared back at him coldly, tight-lipped and grim.

"All right," he said weakly. "All right, I'll take it, but it's a shame, by the living Christ, it's a shame!"

Tom took out his purse and began to count out the money. Suddenly, Andre gripped Stephen's arm.

"Look who's just arrived!" he whispered.

Stephen turned.

There, turning into the square, was the green-and-gold coach of the Arceneaux. Stephen turned and walked over to the hitching rail where Prince Michael was tethered. Releasing him, he swung into the saddle. Andre was a step behind him.

"You aren't running away, are you, Stephen?" he demanded.

"No," Stephen said grimly. "But Miss Arceneaux has looked down on me for the last time. This time she is going to look up!"

He reined Prince Michael in sharply so that the palamino danced sidewise as he drew alongside the coach.

"Monsieur Fox," Pierre Arceneaux said. "Don't tell me you're buying Negroes!"

Stephen saluted the two girls, then turned at once to the old man.

"I'm afraid so, sir," he said. "I've just bought the whole lot."

"The whole lot," Odalie pouted. "What a shame!"

Pierre Arceneaux grinned wickedly.

"I had my eye on that mulatto wench of Waguespack's. Odalie wanted her for a personal maid."

"Then, mademoiselle, permit me to make you a present of her."

"That's quite out of the question, sir," Odalie said primly.

80

"You know quite well I couldn't accept such a present from a man!"

"I'll buy her from you, Stephen," the old man said.

"She's not for sale," Stephen said. Then a little twinkle stole into his eyes. "But I just might wager her against a thousand in our next little game, sir."

"Done!" Pierre Arceneaux declared. "Wednesday night at Maspero's."

"Right," Stephen said.

"What," Odalie asked, "does a gambler need with blacks?"

"Perhaps to gamble with, mademoiselle," Stephen said. But Tom Warren was riding up.

"Pardon me, ladies," he said. "Shall I take the Nigras out to your place, Mister Fox?"

"Yes," Stephen said. "But don't put them to work today. Let them rest. Let them kill a hog or two and eat their bellies full. Hugo didn't treat them any too kindly. They'll need time to recover."

"As you say, sir. Goodnight, ladies; goodnight, sirs."

The long line of Negroes filed past to the carts waiting across the square. As they passed, an old woman suddenly broke from the line and ran up to Stephen. She caught at his stirrup and looked up at him breathlessly.

"Maître," she cried. "Good maître! You good man, the good God bless you sho!"

"Thank you, Tante," Stephen said. "What do you call yourself?"

"Caleen," she said. "I will serve you well, master!"

"Very well, Tante Caleen; run along now with the others."

"You have a way with Negroes," Pierre Arceneaux declared. "That's good. They'll work well for you."

Aurore had stretched out a slim hand and was gently stroking Prince Michael's satiny coat.

"What a lovely horse," she said smiling. "I don't think I've ever seen one quite that color."

"They're rare," Stephen said. "I'm glad you like him, mademoiselle."

"So," a heavy voice said. "The grand Monsieur Fox on his elegant horse conversing with elegant ladies!"

Stephen only half turned.

"I'd thank ye to be more civil, Waguespack," he said coldly.

"Oh, I'll be civil, I'll be most civil," Hugo said. "I'll observe all the niceties necessary in the presence of a gentleman rogue."

"Ye're drunk," Stephen said. "I want no quarrel with you, Waguespack."

"Yes, I'm drunk. I'm verree drunk; but I'm not a fool! Think you I don't know it was your Tom Warren who spread that lying rumor about my slaves being from Santo Domingo!"

"I know nothing of that!" Stephen said. "And I must trouble ye to remember that there are ladies here."

"Ladies?" Hugo mumbled. "Ladies? Oh, yes, there are ladies in Louisiana, are there not? All beautiful and spirited. A trait no doubt inherited from their famed ancestors, the correction girls!"

Old Arceneaux's mouth came open with an explosive outrush of air. Andre, who was just at that moment riding up, took off one of his gloves and reined in toward Hugo. But Stephen stopped him with a lifted hand.

"One moment," he said calmly. "Our friend is doubtless guilty of a slip of the tongue. Ye meant casket girls, did ye not, Hugo?"

"Did I? Perhaps so. I am confused. 'Twas the manners and behavior of the belles of Louisiana that led to my error."

"Very well, Hugo," Stephen said wearily. "Ye win. I'll meet ye at any time and place ye see fit. Ye'll spare me the tiresome business of slapping your face, will ye not? My seconds will call on ye to arrange the details, *Au 'voir.*"

"'*Voir!*" Hugo grunted. "You'll make a very pretty corpse."

Stephen turned again to the carriage.

"Monsieur Fox," Arceneaux roared. "I demand the honor of seconding you!"

"And I also," Andre said quietly.

"Thank you, gentlemen," Stephen said, then to the girls who were sitting breathless and round-eyed on the edge of their seats, "Your forgiveness, ladies; this episode was not of my choosing."

Aurore suddenly stretched out her hand and laid it on Stephen's arm.

"Don't," she said. "Don't meet him!"

"Don't be silly," Odalie said sharply. "He has to meet him now!"

"But he might be killed!"

"Then," Stephen murmured, looking at Odalie, "the world will have lost a gambler, a blackguard, and an ogler of women." He swung Prince Michael in a circle and trotted off in the direction of home.

"I don't like this," Andre blurted. "I don't like it at all."

"Why not, Andre?" Odalie asked. "Monsieur Fox seems perfectly capable of taking care of himself."

"With a *rapier*, or *clochemarde*, or even a saber, yes. But I'll wager that Hugo will choose pistols and the fat swine is reputed to be a deadly shot, while Stephen . . ."

"Is a poor shot, Andre?" Aurore's voice was taut with concern.

"That's just it: I don't know. I never had occasion to find out. He may be a poor shot, or he may be an excellent one; but it's desperately late to be discovering it. Shall I meet you within the hour, sir? 'Tis a long ride to Waguespack's."

"Yes." Then lowering his voice to a whisper, he bent toward Andre's ear: "Think you we can arrange for the small swords? I like that red-headed devil!"

When Andre returned to Stephen's rooms, it was after midnight and Stephen was sleeping soundly. By the time he had awakened Georges, Stephen's manservant, and the two of them had shaken Stephen awake, Andre was in a thoroughly bad humor.

"Sleeping!" he cried, "*Mon Dieu!* While that swine Hugo plots how to kill you. He insists upon pistols, Stephen, and we could not dissuade him!"

"Why did ye try? No harm can come to me. I'll pink him a bit—a ball through the arm, or perhaps the knee cap to give him an illustrious limp, and that will be the end of it."

"But suppose it's you . . . ?"

"A chance I'll have to take. What is it, Georges?"

"It's a *Neg'Mericain* of Monsieur Warren with a message!"

"Send him in," Stephen said.

The Negro stumbled into the room, his black face glistening with sweat and his chest rising and falling in great animal-like pants.

"What is it?" Stephen said sharply. "What do ye want?"

"Mas Warren say come quick!" the Negro gasped. "Yo' warehouse done cotched fiah!"

Stephen was out of the bed in an instant, drawing on his trousers.

"Saddle Prince Michael," he said over his shoulder to Georges. "How is your horse, Andre?"

"Blown. I've done thirty miles today. Get along with you. I'll join you as soon as I can."

When Stephen came out of the doorway, Georges was already waiting with the horse. The sky toward the river was an angry orange red. Stephen could hear, as Prince Michael thundered through the dark streets, the brazen clangor of the bell in the Saint Louis Cathedral warning the sleeping city. The four clumsy engines from the Dépôt des Pompes at the Cabildo must already have reached the scene, he decided, and by now the fools would be fighting over which one got there first and won the fifty dollars!

He burst suddenly out of the gloom of the old city into the full glare of the fire. There was a great crowd milling about, trying to follow the directions of some twenty fire commissioners who were all waving their white truncheons and giving quite contradictory orders. A bucket brigade had been formed, and one of the four engines had actually gone into action—the oldest one of the lot—and its feeble stream, sent up by a hand-operated pump worked by four strong men, curved to earth yards short of the burning building.

There was a compact crowd of men near the front of the warehouse, and Stephen could see Tom Warren towering over all the rest. He reined Prince Michael in and dismounted, striding over to the little group.

"Well, Tom?" he said.

"It was set, Mr. Fox," Warren said heavily. "Deliberately and maliciously set. This here Nigra . . ."

Stephen followed the pointing finger downward. The Negro was stretched out at Tom Warren's feet. Half a glance told Stephen he was quite dead.

"Ye shot him?"

"Yes. He was coming out of the warehouse with the torch in his hand."

"I gave ye credit for more head, Tom. Now we will never know who sent him."

"There were another one," one of the other men put in. "He run out jest afore this one come out. I seed him."

Tom Warren turned toward the speaker and his little eyes held for a second.

"No," he said coldly. "You're mistaken. There was only one."

"I coulda sworn—" the man began doubtfully.

" 'Tis of no importance," Stephen said. "The question is, who sent him?"

"Thas right," the man declared. " 'Tain't likely the nigger burnt yore warehouse for his own amusement."

Stephen started to speak, but the sound of hoofs pounding through the street behind him caused him to turn. Andre dashed up to the group as fast as the ancient nag he'd rented from a public stable could bring him. He swung down from the saddle before the horse had stopped moving, lost his balance and fell to his hands and knees a scant yard from the dead Negro. He did not get up at once, but crouched there looking from the body to the burnt-out torch that lay inches from the outstretched fingers of the dead man's hand. Then, slowly, he straightened.

"I think," he said clearly, "that you need not be lenient tomorrow, Stephen."

"But we have no proof," Stephen said.

"Who else could it be?" Tom Warren asked.

"Who else?" Stephen echoed, and turned his face toward the flames that were billowing upward, pushing the night back, bloodying the sky.

Under the oaks in the morning, it was cool and green. The sun was struggling with the mist, and everything was touched with unclarity, like figures in a dream landscape. Hugo took the pistol from Jacques Fabre, who had started life as Jacob Weber, and squinted along the barrel.

"A good piece," he grunted. "'Twill throw true. I will try to leave your visible parts unmarked, sir, so that your elegant ladies can kiss you goodbye without horror."

"Thank you," Stephen said, and walked very slowly to the marked place.

"You know the terms, gentlemen," Doctor Lefevre said. "You're to fire one shot each at the count of three. If neither of you is hit, you may reload and fire again, or you may choose the wiser course and consider yourselves satisfied. Are you ready, gentlemen?"

"Yes!" Hugo said, "Yes!"

"Yes," Stephen said very quietly.

"One!" Doctor Lefevre said; and Hugo jerked his pistol level, aiming carefully. Stephen left his pointing earthward, dangling at his side. *Mon Dieu!* Andre and Arceneaux said in the same breath. "Why doesn't he . . ."

"Two!" Stephen's pistol remained unmoved. Hugo pulled the hammer further back with a click that to Andre seemed loud as a shot.

"Thr—" Doctor Lefevre began, but the rest of the word was lost in the crack of Hugo's pistol. The whole world was suddenly a sick dizziness to Andre, but when it cleared, Stephen was still standing there, swaying a little, but inch by inch, with deliberate, terrifying slowness, his pistol came level, pointing at Hugo.

It was still in the clearing under the oaks. A single leaf that had clung all winter long to its naked branch dropped down and brushed Andre's cheek. He jumped at the touch. Still Stephen did not fire.

The little beads of moisture began collecting on Hugo's forehead and running down into the corners of his loose, flabby lips. He stood there unmoving until at least the morning damp of the earth stole up his legs and into his spine. Then the shivering started, the whole gigantic fatty mass that was Hugo's body trembling all over so that even Stephen, thirty yards away, could see it through the drifting smoke and the haze and the red curtain closing down over his left eye where Hugo's ball had ploughed along his temple and laid open his scalp.

There were three things he could do, Stephen decided without haste. He could point the muzzle of the dueling pistol skyward and spare Hugo with a grand gesture. But such opera bouffe theatricality was French and he would have none of it. Or he could fire his shot straight downward into the earth and give Hugo back his miserable existence with abysmal contempt; but that, too, was a gesture and Stephen despised all gestures. Or he could deliberately miss Hugo, throwing so close that the quivering hulk of nerves would carry with him always, branded on his brain, the whistle of the passing ball.

So it was, that at the exact moment when Andre, unable to contain himself longer cried out:

"For God's sake, man, fire!" that Stephen carelessly, without seeming to take aim, pulled the trigger, the muzzle pointed slightly to the left, far enough to miss Hugo as he now stood, but not far enough to miss the huge hulk as Hugo threw himself downward and to the left to avoid the anticipated path of the ball. Then the big man was hanging there, like an oak does when it is cut almost through but cannot yet yield to the ax, and fall. He opened his mouth to say something, but the blood gurgled up through his throat and he went over backward against the earth, his head making exactly the same sound as a log would have, striking the ground.

Doctor Lefevre knelt briefly.

"I think, gentlemen," he said as he rose, "that the less said about this affair the better—considering the unusual features of the occasion."

"What do ye mean?" Stephen asked coldly.

"The length of time between shots," the doctor said. "The abundant opportunity you had to spare this man's life with honor—to wound him slightly, or to let him go free. I came to see a duel, not an execution!"

"You'll take that back!" Andre cried. "Or I'll demand satisfaction."

"Softly, Andre," Stephen said. "There has been enough blood letting for one day. The good doctor is entitled to his opinion. And now, sir, if I may trouble ye to staunch this scratch, I have work to do."

V

Minna Waguespack sat huddled up before the fire weeping. Outside, it was raining—a hard, steady downpour, slanting down across the windows. Now and again a gust of wind caught itself in the rain and whipped it against the windows in a lacy spray and all the shutters banged. But most of the time it was silent— a vast, echoing silence into which the rain fell sullenly, and in which the slow drip of the water through the leaky roof, and the occasional whimper of a hungry child was lost, unheard. Minna cried soundlessly without change of face or expression. The rain kept up its slow, unceasing whispering. And the ancient door groaned on its one remaining hinge until at last the wind slammed it shut.

It was one of the smaller children who first heard the clop of the horse's hoofs in the muddy courtyard. She jumped from her place at the corner and ran screaming to her mother. Minna held her close against her ample bosom, feeling the pounding of the tiny heart under the thin ribs.

"Hush!" she whispered. "Sit still!"

She sat there holding the child, staring at the door. The other three children huddled around her, and the smaller ones began to sob aloud.

Pray God he's not drunk, Minna thought.

But the footsteps that clumped down from the horse and strode slowly, painfully almost, across the gallery were lighter than the heavy boots of Hugo, and when the light, almost gentle knocking came through the door, Minna released the child with a sigh.

"Who is it?" she called.

"Herr Fox," the clear baritone answered. "Let me come in!"

Minna sprang to the door and threw it open. Stephen stood swaying in the doorway, his face drained of all color, hatless, with the water streaming down from his tangled coppery hair across a sodden bandage. Where the water had touched the bandage, it was tinged with crimson, creeping along the line of Stephen's jaw.

"*Ach Gott!*" Minna cried. "You're hurt!"

"A scratch," Stephen said. His eyes sought and held hers. "Your husband, Minna—is dead. I've killed him."

The blue eyes widened endlessly. The rain blew down the chimney and hissed into the fire.

"Dead," Minna whispered. "Dead."

"Yes," Stephen said awkwardly. "There was a duel. I—I tried not to hit him but he moved. If there is anything . . ."

But Minna was looking at him closely.

"You're hurt," she said. "Bad hurt. Sit yourself down while I for you hot rum punch make. Otto! Bring you here a chair."

"But you don't understand, Minna. Hugo is dead. I've killed him!"

"I understand. You have Hugo shot. He is dead."

"Don't you—don't you care?"

"Yes. Hugo I loved. Very much I loved him. He was hard, and sometimes he a beast was, but he was also a man. But this thing I for a long time expected have. If not you, then someone else. Always with the men he was quarreling. What happens, happens. For this thing I am sorry. And most of all am I sorry that it had to be you."

"Minna," Stephen said, "I haven't much money left, but what I have is yours. Ye can stay here if ye will or I will give ye a

90

note for this place, payable out of the first crop I make. And the children, for them I'll send ye money as long as I live."

"You're good. . . . But no, it is too much. Pay for me and the children the passage to Philadelphia. I have there an uncle who me in his business wants. He runs there a bakery. He long ago told me not to marry Hugo, but I young was, and a fool."

Stephen sipped the fiery liquor, feeling its warmth curling somewhere deep in his middle and the strength flowing back.

"When wish ye to go, Minna?" he asked.

"Tomorrow! There is nothing to do—we have nothing to pack."

"Then I'll send a coach for ye," Stephen said rising. In the doorway, he paused. "I have your forgiveness, Minna?"

"Yes," she said. "Go with God!"

By the time that Stephen got back to Harrow, after leaving Minna and her brood, the warmth had left him and he was shaking with weakness and the chill. Tom Warren was waiting, surrounded by a huddle of wet, thoroughly miserable Negroes, shivering in their ragged clothing.

He pointed to a row of open-faced lean-to's, from which blue wood smoke was rising, only to be beaten back to earth by the rain.

"That's the best I could do as yet, sir," he said. "What with the rain and all."

" 'Twill have to do, Tom," Stephen said wearily. And then with a wry smile: "Which one is mine?"

"God forbid!" Warren declared. "You're coming back to town with me. Why, in your condition 'twould mean your death!"

"I'll chance it, Tom," Stephen said. " 'Tis too late, and there's too much to be done. But I have a commission for ye. Hire a coach and bring it to Waguespack's place by eleven tomorrow morning. And book passage on a steamer for Minna and the children. Give them a thousand to tide them over. I'm paying them for the place."

"You're over kind, Mister Fox. Seems to me that Waguespack's children are no concern of yours. After all, you held his note . . ."

"Please do as I ask," Stephen said sharply. "Bring Jacques

91

Fabre along to draw up and witness the papers. They'll have to be done in German and French and Fabre knows both."

"All right, sir, but I protest. You're being unwise. Your debts now are upward of fifty thousand and your assets practically nil. I've held aside enough to pay for whatever machinery you'll need and added a bit of my own . . ."

"Thank ye, Tom. I shall not fail ye."

"You'll need an overseer for the Nigras."

"Not yet. I'll do my own driving. But get along with ye, Tom; it grows late."

"As you say, sir. But try to keep warm and dry. I'll bring Doctor Lefevre . . ."

"No. I need no damned sawbones! Now will ye go!"

Tom Warren touched his hand to the brim of his hat and, mounting his horse, trotted away in the direction of New Orleans.

Stephen stood there in the pouring rain and looked over his land. It came to him then that never in all his life had he seen a more dismal sight. The slate-gray sky clamped down like a lid no higher than the tops of the oaks, and the palmettos, waving their fingers in the wind, seemed a thousand hands lifted in derision and accusation. From the Negroes around him came something like a moan, half whispered so that he felt it as much as he heard it.

"Get ye inside," he said harshly. "And warm yourselves!"

"*Mo ganye faim,*" an old black wailed. "I'm hongry!"

"And ye'll stay so till morning," Stephen told him. "Now inside with ye, at once!"

He bent his head and entered one of the lean-tos. A smoky fire burned fitfully at the entrance, struggling bravely with the damp wood. He lay his cloak down upon the wet earth, and stretched out beside the fire, his head throbbing like all the hammers of hell, and his stomach sick to nausea with hunger and weakness. He closed his eyes, but opened them almost at once. From outside there had come a faint whimper. Looking out, he could see the mulatto girl that Odalie had wanted to buy and old Tante Caleen. They were soaked to the skin and shivering all over. This was the lean-to that had been built for them.

"Come in," he said. "Don't stand there like a pair of dolts! Ye're no good to me dead of lung fever!"

The girl looked at Caleen timidly. The old woman nodded. Then the two of them came in past the fire, almost extinguishing it with the water from their garments.

The old woman searched in the back of the lean-to until she had found a few twigs, but they were too few and too damp. So she got up without a word and went back out into the rain. Stephen saw her disappearing into the gloom of the gigantic oaks. She was gone almost a half hour, but when she came back, her arm was full of twigs and fagots that were comparatively dry. She had dug them out from under the overhanging branches and roots which had sheltered them from the rain.

In a little while, she had the fire blazing merrily, so that Stephen could feel the stiffness and the cold stealing out of his limbs. The lean-to was filled with the smell of steaming clothing. In one corner, the mulatto girl sat with her head buried against her knees and wept. Stephen paid her not the slightest attention. He was watching the old woman.

One of her black, spidery hands went down among the folds of her garments and came out with a knife. With it she sharpened a stick into a point. Then again she was gone, out into the rain that was lessening now into a cold, miserable drizzle. Stephen put his aching head again against the collar of his cloak.

Tante Caleen was a long time coming back this time—more than an hour, Stephen guessed. She walked in a stooped-over position, holding her apron up with one hand. It seemed to be filled with something. In the other, she held a small iron pot she had brought from the supply wagon. Bending down, she placed the pot on the fire. Stephen could see that it was half filled with water. Then she loosed the tail of her apron, and several dozen crayfish dropped into the pot. Also into the pot went salt brought from one of the wagons and wild sassafras leaves and wild pepper. Then the old woman sat back contentedly and waited for the pot to boil.

When it was done, she took out a crayfish, broke off the head and sucked the meat from the shell, nodding her head to Stephen

93

to indicate that this was how it was to be done. Then she pointed at the pot.

"Eat, master," she said. "It is good."

Stephen sat up and followed her example. He found the meat amazingly good and well-seasoned. He kept up his eating until he noticed that the mulatto girl was regarding him with big, round eyes.

"Sorry," he grinned. "Have some. And ye, Tante Caleen."

He felt immensely better almost at once. Only the slow, dull throbbing of his head remained to remind him of the events of the day. He stretched himself out on his cloak and slept.

When he awakened, it was to find his head being bathed very gently with a warm, soothing liquid. Tante Caleen then took a strip of cloth, torn from one of her petticoats, and bound up the wound, pressing an odd sort of leaf inside the bandage against Stephen's torn flesh. Stephen could feel it drawing out the inflammation and the fever. He felt stronger.

"Thank ye, Tante," he said. "Ye're the best of the lot!"

Outside the lean-to, the rain had stopped.

He looked out of the opening and saw that the sun was already up, over the river. He got up, and called all the Negroes together.

"We must work hard," he said. "Nobody is to be beaten. Ye obey my orders promptly and all will go well. If not, I'll sell ye back to the Germans." Then he sent a Negro to the supply wagons to bring back a sack of corn meal, and put Tante Caleen and the other women to work, making corn bread. The children he sent to dig crayfish from their castlelike mounds near the river. When they had gathered a plentiful supply, Tante Caleen and two other women put them to boil in a huge iron pot. In an amazingly short time the flat slabs of corn bread were done, sooty and covered with ashes, to be sure, for they had been baked on flat stones thrust into the fire. Then they were passed out to the slaves, who crowded around the pot, blowing on their bread and shifting it from hand to hand, and scalding their fingers as they scooped up the crayfish.

Stephen sat on a fallen log, a little apart from his people, and Tante Caleen brought him his breakfast. It was exactly the same as the others—ash-filled corn bread and crayfish. When the Negroes had eaten, Stephen stood up again.

"Ye men," he said. "Go to the wagons and get axes. Start in here, next to the river, and clear the land in squares. Ye understand me?"

Some of the Negroes nodded, but others looked blank, so Stephen repeated his orders in French. Then they filed away, toward the wagons and the ox carts, and stood there in line while a gigantic black passed out the axes and saws.

"They've been well-disciplined," Stephen decided. "And that big one, he has the makings of a leader. Ye there!" he called. "Come here!"

The big Negro ambled over, looking down upon the white bandaged head of his master.

"What are ye called?" Stephen demanded.

"Achille, master," the Negro replied.

"Well, Achille, ye're captain here. When I'm away, ye're to see that the work goes forward. There must be no laziness and no shirking. Take these men and clear away the palmetto first. Afterwards ye may start on the trees."

"Thank you, master," Achille smiled. Then he turned fiercely to the others: "I'm the captain!" he growled. "You work good for me, yes!"

The others looked at him and grinned; but almost at once the air began to ring with the sound of the axes and scythes.

"Ye others," Stephen said. "Come with me to your old place."

Instantly the Negroes set up a loud wailing and huddled together.

"Don't fear," Stephen said. "Waguespack will never beat ye again. Come now—off with ye!"

They walked behind the horse single file, chatting among themselves in the gumbo patois of the islands, but Stephen rode silently, his head bowed in thought.

When he rounded the bend in the road, he saw the coach already drawn up before the door, and on the gallery Tom Warren and Jacques Fabre waited. Fabre's round face was drawn up in as grim lines of disapproval as a man of his naturally jovial nature could muster, and his pudgy hands toyed nervously with the end of a sword cane he had prudently brought along.

Stephen swung stiffly down from Prince Michael, who was sadly in need of grooming. Stephen, too, was rumpled and unpressed, and two days' growth of fiery whiskers mottled his fair skin.

"Good day, gentlemen," he said. "Is everything ready?"

Jacques cleared his throat.

"I'm not quite clear," he said in his stiff, Teutonic French, "exactly what the nature is of the services you require of me."

"Business," Stephen said. "I will render a document in French and then again in German. Ye will write it for me, Jacques, and ye and Tom will witness it. Whereas . . ." he began.

The pudgy fingers flew over the paper. As he wrote, the lines began to disappear from Jacques' fat face. Suddenly he threw down his pen and stretched forth his hand.

"Sir," he started, "may I have the honor of calling you my friend? This generosity—this largeness of heart and soul—this . . ."

"Easy, Jacob," Stephen said. "'Tis no more than I ought. And I shall be glad to count ye as a friend. I have all too few."

"'Tis only because they do not know—" Jacques began, but from the door there came the sound of knocking. Stephen, who was nearest, got up and opened it. He fell back a step and bowed.

In the doorway, Aurore Arceneaux stood, trim in a deep green riding habit, her hazel eyes widening as she looked at Stephen.

"I hardly expected to find you here!" she said. Then she turned to where Minna sat dressed for traveling, with her bags and children gathered around her.

"So," she said. "Not only do you kill the father, but you dispossess the wife and the little ones!" Her eyes clouded suddenly and she swung toward Minna. "You poor dear!" she said, and turned again to face Stephen, the great tears caught like diamonds in her long lashes; "Oh, Monsieur Fox," she wept. "I never thought, I refused to believe . . ." Then as he stretched out his hand to touch her shoulder: "Don't touch me!"

Minna sat very still her blue eyes wide with incomprehension. Tom Warren frowned, looking at Stephen; then, very clearly in the silence, in his queer, Germanic French, Jacques Fabre began to read the document. Aurore stood very still, listening. Only her eyes were alive, smoldering back of her long lashes. Then the affected voice lisped into silence, she walked up to Stephen.

"Forgive me," she whispered. "I knew all the time that you couldn't—that never could someone like you— Oh, I listened to Odalie and the others calling you 'the executioner' and 'black-hearted Stephen' until I was half out of my mind . . ."

Stephen was looking past her out of the half opened door.

"Why does Odalie hate me so?" he said at last.

"Because she loves you," Aurore said, and her voice was very small and soft. "Because you aren't a thing to be whipped around her little finger, but a man. Because if ever once she let herself go . . . Please express my heartfelt sympathies to Madame Waguespack. I understand she doesn't speak French, and I have no German. Good day, gentlemen—and please forgive my outburst."

"There's nothing to forgive," Stephen said. "If ye can wait, these gentlemen are riding into town . . ."

"No," Aurore said; "I should have been back hours ago! *Au revoir.*"

VI

RIDING out to Harrow, early in the summer, Andre felt that the sky was dropping down over his head. The heat came up from the road in simmering waves, and the horse's coat was glistening with sweat. Up above, the sky was high and cloudless, coming over the tops of the oaks like an inverted bowl of steely blue, so clear and far that it was almost colorless, the blue washed out by the avalanche of sun. The spanish moss trailing from the oaks was dry as hay, bleached white by the heat.

"*Mon Dieu,*" Andre murmured, "what heat!"

He wondered idly if Stephen were angry with him. Not since the day of the duel had he and Stephen met. He shrugged his shoulders listlessly. He must chance Stephen's anger, that was all.

Farther on, the branches of the oaks came down very low and close over the road. In the shadow it was cooler. An arm of one of the lesser bayous came up close to the road. The water was black and fetid. On it a small *piroque* drifted. Andre could see the Acadian boatman lying in the boat, his straw hat pulled down over his face, fast asleep.

"These 'Cadians!" Andre grinned. "They have no love for work."

The road was curving now, and Andre could recognize the place despite the blasting it had taken from the heat. This was the beginning of Harrow, though it was yet two miles to the grove in which Stephen intended that his manor house should stand. Andre kept on slowly, not daring to urge the horse to greater speed on such a day.

Then at last, the fields were coming into sight. Andre pulled up his horse with a gasp. Stephen had nearly half of the visible acreage cleared and under cultivation! But now there was no sound of axes in the woodlands, although mounds of cordwood lay stacked high all the way down to a freshly built steamboat landing. The lean-tos that Andre had heard about from Tom Warren were gone, and long rows of cabins made of slashed cypress board housed the slaves. Under the stately oaks, Andre could see a rude oaken house, larger than the others, but just as crude.

"So," he said to himself, "so this is Harrow!"

He rode on past the house and out into the fields. Under the glare of the sun he saw a little black knot of figures moving up and down the rows. He rode toward them, skirting the rows of cane. As he came close, he saw that one of the figures was white, the hands and arms covered with freckles.

"Mon Dieu!" he said. "So it's true!"

"Andre! I thought ye were sick or dead!"

"But no! Stephen, Stephen! What on earth—*Ma foi*, how terrible you look!"

Stephen grinned, the great scar on his temple glowing scarlet, angling upward into his red hair. It gave him a curiously diabolical look, twisting his whole face into a mocking Mephistophelian cast. Above his fair brows, which the sun had bleached almost white, the skin of his forehead was peeling off in angry red strips. He pushed back his wide-brimmed straw hat like the ones the Cajuns wore and laughed aloud.

"What are they saying about me in New Orleans?" he asked.

Andre said slowly, "They no longer blame you for the duel; they have discovered you are mad."

"Mad!" Stephen said, and his laughter rocketed skyward. "'Tis late they are in discovering it, don't ye think? I knew it all the time!"

"'Tis no joke, Stephen. They say you live in a hovel, and work in the fields with the blacks. And that sometimes at night you work all night alone, after the blacks have finished for the day."

"And for that I am considered mad? Listen, Andre, I owe more than seventy thousand dollars for the land and supplies and machinery. I have machinery coming down the river from Cincinnati this minute. When it comes, I shall have to pay the steamboat captain five thousand dollars. But, thanks to all the saints, I have that now."

"How? Does money grow on the trees at Harrow?"

"No—but it comes from trees. Ye've seen my landing? And the stacks of cordwood?"

Andre nodded.

"Practically every other steamboat on the river stops here for fuel. By the end of the summer I'll have sold seven thousand dollars' worth of wood. And the supply, my good Andre, is practically inexhaustible. But ye, where have ye been hiding? Or are ye among those who think me mad?"

"No, Stephen, 'tis not that. Papa forbade me your company at first, but the storm has settled now. But even that could not have kept me. The truth is, I've been spending the summer in vain pursuit of Aurore. Even Papa approves. In fact, everybody approves—except Aurore."

"Poor fellow," Stephen said. "Come, let us go up to the house for a drink. By the way, how is Odalie?"

"Still running ahead of the pack, if it is any comfort to you. Rumor has linked her name to half a dozen beaux, but as usual it came to nothing. You know, Stephen, I think she's waiting for you. Twice now, she has asked after you. Says you're the most interesting man she's ever met."

"I understand," Stephen said, "that it was she who coined that 'black-hearted' phrase."

"I wouldn't doubt it. You irritated her no end by not falling at her feet like so many others. Why don't you take a day and come in to see her?"

"Too busy," Stephen grunted. "Ye may tell Mademoiselle Odalie for me that if she wishes to see me, she knows the way to Harrow."

"I'll do just that," Andre grinned. "If only for the pleasure of seeing her fly into a rage. But what on earth is that?"

He pointed to a new building standing almost completed some distance behind the house. It was of fresh red brick, and gleamed brightly in the afternoon sunshine.

"The sugar house," Stephen said. "'Tis waiting only for the machinery that I ordered. I'm having steam crushers, Andre."

"And what became of the machinery you got with the Waguespack place?" Andre demanded.

"Five stone crushers driven by mule power. A stone millwheel revolved in a circular stone trough by an ancient mule walking around and around. Ye gods, Andre, what could I do with that?"

"Steam. You're very modern, Stephen."

"Monsieur Coiron has had it since '22. All the bigger planters are putting it in. But here we are—up with ye, lad. I'll have Georges bring us wine up from the spring."

They sat in the bare-boarded room. The sun poked fingers of light through the cracks, and the shuttered windows were without glass or screens. Andre sipped the cool wine and looked at his friend. Stephen's face was freckled more than ever from the sun, and here and there were the broken blisters of sunburn. The lines about the eyes were deeper, and the whole face seemed older somehow, older and quieter and more certain.

"You've changed, Stephen," Andre said.

"Time and hard work . . ." Stephen said. "This year and the next, Andre—by then I will have made it—or I will have failed. Now at the moment I'm not sure I care."

Andre rose.

"You won't fail, Stephen. Whether what you'll win is worth the struggle, I don't know; but you won't fail." He walked to the doorway. "I must be going now," he said. Then he paused, grinning wickedly. "I'll deliver that message," he said.

One day fused into the next, so much the same that Stephen lost all track of time. The steaming, tropical rains fell and wet the earth. An hour later the sun was out and the water rose up from the earth leaving it parched and baked. In the bayous the alligators sunned themselves. The cypress stood in the black water and the frogs sang basso choruses. All night the insects made sleep a living hell.

But the cane grew, and the cotton that Stephen had planted on some of his newly cleared back lands. The machinery had come from Cincinnati, and a mechanic had set it up in the sugar house. All the kettles had been set up and were ready. In the cooling room, the tanks were completed, and the big wooden paddles were already cut waiting for the Negroes to pick them up and start stirring the syrup until it crystalized.

Stephen worked in the fields like a Negro and wondered if Andre had delivered his message. The cane grew tall in the fields and bowed all together to every passing wind. The cotton fields were white with bursting pods. All day and far into the night the Negroes picked, piling up the cotton in bales by the steamboat landing. Only the rice crop failed, for lack of sufficient water.

Then it was Fall and almost time for harvesting the cane. The heat was moderating, and the work lessened. Stephen rode through the fields, next to the road, on Prince Michael. He was hatless, and his shirt was open half way to the waist. The breeze up from the river blew across his face and stirred his coppery hair. He pulled Prince Michael to a stop and looked out over the expanse of his fields. *His* fields! the cotton crop had brought in nineteen thousand dollars. And when the sugar was sold . . .

He stiffened suddenly, listening. From the roadway came the unmistakable sound of hoofbeats. He stood up in the stirrups and turned. A horse was coming up the road, and as it neared,

102

Stephen could see that the rider was riding side saddle. Now the horse was almost upon him—a sleek black mare, beautifully groomed. But Stephen was looking at the rider and his blue eyes were very pale and bright in his sun-whipped face.

"Odalie!" he said.

"Yes, monsieur. The mountain is come to Mohammed. I got your message, months ago . . . so at last I decided to accept. Aren't you glad to see me?"

"Immensely," Stephen said. "I'm flattered and honored."

"You needn't be. Perhaps I came to see the mad planter who holds one of the largest and richest plantations in Louisiana and yet lives in a shack."

Stephen was looking at her, watching the sun touch the midnight masses of hair with golden highlights, watching the eyes into which all light seemed to have passed and drowned, leaving only a flicker now and then to break the surface. Odalie had skin as fair as a Scandinavian's, against which the heavy waves of gleaming jet broke with double force. Watching her mouth moving, the lips not pink, but red—wine-red and petal-soft—Stephen was lost so that the mockery passed by him unheard.

"So," she said, and a little huskiness crept into her voice, "you still stare."

"At ye, yes!" Stephen said.

"Come, show me the place. Andre has told me all about it. I want to see your shack, next to your magnificent sugar house."

"Ye're insolent," Stephen said. "Ye'll need a check rein and a strong hand on the whip. What if someone saw ye here like this?"

"But no one did, monsieur—nor will they. You have no need to trouble yourself about *my* reputation. Is this the road to your manor?"

"Yes. Have ye no fear of a madman?"

"None. Are you going to show me your place?"

"Yes," Stephen said. "This way, mademoiselle."

They rode through the waving sea of cane toward the rude house in the grove. As they neared it, Odalie reined in her horse,

103

looking from the rough planking to the smooth pink outlines of the sugar house that stood behind it at a distance.

"*Mon Dieu!*" she said at last. "You *are* mad!"

"Ye doubted it?" Stephen said.

"Yes. Aurore told me what you did for Minna Waguespack. Every one doubted that story. But I didn't. Aurore doesn't lie."

"Yet no one believed her," Stephen said, one corner of his mouth curving upward into a smile.

"They doubted her credulity, not her honesty. They said you duped her. After all, you do have a certain charm."

"Thank ye," Stephen said. "And now may I show ye my steamboat landing?"

They turned their horses toward the river. As they approached the road that paralleled it, Odalie stiffened suddenly, drawing her horse to a stop.

"What ails ye?" Stephen demanded.

"I hear a coach," she said.

Stephen sat very still listening.

"Ye're right," he said. "Into that cypress grove, there. Quickly!"

They moved forward at a trot, but just before they reached the shelter of the trees, the coach rounded the bend in the road so that to its occupants the horses were clearly visible. They both leaned forward at the same instant, urging the horses into a gallop. Then they were gone, into the thick tangle of the underbrush.

"Sacred Mother of God!" Odalie whispered.

"Think ye they saw us?" Stephen asked.

"I don't know. But I know one thing. That was the Cloutier's coach—and Aurore was in it!"

"Ye saw her?"

"No. But she's visiting them. They're probably taking her out to their place."

"So now ye're compromised," Stephen grinned. "What say ye to that?"

"My father will probably kill you," Odalie said. "Or worse still, he might insist upon your marrying me."

"Is that so terrible?" Stephen demanded.

104

"To live in these wilds—in a shack—with a madman? I'd hang myself first!"

Stephen touched Prince Michael lightly so that he moved in very quickly with a dancing step. Odalie was very close beside him—so close he could smell the perfume in her hair. Then abruptly he leaned down and swept one arm around her shoulders holding her hard against him.

She looked up at him, her eyes very wide and very black, so that looking into them was like gazing into primordial night before light was. Stephen kissed her then, twisting his mouth cruelly against hers, bending her backward so that her little hat fell off and lay among the palmettoes unnoticed. He could feel the soft roundness of her breasts, lifted high by the whale-bone stays, and through them, the quick fluttering of her pulse, like captive wings.

Her hands were against his chest, pushing hard. He released her quite suddenly, seeing the light dancing in her black eyes and the corners of her mouth trembling.

"You—you—" she began.

"Blackguard" Stephen suggested. "Executioner?"

"No," she said, "I don't know the word. But now I know I'd better be going."

Stephen grinned, the scar standing out like a scarlet brand.

"Ye will make a fine mistress for Harrow," he said. "Ye have spirit. I like that in my horses—and my women. *Au 'voir.*"

Odalie half rose from the side saddle, and struck out with her crop, swinging it sidewise with all her force. It caught Stephen high on the side of his face, crisscrossing the scar left by Hugo's bullet.

"Ye little witch!" Stephen said very softly, as he watched the black mare swinging around the curve, out of sight. . . .

The coach of the Cloutier family was approaching the gates of Rosemont plantation.

"I still say that was a woman with that wild Stephen Fox," Henriette Cloutier persisted. "A man wouldn't ride side saddle!"

105

"But no decent woman would do a thing like that," Clothilde Cloutier said. "And none of the other kind have horses—so there!"

"What do you think, Aurore?" Henriette demanded.

"I think," Aurore said slowly, "that I have a terrible headache, and that we shouldn't discuss things that don't concern us."

"You poor dear," Clothilde said. "Why you're as white as a sheet!"

"Tante Suzette will fix that as soon as we get there," Henriette said shortly. "But it was a woman, wasn't it, Aurore? You saw her first!"

"Yes," Aurore said softly. "Yes, it was a woman."

Tante Caleen was waiting for Stephen when he rode in, her wide nostrils lifted to the air.

"Maître shouldn't ride through the brush," she said severely. "You have now a mark on your face!"

"Damn!" Stephen said without heat. "Ye're a bossy old devil, Caleen. I sometimes wonder if I own ye, or ye own me."

"We own each other," Tante Caleen said calmly. She lifted her face skyward again and sniffed the air.

"I smells wind," she said, "big wind. The grand tempest come from the islands."

"Ye're crazy," Stephen laughed. "We don't have tropical storms this time of year!"

"The grand tempest!" Tante Caleen repeated stubbornly, "the very great storm!"

Stephen eyed her narrowly. Tante Caleen was seldom wrong. Her knowledge of the weather was positively uncanny.

"How long?" he asked.

"Two, three day, but she come!"

Again Stephen stood up in the stirrups.

"Achille!" he roared.

The big Negro came running through the cane, his eyes wide. "Yes, Maître?" he said. "Yes?"

"Get the cane knives out. And the wagons! We're harvesting now."

"But maître—it is now too soon—the stalks they is not yet so high . . ."

"Do as I tell you, Achille!"

"Yes, maître!"

In half an hour all the Negroes were busy, working down the rows, the cane falling before them. The wagons moved in and out of the fields, hauling the cane to the sugar house, from whose tall chimney the black wood smoke was billowing. There the sweating Negroes placed the cane on racks, watching with awe as it was whirled up and crushed by the rollers. The juice ran down the pipes into the kettles, going first into *le grand* where it was boiled until it began to thicken. Then other Negroes, especially trained for the work, dipped it out with buckets swung on long poles set in rowlocks, into *le prop*, then into *le flambeau*, then into *le sirop*, and last of all into the small, fiercely hot *la batterie*.

Stephen watched them pushing *la cuite*, the thickened syrup already beginning to crystalize, into the cooling room or purgery. There the slaves diluted it with vinegar and lemon juice, pouring it into vats where the fat Negroes stirred it with the paddles until it crystalized. The hogsheads began to pile up in the cone drip line, where they were suspended to let the molasses drip out into the vats below.

Three days later, the cane was all in. And almost to the minute, just as the wagons were dumping the last of the crushed cane stalks, called *bagasse*, into the river, the black clouds came massing in from over the gulf and the first light gust of wind began to whip through the still uncut fields of the neighboring planters.

When the storm was done, the fields were flattened as if by the hand of a giant. Many planters were completely ruined. But when Stephen Fox walked out of the offices of the factors in New Orleans his eyes were dancing in a face deliberately kept grave and still.

He had sold his crop for a little short of one hundred thousand dollars.

VII

Aurore was sitting by one of the windows at the Arceneaux town house in Conti Street. Her fingers were moving rapidly, looping the fine thin strands of thread over a series of pins stuck into a piece of cork. Outside it was raining, the thin miserable drizzle so characteristic of winter in New Orleans. Across the room Odalie was putting fresh sachets of Vetiver in the *armoire*.

Aurore raised her head, looking out through the window past the gallery. But the iron scroll work interfered with her vision; she could see nothing.

"Expecting Andre?" Odalie asked.

"Yes."

"Why don't you consent, Aurore? Andre is a prince. He'd make you a wonderful husband."

"You're right," Aurore said slowly. "Andre is kind and generous and handsome. Only—"

"Only what, Aurore?"

"I don't love him."

Odalie's fingers toyed with the fine linen she was scenting.

"I see. There is someone else, perhaps?"

"Yes."

"Who?"

"That is my affair, my dear sister. I mean no offense, Odalie. I just can't talk about it. It's no good, and nothing will come of it . . . ever."

Odalie crossed the room and put her arm around her sister's shoulder.

"Poor little one," she said.

"It's nothing," Aurore said brightly. "And you, my dear sister, have you tossed your stays on top of the *armoire?*"

Odalie threw back her head and laughed, a clear tinkling sound, like the breaking of small pieces of ice. Then she stopped suddenly and the laughter was all gone, as though it had never been.

"I am growing old," she said as though talking to herself. "I'm twenty-two. All my friends—and most of yours—Aurore, have been married for ages."

"You've had hundreds of beaux," Aurore said.

"They—they bother me. I don't like being touched or kissed or fawned at. There's something—well—private here," she touched her breast, "something inviolable. And men are such beasts!"

"Odalie!"

"I shock you? I'm sorry. But it's true."

"I'm wondering," Aurore said softly, "just when you discovered that bestiality. Was it in October perhaps?"

The black eyes were wide and dark.

"What do you mean, Aurore?" The contralto had a slight rasp to it, very slight—almost unnoticeable.

"Nothing." She looked up at her sister, her hazel eyes clear. "Satine's coat shines like ebony, doesn't it, Odalie? Especially when she's just been groomed. You can see it a long way off."

"There is a connection between these riddles?" Odalie demanded.

"Is there?" Aurore asked.

Odalie opened her mouth to say something, but Zerline was coming into the room, her yellow face alight with pleasure.

"Monsieur Andre, Mademoiselle Aurore," she said. Zerline liked Andre—all the Negroes did.

109

"Oh, bother!" Odalie said and turned to leave the room.

"Don't go, Odalie!" Aurore said, springing up like a kitten. "I am sorry. I was being spiteful and mean. Forgive me, won't you?"

The black eyes narrowed until there was no light in them, no light at all.

"There's nothing to forgive, Aurore," she said very coldly. "I don't know what you're talking about."

Andre came into the room, his young face beaming.

"Good day! Good day!" he exclaimed. "Ah, how happy I am to see you!"

"You seem in good spirits, Andre," Odalie said.

"I am. I've just come back from visiting Stephen at Harrow. The news there is good—very good."

"You mean to say that he is there now—in midwinter?" Aurore demanded. "Everybody . . ."

"Comes into town for the winter," Andre finished for her. "But not Stephen. He makes a point of not doing what everybody else does."

"Why don't you bring him along sometime," Aurore suggested calmly.

"He thinks that he is in disfavor in this house," Andre said. "I've tried to tell him . . ."

"He's right," Odalie said sharply. "You must not bring that mad man to this house!"

Andre gave her a long, slow look.

"You need not trouble yourself, Odalie," he said. "He has no intention of coming."

"Odalie is cross, Andre," Aurore said sadly. "I'm afraid I angered her."

"I'm sorry," Andre said. "I didn't know . . ."

"It's nothing," Odalie said. Then: "Why does he stay on the land in the wintertime?"

"He is clearing it. By spring every inch of it will be ready for cultivation. And he is building— *ma foi*, what a long tongue I have!"

Aurore leaned forward eagerly.

110

"What is he building, Andre? You can trust us."

"I might as well tell you," Andre said. "He's building a house —the grandest mansion that Louisiana has ever seen. I rode out with Monsieur Pouilly today. The foundations are already laid. I've seen the plans. 'Tis a wonderful house, Aurore—such a house as will shape generations of men."

"But he has no wife," Odalie said. "Where are these generations to come from, Andre? Are they all to be Minerva's and spring full-armed from Monsieur Fox's Olympian brow?"

"No, my precocious one," Andre said softly, "Stephen will take a wife—and she'll be the girl of his choice, I'll wager you."

"Perhaps," Odalie murmured. "But if it happens that this girl thinks otherwise?"

"The good God help her. For she'll be subjected to such a courtship as was never seen before on land or sea!"

"It seems to me," Aurore said quietly, "that you know a great deal about the state of mind of this mysterious fiancée of Monsieur Fox's."

"Oh, bother!" Odalie said again, and walked away with great dignity through the doorway.

Andre looked after her.

"Your sister seems to be of a divided mind," he said to Aurore.

"Yes. She loves him, I think. But she doesn't know it yet. And she's afraid—terribly afraid—"

"Of Stephen?"

"Yes—and of love itself."

"Why?"

"I don't know. Perhaps it's because she's so beautiful. It's given her a kind of mastery—that beauty. Odalie likes mastery. She doesn't want to surrender. And love, for a woman, is surrender. Or perhaps she is really cold—frozen all the way through. I don't know, Andre. I simply don't know."

"When I was in Switzerland," Andre said slowly, "on my Grand Tour, I saw glaciers frozen over volcanoes. But you, my sweet, are you also afraid of love?"

"No, Andre, I'm not afraid."

"Then—Aurore—oh Aurore!"

111

"No, Andre, no. I wish I did love you. God knows I should. you've been generous and patient and kind . . . but . . ."

"But what, Aurore?"

"I can't. I just can't."

"I see," Andre said slowly. "There is someone else. My felicitations, Aurore, to this very fortunate man, whoever he may be. Is the date set, perhaps?"

"No, Andre, the date is not set. The date never will be set." Aurore laughed suddenly. "I shall be Godmother to all your children, and they'll call me Tante Aurore and laugh at the little, dried-up old spinster whenever they hear her say: 'Once I was in love . . .'"

Andre's brown eyes were very dark in his handsome face.

"You too!" he whispered, half to himself. "I think sometimes he is a devil—so easily he does things like this—without lifting a hand. Without caring—without even knowing. By the good God, he'd be better dead!"

"Andre, no! You mustn't!"

Andre's eyes came back from vast distances.

"You're right," he said. "I couldn't. 'Twould be like killing another part of myself. Your forgiveness, Aurore, for this and all my past intrusions. Good night, *Adieu,* Mademoiselle Arceneaux!"

"But, Andre, you'll call again. You're welcome any evening . . ."

"To come and sit and look at you and torture myself? No, Aurore. This is the end. Good night, Mademoiselle the Godmother of the children I shall never have!" Then he was gone, striding through the doorway, his back very stiff and proud.

VIII

THROUGHOUT the long winter the work went forward. The tall sailing vessels came riding into the harbor below the city, their holds bulging with goods. And always there were consignments for Stephen Fox, gentleman planter. Lumber—teak from the tropics for balustrades that would resist the eternal damp of the bayou country, hardwoods for flooring, rich darker woods for inlay patterns. Furniture, turned out in the ancient shops of England and France, patterns shaped by the hands of the finest craftsmen of the continent. Days, weeks, months of loving care had gone into their making, until now they stood in satiny beauty under their protective tarpaulins, waiting in the dark warehouses of New Orleans until Harrow should be finished. From Ghent, and Antwerp, and Brussels came gigantic crystal chandeliers, their myriad diamondlike facets carefully packed away in layer upon layer of straw. Red flagstone from Spain. Tile from Morocco. Vases, urns. Brass and copper knockers and doorknobs that gleamed like gold in their boxes. Carpets from the looms of Holland, rugs from far off Persia. Candelabra of silver. Solid silver services with tracings of leaves and vines in gold. All this waited in the warehouses, while the walls of Harrow grew.

Now, at last, Stephen was too busy for his fields. So the planter Wilson, he who had married a Prudhomme, was summoned from his failing swampy lands and set over the slaves. A house was built for the Wilsons, finer than most of the manor houses of the region, and Stephen and Pouilly shared rooms in one wing of it. Madame Wilson was a gracious hostess, whose admiration for the employer of her husband caused that thin, stooped little man no end of worry.

Day and night the work went on, under the hands of skilled slave labor bought in the West Indies by Stephen's agents and brought into Louisiana by special permission. Pouilly became accustomed to being aroused at any hour of the night to discuss some new idea of Stephen's. Most of them he put down gently but firmly as impractical, for Pouilly came of a long line of distinguished architects, but some he adopted, not a little pleased at Stephen's flair for graceful detail.

Andre practically lived at Harrow, quarreling busily with Stephen over points in the design.

"Classic Greek," he cried. "But of course of course! But still that is no reason why you could not introduce a little iron work on the galleries! Just a touch of Louisiana, a slight touch."

"No," Stephen declared. "Nothing of Louisiana. 'Tis for myself I am building, Andre. Iron work! What kind of bastardy that would make. Look ye, lad. Here a great gallery across the front, and around the two wings. And above it, another. The columns going straight through, supporting the roof. Corinthian columns, Andre, with leaves and grapes and vines at their tops. And at the wing ends of the upper gallery two great curving stairs of teak, so that one can alight from one's coach and go at once to the high porch, from whence ye can see the river."

"Good," Andre said. "It's good, I have to admit. Painted white, of course?"

"Yes. And with a roof of green tile. Forty rooms, Andre, ye can see the sweep of it!"

"I see you've cut down some of the oaks."

"Enough to make a drive. A long straight drive to the river road, with the branches of the other trees making a canopy. And

114

here, at the gate, it branches off into two forks, and swings in great curves up to the patio from two directions. The works go fast, Andre."

"So I see. Isn't that a coach on the river road, Stephen?"

"Yes."

"That's odd. There's nothing out here—that road is rarely used. I don't recall seeing a coach on it in years. Except the Cloutiers, of course, going out to Rosemont. I don't see why. . . ."

"The road *was* rarely used," Stephen observed drily, stressing the "was" so slightly that Andre had to turn and look at him before he got the meaning.

"You mean that it is used now?"

"Yes."

"I still don't see . . ."

"Harrow," Stephen said simply. "There is nothing like it in all the South, Andre. Even unfinished as it is, there is nothing like it. And so the coaches pass and pass again, and the horsemen. Some of the latter even turn up my alley of oaks and ride up to my courtyard. Then they sit there and watch the work going forward. And if I should happen to pass, how friendly they are, all of a sudden."

"You're not bitter, Stephen? That Waguespack affair is almost forgotten."

"No. I hold no rancor. Ye know, Andre, Aurore has ridden past here at least once to my knowledge. But Odalie apparently still holds her ancient grudge. Come. I want to show ye my bachelor quarters and my dovecote."

Andre brushed away the grimace of pain from his handsome face and followed his friend.

"But really, Stephen," he said. "This is too much! Dovecotes *and* bachelor quarters. I have seen one or the other flanking a manor house; but both—this is an extravagance!"

"I can afford extravagances, now," Stephen said. "This is the kitchen house. I took your advice, ye see."

"Good. Stephen—"

"Yes, Andre?"

"I have had no wine, I swear it. But my imbecilic ears persist in hearing music!"

"Ye are not mad—yet," Stephen grinned. " 'Tis music, all right. Come."

He walked ahead of Andre, his long legs devouring the distance until he stood before what appeared to be a rude slave cabin. Only it was larger than the other cabins, Andre saw; and it was so crudely constructed that it was evident that it was a temporary structure, designed to be torn down when it had served its purpose. From it came the strains of music; limping, halting, often off key, but music nevertheless, being played with a certain verve despite its inaccuracies.

Stephen pushed open the door. Entering, Andre saw a dozen slaves seated at musical instruments, while before them a lean, old Frenchman was tearing his hair."

"Dolts!" he shrieked. "Imbeciles! Name of a name of a diseased pig! Thus it goes, thus!" He seized a violin from the nearest Negro and began to play a measure, very cleanly, with perfect phrasing, and a clear bell-like tone.

Stephen closed the door very quietly, and they walked back toward the house.

"What on earth—" Andre began.

"There will be dancing in the great hall, Andre, come this harvest. And my men must be ready. Some of them are surprisingly talented. Du Castri is a musician of violent temper, but he is a good teacher."

"Tell me, Stephen, is it true that when the blacks are done you work all night alone upon the walls?"

"No," Stephen smiled. " 'Tis true I often walk over the grounds and the scaffolding of a night. But I do nothing—in this I have no skill."

"Dine with me tonight in New Orleans," Andre said. "You are in need of divertissement. Harrow will come to naught if you kill yourself building it."

"No," Stephen said softly. "There is so much to be done and so little time, Andre. Ye'll forgive me if I don't divert myself for a while yet."

116

"You're lucky, Stephen," Andre declared. "Everything you want you get. And some things you don't want you could have for the snap of a finger. I sometimes wonder if there isn't truth in some of the stories they tell about you."

Stephen's left eyebrow rose mockingly, and the scar glowed along his temple.

"And how do they explain my luck?" he said.

"Tante Caleen. Everyone knows she's a *Mamaloi* . . ."

"A what?"

"A *Mamaloi*—a sort of high priestess of Voudou. Through her you're said to have a direct connection with the devil."

Stephen leaned against a piece of the scaffolding and laughed until his face was wet with tears.

"Divertissement!" he choked. "Ye're all the divertissement a man could need! No doubt Tante Caleen and I circle the Cabildo's roof in the dark of the moon on the same broomstick. Beware, Andre! 'Tis thinking I am of changing ye into a fine he goat and sending ye out to eat the mayor's winter underwear!"

Andre joined in the laughter.

"It is ridiculous," he said. "But you are lucky, Stephen. By the way, where is your old witch now?"

"In the fields, I'd say, talking to Achille."

"She seems fond of your Number One man—odd, isn't it?"

"Not at all. Achille is her son."

"No! You mean to say that some man, even a black, Stephen, slept with that old horror?"

"She wasn't always old, Andre. In fact, she may have even been attractive in an African sort of way. Her life hasn't been exactly pleasant. It seems she came to New Orleans while she was yet a girl—many years before the insurrections that Tom Warren credited her with having a hand in fomenting."

"He is a queer one, your Tom Warren," Andre observed.

"So I am beginning to learn. There's no question of his fidelity to my interests, but some of his methods—but we were talking about Tante Caleen, were we not?"

"Yes. You were saying that her life was hard."

"It was. Achille's father was a black from Kentucky or Tennessee. She isn't sure which. Anyway, he was one of the leaders of the revolt of '95, and was the last of the twenty-three blacks to be hanged. They honored him by performing the execution before the parish church at New Orleans."

"So Tom Warren wasn't entirely wrong!"

"Only in his geography. And Tante Caleen is unusual. I sometimes think that she only tolerates all whites as mere children in the eyes of her ancient wisdom."

"Then she is a witch?"

"Rot. Come—Georges has our supper ready by now, and there is still much to do."

By the Spring of 1827, the great mansion of Harrow was substantially finished. Throughout the Summer, the work on its interior continued. The river road was crowded with wagons bearing from the warehouses of New Orleans the treasures that Stephen had accumulated for his manor. Steamboat after steamboat put in at his landing, bringing furniture, draperies, fixtures, machinery. Then for many days the slaves were busy with the painting, until the great house gleamed white among the somber oaks. From the first it had a majesty about it—a regal air of pride and lofty disdain. Try as they would, neither the Creoles nor the Americans could disregard it, and even their contemptuous title, "Fox's Lair," bestowed upon it while it was in the early stages of construction, died when they saw the completed house standing in all the austere purity of the classic Grecian line.

Stephen bought their gardener Jupiter from the Prudhommes for the amazing sum of three thousand dollars. The old black had magic in his fingers; whatever he touched grew and flourished.

"I got planters' hands, me," he was fond of saying. "What I plants she grows, yes!"

So in the courtyard, the pink, lavender and white crepe myrtles glowed softly; the red and white oleanders blazed. The yellowish pink mimosa hung low over the crystal ball on the pedestal, and the feathery green and gold acacia shredded the light of the afternoon sun. There was the cape jasmine, and the heavy waxen blossoms of the magnolia fuscata; there were the cruel spines of the yucca with its crown of creamy flowers. There were rambling roses and bush roses with buds like blood drops, lilies whiter than mountain snow and, over everything, the lush creeping fragrance of honeysuckle, heavy above the red flagstone walks. What Jupiter touched grew.

When it was all done, and the sugar-making season had begun, Madame Wilson was summoned to the manor and put to work penning, with her graceful flourishes and much-envied curlicues, the invitations to the grand ball that was to mark the official opening of Harrow.

Andre took up his residence in rooms that Stephen had ordered perpetually reserved for him, and the two of them worked out to the last detail this formal assault upon the ancient society of New Orleans.

"But suppose they refuse you, Stephen," he worried. "Suppose they don't come."

"Don't worry," Stephen declared drily. "They'll come. I'll wager ye a thousand dollars they'll come."

So the invitations went out to the Marignys, the Cloutiers, the Lambres, the Prudhommes, the Metoyers, the Sompaynacs, the Robieus, the Greneaux, the Lascals, the de Mandervilles, the Dreaux, the de Pontablas, the Rouen de Villerays, the d'Arensbourgs, the de la Chaises, the Lafrentières, the Labedoyères, the Beauregards—and the Arceneaux.

They went, too, to the Wilsons, the Claibornes, the Roberts, the Smiths, the Thompsons, and the Walters.

Andre and Stephen stood watching the messengers start out, Georges and Ti Demon and Achille, mounted on sleek horses, in new, well-cut liveries, their black faces bursting with pride. Then Andre and Stephen went back to Harrow—where Lagoaster, the great quadroon tailor, waited—to be fitted with new evening clothes made from materials brought from Scotland by fast clipper.

119

In the mornings, Stephen and Andre and sometimes Tom Warren, accompanied by their Negroes, rose before dawn and rode into the bayou country to shoot waterfowl. At night, they came back laden, and the birds were turned over to Tante Caleen to be hung in preparation for cooking.

For the messengers had returned triumphant.

"They coming, yes!" Georges crowed. "All the true gentlemen!"

"And the grand dames, too," Ti Demon echoed. "We see 'em all, us!"

Now, for a whole week, Harrow was a gigantic madhouse. Tante Caleen was over everything, regally ordering Stephen and Andre out of her way as curtly almost as she did Georges and Achille. Suzette, the mulatto girl who had shared the lean-to with Stephen and Tante Caleen on that first day at Harrow, was put in charge of the marketing. First of all she had to purchase fresh calves' feet with which Tante Caleen made gelatin. These were stripped of the tough outer layer then cut into sections and pounded and ground into a powder. Then Tante Caleen added hot water and sugar and a drop or two of cochineal for the pink jelly, thickened lemon juice for the yellow, and the strained juice of scalded spinach for the green.

Weeks before, a steamboat had left the northern reaches of the Mississippi, its hold filled with a rare and expensive luxury —ice. Packed in straw to slow its melting, much of it arrived at Harrow to be placed in a zinc-lined box búilt to hold it—and nothing else—in the pantry. The surplus was buried in a cool, strawlined cellar, dug near the brook that ran through Stephen's land. The gelatin was placed upon ice and left to solidify; then Tante Caleen turned to more important things.

From the city Suzette had brought refined sugar, which, unlike the crude, open-kettle sugar made and used on the plantations, was white instead of brown. It came in coneshaped loaves of stonelike hardness and for days Harrow resounded to the pounding of Caleen's mallet, hammering it into chips, then into powder fine enough to be used in the cakes and delicate pastries she was baking.

The smoke stood up straight from the great chimney of the

kitchen house on the last day, only a few hours before the guests were due. Caleen supervised the cooks as they pushed the ovens with their hollowed-out tops filled with live coals into the great fireplace. In the smaller pots on the trivets the *roux* and gravies and soups and gumbos simmered. Across the front of the fourteen-foot-wide fireplace, the game—venison, wild hog and wild fowl—turned on the spits, the rich juices dropping into pots set on the hearth below.

Under the watchful eye of the older women the candies had been made, petals of orange blossoms and of violets dropped into boiling syrup, then allowed to harden upon waxed paper. Outside the big house, the strongest slaves on the plantation were taking turns whirling huge cylinders in tubs of ice. These contained the ice cream which had been made by boiling whole vanilla beans in sweetened milk, and since the tubs had no handles or inside fixtures of any kind, the making of ice cream was the hardest kind of work. Ruefully the men blew on their freezing palms, but Tante Caleen was everywhere, her tongue keener than any lash.

Georges was sharpening the carving knives by rubbing them on a hardwood board covered with powdered brickdust. Girls and women were carrying the sherbets and gelatins and charlotte russes down into the ice cellar, so that they would remain firm until needed. The cooking went on. In the pantry the mountainous layer cakes were being iced with much licking of fingers. Girls were weaving strips of orange peel into dainty little baskets, which were then dipped into boiling syrup and set aside to harden. Afterwards they were filled with bonbons and nougats and pralines.

Stephen himself supervised the placing of the wines and liquors on the side table. Madame Wilson was in charge of the decorations, but even here Tante Caleen made abrupt and pointed suggestions. Jupiter filled the costly urns and vases with flowers, and garlanded the magnificent curving staircase with pink ramblers and bloodcolored garden roses for a full three flights of stairs.

The house servants were instructed and instructed again. Their livery was new from the skin out. Two little beturbaned *negrillons* took their places on each side of the great tables, with their hands on the golden cords which moved the huge swinging fans. And the butler, who could read, stood at the doorway to take the cards and call out the names of each entering guest. Now, at last, everything was still, waiting. . . .

But it was not alone at Harrow that preparations were being made for the grand ball. At Rosemont, the Cloutier's plantation, Cloutier, himself, had taken the invitation from the basket of Georges.

"What is it, dear?" Madame Cloutier demanded.

"The infernal impudence of the man!" Cloutier spluttered, "this Fox inviting us to a ball at his place. You tell your master . . ."

"That we accept with pleasure," Madame Cloutier said.

"What!" Cloutier roared.

"Don't be unnecessarily stupid, Louis," Madame Cloutier said calmly. "We have two unmarried girls, and you yourself said that Monsieur Fox was on his way to becoming the richest man in the state."

"You'd sanction a connection with that . . ."

"I find him quite a charming gentleman. I didn't mention it before, Louis, but some weeks ago the girls and I took occasion to drive by Harrow. I tell you, Louis, a finer house does not exist! Girls! Come down! I have a surprise for you!"

Henriette and Clothilde came bounding down the stairs. They were both big strapping girls whose lack of grace was a sore trial to their parents.

"Monsieur Fox," Madame Cloutier announced, "has invited us to Harrow!"

Thereupon the Mademoiselles Cloutier let out such a piercing squeal that Georges backed hastily toward the door.

"No, no," Henriette cried. "We must see the other invitations. I'm dying to know who else will be there!"

The three women then proceeded to go through the entire basket, murmuring over each name.

"Odalie Arcenaux," Madame Cloutier said grimly. "That is not too good. Clothilde, you have a tan. Starting tonight, you're sleeping every night with sour buttermilk on your face."

And that same night, she pounded her beef marrow until it was fluid and poured in the thick, ropy castor oil. Henriette gagged at the odor, but Clothilde stood by while her mother scented the snowy concoction with patchouli and oil of bergamot. Then she rubbed it into the thick black hair of her daughters, and screwed each lock up into curl papers so tightly that the girls howled with pain. Afterwards she smeared lip salve made of white wax and sweet oil on their mouths and marched them off to bed, equipped with a bowl of thick, vile-smelling sour buttermilk to lighten their naturally dark Creole complexions.

At the home of the Arceneaux, Aurore passed the invitation wordlessly to her sister. Odalie read it and her black eyes met Aurore's clear hazel ones.

"You're going?" Aurore asked softly. Odalie didn't answer. Instead she walked to the window and looked up river toward Harrow, miles away and out of sight around many a river bend. Then very slowly she turned back to her sister.

"Yes," she said; "yes—I'm going . . ."

As the night of the ball approached the air of the bayou country seemed electrified. Calls were being exchanged for no other reason than to discuss the mysterious Monsieur Fox, who was so patently English and yet spoke French better than the Louisianians themselves. All the old stories were brought out and passed from mouth to mouth, gaining force and brilliance with each retelling. Stephen was a bastard son of nobility exiled to the New World. Stephen was a notorious gambler, blackguard and confidence man who had seduced the wife of the poor.

simple, but in retrospect, exceedingly noble, German planter, stolen his lands, and climaxed his villainy by slaying the much-abused man in a duel. "Why 'tis said he regularly sends money to Madame Waguespack in far-off Philadelphia. And why not, my dear, since no less than two of the youngest children have red hair!"

So the matrons of New Orleans and of the great plantations rocked and talked, watching each other out of the corners of their eyes to see what effect their words were having. But even as they mouthed the latest scandals about the notorious cases of witchcraft on the Fox plantation led by Caleen, a known *Mamaloi*, they were hastening their departures, smiling their *adieus* and rushing home to lace their daughters unmercifully into corsets with stays of whalebone and a piece of applewood three inches wide up the front, which permitted no deviation from the posture demanded of a gentlewoman.

The sale of rice powder reached unprecedented heights. Many perfumers had their stocks entirely depleted. And in Chartres Street, Mesdames Pluche and Ferret forgot their ardent commercial rivalry to join with Olympe, the very fashionable milliner, in a little celebration over the unexpected business boom in the sale of Parisian imports of gowns and hats.

Andre remained at Harrow for the entire week preceding the ball. On the night of the festivities, he and Stephen dressed in the north wing with the assistance of Georges and Ti Demon. The two valets were at dagger's points, falling over each other in their zeal to see that their masters would be unrivaled. The ruffles on the white silk shirts had been starched until they stood rigidly out from the two broad bosoms, and the new, dark cut-away coats—identical in every respect from their buttons of mother pearl, to their brocaded tone, a maroon so dark and rich that only when the light struck it did the color appear—had been brushed and brushed again. The waistcoats were crème, with embossed patterns of *fleur de lis*, and the stocks were of white

124

silk, so soft and clear as to appear bluish. Their boots had been polished until they reflected the light of every candle.

And now the valets were busy with their masters' hair, brushing it into glossy ringlets upon the imperious young heads, and smoothing the long sideburns that came down the entire length of the firm yet mobile jaws. Truly, Stephen and Andre were matching foils on this night, the dark, wonderfully handsome Creole setting off the lean, fair Irishman to unusual advantage.

"You're shaking," Andre observed as Stephen took a glass of wine from the hand of Georges.

"Of course," Stephen said. "I'm as jumpy as a filly. But never ye fear, Andre, I'll carry it off. This means everything to me."

"Why? The people whom you've invited are insufferably stuffy. You're twice the man of any of them. To go to all this trouble and expense . . ."

"For them? Ye wrong me, Andre. For one only. Afterwards they may drown themselves in the Mississippi, but I will have Odalie." His hands stroked the great pearl briefly. "I can wear this now," he said.

"Of course. But, Stephen, why are you seating me next to this Miss Rogers? I don't know her."

"Wait and see," Stephen grinned, one eyebrow lifting mockingly. And for the thousandth time Andre observed how the great scar added oddly to his attractiveness, lending an air of diablerie and insouciance to his face.

Ti Demon came running into the room at that moment, his big eyes popping from their sockets.

"They come, yes!" he cried. "I see the coaches, me!"

"We'd better go down," Andre said.

"Right," Stephen said, and downed the glass of wine in one gulp.

The stairway made a tremendous spiral going down. At this height, the magnificent crystal chandelier, blazing with hundreds of candles, was below them, and through its dazzling facets they could see the servants taking the wraps of the first arrivals. Inside the ballroom, the slave orchestra, perfectly trained now, struck up a tune. Importantly the butler bawled out the names.

Stephen and Andre stood in the vast foyer greeting the guests. With them was Madame Wilson, who, by reason of the fact that she was born a Prudhomme, was socially acceptable enough to act as hostess, despite her mésalliance with a Yankee overseer. Outside on the curving drive, the footmen were opening the doors of the coaches and Stephen's slaves were guiding them away to the stables, where every horse was watered and fed.

As the guests entered, the thin, formal smiles brightened. The men took Stephen's offered hand firmly, and the women simpered as he bowed low over their gloved fingers. Andre stood a little apart, watching the show.

"Pure theatre," he murmured. "*Ma foi,* what an actor that Stephen is!"

"Meestuh and Meestress Rogers!" the butler bawled. "And Mees Amelia Rogers!"

Andre leaned forward suddenly, and his dark eyes were alight.

"And I accused him of lacking subtlety," he whispered. "And often of having no heart. This is a thing deliberate—to repay me for Aurore. And name of a name of an angel in heaven, what a payment!" Then he was moving forward in response to Stephen's nod toward the tall girl whose walk was the waving of a young willow in a spring wind, and whose hair was silvery white gold throwing back the light of the candles like a halo. The face was kind too, and heartbreakingly lovely, and as he moved toward her, the blue eyes were widening endlessly, fixed upon his dark young face.

Then all the guests were in the great hall—all the guests, even the Cloutiers who had deliberately come late—except the Arceneaux. Stephen was glancing nervously toward the door. The Americans from the Faubourg Saint Marie were gazing with frank curiosity and open admiration at the magnificent appointments of Harrow; but the Creoles were watching Stephen. Then at last the butler was swelling out his chest importantly:

"Monsieur le Vicomte Henri Marie Louis Pierre d'Arceneaux!" he cried. "And the Mesdames Aurore and Odalie Arceneaux!"

Stephen made a gesture to hide his face, but everyone in the vast room saw the blaze of pleasure light his eyes. Madame

126

Cloutier's face was a study in frustration, a look reflected in lesser measure upon the countenances of most of the attendant mothers present.

As the maid servant took away Odalie's wrap, something between a breath and a sigh rose from the lips of the men in the hall and hovered in the air like an echo.

Somehow, all the lights of Harrow seemed to have descended upon the girl as she stood in the foyer beside her father and sister, so that the pearly whiteness of her face and throat and arms seemed to float in a soft haze. With invention that gained daring by its very simplicity, she had defied convention. Her hair was not—as was the hair of every other woman in the place—parted in the middle and tortured into small bunches of curls above her ears; she had simply had it brushed and allowed it to fall in heavy midnight masses about her shoulders, over the gown of ancient French lace cut in extreme décolleté. And when Stephen bent wordlessly over her hand, she smiled, a slow, deep triumphant smile implicit with the luxurious mastery of surrender.

The music had begun now, and the dancing. Touching Amelia's hand lightly, Andre swung into the swirling sweep of the waltz, lost forever, knowing it, and glorying in the knowledge.

"All my life," he whispered, "I've been waiting—for you. Without knowing it, I've been waiting."

And the blue eyes beneath the ash-blond brows looked calmly into the dark face that was as handsome as a young god's and there was no coquetry in them, only pure candor and trust and acceptance.

"I'm glad," she said clearly. "I'm very glad—that you waited."

With amazing control, Stephen made the rounds of the young women, smiling at them, whispering flattering words into each ear. But when Odalie was his partner it was different and every mother knew that the rice powder had done no good, and the perfumes had done no good, and even the vigorous rubbing of the leaves of the wild mullein against creamy cheeks to make them glow softly had been in vain. The tall young man with his scarred face, which looked curiously like the countenance of a Lucifer so shortly after the fall that the brow of the angel still shone through the handsomely satanic cast of features, moved through the measures of the *contre-danse* with a trancelike grace, and the eyes of Odalie, gone back to the dim ages before light was, never left his—never for an instant.

Then it was midnight and the guests were following Stephen into the great dining salon, where the gigantic tables of carved mahogany had been placed end to end in semicircle. When they had been seated, the procession of servants bearing the turkey, goose, chicken, venison, and wild hog began. The guests could no more than touch a little of each course, staring all the while at the flowers trailing from the silver *epergnes* in the center of the tables, and at the side tables where the salads, salamis, gelatines, huge pyramids of iced cakes and mountains of sponge cake snowed under whipped cream and dotted with cherry stars stood. And upon others the cold meats waited untouched, and the snowy mounds of ice cream. The wines glowed richly in their cut glass decanters, labeled with a leaf of beaten gold upon which had been inscribed the name and age. And for favors, each lady found herself in possession of a little basket of candied orange peel filled to the brim with the sugared petals of rose, violet and orange blossoms.

Behind each chair the waiters moved like ghosts seeing that no one of the beautiful crystal goblets with their tracings of vines and leaves in gold went for an instant unfilled.

And Stephen was bending toward Odalie, his pale blue eyes aglow in his face, his lips moving, saying the proper little pleasantries suitable for the time and place, but his words were as nothing, lost, unheard, against the naked clarity with which his eyes were speaking.

Looking at him, Odalie's hand trembled as with a sudden chill, so that she dropped her spoon. Instantly a tall black was bowing with a replacement on a tiny tray.

"They're—they're well-trained, your servants," she said.

"Yes," Stephen said. "So must it be with my servants and my horses and everything which is mine. But ye're trembling. Are ye cold?"

"No. I think I'm a little afraid."

128

"Of what? There's no one here who would harm ye."

"Not even you, monsieur?"

Stephen smiled wickedly.

" 'Tis just possible I might," he said thoughtfully. "I have not yet had my revenge for that blow ye struck me."

"You would take vengeance upon a woman?"

"Yes! But 'twould be a vengeance of my own choosing—which, possibly, she might even enjoy . . ."

"You're eloquent," Odalie said. "If I believed . . ."

But the butler was bending over Stephen, whispering:

"A man wants to see you, maître. Outside on the terrace."

Stephen made a gesture of extreme annoyance.

"He insists, maître. I tried to send him away, but he said to show you—this."

And in the butler's hand the golden snuff box gleamed dully under the flickering candles. Stephen rose at once, murmuring:

"A thousand pardons, mademoiselle. Ye'll excuse me?"

"Of course."

Then he was gone, striding through the great hall. Odalie's eyes followed him until he passed through the doorway out of sight.

Outside on the gallery, Stephen hesitated a moment. Then he saw the brief glow of redness as the big man standing at the foot of the great curving stairway drew upon his pipe.

"Mike!" Stephen cried and went bounding down the stairs to where the giant riverman stood.

"Aye, me little redhaired cockeroo!" Mike bellowed. "And 'tis thinking I was that yez had forgotten an old friend!"

"Never," Stephen said, then with only the slightest hesitation, he added: "Come in and join the party. I have more good Irish whiskey than even ye could drink!"

Mike drew in on the battered corncob pipe, and his big bass voice was curiously soft.

"Yez be all I thought ye," he rumbled. "All man—and all Irish. To keep a friendship yez would spoil all yez worked for, wouldn't yez? Ye'd take me in amongst all those swells and let them know yez associated with river scum, and mayhap lose even yer fine lady. No, 'tis too much. I'll come ag'in t'morrow." He turned away abruptly.

But Stephen caught him by the arm.

"How came ye from town?" he demanded.

"On me own two feet," Mike growled. "And, by God's Grace, they'll take me back ag'in!"

"No! Ye're staying here tonight. Ye don't have to join the party if ye don't want to; but ye're staying."

"All right," the big flatboatman said. "Indeed 'tis weary I am, by all the Saints. Send that fat, sassy Nigra of yourn that tried to turn me away, to let me in by the side door and I'll go straight up and sleep."

"No," Stephen said flatly. "The side door is for tradesmen and Negroes. My friends come in the front. Come."

"But them swells . . ."

"Can take it and like it. Ye're worth any ten of them. Come."

Then taking Mike Farrel's big arm, Stephen led him up the stairs and through the doorway. As they passed through the hall, Stephen nodded curtly to a waiter. The black came at once to his master's side.

"A bottle of whiskey," Stephen said, "up to the North Wing rooms for this gentleman. And when ye bring it, stay a bit to see if he wants anything else."

"I had me a Nigra," Mike said suddenly. "He were a queer little fellow, always shaking like a leaf and mutterin' to hisself about some big fire and shootin' and burnin'. He were a runaway. They caught him up near Natchez, yez ken, but nobody ever claimed him."

"What became of him?" Stephen asked.

"Me money ran low, so I had to sell him," Mike said. "'Twas a pity, because he had a mortal terror of New Orleans. He cried like a child. Shook me up a bit—he were a good Nigra."

"Tomorrow we'll ride into town and buy him back," Stephen said. "Ye'll be comfortable here. Jean will bring ye whatever ye want."

"Aye. Now go back to yer guests like a good lad. But don't fergit that whiskey!"

When Stephen came back into the salon the whispers of the few guests who had seen Mike pass the open double doors stopped abruptly. Odalie looked at him inquiringly.

"A relative of yours?" she asked mockingly.

"No," Stephen said softly. "I am not so fortunate as to have such a kinsman. 'Tis merely a riverman who once saved my life, and one of the finest men to whom the good God ever gave breath." His eyes rested upon her warmly. "Ye're beautiful, Odalie," he said. "Much too beautiful."

It was just at that moment, when the crimson was mounting into Odalie's cheeks, that Andre lifted his eyes from the face of Amelia. His glance traveled from the lovely animated tableau that Stephen and Odalie made to where Aurore sat across from him, not listening to the desperate efforts of a young American to gain her attention, her eyes upon Stephen, watching his every move as he bent toward Odalie. And Andre was conscious of a feeling very like pain, although Aurore's perfectly controlled features showed exactly nothing.

"Andre," Amelia whispered, for so far along had they gone in the space of an evening.

"Yes," he answered absently. "Yes, Amelia?"

"You were in love with that girl once, weren't you?"

Andre turned to her.

"Yes," he said. "Yes I was."

"She is very beautiful. Are you quite sure . . . ?"

"Quite," he said. "Time did not exist before tonight."

"I'm glad. She is so lovely. More so than her sister—though in a different way."

"You—you see that too?"

"Yes. I should like her for a friend, only I should be afraid."

"Don't be," Andre said. "Don't be—ever."

Afterwards the music started again and the dancing lasted until dawn. Then the waiters were bringing the plates of gumbo and scalding cups of black coffee and one by one the guests took their leave. Odalie lingered after the others, her black eyes curiously luminous in her fair face.

131

"And if I call," Stephen was saying steadily, "ye will receive me?"

"Yes," she said. "I shall always be at home—to you."

Waiting for her in the coach on the red flagstone drive, Aurore knotted her handkerchief into a damp ball; but even when Stephen bent low over Odalie's hand she held back the tears that trembled scaldingly under her eyelids. There were miles to go before she could weep.

IX

Tʜᴇ morning after the great ball, Stephen caused horses to be saddled for Mike Farrel, Andre, and himself. Leaving the slaves busy with the house-cleaning under the direction of Madame Wilson, they rode down Stephen's alley of oaks toward the river road.

"Ye remember the dealer to whom ye sold your black?" Stephen asked Mike.

"Yes. And he be a fair one by all accounts. 'Tain't likely he could sell pore Josh yet anyways."

"Why not?"

"Nobody'd buy him," Mike chuckled. "That's why I was able to git him in the furst place. He were so pore and puny, yez ken. They almost give him to me. Still, he were a good Nigra. Gentle-like and very mindful of me orders. I niver had trouble out of him."

"We'll have him back," Stephen said. "Never ye fear."

But Andre sat very still on his horse's back, his dark eyes clouded with distance.

"Andre!" Stephen barked.

"Wha—what is it, Stephen?"

133

"Nothing," Stephen laughed. " 'Tis only that I wanted to wake ye up. How did ye like the lean American female?"

Andre looked at Stephen and his eyes were very clear. Something like a slow smile played around the corners of his mouth.

"I'm eternally grateful to you, Stephen," he said.

"So," Stephen said, his brows rising mockingly. "Ye weren't displeased after all?"

"Far from it," Andre said. "So far, indeed, that you've got to ride with me to her father's house today when I ask his permission to call upon her. And tonight I visit my father, Stephen."

"Ye're in his bad graces, of course?"

"Not so much as before. Since I became serious enough to seek me a wife, his disapproval has lessened considerably."

"Good. And the purpose of your visit?"

"I'm going back to work, Stephen. I'm going to become a planter. After all, La Place des Rivières will be mine one day . . ."

"Ye Gods!" Stephen roared. "This is serious. Ye mean to tell me that in one night ye become so smitten with Amelia Rogers that ye're going to work?"

"I'm going to marry her, Stephen."

Stephen put out his hand.

"Good," he said, "I'll give ye back that wager that ye've lost to me as a wedding present and add something useful to boot. But what about Aurore, Andre?"

Andre's brows knit together and his eyes were troubled.

"I loved her," he said slowly. "Perhaps I love her still. I don't know, Stephen. All I know is that if she returned my affections —even a little—I should be greatly troubled. But she doesn't— so I guess my way is clear."

"Aurore is a queer one," Stephen said. "She has always treated me with the greatest of kindness."

"You know, Stephen," Andre snapped, "sometimes you're positively an imbecile!"

"I don't doubt it," Stephen grinned. "But about what am I being imbecilic now?"

"Oh, nothing," Andre growled.

134

"This big shindig of yours," Mike asked. " 'Twere a big success, lad?"

"Yes," Stephen said. " 'Twas quite a success, Mike."

"With whiskey like that, how could ye help it? Yez told me ye'd
do it, and from the furst I believed yez. A planter, and the biggest
in the state, I hear."

"Well—not quite—old Arceneaux has more land and the
Cloutiers have as much. But I will be, Mike, and soon."

"Arceneaux," Mike rumbled. " 'Tis to his filly yez be plannin' to
git spliced, I'm told."

"Ye're told! By our Lady, Mike, ye've got an uncommonly large
store of information about my affairs!"

"I take an interest," Mike grinned. "Yez are like a son to me,
lad. I must see this gel someday soon, so as to make me mind up
whether or no I'll give me consent. I want yez happy, Stevie."

"Then put your foot down, Mike," Andre said suddenly, and
his tone was only half jesting. "Don't let him do it!"

Stephen looked at him keenly.

"Why don't you like Odalie, Andre?" he asked.

"I do like her, Stephen. No one could dislike so gorgeous a
creature. 'Tis only that sometimes I think she has no heart."

"She has," Stephen said. "But 'tis frozen. I'll thaw it out for
her, never ye fear."

"I hope so. But how did you learn so much about him, Mike?"

"His Nigras," Mike chuckled. "They've all got tongues like bell
clappers when yez kin unnerstan' their talk. Most of 'em don't talk
English so good."

The three of them rode down the river road toward New
Orleans and as they passed an occasional coach or landau or
cabriolet, the occupants saluted them familiarly.

"You've arrived, Stephen," Andre declared. "You're now the best
known planter in bayou country. How does it feel?"

"I don't know," Stephen said slowly. "I think it could become a
burden—a very great burden."

"You're right. Your life is now no longer your own. What you
do will be watched and commented upon and imitated. I'll wager
that within five years there will be a dozen copies of Harrow

135

standing along the river. We Louisianians are used to luxury, but not to magnificence. Today they'll make the rounds in New Orleans. They'll go from house to house to talk about the ball. They'll indulge in no end of bon mots at your expense, but the mother of every marriageable daughter for miles around is probably already planning a soirée to which you can be invited —even those who were not asked to Harrow."

"They'll waste their time," Stephen declared.

"I don't doubt it. Odalie will marry you now. Not even she can withstand the temptation of becoming the greatest lady in the state. Besides, you're a handsome scoundrel. I only hope she makes you happy."

"She will," Stephen declared. "Don't trouble yourself, Andre."

After miles of riding they came to the streets of the Faubourg St. Marie, the American section of New Orleans. They wound through them slowly on their tired horses until they came to a slave mart. The block was empty and deserted and the house behind it was closed.

" 'Tis late we are," Mike grumbled.

But Stephen had dismounted and was knocking smartly on the closed door with his crop.

After a moment, a lean, tanned Kentuckian pushed it open.

"Good day, gentlemen," he said. "What kin I do for you?"

"Ye have a black," Stephen said, "bought yesterday from this man. Have ye sold him yet?"

"No," the Kentuckian said gravely. "And I doubt that I can ever sell him. You've got a persuasive tongue in yer head, suh, to sell me such a Bumbo. Why didn't you tell me he was crazy?"

"Yez didn't ask me," Mike grinned. "Anyways we've come to buy him back."

"There's a little matter of the expense of feeding and lodging him," the slave trader began. "I'll have to ask you . . . "

"Don't worry," Stephen said. "I'll give ye fifty dollars above what ye paid for him. Come, let us see him."

"Very well, suh," the Kentuckian said, and went back into the house that served him as home and place of business and sometimes even as a slave pen. After a moment he was back, leading

136

not one Negro but two. The first was a small, illformed, and very much undernourished black. He was trembling from head to foot, and great tears streaked his thin cheeks.

"Don't let him ketch me," he wept. "Don't let him ketch pore Josh."

"Don't worry," Stephen told him kindly. "Ye're in good hands now."

"Dey'll send me back," Josh wept. "Dey'll send me back to Mas Tom. And he'll kill me jes like he done pore Rad. Don't let them do it, Mas Mike, please don't let them!"

"He's sick, poor devil," Stephen said. "All right, we'll take him. Here's your money." He counted out the crisp banknotes to the slave trader.

"Beggin' yore pahdon, suh," the Kentuckian said. "But since you seem to be in the market for unlikely Bumbos, I thought maybe . . ."

Stephen looked at the second slave closely.

"Hmmmm," he said, "a girl. What think ye, Andre?"

Andre looked at the slave girl closely.

"*Ma foi,* but she's beautiful!" he said.

Stephen looked at the girl again. She was tall, with a small rounded head on a long graceful neck. The hair was closely cropped, so that it fitted her head like a wooly skullcap. But her body was all grace, slim as a young willow, with small conical, up and outthrusting breasts.

Her skin was black velvet. Stephen glanced over the long ebony thighs, but half-concealed by the shiftlike garment she wore, to the slender curving hips and the waist as small as a child's. Then he looked into the face with the small nose, thin almost as a Caucasian's, and the slanted, half-closed sloe eyes, smoldering yellow-brown under the heavy lids.

"Ye're right," he said at last to Andre. "She *is* beautiful. I did not think it possible of a black, but this girl is as lovely a woman as ever I have seen. All right," he said to the slave trader, "I'll buy her. How much do ye want?"

"Wait a bit, suh," the Kentuckian said. "I've sold Nigras heah in Nawleans fur nigh onto fifteen yeahs. I got a reputation fur

137

square dealing. I don't want you to buy a pig in a poke. This heah gal is bad."

"Bad how?" Stephen demanded

"She's a livin' fiend. She try to kill anybody what come near her. She jus' ain't tamed yet. I got her off a Portugee straight out of Africa."

"Give her to me, Stevie boy," Mike said with a grin, "and I'll have her tamed by morning."

"I don't doubt it," Stephen said. "But I want no little yellow *negrillons* on the place. Beside, I was buying her for a wife for Achille. She has no physical defects?"

In answer, the tall Kentuckian seized her jaw and tried to force open her mouth. She reared back, her mouth clamped shut, little animal noises coming from the depths of her throat. Angered, the Kentuckian slapped her lightly across the face. Instantly her lips bared her gleaming teeth, filed to little dagger points, and her long neck was like a serpent, striking. There was a little flurry of motion; then the slave trader let out a yell. The girl's head was bent over his hand, and the pointed teeth had gone through it to the bone.

The three men sprang forward. It took all three of them, including Mike's gigantic strength, to force open her mouth and release the trader's hand.

"You bitch!" he cried. Then he lashed out with his foot, the kick catching her high on the thigh and sending her to the ground. She was up at once, nails and teeth bared, her eyes gleaming yellow like a leopard's. But with a speed amazing in one of his bulk, Mike was upon her, pinioning her arms.

The slave dealer stood before them, trembling with fury, holding his hand from which the thick blood was seeping up through a small semicircle of deep, rounded punctures.

"I'll kill her!" he said. "I'll kill the black bitch!"

"No," Stephen said clearly. "I'll give ye three hundred for her as she stands. My man will call for them in the morning with a wagon. I want no whip marks on her, sir!"

"All right," the Kentuckian growled. "At least you know what

138

you're gitting. Kin I have the big fellow help me git her back in?"

Stephen nodded to Mike and he pushed the girl through the door, kicking and squirming all the while.

"You're mad," Andre declared.

"I think not," Stephen declared. "She can be tamed, but that's not the way. Come, let's go down to Maspero's for dinner, then we can discuss our plans for the evening."

Sitting at one of the little tables at Maspero's, eating the steaming *bouillabaisse* the three of them talked little. Andre's mind was busy and troubled. Would his father take kindly to his marriage to an American girl? Perhaps when he saw Amelia— but the old man was so confounded stubborn. And Colonel Rogers—some Americans were frankly prejudiced against the French. Still with Stephen's help. . . .

"You're calling upon Odalie tonight, Stephen?" he asked.

"No."

"But I thought . . ."

"Think again, Andre. Shall I go running to her the minute she acquiesces just a little, as if I were overwhelmed by the honor? Ye know me better than that. Let her wait a bit—and wonder."

"You're right, of course. Never give the whip hand to a woman, particularly such a woman as Odalie. But tell me, Stephen, how did you come to meet Colonel Rogers?"

Stephen laughed.

"On the steamboats," he chuckled. "I used to play poker with him. Let me tell you, Andre: never gamble with him. He is the best poker player in the entire Mississippi Valley. He used to beat me regularly—which is probably the reason he is so fond of me."

"Then he is fond of you?"

"Who ain't?" Mike growled. "Everybody likes Stevie."

"I'm flattered," Stephen mocked. "Yes, Andre, the colonel is quite fond of me. Told me once that he'd marry Amelia off to me if I ever made a gentleman out of myself."

"Was that one of your incentives?"

139

"No. Amelia was never overly impressed with me. But where does all this lead?"

"To your coming with me to call upon the colonel this afternoon."

"Gladly. When do ye wish to go?"

"Now—as soon as you've finished, I mean."

"How hot ye've blown all of a sudden! Don't ye want to think this over, Andre?"

"Ten years of thinking would do no good. I've got to have her, Stephen. You should understand that."

"I do," Stephen said gravely, rising from his seat. "Let us be off, then."

They left the Vieux Carre and rode northward to the Faubourg Saint Marie. On Phillips Street, Stephen reined Prince Michael in before an American Gothic house with huge verandas and oddly assorted spires and gables projecting from the roof.

The three of them dismounted. Stephen strode upon the veranda and knocked boldly. The others followed him at some little distance. Then the door flew open.

"Stephen!" the great voice roared. "Come in! Come in, my boy! Who is this blasted Frenchman you introduced my daughter to? She can talk of nothing else—and you know I cannot abide foreigners!"

Stephen laughed.

"Permit me to present him," he said. "This is Andre Le Blanc, a very blasted Frenchman at the moment."

"Good day, sir," Andre murmured politely.

"Hmmm," the colonel said, "not a bad-looking lad in an oily sort of way. Where were you born, Mister Le Blanc?"

"In the United States of America, sir," Andre said stoutly. "In the territory of Louisiana."

"But you're French?"

"You honor me, sir. Yes, I belong to the race whose courtesy is celebrated throughout the world."

"I stand rebuked," the colonel said smiling. "I didn't mean to be discourteous, but I guess I was. And who is this?"

"Mike Farrel," Stephen said. "My biggest and best friend."

"Then, gentlemen," the colonel said. "What shall it be? Rye, scotch, bourbon, port, sherry?"

"Bourbon," Stephen said. "And we'll drink to fair Kentucky."

"Good," the colonel boomed. "Josias!"

Sipping the drink, the colonel looked at Andre from under his thick, bushy eyebrows.

"You're a man of substance, aren't you, Mister Le Blanc?" he asked abruptly.

"My father's plantation is one of the largest in the state," Andre said stiffly.

"And I am right in assuming that the purpose of this visit is to gain my permission to pay court to my daughter?"

"Yes," Andre said, "it is."

"You're a friend of Stephen's," the old man said, half to himself. "That means a lot to me. You know, Stephen was the first honest gambler I ever met on the river. I thought it was a fluke when I beat him, because river sharks always deal from the bottom and ring in cold decks and palm a brace of spare aces. But not Stephen—he played me square and lost. He never could beat me, but he could beat damn near everybody else."

He turned abruptly to Stephen.

"Well, lad," he growled. "What do you say? Shall we let him call upon 'Melia? I rather fancied *you* as a son-in-law."

"Suppose we let Amelia decide," Stephen said smoothly. "After all 'tis she who will have to be troubled with a husband."

"Right," the colonel said, then: "Oh 'Melia!"

Then Amelia was coming down the stairs and Andre was standing up, frozen, all of life caught up in his eyes.

"Andre!" she whispered, and Stephen thought he had never heard so much gladness in one voice. "Father—Andre—I—I see you've met," she finished lamely.

"It seems to be out of our hands," Stephen whispered loudly to the colonel. "What say ye to a hand of Twenty-one? In the drawing room, of course, so we won't be drowned in sighs."

"All right," the colonel growled. " 'Melia . . ."

"Yes, father?"

"Shall I let this young man call upon you? Think carefully now!"

"Father—please let him!"

"All right. Mister Le Blanc, tell your father that I'll call upon him next Friday afternoon. Come, Stephen, and you Mister Farrel. You said poker, didn't you, lad?"

"I did not!" Stephen laughed. "Never in my right mind would I play poker with ye." He bowed mockingly toward Andre and Amelia. "Bless ye, my children," he murmured, then followed the colonel and Mike through the doorway.

"Ye know, Mike," Stephen said, as the three of them were riding back toward Harrow, "I think I'd better keep your Josh. He seems badly in need of care. I'll give ye another black in his stead and turn him over to Caleen for treatment."

"Awright," Mike grinned, winking his one eye at Andre. "Yez will give me my pick?"

"Of course."

"Then I'll take that gell"

"No," Stephen laughed, "at that I draw the line. She would be only a burden to ye in your wanderings. I'll give ye a man-servant, and ye may have your choice, saving only Achille and Georges."

"Keep yer Nigras," Mike said. "They're more trouble than they're worth. Just save a bed and a place at yer board for old Mike like we agreed."

"I haven't forgotten," Stephen said.

Andre half rose in his saddle and pulled his horse up short.

"I turn here," he said.

"And where are ye going?" Stephen demanded.

"Out to our place," Andre said, "for the second of my three ordeals."

"Three? Two, I understand. Colonel Rogers—that's done with. And now, your father. But the third?"

"On Sunday I call upon Aurore," Andre smiled wanly. "I swore eternal celibacy because she would not marry me. Now I must recant."

Stephen laughed aloud.

142

"'Tis hasty ye were, I'm thinking," he chuckled. "But wait for me on Sunday, and I'll go with ye. The interval will be long enough by then."

"Agreed," Andre said. "*Au 'voir*, gentlemen."

"A foine lad," Mike declared as they rode away. "I even fergit he's a Frenchy."

Back at Harrow, Stephen found the great house in perfect order. And already there were a half dozen visiting cards upon the table in the hall. There was a note asking him to dine at Rosemont with the Cloutiers; his presence was requested at three soirées.

Some of these he must accept, Stephen decided regretfully. It would not do to drop completely out of the fashionable world until after he had brought Odalie back to Harrow. Even then, perhaps, he would have to entertain and be entertained occa-sionally. Odalie was hardly one to hide her light under a bushel.

He went up to his rooms, stripped and bathed with Georges' assistance. Then he ate alone in the great salon, his meal con-sisting of a pot of black coffee, a crust or two of brown bread, and a bit of strong cheese. It was confounded lonely to eat thus in so huge a room. The manservant's footfalls echoed in the distance. He'd be damned if he would eat here again. Georges could bring his meals up to his rooms in the North Wing. And now he must ride out to the sugar house to supervise the sugar-making.

He called a servant and ordered a fresh horse. Prince Michael was pretty well blown by so long a ride. Then he started out, his head busy with plans. Soon he must erect an earthen wall against floods. The fields adjacent to the river were uncomforta-bly low. And this matter of a wife for Achille—perhaps La Belle Sauvage would do. Achille was now in his prime—a giant of a black, intelligent and capable of carrying out the most exacting task without supervision. 'Twould be well to preserve that strain; but as yet Achille seemed to pay scant attention to any of the women. Stephen wondered idly what Achille's father must have been like. Deuced odd name he had. What was that that Tante Caleen had called him? Oh, yes—Inch—Big Inch. Hanged before

143

the parish church in New Orleans. Yet there was no trace of rebelliousness in Achille. Caleen had reared him well.

The smoke came up from the big chimney and inside the sugar house the slaves worked busily, dipping the syrup out from vat to vat with the buckets on the ends of the long poles set in rowlocks. The sweat glistened on the fat black faces. Sugar house blacks were always fat, Stephen observed; something about the nature of the work itself did it. Surely they ate no more than the others. Perhaps they breathed in sugar through their pores.

Then Achille was coming forward, his white teeth gleaming in a smile doubly bright against his sweat-glistening face.

"How goes it, Achille?" Stephen asked.

"Good—ver good." Achille was assaying English, now that he knew that Stephen preferred that difficult tongue. "We make much sugar, yes!"

"Tomorrow I have an errand for ye. Go down to the St. Marie section to the small slave market—ye know where it is?"

"Yes, maître—I means 'yes, suh,' I knows."

"Take a wagon and bring back two new blacks I've bought. And take Roget and Henri and Gros Tom with ye. Ye'll need help with the wench or I miss my guess. By the way, Achille, look her over well and see how ye like her. She's intended for ye if she suits your fancy."

"Yes, maître," Achille said a little doubtfully. "I take a look, me."

"Ye're a confirmed woman hater, aren't ye, Achille? I can't say that I blame ye."

"They talks too much, the wimmins," Achille grinned. "Always they have the big mouth, yes!"

"Yes," Stephen laughed. "Well, keep them at it. I must ride out to the South fields to see how the late harvesting goes."

Up at the big house, Mike Farrel lay half asleep in the huge bed. Suzette was tiptoeing through the room, busily dusting the furniture. Mike raised up on one elbow.

144

"Come here, gel," he said softly.

The dark eyes widened in Suzette's soft yellow face. She hesitated fearfully.

"I said come here," Mike repeated in the same low voice.

Timidly, Suzette took a step forward—then another. A safe distance from the bed she stopped.

"Monsieur wants something, yes?"

"Yes," Mike declared. "Yez catch on fast. A little closer so's I kin whisper."

Suzette's warm red lips rounded into a little O of curiosity. She walked over quite near to where the big man lay. He smiled disarmingly, but his huge arm shot out suddenly, with all the speed and power of a grizzly striking.

Suzette screamed—a high, edged sound, hanging on the air. Mike clamped a hairy paw over her mouth. Suzette reacted instantly from pure instinct. She kicked with both feet at the same time and brought her long nails upwards so that their points went raking across Mike's forehead and into his one good eye. Mike released her instantly, bellowing with pain. Then she was gone from the room and down the stairs—a doe, buck pursued. In the pantry she hurled herself upon Tante Caleen, sobbing and fighting for breath.

"Tante Caleen!" she wept. "That beeg one, heem— Oh, Tante Caleen!"

"Hush, chile," old Caleen whispered. "It been like that, yes. Always it been like that. 'Tain't no good to fight. Your mamam, now you—mebbe your child, yes."

Suzette drew herself up very stiffly and the sobbing stopped.

"No," she said. "No."

Caleen looked at her; but when she spoke it was to herself she talked, not to the girl.

"Long time nobody talk like that," she said. "Not since my man, Inch. I wait for somebody like him, yes. I think mebbe Achille. But he grow up easy with no fight in him. Now I gits me somebody, and look what I got! Little yaller gal!" She snorted in disgust. Then her fierce old eyes softened. "Awright, Suzette," she said calmly. "He don't tetch you, him. I fix him, yes!"

145

On Sunday, Stephen dressed with unusual care. Georges worked over him busily, bringing out the new dark green coat, never before worn, the pale wine-colored waistcoat and the crimson stock. Stephen's breeches were fawn-colored and his boots a glossy brown, and Georges exclaimed proudly over each new article of attire. He shaved off the fiery stubble from his master's lean jaw, skirting carefully around the great sideburns.

Into the steaming water in the great oaken tub, he threw a concoction of Caleen's, a perfume that smelled of pine woods and autumn and the good clean smell of dry leaves burning. Then he stood by with big towels while Stephen bathed. Afterwards he assisted his master in dressing.

"When that lady see you now," he beamed, "she git up on Prince Michael behind you and come home with you tonight, her. I bet you, yes!"

"Ye're an optimist, Georges," Stephen said drily, and, taking his tall hat, his gloves and his riding crop, he went down the stairs.

Outside Achille waited with Prince Michael. The big palamino had been curried and groomed until his coat shone like satin. Seeing Stephen, he whinnied softly.

"Easy, old boy," Stephen said as he swung into the new English saddle. Then he looked down at Achille and smiled.

"Ye've done a good job," he said. "How d'ye like the new wench?"

"She wild, that one! She wild, but I tame her—she something, her!"

"Then ye find her to your liking? Good. I was beginning to think ye as hard to please as Caleen. Take good care of things until I get back. Report anything out of order to Mister Wilson."

He touched his riding crop to the brim of his hat and was off in the easy rolling gait that Prince Michael could keep up for miles.

Andre was waiting for him at the fork of the road that led out to his father's plantation. His young face was gloomy and there were lines of fatigue around his eyes.

Stephen whistled.

146

"By Our Lady!" he laughed. "Ye have been working, haven't ye?"

"Yes," Andre said. "That was not bad. Dear Papa is pleased as punch with me. But what I have to do today . . ."

"Don't worry," Stephen declared. "I'll wager ye'll find Aurore vastly sympathetic. She's like that. But how did the visit from Colonel Rogers affect him?"

"That was amazing! Papa took him all over the place, all the time deploring the enmity between the Creoles and the Americans. And I swear to you, Stephen, I never before heard him use the word American without adding pig to it, so that it was one word when he used it. Then he ordered Sarah to prepare a sumptuous dinner for the Colonel—and you know how stingy papa is. Afterwards they played *vingt-et-un,* and papa beat the Colonel. I strongly suspect the Colonel let him do it, for papa is no card player. And they parted the best of friends."

"Then papa approves of Amelia?"

"To the extent that he is almost competition! Last night I called on her briefly, and papa insisted upon accompanying me, stating that he wished to see how his daughter-to-be looked. And when he saw her—!"

"He fell down upon his face?"

"Exactly! How did you know?"

"Amelia has that effect upon men. I knew her before, remember."

Andre's expressive young face clouded.

"Only as a friend, lad. Besides, I don't like blondes."

"I think that was it. Golden hair is a rarity among us—and Amelia is lovely. Papa kissed her—a privilege I have yet to gain. The old devil!"

Stephen leaned back in the saddle and rocked with laughter. Andre grinned at him slowly.

"We turn here," he said. "You've never been out to Bellefont have you?"

"No, whenever I saw the Arceneaux they were always at their town house in New Orleans."

"Bellefont is something. It is as large in acreage as Harrow, but

147

it lacks so magnificent a manor. Odalie should be well disturbed in mind by now over your failure to pay immediate court."

"I shall make up for my tardiness with my ardor. How far is it now?"

"Only about two miles. You should be able to see it in a little while.'

They rode on in silence. The two miles slipped away under the hooves of the thoroughbred horses. Then they were turning into the big iron gates.

Instantly there was a great scurrying among the little *negrillons.* They ran toward the big house shouting:

"Monsieur Andre comes! Monsieur Andre and a strange gentleman! Ver' fine on a horse like yellow cream and with hair like fire! I seen him, me!"

The old groom was there at the foot of the stairs waiting, bowing grandly, with his battered old hat in his hand.

"Goodday, Messieurs," he beamed. "I take the hosses, no?"

Stephen and Andre dismounted, throwing him the reins. Then they went up the stairs and into the big house where another ancient Negro took their hats, cloaks and gloves.

"The Mamzelles be down directly," he said.

The two young men waited, saying little. Then there was the light whisper of footsteps on the winding stairway, and Aurore came down into the hall.

"Andre!" she said. "And Monsieur Fox—how nice!"

Andre's face was scarlet under his tan, but Stephen bowed calmly over her hand with all the grace of a dancing master.

"But I thought you were angry with me, Andre," Aurore teased as she led the way into the drawing room, "I thought you swore never to call again."

"I—I came for a reason, Aurore."

"Oh—how mysterious! I am dying of curiosity."

Andre looked at her and took a deep breath.

"I want to be released from my promise not to marry!" he blurted.

Aurore looked up at him and shook with laughter.

148

"But, of course, my poor friend! The Mademoiselle Rogers is lovely. I trust you'll be very happy."

"Then you knew?"

"Yes, Andre—I and everyone else who was at Harrow that night. I have never seen a man so smitten!"

"It is only because you—are you sure you won't change your mind, Aurore?"

Aurore looked at him and her voice was very quiet.

"Never, Andre," she said, then again the teasing note crept into her tone. "Suppose I were to change—what would you do then, my Romeo?"

Andre's face was such a study of perplexity that Aurore and Stephen both laughed.

"Don't worry," she smiled compassionately. "I shan't change. My congratulations, my friend—I wish you every happiness."

Stephen made a little gesture of impatience.

"Odalie will come down in a moment," Aurore whispered. "She has been sulking all week because you hadn't called. But don't tell her I told you! Come, Andre, we must leave them alone. Besides, I want to enjoy the little of your company that is left to me."

Stephen's hand went into his pocket and came out with the massive gold watch that wound with a key; but before he had time to open the case to look at it Odalie came through the door. Stephen stood up and went forward to meet her, his eyes lighted from somewhere within with a flame that leaped and danced as he looked into her face.

"Goodday, monsieur," Odalie said. "I was beginning to wonder if you had forgotten your promise to call."

Stephen smiled, one eyebrow lifting mockingly toward the scar.

"Would ye have cared?" he asked.

Odalie's black eyes widened and the gardenia paleness of her skin took on a faint trace of color. But when she spoke her voice was steady.

"Yes," she said. "I would have cared. Won't you sit down? It's awkward to stand and talk."

Stephen sank into a great chair facing her.

"Ye've changed," he said.

"No—it's you who have changed. I am still the same."

"As in the days when ye hated me and thought me a black-guard and a despoiler of women?"

"I never hated you."

"Call me Stephen. 'Tis over late now for formality between us, don't ye think?"

Odalie looked at him a long time. Then very simply, her voice sunk almost to a whisper, she repeated:

"I never hated you—Stephen."

"I'm glad. I was never one to care too much what was said or thought about me, but what ye said or thought—that was a different matter. Ye cost me many troubled nights, Odalie."

Odalie smiled slowly. Watching the wine-red lips moving, Stephen knew suddenly that all the sunblasted days in the fields, all the nights of sleepless scheming, all the work and waiting and worry were nothing and if they had been multiplied a thousand-fold they would have been still an insignificance against the gaining of this woman.

"You know, Stephen, I'm glad of that," she said smiling. "It pleases me to know that I meant more to you than—than a horse, perhaps."

"My God!" he exploded. "Is that what ye thought?"

"Yes. You seemed a bold devil—utterly careless and reckless of anything or anyone that you wanted. I was unaccustomed to being looked at appraisingly like a slave girl. And whenever you spoke you made a mockery. I kept thinking: 'Who does he think himself that he should look at me thus?'"

Stephen threw back his head and laughed aloud.

"Yet there were many men, very many men who looked upon ye with humility and awe and worship—and ye married none of them."

"I have not married you, Stephen!"

"No—not yet. But ye're going to. Ye know that, don't ye?"

"You're impertinent! If you mean that for a proposal my answer is . . ."

"Wait a bit, Odalie. Do not spoil things because of annoyance at my boldness. That, I cannot help. 'Tis the way I'm made. There is too much between us now—far too much."

"What is there between us, monsieur?"

"Stephen."

"Oh all right—Stephen." Then: "But I see nothing between us —nothing at all."

Stephen looked at her and his face was still and unsmiling. Only his eyes were alive—moving like the strokes of an etcher's pen, short, swift and unbelievably deft, limning her image as she was at that instant forever on his brain. His voice was very deep when he spoke.

"There is Harrow."

"Harrow?"

"Yes. Always I've had the dream of it—the great white house of which I should be master. But 'twas ye that shaped it into reality. When first I saw ye, in the Place D'Armes on the day that Lafayette came, the dream became more than a dream—it became a need, a necessity—an obsession. And for the first time it was a means toward an end rather than an end in itself. Ye were the end, Odalie. Harrow was no longer important then—it was the mistress of Harrow that mattered."

"You—you built Harrow—for me?"

"Yes. I could not have built it without ye. A house yes. Even a great house, perhaps. But not Harrow—not as it is now—sitting there under the oaks waiting, every line of it with ye built into it. And until ye come it will have no life. Only ye can bring it completion."

"I—I don't know what to say . . ."

"Nothing yet. I shall be patient. I'll endure all the necessary formalities of a courtship. But it must end thus. It must, Odalie." He stood up and she rose too, her eyes very wide and dark, searching his face. She laid a hand upon his arm. It trembled so that he felt it, through his coat.

"I think," she said, "that never before was a woman so honored."

Again the little glint of mockery stole into Stephen's eyes.

151

"Then why do ye tremble?"

"Because I am afraid. I have never been afraid before. Other men I could turn aside, but not you, Stephen. You're so direct and terribly simple and yet so endlessly complicated at one and the same time . . ."

"Yet I am nothing to fear."

"I—I've made a sort of obsession of privacy, Stephen," she said, but she was not looking at him. Her eyes were turned inward as though she were searching her own mind. "I've enjoyed being— well—cool and aloof—it made me different somehow. And I think now that it provoked men into greater efforts. I've never liked being touched, not even by my father. And even Aurore doesn't kiss me. She knows I don't like it. While in marriage— to such a man as you. . . ." Her eyes were suddenly bright with dismay. "*Ma foi!* What am I saying?"

Stephen's expression did not change.

"Ye will find me patient," he murmured. "And very gentle."

He bent over her hand, they strode through the door.

She was still standing there, looking after him, her face bathed in crimson when Aurore came in.

"What ails you?" the younger girl demanded.

"I said the most awful—the most unladylike things. Oh, Aurore!"

Aurore came up to her and put her arms around her waist.

"Don't trouble yourself, my dear. He didn't seem to mind. You shall be mistress of Harrow—and that is something."

"Mistress of Harrow," Odalie repeated after her, and her voice was filled with something very like glory.

X

Stephen closed the huge ledger book wearily. It was long past midnight and a new year had come in with the crying winter rains. Tomorrow—not today—since New Year's Day had come in while he sat poring over the multiple entries in his big book of accounts—he would ride into New Orleans and make the rounds of the great houses of the city bearing gifts to some of his closer friends. Stephen wondered idly why New Year's Day was the day of giving in the Bayou country instead of Christmas as in the other American states. 'Tis the religion, he decided. To the devoutly Catholic, predominantly French lower half of Louisiana, Christmas was strictly a holy day and the fun and festivity was reserved for New Year's.

He would stop at Andre's house and salute him and his bride of one week in foaming egg nog. Strange to think of Andre—gay Andre, frivolous Andre—married and working hard to carve out a place for himself and Amelia. Old Le Blanc was literally coming apart at the seams with pride. Already, to Amelia's acute embarrassment, he was talking of a grandson. Stephen remembered the faces of the young couple at the ceremony. Never had he seen such tenderness upon the face of a man—it was almost

153

reverence. And Amelia, lifting her face to her new husband to be kissed, had been as beautiful as an angel. Somehow, afterwards, the emptiness of Harrow had become unbearable—the servants tiptoeing through the vast, high-ceilinged rooms like ghosts had become even quieter to avoid his increasingly irascible temper.

Odalie must give him an answer. Today the date must be set. This delay, this dilly-dallying must end. Clearly she loved him— she admitted it quite honestly, but always added, "I must have more time, Stephen, to get used to the idea." She let him kiss her—quick, brushing kisses—very cool and swift, ..er hands always pushing against his chest in half protest. Stephen was going mad with wanting her, watching her cool loveliness which even in his arms was just out of his reach. "By all the fruits of Tantalus," he said, standing up, "today it ends!"

He went to the window, high up under the roof and looked out. Far off to the left he saw a fire burning despite the steady cold drizzle of rain. That must be Caleen, brewing her herbs.

As he went down the stairs from his garret study, his mind wandered over a number of people. How was Achille making out with La Belle Sauvage? So far, the big black's courtship had proved as futile as his own. That wild Negress was becoming tamer under Caleen's wise old hands, but she was still a savage thing—as beautiful as a black panther, and just as dangerous. And Tom Warren—where the deuce was he? It had been a year and a half since he had visited Harrow. It was rumored that he was growing vastly rich down in New Orleans, with a finger in half a dozen deals, some of which were distinctly mysterious. Josh, the feeble half-mad Negro he had bought for Mike—not an unprofitable deal at that. Josh was a wonderful fisherman, and his skill as a gardener was only less than Jupiter's own. Still he was always talking about "de big fiah, down by de ribber when pore Rad got kilt." Not much sense to it, this talk, but there must be something behind it to make the poor black so afraid.

And Mike. The big riverman stayed on at Harrow month after month, growing ever more quarrelsome and moody and staying sober for shorter and shorter periods. Stephen was beginning to fear for his sanity. At least twice a week they would hear him

154

roaring in his rooms, and entering find him threshing about con-vulsively in the throes of a drunken nightmare. Caleen, he swore, caused these black and vivid dreams.

Even now, as Stephen came down the stairs, Mike was coming out of his rooms, all his belongings slung in a little bundle on his back. His one good eye was wide and staring and his breath was coming out in short, sharp animal-like pants.

"Where on earth are ye going?" Stephen demanded.

"Away from here!" Mike bellowed. "Away from this divil-cursed, hag-ridden place of yourn! I'll never spend another night here!"

"Softly, Mike. Never is a long time," Stephen said. "What's troubling ye now?"

"That old black witch! Yez saw a fire in the brush?"

"Yes—but what has that . . ."

"Caleen sot it! I followed her. And yez know what she was doing? She had made up me image in clay—remarkably like me it were. Me own mither woulda recognized me at once. And she were a stickin' pins in it and a mutterin' curses!"

Stephen laughed aloud.

"And for that ye go chasing off in the pitch blackness with a rain falling? Don't be a fool, Mike!"

"A fool, yez say! Yez want me to become a blitherin' idiot with no wits in me head? She cuts off the head after and tosses it in the fire! I tole yez 'twas her who sent those dreams!"

"Why," Stephen demanded, "should Tante Caleen want to harm ye?"

"Because she hates all whites—even yez, Stephen—and because of the little yaller wench of yourn."

"Suzette?"

"Yes. I tried several times to git her to bed down with me—just a wee bit of sport, Stephen, 'twould do her good in fact. But she runs to Caleen and the old divil starts in to save her from me—with her spells and curses and clay dolls!"

"And ye're running—from that?"

"Yez be damned right I'm running! I will not have me mind destroyed whilst I sleep!"

155

"This will stop, Mike," he said, "this Voudou business. I will see Caleen at once. I promised ye that Harrow would be another home to ye. I mean to keep that promise. And I shall need your help often in the future. I've plans for both of us."

"What kind of plans?" Mike growled darkly.

"A steamboat line of my own—with ye as captain of my fastest packet. 'Twill be many years before I can do it—I am in debt up to my neck for the house and its furnishings; but when I do I want to be able to put my hands on ye."

"That yez will, me foine lad! Why I know the river like the back of me hand. But I think still I'll go up to Natchez until the old witch has forgotten this affair. I'll be back to Harrow often, niver yez fear."

"As ye will," Stephen said. "But do not stay away too long. I shall take Caleen in hand this night!"

Outside in the oak grove, despite the partial shelter from the great trees, the rain was like needles of ice. Stephen walked rapidly towards where he had seen the fire, wrapping his greatcoat about him and bending his head before the wind. After ten minutes of pushing through the brush he came to a little clearing.

Caleen was sitting in the middle of it, crouched before a flickering fire which seemed to burn all the brighter as the rain drops hissed into it. Slowly, and with great ceremony, she was dismembering a doll of clay and tossing it into the fire. Little remained of it now. She was crooning a weird dirgelike song.

As he stepped noiselessly toward her, Stephen noticed another doll waiting at her side. It was crudely done, but he had no trouble recognizing it. This was La Belle Sauvage, the beautiful black girl he had purchased for Achille. Evidently, when she had finished her incantations against Mike Farrel, Caleen meant to go to work on the girl.

"Caleen!" Stephen said sharply.

"Maître!"

"What is the meaning? Ye would harm Mike Farrel with your witchery? And the girl, what mean ye to do to her?"

Caleen looked up at him, and there was no fear in her bloodshot, anciently wicked eyes.

156

"There some things, maître, no good for whites to know. I take care of Harrow and you, maître. I see that no harm come to you, me."

"Ye're lying!" Stephen declared flatly. "Tell me, what mean ye to work against the girl?"

"Nothing, maître. I only fix her so that she love my Achille. He crazy mad for her, him. So I fix."

Stephen walked up to the fire and kicked it apart, trampling on the embers. They flared up again with uncommon stubbornness. When he had the last one out he turned to Caleen.

"I've never had one of my people whipped," he said slowly. "But by heaven, Caleen, if ye continue this witchcraft, I'll send ye up to the Calaboose and order thirty lashes! Ye hear me now?"

Walking away, Stephen realized that on the rare occasions when, as now, Caleen was humble, her humility had a fine excess to it—so slight as to be almost unnoticeable, yet just enough to hint at mockery. He dismissed her from his mind with a shrug. There was nothing anyone could do with Caleen—nothing at all.

Back at Harrow, he stripped off his wet garments and plunged between the icy sheets. Of course he could have summoned a slave with a warming pan, but that would have cost him another half hour of sleeplessness and the hour was already late. Gradually the heat of his body warmed the bed, but it was a long time before he fell asleep. Even then, he was troubled by swift, utterly senseless dreams. He twisted and groaned in his sleep. The dreams swept through his mind in an endless train, yet the instant they had gone he forgot completely what they were about. Only the feeling of cold persisted—cold and horror and a nameless dread. It was as though icy fingers were clutched around his heart, freezing it into immobility. He let out a cry so short and sharp that it awakened him. A cold wind, laden with the icy lances of the rain, blew in the open window, and he had kicked the covers off. His whole body was covered with goose pimples.

He drew the cover back up over himself and pulled the bell cord that summoned Georges. When the valet appeared, Stephen ordered him, through chattering teeth, to bring black coffee and hot buttered rum. Georges ran from the room, his eyes wide and frightened.

"Maître sick!" he babbled to Caleen. "Him face like death!"

The old woman stopped her work and took the coffee pot which was gurgling softly on the hearth. Then she prepared the spiced rum punch and went upstairs to Stephen's bedchamber.

"Who the deuce sent for ye!" Stephen chattered. "Are ye all mad in this house?"

Caleen did not answer. Instead she laced a cup of black coffee liberally with the rum and held it to his lips.

"Drink," she commanded calmly.

Stephen drank, glaring at Caleen all the while. As if by magic the trembling ceased as the chill departed from his limbs. Caleen put the bowl of steaming rum punch by the bed.

"Drink it all, maître," she said. "It do you good." Then she was gone from the room, leaving Stephen staring after her.

"She is positively uncanny," he muttered, then turning to Georges: "Come, man, bring me my clothes!"

Stephen drank the rest of the rum punch while he dressed. It warmed him all over and made him feel cheerful again. Dreams, posh! It was just that he had overtaxed himself, that was all. Running a cane plantation was no simple business. As valuable as was the advice of Andre, old Le Blanc, and even the celebrated de Bores, there were some things a man could only learn by doing. He had made his mistakes as the big ledger plainly showed. Of course, he would survive and even make a small profit; but it was small, and although there were no longer any debts outstanding against the land, the house had set him back for years. This business of Odalie was a vexation, too.

He ate a light breakfast and set out, accompanied by Georges. The Negro had huge saddle bags slung across his nag and they were full of gifts. The first stop was the Cloutiers. Madame Cloutier had been wonderfully kind and, besides, she was a power to be recognized in the social life of New Orleans. Until he was safely married to Odalie, Stephen realized the necessity of keeping the good will of the guardian matrons, however irksome he found it. The Arceneaux' lack of a mother to provide the proper chaperonage was a fruitful field for scandal, especially coupled with old Arceneaux' unbelievably advanced ideas as to the personal liberty of his daughters. It would pay, then, to keep the longest tongues wedded to his service; and no one possessed a longer or more venomous one than Madame Cloutier.

Stephen stopped first at their ancient town house because he could plead as an excuse for his limited stay the fact that he had many more calls to make, and thus rid himself as early as possible of the burdensome society of the daughters Cloutier, who still attempted, under the heavyhanded management of their mother, to compete with Odalie for his attentions. At that, it was far longer than he intended before he was able to bow himself out of the salon where the brandy and whiskey stood in cut-glass decanters upon the sideboard, and the cornets of bonbons and dragees were scattered recklessly about. These were supposed to be gifts from admirers, but Stephen easily recognized in their characteristic lack of grace, the not so very fine hand of the Cloutiers themselves.

Still, it was an ill wind that blew nobody good. Now he could excuse himself from visiting houses which he had no desire to in the first place and dispatch Georges with the presents and his cards. Andre he would visit and after that Odalie. He sent Georges on his way, and turned Prince Michael toward the house of the Le Blancs. Ti Demon open the door for him, his small black face glistening with good cheer, much of it, Stephen guessed, alcoholic.

"Monsieur Fuchs!" Ti Demon called out. The proper pronunciation of Stephen's name came with difficulty to French tongues, and none found it more troublesome than the Creole Negroes. Most people simply translated it so that it became Etienne Reynard and let it go at that.

But Andre was coming toward him now, both hands outstretched, the happiness on his face outshining the candles.

"So," Stephen said, "it goes well with ye—this marriage business!"

159

" 'Tis beyond all paradise!" Andre declared, "and I owe it all to you, Stephen. I never would have met her—and she is the sweetest and the loveliest and the best . . ."

"Andre! Who is it, dearest?"

"Stephen," Andre called back. "Please come down and greet him. He's coming to see whether you throw pots and pans at me yet."

"But of course I do," Amelia said as she came down the stairs. "Although my aim still isn't very good. I'll improve with practice though." She came up to Stephen and gave him her slim white hand. "Thank you, Stephen," she said softly.

"For what?" Stephen demanded with mock brusqueness.

"For my Andre. For all the happiness in the world."

"I won't accept it now," Stephen laughed. "In six months or a year I will see if ye are still grateful. Then I'll accept your thanks."

"Make it ten years," Andre said, "or fifty and still you'll find me the happiest of mortals. But how goes it with you and Odalie, Stephen?"

Stephen shrugged expressively.

"Poor man," Amelia said. "I should like to call upon this Odalie of yours. I think I'd give her a piece of my mind."

"Have ye no eggnog for an old and tired man?" Stephen put in smoothly. "And ye used to make grand plum pudding, Amelia —'twas like a taste of London to me."

"Father brought Stephen home to our place in Kentucky once," Amelia explained. "He was always collecting odd characters. Not that you were odd, Stephen. In fact I thought you wonderful. I remember falling quite horribly in love with you. But you treated me like a child."

"Thank the good God," Andre said. "Forgive our thoughtlessness, my friend—this way, please."

Sipping the foaming eggnog and eating the steaming pudding, Stephen was conscious of a feeling very closely akin to pain. To see so much happiness hurt. It wasn't envy—at least not malicious envy. Rather it was the bitterness of contrast. He who had

160

worked and suffered had gained exactly nothing, while Andre's joy had been handed him on a silver platter, as it were. He put down his glass and his plate and stood up.

"I must be going now," he said.

"So soon?" they chorused.

"I go to call upon Odalie. Tonight I have hopes . . ."

Andre put out his hand.

"Every happiness, Stephen," he said. "You deserve it."

"Thank ye," Stephen said soberly. "A happy new year to ye both." He turned abruptly on his heel and marched toward the door.

As he approached the town house of the Arceneaux, Stephen could see the candles ablaze in every window. He dismounted and gave the reins to a groom. Then, taking a small package from his pocket, he strode up to the door. It was flung wide at once to his knock, and the old butler bent low before him, taking his hat, his greatcoat and his gloves. Stephen followed him into the salon, where a half dozen Creole youths were clustered about Odalie and an equal number about Aurore. The great scar on the side of his face flared scarlet. Plague the luck! It had never occurred to him that he wouldn't have Odalie all to himself. All these oily little bounders . . . But Odalie had detached herself from her admirers and was coming forward to greet him, a smile of pleasure lighting her face.

"Stephen," she said. "I thought you never were coming."

"I can see how bitterly ye missed me," Stephen observed drily.

"Oh, these boys? They're old friends, Stephen, nothing more. You must not take offense."

"Nor have I," Stephen said. "'Tis just that I wanted very badly to talk to ye alone. Oh, well—some other time perhaps."

"No, Stephen. We'll go into the little room. You've come such a long way and I—I like talking to you, alone."

"That's encouraging. I was beginning to think I gave ye the horrors."

Odalie made an impish face at him and took his hand. As they approached the others, all the young men stood up. Stephen knew most of them, but one young man was distinctly strange—an uncommonly handsome lad with boldness and diablerie written all over his finely chiseled face.

"You'll excuse me for a while, won't you, gentlemen?" Odalie asked. "There is a matter that Monsieur Fox and I must discuss."

"Oh, we were about to go anyway," they chorused politely. "Besides, what chance have we against the formidable Monsieur Fox?"

"I'm flattered, gentlemen," Stephen said mockingly and made them an exaggerated bow. They returned it with rare good humor and proceeded to the hallway where the butler waited with their hats and canes.

But the strange lad lingered a moment after the others. He walked boldly up to Stephen.

"You will pardon me, sir," he said. "But I have heard so much of you since my return that I desire to make your acquaintance. My name is Cloutier, Phillippe Cloutier."

"Ye're the brother of Henriette and Clothilde? By our Lady, how different ye are! One would never suspect the relationship."

"Monsieur intends that as a compliment?"

Stephen laughed. "Either way I'm wrong, aren't I? Your pardon, Monsieur Cloutier. I had no wish to offend. 'Tis just that your family seems the soul of honor and respectability while ye have the look of fine roguery about ye. I like the look—'tis becoming to a man."

Phillippe Cloutier smiled.

"I am the black sheep," he admitted. "'Tis the reason for the long extension of my grand tour. But I trust I shall see more of you, sir."

"Dine with me at Harrow," Stephen invited. "I knew Paris well —there are many things I would like to ask ye about."

Phillippe made him a low bow, and bent for a moment over the hand of Odalie. Then he turned and followed the others.

"Birds of a feather," she murmured. "The two of you seem cut from one cloth."

She opened the door to the smaller guest room and led Stephen toward a Louis XIV divan. But Stephen did not sit down.

"Odalie," he said. "Ye know what I want to ask ye?"

"Yes, Stephen."

"And your answer is?"

"Stephen I . . . I don't know . . . it's all so strange . . ."

He stood looking at her, the candle light dancing like fire in his eyes, his jaw set, the great scar visibly reddening.

"Come here, Odalie."

"But, Stephen . . ."

"I said come here." The words were very quiet. Odalie got up and came over to him. He slipped his arm lightly, loosely, around her waist and stood looking down into her face.

"Ye're beautiful," he said, "enough to drive a man to despair. But I have worked too long, and waited too long. I am not waiting longer." He bent his head down and locked his lips expertly against hers. At once her hands came up against his chest, pushing him gently away as always. But his arms tightened, so that she would have cried out in pain had she been able. But her mouth was against his, stopping her cries, stopping her breath. She hammered at his chest with both hands, but he drove his iron hand inward at the small of her back so that her body ground against his warm and soft through all the layers of clothing. And then suddenly the hammering stopped. Her lips softened and parted and the sweet young breath came sighing through. He felt her move, straining upward against him, and her arms stole softly around his neck. They were velvet soft where they touched, but they burnt him like a brand. Abruptly he released her.

She fell back, her black eyes as wide as the night, dancing suddenly with the diamond brightness of her tears.

"Stephen," she whispered. "Stephen . . ."

"When?" he demanded sternly.

"In the Spring," she said.

"The twenty-fifth of April," Stephen said softly. "The anniversary of the day that I first saw ye."

163

"Yes," she said. "Yes . . . Oh, Stephen . . ."

At once he was at her side, locking her again in his arms. Strange how strong they were, she found herself thinking, like bands of steel for all his slimness. And again she lifted her face upward to meet his kiss, then the thinking stopped altogether.

XI

THE wind that swept down over the face of the Mississippi on the night of April 25, 1829, was a laughing wind. It raised little wavelets which the moon caught and topped with silver. It caught the fat, fleecy clouds and spun them out into fine tendrils of lace so thin that through them the watchers on the levee could see the stars. The moon had tangled itself in the oak branches and was spilling silver over the alley of trees that led up to Harrow. And the great house itself was ablaze with light.

On the levee, on the galleries, on the belvédère the Negroes watched and waited for the new yellow maple coach of their master to turn from the river road into the oak alley bringing Stephen Fox back to Harrow—Stephen Fox and his bride. Achille and Georges waited upon the newly built levee from which they could command a view of the river road unbroken for almost a mile. Achille had his ancient shotgun in his hand, and now as the sleek brace of roans rounded the bend, pulling the coach at a spanking trot, he freed his arm from Georges' sudden grip and fired the cannonlike weapon into the air.

At the sound of the shot, the cries and laughter burst from the throats of all the Negroes. The house servants with their blue

165

kerchiefs tied about their heads came thronging out upon the galleries, talking and laughing in an excited but subdued babble. And all the field hands converged upon the house, bounding along as fast as they could run, waving the red kerchiefs that distinguished them from the house servants and letting their laughter roar up from throat and chest and belly.

The instant the coach stopped it was surrounded. The liveried footman climbed down from his high perch, bustling importantly and laying about him freely with his cane, clearing a path for his master.

Stephen got down through the door which the footman had opened and extended a hand into the darkened coach. The slaves held their breaths as the slim white arm stole out and took his gently. Then Odalie stepped down upon the little half step, and they crowded in closer, their eyes shining whitely in the darkness.

Odalie hesitated fearfully.

"Speak to them, my darling," Stephen whispered. "They've all come to see ye."

All Odalie could manage was a feeble: "Good evening, my people," and the air was rent with a great gale of excited laughter and chatter. Then Stephen swept her up into his arms so that her dainty silken slippers should not touch the earth, and marched with her through the cheering crowd up the sweeping flight of stairs and into the great hall of Harrow, with all the house servants trailing behind them.

The field Negroes crowded near the door, but they came no closer, all of them packed in a great semicircle around Harrow. All of them—except one. In the shadows of the oaks La Belle Sauvage lingered, her great yellow-brown eyes glowing in her velvety black face. Clad now in the Mother Hubbard garments of a slave woman, her carriage was still regal and her beauty was a source of trouble to all the younger slaves upon the plantation. Coming away from the door, Achille saw her there, lurking in the shadow, and moved toward her silently. Tonight was the night for nuptials for the good young master—why not then for him? No longer did La Belle Sauvage fight and claw at him with her

166

daggerlike nails; but her method of eluding him now was even more maddening. She simply looked through him and passed him as though he did not exist. But tonight as he stood trembling beside her, she turned and looked at him. Then at last she spoke.

"Slave Nigra!" she spat, and turned and walked away from him, swinging her hips like a queen. The rage mounted up in Achille's throat until it was brine and black bile and fire. He came up to her and caught her by the shoulder, spinning her around to face him.

"You my woman!" he said. "I your man, me!"

La Belle Sauvage looked at him and her full lips curled contemptuously.

"You no man," she said flatly in the horrible mixed gumbo French she had acquired. "My tribe man no make slave. Warrior him die, but him no make slave. Even woman no make slave—die first, killee self first. In my tribe never no slave."

"You slave, you!" Achille cried. "What for you think no, girl? You slave just like me, you!"

"No slave," she taunted. "No work—no bow down. Sauvage still princess. Make slave I kill me, yes!" Then she turned and walked away in the direction of the cabins. Achille walked along beside her, his brow furrowed with thought. She had no right to say that, her. She had no right to make him feel like a dog or a horse or any owned thing. Yet he must have her, with all her arrogant beauty that was like a night without stars.

They were passing his cabin now. Achille's little eyes narrowed. He looked at the girl out of the corners of them. Then all at once without any warning he swept her up as lightly as a leaf into his arms. She kicked out and tore the skin of his face into ribbons, but he shouldered his way into the cabin with her and kicked the door shut behind him.

Up at Harrow, Stephen fingered the long-stemmed goblet of wine. He was in his dressing gown and the wine remained untouched. His eyes swept ever again toward the closed door behind which he could hear Odalie moving up and down—hear her footsteps moving and the soft rustling swish of her wedding garments as she removed them. This was maddening, this waiting. And when at last her voice came trembling through the door, very high and edged and frightened, he stood up so suddenly that the glass crashed to the floor. Where the wine touched, it left a stain like blood.

Then he pushed open the door gently and stood with his back rigid against it, staring at her. Her gowns was of lace net and silk and her hair was all darkness against the candles. She stood there trembling so violently that he could see it even across the vast bedroom and, as she turned her head half away from him, he could see the great tears spilling over the incredibly long lashes, gleaming like diamond drops in the candle flame.

"My God!" he whispered. "My God, but ye're beautiful!"

Then he was striding across the room with long slow steps toward where she stood, shivering as from an icy wind.

"I'm afraid!" she wailed, as he drew her gently to him, "Oh, Stephen, I'm so afraid!"

"Don't be," he said. "Ye've nothing to fear." Then he bent and kissed her lips softly. They were so cold that they burnt him. He kissed her once again, harder, but this time the hands came up against his chest pushing against him.

"Stephen!" she said. "You said you'd have patience! You promised, Stephen, you promised!" Then she struck out wildly with her fists, hard against his chest, his shoulders, his throat.

Stephen's fair brows knitted together, and the scar was a brand of scarlet. Something very like to madness exploded in his brain. The years of waiting, of work, of anguish of mind and heart—for this! His lips came away from his teeth in a grimace of agony. He jerked her to him so hard that the single cry: "Stephen!" broke in half upon her lips. Then just as abruptly the rage was gone and the desire and in their place was an icy, echoing emptiness. He released her quite suddenly and spun on his heel. In the doorway he turned.

"Goodnight—Madame Fox," he said. Then he turned through the door and was gone.

Odalie lay weeping across the great bed. She had intended to submit. She wanted to be a good wife—she wanted to give Stephen tall manly sons with hair like foxfire and an arrogant lilt to their walk; but this thing—this horror of being touched—this dwelling within the sanctity of her person was too strong. The fear was too strong and she could not let go. After a time her sobs quieted. She stood up and crossed the room. At the door she hesitated—then at last she pushed it open.

The hallway was vast and dark; she trembled like a small woods creature crossing it. On the far side the light from the candles in Stephen's room edged the door with silver, and laid a line bright across her face from forehead to chin. In it, the one of her eyes that it touched swam with tears that caught the light like jewels. Then at last her hand came down upon the knob and she was twisting it, pushing the door open with sudden strength.

"Stephen. . . ." she whispered.

He looked up from his long white pipe of Irish clay and the hardness went out of his eyes.

"Yes?" he said and his voice was gentle. "Yes, my dear?"

"I've come to be your wife," she said. "If you still want me—after that . . ."

He put down his pipe carefully and stood up.

"Still want ye," he said. "Still want ye? Oh, all ye blessed saints in heaven!"

She took a half step forward and the next instant she was in his arms.

Afterwards, it was very quiet at Harrow. There was no sound except the quiet rustle of Stephen's breath as he lay sleeping, one arm around the shoulders of his bride. But Odalie was awake, lying there in the crook of her new husband's arm, and her silken pillow was sodden with her tears. This—this was marriage! This was how a man expressed the tenderness that was within him and the devotion. Then human beings *were* animals after all and no better than the other animals despite all the lace and perfume and poetry . . . lace and perfume and poetry leading up to this! And there were years of this before

169

her, years of steeling herself to submit, of shaping herself into a dutiful wife. Yet she must . . .

She raised up and looked down at Stephen's sleeping face, clear in the moonlight that was pouring in through the window. The scarred side was turned down next to the pillow and sleep had eased and softened all the lines, until his face was as she had always imagined the face of an angel, strong and beautiful in its manhood, with the cynicism and the mockery erased. The great red ringlets curled damply over his high white forehead and the lines of pale pink freckles curved over the bridge of his nose.

"I love you, my husband," she whispered. "For you I'll be patient and submissive and try to comprehend." Then very softly, she began to pray.

Stephen waited at the foot of the stairs as Amelia and Andre alighted from their landau. It was still early in the summer and the blasting heat of the bayou country had not yet made itself felt. Amelia was cool in her summer dress of thin India muslin, despite the great ham-shaped sleeves, and the numerous petti-coats. Her face, under the big straw hat, was radiant. She waved her little ruffled parasol at Stephen and smiled. Stephen smiled back and bowed grandly over her white gloved hand. Andre strutted about like a turkey cock, looking for the moment so much like old Le Blanc in one of his more expansive moods that Stephen laughed aloud.

"So!" he laughed. "Already I am to become a godfather!"

"Stephen!" Amelia's face was stricken. "How on earth did you know?"

"My apologies, Amelia. I didn't mean to be so indelicate. But look at him, will ye—what else could make him strut so? And your face, my dear—it has the look of the angels."

"You won't tell your wife?"

"Of course not! But come—she's been on pins all day waiting on ye two."

Going up the curving stairs, Andre looked at his friend.

Stephen's face was still, and the laughter had gone out of his eyes.

"Stephen . . ."

"Yes, Andre?"

"How goes it with you? You're happy, my old one?"

"Divinely."

Ma foi! Andre thought. Never have I heard it said with less enthusiasm. Still, one never can tell about Stephen. He flies hot and cold with little or no provocation.

Odalie came out on the gallery to greet them. Her dress of flowered chintz was cool and sweet, and her black hair, worn loose despite the fashion because Stephen liked it so, blew lightly away from her shoulders in the summer breeze. She extended both her hands to Amelia and the smile on her face was genuine.

"I'm so glad," she said, speaking in English with only the faintest trace of an accent. "I've been looking forward so to meeting you. Of course we did meet before—but there was such a crowd, and we had no chance to talk. Come in, my dear. I was beginning to think you'd never come."

"We've been so busy," Amelia murmured.

Stephen glanced at her with one eyebrow arched until it almost touched the scar.

"That ye have!" he laughed. "Of that there is now no further doubt!"

"Stephen!" Odalie said sharply. "Please forgive my husband, Madame. At times he has the most abominable manners." She linked her arm through Amelia's and walked ahead of the men.

"You're so beautiful," she said warmly. "Stephen literally raves over you—and now I see why. Of course I've seen the German girls from Law's Coast—but such hair and eyes as yours! How I envy you!"

"It's like old straw," Amelia declared. "Andre often repeats what your husband said when first he saw you: 'Hair like midnight cascading from God's own heaven, unlighted by a star.' And so it is."

"Stephen said that? Strange he never told me. I like it though,

171

that phrase. I'll remember it. Thank you very much, Madame Le Blanc."

"Please call me Amelia. I hope we're going to be friends."

"But of course! And you must call me Odalie. But here we are. You must sit there across from me, so we can talk. It's been ages since I've talked to a woman other than the slaves. And you can scarcely call that conversation, can you?"

"But your sister?" Amelia asked. "She comes to see you often, doesn't she?"

Odalie's lovely face clouded.

"No," she said. "No she doesn't. In fact, she's visited us only once since we've been out here. Of course, it is a long ride . . ."

They took their places at the table and the slaves brought the gleaming dishes. While they ate, Odalie kept up a running fire of small talk, but Stephen said scarcely a word. He sat back in his chair watching her, and his eyes were somber.

She's too eager, Amelia decided; she's trying too hard to be pleasant. She isn't like this really. I had the feeling before that she was rather reserved. Still, I shouldn't make rash judgments.

Andre cleared his throat.

"Everything goes well, Stephen?" he got out.

"Everything."

There was a little pool of silence in which the clinking of the knives and forks sounded too loudly.

"You've heard about Tom Warren?" Andre tried again.

"No," Stephen said. "What about him?"

"He grows richer by the minute. I don't know how he got his start. 'Twas rumored that he made a killing in wheat at first, but that couldn't be for all his wheat burned in that warehouse of yours, didn't it?"

"Yes," Stephen said. "It did."

"Strange. I heard it from people who should know. You don't see much of him, do you?"

"He hasn't been out to Harrow in nearly two years. I guess he's busy. Someday I'm going to look him up—when I get the time."

"But you do have many visitors here, don't you?" Amelia asked.

172

"Quite a few. Young Cloutier is the most frequent. I think he'd like to relieve me of my wife," Stephen said wickedly, "so I watch him most closely!"

"Must you say things like that?" Odalie snapped. "You'll have Amelia thinking . . ."

"That ye're the loveliest creature on earth and no man can resist ye? Why not, my dear? 'Tis true."

"Stephen, you're positively the worst . . ."

"You wouldn't love him if he were a saint," Amelia observed gently. "I think I should be horribly bored if Andre weren't such a devil!"

"You see?" Andre said with a laugh. "The truth will out."

"So it will," Stephen smiled. "Marriage reveals so many things. By the way, Andre, I married my Achille off to that African wild-cat—at last."

"I saw him when we drove up," Andre said. "Is that why he looks so morose?"

"Yes," Stephen laughed. "She gives him not a moment's peace. She's either being terrifically affectionate or throwing him out on his ear—all in the space of an afternoon! Poor fellow! At least he's never bored."

"And you, my dear," Odalie murmured softly. "Are you bored?"

"Of course not," Stephen declared stoutly. "How could I be?"

"I was merely wondering, darling. But come, Amelia, let's go up to my rooms and leave the men in peace. I want to talk more freely than we can here."

The two women rose. Andre and Stephen got up with them. After they had gone, Stephen turned to the sideboard.

"Whiskey?" he asked.

"No, port," Andre said. "Well, Stephen, how does it feel to have succeeded in all your aims? Your head must be in the clouds."

"I don't know, Andre," Stephen said soberly. "It takes a bit of getting used to—this marriage business."

Andre raised the glass of ruby-colored liquid.

"Your health, my good friend—and your happiness."

Stephen studied him over the small amber-colored whiskey. Then, smilingly, he raised his glass.

173

"To the coming heir of the Le Blancs," he said. "May he be all that ye've hoped for."

"Thank you, Stephen," Andre said. "A son—it must be a son, Stephen. That's something to think about. It makes me feel old somehow—and curiously humble. What can I say to him? What can I teach him? Still—a son. 'Tis a wonderful thing, Stephen."

"Aye," Stephen said, and his voice had such a huskiness to it that Andre turned and stared openly into his face. Stephen paid no attention to his friend's look. Instead he gazed out of the big window over the rolling fields that stretched away mile after mile out of sight. Strange how empty they seemed—how empty and desolate and futile. Conscious of the deepening silence between them, Stephen turned at last to Andre.

"Aye," he said again very softly, " 'tis a wonderful thing, Andre, a very wonderful thing."

It was no good to stay after that. So as soon as courtesy permitted Amelia and Andre said their goodbyes and took their leave of Harrow. Riding away in the landau, Andre looked at his bride. Amelia's lovely face was troubled. The miles rolled backwards under the hoofs of the horses, but neither of them spoke. Finally, as they were turning into La Place des Rivières, Amelia turned impulsively to Andre.

"Kiss me," she whispered.

Andre bent and kissed her very gently, touching her lips lightly, lingering a long moment, then drawing his face away slowly. She nestled her head against his shoulder.

"Andre. . . ." she said.

"Yes, my angel?"

"I feel so sorry for them—both of them."

"Aye," Andre said slowly. It was an expression which he had never before used.

After Andre and Amelia had left Harrow, Stephen went up the stairs to his rooms. He set his dress in order, and picked up his hat and gloves. As he gave one last look into the mirror,

174

Odalie turned the gleaming brass knob and stood there in the doorway.

"You're not going out again?" she asked.

"And why not, my dear?"

"No reason—only it's so lonely here."

"I didn't think ye particularly enjoyed my company," Stephen said.

Odalie shrugged.

"You wouldn't believe the truth if I told you," she said. "But might I ask where you're going?"

"Ye might," Stephen said tartly. "Although it seems scarcely becoming of a wife to question her husband's doings. I go to the city—to be exact to the corner of Orleans and Bourbon Streets —to the gambling house of one John Davis, of whom ye've no doubt heard."

"Must you go, Stephen?"

"Don't worry. I shan't lose, if that's what's troubling ye."

"No—it's not that. It's just that I see so little of you, and we've been married only a little more than two months."

"And that bothers ye?"

"Yes." She lifted her face up to his, moving very close to him so that he could smell the perfume in her hair. When she spoke again her voice had just the trace of a quiver in it.

"I want to have a baby," she said.

Stephen's eyes were very pale in his lean, scarred face. He put down his hat and his gloves slowly, and took her by the shoulders, gently with both hands.

"But ye hate my touching ye," he said. "In my arms ye tremble like a wild thing—frightened almost to death."

"I know—and of that I'm horribly ashamed, Stephen my husband. Perhaps I shall change . . . I . . . I don't know. Only I want you to have your son, Stephen, with his hair like sunflame and the hot, sweet arrogance in him. Is that so strange, my husband, since however I am—however wild and frightened and shy—I love you with all my heart?"

"Holy Mother of God!" Stephen whispered.

"It's all right," Odalie said softly. "Go away to your gaming."

But Stephen's arms were around her, holding her against his heart. She could hear it hammering there, like a muffled drum.

"No," he said. "No—I shan't go."

Then effortlessly he swept her up into his arms and walked with her through the doorway. But afterwards it was the same: with all the rigidity and trembling and cold hurt-frightened tears. Stephen got up without a word and began to dress himself rapidly.

"Stephen!" The word was half a sob.

"Yes," he snarled. "Yes, I'm going!" Then he strode from the room and his boots sounded clearly on the stairs going down. . . .

Day after day as the Summer came on the heat mounted. The sun rose over the fields of Harrow, white in a steel-white sky from which even the blue had been blasted by the never-ceasing heat. The swamps began to dry up from the lack of water, and sandbars showed through the waters of the Mississippi. In the high-ceilinged rooms of Harrow the heat was lessened, but even there it hung like a tangible weight, pressing down upon their heads. Looking out of her window, Odalie could see the dwarfed stalks of cane standing up bare and brown in the naked fields.

Stephen was down there, moving through the fields as though the heat did not exist. She could see the gleam of his bright hair even from where she sat. He was working like mad, driving himself and the slaves to exhaustion in his efforts to save the crop. There was a line of Negroes moving in from the river, with staves bent across their shoulders, from which were suspended oaken buckets filled to the brim with river water. This, Odalie had never seen done before on any of the great plantations. By this means, desperate and heartbreakingly slow, Stephen was keeping some of the cane alive until it should rain again.

He was never at home anymore. For weeks Odalie had not seen him eat more than a crust of bread. The freckles on his fair face increased but he did not tan. Instead, his face grew daily leaner and harder and his eyes receded into the sockets ringed with

176

bluish shadows. He spoke seldom and then in monosyllables, with the corner of one lip curling a little and one eyebrow climbing upward toward the scar which shone with demonic clarity upon his forehead.

At night, after a day of work which left even the big Achille spent and panting, he would bathe and dress himself and ride away toward New Orleans. Toward Odalie he was grave and exquisitely polite. But he did not come near her again. Sometimes she could feel his eyes upon her, blazing like the eyes of a hawk; but when she turned, he would merely nod and continue upon his way.

Watching him now, Odalie could feel the pain lying upon her heart like a weight of lead. Such a man as this she had and now between them was this thing intangible but none the less real, against which she seemed powerless to fight. All she could do now was to kneel at her casement and look out at him and pray to the Virgin to send the rain before the crop was ruined.

She rose suddenly from her seat. Then, suddenly, the weakness and the nausea which she had noticed several times before of a morning was upon her: this time far stronger than before. She took a tentative step forward, then she was hanging there, swaying on her feet, the blackness pressing in upon her eyes.

"Zerline!" she got out, but the yellow maid servant she had brought from Bellefont was far away, out of hearing. She could feel herself loosening at the knees, the floor coming up to meet her slowly. Then she screamed out: "Zerline!"

But it was not her maid who came flying through the door to catch her in her arms and ease her gently to the floor; it was Caleen. Odalie was afraid of Caleen. The old woman had a look about her of such bland and competent evil that the thought of being touched by her was a chilling one, but now Odalie clung to her gratefully.

"Easy, mistress," Caleen said. "I take you where you kin lie down, me."

Then with one spidery black arm about her mistress's waist she led her to the big bed.

"Wait," she said, "I bring you something, yes."

177

"Thank you," Odalie whispered. Then: "Oh, Caleen, I'm so sick!"

"It does that, yes. Great lady not like field woman. The master is ver' glad, him, I bet."

"I—I haven't told him. I wasn't sure."

"Well, you sure now. You can tell him now, yes!"

"Please, Caleen, the medicine—whatever it was you were getting. I'm going to be sick!"

Caleen scurried from the room. Odalie sank back upon her bed, pressing both hands over her eyes. She kept quite still, not daring to move, lest the precarious equilibrium she was maintaining with the thick tide of nausea be upset. Then there were footsteps sounding clearly on the stairs, pausing a moment outside her open door, approaching her bedside.

"Caleen?" she whispered hoarsely.

"No," Stephen's voice came down to her. "'Tis not Caleen. What ails ye, my dear?"

"I'm sick, Stephen. I—I can't retain my food. I—think— Oh, I don't know what it is . . ."

"Shall I call a doctor for ye? All this heat and the air is very bad. They say Dr. Terrebonne is an excellent physician."

"No, no—Caleen is taking care of me. Besides, I feel much better now—since you came. Stay and talk to me a while, won't you, Stephen? I—I've been so lonely."

There was the scraping of a chair as he drew it up beside her bed. Odalie kept her hands pressed tightly over her eyes. Then Caleen came through the doorway, bearing a steaming tea that smelled strongly of mint leaves and lemon.

"Men," she said with mock severity, "always make trouble, yes. You go way from here, maître! Already you done enough, you!"

"I've done enough?" Stephen growled. "What the deuce do ye mean, ye old witch?"

"Her," Caleen pointed, balancing the tray on one hand. "all your fault, yes!"

Stephen turned to Odalie.

"What on earth is she talking about?" he demanded.

178

But the waves of color were chasing one another across Odalie's face.

"Don't you know, Stephen?" she asked gently.

"Don't I know what . . . Odalie! You don't mean."

"Yes, my husband, I do mean. And I am so happy that almost I could die of it."

The chair went over backwards with a crash, and Stephen was on his knees beside the bed, gathering her into his arms. Then Odalie nestled her head against his shoulder and loosed her tears.

"Why do ye cry?" he asked. "'Tis a thing for joy and laughter, not for tears!"

"Because I'm happier than I can bear. Because you take me in your arms and do not turn away as though you hated me. And because there will be a son for Harrow."

"A son for Harrow," Stephen repeated after her. Strange how right the phrasing was: not his son, nor hers, but Harrow's— a son to be shaped by the house into the finely tempered image of a gentleman, who would grow with it until at last he became master of it, until his son came, too, to manhood. And so it would go, for endless generations, until the house should become weathered and old and the family ghosts should whisper about the halls. Harrow. This was it. Completion. Fulfillment.

He looked out the window to where the sun was smashing the earth with hammer blows, wave upon wave of heat. Odalie stirred in his arms.

"What is it, Stephen?" she whispered. "You seem troubled. You are sorry about this?"

"No. Only 'tis thinking I am that if this heat does not abate soon, 'twill be a poor heritage that the lad will come into."

"As bad as that, Stephen?"

"Yes. But don't trouble yourself, my darling. I shall win now even if I have to ring in a cold deck. Caleen! Don't stand there like a dolt! Bring your mistress her tea."

"Yas, maître," the old woman grinned. "I bring it, me."

"Ye're not to leave her side," Stephen said sternly. "Not for an instant! She is not to walk in the sun, nor exert herself in any

179

way. Anything she wants, ye will get for her and promptly. Leave nothing to the hands of these flighty yellow wenches. I'm holding ye responsible, mind ye!"

He turned again to his wife.

" 'Tis becoming to ye," he smiled. "Never have I seen ye with finer color." He bent and kissed her gently. The kiss was light and tender, and Odalie realized suddenly with a vast relief that there would be no more passion in his caresses—not for a long time now. And almost at the same time she was conscious of a feeling of shame at her relief. It must be a boy, she decided: she must not fail him in that, too.

Stephen kissed her again. Then he stood up.

"I must ride into town," he said, "to arrange a loan. The crop is a failure—even if it rains now, it is still a failure. I'll see Warren—it shouldn't take very much to tide us over. The notes on the house can ride. My credit is excellent hereabouts. Take care of yourself, my darling. Ye must be very, very careful. Follow Caleen's suggestions. She's a wise one for all that she's an old devil!"

Again he bent and kissed her, then he turned and strode through the doorway.

"You hear what the maître say," Caleen said bossily. "I don't want no sass, me! You do like I tells you, yes! And we bring maître fine boy—beeg boy with red hair. But you hafta do like I say!"

Odalie smiled indulgently.

"Yes, Caleen," she said, "I'll be good."

Riding toward the river road, Stephen met old Josh, coming back from the river with a string of fish. They were tiny, hardly worth the trouble; but with the heat and low water they were the best that Josh could do.

"Howdy, Massa Stevie!" he called out as the big palamino approached him. "I bring you some little fishes. Not much good, but deys all I could kotch. Hit so blame dry, you knows."

"Take them up to the house and give them to Caleen," Stephen told him. "Ye're much improved, Josh; ye don't shake anymore. Still afraid of fire?"

"Yassuh, I'se powerful scairt of hit yet. But I'se gittin less scairt all de time. I'se gitting strong now."

"So I see," Stephen said gravely. "So strong, in fact, that I think I'll put you to work in the fields."

"Oh, Massa Stevie, you wouldn't do dat to poor Josh! I'se a old man! Dat heat out dere would kill me sho!"

"Don't worry, Josh," Stephen laughed. "Ye're far more valuable as a fisherman. Have you seen Achille?"

"Him down by de levee making dem Creyole Nigras tote water. Ain't gonna do no good now, Massa Stevie, hit too late to save de crop."

"I'm afraid ye're right, Josh," Stephen said. "Well, hurry along with those fish."

As Stephen stopped Prince Michael at the foot of the levee, the big black came scrambling down to meet him, his face glistening with sweat.

"You go way for long, master?" he asked.

"No," Stephen said; "I'll return by nightfall. How goes it, Achille?"

"Them Negres lazy, master. But I make them work, me."

"Ye report everything to Mister Wilson, of course?"

"Him sick. Caleen say him goin' to die."

"What! And none of ye said a word! Even Madame Wilson did not so much as send me a note."

"She half crazy, her, with all them children, master. Maybe her fergit."

"I'll ride by there," Stephen said. "But how goes it with your family, Achille?"

"That wild gal she make me crazy, yes! Her *enciente* now. No beeg belly yet, but soon. All time she fight me like wildcat. Then afterwards she kiss me like fire. She something, her!"

Stephen turned away from the road to the big house of his overseer. Wilson never had been much good, he reflected. Achille had done most of the work. Still, it was necessary to have some

181

white man over the Negroes lest they become unruly; 'twould be a pity if Wilson were to die. He was a good man, in his odd, timid way.

Stephen swung down from Prince Michael and strode up to the gallery. It was, he noticed, in a sad state of repair. He lifted his crop to knock upon the door, but then, at that moment, his ears were struck by a chorus of wailing. Stephen pushed the door open softly and went in, holding his hat in his hand. Seeing him, Madame Wilson threw herself into his arms, sobbing violently, while three or four small Wilsons clutched his knees and howled.

"There, there," Stephen said. "There, there."

When he left the house, Stephen had undertaken the expense of the funeral and made Madame Wilson a present of the house, as long as she cared to reside at Harrow. Harrow—deucedly appropriate that name. Truly it harrowed a man's soul with trouble often enough.

Thinking thus, he rode along the highway with his head bent upon his bosom. A son for Harrow. That put quite a different shape upon things. As hard as he had worked, now he must work harder. The plantation must be put on a firm basis for all time. The debts must be cleared and operational costs decreased so that never would his son want for anything. He must have everything and the best of it. Care, tutorage—a university education. Which should it be—Oxford or Cambridge? Then there was Edinburgh—not to be sneered at by any manner or means. But he must be trained for leadership. The Foxes were here in this new world to stay. And not merely to stay—to lead it, rule it, leave their mark upon it. Having no ancestors, he told himself, I am become one. The thought pleased him. He straightened in his saddle, gazing down the road.

As he did so, he noticed a horseman bearing down upon him, sitting in the saddle like a centaur. That would be young Cloutier —nowhere in the state was there a better horseman. As the two riders closed the gap between them, the young man's face lighted in a rueful smile.

"I was bound for Harrow," he said. "I expected to find you

182

there. But now that I see you're not. . . ." He reined in his horse. The sleek animal sidestepped like a dancer.

Stephen looked at Phillippe Cloutier. Truly the lad was a handsome devil. But this rôle of dancing attendance upon Odalie was not a thing suitable for Louisiana. Yet Odalie obviously enjoyed his company. Perhaps she would have been happier had she married such a man—with grace and distinction implicit in his bearing, and of her own kind.

Stephen smiled suddenly.

"My absence is no cause for ye to change your intent," he said. "Madame Fox will be glad to see ye. And anything that brings her happiness is not displeasing to me. Ride on, lad. Ye're always welcome at Harrow."

Young Cloutier studied the lean face before him. Was this mockery? There was no trace of irony in Stephen's tone. But the twist of lip and play of brow and eye made everything that Stephen uttered suspect. Not a man to trifle with—this. But Odalie—Odalie! If only he had come back to Louisiana two years ago. Well—he hadn't. He was here now—two years and more too late. And nothing—not the laws of man nor the doctrines of the Church nor even the fear of Stephen's wrath could stop him now. This thing was here, and there was no solution to it. What must be must be, if he wrecked half a world.

He bowed slightly from his hips.

"Thank you, monsieur," he said. "I'm glad you don't find my visits a burden."

"When they become one," Stephen said evenly, "they will end. 'Voir, Monsieur Cloutier."

Phillippe lifted his hat and the clatter of horses' hoofs rang sharply upon the sunbaked road.

Stephen dismissed him from his mind almost at once. Whatever Phillippe's intent might be, he was aeons from its accomplishment. There was this about Odalie—a husband of hers would never wear horns. He slowed Prince Michael to a walk. No need to kill the beast in this heat. God and Our Lady, what a distance it was!

Later, winding through the streets of the Faubourg St. Marie,

183

Stephen was struck with the desolation and squalor of the place. The Americans produced most of the wealth of New Orleans. They were thrifty, enterprising people. Yet the council, firmly in the hands of the Creoles, calmly and persistently vetoed any appropriations to improve the place. The revenues from the Saint Mary district more than doubled those of any other section; yet the streets remained unpaved, and the wharves were rotting away. No wonder the Americans were up in arms against anything French—whom already they were beginning to outnumber. This racial quarrel would come to bloodshed yet, Stephen reflected soberly. And he and Andre and the hundreds of others who had married across the line would be caught in the middle.

Still, to leave the drainage in such a state! The stench was enough to sicken a man. And the yellow fever killed hundreds yearly. Yet the Creoles, when this was pointed out to them, only shrugged. Yellow Jack was a "stranger's disease." They did not die of it. Used to the climate, habitually drinking wine instead of water, they lived calmly through epidemic after epidemic, while the raw Irish immigrants on Rousseau Street dropped in their tracks like flies, and the Germans died and the English and the Americans were decimated. Damn the Creoles anyway! Except, of course, Odalie and Aurore and Andre and old Le Blanc and Pierre Arceneaux.

Prince Michael's hoofs raised little clouds of dust in the street. Stephen rode on, holding a fine handkerchief to his nose. The carcasses of dead animals lay rotting in the streets, and the garbage lay in stinking month-old mounds. And when it finally rained, conditions would only become worse. Every street would become a sea of impassable ooze, if it were not actually flooded. No wonder the Creoles called their street blocks *ilets*; the name was undeniably appropriate.

In the *Vieux Carre*, conditions were a trifle better. But only a trifle. Apart from their own persons, the French were not a cleanly race. Here, to be sure, were streets paved with cobblestone, or cypress blocks, or brick; but they were narrow and dark, and in them the heat was doubly oppressive. Even the main thoroughfares were so narrow that two coaches could not pass abreast.

But at least the overhanging galleries did provide some relief from the sun.

Turning into Chartres Street, Stephen stopped before an imposing edifice. Identical in style to all the others, it was a veritable skyscraper—four stories tall. Glistening in its newness, it made the other establishments in the street seem shabby by comparison. Truly, Tom Warren must have struck it rich. Land on Chartres was impossibly dear. Most of it was owned by Creoles who had turned their backs upon Louisiana and gone back to France to live off the rentals that property in the new world brought them. Their fees were high, and their rental agents, by and large, an unprincipled set of scoundrels. Yet Tom Warren had bought and built here, where one hundred feet of frontage had often brought as much as fifty thousand dollars. Well, he had done Tom favors in the past; 'twould not be amiss to ask one now.

He climbed down from Prince Michael and went into the doorway. One of the half dozen clerks who were busy with their pens at the high desks scurried away into an inner chamber to summon Tom Warren.

The big man came out, frowning a little; then, seeing Stephen, his face cleared. He took a step forward, stretching out his hand.

"Stephen!" he said. "'Tis good to see you again. Come into the office—this *is* a pleasure."

Stephen took the offered hand and looked at Tom Warren. He's put on flesh, he decided. Dresses better, too. And it's "Stephen" now. Always before it was "Mister Fox." Still the man has grown in importance. I can hardly expect diffidence from him now.

"Ye've prospered," he said, as he followed Tom Warren into the well equipped inner office. "I'm very glad."

"Thank you," Tom Warren said. He picked up a small wooden box from his desk. "A segar?" he asked, his little eyes shifting rapidly from the box of twisted Cuban tobaccoes to Stephen's lean face.

"No, thank ye," Stephen said. "'Twas scarcely civil of ye not to visit us at Harrow, Tom."

"I know. But I've been infernally busy. You'll forgive an old friend, Stephen. Yet, I don't recall seeing you at my house for nearly three years now."

"Ye never invited me, Tom."

"It never occurred to me you needed an invitation. My house was always yours, Stephen. But to what do I owe the pleasure of this visit?"

"I need your help," Stephen said bluntly. "I'm in trouble. Cane needs water—lots of water, and ye know how this summer has been."

"Do I! I've suffered losses all down the line. But anything I can do—how much do you need, Stephen?"

"Fifteen thousand. And I'll need it until next harvest. Ye can fix what rates ye will."

Without a word, Tom Warren took up his pen. Then from the drawer he drew a cheque book. Scarcely glancing at Stephen, he wrote rapidly. He sanded the cheque, dusted it off and passed it to Stephen.

Stephen's fair brows rose. The cheque was for thirty thousand dollars.

"I asked ye for fifteen only," he said.

"You shouldn't figure so closely, Stephen," Tom Warren observed. "I've had dealings with many planters lately, and I know the expense of running a place."

"And what are your rates?" Stephen asked.

"To you—none. And the date of repayment is left to your judgment. I have no need of the money. Take what time you will."

Stephen stood up.

"Ye're a good friend, Tom," he said. "But I shall repay ye at the next harvest—and with interest too. And now I must ride back to Harrow. I've been gone overlong. A thousand thanks for your kindness."

Tom Warren put a sulphur match to the end of his segar. The fragrant blue smoke drifted through the room.

"Stay a bit," he urged. "And dine with me. A man should not ride so far with his belly unfortified."

"No," Stephen said, "I must be going. But your standing invitation to Harrow remains. This fall the hunting will be poor, no doubt; but ye can enjoy what shooting there will be."

"I'll try hard to come," Tom Warren said. "But do not hold it against me if I do not. 'Twill be only because I can't. My regards to Madame Fox. I hear she is the loveliest lady in Louisiana. You're a lucky man, Stephen."

"Thank ye," Stephen said, and took his leave. Whatever might be said about the sharpness of Tom Warren's dealings there was no denying that he had a heart.

There was really no reason for his rushing back to Harrow, Stephen decided as he left the bank after having deposited Tom Warren's draft. Odalie was probably pleasantly occupied with Phillippe Cloutier, so that she would not mind his staying away. It would be pleasant to drop in upon Andre and Amelia, but their happiness always evoked the pangs of comparison. Beside, Amelia's figure must be considerably altered by now, and she, as a consequence, reluctant to receive visitors. Why not then drop in at Bellefont, and lunch with old Arceneaux and Aurore? The idea was an appealing one. Stephen was genuinely fond of both his in-laws. Aurore, he reflected, was a lovely girl. Strange that she had not married. She must be in her twenties now—she was a full three years younger than Odalie. She'd had her share of beaux, but about them she seemed even more reticent than Odalie. Odd, this trait, in the daughters of old Pierre. The old man had an eye for beauty and there was nothing cold about *him*. Madame Arceneaux must have been an iceberg!

Aurore was standing on the broad gallery looking out over the drive as Stephen rode up to Bellefont. She came down the stairs to greet him, a tiny smile curving the corners of her mouth. Odd that a smile could convey the impression of sadness, Stephen found himself thinking. Yet what could a lovely creature like Aurore know of sadness? She put out her hand to be kissed.

"My dear little sister," he said, bending over it. "I came especially to see ye."

"That would be nice," she said, "if it were true. But I'm afraid you've wasted your visit, Stephen; father isn't here."

"So? Then ye object to exchanging a pleasant word or two with your superannuated brother-in-law?"

"Not at all. In fact, I'm very glad to see you. It's nice that you're 'family' now, Stephen."

"Why?"

"Because I couldn't sit and talk with you without father here if you weren't. You know that, Stephen."

"Aye. Never have I known a place with more cursed conventions! Ye grow more beautiful daily, Aurore. Ye tempt me to embrace the Moslem faith and become a Turk."

"Why, Stephen?"

"Because then I should be allowed four wives. However, if ye would have me, I think I should be most content with two!"

"Stephen!" Aurore laughed. "Of all the unconventional ideas!"

"Do ye like the idea, Aurore?"

"Of course not! I think it's perfectly scandalous! And, besides, Odalie wouldn't stand for it."

"How could she help it, if it were the law? But I'm hungry, Aurore. Might I not have some coffee and cake?"

"Of course, Stephen! Is that all you want?"

"Yes—I don't eat very much."

Following her into the house, Stephen was struck by the grace of her walk. She grows more like Odalie every day, he thought; the coloring is different—still they are much alike. But Aurore was turning into the dining hall and the dim light edged her profile briefly. Stephen found himself confronted with the necessity of reversing his judgment. Odalie and Aurore were nothing alike: there was only the family similarity; but in all else they were actually different.

Stephen looked at her over his steaming cup. The look was hard, intent. The small smile on Aurore's face wavered. Then abruptly it died. The spoon in her hand came to a halt in midair. And her eyes, meeting his, were utterly naked.

Stephen's forehead creased into a frown, and his fair brows knit over the bridge of his nose. He shook his head slightly as if to clear it. It was the motion which released her. She stood up quite suddenly, the russet tides spreading over her face.

"I—I don't feel well, Stephen," she said. "You'll excuse me, won't you?"

"No," Stephen growled. "Something in your look puzzled me just then. What is it, Aurore? What's troubling ye?"

"Nothing—really, it's nothing, Stephen. The heat and all—please let me go!"

"Not until I have your promise to visit us more often at Harrow. We've missed ye sadly."

"Oh, I'll come! I'll come! Please excuse me now, Stephen. I really must lie down."

"Very well." Then a mischievous glint came into Stephen's eyes. "But first ye must salute me with a sisterly kiss, or else I shall not budge from this spot."

He stepped forward and caught both her hands at the wrists. Her arms were warm and soft, and he could feel her pulse pounding against the palms of his hands.

"No, Stephen," she said, and her voice was very quiet. "You mustn't."

"And ye said I was 'family'," Stephen mocked. Then he leaned forward suddenly. But she turned her head very rapidly so that his kiss brushed lightly across the corner of her mouth.

"That wasn't much of a kiss," he laughed. "But 'twill have to do for now. Goodday, my dear sister." His bow was unnecessarily deep, and his laughter floated back after he had gone.

Aurore sat very still, rubbing the corner of her mouth with the back of her hand. She rubbed it for a long time and very hard until it began to swell. But even then, through the numbness and the bruise, she could still feel the light brushing pressure of his lips on hers.

Riding away, Stephen's brows were furrowed, but his mouth was smiling.

"They're cold, both of them," he mused. "But she less than Odalie. I wonder—yes, I wonder . . . "

XII

ODALIE sat in the *chambre-à-brin*—the little screened enclosure on the corner of the great gallery—talking to Phillippe Cloutier. It was necessary for her to have fresh air, but the fierce *maringouins*—the huge mosquitoes of the bayou country—would have devoured her alive if she had not had the protection of the screening.

Strange that Stephen had not yet returned. He should have been back a long time before now.

Phillippe's heavy black brows came together in a frown.

"You love him, this husband of yours," he observed drily.

"But of course. Why else would I have married him?"

"Why, indeed? This foreigner—no, that's not the word. The Germans have a better—I learned it on my grand tour. *Auslander.* It has the proper harshness."

"Need one be harsh?"

"Yes! These Americans! Enterprise, push, boorishness—and you, married to one of them! Oh, I admit that he has better manners than most of them, but you're a Creole, my dearest— and Creoles don't mate with barbarians!"

"But since I've already married my barbarian, my dear Phillippe, I don't quite see . . ."

"You could not love another man?"

"You, for instance? No, Phillippe, I couldn't. There is nowhere on this earth such a man as he."

"You're mistaken," Phillippe said. "I'll prove you're mistaken!" He bent forward suddenly and swept her up into his arms. Then very slowly and with great deliberation he kissed her, hard upon the mouth.

Odalie did not resist. She stood very quietly in his arms and allowed herself to be kissed; but she made no response—no response at all.

When he released her, she looked at him with eyes that were very wide and dark. But when she spoke her voice was calm.

"I'm sorry you did that," she said.

"Why?" he demanded.

"Because I've enjoyed your company so much, Phillippe. But now I must ask you to go and never come back again."

"You're being unfair," he said. "Monstrously unfair."

"Perhaps. I don't know. I'm no judge of such matters. It grieves me to send you away, Phillippe. I shall miss you. And if I ever—by word or gesture—led you to think that I would permit such liberties, please forgive me, for it was not my intention to. Goodbye, Phillippe."

He bowed silently. One dark eyebrow climbed sardonically toward his heavy black curls. Seeing it, Odalie smiled a little.

"Now I know why I liked you so," she said. "Except for the difference in complexion, you look quite a lot like Stephen. There is in you both the same quality of arrogance and recklessness and mockery . . ."

"You might have spared me that, Madame," Phillippe said, and went down the stairs.

Odalie sighed. Poor Phillippe! She had not meant to hurt him. He was a very handsome lad—very lean and hard and polished like a rapier blade, a true gilded youth of the Parisian school. For a moment she wondered how it would have been if he had come back two years ago. Then she stopped abruptly, shocked at her own thoughts. She looked down the alley of oaks and saw Phillippe riding away.

After a moment or two, she turned to leave the screened enclosure, but as she crossed the gallery, Achille came up the stairs, holding his hat in his hand.

"Mistress," he began.

"Yes, Achille?"

"That Mister Wilson—he ups and dies, him. Maître say I tell you right away, but I fergit. Anyways, they all cry very loud down there, yes. Mistress come?"

"Yes, Achille. Go and hitch the little cabriolet. When you have finished, bring it around here. Be quick now." She went into the house and called Zerline. When the girl came, Odalie ordered her to gather up all the foodstuffs left in the house. Then, slipping on a sunbonnet, she started for the Wilsons' with Achille at the reins.

The house of the overseer was dirty and ill-kept. Odalie went to work at once with the help of three slave women. The children were bathed, dressed in clean linen and fed. The house was swept and dusted. And poor Madame Wilson, prostrated by her loss, found the wine and small cakes vastly stimulating, and sobbed out her gratitude upon her mistress' shoulder. Between sobs, she dictated to Odalie a list of relatives who were to be invited to the funeral. And, since it was far too late to have the invitations engraved as was customary, Odalie wrote out the melancholy little notes in her own fine hand. Then she dispatched Georges on horseback to distribute them. The funeral must be held early tomorrow—before the blazing sun advanced too far above the horizon. Mister Wilson had been rather too long above ground now for this heat.

Coming back from the city, Stephen found her still at the Wilsons', busily engaged in half a dozen tasks at once. He stood in the doorway, dusty and stained from his ride, his face reddened by the never-ending sun.

"Odalie!" he said sharply. "Have ye taken leave of your senses?"

"I'm so glad you're back," she said brightly. "There are so many things to be done . . ."

"None of which ye shall do, my girl. Get ye up this instant and ride back to the house. So it's working ye are! Working and looking into the face of the dead while ye carry a child! Where is Caleen? By all the saints, I shall have her thrashed for letting ye out of her sight!"

"But Stephen, somebody had to help these people! I felt it my duty . . ."

"Your duty, my dear, is to yourself and this child. Come now."

"Sometimes, Stephen," Odalie said tartly, "you're positively impossible!"

The following day the inconsequential Mister Wilson was laid to rest with ceremony. And Madame Wilson and all her brood left Harrow for the great Prudhomme estates, having declined with thanks Stephen's offer of a permanent home at Harrow. Stephen spread a huge table to all the legions of Prudhommes —seemingly there were no other Wilsons in existence—and their grief at their daughter's loss had little effect upon their appetites.

"The only sadness there," Stephen whispered to Odalie, "lies in their recognition of the fact that 'twill be impossible to marry her off again. What a crew to feed! Can't say that I blame them."

Throughout the fall the heat continued. The smokestack of the sugar house stood up straight and tall, but no smoke came out of its gaping mouth. There was no cane for the sugar. Had it not been for Tom Warren's loan, Stephen would have had to sell some of the land to meet his notes, but as it was he was able to ride over into winter with a comfortable margin of security.

The heat was a great burden to Odalie. Delicate by nature, she continued to have sieges of nausea and fainting. No longer could she walk abroad now. Swollen ankles and knees kept her abed most of the day; and her now misshapen figure was a source of endless worry to her. She was constantly in tears, fearing the permanent loss of her former litheness, storming at Stephen, swearing she hated him, accusing him of cruelty and worse, vowing to leave him forever.

All this Stephen bore with great patience—especially after the heat had abated early in the fall. For now the driving fall and winter rains had set in, and he knew that next year the crop would be good. Odalie would be occupied with the child, and would, therefore, give him little trouble.

The winter went by slowly. Never, it seemed, would the icy rains cease. Stephen rode out once or twice, wrapped in his greatcoat, to inspect the levee. By spring, he suspected, they would need all its strength. When the snows of the Northern Territories had melted, and the spring rains begun, it was no telling what height the river would reach. On these tours of inspection, he stopped at the slave cabins to see after the welfare of his people. It was troublesome not having an overseer, but Stephen was determined not to hire another until he had found a man whose qualifications were really suitable. One by one he entered the cabins, checking them for warmth and dryness, and also for cleanliness. Many a black was put to work with broom and mop in the middle of the night because his master, visiting unannounced, found the cabin offensive to his nostrils.

One of the last cabins to be visited was that of Achille. It was scrupulously clean, and the big slave had made rude furniture for it, fashioned, as far as Stephen could see, in imitation of the furniture up at Harrow. On the bed La Belle Sauvage lay, moaning softly.

"How goes it with her?" Stephen asked.

"Bad, maître. You think she lady, her! She suffer like lady—not easy for her like field woman."

"Sauvage princess," the girl on the bed got out between moans. "No field woman, me! No slave!"

"Hush," Achille growled. "You don't talk like that to maître, no!"

" 'Tis nothing, Achille," Stephen said. "They all want a bit of humoring when they're like that."

He looked up from the bed toward the rough stone mantel.

194

On it two candles flickered, and between them was a little carved wooden figurine. Stephen looked at it, his brows rising. The figurine was of some dark wood, and had been carved by the hand of a masterly craftsman. It was something out of Africa, Stephen decided, some fetish or tribal god. Walking over to it, he picked it up in his hand. God and Our Lady, how hideous it was! Holding it there loosely in his palm, it seemed almost obscene. He turned to Achille.

"What is this?" he demanded.

"Wanga!" Achille muttered uneasily. "Powerful Wanga—maître mustn't touch!"

"Ye worship this monstrosity, Achille?"

"I Catholic, me," Achille declared. "Same as maître . . ."

"But the girl?"

"Her still wild, maître. She no understand, her."

"I see. Belle . . ."

The great yellow brown eyes glowed up at him.

"Ye must not worship this thing," Stephen said calmly. "'Tis only wood. It has no power over ye. See, it burns like any other wood."

He tossed it lightly into the fire. La Belle Sauvage sat straight up on her bed and made the cabin quiver with her screams. Strongly but gently Achille pressed her back upon the bed.

"Maître go now," he said. "She have fits sho. Best that maître go now."

"Ye're right," Stephen said. "Sorry that I disturbed her."

Wrapping his greatcoat about him, he went out into the driving rain. He walked slowly toward Harrow, disregarding the rain completely, his brow furrowed with thought. I should have Father DuGois come out and teach them, he thought; but what would he say to my own laxity? 'Tis troubles enough I have without having my soul looked into. He sighed and plodded on through the rain.

As he approached the house, he saw a horse standing near the foot of the stairs. The animal was evidently spent, for it stood with its forelegs wide apart, and its belly heaving. Coming closer, he could see the rain steaming up from its sides.

"Poor fellow," he said. "Ye've been cruelly used this night. I wonder who on earth . . . ?"

He started up the great stairs, but as he neared the top, the doors swung open and the warm yellow light poured out.

"Maître," Georges' excited voice called. "Guess what! You never guess, maître—never in a hundred year!"

Then Ti Demon was shouldering Georges aside, his big white teeth gleaming in a huge grin.

"Monsieur Andre tell me bring you this," he chuckled. " 'Portant message. Very 'portant!"

He extended a rainsoaked piece of paper to Stephen. Stephen opened it and read:

"My dear Stephen:

"It's a son and heir! He is beautiful beyond belief—with Amelia's hair and eyes and the set chin of the Le Blancs. Papa has gone insane with joy. I am taking the liberty of naming him Stephen, after you, my old one! We are eagerly awaiting your visit.

"Andre"

Stephen's pale eyes were very clear, and a little smile played about the corners of his mouth. So soon? he mused; why 'tis but February. Andre a father—quite a strain upon the imagination, that. He turned to Georges.

"Take Little Devil up to your quarters and give him dry clothing," he said. "Also ye may open a bottle of Tafia; but if either of ye becomes quarrelsome, I shall have ye both soundly thrashed. And see that his horse is stabled and fed." He spun on his heel and marched in the direction of Odalie's room.

"How are ye, my dear?" he asked as he crossed to the bed upon which she was lying.

"What do you care?" she stormed. "You got me like this! And now you stay away forever and care not if I die!"

"Softly, my dear," Stephen said. "Ye should not excite yourself so." He sat down beside the bed. "Andre and Amelia have their wish," he told her. "It is a son at La Place. They've called him Stephen in my honor."

"Oh, Stephen, they can't! You mustn't let them!"

"Why not? The name will not harm the lad."

"But, Stephen, what on earth will we call *our* baby?"

"Holy Saints! That I had forgotten. That does put a different face on things, doesn't it?"

"Stephen . . ."

"Yes, darling . . . ?"

"Would you—mind very much if I called him Etienne? I know you don't like French names, but after all the meaning is the same. Besides it is what I would have called him anyway—my little 'Tienne, even if you'd named him Stephen."

"Suppose it is a girl?" Stephen grinned. "What then, Odalie?"

"Oh, Stephen, no! It can't be! I'd die if it were only a girl!"

"Ye'll love and cherish it, whatever it is," he said gently. He kissed her and got to his feet. "Call it whatever ye like," he said softly, and crossed the room to the door.

The ice left the rains, and they were warm with fragrance. The spring came whispering in with rains that probed like warm fingers into the black earth. And where they touched, the earth greened and blossomed. Already the cane was up, taller than it usually was by midsummer, and the cotton stalks clustered over mile after mile of fields. The river, swollen by the months of rainfall and the melting snows of the North, was growling a few scant feet below the top of the levee, and Stephen found it necessary to have his Negroes patrol the earthern wall day and night lest an unexpected break catch them unawares.

Now that it was almost time for her travail, Odalie found herself surprisingly well. Except for the heaviness and fatigue, she was not much troubled. The nausea and dizziness had disappeared and time, weighted with idleness, hung heavy upon her hands. Often now of an evening she was driven into New Orleans in a heavy coach, to attend the theatre. Heavily veiled, she would descend from the coach at a private side entrance of the Théâtre D'Orleans, and being met there by a special attendant, she would be conducted up a hidden stairway to the *Loge Grille* that Stephen had ordered reserved for her. Sitting there behind the lattices that enclosed her box, hiding her from the public eye, she could enjoy the new series of light operas that John Davis had introduced. Often, indeed usually, Stephen went with her, but when he could not, Georges and Caleen and often Zerline were at her side every instant that she was away from Harrow.

Sitting beside her late in the spring, Stephen peered through the lattices at the stage. *La Dame Blanche*, he decided, was but an indifferent opera, and the singing less than fair. Still, if it pleased Odalie . . . He glanced at her out of the corner of his eyes. Her face was very white—unnaturally so, and there was a noticeable grimace of pain hovering about her mouth. He stretched out his hand, and she caught it suddenly. Her grip was fierce, the fingers biting into his arm.

"Stephen," she whispered. "I—I don't think I'd better wait for the ballet."

He stood up, taking her arm.

"So," he said, his voice all concern. "It's come?"

"Yes, Stephen—it's come—and we'd better hurry!"

"Doctor Terrebonne's is but a few blocks beyond. I can take ye there. . . .

"No, Stephen, no!"

"Why not? 'Tis the safest thing to do."

"Harrow, Stephen—he must be born at Harrow! We cannot cheat him of that!"

Stephen bent and swept her up into his arms. He went down the stairs to the waiting coach.

"Harrow," he said to the coachman. "And be quick about it! Georges!"

"Yes, maître?"

"Get ye over to Dumaine Street and tell Doctor Terrebonne that we shall expect him at Harrow within the hour. Tell him it's urgent—very urgent. Be off with ye now!"

All the way on the long drive out to Harrow, Odalie held

Stephen's hand tightly. Never did she permit the slightest moan to escape her lips, but at times her grip tightened, tightened until her knuckles whitened visibly from the strain and a fine dew of perspiration filmed her brow and the corners of her mouth.

Stephen drew her head down upon his shoulders and tried as much as he could to protect her from the jolting, swaying motion of the coach. "Damn this road!" he muttered each time the wheels dug into a rut.

Then they were swinging up the alley of oaks before Harrow. The coachman brought down his whip sharply across the laboring animals and they broke from their trot into a headlong gallop. It was the first time they had ever felt the lash. The coachman pulled them up before Harrow, sawing their mouths so cruelly with the bits that they reared and the whole coach bucked and shivered.

"Damnation!" Stephen thundered. "Do ye want to kill us all?"

Slowly the terrified horses quieted. Stephen leaped to the ground. Then he put his arms inside the coach, and Odalie sank into them. He went up the stairs very fast yet very smoothly, only to find old Caleen waiting at the top.

"The grand chamber is ready," she said, "but the water is not yet to a boil. Soon it be ready, yes. The maître be very careful. I take care of maîtresse, me."

"How the devil did ye know?" Stephen demanded.

Caleen smiled.

"Caleen have ways," she said mysteriously. In truth she had been watching from the belvédère and had seen the coach thundering up the river road. Only one thing, she knew, would make the master drive so fast with the young mistress aboard. But never would she tell him that. Better to have him believe in her mystic powers.

Stephen carried Odalie into the master bedroom, and lay her gently on the great, canopied bed. Then Caleen and Zerline undressed her, moving very slowly and gently. Stephen paced the floor in a black fury. Why the devil didn't that cursed sawbones come? Odalie's face was twisted, but not a whimper did she permit to escape her lips. She stretched out her slim hand to

Stephen, and he knelt beside the bed, his face so drawn that the great scar was livid against his pallor.

"It is nothing, my husband," she whispered. "I am all right. Do not worry so . . ."

Then her face was contorted in a grimace so acute that Stephen sprang upright.

"Georges!" he roared, then turning to Zerline: "Get Georges! Tell him to ride at once to the city and fetch that damnable doctor! Tell him to ride Arrow and I care not if he breaks his wind and limbs so long as he reaches Dumaine Street within the hour. Get on with ye now! Move!"

Zerline was out of the bed chamber at once, her skirts swirling as she ran.

"Not Arrow, Stephen," Odalie whispered. "Give him some other mount." She knew well how Stephen loved the sleek black stallion he was grooming for the fall races at the Metairie Track.

"There is none here half so fast," Stephen said. "Rest quietly now, my darling—ye must conserve your strength."

An hour and a half later, Doctor Terrebonne arrived. Stephen was hard put to conceal his impatience at the delay. But the fat little Creole physician was filled with such bustling good humor and confidence that it was easy to relax in his presence.

"Ah, monsieur," he said merrily. "I can guarantee you a fine son, perhaps, but I cannot swear that if this pacing and gnawing of nails and palpitation of heart does not cease that Madame will not find herself a widow this night. You have whiskey?"

Stephen nodded.

"Good. Go then and get splendidly drunk, but stay out of my way. I will brook no interference. I will need the assistance of a woman—one with strong nerves. None of these young wenches now."

Stephen inclined his head dumbly toward Caleen.

"Come," Doctor Terrebonne said, then smiling broadly, he added: "Perhaps I shall have need of a witch!"

The examination took agonizing aeons of time. Stephen stood outside the door of the bedchamber and waited, rigid as a statue. When, at last, the little doctor came out, Stephen strode forward to meet him.

The physician's round, owlish face was grave. Stephen looked at him wordlessly—unable to speak.

"I want you to dispatch a man to the house of my colleague, Lefevre. Tell him to take over my practice for tonight. I'm remaining here."

"It—it's that bad, doctor?"

"Yes," Doctor Terrebonne said. "It's that bad."

"God and Our Blessed Mother!" Stephen whispered.

"She is not built for childbearing. She is too slim in the flanks and the child seems unusually large. And again, like so many of our patrician Grand Dames, she is too delicate. If she survives this one, it must be the last. Remember that."

"If she survives— My God, man, do ye know what ye're saying?"

"Yes," the doctor said, "yes, I know. You must get a grip upon yourself, monsieur. 'Twould be a pity to leave Harrow tenantless in a single night. You have a chamber where I can rest?"

"Yes," Stephen said, not even looking at the physician. "Yes. Zerline, show the doctor to the North Wing."

Throughout the entire night, only Doctor Terrebonne slept and he only at intervals. Odalie's agony was a fearsome thing. Watching her Stephen found almost unendurable. He went to her bedside a thousand times, only to be driven away by the pain etching her fine mouth and eyes. When he was away he cursed himself with all the foulest terms he had acquired in his years of wandering. But when he was beside her he prayed silently to the Blessed Virgin to preserve and protect her and the unborn child.

All through the next day the anguished labor continued with scarcely an interval between the black tidal waves of pain. Odalie was quietly, persistently praying for death. This, then she told herself, was how life came into the world, this monstrous, obscene agony without relief or succor.

Toward morning of the following night, the exhausted little doctor was sleeping fitfully in his chamber while Caleen watched by her mistress' side. Outside the room, Stephen paced up and down like a caged beast, ten feet in one direction, then back again, never changing his stride. Suddenly, Odalie moaned softly—a sound too low to carry over a yard of space. Caleen bent over her mistress, writhing on the great bed. There was no time now to summon the doctor. And to call the maître was worse than foolish—what must be done, must be done now— alone.

Fifteen minutes later, Stephen's stride was arrested abruptly. He stood there, perched grotesquely on one foot, the other still poised in midair. From the chamber came a series of sharp slaps, then a thin ragged wailing. It caught on, became steadier, a lusty, full-lunged howling that filled even the great hall. Stephen hung over the brass knob, too weak even to open the door.

Then the gigantic form of Achille was shouldering past him, his eyes glazed over and sightless, oblivious to everything.

"Caleen!" he roared; "you come now! The baby he come. come, Caleen, for God sake come, you!"

Caleen's voice was like ice, as she faced her son.

"Git out of here, you!" she said very quietly. "Before you kills the young maîtresse! Negress no die and if she do die, good! I comes when I can. Go you!"

Achille stood trembling before his mother's wrath, the great tears streaking his black face. Then, without a word, he turned and left the room. Stephen came in the door past him, white and shaking, bending over the still form of his wife.

"Is she . . . " he quavered. "Is she?"

"Maîtresse be all right," Caleen said sternly. "Now you git out here too, and git that damn little doctor!"

When Doctor Terrebonne came out of the bedroom, his round face wore a look of astonishment.

"Name your price for that old Negress," he said. "I'll give you whatever you want. Never in all my years of practice . . ."

"There is not that much money," Stephen said happily. "Not now—not in the whole world."

"You have a perfect son," the doctor said. "You can see him now if you will."

"If I will!" Stephen growled. "Ye should try to stop me!"

As they entered the room, Caleen picked up the baby and approached them. Stephen bent over his son, now sleeping peacefully in the old woman's arms. He drew back a little startled.

"By the saints," he said. "How ugly he is!"

"They all are at first," Doctor Terrebonne declared. "In fact this one is uncommonly handsome—as babies go."

"Then I have no wish to see more of them," Stephen declared. "Look ye, he is as red as a tomato! And what a mass of hair he has!"

"Black like his mother," Caleen declared. "But him got eyes blue like yours, maître."

"Good!" Stephen laughed. "I was on the point of disowning him."

"The maîtresse, her wake now," Caleen said. Stephen turned away from the child and knelt beside the bed.

The doctor glanced at Odalie.

"That's odd," he declared. "She seemed to be sleeping peacefully—as if nothing in the world was wrong with her."

"I give her something," Caleen said.

"What was it?" Doctor Terrebonne demanded. "If I had that I could cut childbirth deaths in half. What is it, Caleen? How do you make it? Where do you get the ingredients?"

"Secret!" Caleen snapped. "No good for white man to know!"

"So," Odalie was whispering, "I didn't die after all. I wanted to. I prayed to the Virgin for death . . . the child, how is it, Stephen?"

"Perfect," Stephen smiled. "A son, as ye wished. And ye're going to be all right . . ."

"May I see him? Let me hold him, my little 'Tienne. Where is he?"

Caleen bent and placed the sleeping child in Odalie's arms.

"How beautiful he is," she whispered. "He pleases you, my husband?"

"Beyond comprehension," Stephen said. "Now ye must rest. 'Tis a frightful siege ye've undergone." He bent and kissed her,

203

lightly, upon the mouth. There was the taste of blood upon her lips, where she had bitten them through.

"Stay with her, Caleen," Stephen ordered.

"Maître permit I call Zerline? Her all right now, the maîtresse. I want to see after the baby of Achille—my grandson. Maybe him die, yes, with no one there."

"My God," Stephen said. "I'd forgotten. Come, I'll go with ye. 'Tis safe to leave her now, Doctor?"

"Safer than to stay. You'll only upset her. I'll follow you shortly and have a look at the little Nigra. There is an atmosphere of fertility here at Harrow. I must be off before I contract the disease. There are five sons Terrebonne now; that's enough!"

Going down the road toward the slave cabins, Stephen could hear the booming of the river. The top of the levee was almost awash and the waters talked with dark voices. Stephen looked upward to see if the slaves were still patrolling his wall of earth. 'Twould not do to have a crevasse now—Odalie could not be moved. As he watched, he saw a stooped black figure silhouetted against the sky. Old Josh, he recognized. The old Negro was a good slave for all his lack of strength.

As fast as he walked, Caleen was ahead of him. She flung open the door of the cabin and went inside. Stephen followed her, holding his handkerchief against his nose to keep out the dark, fetid smells of birth. La Belle Sauvage lay upon the rude bed with an infant cradled in her arms. The child was of an inky, bluish blackness, large and sound of limb. Looking closely, Stephen could see it had something of its mother's striking dark beauty.

"A son?" he asked.

"A manchild," Sauvage whispered. "A warrior for his people!" She began to chant a wild, savage song to the baby. Stephen found it unpleasant, somehow.

Achille's face was split by a pleased grin.

"All by herself, she have him yes! She bite the cord through with them cat teeth. I tell you, maître, her something, that one!"

Stephen was examining the child.

"He is a fine one, Belle," he said. "Ye've done well. Never have

204

I seen a better. This one, Caleen, is to be kept apart from the rest. I want him trained as a manservant for my Etienne. It will be a good life for him—he will be taught many things. And never will he have to labor in the fields."

Caleen smiled slowly. But Sauvage was coming erect in the bed, holding the child to her naked breast.

"My child no slave!" she said. "Him prince—warrior prince! Him killer of lions and master of men! Him nobody servant, nobody slave!"

"Hush, girl!" Achille growled. "We do like maître say, yes!"

Stephen smiled.

"'Tis not so harsh a fate, Belle," he said gently. "Here, let me hold him."

"No!" the girl screamed; "no touch! No lay hands on him, no!" Then like a great cat, she had sprung from the bed and was dashing for the door. Achille sprang after her, and Stephen and Caleen followed more slowly.

But the great, clumsy black was no match for Sauvage's lithe swiftness. Watching her as she ran, her slim body innocent of clothing, Stephen realized again that here was an unmatched beauty. Then, he too gave a short cry, and took up the chase. For La Belle Sauvage was headed straight for the levee, straight for the river.

She went up the incline like a black panther, with effortless, cat-like grace, the long, ebony legs shooting out, and the earth flowing backward under the slim feet. Still holding the child, she stood for a moment atop the levee, her belly sucked in to make a curving hollow, and the high, up and outthrusting, conical breasts pointed and flaring. Then old Josh was coming toward her, his wizened hands outstretched.

"Stop her, Josh!" Stephen roared.

The old man grappled with the savage girl. There was a brief flurry of motion, and Sauvage tore free. She stood upon the levee, outlined sharply against the light, and lifted the child high above her head.

"Him manchild," she chanted, "him warrior! Him die, but him never no slave!"

Then Achille was upon her tearing the child from her grasp. Stephen was but a step behind. Together, they dragged the crying infant from Sauvage's arms. The girl fell back, her eyes like yellow coals in her glistening black face. Then, with a cry, she whirled and threw herself out and down into the swirling yellow water. It rose like dirty yellow wings as she went in, then it fell back, and the current howled like a living thing.

Achille thrust the child into Caleen's arms. But Stephen lunged forward and grasped the big Negro about the waist.

Josh caught the big man's arm, and Caleen, placing the baby tenderly upon the muddy earth, tightened her ancient arms fiercely about his neck.

"Lemme go!" he wept. "She drown, her! She drown, sho!"

"And so will ye, ye fool!" Stephen said. "There's no saving her now."

Fifty yards downstream, Sauvage's head broke water; then the swirling yellow torrent rode over her. The sound of the river pounded upon their eardrums. Caleen picked up the child.

Then they all went down the levee together. Achille's big hands hung loosely at his side, and the tears streaked his black face. Stephen put a hand upon his shoulder.

"Trouble yourself not about her," he said. "She was never the one for ye. I will get ye another—gentle and comely, better for ye and the baby."

Achille did not answer him. He went on down the road to the cabins, his great body shaken with sobs, like a child.

And old Caleen held the baby, her ancient eyes veiled and crafty. "Inch," I will call him, she mused. "Little Inch," after his grandfather. Never such a one will he be like Achille, but a man, him. His body will they enslave, yes, but never his mind and his heart. I will teach him, me. And in him the blood of his grandfather and of this girl. A man, him. A warrior, yes! She smiled slowly to herself.

Stephen saw the smile.

"At what do ye laugh, ye old witch?" he growled. "However much ye hated her, 'tis a bad thing to smile thus!"

" 'Tis nothing maître," Caleen said humbly. "I do not smile."

206

XIII

THE year 1831 was a good one throughout the Bayou Country. The great plantations grew and prospered. And of them none grew richer or greater than Harrow. Twice during the year, Stephen Fox found it necessary to purchase new slaves. The law of 1808 forbidding the further importation of African blacks had not yet had serious effect upon the supply, so now there were nearly fifteen hundred Negroes laboring on the broad acres of Harrow.

Stephen paid off his debts to Tom Warren and the various factors and invested money in newer and finer machinery. He opened accounts with two of the largest banks in New Orleans; but the bulk of his profits he sent away to far-off Philadelphia.

"Your Louisiana banker," he remarked to Andre, "is like your Louisianian generally, long on emotion but short on prudence and foresight. For monetary affairs, give me a vinegary Yankee every time."

Little Etienne Fox, at the age of one year, was already trying his first steps. His coming had changed everything at Harrow. All life at the plantation was geared to revolve around him: Caleen watched his waking movements, and was on her feet at his lightest whimper in his sleep. Odalie forgot Stephen existed in her preoccupation with the child; Aurore Arceneaux's visits increased and old Pierre fairly lived at Harrow.

Etienne was undeniably a striking child, though no one but his mother thought him beautiful. He had reached far back among his swarthy Mediterranean ancestors for a complexion that was as dark as a mulatto's, and inky hair that curled in great masses above his forehead. It was only when he turned and fixed a visitor with his long, level glance that the gasps of astonishment and the excited comments about his beauty began; for Etienne had Stephen's eyes, and their pale blueness was doubly set off by the darkness of his skin. Even as a baby, he was a quiet child, little given to laughing and cooing. He cried seldom, too, and seemed to live always in a world apart.

As soon as the babies could crawl, Andre and Stephen brought the two heirs of their respective fortunes together. Little Stephen Le Blanc, oddly enough, was as fair as Etienne was dark, and the two of them made the same sort of pleasing contrast, in reverse, as their fathers had before them. But babies, the new fathers soon discovered, are individualists. Any toy picked up by the one became the instant target of the other's affections, to be yanked away at the earliest possible moment.

Amelia and Odalie, too, found themselves bound together by the common experience of motherhood. On the part of Odalie, the friendship was warm and genuine; she grew to depend upon the levelheaded judgment of this odd American girl and to admire and cultivate her ways. Amelia, however, recognized that her own feeling toward Odalie was one of sympathy much more than it was of liking or of friendship. To her, the lovely Creole was no less enslaved than the meanest black woman on the plantation; and the chains that bound her were no less firm for all their being the intangible links of tradition, custom, and age-old habits of thought. Stephen, Amelia concluded, with the peculiar sense of guilt that came when she permitted herself to think of him at all, was such a man as any woman should be eternally grateful to have as a husband; yet Odalie's relationship toward him seemed to be that of a dutiful wife rather than a vibrantly loving one. Dutiful—ye Gods! How could anyone be dutiful toward Stephen?

And, although her contacts with Aurore were far fewer, Amelia liked the younger girl better than she did her cold, imperious sister. Half a glance sufficed to let her know what Aurore's trouble was and her heart went out to the lovely young girl whose face held the sad sweetness of an angel. Amelia went out of her way to cultivate Aurore, with some success; for soon Odalie was complaining that her sister spent more time at La Place des Rivières than at Harrow.

Thus matters rested when Mike Farrel chose to put in his appearance one more time at the big plantation.

"The trouble is, yez ken," he said to Stephen, "that nobody wants an old flatboatsman any more. The packets kin do the job almost as cheap and twice as fast. And they kin go it upstream as well as down. I've lived too long. 'Tis the drydocks and dryrot for me, me lad."

"Nonsense," Stephen told him. "Ye'll make as fine a boat captain as ever was seen upon the river. 'Tis high time we started upon that business anyway."

Then, having assigned Mike quarters at Harrow, the two of them rode down to New Orleans to consult with Tom Warren. By the early spring of 1832 there was a fast new steamer upon the river. Odalie was present at her launching, christening her the *Creole Belle*. She was a swift packet, with high twin stacks at the front and palatial appointments.

Mike avidly undertook the business of learning steam navigation. His knowledge of the river was superior to that of most of the river captains, but his ignorance of machinery was an obstacle to be surmounted. He fretted under the restraint of taking instructions from young whippersnappers, but doggedly he studied and applied himself until the steamboat men were forced to admit grudgingly that here was a formidable rival. On her first trip under Mike's full command, the *Creole Belle* came within minutes of breaking the upriver record to Cincinnati.

While in port, Mike continued to live at Harrow. No longer did he feel humiliated to accept Stephen's bounty. He was a person of importance now, a river captain; and he dressed and lived the rôle to the hilt. He felt freer than ever to indulge himself in his fondness for good liquors and mulatto wenches. This, Stephen found it necessary to check, for Mike was in a fair way toward demoralizing the entire plantation. He suggested with quiet good humor that it would be better if the big Irishman indulged in his peccadillos elsewhere and the whole thing would have ended there if Odalie had not chosen this moment to interfere.

"I won't have him here!" she stormed. "He is a great beast, this friend of yours! Why cannot he leave the girls alone?"

"Softly, Odalie," Stephen said. "This thing is a matter for my handling. 'Tis unseemly of ye to concern yourself with it."

"Unseemly! There are two near-white babies in the infirmary now and Harrow is becoming the talk of every great house for miles around. There are some who would say that some of these children are yours, Stephen . . ."

Stephen stood up, his fair brows coming together over his nose.

"That's enough," he said quietly. "If I choose to have Mike stay at Harrow 'tis my affair, and, by all the saints, he stays!"

"Oh, you!" Odalie exploded, and marched from the room. She went up the stairs to her bedroom, and picked up the sewing she had laid aside. Her head ached abominably. A glass of ruby port chilled with ice would help that. *Ma foi*, how hot it had grown already! Although it was scarcely midsummer, the heat was unbearable. She pulled the bell cord. Zerline was uncommonly long in coming. When she came into the room, Odalie looked up with an expression of annoyance.

"Must you be so slow?" she demanded. "'Tis all of a quarter hour since I rang."

"I'm sorry, maîtresse," the girl whispered. "What is it that you want?"

"Can't you talk above a whisper?" Odalie said fretfully. "What ails you, girl? Of late you seem totally lacking in spirits. Are you ill?"

"No, maîtresse," Zerline said; "No, I'm not ill—maîtresse desires?"

"A glass of port—chilled, and for heaven sakes be quick about it. My head is splitting."

Zerline turned and walked toward the door. She walked, slowly, almost heavily, with nothing of her usually spritely gait. Odalie looked after her curiously. Then Zerline was turning through the doorway.

"Zerline!"

"Yes, maîtresse?"

"Come back here!"

The girl turned slowly. As she approached, Odalie could see the tears standing in her eyes.

"You've put on weight," Odalie said, her black eyes narrowing. "And all of it about the waist too. Zerline . . ."

"Oh, maîtresse," the girl wept. "Maîtresse!"

"Who was it, Zerline? Come, girl, pull yourself together! Who was it?"

"Heem, maîtresse knows—heem. Suzette, she runs, her—and fights; but I am not so fast as Suzette, me. Many time I run away; but one time I am too slow—and he is so strong like a bear, him."

Odalie stood up slowly, the headache gone, forgotten.

"Go downstairs," she said softly, "and put yourself in the care of Caleen. Tell her that you are to receive the best of everything. She is not to reproach you."

Zerline looked at her mistress with eyes filled with tears of adoration.

"Maîtresse too good," she whispered. "Now I get you that wine first, then I go."

"Forget the port, Zerline. I don't need it now." She went out the door and down the stairs.

Stephen had not yet ridden out to the fields. He was busy in the great ledger book, recording the births of six male slave children, the sale of a thousand bales of cotton held over in his warehouse from last harvest, and the figures on the comparative

211

yield of purple and striped cane as against the old Malabar variety. Hearing Odalie's step, he looked up.

"Stephen . . ."

"Yes, my dear?"

"Stephen, I must ask you to have that man leave Harrow."

Wearily Stephen closed the big ledger.

"Didn't we discuss that matter this morning?" he asked softly.

"Yes, but . . ."

"My answer is still the same, my dear. I can see no reason for changing it."

"Well, I do! Perhaps you care not if he fills up the place with mulatto children! Perhaps that is nothing! But when he goes so far as to violate my own personal maidservant, it seems to me high time to call a halt!"

"Mike did that?"

"Yes."

"I must warn him to confine his activities to Girod Street. This is not a thing to be tolerated."

"Exactly. That's why you must have him leave."

Stephen looked at her.

"That—no," he said quietly. "Mike has a home here for life. I gave him my word."

"Either he goes," Odalie declared. "Or I do!"

Stephen shrugged.

"The only choice in that matter," he said, "is up to ye." He stood up, taking his hat and his riding crop in his hand.

"*Adieu,* my dear," he said. "I have work to do."

Odalie watched him striding away in the direction of the stables. Her face was still. Only about the corners of her mouth was there a trembling, so that a person, watching, would have been unsure whether or not she were going to laugh or cry. Then she turned back into the house.

"Georges!" she called.

Stephen's valet came out of the pantry. His face bore a guilty look, for he had been spending the better part of an hour trying to kiss Suzette, while she only laughed at him. He'd get her yet, though. She couldn't do him that, no! She'd be his wife and soon.

"Yas, maîtresse?" he said.

"Georges, have the coach hitched. Get Caleen—and Zerline, too. Tell them I want them here at once!"

"Yas, maîtresse," Georges said, and his voice was frightened. Never had he seen the young mistress look like this before, never. He scurried away to fetch the others.

Two hours later, the yellow coach rolled away from Harrow toward New Orleans. In it were Odalie and little Etienne, Caleen, Zerline, and Jean, a manservant. Zerline was crying softly; but Odalie's face was pale and still. Old Caleen stared blankly out of the window.

How would he be—this grandson of hers that she was leaving behind? Little Inch—blood and bone and breath of his grandsire. Oh, well, she'd come back again; there were so many things to teach this little one, so many arts, crafts, subtleties: He must outwit his enemies as she had for so many years outwitted them. In seeming surrender, he must conquer.

The coach rolled on through the gathering haze of early August. On the table in the great hall the note gleamed white, there against the fine old yellowed fabric. And the night came down in a vast stillness.

When Stephen came back to the house, Andre was with him. The young Creole had ridden over from his own plantation and joined Stephen in the fields. They had talked of many things as they rode through the rows of cane: the sickening corruption in municipal politics which Mayor Denis Prieur seemed powerless to check; the rapidly disintegrating situation between the Creoles and the Americans in the bitter tax and governmental control dispute; the weakening influence of the church under the onslaught of the Protestant sects, particularly the Presbyterians with their powerful speaker, Clapp, especially since Father Antoine had died in 'twenty-nine.

"And what a funeral they gave him!" Andre said. "Why, even the Freemasons attended as a guard of honor, and you know how they regard all things Catholic."

"Aye," Stephen grinned maliciously. "But how much greater a burial did they give that pirate, Dominique You, the next year?

213

Why, if ye recall, the Mayor declared a holiday. And of the two men which was the greater? 'Tis always Barabbas the people want!"

"You have much right in that," Andre said sadly. Then his handsome face lighted with a smile. "Here we are talking like old men, when 'tis only a few short years since we stole the fat drunkard's pants . . ."

"Seven years, Andre."

"Seven? *Ma foi*—so many? It seems but a day."

"To me it has been a long time—a hellish long time."

"You're not happy, my old one?"

"No, Andre, I'm not. I've gained everything I wanted. My lands, my big house, my bride—and my son. Yet there is but an emptiness here. I think sometimes I should have caught the next upriver packet that day we watched Lafayette."

"Stephen!"

"I'm sorry, Andre. We have had some times together, haven't we?"

"But yes! Remember in 'twenty-eight when we patrolled against the threatened slave insurrection?"

"Aye—the Nigras had a time of it then."

"And that same year we went down to the Place D'Armes to see Andrew Jackson. And those two little fillies, you remember, Odette and Jeanne—they both wanted you; why, Odette pouted for the better part of an hour before I convinced her that I wasn't a bad fellow really."

"Softly, Andre," Stephen grinned. " 'Tis best not to recall those scrapes—at Harrow even the trees have ears. Well, here we are."

Andre dismounted.

"Amelia wants a town house," he said, "but I postponed the construction—there's too much sickness in the city now. You know, Stephen, this year even the Creoles are dying—and yellow fever never used to bother us."

"Then perhaps ye will consider cleaning up that filthy hole of a town. No wonder it's a plague spot; why, right now ye can smell New Orleans three miles against the wind. Carrion, vermin,

214

sewage. By our Lady, do they all have to die to become con-vinced?"

"Apparently—more than three thousand have perished now, and the summer is yet not half spent."

They went up the stairs and into the great hall. Stephen went to the bell cord and rang for Georges. Then he turned and walked back toward his friend. As he passed the little table, the note caught his eyes. He picked it up, and tore open the envelope. His pale eyes moved in swift little jerks over the page. Andre stood there, watching Stephen's face.

"What is it?" he demanded. "Why do you look so?"

" 'Tis Odalie," Stephen said very quietly. "She's left me—she's gone back to her father's house in New Orleans."

"You're riding after her, of course?"

Stephen looked at his friend and the corner of his lip curled upward in a half smile."

"No, Andre," he said, "no, I'm not."

"But, Stephen . . ."

"My dogs, my horses, my blacks—and my women—obey me, Andre. She will come back. I shan't lift a finger—but she'll come back."

Pierre Arceneaux greeted his daughter heavily when the coach stopped before the high town house. He had aged greatly in the last three years, so much so that the burden of managing Belle-font had become too great for him. So it was that now for months at a time he retired to his three-story town house that was one of the wonders of New Orleans, and left the management of the plantation to assistants. Now as he greeted his elder daughter his face was lined and grave.

"I have no doubt that you know what you're doing," he said, "but any dissolution of the marriage contract grieves me. How-ever, come in, child; you're always welcome."

Followed by her retinue, Odalie got down from the coach and walked into the house.

"Take the coach around to the south end," old Arceneaux said wearily. "My groom will attend to the horses." Then he followed his daughter into the house.

Odalie had gone at once to her rooms on the second floor. Slowly the old man climbed the curving stairs. The crystal chandelier with its chimes of cut quartz was still, unstirred by any breath of air, and the heat was like a physical weight, pressing down upon his head. Outside Odalie's door, Pierre paused until he had regained his breath.

"Go down," Pierre said to Jean, "and tell Jules to bring us wine." As the Negro left, the old man sank down upon the nearest chair. "I am not well," he complained. "The years have left a heaviness in me."

"Nonsense, father," Odalie said. "You look like a stripling."

"Thanks, but it isn't so. Odalie . . ."

"Yes, father . . ."

"What if I sent a messenger to Stephen asking him to come and discuss this difficulty? To my mind he has done well with Harrow. Perhaps the nature of your complaint will not seem so serious upon re-examination."

"No, father. I'll never go back. What's done is done."

"You're being very foolish, my girl. Stephen has grown in Louisiana. There are those who say he'll reach greater things yet."

"I don't doubt it. Stephen has ability. Only he has no sense of the fitness of things. If he prefers his big brute of a river captain to me—why, then let the two of them stay up at Harrow without me." She rose and crossed the room.

Down below, the alley was all but deserted. As Odalie watched, a wooden ox cart groaned through the narrow street below the gallery. It was piled high with something, the exact nature of which Odalie could not discern, since its contents were covered with canvas. But as it passed beneath her, the heavy stench rose up and struck her in the face. She put her handkerchief to her nose, and leaned out of the window. Then she was jerking her head back in, turning to Pierre.

216

"What is it?" the old man demanded.

"That wagon—" Odalie said. "Father, am I mad, or is that a human leg I see sticking out from under the canvas?"

"You're quite sane," Pierre told her grimly. "They pass this way every day."

"*Mon Dieu!*"

"Yes—more of them every day—with the unclaimed and name-less dead stacked up like cordwood. The whole world seems to be dying, Odalie."

"But, father, what on earth—why?"

"The fever, again—and worse than ever before. This time it's sparing no one. Even the blacks are dying and they've always been immune to it. Still want to stay in New Orleans, Odalie?"

The tall girl faced her father.

"I'll chance it," she said; and went on with her unpacking.

Throughout the rest of the summer, the deaths continued to mount. Odalie forbade Caleen to take little Etienne out even for air. The boy fretted in the sweltering heat of the house. At night, no one slept. The boy cried fitfully. And Zerline, heavy with child, tossed upon her cot, her lips swollen and covered with blisters. There was a headlong rush to leave the city. By October twenty-fifth, only thirty-five thousand people were left out of New Orleans' normal population of more than eighty thousand souls. Still Odalie held on grimly.

On the night of October twenty-eighth, Odalie was shaken awake by Caleen's horny old hand.

"Maîtresse come," she said. "Zerline, she dying, her!"

Without bothering even to don a robe, Odalie ran down the dark hall in her nightdress. The mulatto girl was twisting on her cot, locked in the most violent convulsions.

"Get Jean," Odalie said. "Tell him to ride for Doctor Terre-bonne. Come, Caleen, we've work to do."

Caleen shook her head.

"Too late," she said. "Her die sure."

217

"Isn't there anything we can do?"

Again Caleen shook her head.

"Nothing," she said. "Nothing. Her die."

Doctor Terrebonne did not reach the house of Pierre Arceneaux until six o'clock the next morning. By that time Zerline had been dead almost eight hours. Neither Jules nor Jean, the Negro menservants, had been able to find a priest. At the last, Odalie had knelt beside the unconscious girl and whispered as much as she knew of the sacrament of Extreme Unction, adding in the places where her memory had lapsed, her own fervent prayers.

When the little doctor came into the room where the dead girl lay, Odalie scarcely recognized him. His face was covered with a thatch of iron-gray beard. His clothes hung loosely like bags from his once ample form, and his eyes were streaked with fiery red, peering out from great blue hollows.

"You come too late," Odalie said.

"I know. I am always too late now. Merciful God! As if the fever were not enough . . ."

"Not enough? You mean that there is something more?"

"Cholera. If there is a man alive in New Orleans when the hot weather abates he should thank the divine intercession of all the saints!"

"Doctor," Odalie said. "Surely you exaggerate."

Doctor Terrebonne was writing in his little book of records: "Name: Zerline; Race: Colored; Slave to Madame S. Fox; Age: Twenty—" He looked up at Odalie's words.

"Madame," he said, "I can only suggest that you have your horses hitched to your carriage now—this instant—and drive out of New Orleans at a gallop. Good night, Madame. I will have the dead cart call for the remains."

"The dead cart?" Odalie whispered. "You mean that horrible wagon with—oh, my God!"

"Exactly. One will pass this way before noon. I shall have the driver stop."

"No!" Odalie said. "She will have decent Christian burial—and masses for the repose of her soul."

218

"If Madame can find a priest—most of whom are dead by now, because of their unswerving devotion to the cause of ministering unto the sick. Asiatic cholera is no respecter of clerical garb— and if Madame is willing to undertake the labor of grave-digging with her own patrician hands . . . Good day, Madame." He left with a curt bow, already hurrying to his next call.

He's mad, Odalie thought; then she turned and went back into the room where Zerline lay. Carefully, she and Caleen wrapped the bloated figure of the girl in a winding sheet then, summoning Jean and Jules, they had her lifted tenderly into the carriage. Arming the Negroes with spades, they set out for the burial ground. As they were leaving the house, the dismal ox cart turned into the street. The driver was a black, hideously pockmarked from smallpox.

"Bodies?" he croaked: "Any bodies? Out wit your daid!" And behind him Odalie could see that the cart was uncovered, the bodies strewn about like curiously lifelike puppets, piled up so high that here and there a head hung over the side, lolling loosely on the neck. Then the cart plodded past, and the stench rolled into the coach windows. Holding her kerchief to her nose, Odalie looked back. One fat old man had fallen from the cart, save for one foot that was entangled in the railings; and as the cart moved, he bumped on the cobblestones like a thing of rubber, his bald head stained with dust.

"Bodies," the driver called. "Bodies! Out wit your daid!"

The sky hung low over the city like a grey iron lid, and no slightest wind stirred. As they passed through the deserted streets, they saw houses boarded up; these, Odalie realized, were the homes of those who had first left the city. But as they went on, other deserted houses stood with doors and windows opened and the furniture undraped. Time and again she had to turn her head to avoid the sight of a sodden bundle of rags lying amid the filth of a gutter—sodden, shapeless bundles that had once been human beings.

They drove, unopposed, into the gates of the cemetery. The coachman drew up his pair just inside the door. Leaning out, Odalie could see the great open trenches into which the death

219

carts were dumping their loads. There were dozens of freshly
dug graves; but now, apparently, even the grave diggers were
fled, for, at their approach, two or three carrion crows flapped
heavily up from the open graves. At one place there were mounds
of the dead, where the drivers of the dead cart, careless, or heed-
less of the fact that here there was no trench, had simply spilled
their cargoes out upon the ground.

Odalie pointed to a clear spot and the two Negroes went to
work. When they were done, they laid the body gently in the
earth, and waited bareheaded while their mistress said a prayer.
Then, at last, they covered Zerline with the rich, black earth and
turned again homeward.

Long before they reached the house, night had fallen. The
coachman slowed the horses to a walk, and they went down all
the dark streets leading toward the house. But as they reached
the center of the city, they went faster; for here the streets
were garishly illuminated with burning barrels of pitch and tar,
by which means the medical authorities sought to purify the air.

Again Odalie put her head out of the window. On the corner
a cask of pitch was blazing, the great flames shooting straight up
into the air, unstirred by any wind; and above them the sooty
black smoke clouds billowed. From the opposite corner the roar
of a cannon split the night open from one end of the street to the
other. The horses jumped and reared. The coachman lashed them
savagely, fighting for control. The coach rocked and pounded
through the dark streets, the horses gathering speed everytime a
cannon boomed. Odalie sat in the swaying coach and prayed that
the explosions of artillery would indeed change the air currents
so as to drive away the malignant vapors that were rapidly con-
verting New Orleans into a city of the dead.

When at last, bruised and sickened, aching in every muscle,
and holding on tightly to her shocked nerves, Odalie reached
her father's house, she was met at the door by a slave.

"Maîtresse," the woman said. "The baby him sick, yes. Your
papa sick, too, him. Mebbe they die."

Without a word, Odalie shouldered her aside and went up
the stairs two at a time. In his little bed, Etienne twisted sound-

lessly, his naturally dark face flushed a deep mahogany red. Odalie put a hand to his forehead. It was so hot that she drew her hand away with an involuntary cry. Then she ran from the room toward her father's bed chamber, calling to Jules and Jean as she went.

The old man lay unconscious and shrunken upon his bed, his eyes wide and staring, and his breath coming out in feeble puffs and whistles. In one glance Odalie saw that there was no hope for him, the look of death was already in his face and his breath was weakening.

Even as she stood there, the proud old eyes opened suddenly. "Get Father Antoine," he whispered. "I have sins to confess— many sins. . . ." Then he sank back upon the bed. No need to tell him that the old Spanish priest had been dead these three years. No need to tell him anything—no need to do anything but kneel beside his bed and say a prayer for the tranquility of his soul. Pierre Arceneaux was dead.

Dry-eyed, Odalie came out of the room to meet Caleen in the corridor.

"I sent Jean for the doctor," the old woman said. "I told him to ride fast, him. The baby is ver' sick, yes!"

"Father," Odalie said, "Father. . . ." Then she bent her face against Caleen's shoulder and cried aloud, dry, racking sobs, utterly without tears. Caleen patted her gently upon the back and stroked the thick black hair.

"Don't cry, maîtresse," she said. "He good man, him. The Virgin and all the saints pray for his soul, yes. He don't stay one hour in purgatory I bet you."

An hour later when Jean returned, he and Jules started to work in the courtyard, tearing up the flagstones to make a grave for Pierre. Odalie had decided not to risk another trip to the graveyard. Sitting in her room holding the fever-racked body of little Etienne in her arms, she could look out of the window and watch the two Negroes working, their pickaxes rising with a dull gleam in the flickering light of the torches. Behind the house, on the street side, the barrels of pitch and tar cackled fiercely, hurling their flames straight up, higher than the houses. Now and again from the distant parts of the city, a cannon boomed; then another and another until the whole night echoed with the crash of artillery. Even now, as she watched the slaves, the police were setting up a twenty-four pounder on the corner nearest to the house, beneath the swinging chains of lanterns. When, a half hour later, they fired it off, the whole house shook and all the windows rattled. In her arms, little Etienne was thrown into convulsions by the explosion. Still holding him, Odalie dashed to the window, and tore it open.

"Stop it!" she screamed. "Stop it, for the love of God!"

But the roar of the great field piece drowned out her words. Odalie hung out of the window holding the child, and the acrid smoke from the gun stung her eyes and throat. She opened her mouth to cry out at them again, but the dead carts were turning into the street, not one but many of them, stretching out of sight around the corner. Odalie closed the window and sank back into her chair, cradling the sick child to her breast. The cannon crashed. In the courtyard, the pickaxes bit into the earth. The pitch barrels crackled, the great flames roaring up past the windows, and the smoke hanging heavy and black like a pall over all the city. And in the intervals of silence the wagons of the dead creaked endlessly by in the nightlocked street.

"Holy Mother of God," Odalie prayed. "Holy compassionate Mother of God . . ."

Then Caleen was coming into the room leading a strange doctor.

"I am Doctor Lefevre," he announced a trifle pompously. "My colleague, Doctor Terrebonne, died this afternoon of the cholera. May I see the child, please."

Without a word, Odalie passed Etienne over to him. The doctor laid him upon the bed and began his examination. Finally he straightened.

" 'Tis not the cholera," he said, "for which you may be grateful. He has yellow fever. We may be able to pull him through."

He sat down and pulled from his bag a great array of small vials and powders.

"Tisanes, cataplasms, and purgatives," he announced. "We shall try them first. Tonight you will administer seven grams of Julap, and four grams of calomel. If he is not improved by morning, we will try a spoonful of croton oil with three drops of mercury."

"My God!" Odalie whispered.

"That should break the fever. Afterwards we will continue treatment with calcined magnesia, olive oil and juice of citron, alternated with ptisan of tamarind, cassia and cream of tartar. . . ."

"But he is only a baby . . ."

"You want him to live, don't you?" the doctor said sternly.

"Yes," Odalie said, "yes."

"Then do as I say. 'Tis fortunate it is not cholera. About that, medical science knows little. But we know the causes of yellow fever, hence we can cure it. You see, Madame, the stagnant water around the city becomes heated by the sun and evaporates into the air, which is then saturated with aqueous vapor. When the temperature diminishes, the water vapor descends to the surface of the earth bringing with them miasmata formed by the decomposition of certain bodies under a favorable state of the atmosphere. When these are absorbed through the pulmonic passages, yellow fever results."

"Yes," Odalie managed, stunned by this barrage of medical terminology. "But will he live?"

"Of that no one can be certain. Much depends upon the patient." He stopped, smiling wryly. "I once saw Monsieur Fox fight a duel. He stood without moving, without even lifting his pistol, and allowed Monsieur Waguespack to fire at a perfectly stationary target. Then, badly wounded, he sighted slowly and carefully and brought down his man. With the inheritance of such courage, this child should certainly survive. Good night, Madame Fox. I'll call again tomorrow."

Doctor Lefevre kept his word. He called daily at the Arceneaux mansion, often neglecting other of his patients to do so. The great beauty of Madame Fox, marred as it was by the sleeplessness and weeping, was still enough to move a man of stone, much less a still young and somewhat impressionable doctor. But little 'Tienne got no better. Pierre Arceneaux slept the long sleep beneath the flagstones of his courtyard, and Jean and Jules, too, were now laid in death before the door of the stables. Every day someone of the household died.

Finally, Doctor Lefevre looked down upon the barely breathing child in whom the fever still mounted.

"There is but one hope," he said, looking up at Odalie. "Sometimes the fever is cooled by a diminution of the blood. We must bleed him."

"No!" Odalie cried. "No!"

" 'Tis the only way, Madame," the doctor said patiently. Odalie looked at him, her black eyes widening; then, turning her face to the wall, she nodded silently. Doctor Lefevre stood up and opened his satchel. His face was haggard with sleeplessness, and his thin fingers shook. But he took out the instruments and laid them upon a cloth. Old Caleen watched him, her eyes blazing in her black face. The doctor bent over Etienne, scalpel in hand.

"No!" Caleen screeched. "No! you no cut him, you!" She sprang forward and gathered little 'Tienne into her arms. "Maîtresse gret fool!" she stormed. "We go back to Harrow, now! And I cure him, me! No great fool of a *docteur* kill my baby! Come now, maîtresse. Come!"

The doctor glared at the old woman, but Odalie followed her helplessly out of the room. An hour later, they were on their way back to Harrow on horseback, since there were no longer any slaves to hitch and drive the carriage. Caleen rode behind Odalie on the single ancient nag, the baby cradled in her arms.

Four hours later they reached the plantation. Old Josh spied them from the levee, and dashed off to inform his master. So it was that when they turned up the oak alley before Harrow Stephen was waiting.

"So," he said. "Ye've come back."

"I have brought you back your son," Odalie said with great dignity, "so that he may die in the house of his father."

Stephen looked at the tiny bundle of skin and bones that had once been a healthy, prattling child of almost three years.

"If he does," he said grimly, "God and Our Lady forgive ye, for I never shall!"

Then, taking Etienne in his arms, he marched up the steps and into the house.

XIV

For the next four days Harrow was a gigantic madhouse. The work in the fields was totally neglected. The field Negroes hung around the big house day and night, watching the windows from which the lights never vanished. Even old Josh sat no more on the levee, absorbed in his eternal fishing; instead he stationed himself at the foot of the great stairs, waiting for news of the young boy. The house servants moved about like ghosts, fear written all over their sleek brown and yellow faces. For the maître was consumed with an icy, deadly soft-spoken rage. They knew it and they started at the sound of his too carefully controlled voice.

Old Caleen was in complete charge of everything. "Doctors, posh!" Stephen said. "Dirty, murdering sawbones! Caleen knows as much as any ten of them. Ye do as she tells ye and be damned quick about it!"

So it was that the strongest hands on the plantation found themselves pulling on the cords that moved a great overhead fan, under which the child's crib had been placed. Sheets wet with the coolest water that could be found, were constantly wrapped around the sweltering little body. And Caleen stubbornly, persistently got drop after drop of orange juice, lemon juice, lime juice down the parched little throat. The precious ice was brought out from its deeply buried storage place and wrapped in thin cloths which were then placed upon the boy's blazing forehead. Inch by inch, Caleen fought the temperature down, and kept the slender thread of life from snapping.

On the morning of the fourth day, Little Inch was standing by the crib. His coal-black, chubby body was clad in a cast-off shirt that came down to his fat, dimpled knees. And his bright shoe-button eyes rested fearfully on the face of his little master.

" 'Tienne die?" he asked.

Caleen bent forward suddenly. Slowly she extended a trembling hand. Etienne's body was wet from head to foot; but this time from his own sweat. And his forehead, where Caleen's fingers rested, was cool to the touch, and entirely free of fever.

"No," the old woman said. " 'Tienne no die! He getting well, him!"

Stephen, dozing fitfully in the big chair beside the bed, came awake at once at her words.

"What's that?" he said. "What did ye say, Caleen?"

"Look," Caleen pointed. "Fever all gone. He sweats, him. He better now—soon he be all right, yes!"

"Holy Blessed Mother of God!" Stephen whispered, looking down at his son. Then, raising his head, he called out: "Odalie!"

Odalie came into the room, all color gone from her face, even her lips white, defined only by their contour. Her black eyes swept from the face of her husband to the tiny form lying peacefully upon the crib.

"Is he—is he . . . " she managed; but the child opened his blue eyes.

"*Mo ganye faim,*" he whispered. "*Mo ganye faim.*"

Odalie took a half step forward, and fell into Stephen's arms. He let her weep there against his chest, until the ruffles of his shirt front were sodden with her tears. Holding her there, close against him, he raised his eyebrows at Caleen.

"What on earth is he saying?" he whispered.

"He say him hungry. That Negre—Gumbo French. He hear

227

me talk and Little Inch. Now I go get him soup, me." She slipped from the room.

"Stephen," Odalie said, "Stephen . . ."

"He lives, Odalie. That's all that matters. Ye can forget the harsh words. And in the growing, he will need both a father and a mother. Our differences must not be permitted to affect him. Ye can find it in your heart to tolerate an old boor for a little longer, can ye not?"

"Tolerate?" Odalie said. "Oh, Stephen—Stephen, why can't you understand?"

"I think I do," Stephen said. "Come, we must leave him alone to sleep now." They went over to the crib and looked down. Etienne was sleeping like a tiny angel. Then they tiptoed from the room.

"Who'd ever have thought what a treasure I was buying in that old witch?" said Stephen.

Then they went down the stairs and into the dining hall.

Mike Farrel called the next day from his rooms in the city to pay his respects to the mistress of Harrow. He stood before Odalie, twisting a big kerchief nervously in his powerful hands.

"I come to ask your forgiveness, me lady," he said. "Yez have no use for the likes of me, I ken, and rightly, no doubt. But if Stevie's wee one had died, I would have felt myself a murderer."

Odalie watched him, completely at ease, smiling a little.

"I never thought yez would take on so about the wenches," he went on. "Yez have me word I'll never trouble yez again."

"You're welcome at Harrow," Odalie said softly. "I ask only your word that you will leave the servants alone. Stephen dotes on you. Please come whenever you will."

"Thank yez, me lady," Mike said, and bowed himself out with great dignity. By virtue of his new position, Mike was bidding fair to become a gentleman. Even vanity had its point, Odalie decided.

Before the middle of winter, Etienne was running around the house as vigorously as ever before. Only he seemed to have retreated into his own private world of childhood, into which he permitted only the slightest glimpses. Little Inch was constantly at his side, but Andre brought little Stephen less and less frequently to play with him.

"They have brought forth a monster!" he confided to Amelia. "The last time 'Tienne wanted to play the Spanish Inquisition, with our Stephen, of course, as the victim of torture. This time, he was Jean LaFitte, the pirate, ready to extort ransom by putting out little Stevie's eyes. I tell you the boy is mad!"

" 'Tis the after effects of the fever," Amelia said gently, cuddling their third child to her breast. "He will get over it."

"He has a sickness of mind," Andre insisted. "Like that La Laurie woman who tortured her slaves."

"You don't have to take our son to visit him," Amelia said. "After all, Stephen never brings him here."

"That's true," Andre mused. "I wonder why?"

Late in March of 1836, Stephen met Andre at the fork of the river road, and the two of them rode in to New Orleans. Andre was afire with enthusiasm.

"Don't you see, Stephen?" he demanded. "This means everything to us. As soon as Texas wins her independence—and she will win it, never you fear—we must annex her!"

Stephen smiled.

"Softly, Andre," he said. "The people of Texas may have something to say about that."

"The people of Texas! Why, they are as eager for annexation as we! Don't you see, Stephen, out of Texas we can carve five slave-holding states—more than enough to counter-balance the Northwest Territory?"

"Aye," Stephen said grimly. "And 'tis a thing that troubles me: this race between us for more lands, more peoples, more votes. I have good friends in Philadelphia and New York. Ye know I go to Philadelphia once each year to settle my accounts and arrange future transactions. And now there is much bitterness because of this thing."

"Filthy money grubbers!" Andre said. "They dare to point at us in scorn because of slavery. Everybody knows that slavery is the natural order of things, ordained by God. Why, the blacks themselves have benefited by it. We took them out of ignorance and savagery and gave them useful work, and care and kindly treatment. Why, the thing is just right—simply and beautifully right—on the face of it."

Stephen threw back his head and laughed aloud.

"How I envy ye your Louisiana faculty for self-delusion!" he chuckled. "Slavery is a very convenient and pleasant system—for us. But I've often had qualms over the rightness of a system which permits me to sell a man as though he were a mule. Still, I have my leisure, which I haven't earned, and my wealth, which I don't work for—so I cannot complain really."

"Stephen!" Andre's voice was thick with shock. "You talk like an abolitionist!"

"Forgive me, my lad," Stephen smiled. "I couldn't resist needling ye. We'll talk no more of this."

"But we will," Andre declared. "And you may tell your Yankee friends that if they interfere we shall leave them and continue on alone in our own way."

Stephen was no longer smiling.

"Aye—there is talk of that now," he said. "Not much yet—just a whisper. But it will grow. 'Tis a terrible thing, this secession business. Can a hand declare itself independent of the body? Or a foot or an ear or even a head? Sever them, and blood will flow. I tell ye, Andre, that what we have here in America is something new in the world. 'Tis not a loose collection of sovereign states bound by the flimsy paper of a treaty which can be nullified at the whim of any one of them. This is a people's government—the truest republic the world has ever seen."

"Yes, but when a state sees its rights interfered with . . ."

"States have no rights! Only the people have rights. There must be conciliation between us. We must not destroy the brightest hope of human freedom of all the ages. We cannot ram slavery down their throats, nor can they force us to give it up.

But we must get along with each other. The union must be preserved."

Stephen paused and looked out toward the river. "I've seen a goodly part of this land of ours, Andre," he said softly, "and there is something about it different. I cannot tell ye what it is, exactly. 'Tis the vastness of it, perhaps; the bigness of tree and hill, the sweep of plain, the might of its rivers. 'Tis a big land, Andre, for big men to carve out and build and conceive the shape of human destiny . . ."

Andre was looking at Stephen in awe.

"*Ma foi!*" he declared. "Never before have I seen you so moved!"

Stephen smiled wryly at his friend.

" 'Tis only that I've been in most of the rat holes of this earth, and I've been hunted by the keepers of rats. 'Tis here, and only here, that a man can breathe. But enough of this for now."

They rode along in silence. The road stretched behind them bare and white, and the clop of the horses' hoofs alone broke the stillness. Then, at last, they were turning off Gravier Street into Magazine. Before the new three-story building they dismounted, throwing the reins to a Negro boy. They went into the bar room, and had small whiskeys, then they walked out into a glass-covered courtyard.

"Banks Arcade," Andre said in a low voice. " 'Tis only three years old, but I'll wager that more expeditions have been organized here than in any other place in the city. Look, Stephen! That's Governor Quitman, and Senator Henderson from Mississippi. They've always had a hand in this Texas business. . . ."

Stephen lifted a hand. An orator was reading from a document in the middle of the courtyard.

" 'I shall never surrender or retreat,' " the orator intoned.

The crowd roared, drowning out his words.

" 'If this call is neglected, I am determined to sustain myself as long as possible and die like a soldier who never forgets what is due his own honor and that of his country—VICTORY OR DEATH. Signed, William Barret Travis, Lieutenant Colonel, Commanding.' "

231

Every man in the courtyard was on his feet, his head bared. The voices beat upward against the glass roof of the courtyard in a thick, hoarse wave of sound. The orator lifted his hand for silence.

"That, gentlemen, was the last message from the Alamo. Colonel Travis died there, and Davy Crockett, and our own Jim Bowie!" He waved both hands to stifle the impending applause. "Gentlemen," he said solemnly, "Thermopylae had its messenger of defeat; the Alamo had none!"

The roar of the crowd was a thing to be felt. It pulsated upon the air in wave after wave for a full ten minutes. Before it had entirely died, Phillippe Cloutier sprang to the rostrum.

"I offer my services, sir," he said. "I will endeavor to raise a company of men and outfit them at my own expense!"

Instantly the cries went up.

"I'm with you, Phillippe!"

"Take me!"

"Me!"

Other men of wealth and prominence followed Phillippe to the rostrum. In half an hour, twelve companies had been started on the way to organization. One hundred and fifty thousand dollars had been pledged to the cause of the new Republic. Stephen and Andre had both signed notes for ten thousand dollars apiece.

XV

B<small>Y THE</small> end of May, 1836, the rebellion of the people of Texas
against Mexico was over. Santa Anna had been captured at
Jacinto, and Texas was free. In September, the treaty of Valasco
was signed, and the Lone Star Republic took its place among the
nations. Of the hundreds of Louisianians who had taken part in
the revolt, some were dead, but the vast majority were back in
New Orleans, boasting grandly of their exploits.

Some, however, chose to remain in Texas and become a part
of the new land. Among these was Phillippe Cloutier. He had
risen high in the councils of the new republic. He had been
wounded in battle, had covered himself with glory, and now,
at thirty, was revered by the lean, long-limbed sparse-spoken
men from whom he differed so greatly. But there were none who
knew why he often turned his face eastward toward the Sabine:
better the sweep of plains and the waters moving between him
and Odalie; better a new life, in a new land.

In New Orleans, the suggestion of councilman Peters had been
adopted. New Orleans was now, in reality, three cities, each
actually independent of the others, bowing only on paper to
one mayor. And now that she was in control of her own finances,

the Faubourg Saint Marie forced rapidly ahead of the others. Wharves and warehouses were built, businesses sprang up like mushrooms and prospered. The twangy Western speech and the softly slurred Southern English were now heard on the streets more often than French. The Creoles were still to elect four more mayors, but afterwards never again would a mayor of New Orleans be aught but an American. The day of the descendants of the Dons and of the French was over.

And in January of 1837, Stephen Fox was thirty-seven years old. The years had changed him little, except to add a fine network of lines at the corners of his eyes, which, even when he was looking directly at a person, gave him the appearance of peering into far distances. His speech had mellowed and slowed, and taken on some of the drawling music of the South. But his body was as lean and as hard-tempered as a rapier, and as full of a deadly grace. He rode to the hunt, and jumped his horse over the highest barriers; he shot, and fenced, and gambled with the best. But he refused to be drawn into any of the countless duels that the fashionable young blades of the day thought necessary to the maintenance of their honor as a gentleman.

And more and more he became interested in politics. He stood for the city council and was elected from the Orleans district, the old French Quarter where he held property, although he was not a Creole. In 'thirty-seven, his name was being mentioned for both the state legislature and the mayoralty. In this city where municipal corruption was so much the order of things that it called up no mention, Stephen's political activities were a cause for wonder: he was now the greatest landowner in the state, both because of the additions to Harrow, and because of his management of Bellefont held in trust by him for his wife and her sister after the death of Pierre Arceneaux. Certainly, he had no need to fatten his purse from the affairs of state; why then should he trouble himself?

"We are shaping a new life," he said to Andre, as the two of them sat over *café noir* at Harrow. "And I would have a hand in it. Texas will come in, and after that the Californias. Ye were right about that. This land will sweep from sea to sea and there will be no power on earth that can touch her."

Andre smiled, his small mouth half lost in his round apple cheeks.

" 'Tis odd to hear you speak of power, Stephen. I've often heard you fairly bristle against the despotisms of the Old World."

"A power for good. The power of free men acting in just causes. 'Twill shake the earth, Andre."

"You're right there. If only we are not interfered with. If only those money grubbers of New England will hush their pious nonsense! That's the main reason we must have Texas, Stephen. We've got to have more weight than they in Congress."

Stephen picked up his longstemmed clay pipe.

"Aye," he said grimly, "there's the danger. There's the rock on which the Union might split."

"Then let it! With our lands and our slaves we can be the wealthiest nation on earth—and the most powerful, without them!"

Stephen looked into the earnest face.

"No, Andre," he said. "There ye're wrong. If it comes to that, 'tis we, not they, who will fall. In all the South we could not cast as many cannon as they could in one of their cities. We could never muster as many men. And behind us we would leave the brooding mass of blacks ready to spring the minute our backs are turned."

"We're better fighters," Andre declared hotly. "One gentlemen is worth any ten merchants! We'd have allies—England would come in with us, and possibly France. And the blacks would never revolt—they're like children, lacking either the mind or the heart. Besides, they've been kindly treated and they love their masters."

"I don't know," Stephen said, but Odalie's voice, trembling with anger, interrupted him.

"Stephen!"

Wearily Stephen put down his pipe.

"Coming, my dear," he said.

He got up and Andre rose with him.

235

"I must be going," the younger man said. "Amelia is over-burdened with the children, and there are some monetary affairs I must attend to."

Stephen nodded, and the two of them walked out into the great hall.

There Odalie met them, and clutched Stephen's arm.

"Wait," she said to Andre. "I want you to see how my husband rears his son!"

They crossed the hall and stood outside the opened door-way. Odalie pointed. There, seated across the table from Little Inch, was the seven-year-old Etienne, a hand of cards fanned out in his grimy little paw. Little Inch's black face was furrowed.

"Deal me 'nother un," he said.

Odalie started forward, but Stephen's hand was firm on her arm. His face, watching his son, was gleeful, the great scar above his eye glowing in the morning light.

"Two picayunes?" Etienne asked.

"Done," Inch declared.

The play went on, until at last there were five picayunes on the table and each boy had four cards face up and one face down before him. Odalie was trembling with fury, but Stephen's face was lighted with a grin of pure diablerie. Standing on tiptoe, he could see that Etienne had a beautiful run: three Jacks and a Queen exposed; but Little Inch had three tens and an Ace. Etienne turned his covered card and laughed aloud.

"Pay up," he said in French. "I've got a full house!"

But Little Inch's white teeth glistened in his black face.

"Gotcha 'Tienne!" he said, reaching for the coins. "I got four o' a kind!" He turned the fourth card up, showing the fourth ten-spot. Etienne glared at the two hands, frowning over the four tens and his own three Jacks and two Queens. Then with all his force he brought his fist down on Inch's fingers, smashing them against the table. The picayunes rolled over the floor. Little Inch howled. And before the three spectators could cross the room, Etienne had the little black boy down on the floor and was pounding him in the face with both fists.

Stephen dragged his son from the prostrated slave. Little Inch got to his knees, but a well-aimed kick sent him sprawling.

"'Tienne!" Stephen roared. "Have ye taken leave of your senses? Get ye down and pick up the chips!"

Sullenly Etienne obeyed.

"Now give them to Inch, and up with ye to your room! By all the saints, I will not stomach a bad loser!"

"You see," Odalie wept, turning to Andre. "Not a word against the gambling! And 'Tienne must humble himself to a slave, because of his father's peculiar conception of honor! Here, Inch!" she said, "give me the money. Now go to Caleen and tell her how wicked you've been. Go now!"

Little Inch looked at her with his mouth opened, and the great tears streaked his shiny black face. Then, like a frightened animal, he scurried from the room.

"My apologies, Andre," Stephen said, "for this exhibition. Ye'll excuse us, my dear?"

Odalie nodded mutely. The two men walked toward the door.

"He is difficult," Stephen said. "His whole life is spent in plaguing me and his mother. He refuses to speak English, and when I force him to, his accent is execrable."

"Patience, Stephen," Andre said. "The boy will outgrow it. Too bad he's an only child. There's nothing like a crew of brothers and sisters to knock the deviltry out of them."

"Ye should know," Stephen laughed. "How many are there now at La Place?"

"Five," Andre grinned. "And, by all the saints, that's all there'll be!"

Stephen laughed aloud.

"I doubt it," he said. "Any way, next month is 'Tienne's birthday fête. Ye and Amelia must come and bring the brood—all of them."

"We'll be here," Andre said. "Now I must ride to town and settle my accounts in the forty different varieties of worthless money."

"Aye, that's no good. Every bank in the city issuing its own money, and now the business houses have taken it up, and even private citizens. 'Twill mean only ruin, Andre."

"Yes," Andre snorted. "You could pass the label from an olive oil bottle: 'tis greasy and it smells bad, and it has writing on it! *Voir*, Stephen."

"*Adieu*," Stephen said. "I must go up to my rooms in the North Wing and rest for an hour. I've had no sleep these three nights."

Andre's eyebrows rose. The North Wing was the bachelor quarters. The bridal chambers were in the South Wing.

" 'Tis none of my affair," he said, "but how long have you slept in those rooms?"

"Since 'Tienne's birth," Stephen said gravely. "My wife's health has been delicate since the child."

"I see," Andre said; then to himself as he strode down the stairs: "Seven years, *Ma foi!*"

The morning of Etienne's birthday dawned bright and clear. From all parts of the city and all the great plantations the crowds began to gather. There were many traders and merchants and business men among them, and many working men, for Stephen Fox's philosophy of democracy had become a thing very real to him, for which he was willing to brave the ill-concealed sneers of his fellow planters.

Most of the young men came on horseback, but the court-yard was filled with carriages too, and the halls echoed with the laughter and shouts of the children. On the lawn before Harrow, a great table had been spread. Etienne sat at the head of it, while Little Inch, costumed in turban and silken pantaloons like a Turk, stood behind his master to fulfill his every wish. Inch did not smile now, despite the gaiety. He had learned his lesson well. When he had gone to Caleen with the story of his latest beating at the hands of Etienne, she had taken him in her arms and whispered to him softly.

"We can't win by fightin', us. They too strong. We got to be clever like a swamp fox. 'Tienne tell you to do something, do it.

Do it, too quick. Be polite, just a little too polite. Think fast—think good. We outsmart him. Master ain't always the best man —sometime the slave win if he smart, him. You learn. Learn to read and write and figger. But keep your mouth shut. Learn everything white man knows. Grow up strong in the back like your Grandpère, Big Inch, and smart in the head like me. Someday freedom come. Someday you be maître, I tell you! 'Tienne wash your feet then! You wait, you!"

Before the table a straight-away had been marked off. And above it small rings were suspended from cords. The sons of the planters gaily attired in the costumes of knights, thundered down the stretch and attempted to spear the rings with their long lances. The lad who brought in the greatest number of rings upon his lance was crowned King of the Tournament, and won a kiss and a prize from the Queen of the Lists, who today was the youngest of the Pontabla girls, selected by popular acclaim.

Etienne watched the sport glumly, toying with his rapidly melting ice cream. Nothing could win a smile from him. He was secretly thoroughly enjoying the bleak misery on his mother's face and his father's constant frowns.

Now the rings were taken down and a tough old goose suspended by the feet above the course. Now it was the turn of the peasantry. Tradesmen, businessmen, laboring men, kicked their nags down the stretch and attempted to yank off the ancient bird's strong old head. One by one they failed. Finally a fat Creole carpenter got a good grip on the goose's neck. He gave a tremendous yank, but the stout neck held, and the carpenter was jerked from his horse to roll ignominiously in the dust.

Etienne laughed until his cheeks were wet with tears. And when the fat man arose and limped off the course, blasting the air with lurid patois profanity, the boy rocked back against his chair, unable to speak.

Odalie sighed with relief at the sight of her son's happiness, and thereafter the party went smoother. Etienne was showered with gifts. He received them with the bored disdain of a young prince, to whom all homage was no more than his due. But finally when Stephen's gift was brought to him, he straightened up, his blue eyes alight in his dark face.

It was a pony, a fat, shaggy little animal, fully equipped with saddle and bridle. At once Etienne got down from his place; but Stephen lifted a warning hand.

"Not until afterwards, lad," he said. "First ye must say a word of thanks to all your guests."

Sullenly Etienne stood.

"A thousand thanks to you all," he said rapidly in French. Then he sat down again. The American tradesmen looked at him blankly.

"Now in English," Stephen said.

Etienne shook his head, and clamped his lips together.

"I spoke to ye, 'Tienne!" Stephen said evenly.

Again Etienne got to his feet.

"Thank—you—all—ver' much," he said slowly, then: "'*Meri-cain Cochons!*"

A little titter of laughter ran through the ranks of Creoles. Here and there an American frowned.

Stephen leaned forward.

" 'Tis ye who are a pig, my lad," he said softly. "Now get ye to your room and await me. But excuse yourself properly before ye go!"

Etienne mumbled a jumble of French and English that nobody understood, and left the table. As he passed down the lawn, Stephen Le Blanc touched his arm.

"May I ride him, your pony, 'Tienne," he demanded breathlessly. "May I?"

Etienne turned toward him.

"If you touch him at all, I'll kill you!" he barked and ran into the house.

Stephen ordered the Negroes to bring wine, and afterwards the adults retired to the great hall. The slave orchestra struck up a tune, and there was dancing. But it was no good. Not even the wine could bring true good feeling. One by one the guests made their excuses and left. Only a few lingered.

Stephen was dancing with Aurore, holding her as lightly as a

240

breath as they swept through the great curves of the waltz. There was a rare, elusive perfume in her chestnut hair, and her hazel eyes under the long lashes were alight with sombre fire.

"Ye're beautiful, my little sister," he whispered. "And ye grow more so daily. I wonder at the stupidity of these lads . . ."

"It's not their fault, Stephen," Aurore said. "I am naturally an old maid—too finicky to please a man. But I like dancing with you."

"Nonsense. There is more to it than that. Someday I'll find out the reason for your demi-nunhood. Or perhaps ye care to tell me. What is it, Aurore? Why have ye never chosen to grace some lucky man's board?"

"From me you'll never know. I wish I could tell you. But it's better that you do not—that no one knows. Please, Stephen, do not pry into this thing."

Stephen led her back to her place and bowed over her hand.

"As ye will, little sister," he murmured.

When all the guests had gone, Stephen strode up the stairs to Etienne's room. Without knocking, he pushed open the door and went in; but the room was empty. He stood there, frowning a moment, then he turned and went back down the stairs and out into the courtyard. Neither Etienne nor the pony was in sight. Stephen bent down, staring at the soft earth. The tracks were there, small and well-shod, and they led off toward the cypress wood. Stephen followed, swearing softly under his breath.

Before he reached the clump of woods, he heard the high, shrill whinny of the pony. It was squealing in anguish, and sharp and clear above the sound came the singing whine of a whip. Stephen ran forward. Just inside the screen of branches the pony was tethered. He was rearing and plunging like a wild thing. And beside him, just a little way off, Etienne stood, the long black snake whip in his hand. Even as Stephen ran forward, Etienne lifted the whip. The long lash sang through the air and bit into the pony's rough coat. The little animal squealed pitifully.

Then Stephen was upon his son, tearing the whip from his

241

hands. He stood back, looking at the boy, the great scar on his forehead glowing scarlet with anger. Etienne was covered with mud and dust, and a thin trickle of blood stole down from the corner of his mouth. Stephen looked at the pony. It was covered all over with stripes. In one or two places Etienne had drawn blood.

"Ye little beast!" Stephen roared and lifted the whip. Etienne stood without moving, without flinching, his pale eyes steady upon his father's face. Stephen lowered the whip slowly, without striking his son; then, with a quick motion, he broke it across his knee, and flung it way into the underbrush. Without another word, he turned and strode back toward the house.

Etienne stood looking after him, his blue eyes bleak in his dark face.

"Father," he whispered. "Father."

But Stephen walked on, unhearing. Slowly, Etienne moved after him.

Inside the house, Stephen walked dully into his study. He paused to light a candle, for already the dusk was gathering, and turned to the row upon row of leather-bound volumes that lined the walls. Here were the great Greek writers, and the Latin. He stood there, frowning a moment in indecision, reading the titles: Aristophanes, Sophocles, Homer, Euripides, Horace, Plato, Seneca . . . Then he stretched forth his hand. There was a little scurrying noise behind him, and he whirled. Little Inch stood frozen there, the whites of his eyes showing grotesquely in his black face.

"Inch!" Stephen said. "What the devil do ye here?"

"I—I was reading, maître," Inch stammered. "Please, maître, I go now. Don't beat me, no?"

"Reading?" Stephen said. "By all the saints! Who taught ye to read?"

"Grandmère—an' Jean-Jacques, maître's butler—an' 'Tienne, a little. Please, maître . . ."

Stephen bent and picked up the open book from the floor. It was Molière, a bound volume of the plays. Stephen pointed to a passage.

"Read," he commanded.

Inch read the passage, clearly, and with good accent.

"Now," Stephen said. "Tell me what it means—in English."

Little Inch interpreted the hypochondriac's troubles from *Le Médicin Malgré Lui.*

"A black," Stephen said half to himself. "Yet one with a mind. Miracles never cease. Inch, ye listen to me."

"Yas, maître?"

"I like this, your knowledge. But when ye would have books, come to me and ask for them. There are many things which are no good for ye to read—'twill cause only trouble and confusion in your mind. From now on, ye are to read only what I select; there will be no lack of books, I assure ye, but they will be the right ones. Here, take this one, and ponder over it. When ye have finished it, I shall have a report from ye over its meaning. Ye may go now."

Inch showed his white teeth in a gleaming smile and scurried from the room, clutching the catechism Stephen had given him in his little hand.

Stephen turned again to his books. But Georges was coming into the room, pausing there before his master.

"Well," Stephen said, "what is it, Georges?"

"Monsieur Andre, maître—outside on the terrace. He wants to talk with you."

Stephen made a little gesture of annoyance and put the book back in its place. When he reached the terrace, he saw the rotund figure of Andre Le Blanc pacing nervously back and forth.

"Andre," Stephen said. "What ails ye, man?"

"I'm in trouble, Stephen—terrible trouble. I need your help."

"Then ye have it. Stop pacing like an animal and tell me what this is all about."

"The Second Bank of the United States—this morning it withdrew all its deposits from its fiscal agencies. Then later in the morning, the Bank of England contracted its credits. They're asking for gold, Stephen."

"My God!"

"By midafternoon, while we toasted your son's health, fourteen banks had failed. And all my creditors are calling in their notes at once. 'Tis a ruined man you see before you, Stephen!"

"These notes, they're against the lands of La Place, itself?"

"Yes," Andre said miserably. "By nightfall, Melia and the children will no longer have a roof over their heads!"

"Will ye cease your sniveling! I have no ready cash—my accounts were in the Second Bank too, ye ken; but I will give your creditors a lien against as much of Harrow as is necessary. . . ."

"No, Stephen, never in honor could I permit . . ."

"Silence! We shall not lose the land. Ye know well I kept the bulk of my accounts with Hammerschlag in Philadelphia. I have enough and to spare to tide us both over."

"That is if the Philadelphia banks do not fail, Stephen. I understand this thing is nationwide."

"About that we shall worry when we find it true. Come into the house, Andre. We must discuss this thing with Odalie, since her holdings, too, are involved."

The two of them went into the house, and Stephen ordered wine and sent Georges to fetch Odalie. When she came, Stephen went straight to the point.

" 'Tis the panic, my dear, which I've feared. The currency is worthless, having no gold to back it up. Andre, here, is in a fair way to be ruined. There are debts outstanding against all his estate. Have I your consent to pledge the outlying lands against his notes?"

Odalie did not even hesitate.

"Of course," she said; "we have more land than we'll ever need. Pledge Bellefont—I'm sure Aurore will be agreeable, she's so fond of Amelia."

"Ye understand that we are in a bad way ourselves? The Second Bank failed this morning. We have no money here."

Odalie stood up.

"Don't talk like a Yankee, Stephen," she said. "There are other things in the world beside money."

"Thank ye, my dear." He pulled on the bell cord and Georges appeared.

"Pen and paper, Georges—and the sand box."

When Georges returned, Stephen took up the pen and wrote:

"To whom it may concern,

"I, Stephen Fox, do hereby pledge and commit certain of my lands, vs: The entire southern tract, lying nearest to New Orleans, and the plantation of Bellefont, as security against the debts of Andre Le Blanc of this parish, my friend and associate. Done by my own hand, at Harrow, May 13, 1837, Stephen Fox."

"I don't know about the legality of this. We shall need witnesses. And as Odalie is my wife and ye are both party to it, neither of ye will do. We'd best ride into the city, Andre. Ye'll excuse us, my dear?"

Odalie nodded. Stephen and Andre stood up, but as Stephen waited for his hat, gloves and crop, a horseman came pounding up the oak alley toward Harrow at a full gallop. He leaped from the horse, flung the reins to the astonished Georges and ran up the stairs, two at a time.

"Tom!" Stephen said, "Tom Warren! So it took a panic to make ye visit Harrow!"

Tom Warren's face was haggard.

"I need money, Stephen," he said. "Much money. I'm in a hellish fix!"

"Softly, Tom," Stephen said. "So are we all."

"Not the kind I'm in. I—I speculated a bit with monies that were not actually mine. If I cannot restore them by tomorrow noon, 'twill mean prison for me."

Silently Stephen extended the note he had just written.

"I was coming in for ye to witness this," he said simply.

Warren's eyes ran rapidly over the page.

"So," he said. "You've tied up all your visible assets for this man. And now you're powerless to help me. A fine friend you've proved yourself, Stephen Fox!"

"I'm sorry, Tom. Money I have not. But this of prison is nonsense. My word alone, pledged against the restoration of the monies is enough to keep ye out. Then, afterwards, ye could

245

manage Harrow for me. Since Wilson's death, I have needed such a man as ye are. 'Tis no great honor, I'll admit but . . ."

Tom Warren looked from one to the other of them.

"Give me the paper," he said at last. "I'll witness it."

When Tom Warren had signed the paper and had drunk the wine a servant brought, the three men went down the great stairs together. At the foot of the stairs, they stood for a moment in talk, then Andre swung his great bulk aboard his horse and started away. But ten feet down the alley he encountered old Josh, coming home from the levee in the early dark, a string of fish glistening in his hand.

"Evening, suh," he grinned, taking off his battered hat and bowing, "Nice evening, ain't it?"

"Those are fine fish," Andre observed, then calling back to Stephen: "Do you mind if I take some of them?"

"Not at all. Take the whole string." He and Tom Warren strode over to where the old man stood, holding his catch.

Then old Josh's mouth was gaping open, and his knees were knocking together quite audibly.

"Doan let him git me!" he moaned. "Please, Mas' Stevie, doan let him git me!"

"Don't let who get ye? What ails ye, Josh? Have ye gone mad?"

Josh was almost speechless with terror.

"Dat's Mas' Tom!" he quavered. "Dat's de one who kilt poor Rad! He tried to kill me too, but he missed! Please, Mas' Stevie!"

Stephen turned to Tom Warren.

"What's he talking about, Tom? He appears to know ye, truly."

Tom Warren's little piglike eyes were shifting rapidly in his big face.

"I don't know," he said. "I never saw the Nigra before. I think he's mad."

"What's this all about, Josh? Speak up, man, nobody's going to harm ye."

"Us moved de wheat like he done tole us to. Me'n' Rad moved all dat wheat outa de warehouse down by de river. Den we took hit cross town in de wagon. We musta gone back and forth a

246

hundred times. After dat he tole us to sot dat warehouse on fire an' we done dat too. An when po Rad come out—Mas' Stevie!"

Stephen whirled, but the blast of the pistol leaped out between him and Josh. The old black hung there clawing at his throat where the ball had gone through; then he went down on his face in the dirt and they could hear his breath gurgling out through the opening the bullet had made.

Stephen started toward Tom, walking very slowly. Andre sat paralyzed upon his horse, watching him. Again Tom Warren lifted the pistol. It was a squat, ugly affair with four barrels mounted in pairs, one above the other.

"Easy, Stephen," he said. "I still have three shots, remember."

"It matters not if ye have a hundred," Stephen said, and lunged forward all at once so that the pistol made a mushroom of flame and smoke squarely against his chest, and his fingers, as he fell, clawed loose the buttons of Tom Warren's waistcoat. Tom Warren leveled the pistol at him as he lay there, but Andre was kicking his horse forward, unsheathing the swordcane as he came.

The big man whirled, firing as he turned, but Andre ducked low along the horse's neck and ran the point of the sword through the wrist of Tom Warren's hand with a deftness born of long practice. Tom dropped the pistol and ran clumsily to his horse, holding his wrist tightly with his left hand as he ran. Then he was tearing the reins loose from the hitching post and dragging himself atop the horse.

But Andre was not following him. Instead, he was bending over Stephen, ripping the clothing away with the bloody blade of his sword, and staunching the gaping wound the slug had torn low on Stephen's left side. It had gone completely through Stephen's lean body, too low to strike the ribs, and too far to the side to puncture the internal organs. But it bled frightfully. Andre stuffed his own fine linen handkerchief into the wound, then with difficulty he lifted his friend and started up the great stairs.

Above, Odalie had heard the shots, and had come running out on the gallery. But the now heavy darkness prevented her from seeing much until the fat form of Andre, struggling like a beetle

247

with a far too heavy load, appeared half way up the stairs with Stephen swinging inertly in his arms. Odalie opened her mouth to scream, but only a whisper came out.

"Stephen!" she said, "Stephen!"

Then she was cradling her husband's head in her arms and the two of them got him to the bedroom. And not until Caleen had reached the bedside and taken full charge, did Odalie slip quietly, easily to the floor in a dead faint. Caleen stepped over her without even a downward glance, and went on with her work. There was the water to be heated, and the fresh cloths, and the herbs to be brewed against infections. She worked with lightninglike rapidity, until at last the thick stream of the blood slowed and stopped. Stephen lay back against a pillow, his pale skin almost transparent. But a thin mist of sweat dewed his brow, and his breath sounded ragged and slow through the room.

"He be all right now, Monsieur Andre," Caleen said, "soon's I get some soup in him—make more blood. Hafta wait, though. It would kill him now, yes."

Andre lifted Odalie from the floor and crossed the hall to another bedroom. Then he summoned Suzette, and the two of them worked on her until her eyelids fluttered open.

"Is he—is he . . ." she said.

"No," Andre said. "He is not dead—in fact he's going to get better."

He stood up, and his round face was grim.

"Now, if Madame will excuse me, I have work to do."

After he left Harrow, Andre stopped only briefly at La Place des Rivières. He went up into the great study that had been his father's and took down a long mahogany case. When he opened it, two slim-barrelled dueling pistols, rich with silver mountings, gleamed in the dull light. Slowly and carefully he cleaned both of them, then loaded them, ramming the ball far down against the charge, wrapped in its linen wadding, and setting the percussion caps in place where the great curving hammers on the sides of the pieces would strike them truly. In his pockets he put additional charges, and a small bag of shot. The primings he put in a small waterproof box. As he turned, he realized that Amelia had been standing behind him for a long time, watching his every move.

"You—you've quarrelled with someone," she said, and her voice was high and breathless.

"No," Andre said softly. " 'Tis no quarrel of my own, Melia. But Stephen Fox lies at the point of death, shot down by a man whom he trusted. He carried no weapon, Melia. Will you see that Ti Demon and some of the other blacks are sent to all the neighboring plantations? Tell them to meet me at the point of the Bayou in four or five hours. 'Tis there that the murderer is most likely hiding. I go to the city to report this thing, and to seek Mike Farrel and other friends of Stephen's."

"You'll have wine before you go—or coffee?"

"Neither. Goodnight, my dear."

He leaned forward and kissed her lightly. But she caught his arm and clung to him a moment. Then she released him, and her eyes were bright with tears.

"Aim true, Andre!" she said. And he strode through the doorway murmuring thanks to the blessed saints who had given him such a wife.

With a fresh horse, it was no great ride to New Orleans from La Place. Andre stopped first at the house of Judge Joachim Bermudez and made formal report of the crime. At once the old jurist was pulling on his coat and taking down his pistols.

"But, sir," Andre protested, " 'tis hardly fitting in your position and at your age . . ."

"Silence, lad!" the judge barked. "If the wretch is captured I'll see that he gets a fair trial—there upon the spot. And no law exists governing how short the interval between the passing of a sentence and its execution may be. Quiet now, before you wake Madame."

At Maspero's, Andre stood in the middle of the barroom and told his story. When he left, every man in the place filed silently out behind him; for there were not many there whom Stephen had not befriended in some way. And they dispersed to their homes, to rejoin the procession later armed with sabres, *cloche·*

249

mardes, rapiers, fowling pieces, and every sort of pistol made. Andre rode alone into the Swamp.

He rode from den to den and entered them boldly. The fierce riverboatmen looked at him curiously. The footpads appraised his fine dress, but the butts of his great pistols, protruding in plain sight from his belt, were ample discouragement to those who would do him violence. The painted slatterns smiled at the plump young man with the grim face, but he paid them no attention, entering very quietly, looking around each of the combination gambling house-saloon-bordelloes, and leaving just as quietly.

Finally at Mother Colby's Sure Enuf Hotel his quest was rewarded. There, before the dealer's box in a Faro game, half sunk in a drunken stupor, Mike Farrel sat. Andre crossed to him at once.

Mike looked up with his one good eye and grinned broadly.

"Out for a night of sport, lad?" he asked. "Sit yez down and join me. 'Tis Buckin' the Tiger I am, but me luck is terrible. Waiter, two whiskeys!"

"There is no need for that, Mike," Andre told him. "We have need of you at Harrow."

"Yez be making sport with an old man? 'Tis nothing I kin do for so fine a broth of a lad as Stevie."

"But there is," Andre said. "This night Tom Warren shot Stephen without just cause, and I fear for his life."

Mike was on his feet then, his horny hand gripping Andre by his beruffled shirt front.

"Don't lie to me, lad!" he roared.

Mildly, Andre pushed his hand away.

"Why should I lie?" he demanded. " 'Tis the truth, Mike. I saw it happen."

"Maw!" Mike bellowed.

"Yes, son?" Mother Colby said.

"What have yez here that will shoot or chop or rip out a man's guts?"

The old harridan grinned. Then she went behind her counter and came out with an ancient flintlock pistol as big as a small musket, various types of slung shot, sand bags, and blackjacks,

250

and an enormous Bowie knife whose edge had been honed to razor keenness.

Mike picked up the pistol and stuck it in his belt. Then he ran a horny thumb along the blade of the knife.

"Awright, lad," he growled. "Lead me to him!"

When they reached the edge of the bayou, the whole road was crowded with horsemen. They sat very quietly on their mounts and waited. Here and there a horse whinnied, or a hoof came down on the road with a heavy clop, but most of the time the stillness was broken only by the heavy breathing of the tired horses, or the clink of a weapon.

The moon rode in over the cypress trees and the road was silver. Andre and Mike rode up to the waiting men, shifting black shadows against the blacker shadows of the trees. The horses broke abruptly, and the crowd milled about in a semicircle around the newcomers.

"We'd best dismount," Andre said. "'Tis no fit footing for horses. He was headed this way when I saw him last. We'll need lights, I think."

Instantly two riders started up the road at a gallop. In a few minutes they were back, bearing pine knots. They lighted them and passed them out to the riders. Then all the men moved very quietly into the marshland, the flaring torches edging the darkness with dancing light.

At once Mike took the lead, murmuring to himself in a throaty bellow. They went on in through the underbrush, scattering in a dozen different directions, so that the diverging lights danced like great fireflies in the woodland. Then Mike was bending close to the earth, the rumblings in his throat deeper, until they had the sound of a trailing animal.

Then there was a place where the underbrush was broken down as though a heavy form had fallen through; and beyond that the saw grass was trampled. Here was a clump of palmettoes bent aside; the thin tendrils of a vine lay tangled on the trail where they had been torn down when they interfered with a man's passage. The men were silent, and their breaths came out loud in the stillness.

251

Then the ground was no longer firm under their feet, but a green ooze that sucked audibly with every step. Here where they were, the cypress trees bulged at the roots until the trunks resembled gigantic ninepins. And the water was black and fetid. But they went on, with the trailing streamers of Spanish moss brushing like damp wings against their faces.

"Damn," an American said. "He had his guts to come in here!"

The waters of the bayou itself were ahead now, black with an utter lightless blackness. They stood on the oozy, infirm banks and stared out over the water. Then Mike was lifting his hand for silence. They bent over, listening. The sound came riding in over the bayou, far away and faint, but very clear. Someone was walking in the shallows. They raced along the bank, their feet sticking with every step in the gumlike mud, until at last they saw him, walking with his head down, holding his wounded wrist around which a white cloth showed.

With a roar like a bull mastiff, Mike was in the water. Where he went in, the blackness was broken, and the water rose up like white wings around his heavy thighs. Then he was racing forward, churning the water into a foam, his great bellow echoing.

Tom Warren turned, holding the pistol in his left hand. He fired, and the orange yellow flame split the night open. There, where the branches of the trees roofed the narrow arm of the bayou, the crash of the pistol was deafening. Mike made no gestures toward the weapons in his own belt, but came on forward. Three times more Tom Warren fired, but Mike plunged on in, shaking his massive head and roaring. Then his big hairy paws were gripping Tom's shoulders and the two of them went down into the bayou. The black water boiled, hiding the two men. . . .

On the bank, all the men held their fire. Then the boiling ceased, and Mike's head rose above the waters, but his arms were still beneath it, the muscles tense with strain. Again the water was thrashed into whiteness, but Mike held on, the big veins on his forehead standing out and throbbing in the glare of the pine torches. But now, at last, the water was still. Mike stood up and walked slowly through the trailing waters. Heavily, he climbed the bank.

The men crowded around him. Leaning forward, Andre saw the bloodstains on his shirt front.

"You're hurt!" he said.

"Fleabites," Mike growled, then looked out over the still waters. "Let the bayou have him," he said. He turned away from the bayou and started back the way they had come. And one by one, without saying anything, the men followed him.

On the road again, they mounted their horses and turned them toward their various homes. But Mike headed toward Harrow.

"You're hurt, Mike," Andre said; "badly hurt. You have need of a doctor!"

"Hold your tongue, lad," Mike said. "First I'm gonna see after Stevie. These little pinks kin wait. Are yez coming?"

"Yes," Andre said; "yes, I'm coming."

Up at Harrow, the lights blazed from every window. All the field hands stood around the big house, staring open-mouthed at the door. Some of the Negroes were weeping.

As Andre and Mike turned their tired horses into the alley of oaks before Harrow, a sleek black mare shot past them at a gallop. Leaning forward Andre saw that the rider was a woman, mounted sidesaddle, her long hair loose and blowing behind her. He kicked at his horse's sides, but there was no more speed left in the animal. The girl drew her mount up before the great stairs, sawing at its mouth so savagely that it reared, almost unseating her. Grimly she fought for control of the excited animal.

But Andre had reached her now, and was pulling on the reins with all his weight. Slowly the mare quieted.

"Aurore!" Andre whispered.

The girl swung down from the saddle, pushing her chestnut hair out of her eyes.

"How is he, Andre?" she demanded. "Don't tell me he's . . . Oh, no, Andre! Don't tell me that!"

"Softly, Aurore," Andre said. "Your sister's husband is neither dead nor dying. Come, I'll take you inside."

Aurore smiled at him, but her eyes were bright with tears. "My sister's husband," she murmured. "Thank you, Andre. I needed reminding, didn't I?"

Silently Andre offered her his arm, and they started up the stairs together. But there was a noise behind them, and they whirled, looking downward.

Mike Farrel hung half over the balustrade, shaking his head back and forth. Instantly, Andre released Aurore and ran back down the stairs to the big man.

"I'm a trifle spent, me lad," Mike said. " 'Tis nothing, yez go ahead with the lass."

But Andre had one arm around the big man's waist and was beginning to help him up the stairs. Aurore came down at once, and put her small arm around him from the other side. Together they helped Mike up the stairs. When they were inside, Andre called slaves and had Mike carried to his old rooms, ordering them to dress his wounds at once.

Then he and Aurore went to the master bed chamber. Outside the door Little Inch stood guard, his eyes red with weeping. Beside him, in the big chair, 'Tienne sat, his blue eyes fixed cold and unmoving on the closed door. Gently Andre pushed it open, and the two of them entered. The room was plunged in semidarkness, and Odalie was kneeling beside the bed, her face burrowed in the linen, her whole body shaken with sobbing. Aurore's fingers were ice brands, biting into Andre's arm.

On the other side of the room, Caleen stood. Her face was a grotesque death mask out of Africa. Andre turned toward her, his eyebrows rising.

"Maître worse," she said simply. "Docteur say him die soon."

Aurore turned to Andre and buried her face against his shoulder. He put up his hand and stroked her lovely head. Then she lifted her face, until her lips were almost touching his throat.

"If he dies," she whispered, "if he dies . . ." She pillowed her face against his throat. Where her tears touched, they scalded him.

But Caleen was speaking again.

254

"*Docteur* great fool," she said. "Caleen kin cure him, yes! I make him better in one hour, me."

"Then for God's sake, do it!" Aurore cried.

"All right," Caleen said, "you leave the chamber—you an' Monsieur Andre and maîtresse. Leave nobody here but me and maître. Then I cure him, me."

"What sort of wickedness is this, Caleen?" Andre demanded.

"Oh, Andre," Aurore said. "Let her try it, please let her try it!"

"All right," Andre said reluctantly. "But no witchcraft, Caleen!"

Caleen smiled blandly, and bent down to lift the half-dazed form of Odalie from the bed. Andre and Aurore supported her between them, and the three of them went through the doorway.

When they had gone, Caleen closed the door behind them and crossed to the great canopied bed. Then she crossed herself and bent over the still form of her master.

"Maître," she crooned in a slow, singsong voice. "You not happy—Caleen knows. But sometime you be happy, yes. Don't die, maître—sometime you be happy. Easy to die, maître, don't take no heart for that, no. Easy to die; but hard to live, yes. Hard to live when life ain't no good, and no joy in it. But you got son, maître—you got strong fine son, you. Live for him. Make him strong like you, brave like you. Make man out of him, yes. Cowards die; cowards give up, run away. Brave men don't die, them; they live, yes!"

Over and over she talked to him, whispering the words very low, stringing out the intonations until she was half singing them, watching his face. Then slowly, the grey tide was stealing out of his cheeks, and the faint flushes of color stealing in. While she talked, his breathing evened; but she kept it up, repeating the words over and over again:

"Don't die, maître; you can't die you! You got too many lives in the hollow of your hand. Don't die, maître, don't!"

Then Stephen was breathing very steadily, and something very like a smile played about the corner of his lips. Caleen tiptoed to the door and opened it. Odalie, Aurore and Andre trooped in, walking over to the bed. They looked at Stephen, then with a single motion they turned and faced Caleen.

"You old witch!" Andre said. "You blessed old witch!"

255

Afterwards, Stephen's recovery was steady; but it was many weeks before he could leave his bed. While he lay there, fretting against his inactivity, Andre ran both Harrow and La Place. Aurore moved into Harrow and assisted Odalie in the nursing of Stephen and Mike Farrel, who had three bullets in his gigantic chest. The big man was an easy patient, following Aurore's every move with his worshipful eyes. But Odalie's voice was often cold, speaking to her sister, and in her eyes was a little look of puzzled hostility.

The crops that year were good, so that despite the unsettled condition of the country's finances, Harrow made money. Andre was able with the help of Stephen's note to obtain extensions from his creditors, and by fall La Place was paying off its debts. But the city recovered slowly from the panic; most of the banks remained closed, and many ambitious projects started in the early part of the year had to be curtailed or abandoned.

By the time that the great clouds of smoke were billowing up from the tall stack of the sugar house, Stephen was on his feet again, moving restlessly about the plantation like a pale ghost. His thinness was painful to behold. His eyes were very deep and ringed with blue circles and his gait was halting and slow. But Andre, watching him, was conscious of something else—a thin, brittle edge of bitterness that shone through every word he spoke, every gesture he made.

The words were few enough, God knows. He retired for hours upon end into his study, where he summoned Little Inch to read to him. The slightest effort, even reading, fatigued him unduly, so that the small slave boy found himself possessed of an unbelievably rich world of knowledge. Together they went through Plato's *Republic*. Stephen stopped the boy for long minutes at a time while he weighed this or that principle of the philosopher against the happenings of the day.

For the battle against the annexation of Texas was being fought in Congress with ever-mounting bitterness. Here it was that slave owner and free soiler had at last crossed swords, and the intensity of the debate was casting ominous shadows against the skies of the dawning day.

"One of us will have to give in," Stephen said to Andre. " 'Tis we or they. They cannot permit the power of slavery to spread; and we cannot permit them to abolish it."

"Then there will be two nations in this hemisphere," Andre declared. "We shall go our way, and let them go theirs."

" 'Tis an absurdity, Andre. Two weak nations eternally at war instead of one great one at peace. Don't ye see, lad, that nothing could compel them to return our runaways were they a separate nation? Nor could we count on their trade, despite their nearness to us. The only thing that we could count upon would be their eternal hostility, their eternal determination to destroy us."

"You're morbid," Andre laughed. "What you need is a change."

"That I do not doubt," Stephen said.

Throughout the winter, Stephen continued to gain strength. By spring he was riding over his lands again, leaping his horse over the barriers with a hard, studied recklessness. He fairly lived on Royal Street in the palatial gaming houses. He lost princely sums to the wicked dealers' boxes of faro, and the spinning wheels of roulette; but at the gaming tables, with the cards in his hands, he was invulnerable. He seemed incapable of losing, no matter how carelessly he played. Andre watched him with growing concern. Something must be done about this, he decided, and that right soon.

"Stephen," he said one evening as they rode toward La Place. "How would you like to attend a ball?"

Stephen looked at him with a grimace of acute disgust.

"This from ye!" he snorted.

"I mean no ordinary ball," Andre said slyly.

Stephen raised one fair brow.

"Have you never heard of the *Bals du Cordon Bleu*?"

"So that's the way the wind lies!" Stephen laughed. "Ye propose to obtain me a mulatto wench? What a wickedness!"

"I propose to let you see them—that's all. Any objections?"

Stephen looked at him, one corner of his mouth curving into a smile.

"No," he said; "no objections."

XVI

NEXT to the Théâtre D'Orleans on Orleans Street between Bourbon and Royal stood the Orleans Ballroom. As Andre and Stephen rode up to it on a spring night early in 1838, it was ablaze with light, and the sound of music and laughing voices floated downward into the street. Stephen sat for a moment on his horse, looking at the low, ugly two-storied building.

" 'Tis not much to look at," he remarked.

"Wait until you see the interior," Andre said. "Come now, we'd better hurry."

"Why?" Stephen demanded.

Andre laughed.

"You'll find three quarters of the gentry of New Orleans inside," he said. "Last year, the *Cordon Bleu* conflicted with one of our own balls. I spent the entire night dancing—at Melia's suggestion—with various deserted females. The men were all here."

Stephen swung down from the horse.

"I don't share your eagerness," he smiled. "Your mixed-strain wenches don't seem particularly remarkable to me."

"We shall see," Andre said. "Come!"

258

They went in through the low wide façade. In the vestibule, they surrendered their hats, cloaks, and gloves; and Andre paid the admission fee of two dollars apiece. Then they went up the stairs into the ballroom. Stephen stopped just inside the door and looked around him. Above his head, the gigantic crystal chandeliers, almost as costly as the ones at Harrow, swung low over the dance floor. In niches around the walls stood statues which would not have disgraced a hall at Versailles, and paintings which Stephen's practiced eye recognized at once as being originals. The walls were paneled with fine woods, and inlaid with even costlier ones.

On the magnificent dance floor, constructed, Andre had told Stephen, of three thicknesses of cypress topped by a layer of quarter-sawed oak, the young, and not so young, gentlemen of New Orleans were dancing. Half a glance told Stephen that almost everyone he knew, and many men unknown to him, were here; then his gaze traveled on to their partners. He stopped, frowning.

"Lovely, aren't they?" Andre said.

Stephen stifled a yawn with the back of his hand.

"Of course they're pretty," he said. "Why shouldn't they be? Ye've been busy for generations improving the strain. I don't see how Frenchmen ever grow anything, ye're so busy in the slave cabins. Gad, what a taste for dark meat ye have!"

"I won't let you anger me," Andre grinned. "Besides, you haven't seen anything yet."

"I'm on pins," Stephen growled. "What the deuce is so enjoyable about this? 'Tis just as stuffy as some of the fashionable balls ye've taken me to. The girls are prettier, that I'll admit; but those fat old yellow mothers of theirs seem to be watching them like hawks."

"You don't understand. For them the connections they make here are as honorable as marriage. They never desert a protector or betray him. And when it comes to love—*Dieu!*—they've forgotten more than our women ever knew. Of course the mothers watch. They'd object to an unwise connection as strenuously as would a white mother to an unwise marriage."

"Let's make the rounds," Stephen said. "I'm wearied to tears with standing here."

The two of them moved off, circling the ballroom. The girls watched them from behind their fans, commenting in whispers as the two richly attired men passed. As they came abreast of the stairway, Stephen stopped, his slim fingers tightening on Andre's arm.

"I think," he said slowly, "I think I see what ye mean!"

Andre looked up. A group of quadroon and octoroon girls were coming down the stairs. There was no need for Andre to ask which one Stephen meant. The others might as well not have existed.

She was taller by half a head than any of the others, and her skin was darker, a clear, light golden color, gleaming against the ivory white tones of her companions. But it was her hair that made her stand out—instead of the usual midnight curls, spun in ringlets over each ear, she wore it loose—a tawny mane of chestnut, lightening to pure gold in the highlights, with over-tones of auburn that ran like flame through the waves whenever she tossed her head.

Stephen was standing on the last step when she reached it. As she neared him, he put out his hand and touched her arm.

"Tonight," he said, "ye're dancing with me—and with none other. Ye understand that?"

She turned toward him without speaking, and the heavy lids widened over eyes that were as cool and green as the sea.

"You had better ask Madame my mother, monsieur," she said. Her voice was deep and rich. Stephen thought it sounded like the tones of a soft, golden gong.

Stephen looked her straight in the face.

"To hell with Madame your mother," he said clearly. "Ye're dancing with me."

The full, wine-red lips widened slowly into a smile and little flakes of gold danced in the sea-green eyes.

"And after tonight?" she said.

Stephen lashed her with his glance, letting his eyes wander over the gown which was cut in extreme décolleté, the sleeves falling away from the shoulder, a frill of fine old lace barely covering her breasts, the bodice clinging to every inch of her incredibly slim waist.

"Ye may call the turn," he said; "I'll play the fiddle."

He swung her away into the dance, gazing down into her face. She lifted it to his, until her lips were almost touching his throat. A perfume floated up from the chestnut, russet, golden hair; it was elusive, but subtly, insistently provocative. Stephen's thin nostrils flared. He looked down at her eyes, but they were closed, the sooty lashes curving out and away, unmoving. Stephen found these black lashes odd, in conjunction with the rest of her coloring; but as they swirled under the chandeliers, he saw them gleam golden at the roots, their darkness a trick of the light and shadow of the ballroom, so that their colors were constantly shifting. Now they were dull gold; now lightless, inky black; but most often they were a changing combination of the two.

Stephen took her arm and swept her from the dance floor. They went out on the gallery which overlooked the gardens in the rear of the Saint Louis Cathedral. The night was a clear one, a purple sky dusted over with stars. There over one of the spires of the Cathedral a thin sickle of a moon blazed silver, with a great halo of white around it.

That means rain, Stephen thought irrelevantly. And this means I am mad . . .

He caught her by both her soft, rounded shoulders and held her away from him at arm's length. The moonlight caught in her hair, in her lashes. Stephen drew his breath in sharply.

"Ye're lovely!" he said. "God, but ye're lovely!"

"Thank you, monsieur," she murmured, and the overtones of her rich, throaty voice lingered a moment after she was silent, like the echoes of a golden gong. Stephen listened to them a moment, straining his ears against the silence. Then he drew her to him.

Her face was lifted to his, and the wine-red lips softened and parted. As he kissed her, Stephen could feel the sweet young breath sighing through. The kiss was light at first, light petal soft, and lingering. She rolled her head ever so slightly upon her neck so that her lips caressed his, sweet and warm and parted.

261

Then something like madness flamed in Stephen's veins. His arms tightened ferociously about her slim waist, until a little cry of pain was locked somewhere deep in her throat, then one hand swept upward to the back of her neck, and his fingers were bruising her flesh.

Then abruptly, he released her. But instead of stepping back, she rose on tiptoe, her arms limp at her sides, her lips touching his so lightly that almost they did not touch at all, swaying there as if suspended by a breath. Stephen put his arms again about her waist, and she lay back against them, her eyes closed, her breath sighing through the stillness.

Again Stephen drew her to him, but this time she did not lift her face, but hid it in the hollow of his neck, so that he could feel her warm breath making little whispers against his throat.

"My dear . . . " Stephen said.

"Yes, monsieur?"

"What is your name?"

"Desiree," she said. "Does monsieur like it?"

"Like it? 'Tis perfect. And now 'tis time I had a word with Madame your mother. If ye'll be so good as to conduct me . . ."

Desiree took his arm, and the two of them went back into the ballroom. The girl led him straight across it until they reached a tall, middle-aged quadroon, sitting regally in one of the great chairs. At once, Stephen saw where Desiree got her beauty. The mother, though aging and putting on flesh, was still a rarely beautiful woman. She looked from Stephen to her daughter, her dark brows rising.

"This gentleman wishes a word with you, *Maman*," Desiree said. The woman turned her gaze to Stephen, waiting like a queen for him to speak. Stephen found her gaze disconcerting. To be looked at like this by a Negress—even an almost white Negress—was, to say the least, a new sensation. He hesitated. Seeing his perplexity, Andre crossed the room and stood at his friend's side.

"Permit me, Madame," he said politely, "to present my friend, Monsieur Fox. Your name is, Madame?"

"Hippolyte. Madame Hippolyte. Is Monsieur Fox of the plantation Harrow?"

"Aye," Stephen growled. "How did ye know of Harrow?"

Madame smiled.

"Everyone knows of Harrow, monsieur." She leaned forward, her smile pleasant and inviting.

Stephen cleared his throat. But this was a new thing: this shameless willingness to sell a daughter into concubinage. There were many men they could marry. He knew quadroons like the Logoasters, the Dumas, the Lascals and two dozen others who held great plantations and lived as richly among their slaves as any white. A girl like Desiree . . . any man . . . any man at all. . . .

"I take it that monsieur wishes to form a connection with my daughter," Madame Hippolyte said.

"Aye," Stephen said stiffly. "That is my intent."

"Monsieur is a man of wealth," the woman said.

"Sufficient to compensate ye for the loss of your daughter," Stephen said drily.

Madame Hippolyte flushed darkly.

"Monsieur does not understand. There is not that much money in all the world. Desiree is not for sale like a black slave. I simply wanted to assure myself that my daughter would be amply provided for."

"In that you need have no further concern," Andre told her. "Monsieur Fox is the richest man in Louisiana. Desiree will live like a princess. You will of course accept some token of his esteem . . ."

"Not one cent," Madame Hippolyte said firmly. "But if Desiree wants him . . ." She looked at her daughter. Desiree looked back at her, the sea-green eyes unclouded. Wordlessly, she nodded. Madame sighed.

"Shall we discuss the terms, gentlemen?"

"Yes," Stephen said, "anything ye will."

"Monsieur will provide a house for my daughter down by the ramparts. It must be richer and more beautiful than any other on the street. He will further provide her with a maid servant and a cook. He will see that she is suitably attired at all times. He will visit her with discretion, so that no scandal will be attached to her name or his. And any children born of this connection he will fully provide for, educating them in the same style as whites. And, further, monsieur is not to see Desiree or have any further contact with her until this house is completed. Then, I shall send her to him."

Stephen's fair brows met over his nose, and the great scar flamed on the side of his forehead.

"Ye're mad," he said.

Madame Hippolyte shrugged.

"Careful, Stephen," Andre whispered. " 'Tis best to humor her."

"Aye," Stephen said. "I can see that here ye have the whip hand. Very well, I shall abide by those conditions. Construction will begin tomorrow!"

He touched Desiree's hand and swept her away in a waltz. She followed him effortlessly, gazing intently into his face, her eyes very wide and green with the tiny flakes of gold swimming in their depths.

"Why do ye watch me so?" Stephen demanded.

"Monsieur's eyes are very blue," she said simply, "and his brows are almost white. And there is a great scar upon his forehead from a duel."

"What else?" Stephen laughed.

"His hair is like fire. And his lips make mockery. He is very handsome with a wickedness about him. You see, I wanted to remember."

"Why?"

" 'Twill be so long before I see you again. I could die almost. But then I couldn't come to you, could I? I will live for that—no matter how long it is."

"Never will a house be built faster," Stephen said. "Come out upon the gallery with me."

"No, monsieur."

"Why not, my little Desiree?"

"I do not wish to betray *Maman*. With you, I have no will."

Stephen smiled.

"I shall be patient," he said. " 'Twill be a great happiness having

264

ye." Then, as she smiled at him, the great curving lashes closing over her eyes, he whispered: "Nay, more—'twill be a glory!"

When at last the *Bal du Cordon Bleu* was over, Stephen surrendered Desiree to her mother. Then he and Andre left the ballroom together. Outside it was very clear, and the horses' hooves rang in the silent street. Others saluted them as they rode away, grinning mockingly at Stephen as though glad to find in him at last a common weakness. But Stephen paid them no heed, sitting bent over in his saddle, the reins loose in his hands. His pale eyes were fixed on vacancy, glazed, unseeing.

Andre rocked his plump form back in his saddle and laughed aloud.

"So," he chuckled. "You've taken on the *placée* you swore you'd never have!"

"She's beautiful, Andre," Stephen said.

"Yes! In that you have right! Your Desiree is a creature to stop the breath and send the mind reeling. But you must be careful, Stephen. Odalie must never know."

"Odalie," Stephen said slowly. "Oh, yes, Odalie. Do you know, Andre, for the moment I'd forgotten her?"

"I don't doubt it. But she has no cause for complaint. You've treated her well, Stephen."

"Aye," Stephen said. " 'Twas a mistake—our marriage. But it cannot be undone now. I shall take whatever joy there is left for me in life and make the best of it. Come, lad, 'tis a long way yet."

Early the next day, the ox carts bearing the cypress boards turned into Rampart Street. Stephen sat in a little closed carriage across the street and watched the Negroes erecting the framework of the house. Monsieur Pouilly stood on the *banquette,* directing them. The little architect was Gallic to his finger tips. He found this commission vastly stimulating. A man of discretion, Monsieur Fox, he thought.

Satisfied, Stephen ordered his coachman to drive on. As they turned into Canal Street, Stephen was amazed at the change in it. Businesses were springing up all along its length, and now a horse car, with its pyramid of steps leading up to its upper deck, clattered along a set of freshly laid rails. A year ago, the absentee landlords who held the property on Chartres had raised their already outrageous rents, and a general exodus had resulted. Now, day by day, Canal was gaining the ascendancy. Lying as it did between the first and second municipalities, it was of easy access to both American and Creole. Stephen looked again at the horse car. He had drawn aside the curtains of the carriage to let the sunlight in. Now he straightened. A woman had waved to him from the upper deck. As he drew abreast of the car, he saw that it was Aurore. She signaled for the car to stop and climbed precariously down the one side of the pyramid of steps.

Stephen got down at once from the small carriage, and assisted her to the ground, then up again into his little cabriolet.

"So, Stephen," she laughed. "You've grown too old for horse-back? 'Tis odd to see you in a carriage."

"Yes," Stephen smiled. "My old bones give me many a twinge these days. Where were ye going, little sister?"

"Oh, I'd finished my shopping. Take me out to Harrow with you—if that's where you're going. I haven't seen Odalie in ages."

"With pleasure, Aurore. Ye seem in high spirits today. There's a glow to your cheeks. It makes ye lovelier, if such a thing is possible."

Aurore tapped him playfully with her parasol.

"You're wicked, Stephen," she said. "But in a nice way. 'Tis thoughtful of you to pay compliments to an old maid."

"Ye'll marry yet," Stephen said. "That I'll wager ye."

"But no one will have me, Stephen. I'm twenty-nine years old. Who wants such an old wife?"

"Tempt me further and I'll play Turk," Stephen growled. "Ye'd make a lovely addition to my harem."

"Then you have a harem? I'd long suspected it. But don't rush me into this; I think I should like to be number ten. Yes—the tenth—and the last."

Stephen looked at her. Aurore seemed scarcely more than a girl. Her brown hair curled softly over her ears, and her hazel eyes, looking at him, seemed oddly tender. Gazing at her,

266

Stephen suddenly remembered Andre's words on that April day, long ago: "For my part, you've chosen the poorer one. Aurore is much more beautiful . . ."

"Ye are," he said aloud. "By all the saints ye are!"

"I am what?" Aurore demanded. "You're making riddles, Stephen."

"Ye're prettier than Odalie. Andre and I used to argue over that point. I see now that he was right."

"No," Aurore said softly. "I'm not—really I'm not. Andre was fond of me then, that was all. Odalie is the most beautiful woman I've ever known."

A silence fell between them. They talked little until they reached Harrow. As they drove up the oak alley, Aurore saw Achille slinking along, his head bent low on his chest.

"What ails him, Stephen?" she asked. "Is he ill?"

"Aye, he is dying of heartbreak. Since that wildcat of a Nigra drowned herself, Achille has been of little use. I've found him half a dozen other comely wenches; but he will have none of them. I fear he will not be long upon this earth."

"Yes," Aurore said slowly. "A person can die of that, can he not? Especially when there is no hope."

Then she had skipped down from the carriage and was climbing the great stairs, walking very swiftly.

Within one month, the little white house by the ramparts was finished. Stephen found his hands were trembling as he dressed himself. He was fresh from his bath, and all his clothing was new and far richer than any he had bought before. Lagoaster, the quadroon tailor, had literally outdone himself this time. Outside his window, the evening was purpling into night, and a necklace of stars strung itself out over the river.

Stephen went down the stairs very quietly past the room where Etienne slept watched over by Little Inch from his own pallett on the floor. As he passed Odalie's room she came out, and stood there staring at him.

"How handsome you are, my husband," she said. "Where do you go?"

"To the city," Stephen said shortly.

"To the city—always to the city! Is there nothing I can do to know that, Stephen. Still . . . if you wish . . ."

Stephen smiled.

"Aye, but there is," he said. "And what it is ye know!"

The tears stood and sparkled in Odalie's eyes.

"Another child would cost me my life," she whispered. "You know that, Stephen. Still . . . if you wish . . ."

"No," he said gently. "Ye're right. Don't wait up for me, I shall be very late."

He went on down the stairs. She stood on the landing looking after him. Then she turned slowly, and went back into her room.

When Stephen reached Rampart Street, a light glowed softly in the little white house. He dismounted, and walked up to the door. As he raised the brass knocker, his hand shook slightly. Then, before he could bring it down sharply, the door flew open, and that wonderfully rich deep voice was whispering:

"Come in, monsieur. I've been waiting for hours!"

There on the mahogany table two candles flickered. The rich, off-white tablecloth threw back the soft glow, and the goblets and silver sparkled. There in a pail of ice the wine bottles stood.

Desiree put out both her hands to Stephen.

He took them gently but held her there at arms' length, looking down gravely into her face.

"Aye," he said at last. "Ye're as I remembered."

"And how was that, monsieur?"

"Unbelievable." His eyes strayed around the little house. Desiree had rearranged it so that it was quietly, elegantly perfect. There was nothing superfluous; nothing in the way. Restful —that was the word for it. None of the stupendous, nerve-tingling magnificence of Harrow, here; but only simplicity raised to the level of an art.

"Ye've done well," he said.

"I'm glad monsieur likes it. Monsieur would have wine?"

"Yes," Stephen said. He sank down into the great chair. Desiree brought the sparkling ruby-colored liquid in a bell-shaped goblet. She leaned over the back of the chair as he sipped it, gazing down upon the fiery mass of curls upon Stephen's head. Here and there was a strand of white at the temples, she saw. Slowly she put out her hands and stroked his forehead. Her hands were warm and very soft. Stephen could feel the tension of nerve and sinew ease under her touch until at last even the little knot of muscle that had gathered perpetually of late above the bridge of his nose relaxed and disappeared. He caught both her hands and drew them downward, turning at the same time and gazing upward into her face.

"There's magic in your hands," he said. "Never in years. . . ."

"Monsieur is unhappy," she whispered. "But there is no room here for unhappiness." She looked around the room. "This was built only for joy."

"Yes," Stephen said. "Ye are very wise, Desiree. Too wise for your years. How old are ye?"

"Sixteen," she said.

"Holy Mother of God!"

"That troubles you, monsieur?"

"Of course."

"Don't let it. We are never young. We cannot afford youth. This wisdom, as you call it, is a thing handed down from mother to daughter for generations. This is what I was born for, monsieur."

Stephen sat very still in the big chair, watching her moving about the table, preparing the meal. There was something unearthly in her grace. He felt strangely at peace. No need to hurry this; better to savor every moment as it passed; better far to let the evening sink into night unhastened, without abruptness or too rude eagerness. Play it out like a perfect hand; God knows he held a Royal Flush.

Desiree served his plate and poured out the wine for him, then she stood behind his chair like a servant.

"Sit," he growled.

"No," she said. "It is not fitting."

"I told ye to sit!"

269

Silently she took her place across the table from him, the outlines of her face softened in the small flameglow of the candles. She kept watching him, the sea-green eyes dancing under the long lashes, fixed upon his face.

"Ye're not eating," he said.

"I'm not hungry, monsieur."

Abruptly he pushed back his chair and stood up.

"Come here," he said.

She came to him very simply, lifting her face to his.

In the morning, in the faint gray haze of just before dawn, when Stephen rode homeward toward Harrow, the air was like wine and all the winds had a singing in them. He felt curiously light and weightless; full of a soft tiredness and a warm contentment. His bones felt hollow with fatigue and his blood ran slow and cool through his veins. His mind was amazingly clear. All the future lay before him, with its outlines sharp and discernible. Etienne must be sent abroad for his education—to England, beyond all reasonable doubt. A husband must be found for Aurore. He stopped for a moment frowning upon that thought, wondering why he found it vaguely unpleasant. If only young Cloutier had not gone to Texas; he would have been ideal. Still there must be someone. And this bitterness growing out of the annexation question must be allayed somehow; though how he or any other one man could halt the inevitable trend of events was more than he could see.

Desiree. This was something else again from what he had thought. She had come to him simply and directly without pretense or shame. And to his amazement, he had found her virginal. Yet, in her, instinctively, love was an artistry. "This is what I was born for, monsieur . . ." This above all—to be to him a salvation from the emptiness of his existence. I had everything but happiness, he thought, and that eluded me.

Over the broad fields of Harrow the young cane stalks bowed altogether to every passing wind, and the cotton was up and greening. High on the skyline, Stephen could see Achille sitting

270

hunched over on his mule, his face half covered by the big straw hat. But the earthen wall of the levee was empty; never again would old Josh sit over his lines, dozing above the ancient river. So many had gone: Zerline, Odalie's maidservant, Pierre Arceneaux, old Le Blanc . . . In the midst of life there was always death. But Harrow would go on, for in the great house slept a manchild. Strange and difficult to be sure: with Gallic fire and Celtic mysticism; but still a lad upon which to pin one's hopes. There would be other Foxes at Harrow—a long dim line of unborn ghosts stretching out to the edge of eternity.

This, all this, because a golden girl with hair of tawny flame had lain in his arms all night and awakened him in the morning with the soft brushing of her lips against his throat? What a foundation to erect such a towering structure upon! He dug his heels into his horse's flanks and thundered up the oak-canopied road at a gallop.

In the weeks that followed, Stephen went almost nightly to Rampart Street.

Odalie's eyes grew dark and ringed from watching for his return. Yet, she had to admit, never had life gone smoother at Harrow. Stephen was almost too goodnatured, smiling easily over nothing, impervious to her worst outburst of temper. Not even Etienne could disturb him. And now at last the boy was beginning to follow his father, silently and afar off, around the great plantation. There grew up between father and son a sort of silent companionship. Etienne began to learn English, slowly and haltingly but entirely of his own free will.

Sitting at the great table awaiting Stephen at the evening meal, Odalie heard him coming through the hall, whistling to himself, in smooth runs and trills as clear as any mocking bird's. Her hands tensed upon the edge of the table. There was something amiss here. He had no right to be so happy—so outrageously, completely happy. He came in the door at a brisk pace and crossed to where she sat, bending to kiss her cheek.

"Stephen," she began.

"Yes, my dear?"

"You never take me anywhere. Friday night there is a ball at the City Exchange. I promised Amelia that we would come."

"Friday night?" Stephen thought rapidly. Friday night was the final Grand Ball of the *Cordon Bleu*. Desiree was expecting him as a matter of course.

"No," he said shortly. "'Tis quite impossible!"

"Why, Stephen?" she leaned forward across the table. "Stephen," she said softly, "who is keeping you away from me?"

The fair brows almost met over the thin nose, and the blue eyes blazed.

"About that, I would not inquire if I were ye," he said. Then he stood up, his dinner untasted. "Very well," he told her slowly. "We shall attend your ball!"

Odalie sat in dumb misery, watching him stride through the doorway, his back very stiff and proud against her glance.

Stephen went down the stairs into the courtyard at the rear of the house and summoned Georges.

"Saddle Prince Michael for me," he growled. Then he stood by the stairs drumming nervously upon the balustrade. When the big palamino was led forth, Stephen swung at once into the saddle and headed for New Orleans.

"That Negre gal must be something, her!" Georges murmured. Georges knew. Such a thing came early to the ears of the Negroes.

When Stephen turned the horse's head into Rampart Street, he was in a thoroughly bad humor. He would have to break a promise, and that he disliked doing. Worse still, Desiree would not cry or reproach him, but incline her head to his decision with no show of whatever she might feel. He swung down from the horse and entered the house without knocking.

Instantly a young man as handsome as Andre had been in his youth sprang to his feet. Stephen inspected him coldly. The youth was fair of skin, with great mases of tawny chestnut hair curling thickly over his high white forehead. Stephen looked from him to Desiree, but the girl was smiling serenely.

"Monsieur," she said, "this is my brother, Aupre. He has just returned from France."

"Your brother?" Stephen growled. "But this one is white!"

The youth flushed darkly.

Desiree laughed, a clear, golden sound.

"'Tis only I inherited the blood of the blacks," she said. "Aupre labors under no such disadvantage."

Stephen looked at the youth. Yes, the resemblance was there; even to the beauty of face and form. This soft boy's face was almost girlish. Stephen relaxed slowly, and put out his hand.

"'Tis glad I am to meet ye, Aupre," he said.

The boy stood before him, as rigid as a statue, his hands limp at his sides. Stephen's fair brows flew together.

"I offered ye my hand!" he thundered. Slowly, the boy put out his hand. Stephen took it, almost crushing it in his grip. Then with a sound very like a sob, Aupre whirled and was gone through the door.

"What on earth . . ." Stephen began.

"Was that necessary, monsieur?" Desiree said. "Did you have to humiliate him so?"

"Humiliate?" Stephen said. "Nothing was further from my intent."

Desiree's eyes were bright with tears.

"He was debating whether or not to return to France," she whispered; "there he knew nothing but liberty. And now this . . . he will go now, and I'll never see him again."

"I don't understand," Stephen said. "What was it that upset him so?"

"Put yourself in his place, monsieur. Suppose you returned to find your sister, flown, unmarried, to the arms of a lover—and that lover a man of another race. What would you do?"

"Aye, I see. Such a one would not live one hour. But since ye think like this—why did ye not marry one of your own men —say a Dumas or a Lagoaster?"

Desiree's face showed disgust.

"They are so disgusting? Why? I've found old Lagoaster a capital fellow."

"They are not men. You do not permit them to be. When they rise up and attempt manhood, you shoot them down like dogs and exhibit their bodies in Jackson Square—like Bras Coupe, remember. To live at all they have to fawn and bow, and permit you the liberty of their homes and the favors of their daughters. I am a woman, monsieur; I can only love a man—not a thing!"

"Holy blessed Mother of God," Stephen whispered. "To live always with a thing like that in your mind—in so young a mind as yours!"

"Forgive me, monsieur. I—I forgot my place. 'Twill not happen again."

"There's nothing to forgive," Stephen said. "I have no wish to hurt ye." He stopped, frowning. "Yet, I'm afraid I must. Desiree, I cannot take ye to the ball Friday night."

The girl took a step backward and her face was stricken. Then instantly she was all composure.

"As monsieur wills," she murmured.

"No," Stephen said gently. "Such submissiveness ill becomes ye. Say what ye will."

"If I do not attend the ball," Desiree said, "tongues will wag. If I go alone, I shall be the laughing stock of the whole quarter. But . . ."

"But what, Desiree?"

"If monsieur will condescend to leave the City Exchange and come to the Orleans Ballroom for just one dance . . . just one . . ."

"I see," Stephen said gravely, but there was a laughing light in his pale eyes. "Ye're a lovely little witch!"

"I wish I were. Then I'd cast such a spell upon you that you'd never leave me."

"Afraid of that so soon, my little Desiree?"

"Yes—horribly. 'Tis my favorite nightmare: that someday a night will fall without you in it. I try to think how it will be to live day after day not hearing your voice or seeing your face. I can't—the thought itself is a kind of death."

Stephen put his arms around her.

"Then why think so?" he asked. "Such a day may never come."

"Oh, but it will. There are oceans of blood between us. There is your loyalty to your own kind. So I have to think about it. I have to steel myself. And already it is beginning."

"I don't like this somber mood," Stephen said. "Ye were made for gaiety not for this."

"Then I shall be gay. Shall I sing for you?"

"Of course; I should enjoy that."

Desiree disappeared into an inner room and came back with a mandolin. Then striking a comical pose she began to sing a satirical patois song about Judge Preval.

"Monsieur Preval, he gave a great ball:
He made the Negroes pay to march in line.
Monsieur Preval, he was captain of this ball;
His coachman, Louis, was master of ceremonies.
In the stable there was so much gaiety
I believe the horses must have been amazed.
There were Negresses more beautiful than their mistresses—
They stole their finery from the *armoire* of Mademoiselle."

Stephen rocked back against the great chair with laughter. The stinginess and other eccentricities of Judge Preval were legend in New Orleans. Desiree tossed aside the mandolin and sat down in his lap, twining her arms about his neck.

"Monsieur is happy?"

"Aye. What a creature of moods ye are!"

"I'm glad. I like for you to be happy. Now you must make me happy."

"How?"

"By kissing me. Kiss me a thousand times. No—a million. Kiss me and never, never stop."

"But that always leads to other things."

"So?"

"Ye little witch," Stephen laughed. "Ye lovely little witch!"

The City Exchange was another of De Pouilly's architectural triumphs, though a sadly curtailed one. At first the architect had planned for it to occupy the entire square bounded by Royal, Toulouse, Chartres, and St. Louis Streets; but the panic of 1837 had put a stop to this grandiose scheme. Now, in 1838, it occupied only the St. Louis Street side of the square. But with its magnificent ballrooms on the second floor and the awe-inspiring rotunda, it was a structure by no means to be sneered at. And on Friday night, most of the first families of New Orleans were in full attendance. The music, furnished by a Negro slave orchestra, was superb; and outwardly at least the ball had an air of carefree gaiety. But as the evening wore on, the number of males present steadily decreased.

Odalie turned to Amelia.

"The men," she said. "They're all going! Never have I seen so many wallflowers—and lovely girls, too!"

"Those Negresses," Amelia snorted. "They've grown impossibly bold. I think that they do it on purpose!"

"Negresses? What do you mean, Amelia?"

"Don't tell me you've never heard of the Quadroon Balls?"

"Yes—vaguely. But they occurred years ago, under the French. . . ."

"They occur now—tonight," Amelia said drily. "They've never stopped."

"*Ma foi!* You mean that the men are leaving these girls to disport themselves with black wenches?"

"Not black ones at any rate. Your Suzette and the one who died in the plague—Zerline? That was the name, wasn't it?"

"Yes."

"They're like that—and fairer. And I'm quite sure they give their filthy balls deliberately on the same nights as ours to flaunt in our faces their power over the men."

"My Stephen would never do a thing like that," Odalie said.

"Perhaps not," Amelia declared. "But I've been wondering for the past half hour where Stephen was—and Andre."

"Amelia!"

"I'm sorry. Perhaps I'm being morbid. Forgive me, won't you?"

Odalie stood up.

"I'm going to look into this," she said.

"And I also," Amelia declared.

The two women moved quietly off toward the stairs. On the first floor, outside the barroom, they stopped.

"We can't go in there," Amelia observed. "How on earth . . . "

"I'll go down and get Georges," Odalie said, "and send him up to inquire after his master."

They went out of the entrance on Royal Street, and walked around to the stables. Georges was sprawled over the seat of the yellow coach, fast asleep.

"Go up into the bar," Odalie commanded, "and tell the maître I'd like to have a word with him."

Georges's eyes were big in his black face.

"The maître ain't . . ." he began.

"You were about to say that the maître isn't in the barroom? Then where is he?"

"Oh, he there, all right; I go tell him, now, me." Then he was off as fast as his legs could carry him.

"He's lying," Odalie said. "They always defend Stephen—the Negroes. They literally worship him."

Amelia said nothing. In a few minutes Georges was back.

"The maître ain't there," he said. "Perhaps he go back upstairs, yes."

"Georges," Odalie said. "Go and call a cabriolet for us. Quickly now."

Georges scurried off, his face grey with fright. Any way this ended, it would be too bad for him—yes, any way at all. . . .

At the Orleans Ballroom, Stephen was dancing with Desiree. Her golden face was radiant.

"I knew you'd come," she whispered. "I knew it!"

"One dance, remember," Stephen growled. "Only one!"

Desiree half closed her eyes so that the long curving black lashes with gold at their roots swept downward, but her lips were smiling. Then she tilted her head back and swung up on tiptoe, whirling expertly so that her lips were like wine flames, inches from Stephen's mouth. The tawny mass of hair swirled backward and out, and that elusive perfume which was almost a part of her floated upward past his nostrils.

Stephen looked down at the soft bare shoulders which were

ivory-white overlaid with thin, transparent gold. And the green eyes were opening, deeper than the sea, wiser than all forgotten mysteries, looking into his.

"I love you, monsieur," she said, "so very, very much!"

Andre was whirling past with a slim quadroon beauty in his arms.

"Time we were off, Stephen," he said warningly.

But Desiree reached up and brushed Stephen's lips lightly with her own.

"To hell with that!" Stephen said. "I'm staying!"

Outside, in Orleans Street, Amelia and Odalie sat in the hired carriage looking at the ballroom. They had been there now for almost three hours. Then, at last, the men were coming down the stairs and into the street.

Abruptly, Amelia stiffened, laying a hand on Odalie's arm. Stephen and Andre were coming down the stairs and walking arm in arm toward the curtained cab. As they neared it, the women could see that they were laughing.

"Drive on!" Odalie said furiously to the driver. The whip slashed down across the thin nag's back, and the cabriolet moved off.

"That's odd," Stephen observed. "I could have sworn that cab was empty!"

When they reached the Exchange, both Stephen and Andre found that their coaches were gone and that they were faced with the painful necessity of hiring horses in order to get back to their plantations.

Stephen smiled a little ruefully.

" 'Tis better that we go to your town house for a few hours' sleep," he said. "No livery stable will be open at this hour."

"Sleep!" Andre groaned. "Oh, my God!"

"Ye're troubled?"

"Stephen, you don't understand. What if they've found out? I only went to that accursed ball on your account. And by now Melia probably thinks I've got a yellow *placée* . . ."

"Then ye haven't?"

"Of course not! Melia is an angel! I've never even looked at another woman since we were married."

"Ye poor fellow," Stephen murmured.

Despite his misery, a thin smile crossed Andre's face.

"In what way am I a poor fellow? Because I'm in trouble now or because I've had no other woman?"

"Both," Stephen said. "But ye have no cause for worry. A bit of exasperation over our long delay—that's all. Besides, ye seemed to be enjoying your night."

"I did; but it wasn't worth this. Stephen, let's try a few of the stables, there might be a possibility . . ."

"Oh, all right. God knows there are many forms of slavery."

To their astonishment the first place they tried was open. The Creole liveryman met them with a smile of bland amusement.

"But of a certainty I am open," he grinned. "I always stay open on those nights that the *Cordon Bleu* conflicts with a ball at the 'Change. There are always many who have need of my services."

So, after having paid exorbitant fees for their use, Stephen and Andre limped homeward on a couple of ancient splayed-shanked nags which could not move above a slow walk.

XVII

ALONG the edge of the bayous, the fronds of the palmettos were like giant hands waving. Here and there the heavy, yellow-white flowers of the yucca moved majestically above the menacing bayonet spines of the cruel plant. The water came up to the very roots of the trees, and where they were cypresses, it was black. The great oaks trailed streamers of Spanish moss that caught the smallest breeze, and the willows sighed, dipping their branches into the water.

It was morning, so early that the mists had not yet left the bayou road, yet Aurore was already up, riding her chestnut mare toward Harrow.

'Tis a very great sin that I do, she thought bitterly; yet it is one for which I cannot seek absolution. No point to confess this that I will always do again and again—that indeed I cannot help doing—and Father DuGois says the sins of the mind are taken no less into account than the sins of the body. I guess I am truly damned. Both in this life and the one to come. But I cannot help loving him. 'Tis a thing beyond my will. And this is the worst of it, this shameless riding out to see him, so early that he will not have had time to have gone into the fields. May the Blessed

Mother of God forgive me and give me strength against this thing. . . .

As she rode up the oak-canopied drive to Harrow, Georges came scurrying out to take the reins. Aurore noticed that his face was strained and fearful.

"Morning, Mademoiselle Aurore," he quavered.

"Is your mistress up yet?" Aurore asked.

"Oh, yas, she up, her. She been up for hours."

That was odd, Aurore decided as she swung down from the horse. Odalie was not overly fond of arising early. And the morning after a ball too. . . .

She shook her head, so that the chestnut curls bobbed, and went on up the stairs. She crossed the great hall and approached the dining room. She was walking rapidly, her mind preoccupied with many thoughts, so that she passed through the doorway and into the dining room before the voices arrested her.

"So," Odalie was weeping. "You've come home to me night after night with your lips still warm from the kisses of your Negress! Filthy, disgusting beast! I wish I could scald off the skin where you've touched me!"

"Ah," Stephen mocked. "That would be a sight. Please do so, my dear. I should like to see what a charming chameleon ye'd make."

"Don't provoke me further, Stephen! Have you no shame? What under heaven could possess you to ride fifteen miles to visit a mulatto wench? Tell me—I'm trying to understand—truly I am."

"That ye could never understand," Stephen said drily. " 'Twould be describing the colors of a sunset to a blind man. And now, if ye've finished this senseless tirade . . ."

"But I haven't finished; I shall never finish it! I must know what this thing is—I must know!"

"That—ye cannot, even if I were so foolish as to attempt to tell ye. But there is enough and too much of this—and I have work to do."

He made a half turn, but Odalie laid a hand upon his arm.

"Never go to her again," she said. "Promise me, Stephen!"

Stephen looked at her, and his pale eyes were blue glacier ice. Then very gently, he disengaged her hand from his arm, and turned to go.

"I shall have her whipped!" Odalie cried. "You know I can! It's the law, Stephen, it's the law."

Stephen turned back to face her.

"Aye," he said quietly. "'Tis the law, all right. But if ye ever dare invoke it, ye know right well who would suffer."

"You—you don't mean you'd leave me for her—for a Negress!"

"And why not? She has been a better companion to me than ever ye could dream of. She is twice the woman, and thrice the wife that ever ye were. Remember this, my dear—no man ever leaves a *good* wife. Think on that, if ever ye think at all!"

He spun on his heel so that his eyes met the stricken face of Aurore, who was still standing, as though frozen, in the doorway.

"No, Stephen," she whispered. "No—this I cannot believe— not of you—never of you, Stephen."

"Thank ye for your trust," he said. "But 'tis true, Aurore. I have a quadroon mistress. I don't try to justify it—what is—is. Good day to ye, ladies."

"Wait, Stephen," Aurore said. "Let me ride with you into the fields."

"I shall not discuss this thing, Aurore!"

Aurore hesitated looking into the pale blue eyes that were like those of a peregrine. Then she turned to her sister.

"Stay with me, Aurore," Odalie sobbed. "I need you."

Aurore crossed the room, and stood beside her sister's chair, one arm around Odalie's shoulders. But her gaze followed Stephen as he went through the doorway. Then she folded her sister against her, and both of them wept, there in the silent room.

Night after night, Stephen rode away to New Orleans toward the little house on Rampart Street where music was and laughter and a slow, insidious witchery that poured fire into his veins and kept it ever blazing. All his instincts, all his better judgement rebelled against this thing, but, for the first time in his life, he was powerless. 'Tis wrong, wrong, wrong! he would tell himself, and the next instant an image of Desiree—dancing a mad gypsy dance, her scarlet skirts swirling about her perfect limbs, or Desiree's lips, moist and warm and parted sighing under his, waiting to be kissed, or Desiree naked in his arms, her body of pale white gold stirring ever so gently so that the long curving sweep of arm and thigh and waist seemed to flow from one position to another each more enchanting than the last—would arise in his mind and groaningly he would commit himself to damnation.

At Harrow, Odalie grew thin and pale from days of scarcely touching food and nights of sleepless waiting. It was on one of these nights, after she had seen Etienne tucked safely abed and seated herself at her window that faced toward the river road, that Caleen came into the room, silently, without even knocking. She must have stood there a long time before Odalie sensed her presence. She whirled, a little half scream caught deep in her throat, one hand pressed against her mouth.

"Do not have fear, maîtresse," Caleen said. " 'Tis only me."

"Well," Odalie snapped, "what do you want?"

"Nothing," Caleen said. "Only to help, if I can."

"You—you want to help me? Why, Caleen? How?"

"I know maîtresse's trouble. The maître run after Negre gal. That's not new, that happens a lot, yes. But maîtresse is good to Caleen, and the good maître is tricked by Negre magic. So I help, me. Somebody got to have sense round Harrow, so I have it, me; ain't nobody else got none."

"All right, Caleen, get to the point."

"I know a wise woman—wise in Negre magic. She can tell maîtresse what to do."

"Not—not one of those Voudou priestesses, Caleen?"

Caleen nodded.

"Yes. She a *Mamaloi*, and a good one, I tell you, yes!"

"Now, Caleen, don't be ridiculous!"

The old woman drew herself up proudly to her full height. Caleen was a tall woman, and she knew how to be impressive.

"Maîtresse ever see Caleen fail? Didn't maîtresse give birth all right when *docteur* say her die? Didn't 'Tienne live, him?

283

An' maître—when he got shot by that wicked old man—didn't Caleen bring him back when already he 'most dead, him?"

"You—you have much right," Odalie said. "Still a *Mama-loi*...."

"She wiser than Caleen. She teach me all I know, her. You see, maîtresse, white man wise, all right; he wise one way; but Negre wise, too; he wise another way—a old, old way. White man can't understand that way. I sing a song, me, out in the kitchen house. Maîtresse hear me sing it a hundred time, but tonight I sing it different, just one sound different; hold one word a little too long, maybe. Cook, her hear me sing it. She hear that one word held too long. She go outside to empty water and she sing it too, her. And she hold that one word too long. Negre passing by hear it, him. He go through all the fields singing it the same way, till finally it go from mouth to mouth and the Negres in the fields next to ours done got it too, them. Then tonight, Negres from every plantation in fifty miles meet me tonight in the black bayous when the moon is dark. Ain't no white man can do that, maîtresse. Ain't no white *docteur*, no white priest can tell maîtresse what to do. Got to fight magic with magic: *gris-gris* with better *gris-gris*. We get maître back—you watch."

Odalie stood up, her dark eyes very clear.

"This woman," she said. "When can we see her?"

"Tonight."

"Tonight? But Caleen it's raining like mad and it's very late and . . ."

"Maîtresse want maître back?"

"All right, Caleen. Go get my things—you know where to find them."

A half hour later, a small black coach rocked away from Harrow through the driving rain. Caleen sat beside her mistress, who was dressed in black and heavily veiled. The rain steamed up from the flanks of the horses and drummed against the roof of the coach, which lurched on at a furious speed through the puddles and ruts in the road. Odalie sat very still, twisting a handkerchief into a damp ball in her hands.

Then, hours later, they were turning into New Orleans, the

284

horses flecked with foam and heaving. They kept on at a trot until they came to the quarter where the free Negroes lived. It was a dark, evil-smelling collection of ruined buildings. Looking out, Odalie shuddered.

Caleen ordered the coachman to stop.

"We get out here," she said. Odalie's black eyes widened. "Come!" the old woman commanded. Odalie stepped down into the inky road.

"You wait here, you!" Caleen said to the coachman.

"Come," Caleen said again to Odalie. "I'll go in front, me. Quickly now."

Odalie lifted the corner of the heavy black veil that hid her face. It was very dark and the rain fell hissing into the mud puddles, stippling the surface of the water. There was no light, and the Negro shanties, blackedged even against the blackness, slanted up at crazy angles. Odalie let the veil fall again and put her slim hand on Caleen's arm. They turned and twisted through a labyrinth of narrow lanes and alleys, covered ankle-deep with mud and icy water. Suddenly Caleen stopped.

"Here," she muttered, "here."

Odalie could feel a great trembling running through her entire body. Now, at that moment, she would have run away, twisting down all the dark and muddy alleys they had come if she had known the way. But she was lost. They had turned too often, retracing their steps too many times. Standing there, she could feel nothing but the cold and the fear. There was a vast, echoing hollow in her middle, a gone spent feeling, a weakness in the very marrow of her bones and her blood ran very clear and cold like spring water.

Caleen was knocking now, making a definite rhythm, three times repeated. The door swung open, noiseless on its hinges, and a rich, rolling, midnight bass called out in Gumbo French:

"Who's there?"

"Me," Caleen snapped. "Tante Caleen. *Voudou Magnian!*"

"*Voudou Magnian,*" the voice repeated. "Enter!"

The two of them slipped into a hallway, and the door was shut behind them. There was no light, and the blackness had thickness and texture. It seemed compounded of smoke and foul air and the smell of musk and oil and dark bodies. Odalie's trembling increased so that Caleen could feel it, communicated through the grip of her mistress' fingers on her arm.

"Not the fear," she said. "'Tis nothing."

The man who had admitted them was moving ahead in the darkness. Odalie knew that, although she could neither see nor hear him. Then a hinge creaked briefly, and a slanting blade of yellow guillotined the darkness. The man stood half revealed in the doorway, and now for the first time Odalie could see him. He was a magnificent Negro, more than six feet tall, and proportioned like a Nubian archer. Standing there, the stillness about him had an impact that was almost physical, a sensation of force frozen into quiet which stunned Odalie's senses so that the trembling stopped as if by a word of command.

"Enter," he said again.

They went by him very rapidly into a room illuminated by half a dozen flambeaux. When the smoke had ceased stinging Odalie's eyes, she could see a large mulatto woman seated on a rude throne. Half a glance told her that as a girl this woman had been very beautiful, and even now was still compellingly handsome.

"Closer, my child," the woman said in perfect French. "Do not fear. What is it you desire of Selada?"

Odalie moved toward her. Then she stopped. From a wicker basket before the throne, a full-grown snake had put out its head. Then another and another and another until the petrified Odalie, her arms half strangling Caleen—and the scream she had started to utter caught somewhere deep in her throat—had counted twelve of them.

"My pets will not harm you," Selada said. "Take them away, Tante Caleen, since they frighten our guest."

Calmly Caleen broke her mistress' grip, and picking up the basket, the snakes twining and untwining about her arms, she placed it in a far corner.

"Speak, child," Selada said. "What is it you wish?"

286

Odalie stood before her, her lips moving, but no sound came from them, no sound at all.

"It does not matter much," Selada said, her eyes sweeping over the veiled young figure, resting for a moment on the heavy gold wedding band, then traveling on. "*Voudou Magnian* will speak to me. Your husband, is it not so? I see him and another woman. A woman of the blood of the blacks. I have right, do I not?"

Odalie nodded dumbly.

"I will help you. Hercule!"

The magnificent black man appeared and bowed low before Selada.

"Your servant, Queen," he said.

"Summon the others. We will dance *Calinda*. We must make strong *gris-gris* for Madame."

Hercule was gone as silently as he came. Selada indicated that Odalie and Caleen should be seated. After a moment Hercule was back, followed by twenty-five or thirty Negroes of various ages and colors, including a quadroon girl of sixteen or so who was so beautiful that Odalie caught her breath looking at her. They grouped themselves around the throne and two men only a shade less perfectly developed than Hercule seated themselves before drums which looked as though they had been brought, hundreds of years ago, from Africa.

They began to beat the drums with the palms of their hands, a slow steady rhythm never varying, never ceasing. Odalie could feel her breath coming quicker. They kept it up, over and over again, the whispering, muttering, muted blood-throbbing beat.

Selada made an imperceptible gesture and the beat changed. Faster it grew, faster, louder: low thunder on the dog-skin drums. The beautiful quadroon girl went down the rows between the guests and placed a baked clay vase filled to the brim with Tafia, cane rum, before each of them. They began to drink, and Odalie, fearing to be different, sipped hers once and again as the beat of the drums increased, then again and again until the ice water in her veins changed into warm wine. Then her blood was pounding through her body, and her eyes were bright as the rest, and her young patrician body was swaying with those of the others.

Again Selada waved a hand.

Hercule sprang to his feet and tore off his clothes until he was naked except for a loin cloth. Never had Odalie seen such a man. He dashed to the corner of the room and came back with a serpent. He held it aloft, allowing it to twine around his gigantically muscled arms. He talked and whispered to it, putting it upon the floor at the foot of the throne and squatting before it. At every word the snake swayed back and forth, sticking out its swift, lambent tongue, matching every undulation of the big man's body.

Then at last he stood fully erect, and caught up the reptile. The two drummers increased their mad beat. Two men, as if by a signal, came in with an iron cylinder, blazing with fire.

"*Voudou!*" Hercule shouted, "*Voudou Magnian!*"

"*Voudou,*" the worshippers screamed in echo, "*Voudou Magnian!*"

With a roar like that of an enraged lion, Hercule hurled the snake into the fire. The reptile twisted and writhed in anguish.

The snake worshippers shrieked.

The quadroon girl sprang to her feet. There was the sound of cloth tearing and she stood before Hercule clad only in a chemise. With both feet planted firmly on the ground, her perfect legs spread wide apart, she began to undulate, her body moving only from the hips up, her young breasts moving under the thin garment, in a dance so sensual that Odalie could feel with her hand the pounding of her pulse in her throat.

Hercule advanced toward her until they were standing inches apart and matched her every movement. Suddenly he put forth his hand and snatched away the chemise. The girl stood there washed in the flickering yellow light of the fire, and the muscles of her abdomen rolled independently. The young, proud, up-thrusting breasts made semi-circles in the air, and the little cherry teats were visibly pointing. She threw her head back and her lips parted a little, allowing the breath to come sighing through. Hercule moved closer.

Odalie could feel her own breath coming out in short, sharp, gusts.

Hercule was running his huge black hands over the girl's body now, caressing her lightly as a breath, up over the sweetly curving hips and waist and breasts, moving like great black spiders on the creamy flesh. Then as they tightened, drawing her to him, Selada gave a signal and the drums crashed into silence. The girl hung limply in Hercule's mighty arms. He picked her up as lightly as a leaf and walked through the doorway into the dark.

"Enough," Selada said. "Enough!"

Then she was coming down from the throne, a little glass vial in her hand. She gave it to Odalie.

"A little in his wine or his coffee," she said. "But only a little. It is ver' strong *gris-gris*. Too much might harm him."

Odalie was fumbling in her purse for money, but Selada raised a hand.

"Later," she said. "You may send it by Tante Caleen. One word more. Love is an art. For the woman it must be all giving, nothing held back. Remember that. Your husband, Madame, turned to another woman—why? Was it not because Madame did not come with eagerness to him, but with fear, and trembling and misgivings of heart?"

"Yes," Odalie whispered. "That was it."

"Why, Madame, why?"

"It all seemed—so disgusting somehow. I never knew—I never expected . . ."

"Ah," Selada said, "'twas Madame's thoughts that were wrong. Such were the means for the making of life set by the good God. If Madame could once forget herself, if Madame could for once *want* Monsieur—instead of passively submitting—then Madame would learn that love is the most wonderful gift of God, in which fierceness and tenderness are so entwined that never can they be separated, and abasement linked with exaltation, and pain with ecstasy! Good night, Madame."

Caleen touched her arm and they went back through the doors, through the inky hallway into the cold rain-lanced night.

Could a woman be too good? Was it then this pale reserve, this withholding of self that drove men like Stephen to the dark and sultry passions behind the highwalled courtyards of the little white houses on Rampart Street? What was it then that he shared with a dark mistress that she, his wife, could never know? Mistress. What was a mistress? A quadroon. A woman with a little black blood in her. Not much—just enough to retain the savagery. Did Stephen want savagery? Did he want a woman who matched mood for brutal mood as the yellow dancer had matched Hercule step for step in that wild dance?

She looked at Caleen.

"Could a woman," she whispered, "*want* to do things like that?"

Caleen's eyes widened at the question.

"Unless she do—until she do, she ain't no woman, her. Here the coach. Maîtresse come."

XVIII

ODALIE sat before the mirror between the twin silver candlesticks. I am afraid, she told herself; but the image in the mirror looked back with serene unconcern. Caleen stood behind her, the outlines of her lean frame wavering off into the darkness there in the feeble candleglow. Now she was parting Odalie's hair and brushing it back and down like a nightblack cloud over her mistress' shoulders. Against it, Odalie's face and neck and shoulders were pearly.

"Maîtresse one gran' beauty, her," the old woman said.

"Am I? Truly, Caleen, am I really?"

"No woman so pretty like maîtresse, no. Except maybe Mamselle Aurore and she don't count, her."

"Still, Caleen . . ."

The old woman's black face split suddenly into one of her rare smiles. The yellow, fanglike teeth gleamed dully.

"We fix that us," she whispered. "You watch!"

"Yes," Odalie said. "But how?"

Caleen went on with her brushing.

"Maîtresse do what Caleen say?"

Odalie half turned and looked up into the old woman's face.

"Yes," she said doubtfully. "Yes, Caleen."

Instantly the old woman was swirling the heavy masses of hair up on top of her mistress' head, and pinning them there with ivory hairpins, so that Odalie's neck and shoulders were bare. Then she drifted off in the darkness and was back in no appreciable lapse of time with her mistress' robe.

"Maîtresse come?"

Odalie's eyebrows rose, but she followed the old woman out of the room and into the little chamber where the tiny, slipper-shaped bathtub, brought from France at great expense at Stephen's order, stood. It was just big enough for an adult to sit rigidly upright in.

"Maîtresse disrobe," Caleen said. "I be back in a minute, me."

Slowly Odalie took off her garments until she stood naked, and shivering a little, despite the warmth of the little room. Then Caleen was grunting up the stairs, bending backward under the weight of an immense oaken tub of scalding water. She poured it into the bath, and went back for more. This time, satisfied that she had enough, she bent and tested the water with a horny finger. Then, straightening up, she brought forth a small gourd from the folds of her apron. With one jerk, she pulled the cork out of its neck and spilled the deep violet-colored powder into the bath. Instantly it steamed up in a great cloud, and the whole room was filled with the perfume.

Odalie's black eyes widened. Never, in all her life spent in a country where perfumery was a great art, had she encountered a scent like this. It was not heavy and sweet, but elusive to the point that the senses were unsure of its existence. And yet, apparently, it lingered with quiet persistence, piquing the mind to awareness, insistently. She leaned forward over the tub, drawing it in with deep breaths. Then she stepped back, looking at Caleen. This—this was like wine, slowly, insidiously intoxicating, working in silence so that one was not quite sure at what point one took leave of one's senses. But dimly she sensed how it would affect a man, arousing him slowly, surely, persistently, with a lilting, mocking, unceasing provocation until all the centuries of civilization would be shed like a cloak, leaving only pure brute, pure savage.

"This," Odalie said, "this is a scent for a harlot! Caleen, where on earth . . ."

"Maîtresse fight robber with bare hands, her? Or . . ."

"Or what, Caleen?"

"Or with a *gris-gris* that works?"

"Like that other, Caleen? The one Selada gave me? It only made him sick!"

The old woman shook her head.

"Maîtresse trust Caleen," she said, "I never fail, me."

Odalie's creamy shoulders bowed in assent. She lifted one dainty foot, and tried the water with a toe.

"It's too hot," she wailed.

"Maîtresse get in, her!" Caleen said sternly.

Odalie stepped at once into the tub, and sat down, although the water steamed up around her in a cloud. Caleen knelt beside her, and began to bathe her, laving her all over with a soft cloth, rubbing very firmly. Then afterwards she let Odalie relax in the tub, leaning back against the high slipper back, while the perfume rose up past her nostrils.

"Maîtresse get out now."

Obediently, Odalie stood up, and Caleen wrapped her in the big towels. Even after she was dried, the perfume lingered. Then, clad in robe and slippers, she went back to the bedroom.

"Take off the robe," Caleen commanded. "Lie down on the bed, yes!"

Odalie stretched herself luxuriously on the bed and closed her eyes. She heard Caleen moving away; then again she was coming back toward her.

"Maîtresse drink this?"

Odalie sat up and took the glass; it was a wine that gleamed like amber. Without question, without hesitation, she drank it down and sank back upon the bed. Then suddenly she could feel Caleen's hands, cool and dry as parchment, moving over her body. She opened her mouth to protest, but the wine was curling warm within her, leaving a faint taste of ash and woodsmoke

293

on her tongue's tip, and all her limbs were loosening. She sighed and turned her head aside.

This wrong, Caleen thought. Should sprinkle her with blood from young poulet, too, yes! Got to leave that out, that part, or maîtresse know. But the oil, I use that, me.

She dipped her fingers into an earthenware jug. They came out dripping. The oil was very thin, and it had the same scent as the perfume. Caleen rubbed it gently until it disappeared into the pores of her mistress' skin, working from head to heel over the entire lovely body. Then she began to massage the flesh, kneading it firmly until Odalie glowed all over. She lingered over the breasts, caressing them lightly with the tips of her old fingers until they were proud and pointing.

"Should use feather from rooster," she muttered. "Point 'em up so. So we give bride in marriage in the dark hills of San Domingo. And she go to her man no more a green girl, scared; but a woman, proud, her, with fire in her limbs, yes!"

She bent to her task.

Selada right, but she don't know maîtresse, her. Never from her own mind, could maîtresse change. But I change her, me, by Dambala, by the Virgin, by all the saints!

She leaned close to Odalie's ear.

"Maître a good man, him," she whispered. "But him more. He a devil-saint with blood like fire. You cannot tame him, he only beautiful when wild. He kiss like fire, kiss back like fire. Stay with him, ride wild and free over all the world with him, yes; reach up your hand and touch the blazing sun. You do this, yes; he come back to you!"

Then she was gone, like a gaunt black ghost, guttering the candles as she went.

After she had gone, for a little time, Odalie lay still. Then, like a sleepwalker, she got up and crossed to the mirror, lighting the darkened candles. Her eyes peered back at her from the mirror, black and lightless and velvet soft. Sitting there entirely nude, she began to brush down her hair. Leave it like this, she thought, he likes it loose, he likes . . .

Then she was picking up her clothes from the chair. They

294

were new, every one of them—a white dress with a bodice like a silver sheath, and satiny skirts that billowed endlessly, catching each tiny candle flicker in their glossy folds. And they—the dress, the chemise, and every one of the numerous petticoats—held in them the faint, elusive scent of that perfume. Slowly she began to dress, drawing on the silken stockings, the white slippers, the spray of white lilacs for her hair. Then at last she was almost done, fastening the massive triple string of pearls, with the heavy golden catch, about her neck. She stood back, gazing at herself in the mirror.

The dress fell away from her shoulders, leaving them bare, and her hair rested like a cloud of darkness upon them. She smiled at herself, feeling the warmth stealing slowly and subtly along the hidden surface of her flesh. Then she turned and left the room.

"Pray God he has not gone," she whispered as she crossed the hall. "Pray God . . . "

She stood for a long time before his door. I did this once, she thought, and I failed. I must not fail him, now; no, never again must I fail him—never in all our lives. Then she twisted the doorknob firmly.

Stephen was standing by the window, gazing out over his darkened acres. His fair brows were knit together in a frown, and in the glow of the candles the scar on his temple gleamed redly. He stood there clad in a rich green dressing robe, a long time, unaware of her presence; then at last the scent of her perfume stole into his conscious mind. Slowly he turned, and his pale eyes widened, looking at her.

"Ye're very beautiful, my dear," he said. "Do ye know, I'd almost forgotten that?"

She did not answer him, but stood there, just inside the door, both hands behind her, leaning against the knob. Stephen raised one eyebrow questioningly.

"And ye wear your hair loose. 'Tis a long time since ye've done that. Why? And that dress. Is there a ball?"

"No, Stephen," she said; "there's no ball."

Stephen crossed the room to where she stood, his face half

frowning. When he was close, he lifted her chin with one hand and looked into her eyes.

"What is it, Odalie?" he asked gently. Then he stopped. The perfume came up from her hair, from her shoulders, from the deep vale between her breasts. Puzzled, he bent closer. That perfume—but was there a perfume? There must be, still—how beautiful Odalie is!

Then suddenly, unexpectedly, her arms were sweeping up and around his neck. Her body arched upward against his; blindly, her eyes closed, she sought his lips. Just for a moment, Stephen was lost in amazement; just for a moment, then the perfume was all around his head in a cloud. He kissed her achingly, softly, tenderly. But her hands were locked behind his head, and her fingers were fierce suddenly in his fiery hair. Her mouth burned upon his, the lips slackening, parting. For another long moment Stephen was limp against her, then his arms tightened around the slim waist, until her body ground against his.

Then he broke her grip and stood back, looking at her, his pale eyes dancing. Odalie swayed there at his finger tips, her eyes still closed, and the great tears diamond bright at their corners. He drew her in again, gently against him, her dark head pillowed against his chest.

"I love you, Monsieur my husband," she whispered, "so much I love you—so very much!"

Stephen bent down and swept her up into his arms. Crossing the room, he laid her gently upon his own narrow bed. Then he knelt down beside her, kissing her eyes, her lips, her throat. Odalie's hands were urgent suddenly, drawing him to her. He drew away a little, rubbing his bare chest where his dressing gown had parted.

"Those pearls," he said. Odalie's hands fumbled briefly at the catch. It wouldn't work. Then both of her hands swept up suddenly and caught at the triple strings. Slowly, with Stephen's eyes full upon her, she drew them out and down until they broke. The pearls scattered over the bed, over the floor. There on the rug they picked up the candle glow: tiny blue-white mounds gleaming in the darkness . . .

First in the morning, after the sun was up, the waters of the river were golden. Then the light worked its way across the bayou road, dispelling the mist as it went. It lingered a little over the fronds of the palmetto, then moved onward up the alley of oaks tangling itself like pale fire in all the trailing streamers of Spanish moss. A few minutes later, it washed Harrow with sunglow, so that the great house blazed like a jewel among the somber oaks.

It was the light itself that awakened Stephen, falling across his face through the open window. He lay quite still, blinking owlishly at the strengthening glow. On the floor, between him and the window, there were little points of light, scattered wildly about with a solid iridescence all their own. Stephen studied them carefully. Yes, there was no doubt about it, they were pearls; but how on earth . . .

His arm felt numb. He tried to move it, only to find he could not. There was a weight upon it, pressing it firmly to the bed. Slowly he turned his head, and his fair brows flew upward. There beside him, her head cradled into the hollow of his shoulder, her full weight resting upon his arm, Odalie slept. Looking at her, Stephen smiled a little, remembering. He made no attempt to move his arm, although it ached confoundedly from remaining so long in one position.

"So," he whispered. "Ye came to me at last! Ye came and loved like a hot-blooded young savage and there was no reserve in ye, none at all. Saints and satyrs, what a transformation! I wonder what under heaven caused this? Ye wanted to compete? To win me back? Aye, that was part of it; but what cracked the ice and let the spring floods through?"

He looked out over the disordered room, half-covered with the garments she had discarded.

This was all planned, he decided; even down to that devilish perfume she used. I've been tricked, he told himself; but, by heaven, I like such trickery!

Gently he eased his arm out from under her head. Odalie

came awake at once, and sat up beside him. Stephen waited for her to draw the coverlet up over her body, but she sat there as shameless and as graceful as a woods nymph.

"Good morning, Stephen," she said clearly.

"Good morning, my dear," he said with grave mockery. "Ye slept well, I trust?"

She looked up at him, her black eyes searching his. Then she saw what she sought, the little laughing light dancing far back in his eyes. She bent forward to be kissed, but he stopped his face inches from hers. Then, as if by a signal, they both exploded into laughter.

Afterwards, life was very good at Harrow. Stephen's face lost its perpetual frown; in its place was a look of profound peace. He went no more to the little house by the Ramparts, but spent his days and nights at Harrow. He commissioned Monsieur Pouilly, much to that gentleman's astonishment, to build two magnificent houses: a town house for Odalie in New Orleans, and a cottage on Lake Pontchartrain where they might escape the heat of summer.

And Odalie, although in her middle thirties, grew hourly more beautiful. There was about her a look of completion, of fulfillment. It was during this period that the portrait of her that hangs in the great hall at Harrow was painted. To the day of his death, Paul Dumaine, *père*, spoke of it as his finest work.

"Madame called forth my best," he was fond of saying. " 'Tis not often that one is granted the opportunity to paint such loveliness—and such joy."

Stephen stood watching the artist at work, marveling at his skill, and marveling still more at the sweet, secret glow that transfixed his wife's face.

"Enough," the artist declared. "There is nothing more that I can do to it—'tis finished—"

"Thank ye, monsieur," Stephen said. "Ye've done well. I trust ye will find your commission as satisfactory as I have found your work."

The artist smiled. "That doesn't trouble me," he said. "Painting one so beautiful is reward enough. *Adieu!*" He bowed grandly and took his leave.

Stephen walked over to the raised platform upon which Odalie sat and took her hand. She stepped down, smiling up at him.

"Still I don't understand it," he said, "this change in ye. After all these years ye became what I dreamed ye were. Why, Odalie, why?"

"I don't know, Stephen," she said. "Truly I don't. I think that when I saw I was losing you, I became a woman. It wasn't a conscious thing. So much I've lost—so many precious years."

"We'll make them up, never ye fear."

"We seem to be trying," she laughed softly. "I fear that sometimes I tire you with my ardor!"

" 'Tis a fatigue I like," he said. "Holy angels, but ye're beautiful!"

She made him a mocking little courtesy and the two of them went out into the great hall.

"Stephen. . . ."

"I love ye," he said. " 'Tis this I saw in the Place D'Armes the day that Lafayette came. I'd wondered where it went, what had become of it—that look: the way your eyes are now—like—like . . .

"Stephen . . ."

"What is it, my dear?"

"How would you like another son? Or a daughter perhaps?" Stephen frowned.

"That—no. Doctor Terrebonne said 'twould be extremely dangerous . . ."

Odalie smiled up at him, a slow, misty smile.

"The—the chance must be taken, my husband," she said softly. Stephen's fair brows flew together, and his pale eyes were fierce suddenly.

"No," he said, half to himself. "Ye must be mistaken. It cannot be!"

"The first time, there is doubt. After that—a woman knows."

"Holy Mother of God!"

"Are you sorry, Stephen?"

"No—not sorry, frightened. If Doctor Terrebonne were only alive. I don't trust this Lefevre. He's too young, and too advanced —still we have Caleen. One thing is certain, my dearest, off ye go to bed and stay there till it is time. The last time ye overtaxed yourself in many ways."

"I—I've been a bad wife, Stephen . . ."

"Nonsense. 'Tis only that I lacked patience and understanding. But all that is gone now—'tis over and done with. And what I have now is granted to only one man among millions."

He took her hands and looked down into her face a long, long time before he kissed her.

There in the doorway Aurore saw the look, but when Stephen bent forward towards her sister, she turned away her face. Then, without a word, she turned and went back down the great stairs to her horse and rode away through the sunlight, the tears bright and heavy in her lashes.

But as she turned away from Harrow, into the Bayou Road, Aurore was conscious of another horse, standing quietly in the cypress shade. She reined in, looking curiously at the rider who sat half hidden among the trees. It was a girl—a very young girl— Aurore recognized at once; but one who bore herself on horseback as though she had spent half her lifetime there. She was dressed in a rich green riding habit, but she was hatless, and her hair escaped uncurled down over her shoulders in a tawny mane.

Mon Dieu! but she's lovely, Aurore thought. I wonder who on earth— But something in the girl's coloring struck her. Even those who foolishly slept overlong on the sands at Lake Pontchartrain had not that pure transparent golden tone. She rode in closer.

"Who are you?" she demanded. "What are you doing here?"

The girl turned slowly. Her eyes, beneath her amazingly dark lashes were a cool green. When she smiled, little flakes of gold swam in their depths.

"That shouldn't interest such a great lady as Mademoiselle," she said evenly.

"You're insolent!" Aurore said, certainty crowding hard upon suspicion. "Let me see your hands!"

Calmly the girl stretched them out.

"That is great foolishness," she said, "that business about a bluish tinge at the base of the nails. See, I have none. But for Mademoiselle's information: yes, I am a woman of color—a free quadroon, if you will. And my errand is perhaps the same as Mademoiselle's own—to see that which I cannot have."

"I—I'll have you whipped!"

The girl shrugged.

"So? What will that prove? Only that Mademoiselle is white and rich and powerful—and that the world already knows. I think Mademoiselle could afford to be more gracious."

"You—you were Stephen's mistress!" Aurore said.

The girl laughed, a dark, rich sound—like the echoes of a soft, golden gong.

"Yes," she said. "And Mademoiselle?"

"Oh," Aurore cried, completely beside herself, "you—you baggage!" Then she brought the crop down across her horse's flank and thundered off, down the road.

The girl sat very quietly upon her horse looking after her. Then again she turned her face toward Harrow. It would be a long wait, she knew. Sighing, she shifted her position a little, and half closed her eyes. Then at last she saw the big palomino trotting away from Harrow, angling out toward the fields.

Instantly she started toward him, tapping the big, rawboned stallion with her crop. The horse rolled his bulging, bloodshot eyes and snorted. He had a nervous gait without constant pace or smoothness.

Stephen rode on, his head lifted to the morning sun, whistling a gay tune. But suddenly Prince Michael stopped short in his tracks and whinnied. Stephen half rose in the stirrups, turning as he did so. Almost at once he saw the roan stallion coming

301

toward him at a loping canter; and instantly he recognized the rider.

"Desiree!" he said aloud. "Oh, my God!"

Then she was reining in, turning the big horse so that he presented his flank to Stephen's mount. Stephen's brows were twin white-gold thunder clouds, and his mouth a thin line. Desiree saw the look.

"Forgive me," she said. "But I had to come."

"Why? Ye know well that it will only cause trouble. To ride all the way to Harrow in daylight, pass a dozen plantations of my friends is, to say the least, an indiscretion—it may even be an impertinence!"

Desiree's hands jerked on the reins so that the roan stallion danced.

"I had to come," she whispered. "You would ask me to live all alone in that little house where everything reminds me of you? This morning I pushed aside the curtains to see if there were sunlight, and in them was the scent of your pipe smoke. Last night I sat down to supper, and there was your chair, empty, across from me. No one but you has ever sat in it, monsieur. I walk and walk and walk—back and forth, back and forth. And all the time it seems to me that if I were to whirl suddenly, you'd be there, mocking me, teasing me the way you love to do."

Stephen was silent, but his frown deepened.

"I talk to you just as if you were really there. Sometimes it seems that you are there; my mind is not very clear at times. It's being consumed by this awful hunger for you—the sight of you, the sound of your voice. . . ."

Her eyes were searching his face as she talked, moving very rapidly, her gaze caressing him.

"What is it that ye want?" he said harshly.

"You. I want you to come back to me and set everything straight so that I'll know that I'm alive."

"Do ye not know it now?"

"No. I'm numb. There is no feeling at all except this horrible emptiness. I don't know whether I've eaten or not. I don't know what time of day it is—or what day—or even if it is day. I'm not

302

sure of anything except that I want you and want you and want you until soon I shall die of it."

"Ye're a child," Stephen said evenly. "Ye don't know what ye want even though ye do talk like a woman grown."

"I was never a child. My mother discussed love with me when I was eight years old. I was never allowed dolls or play or even the foolish prattle of children. From infancy I was reared to be only one thing: a perfect mistress for such a man as you."

"My God!"

"I was brought up more strictly than your convent-trained maidens. Of course I was taught to dance and to sing; but I was never allowed to look at a boy. Monsieur knows I was untouched when I came to him?"

"Yes," Stephen said, "I know."

"You would end my life then before it is begun? That is what you're doing."

"There's no help for it, little Desiree," Stephen said gently. "There are others with a better claim on me. I'm afraid 'tis quite impossible."

Desiree's hand tightened upon the reins and the thin nag shied.

"Careful of that horse," Stephen said. "He seems of unsteady disposition."

The girl sat there looking at him, the deep green eyes widening endlessly. Then deliberately she tossed her reins away from her high upon the roan stallion's neck and raised her crop above her head.

"Desiree!" Stephen cried.

But she brought the crop down in a vicious semicircle. The sound of it striking the stallion was very clear. The animal screamed—a high, thin sound—and lunged forward across the fields. Stephen bent low over Prince Michael's neck and urged him forward; but the big palomino was now well along in years and no match for the pain-maddened roan. Desiree lashed the thin stallion without ceasing, driving him onward at ever increasing speed, the reins flapping loosely about his neck.

Before her now was the cane brake, behind which, Stephen

303

knew, was the mill stream, dropping away a full fifteen feet below. Unless that horse was a jumper . . . Stephen brought his own crop down savagely across Prince Michael's broad flanks.

Then the roan was soaring up and out over the brake, as effortlessly as a great bird. Stephen pulled Prince Mike up; never could that great heavy horse make such a jump. But even as the palomino reared, Stephen saw the stallion's forelegs striking the opposite bank. For a brief second they held, then they doubled under him, and he rolled over and over, throwing Desiree clear. The stallion threshed about and screamed like a woman in agony; but the crumpled little figure in the green riding habit was quite still.

Stephen jumped to the ground and slid down into the water. It came up to his thighs. He strode across to where the horse was, the little derringer, which he carried with him always since Tom Warren's attempt upon his life, ready in his hand. Scarcely seeming to take aim, he fired just once, and the threshing and the screaming stopped. Then he knelt down beside the girl, pillowing her head in his arms.

She smiled up at him, a thin trickle of scarlet escaping the corner of her mouth.

"For me," she whispered. "You saved one for me? It has two barrels, hasn't it?"

"Holy Mother of God!"

"Please, monsieur. Inside I'm—all broken. It hurts terribly. Am I not more to you than a horse?"

Stephen slipped his arms under the slight form of the girl; then he straightened, lifted her and started back toward Harrow. Desiree nestled her head up against his chest, and bit her lip to keep back the moans from every jolting step.

Then at last he was going up the great stairs into Harrow. The girl had long since lapsed into merciful unconsciousness. But Odalie had come out upon the gallery and Caleen stood behind her, the two of them watching him coming up the stairs like figures of stone.

When Stephen reached the top stair, Odalie was bending curiously over the still form in his arms.

"Who is she?" she demanded. "What ails her?"

Stephen did not answer. He walked very quietly past his wife, his face set and grim.

"Stephen! I asked you a question! Who is this girl?"

Stephen entered the great hall. Odalie keeping pace behind him. Suddenly she leaned close; then she straightened up.

"Stephen," she whispered. "This is—this is—by the good God! You'd do a thing like this! You'd bring your quadroon wench here—into my house! Sacred Mother of God!"

"Hush," Stephen said. "She's dying."

He laid her in a small chamber in the South Wing and summoned Caleen, who was attending her mistress's hysterics, to do what she could. Caleen examined the girl briefly, with all the native hatred the pure black has for the mixed breed glaring from her eyes.

"She no die, her," the old woman grunted. "Only got t'ree ribs busted, more's the pity!"

"Then do something for her," Stephen commanded.

Caleen looked at her master.

"I no touch her, me," she declared flatly. "Maître have me whipped, all right; but I no touch that little yaller whore!"

Stephen measured her with his glance. Then abruptly he turned away.

"Get Suzette," he said shortly. "Tell her to see that she wants for nothing."

For three weeks Desiree lay upon the little bed, her body swathed in bandages. And in all that time, not one word passed between Stephen and Odalie. The young mistress of Harrow locked herself in her room, and refused to listen to any sort of explanation.

Even Etienne and Little Inch were caught in the upheaval. Everywhere they went they were greeted with tears, or brusque gruff-voiced dismissals, until at last they started at the sound of a step.

When Desiree was well enough to be moved, a small wagon, well oiled and loaded down with bedding, carried her away from

305

Harrow. At the last Odalie came out of her rooms to watch the departure.

"My dear," Stephen began . . .

"No, no!" Odalie cried. "There is nothing to be said! Go to your Negress and leave me alone!"

Stephen's brows flew together over his nose, and his eyes spoke icy fire.

"Thank ye," he said evenly. "Perhaps I will—at that."

XIX

Dᴜʀɪɴɢ all the months of Odalie's second pregnancy, scarcely
a word passed between her and Stephen. She rarely slept and
only a few crusts of bread and countless cups of *café noir* passed
between her lips. This, of course, was no diet to be recommended
for an expectant mother; and Stephen knew it. On several occasions he swallowed his pride and went to her with explanations
and apologies upon the tip of his tongue, only to be rebuffed
before he could utter them.

Finally he gave it up. Stephen was a proud man, perhaps even
an arrogant one; and to make such gestures cost him dearly. So
in pique and in confusion and trouble of mind, he turned once
more to Desiree. Early in the summer, while she lay abed with
her injuries, he visited her almost nightly, and attended to her
wants with an almost womanly tenderness. But after she was
again upon her feet, pale and weak but still full of her spritely
fire, his visits lessened. And when he did come, he talked to her
gravely, and kissed her with calm, paternal affection.

To Desiree, this was maddening.

"Am I a child," she stormed. "Have I grown ugly? Why is it,
monsieur? Why do you no longer love me?"

Stephen smiled slowly.

"I've grown old, Desiree," he said. "And there is enough and too much of trouble already. They say in the bayou country that I am lucky: that whatever I touch flowers. Aye, so it is; but with what a poisonous blossom! I have a house—the greatest in the state—in which I am hated. I have a son, but he is strange and wild towards me. I have much wealth—but no happiness . . ."

"Monsieur also has one thing more."

"And what is that?"

"Monsieur has me."

"And ye have broken your lovely body because of me, and brought down my life around my ears!"

Desiree came around from behind the great chair and knelt like a child at his feet. The tears stood and sparkled upon the long curving lashes.

"Better that I should have died than to have hurt you," she whispered. "You should have had me whipped—like a slave."

Stephen laughed.

"Enough of this foolishness," he declared. "Ye have all your life before ye still. Sing for me. I will not be saddened longer."

Desiree scampered away and was back almost at once with the mandolin. Then striking the chords boldly, she began to sing the saucy crayfish song, in which an American Negro pokes fun at the Creole Negroes' fondness for *les cribresses*.

Stephen leaned back in the great chair smiling at the tricky cadences of the gumbo French. Desiree's fine hands flew over the chords.

Stephen laughed aloud. Desiree's green eyes sparkled, and the little golden flakes caught the light. Then she strolled over and sat on the arm of Stephen's chair, and sang the song through to its mocking conclusion. Stephen roared at the picture of the 'Neg 'Mericain falling over the mounds of crayfish heads piled up around the Creole Negro's bed. Desiree put down the instrument and sat down in Stephen's lap, laughing and tousling his hair with her two hands. Then she kissed him lightly upon the mouth, the eyes, all over his face and neck.

308

Stephen caught at her arms, but she slipped away and ran, laughing, around the little house. Stephen got up and chased her, but she eluded him easily. Finally, weak with laughter, she allowed herself to be caught; but she kept turning her face away from his kisses. Then, growling in mock anger, Stephen seized her chin and turned her face upward to his. He bent down and kissed her gently; but her lips clung to his as lightly as a breath, and inch by slow inch her arms stole upward around his neck. Then her slim fingers were working in the fiery curls on the back of his head, and her lips moved beneath his.

For an instant it was so; then fiercely she swung herself up against him, until her whole body was one long caress: knee and thigh and breast, burning into his blood. She drew back her head a little; but her lips were still so close that they brushed his as they moved.

"Never let me go," she whispered. "Never, never, never!"

It was late in the winter of 1839 when the time came for Odalie to be delivered of her child. Aurore came to stay at Harrow to be with her sister, and Caleen was on duty day and night. Doctor Lefevre had been summoned, and he too took up his residence at the great house. Stephen went no more to the city, but spent his nights in his study, sleepless and troubled.

For Odalie was pitifully weak from long starvation, and her thin form, at best but ill-suited for childbirth, was racked with unceasing anguish. Doctor Lefevre shook his head gravely.

"Frankly," he said to Aurore, "'tis to be doubted that she will survive. Her body is weak enough, the good God knows; but it is her mind that is a major cause of the trouble. There is no fight there—the will to survive. If only I knew what the trouble was . . ."

"I do," Aurore said grimly. "And, by heaven, I'm going to mend it, now!" She strode away from the doctor and crossed the hall to Stephen's study. Firmly she knocked upon the door. There was no answer.

She twisted the knob angrily. It gave and the door flew open. She stepped into the room and stopped suddenly. There at Stephen's desk the candles were guttering in pools of wax, and his bright head was bent over the desk, pillowed upon his arms. She could see the empty cut-glass whiskey decanter, but the smell of the liquor was strong in the room.

Aurore snorted in disgust. Stephen lifted his head and looked at her, blinking at the light streaming in through the opened door. His face was chalky white, and his eyes were sunk far back in his head and ringed with great circles of blue. He sat there like that, frowning, with a look of so great hurt and trouble upon his face that all Aurore's anger vanished as though it had never been.

Always I could forgive him anything, she thought; always I could—even this . . .

"Stephen," she said gently.

"Yes?" he said. "Yes, Aurore?"

"Odalie is worse. There are—complications. You could help her—you are the only one who can now."

Stephen smiled crookedly, the great scar crawling upward into his red hair.

"That I doubt," he said. "God and Our Lady, how she hates me!"

"You deserve it," Aurore declared. "But the fact is—she doesn't. She loves you so much that it is chiefly of heartbreak that she is dying."

Stephen came to his feet at once, his thin nostrils flaring.

"Dying!" he said. "Ye said she is dying?"

"Yes," Aurore said simply. "Please come to her, Stephen."

"Aye," Stephen growled. "Many times now I have tried; but she would have none of me. But one more time, or one million more now, would not be amiss." His fingers toyed briefly with his ruffled shirt front; then he was gone from the room, leaving Aurore staring after him.

In the bed chamber, Stephen bent over the twisting form of his wife. Aurore came and stood in the doorway, unnoticed.

310

"No, no," Odalie whispered. "Go away! Let me have peace at last."

"Odalie," Stephen said slowly. "There is this much to be said: when that girl came to Harrow, she came without my knowledge or consent. I had broken with her long ago—that ye must believe."

On the bed Odalie lay very still, looking up at her husband. "You—you do not lie to me?" she whispered.

"I never lie," Stephen said simply. "Ye know that."

Something like a smile crept across Odalie's stricken face; then abruptly it vanished.

"And now?" she whispered. "And now, Stephen?"

"And now I shall never consort with her again," he said. "That I promise ye."

Her lips widened pitifully into a smile, but her words were so low that Stephen had to bend down his head to hear them.

"Thank you, my husband," she said. "Now no more will I fear it—this business of dying."

"Ye aren't going to die," Stephen said. "Ye cannot—ye must not!"

"I'm afraid I must, my husband," she said quite clearly. "Of that there is no longer any doubt."

Stephen opened his mouth to refute her, but the look was there, visibly, in her face. He gave a short cry and sank down beside her, burying his face in the covers. She lifted her hand feebly and stroked his bright head.

In the doorway, Aurore wept.

Four nights later, Odalie gave birth to a stillborn child—a daughter. She herself never regained consciousness, but died very quietly in her sleep, with Father DuGois kneeling beside her, intoning the prayers.

Looking at Stephen, Aurore forgot to cry. Quietly she left the bedchamber and summoned Georges and Caleen.

311

"You know where the master keeps his weapons?" she said to the manservant, and her voice was very tight and dry.

"Yes, Mamzelle," Georges said, "I knows, me."

"Get them," Aurore commanded, "all of them, and bring them to me, Caleen . . ."

"Yes, Mamzelle, I watch him—never I let him out of my sight. The maître a strange man, him. He do bad things, yes; but his heart good like saint. That Negre gal bewitch him, her—I tell you . . ."

"Hush, Caleen," Aurore said. "Please hush!"

She went into the study and sat down. Her head ached abominably. There was so much to be done . . . The invitations to the funeral must be engraved and sent; a mausoleum must be built, even a cemetery plot selected here at Harrow. There was no doubt that Odalie would want to lie here. She would need help. As she rose, she met Doctor Lefevre coming into the study.

"I gave him a sleeping draught," he said. "I thought it best. He is resting very quietly now."

Aurore nodded dumbly and slipped out into the hall. Moved by a sudden impulse, she climbed the stairs to Stephen's chamber. He lay abed, still fully clothed. Aurore bent over him. In sleep all the lines were softened, and even the patches of white that were spreading above his temples did not detract from the strangely youthful cast of his face.

He turned suddenly, so that the great flaming scar appeared and that side of his face was drawn and tortured. A little cry came from his lips and his lean body threshed briefly. Aurore drew back step by step to the door, then she was running down the stairs. As she ran she whispered to herself, over and over again:

"God forgive me for my thoughts! God forgive me—the Good Blessed God forgive me!"

Amelia and Andre came before daybreak and took complete charge of everything. Etienne and Little Inch were sent to La

312

Place to be cared for until the day of the funeral. Mike Farrel came and dogged Stephen's steps like a gigantic shadow.

"I like it not, that look, yez ken," he whispered to Andre. "Me heart bleeds to see Stevie suffer so. She were a cold high-strung wench that one but, angels above, how Stevie loved her! I'm gonna keep me eye upon him."

And in the cypress grove near Harrow, stone masons were at work building the mausoleum. Because so much of the bayou country is swampy, the custom had grown, since the plague of 'thirty-two, to inter bodies above ground. The resting place Stephen had ordered for Odalie was a magnificent one, with twin stone angels guarding the door and a bench of iron scroll work facing it, on which he could sit and look upon the place wherein she lay. Inside, there was a niche already reserved for him, with his name and date and place of birth engraved upon the headstone. This fact was a source of great trouble to all his friends.

Andre came out of Harrow late in the evening to find Stephen standing there, watching the almost finished work.

"Stephen," he said. "My old one—you must not—'tis a thing that happens to us all . . ."

Stephen's blue eyes were very clear, gazing upon his friend.

"I shall do myself no violence," he said softly. "She would not wish it, and there is still the boy. But God and Our Lady knows 'twould be easier, Andre . . . than to live with my thoughts . . ."

"Nonsense—" Andre began with great relief. But Stephen stopped him.

"I drove her to her death," he declared. "There is a kind of black madness in me . . ." He fell silent, shaking his head. Andre, too, was still; he knew, at least, when a man should hold his tongue.

After the funeral, Harrow was a great, echoing tomb of silence. The servants tiptoed about their work. And Stephen Fox sat for endless hours in his study gazing upon vacancy. Even when he

313

rode out into his fields, he saw nothing. Still, Harrow went on as prosperously as before; for it had long since reached the stage where it ran itself. But throughout the entire bayou country the stories ran from tongue to whispering tongue about the greatness of Stephen Fox's grief.

"He is like a madman," the whispers went. "He sits and stares and does not even hear you when you talk."

"And he goes no more to that place of his in Rampart Street. *Ma foi!* A man must be grieved to give up such a one as she!"

But at last, upon an evening, Stephen dressed himself with the aid of Georges, and rode in toward the city. He stopped for a moment at the sepulcher, then rode on past the rude graveyard at the foot of the levee where the slaves were buried. Achille rested there now and Stephen understood why.

" 'Twas easier to follow, was it not, my old fellow?" he whispered as he paused by the grave of the big slave. "To ye, your Sauvage must have been as much a goddess as my Odalie was to me. There is too much of sadness in life—is there not?—far, far too much!"

He rode on slowly, down the bayou road.

On Rampart Street, in the little white house with the high walled courtyard, Desiree awaited him. As the big almost white horse rounded the corner, she swayed dizzily, her hands tight upon the window sills.

I must tell him, she thought. He cannot leave me now—he cannot!

Then Stephen's knock was sounding from the door, twice repeated clearly. Desiree fought back the feeling of nausea rising in her throat, and smiling invitingly, ran forward to meet him. But when she opened the door, the smile vanished. She stood there a moment, swaying a little as she looked at him; then, very quietly, she said:

"Come in, monsieur."

"Desiree," Stephen began.

314

"Yes?"

"'Tis a hard thing I must say to ye now—the hardest almost that I have ever said . . ."

"Then don't say it! There is still much happiness. . . ."

"No, Desiree—no."

The girl drew herself up proudly. The sunlight came in the window and tangled in her tawny hair.

"I know what you would say, Monsieur my lover," she said softly. "Your wife is dead. And before she died she was grieved by this thing between us. So, in honor, you cannot continue with me longer. That is it, is it not?"

"Aye," Stephen said grimly. "That is it."

"Very well. Against this I can do nothing. There is nothing, perhaps, that anyone could do. But there is this that I must say. . . ." She looked at him, a long, slow look, her eyes very wide and bright with trembling tears.

"Say what ye will," Stephen told her.

"When you go through that door, I shall die a little. And every day that you are gone from me I shall die a little more until I am all dead. And then I shall be happy, but never again until then."

"The house is yours," Stephen said. "And everything in it. I have arranged a settlement upon ye to be paid ye monthly as long as ye shall live . . . Is there anything more that ye want?"

Desiree smiled wryly.

"Only that which I cannot have," she whispered. "Now it is better that you go quickly while I can still bear it. *Adieu*, and may the good God grant you every happiness."

Stephen took a step toward her; then he stopped and, turning swiftly, walked through the opened door. Desiree stood there holding her breath, listening to the sound of his footsteps going and the creak of leather as he mounted Prince Michael.

"He did not kiss me," she whispered. Outside in the street there was the sound of the horse's hoofs moving off through the silence. Desiree stood very still listening, then a sudden wave of weakness and nausea struck her and she went down upon her knees upon the floor.

315

I couldn't tell him, she thought; there was already too much of anguish in his eyes. And now he is gone from me and I feel no pain. Why? By now I should be dying of it. Perhaps it is because my senses are so numbed that I can feel nothing and afterwards I shall wake up screaming. I don't know. God knows I don't know.

She knelt there, staring at the floor. Then feeling the ache in her knees she got up and crossed to the window.

"It shall have red hair," she whispered, "this my son, and eyes like blue ice and a smile that is never quite a whole smile, but always has mockery in it. And I shall watch over him and cherish him and watch him grow more like him who has gone from me each day. And he shall be my life—my whole life." She turned away from the window and walked back into the darkened room.

XX

U P AT Harrow, a stillness lay like a weight upon the whole
land. There was no wind in the branches of the oaks and the
water went by the limbs of the willows so slowly that there
was no whispering as it passed. The fields stretched out over the
rim of the world and the Negroes moved over the acres like
figures in a dream landscape. The work went on: the purple and
striped cane was laid end to end in the black earth and from their
joints the new plants sprouted. It came up and grew tall in
the fields and the slaves worked in and out among it. Then there
was harvest, and the cane knives were brought out and the stalks
fell before their bright flashes, but the Negroes did not sing as
they worked.

Stephen sat upon Prince Michael, watching the harvest. The
wooden wagons creaked through the fields, bearing the cane away
to the sugar house, from whose tall stack the black smoke once
more poured. The crushers were again in action, and the thick
juice ran down bubbly and sweet into the vats below. And
Etienne and Little Inch ran from vat to vat, dipping strings of
pecans into the boiling cane juice and greedily eating this home-
made confection.

Stephen moved over his lands and through the refinery, watching it all, taking in the details with unconscious attention. But his eyes were far away, in those distances from which no one ever returns, and his words grew fewer.

It was upon such a day that Aurore Arceneaux came riding up to Harrow in her small carriage, all her belongings packed in valises upon the top. Stephen rode alongside the carriage and greeted her gravely.

"I've come to stay," she said simply. "Harrow needs a woman's hand, and 'tis no good that the boy goes motherless. You don't mind, do you, Stephen? 'Tis lonely out at Bellefont. Here I might be able to help."

"No," Stephen said. "I don't mind. But ye're still a young and lovely woman. There are those who might think ill of this."

"Let them," Aurore said. "If there are any sinful ideas left in an old spinster of thirty-one years, 'tis time we had them out, don't you think?"

"Aye," Stephen smiled, with almost a twinkle in his bleak eyes. "Perhaps I shall add ye to the legion of women I am supposed to have kept. But come up to the house. I'll have Caleen prepare quarters for ye."

Going into the great hall, Aurore's eyes noticed the tiny evidences of slackening discipline: dust upon the lower rungs of the furniture; the rugs neither beaten nor swept; a lack of freshness in the livery of the servants. These things must end, she decided at once. Harrow must still be the greatest house in Louisiana.

When Caleen showed her to her rooms, Aurore turned to her.

"Get Suzette and the other women, Tante," she said firmly. "We shall have a house-cleaning here."

In a few hours the great house shone like new: the cut-glass glistened and the silver sparkled. Fresh embroidered chair covers appeared; tablecloths glowed whitely in the gentle light. Aurore went in search of Etienne, and found the boy, dirty and unkempt, playing cards with Little Inch back of the stables.

"Come with me, 'Tienne," she said gently. "And you too, Inch."

Wonderingly, the boys followed her into the house. She led

318

them upstairs to the little bathing chamber. Then Inch was sent for water and, under Aurore's direction, scrubbed his young master vigorously. Afterwards, the little black boy was sent away to bathe himself, and Aurore busied herself trimming 'Tienne's great black mane of hair. Then, brushed and combed and dressed in new, fresh clothing, he stood before her for inspection.

"Ah, now you look the gentleman!" she said. "Please go and bring me your books, 'Tienne."

The boy scampered away, adoration glowing in his pale blue eyes. When he returned, Aurore had him read to her. His education, she discovered, was sadly lacking. So, gently, she began to instruct him. She read him the stories dear to the heart of a boy: tales of the heroes of old France and the new, deeds of chivalry and heroism. Many of the stories stressed the idea of *noblesse oblige* so precious to the aristocratic South. A gentleman, Etienne learned, had many more and much greater responsibilities than an ordinary mortal. His blue eyes were grave as they gazed upon his lovely young aunt. Perhaps it would be better after all to follow the much more attractive pursuit of gambling upon the river packets as his father had done instead of attempting to sustain the rôle of a gentleman planter. Still, as Stephen Fox's son, he was already beginning to be admired, respected, and sought after; even Stephen Le Blanc looked up to him as a personage and the Le Blancs were people of no mean importance. This, 'Tienne liked—definitely. There was a certain pleasure in lording it over Inch, but this was not to be compared with the exquisite joy of receiving homage from whites as well. No, Etienne decided with grave precocity, there was no escaping his destiny.

So—after a fashion—life went on at Harrow. Aurore ran the big house with effortless grace. The slaves soon found that her firmness was tempered by a native kindness of heart that went much further in attending to their smallest wants than Odalie's sense of the obligations of a gentlewoman had ever done. Universally the Negroes of Harrow had admired and respected their former mistress; the new one they loved.

But already tongues had begun to wag in New Orleans, that

city in which a certain fine preoccupation with the morals of others had always been a pleasant substitute for too close attention to one's own. In truth, however, it was among Aurore's closest friends that concern was most acute.

"I don't like it," Andre said bluntly to his wife. "I know too well how she feels toward him."

Amelia smiled.

"A fact," she said gently, "to which I am indebted for a very sweet and charming husband."

"Melia!"

"Don't let it trouble you, Andre. I've long since become reconciled to the idea that I was your second choice. Love has very little pride."

"But it isn't true!" Andre spluttered; "I didn't even know you then!"

"And you objected very strenuously to even meeting me," Amelia teased. "You had no use for 'lean, American females.'"

"You've been talking to Stephen. I should shoot him."

"A very dangerous business, my husband. Besides, I'm far from lean and that was long ago."

Andre bent and kissed the soft cheek.

"You're an angel," he said. "Completely an angel."

"No, I'm not. But about this business, I agree with you. Perhaps I should talk to Aurore . . ."

Andre frowned.

"No," he said, "I think not. I doubt that it would do any good. Aurore can be terribly stubborn in her own quiet way."

They sighed and a silence fell between them.

Up at Harrow, Aurore lay awake listening to Stephen's footsteps in the great hall. Back and forth they went, back and forth in a slow measured tread. But at one place they stopped. Aurore knew that this was before the portrait, glowing with unearthly loveliness upon the wall. How many nights had she heard those footsteps now—walking through the darkness and well into the dawn. The lines from Shakespeare kept echoing through her head:

"Sleep no more! Macbeth hath murdered sleep!"

320

The good God knows Stephen had murdered sleep both for himself and her. And in this lay clearly the road to madness. But now, suddenly, frighteningly, there was silence. With fingers so shaken that they could hardly tie a knot, Aurore drew on her robe. Then putting her tiny feet into her slippers, she stole out into the hall. There was no sound but the pounding of her heart like a muffled drum beneath her ribs. But she went forward until she reached the picture. Before it, curled up in a big chair, Stephen slept. Exhaustion had finally done its work.

Aurore leaned close, where the candles glowed softly in the silver candlesticks. There was so much of torment there in the still face that she could feel the pain lying very cold and deep next to her heart, like the blade of a sharp knife. She leaned closer, studying his face. The mouth, so stern and commanding when he was awake, in sleep was pitiful and lost like the lips of a child. Even the mockery was gone and in its stead were only bewilderment and deep abiding hurt.

She had an impulse to smother his face against her breasts and rock to and fro, crooning to him softly. She straightened up abruptly, sure that the drumroll of her heart would awaken him. But still he slept. Again she leaned forward.

"Do not grieve, my Stephen," she whispered. "Never in the world was she worth so much pain. Not she nor any woman. Merciful saints, how ill he looks!"

Stephen half turned in his sleep so that his face was raised a little. Aurore's face moved closer until her lips were almost touching his.

"You kissed me once," she murmured. "In laughter and diablerie—I give you back your kiss, my Stephen. But God knows I mean no mockery." Her lips touched his as lightly as a breath; but involuntarily they lingered and moved caressingly over his. Then without opening his eyes, Stephen's lean arms, hard as corded steelwire, stole upward around her, drawing her downward to him. She struggled briefly, and the pale blue eyes flew wide.

"Aurore!"

"Oh, my God," she wept. "Oh, my God!"

321

He held her firmly in his arms, his eyes studying her face.

"Ye kissed me," he said. "Why?"

"Please, Stephen," she whispered. "Let me go—please, Stephen, please!"

"Not until ye explain this."

"There's no explanation—none that I can give. Forget it happened. Forgive me—and let me go—away from here—miles away from here."

"No," he said gravely. "No. I must understand this thing."

She lay very quietly in his arms. Then she buried her face against his chest so that her voice was muffled and thick with tears.

"I love you," she said. "Always I've loved you—since the day you stood in the Place D'Armes when de Lafayette came. You stood there and stared and stared at Odalie until my heart broke quite in two. I thought you so beautiful, Stephen—like a young god. And since then it has grown worse. Whatever you did— your carelessness, your mockery, your quadroon wench, your loving Odalie—I forgave you, Stephen. I could forgive you anything. I lived only for the precious minutes when I should see you, and between them only in the hope of seeing you again. And now that I am become a shameless thing not fit to associate with decent people will you please let me go?"

Stephen lay very still, but his arms did not move.

"There is nothing left in me of love, Aurore," he said gently, "but 'tis certain I cannot live alone for long. That I know. Already I am unsure between the real and the dreamed. Perhaps in time I can learn again to feel as a man ought."

He stopped, gazing upward at the picture.

"We shall be married at once," he said. "God knows that never before was a man so honored. Ye must know how grateful I am —how simply and humbly grateful."

Aurore lifted her face to his and on her face the tears were cold and wet.

Late in the morning of the following day, the great yellow coach from Harrow rode up the long driveway that curved away from the wrought-iron gates of La Place des Rivières. The usual

322

crowd of Negro children scampered laughingly around it, almost beneath the wheels. Ti Demon met them at the foot of the stairs, his popeyes rolling in his wizened black face.

"Monsieur Stephen and Mam'zelle Aurore," he bawled. Then bowing, he opened the door of the coach.

Stephen stepped down. He was flawlessly attired in the very latest fashion: no longer was his neck encased only in a dark stock; instead a huge cravat of silk crowded the space above his brocaded maroon waistcoat with its roll collar and the high, sharply pointed white collar of the shirt itself. In the great knob of the cravat, the big pearl stickpin gleamed softly. The new coffee-colored clawhammer coat contrasted sharply with the faun-colored trousers, which, unlike those of the decade before, clung to every inch of Stephen's well-turned legs, and were anchored beneath the instep of his shoes with a strap. On his head the tall beaver sat at a jaunty angle, but his face was lined and grave.

He extended his hand into the coach and helped Aurore down. Her face was pale with nervousness above the dress of changeable silk with the tight sleeves. Her chestnut curls bobbed as she stepped down from the coach, but on the back of her neck she wore a huge knot of her own soft hair as an indication of her modernity—a fashion which was not to become general until almost a year later.

Amelia came down the stairs to meet them, her face alight with pleasure and both hands outstretched.

"At last!" she laughed. "I was beginning to believe that you two would never again honor La Place."

"The honor is ours," Stephen said, "that still ye receive us. But truthfully, my dear Amelia, we come to seek your aid."

"So? You plan a party perhaps? I'll be only too glad . . ."

"No," Stephen said bluntly. "A wedding."

Amelia's coral lips formed a soft *O*, but she said nothing, standing there staring at them while her eyebrows climbed toward her ash blonde hair.

Aurore went up to her and put her arms around her neck.

"Please forgive us," she said. "I know how terrible it sounds . . ."

323

Amelia smiled down at her friend.

"I'm glad," she said. "It's unconventional and will make a scandal, but it's the right thing—especially since you've lived up at Harrow all these months . . ."

"Amelia!" Aurore's voice was stricken. "Surely you don't think that I—that we—"

"Of course not," Amelia said. "I know you too well, both of you. But there are others who don't. It was of them that I was thinking. Come into the house. I've already sent Ti Demon for Andre."

The two women locked arms and started up the stairs. Stephen strode along beside them, looking from one to the other.

"I'm glad of one thing," he remarked. "At least ye don't think me a monster, Amelia."

"You're too stupid to be a scoundrel, Stephen," Amelia mocked.

"Stupid?" Stephen echoed blankly. "This from ye I didn't expect!"

"That you could have looked into Aurore's face all these years and not discovered how she worshipped you called for a stupendous amount of stupidity, Stephen. Even Andre knew, and God knows he's not overly bright."

"Thus do American women speak of their husbands!" Stephen laughed. "Perhaps I've done well to escape them."

"Perhaps you have," Amelia smiled. "And then, perhaps you might have been agreeably surprised."

"As Andre was. I envy ye both your happiness."

"Soon you will have no cause to. It's made up of many things, Stephen—deep and abiding love, and mutual trust and respect. There is tenderness in it, too, and a certain sharing of sorrows—but it's wonderful, Stephen, and life is no good without it."

"Aye," Stephen said grimly. "That I know."

"And sometimes you must laugh—without mockery—and at yourself . . ."

"Ye're lecturing me?" Stephen growled in mock anger.

"Yes. You need it. Aurore doesn't. She's an angel. But laughter is important. I shall never forget my poor Andre's face the morning after you took him to that filthy quadroon ball—he was so abject. He thought I was going to leave him—as if I could live two minutes without him, the fat rogue! He looked so pitiful that I couldn't keep from laughing and there the matter ended."

Stephen threw back his head and laughed aloud. But Aurore's face was white and still. Amelia squeezed her arm.

"Forgive me, Aurore," she whispered. "I do talk too much, don't I?"

"It's nothing," Aurore said. "Only I want to forget that he ever belonged to anyone else. 'Tis hard, but I'll manage."

When Andre came in from the fields and was told the news, he fairly danced with glee.

"So," he chortled. "At last, my old one, you begin to develop intelligence. I was on the point of giving you up as hopeless. When is it to be?"

"Tomorrow—with your aid."

"So soon? Well 'tis best at that. We'll have to rush, however. Who will officiate?"

"Father DuGois," Stephen said. "If he will."

"Then we'd best ride into New Orleans and make the arrangements. Aurore can stay here tonight with Amelia. But I must have the honor of buying you your last bachelor dinner. Give me half an hour in which to dress. Now I must go and tell Ti Demon to saddle fresh horses for us."

They rode first to the rectory of the cathedral and sought out the old priest. Stephen had feared that Father DuGois would object, but the aged man's wisdom was in his heart, not drawn from dogma. He agreed calmly.

Stephen's face was still as they left the Saint Louis Cathedral, but at last his eyes were clear and untroubled.

"And now," Andre said, "about that dinner . . . ?"

"Anywhere you say," Stephen told him; "but I fear that I have scant appetite."

The next evening, the yellow coach drew up before the cathedral, and Andre and Amelia and Stephen and Aurore got out.

To their vast astonishment, the stalls were filled with spectators.

"How on earth?" Aurore gasped.

"Negro grapevine," Andre said grimly. "I shall have Ti Demon whipped!"

"Or perhaps Georges," Stephen added. "At any rate, 'tis not to be helped now. Come, my dear."

Father DuGois made the ceremony mercifully brief. Still, in his quiet way, he managed to get so much of beauty into it that at last Aurore's nervousness vanished and her face was transfixed with happiness. When she lifted her mouth to her husband, there in the light of the candles, in an atmosphere filled with the perfume of flowers, even those who had come to mock were stilled.

The four of them left the church together, and the spectators filed out after them into the street.

"We shall go to the town house," Stephen said. "I had Pouilly finish it, but it was never occupied. The wedding supper, unfortunately, will have to be supplied by caterers. Afterwards, we will decide upon a honeymoon . . ."

" 'Tis overlate for that," Aurore declared. "Just being with you will be enough. Afterwards we can go back to Harrow and take up what there is left of our lives."

The wedding supper was a good one, with much wine. Afterwards, Stephen urged the Le Blancs to remain overnight. The house was large enough, he declared, for two loving couples not to interfere with one another. But Andre declined with thanks.

"No house is large enough for more than two upon a wedding night," he laughed. So, immensely pleased and well filled with wine, he and Amelia started homeward in a hired carriage.

After they had gone, it was very still at Bonheure, as Odalie had christened the new house which she did not live to enter. Stephen looked at his bride and hesitated. So much of love was there upon her face and shining out of her clear hazel eyes that he was awed and humbled. She followed him with her glance each time he moved, until the silence grew heavy between them. At last Stephen walked toward her. 'Tis better that it begins, he thought, our life together. Perhaps this will dispel the other.

But as he bent toward her, a sound rose through the windows, a noise of many voices roaring:

"Monsieur Fox left his wife
And took upon himself a nigger
Cut her with a carving knife,
But now he's seeking something bigger—"

Stephen stood there frozen, holding Aurore in his arms. Then, his almost white brows bristling, he crossed to the window. Aurore followed. Down below the house the street was filled with a merry, jostling mob. In their midst they bore a coffin, open, in which an effigy lay. Half a glance told them that this was supposed to represent Odalie. Beside the coffin dangled two effigies, clad in bridal costumes: these were himself and Aurore.

"Stephen," Aurore wept, "Oh Stephen!"

"So he made mock of his wife,
Laughing even as he kissed her
And when she took her leave of life—
At once he married with her sister!"

Stephen's hand went into his pocket and came out with the derringer.

"No, Stephen, no!" Aurore said. "That's not the way."

He turned and stared at her. Then, slowly, he pocketed the pistol.

"Aye," he growled. "I know how to still the beasts! Feed them!"

He left the room and quickly came back with two heavy leather bags.

"This was to pay for our honeymoon," he said. "But there is more where it came from."

Quietly, Stephen opened the window. Then dipping both hands into the leather bags, he scattered silver dollars out over the streets. Instantly the mob stopped singing and began to fight over the silver. When each man had gathered a few, they looked up with rare good humor.

"Good for you, Monsieur Fox," they shouted. "That's a sport! For so much money you can marry my sister!" Then one by one they left the street until it was empty and still.

In the corner, Aurore wept miserably.

Stephen crossed to her and took her again in his arms.

"I'm sorry, my dearest," he said. "But this ye must expect when ye marry a blackguard."

"But I didn't," she whispered, her lips trembling into something very like a smile, "I married a prince. And if he doesn't kiss me soon, I shall die!"

Stephen bent and kissed her gently. Her lips were salt with the taste of tears.

She drew back, looking at him.

"No, no!" she whispered huskily. "Not like that! I'm no longer your sister remember!"

Stephen's fair brows flew upward.

"And how shall I kiss ye, my dearest?"

"Like this," she murmured. "Like this . . ."

A few days later, Stephen engaged a young Creole, a son of a distinguished family, to manage Harrow during his absence. This business finished, he and Aurore took their leave of the Le Blancs and engaged a stateroom aboard a packet bound upriver. By this means they could travel in great comfort all the way to New York via the new Erie Canal. Etienne became a member of Andre's household for the duration of the honeymoon, and set about a career of such extravagant misbehavior that his hosts were many times tempted to write Stephen to cut short his journey and come to their rescue.

For the rest of the summer, the Foxes stayed at a fashionable hotel at Saratoga Springs, making, of course, trips into Philadelphia and New York. And behind the fans of the matrons at the great watering place, the whispers ran. All the old stories were dusted off, repolished and brought out with new and original twists, for among the many guests not a few were

Louisianians and, of these, fewer still had been nodding acquaintances of Stephen's in New Orleans.

But slowly, to his own astonishment, Stephen was being forced to the realization that he was actually happy. Aurore made an enchanting wife. Her own joy laid a glow upon her, so that her soft loveliness became vivid and men looked at her as they had once gazed upon Odalie.

"Prettiest woman here—Madame Fox," the young blades declared. "'Pon my honor she is!"

Even more marked was the change in Stephen. The lines in his face relaxed. He smiled often and freely. And people who, fearful of his scowling countenance, had avoided him in the beginning of the season, now went out of their way to meet him at its end.

Aurore teased him, played with him, laughed at him, and loved him with all her heart.

"Stephen," she said. "Let's pretend I'm your mistress instead of your wife."

"Why?" he demanded. "What on earth gave ye such an idea!"

"Men love their mistresses better than they do their wives."

"Not when they have such a wife as ye," Stephen laughed. "Ye're wife and mistress and good angel and plaguing imp all rolled up in one package. A very sweet package at that."

"Did you," she teased, "say package—or baggage?"

"Aurore! What a word for ye to use!"

"But I am a baggage. I'm your baggage. And I like it very much!"

"Well, so long as ye confine your activities to me," Stephen said, "I shan't mind, too much!"

In the fall, they returned to Harrow, and the great house came alive. There were endless parties and soirées and entertainments. And the gentry of New Orleans came: after all one could not hold flouting convention against such a charming couple as the Foxes. There was one convention, however, that Aurore did not disregard. She waited almost two years, until the fall of 1841, before presenting Stephen with an eight-pound daughter, delivered without the slightest fuss or bother. They called the child Julie.

XXI

I**N MAY** of 1853, Stephen Fox rode through the broad fields of Harrow on a tour of inspection. These trips were frequent, for, although he now had no less than five competent overseers, still he loved the sights and sounds of his own lands. Etienne had been in France for almost three years now, studying in Paris. Behind Stephen, on a shaggy, fat Shetland pony, bu little bigger than a large dog, rode his daughter, Julie. From time to time, Stephen turned to look back at her, and each time his hard blue eyes softened and warmed with pleasure.

At eleven, Julie was already a beauty. The heritage of her father had lightened her hair to a coppery gold, but her eyes were as black as Odalie's had been. Her face, however, had the shape, the softness, and the general expression of her mother's, although there was a look of gentle mischief about her that came more, perhaps, from Stephen.

The whole plantation, while it had grown only slightly in acreage, and was rivaled in this regard by three or four others in Louisiana, was producing almost triple its yield of ten or twelve years before. Stephen had had it completely re-equipped, employing the new multiple-effects process invented by the same

Robert Rilleux who had been for a time in his employ, and the even more revolutionary centrifugal machine which separated in minutes more sugar from molasses than the cone drip method had done in days. The sugar produced at Harrow was now pure white and finely powdered, thanks to the fact that Stephen extensively employed bisulphate of lime for bleaching purposes. His white sugar, as a result, commanded a much higher price on the market than the brown hard lumped product of most of his conservative Creole neighbors.

The land was good to look upon. The cane grew up in the fields and the cloudless blue sky crowned the earth with a dome of sapphire. Stephen looked down upon his daughter and smiled.

" 'Tis something, this land," he said.

Julie looked all around her, her black eyes dancing.

"You know, Papa," she declared, accenting the second syllable of the word French fashion, "I think Harrow is the prettiest place in all the world!"

"Aye," Stephen smiled. "So it is; but 'twas not alone of Harrow that I spoke. I mean the whole land—all of it."

"You've seen it all, haven't you, Papa?"

"No—not nearly. I've never been west of Texas. 'Tis said that the territories of New Mexico and Utah are something to be seen, and the state of California beggars description. And in the Northern states there are great forests and mighty rivers and cities bigger than New Orleans."

Julie's eyes grew round.

"But the people—they're so strange," she said. "And they hate us so."

Stephen looked at his daughter.

"Ye've been talking to the Le Blancs," he said. "In that ye wrong the Northerners. Some of my best friends live in Philadelphia and New York. They don't hate us, Julie—'tis only slavery that they hate."

"Why?" the girl asked. "Stephen Le Blanc says it's a holy system ordained by God. Why should they hate it?"

"My young namesake and godson echoes his father. I call that statement extravagant. But if I were to try to explain the reason

331

why the North hates slavery, I should only confuse ye. It goes a long way back, even into the mentalities of the two regions."

"But I'd like to know."

Stephen frowned.

"I'm not sure I know myself, truly," he said. "But the difference lies in the minds of men. In the North, Julie, the climate is cold and that makes much of the difference."

"The climate?"

"Aye. The blood flows briskly through the veins in a cold land and work is a pleasure. 'Tis uncomfortable only to be still. Therefore, no prejudice ever arose against a gentleman's working."

"But Stephen says there are no gentlemen in the North."

Stephen laughed.

"My godson is no oracle, Julie. Ye must not accept his views without question. In fact, I think ye should see less of him. 'Twill be many years before the two of ye can marry."

"So long? To hear Monsieur Le Blanc talk, you'd think we were already married."

" 'Tis Andre's pet dream. But I want to be sure that the two of ye are really suited. Marriage is not to be taken too lightly."

"But you and mother are so happy."

"Aye. But then your mother is an angel, and 'tis to be doubted that ye are!"

"Now you're laughing at me again," Julie said. "But I don't mind. Go on, tell me more about the North."

"The North? I thought ye'd forgotten that. Well, since no objection to labor exists in the genteel classes, it follows that labor is honorable. Then, too, because of the climate, the North is no place for blacks. They die of the cold. Much of it is devoted to industry, to factories . . ."

"Stephen says—" Julie began, but her father looked at her. She halted abruptly.

"Go on," Stephen said kindly. "What does the lad say now?"

"That the Northern factory workers are far worse off than the Nigras."

"In that, he is not far wrong. But the point is, Julie, that since slavery is unprofitable in the North, 'tis easy for them to oppose

332

it. They do so on moral grounds—that 'tis wrong to buy and sell men like cattle. But if they made money from it, ye'd see how fast they'd change their tune. Their workers live almost in starvation, and when they become old and weak, out they go to die."

"We're good to the Nigras," Julie observed. "I just love Tante Caleen!"

"Aye. Caleen is a wonderful woman. Ye should have known her when she was younger. Here in the South, Julie, we find the system to our profit, so we deify it. And that, too, is wrong."

"Why?"

"There is much that is wrong with slavery, Julie. Ye've never seen the wrongs, because they are not practiced at Harrow. Here we do not whip the Negroes, or sell them away from the plantation or separate families. But those things are done—not so very often, yet they are done."

"Then it is wrong to hold slaves, Papa?"

"That I don't know. If the Negro had the mentality of the white race, I should be forced to say aye. But he seems quite happy and contented with his lot. There have been only the fewest insurrections in this country. Your Anglo-Saxon and your Frenchman on the other hand would gladly starve in freedom than live in comfort as a slave. But perhaps it would be only the greatest unkindness to free the Negro—he would be helpless without a kindly, guiding hand. But enough of this—we're wasting time."

They rode on through the fields where the gangs of Negroes sang as they worked, and the Spring breezes whispered through the cane. Julie looked at her father, splendid on the palomino that he had bred, one of the many descendants of the original Prince Michael. Her face shone with admiration.

"Papa," she said. "Tell me about what you did in the war."

Stephen frowned.

"I rode endless miles," he said. "I ate bad food and drank foul water. And finally I came home to your poor, dear patient mother."

"Oh, Papa!" Julie wailed. "That's all you ever say about it. You must have been brave—they made you a major. Tell me about the battles."

"I remember the morning we landed at Vera Cruz," Stephen said, one white eyebrow settling wickedly down over an eye. "We went ashore in boats—under the guns. The ships had bombarded the town for days. When we hit the shore we charged up in the sand with bayonets fixed, and fingers so tight on the triggers that some poor fellows fired off their muskets and had to rely on the bayonets alone for the charge." He stopped and drew out a short pipe of white clay from his pocket. Then he searched for tobacco while Julie waited breathlessly. Finally he found it, filled his pipe and lit it with a sulphur match. The fragrant blue smoke swirled upward around his head.

"Please, Papa!"

"Eh, what? Oh, yes, when we got to the top what d'ye think happened?"

"You fought the Mexicans," Julie said, "and beat them, didn't you, Papa?"

"Well—not exactly. Ye see, Julie, when we got to the top, there wasn't a soul in sight—not a greaser to Moses. So we just stood there leaning on our guns and cussing and panting like the devil. And there before us lay the whole of Mexico without a Mexican in it!"

"Oh, Papa!" Julie said. "You're mean."

"So I've often been told."

"But you were brave. I know you were. Stephen Le Blanc told me that his papa said you fought at Monterey, Contreras, Churubusio, Chapultepec, and Mexico City!"

"Aye, and I suppose I dictated the terms of Guadalupe Hidalgo? Yes, Julie, I fought at all those places and more—though ye couldn't recognize them from your pronunciation. But there is this to be remembered about war—'tis a bloody, nauseating, murderous business—with no chivalry in it, and no glamor. And that war was outrageously unjust."

"Papa!"

"So it was, little Julie. The Mexican government invited American settlers into the province of Texas on condition that the new immigrants be either Catholic or be willing to submit to conversion. The whole time I was there, Julie, more than two years, I met not one person of our faith. They chased away the good Spanish priests, and abused the Mexican police. When they went in they had no other purpose than to steal the land from Mexico in order to further slave territory. Our army was miles inside of Mexican territory when we were attacked. And I have my doubts as to who fired the first shot."

"But Monsieur Le Blanc says that the treaties—you know, I can't remember all that—that Texas was a part of Louisiana and that Mexico took it!"

"Another example, my dear Julie, of our Southern faculty for perverting the truth. That is one thing about the Northerners, they lie to others, but never to themselves. Your Southerner sits like a Hindu and fascinates himself with his own mislogic before he applies it to others."

"But we're a very honorable people. You know that, Papa."

"Aye—we talk honor until 'tis like the refrain of a musical ditty. But what city of the North would put up with the municipal corruption of New Orleans, which hasn't had an honest election since the French left? Who else would stomach our sewer system? Who else would hush up yearly epidemics because they are bad for business?"

"Papa—why did you fight in that war—then?"

Stephen laughed. "I didn't know all the facts, Julie, and at forty-five I was still young enough to be touchy on the questions of patriotism and national honor. And everybody else was going. Now I wouldn't go."

Stephen half rose in the stirrups and looked out over the fields.

"We'd best be going back now," he said. "Your mother will have dinner ready."

They turned their mounts in a circle and headed back toward Harrow. For several minutes Julie was silent. Then no longer able to resist the temptation to converse with her beloved parent, she began again:

"Papa, do you think I'll ever be as beautiful as Mother?"

"That—aye. Almost ye are now. I only hope that ye develop her character."

"Mother is so wonderful," Julie sighed. "I remember the Sauve

335

Crevasse. You were in Philadelphia at the time, and Mother rode all day and all night directing the Negroes who were working on the levee. Of course it didn't do any good—we were flooded just the same, but Mother was so brave!"

"Aye," Stephen said softly, "I am the most fortunate of men to have such a wife."

They trotted briskly up to the oak alley, but the short legs of Julie's pony limited their speed. When the house came in sight, gleaming whitely among the trees, Julie exclaimed for the thousandth time with pleasure.

"Our house is beautiful—isn't it, Papa?"

On the gallery, Aurore waited.

"Stephen," she called, as her husband dismounted. "A letter just came from Etienne! He's on his way back. He should be here within the week!"

Julie bounced down from her pony and began to dance up and down like a plump, pink-cheeked doll.

"'Tienne's coming!" she cried. "'Tienne's coming! Oh, Mother, how nice!"

Stephen strode up the steps to kiss his wife, and his eyes were filled with joy.

"So," he said, as his lips brushed the soft cheek. "'Twill be good to have the lad back again."

They went in together into the great hall. Inside, Caleen waited. Now so old that she herself had forgotten her years, she had changed but little; she was thinner, and a little more stooped. All the Foxes confidentially expected her to live forever. Now she was smiling, a wide, toothless smile.

"Ah, Caleen," Stephen said. "We will see our lads again. Ye had a message from Inch, of course?"

"Yas, maître," the old woman said. "He wrote me, him. Maîtresse read it to me. He writes beautiful, like a white!"

"Indeed he does," Aurore said. "Do you know, Stephen, that Inch's letter was actually freer from error than 'Tienne's? He writes a lovely, fluent French."

"The lad has a head. 'Tis true of many blacks, I'm told. We did not make the same error as the French did in Haiti and Saint

336

Domingue of attempting to enslave those intelligent ones. We chose our Negroes more wisely."

The dinner went by rapidly, paced by Stephen's gently cynical talk. He poked sharp fun at Aurore and Julie and also the Le Blancs.

"He has become a fanatic, that Andre," he laughed. "Always 'tis politics, politics, politics! A man grows weary of it. The crime of admitting California as a free state. The tardiness of carving up Texas to equal the Northern electoral votes. He is resigned to Oregon because it lies so far North, but when ye mention the District of Columbia, he foams at the mouth! He calls it a direct slap at the South that the capital of the nation should be free soil."

"Well," Aurore said. "Isn't it?"

"Ye too? After all, my dearest, we've gained many advantages. Slavery can be made legal all over the nation."

"Only if the people permit it," Aurore observed.

"Ye're a sharp one! There lies the weakness. They won't permit it. Ye see what their reaction is to the Fugitive Slave Law. Violence. Naked and ugly violence. And it will grow. This system of theirs which aids escaping Negroes—the Underground Railway, I think 'tis called—is but a symptom."

"Then what is the answer, Stephen—secession?"

Stephen frowned, his silver-white brows, from which every trace of the gold of his youth had completely disappeared, knitted together over his nose.

"That—no. The Union must be preserved."

"An unpopular notion, nowadays, my husband. We don't need the North—and they do need us."

"That is typically Southern, Aurore, and typically wrongheaded. They could continue to flourish if we perished tomorrow. While we . . ."

"They have no cotton."

"Aye—but the lands to the South, Mexico, the central Americas, the Argentine have climates in which it would grow as well as here. And already the English are planting it in Egypt and India. But we cannot exist without the products of their industry

337

of which we have almost none. We depend upon England to support us, but England has long ago freed her slaves, and her abolitionists are outspoken and respected. Then, if it comes to that, the North will go into woollens."

"But England depends upon us for nearly all her cotton."

"She will never fight for us, mark ye. She would rejoice to see us destroy the nation in a fratricidal war—then she'd realize her own territorial ambitions in this land."

"Then what must we do, Stephen?"

"Free the Negroes by gradual emancipation—and retain them upon the land under small wages and our patronage. We could limit their movements and control them as well as now, and remove at the same time the squeamish ethical questions that plague the North."

"That would be hypocrisy," Aurore said clearly.

"Admitted. Here in the South we've already raised it to a fine art. But 'tis that or the North will destroy us."

"Never," Aurore said spiritedly. "We could whip them without half trying."

"No, my dearest, we could not. Ye forget how much time I've spent in the North. They could put four men in the field for our one and twenty times the artillery and equipment. And they are no less brave than we. Naked courage no longer wins wars."

He rose from his place.

"Forgive me," he said. "I must ride out again to finish my tour. But one thing more. 'Tis the nation I love, not any one part of it. I would not see it rent asunder. 'Twill stretch, my dearest, from sea to sea, from Canada to Mexico; and already 'tis the last, best hope of man. Never upon earth has the poor man, the commoner, had such freedom; never has there been so much respect for the essential dignity of mankind. The kings and captains revile it because as long as it exists their empires of exploitation, misery and degradation totter, and men everywhere have hope."

Aurore lifted her face to be kissed. But at the last she could not refrain from teasing Stephen.

"Even the Negroes?" she asked.

Stephen looked at her, his pale eyes alight under the snowy brows. The strands of white in his red hair caught the light and gleamed like silver.

"Aye," he said at last. "Even the blacks. We shall find men with minds like Inch's among them, and in the end they will take their part in the nation." Then he was gone, striding through the great hall and out upon the gallery.

Stephen's face was frowning as he mounted his horse. It was one thing to begin a line of thought, but quite another to follow it to its logical conclusion. The Founding Fathers had had no such difficulties: there had been no coldly logical abolitionists to point out to Jefferson, for instance, that when he penned his immortal: "All men are created equal, and are endowed by their Creator with certain inalienable rights; that among these are life, liberty, and the pursuit of happiness—" he necessarily included the slaves who worked his broad Virginia acres. Of course the Negroes were better off as slaves than they would be if freed, but that again was quite a different thing from saying that they were happier than they would have been if they had been left upon their native shores. God knows, they hadn't asked to be brought away from Africa. Then was it really necessary to justify this thing from an ethical standpoint? This was economics —not ethics; and his Philadelphia business friends made no apologies for their sharp trading practices. But the South had been forced into the awkward position of apology, explanation, and defense, and the bitterness of the quarrel was growing hourly. How would it all end? Stephen's head ached at the thought.

Thinking thus, he rounded the curve that brought him in sight of the private burial ground of Harrow. Abruptly his hand tightened upon the reins, for there before him was a short, ugly horse, standing riderless in the road. Stephen reined in closer. There was no mistaking that long head and shaggy coat, nor those short, powerful legs: this was a prairie horse—a mustang, a breed never seen in Louisiana.

Stephen looked on both sides of the road. An instant later, his gaze came to rest upon the rider. He was a tall man with inky black hair, and just now he was standing very quietly before the tomb of Odalie. Stephen swung down from the palomino and approached him. When he was but a yard away the stranger turned. There was the passage of hard, slow years written in that face and the savage erosion of wind and sun, but Stephen recognized it at once.

"Phillippe," he said, "Phillippe Cloutier! So ye've come back again."

"Yes," Phillippe said. "I've come back. But years too late, I see. If I had come before I might have saved her all the misery you brought her. I might even have saved her life."

Stephen looked at him, his blue eyes very clear beneath the white brows.

"No rancor, Phillippe," he said slowly. "The cause of our quarrel rests in peace, and what ye might have done is neither here nor there. Ye had your chance—as good if not a better one than I. She came to me of her own free will. Before she died all our difficulties had been solved or forgiven. I can't submit to your judgment. 'Tis none of your affair and never was. Still I want no quarrel with ye."

"You'll have none," Phillippe said. "What's done is done. Forgive me my harshness. Seventeen years in Texas are no aid to good manners." Awkwardly he put out his hand. Stephen took it firmly.

"Why did ye come back?" he asked. "I've heard ye mentioned to succeed Houston. Ye made quite a place for yourself there."

"Rosemont. Clothilde died a month ago, and Henriette is married and moved to Baton Rouge. My only choice was to sell it, and I couldn't bring myself to do that. Besides there is my daughter to think of."

"Ye have a daughter? That I didn't know. Ye could not have been too troubled about Odalie to have taken upon yourself a wife."

"I took no wife," Phillippe said harshly. "Ceclie is a natural child. Her mother was a squatter's daughter—part Navaho and

340

part Irish—two very savage races," he added with a wicked grin.

Stephen threw back his head and laughed aloud.

"Then ye have trouble upon your hands," he said. "I don't envy ye, Phillippe."

"She is difficult," Phillippe admitted. "That was another reason for returning to civilized territory. Though I can't say that Louisiana is overly civilized—what with your riots and other difficulties."

"Ye mean that Lopez affair? That was something. It brought us to the brink of war with Spain. But that's a long story. Still if ye have the time . . ."

"I'll ride with you," Phillippe said. "I need to be brought up to date upon the affairs of New Orleans. Texas is like another world."

He mounted the short prairie horse and the two of them rode away toward the bayou road.

"The point was," Stephen told him, "that there were many who wanted Cuba free of Spain for commercial reasons and also for possible annexation as new slave territory. But there were still more who were simply spoiling for a fight. So when Lopez came they flocked to him. Ye knew Wheat and Crittenden, didn't ye?"

Phillippe nodded.

"Wheat was captured and released, but Crittenden was executed. The secretary to the Spanish Consul brought back the letters from the condemned man to New Orleans, but refused to surrender them. Then some damned fool wrote an editorial in *La Union*, the Spanish newspaper, describing in detail how Crittenden went to his death, and upholding the Spanish Government. So our good New Orleans citizenry wrecked the offices of *La Union*, and topped it off by doing a neat job upon the Spanish Consulate, burning the Spanish flag and attempting to lynch the Consul. They'd have done that too, but Pepe Lulla saved us from actual war by parading through the streets with a sword in each hand at the Consul's side, thus getting him safely out of town. He later killed four men in duels over the insult to his country's flag. That cooled your New Orleanians' ardor considerably."

"Comic opera, New Orleans style," Phillippe said. "The old place never changes, does it?"

"No, but it grows. Ye've seen the St. Louis Hotel?"

"Yes—and the Saint Charles. I must admit that the food is excellent at both."

"And the wines. We've had a time of it since ye left, Phillippe. We've moved our business section from Chartres to Canal, we've grown to the fourth city in size in the country, we've been visited again by Old Hickory, and by your Sam Houston, and we've fought a war . . ."

"I heard that you bore yourself very well in that. Too bad we never met while you were in Texas."

"Aye. Perhaps then I should have understood the land better. But Texas is a wonderful place."

"'Tis half a world. But go on, what else has happened here?"

"Nothing else of any importance. Ye knew about our panic?"

"Do I? All the loans we were trying to float went haywire."

"Well, apart from the fact that the whole city nearly burned to the ground in '44, and was almost washed away in the Sauve Crevasse flood of '49 . . ."

"But are we becoming civilized? New Orleans boasts of its culture, yet I don't see any signs of its overtaking Paris."

"Ye ask too much," Stephen laughed. "We established a National Art Gallery, and applauded a new singer—Lind, her name is—Jenny Lind. Quite a nice voice. That old rogue, P. T. Barnum, brought her here, but aside from that, and perhaps the new custom of masking in street carnivals just before Lent that some young blades started in '37, we're about the same as before. Last month we were honored by having Pierre Soule, ye know the family—appointed minister to Spain by President Pierce—and that brings ye up to date."

"But what about the people? What's happened to them?"

"I have a grown son who returns this week from his Grand Tour. I wanted him educated in England, but his mother insisted upon France. So after her death, I respected her wishes. I have a daughter, too, who is now almost twelve years of age."

"Mine is sixteen," Phillippe said.

"So? Ye wasted no time in Texas. The Le Blancs have five children of whom two are girls. The Prudhommes continue to repopulate the state, but the Pontablas are dying out."

"And the Cloutiers," Phillippe said sadly. "I am the last to bear the name, Stephen."

"This daughter of yours will carry on the blood at least—and names are not really important."

"No, I guess not—still there was a pride in the name Cloutier in the old days."

They rode on in silence over the vast fields of Harrow.

"I shall need your aid, Stephen," Phillippe said. " 'Tis a long time since I've been in cane lands. I fear the equipment of Rosemont is sadly out of date."

"I shall be glad to help in any way. But come back up to the house. Aurore will be glad to see you."

Phillippe's black brows rose.

"Aurore? What is she doing at Harrow?"

"My wife has every right to be at Harrow, don't ye think?"

"Don't tell me you married Aurore!"

"Of course—why not?"

"No reason—only you seem to have a fatal fascination for the Arceneaux family. Strange I hadn't heard this; but then I arrived in New Orleans only yesterday."

"Ye have no objections, I hope," Stephen said mockingly, "to this second marriage of mine?"

"Would be rather too late if I did," Phillippe declared. "But I must ask to be excused from your invitation for the present. Truthfully, I simply haven't the time. Make my apologies to Madame Fox, won't you? I shall expect you both at Rosemont as soon as the place is put to rights. For that matter I want you to come out before then—I need the benefit of the advice of Louisiana's most successful planter."

Stephen took his hand and Phillippe rode away. Stephen looked after him with a little puzzled frown hovering about his eyes

343

Texas had done something to Phillippe Cloutier. For all his Old World courtliness of speech and manner there was about him now a directness that was completely American, and a suggestion of well-controlled force. Stephen shrugged and turned the horse's head in the direction of the fields. After all, Phillippe's oddities were really no concern of his.

A few days later, the steamer *Le Cygne*, inward bound from France, was towed over the Mississippi bar, and dropped anchor in the harbor at New Orleans. Already there were five ships lying at anchor when *Le Cygne* slipped into line, lying so close together that the four young men upon her upper deck could easily read their names.

"The *Northampton*," Paul Dumaine read gaily, "the *Siri*, the *Camboden Castle*, the *Augusta*, and the *Saxon*. What outlandish names you give your vessels, 'Tienne! Do I say them right?"

Etienne Fox smiled at his friend.

"Your accent is execrable, Paul," he said, "as usual. You should stick to French. Most of New Orleans can still understand it."

"New Orleans!" Paul said. "Father never grew tired of talking about it. I've often wondered why he ever came back to France. There was only one other topic that was more frequently upon his tongue."

"And what was that, Paul?" Etienne asked.

"Your mother. He would run quite out of adjectives attempting to describe her. He kept two dozen paintings of her that he'd done from memory after his return. I always thought them the acme of loveliness, but Father used to weep—quite literally, 'Tienne—at their inadequacy."

"There's one that he did from life," Etienne said. "It hangs at Harrow. You'll see it tonight."

"I know. Father told me about it. He calls it the crowning masterpiece of his career. Until I can equal it, Father says I am no painter."

"Then you're no painter. You'll never be able to touch that one—never!"

The other two men stood a little apart from Etienne and Paul and took no part in the conversation. The face of one of them, a man older by perhaps ten years than any of the others, was somber. He was dressed quietly, but richly, and he wore his clothing well. His frock coat of glistening black broadcloth was pulled back and away from the creamy white doublebreasted waistcoat across which a massive gold watch chain gleamed. Absently he stroked the deep revers of the waistcoat that was cut straight across above his loose-fitting pearl-grey trousers. The huge sloppy bow tie which he wore, as did all of the others, had exactly the correct Parisian effect of studied carelessness so admired by the gentlemen of the 'fifties. But, for all his elegance, his face was troubled beneath the black stovepipe hat.

"What ails ye, Aupre?" Paul Dumaine said with a laugh. "You seem sorry to come back to your New Orleans. You haven't said a word all morning."

Aupre pushed back his hat so that his chestnut curls caught the light.

"I love New Orleans," he said huskily. "But I cannot live here. Someday I shall tell you why—both of you." His glance rested upon Etienne.

Etienne's hand went to the tiny S-shaped scar low upon his left cheek.

"Perhaps Aupre has memories," he said. "Perhaps he has a past such as the one he accuses my father of."

"Forgive me for that, 'Tienne. But your father was such unparalleled material for a play . . ."

"If Monsieur Fox did half the things that your character in Le Planteur de Louisiane was mixed up in," Paul said, "he must have been a most interesting blackguard. And, knowing 'Tienne I'm inclined to believe he could have."

"Oh, father did all that and more," Etienne grinned. "'Twas having it all paraded before the audiences of the Comédie Française that I objected to."

"And your objection was overruled by Aupre's pointed arguments," Paul chuckled.

Again Etienne touched the scar.

"I was always a miserable swordsman," he said. "While

Aupre, here, was the best since old Robert himself. 'Twas a kindness that he didn't kill me."

Aupre smiled slowly.

"I was tempted to. But I must confess to a sneaking sort of admiration for the Foxes. Let's forget all this, shall we, 'Tienne?"

"'Tis forgotten and forgiven. You'll dine with us at Harrow tonight?"

"That, no," Aupre said abruptly. "I don't expect to see either of you during my stay. I shall be damnably busy—settling mother's estate and all—and I must leave again for France within a fortnight."

"So soon?"

"I cannot abide Louisiana," Aupre said harshly. "It gives me the horrors!"

"Who is she, Aupre?" Paul demanded mischievously. "You'll give me her address? Surely she must be quite a woman to sour you upon an entire state!"

"There is no woman," Aupre said. "I swear it!"

Etienne turned to the fourth man who was facing away from the others, staring out to sea. He was a Negro, with a face of polished ebony, but there was little difference in either his dress or his bearing from that of the three whites.

"Inch!" Etienne barked.

"Yes, maître," Inch said softly.

"Is our baggage ready?"

"Yes, maître."

"Then go down directly and bring it up! Here comes the boat now to take us off. Move faster, you scoundrel!"

Inch walked away, his pace but little accelerated by his master's commands.

"Why do you always speak so harshly to him?" Paul asked. "I find your Inch a capital fellow."

"France ruined him," Etienne growled. "He stole away of nights and studied at the Ecole de la Jurisprudence de Paris. Law —no less—the black ape!"

"But if he had an aptitude for it . . ."

"You Frenchmen! Of course you don't see! Wait until you've

346

been in Louisiana for a while, then you'll understand. I grant you that Inch is a capital fellow, and a damned intelligent one; but he must be kept in his place. Have you never heard what happened in Santo Domingo and Haiti?"

"Yes—horrible things, those insurrections, still . . ."

"A black like Inch can become a firebrand. I wish I'd never taken him to France. The French have no sense of the fitness of things. Why they actually looked upon him with admiration. And some of your women—I had to go so far as to forbid him their society."

Paul shrugged.

"We're a rational people," he said. "Such a minor irrelevance as a little pigmentation . . ."

"A little pigmentation!" Etienne snorted. "Why, there is all the difference in the world between the blacks and us! I tell you, Paul. . . ."

Aupre raised a hand.

"Here is the boat," he said quietly. "You have the rest of the summer to shout about that topic; but now we'd best be getting ashore."

Inch came back with the valises, and the four of them went down a ladder into the boat.

"The purser will send the trunks ashore directly, maître," Inch said.

"See that you have some of the men on hand to receive them," Etienne growled. Inch nodded wordlessly.

As they stepped out upon the quay, Aupre bade them an abrupt farewell, and disappeared into one of the streets leading away from the river.

"Odd," Paul said. "Is he always so brusque, 'Tienne?"

Etienne shrugged.

"How should I know?" he said. "You've known him as long as I have."

"No one will meet us?" Paul asked.

"No. I gave no exact date for our coming, Besides, 'twill be vastly more amusing to surprise them. Inch! Go!"

Inch nodded silently and moved off. Paul watched him a

347

minute, then turned again toward the river where the six vessels lay in a line. The quay on which they stood was high as the levee top, so that they could see the ships, which, except for their rigging, were out of sight of a city lying generally below the actual water level of the river. Even as they watched there was a sudden flurry of action aboard the *Northampton*: a group of men came boiling over the sides and into a small boat. Then they were rowing like mad toward the quay upon which Paul and Etienne stood.

"What the deuce?" Paul said, turning to Etienne.

"I don't know," Etienne said. "I've never seen any native of Louisiana display that much energy before. However, we'll soon find out."

They continued to watch the small boat driving through the morning swells until it drew alongside the quay. At once the men in the boat began to swarm up the pilings that supported the quay, like so many monkeys. They looked darkly at Paul and Etienne and went on past them, muttering to themselves. As the last man passed, Etienne took hold of his arm.

"I say," he began. "What's the trouble out there? You men seem to be fleeing the devil himself."

"Wish it 'twere ole Satan, mister; but it be far worse than that. It be yellow jack!"

"Yellow jack?" Paul Dumaine echoed blankly.

"Yellow fever," Etienne explained. He turned to the seaman. "Are you sure?" he asked.

"Sure I'm sure. There be clots of black vomit in the sick bays. The hull damn ship stinks of it. We be the shore crew, mister. 'Tis our job to tidy up them ships out there. An' I tell you, sir; there ain't a ship amongst em free o' the taint. You take the *Siri* there—her captain and several crewmen died and was buried at sea. An' the *Camboden Castle* lost seven men at Kingston, Jamaica an' both of em was inward bound when this thing happened. We didn't know about the *Northampton*, but we're learning fast. Them others come in on the same tow with the sick ones, and I'd lay you my shirt that they be tainted too!"

348

"Hadn't you better report this to the city authorities?" Paul suggested.

"The city authorities!" the crewman snorted. "Helluva lot a good that'd do!"

Paul looked at Etienne.

"He's right," Etienne said. "They wouldn't lift a finger. They never have. Father has been trying for twenty years to get them to do something about the sewage, and you can see for yourself . . ."

Paul glanced downward at the streets leading into the quay. They were littered with filth, dead animals, human excreta, and waste food and vegetables. The stench was formidable.

"Tell me, 'Tienne," Paul said. "When one's dear old grandmère dies in New Orleans, does one also toss her into the gutters with the rest of the débris?"

"I wouldn't swear that we don't. But here's my learned Negro with the carriage. Shall we stop off at the St. Louis for a bite? 'Tis a hellishly long drive out to Harrow."

"No—I have no appetite. I find New Orleans too exciting."

On the drive out to Harrow, Paul Dumaine was all eyes. His father had told him much about the Louisiana countryside; but he was totally unprepared for the reality. The great oaks trailing their streamers of moss, the bell-trunked cypress, sitting in the brackish swamps, the handlike fronds of palmetto, the spines of the yucca, the greenish black waters of the bayou, the endless fields rolling up out of sight over the edge of the horizon, covered with the green cotton plant, the low lands hidden by miles of cane, and the magnificent planters' houses— all these were a source of endless wonder to him.

"What a place in which to paint!" he cried over and over again. "Father never should have left—never!"

Then they were rolling up the alley of oaks before Harrow, and the great white house gleamed softly in the early afternoon sun.

"Ma foi!" Paul said. " 'Tienne, why didn't you tell me that in your own land you were a prince!"

Etienne looked at the house.

349

"This is Harrow," he said softly; then after a moment, he said it again, as though savoring the word: "Harrow. . . ."

High above them on the upper gallery, Julie saw the carriage turning in from the bayou road. At once she started downstairs, running so fast that her skirts made a blur around the lacy pantalettes that encased her plump legs.

"Company, Papa!" she called. "Company!"

"Julie!" Aurore's voice was genuinely annoyed. "How many times must I tell you it's unladylike to scream at the top of your lungs?"

"But, Mother—there's company! I saw the carriage—a hired one, from the city!"

"All right, all right," Aurore said. "But don't shout so. A hired carriage—who on earth . . . ?" Then taking her daughter's arm, she walked down the stairs. As they reached the ground floor, Stephen emerged from his study and joined them. He threw his arm about Julie's shoulder and the three of them went out upon the lower gallery.

Paul Dumaine got down first from the carriage, and Stephen fixed him with a kindly, quizzical glance. Then Etienne appeared and Julie let out a squeal of pure delight and bounded down the steps three at a time. Her parents were close behind her, and for a moment it looked as though Etienne would be smothered in feminine embraces. Stephen stood back and measured his son. Then, when Julie and Aurore had kissed him enough, Stephen took his hand.

"Ye've changed?" he said. "But 'tis for the better, I think. And your friend is . . . ?"

"Father. This is Paul Dumaine, son of the Paul Dumaine who painted mother's picture. He's an artist, too, and a rattling good one, I tell you. Paul, this is my father, my sister, and my step-mother."

Paul smiled and bowed grandly over Julie's hand. Her face was covered with blushes and confusion. Aurore smiled gently at Paul.

"Welcome," she said. "While you are here you must consider yourself a second son."

"You are too kind," Paul murmured.

"Come into the house," Stephen said. "Ye've breakfasted?"

"No," Etienne told him. "Paul here was too excited at our landscapes to eat. But as for me, I'm hungry enough to eat *coushcoush caille!*"

"Sounds horrible," Paul laughed. "What is it?"

"Cornbread and clabber. The Cajuns eat it. But then they can eat anything. They're almost as bad as the Negroes. Come on—don't you want to see your father's masterpiece?"

A moment later, Paul stood before the picture hanging in the great hall. He stood there a long time watching it, his eyes widening.

"*Ma foi,*" he whispered at last. "Could anyone have been as lovely as that?"

"Yes," Aurore said softly. "My sister was every bit that beautiful."

But Stephen shook his head, still a mass of curling foxfire above his snowy temples.

"No," he said. "Odalie was not so beautiful as that. But your father thought she was. Odalie was never so beautiful as Aurore, here; but somehow, she made everyone—including myself—think her the loveliest lady on earth. I think it was she believed herself so. Faith is a wonderful thing."

"If only," Paul said to himself, "I could become half the painter my father was—just half . . ."

"You will," Etienne declared. "But while you moon over that picture, I'm still starving."

They went into the dining hall and sat around the great table of handcarved oak. Presently the Negroes appeared with two steaming breakfasts, and the two young men began to eat.

"Ye have a scar," Stephen said. "Still following my bad example, son? With whom did ye fight?"

Etienne looked up at his father with a slow smile.

"That was in your behalf, Father," he said. "Aupre D'Hippolyte wrote a play about you—a satire. 'Twas all the rage. Aupre is from New Orleans—strange that I never knew him before. Anyway he is one of France's leading playwrights. Every line that he pens is in much demand."

"Ye fought him about this play?"

"Yes, Father."

"Hmmmm—D'Hippolyte—so 'tis De now. He has assumed the aristocratic particle. A fair lad with a girlish face and chestnut hair, 'Tienne?"

"Yes—you knew him?"

"Of course. But I must say ye've become quite democratic, 'Tienne—crossing swords with mulattoes."

"Mulattoes!"

"Aye—but then he's probably a quadroon or an octoroon—I don't know how to draw those nice distinctions in blood lines like a native Louisianian. All I do know is that Aupre Hippolyte has a touch of the tarbrush about him. Ye should have studied his nails."

But Etienne was already on his feet, calling:

"Inch! Inch! Where the deuce is that black scoundrel!"

Inch, at the moment, was down in the kitchen, talking earnestly with old Caleen.

"It was wonderful, mother," he said. "There the people care not if a man is black. They liked me—I went to school, though 'Tienne tried to stop me, and I learned many things."

"Good," Tante Caleen beamed. "You're smart, yes. You talk *comme un blanc*. Now when the time come, you be ready, you! You know how to fight, yes!"

"Mother," Inch laughed. "You're a fraud. You've been talking about freedom and fighting since I was a baby, yet you've done all you could to aid and abet the Foxes."

"I can't fight, me. Don't have the weapons. But you got em, you. Got em in your head where no patterollers kin find em. When the time come you be ready. I don't hate maître and young maîtresse—they good people, them. They treat the Negroes good, yes. I don't hate nobody, me. But it ain't right, Inch, baby, it ain't right. Maître, maîtresse, they don't know that, them. We got to learn 'em, us."

"I see," Inch said. "'Tis a good thought, mother. Man does not live by bread alone. There's pride in him, fierce pride—a certain dignity. You can't allow those things to be destroyed. If you do —you don't have a man any longer—you've got a thing. I can't belong to 'Tienne like his horse! I'm made in the image of almighty God and there is Godhood in me—there is; I won't be reduced to the level of a beast—clothed and sheltered and fed and driven to work by the lash! I'll die first, mother! Perhaps as the old maître is fond of saying, I'd starve if I were free; but, by God, I'd starve willingly, gladly, as my own man. To me this patient paternalistic kindness of maître and maîtresse is more cruel than any amount of whippings could be. I'm a child, they assume, mentally I will always be a child until I am dead of old age! I must be guided, directed, shown how and what to do— even my books must be selected for me for fear of my reading the wrong things—why, I might even get insurrectionary ideas! But I admit of inferiority to no one of any race! And one day, mother, these pale ones will dance to our tune . . ."

"Inch!" Etienne's voice came floating through the corridor. "Where the devil are you!"

Inch stood very still, his clenched, uplifted fist arrested in midair. Slowly he let it fall.

"Coming, maître," he said, and his voice held a break in it, like a sob.

Outside in the hall, Etienne paced back and forth, his dark face clouded with anger.

"Inch," he said. "You will ride into the city for me. Find out where Aupre has gone. I'd suggest that you search through Rampart Street, and all the rest of the quadroon quarter. When you've found him, report to me at once."

"What shall I say to him, maître, once I've found him?"

"Nothing! Don't even let him see you. Just seek out his hiding place and let me know." He turned away muttering to himself. "The pompous, lying, yellow hound!"

"So," Inch murmured under his breath. "You've found out, my good master. I could have told you this months ago—if I had any desire to tell you anything. 'Tis a thing one senses—this kinship of the blood."

He drew on his coat and his gloves and walked out of the house to the stables. It was useless to remind Etienne that he had not eaten. Oh, well, there were places in New Orleans where even a black might find food. Then, too, the chance to display his European finery before the mulatto wenches in the market place was not to be despised. His voice held a note of blasé confidence as he ordered a horse saddled. And the way the groom stared at this black who dressed and talked and acted like a planter's son was a good thing to be savored in the memory on the long ride to New Orleans.

Upstairs Aurore glanced at Stephen reprovingly.

"You shouldn't have told 'Tienne that," she said; "you've upset him terribly."

"He'll get over it," Stephen laughed. "He needed bringing down a peg!"

Two nights later, five horsemen sat very quietly upon their mounts at an intersection of Rampart Street. Three of the horsemen were great, muscular field hands, bearing long staves in their black horny hands. The other two were Inch and Etienne Fox.

"He walks here, maître," Inch said, "on his way back from the law offices. He should pass this way soon."

Etienne said nothing.

Inch looked at his master. I thank you, 'Tienne, he thought, for this show. If there is any one thing more despicable than a white it is one of these yellow ones. He would leave his race, this Aupre; he would marry his Frenchwoman and produce his nearly white children. And he would order me about as his own grandsire was ordered. Yes, 'twill be good to see him brought low!

Precisely at the same time as yesterday and the day before Aupre passed the corner. He walked slowly, with his head bent low, and his brow furrowed with thinking. Etienne stiffened in the saddle, nodding to his men. At once the big Negroes swarmed

354

down from their nags, and Aupre looked up to find himself surrounded.

"What the deuce—" he began; but the biggest of the blacks struck him hard across the mouth with the stave. The slight quadroon went down in a crumpled heap in the mud.

"Help!" he screamed; "Help!" Then seeing Etienne who had reined in closer in order to get a better view: "Help me, 'Tienne, for the love of God!"

Again Etienne nodded. The Negroes rained blows upon Aupre. The staves rose and fell in the dull light of the twelve lanterns swinging from the cross chains. And the slender figure twisted silently upon the ground.

Etienne raised a hand.

"Enough," he said quietly. The Negroes remounted their horses and the little cavalcade rounded the corner out of sight.

Aupre lifted his bloody, broken face out of the stinking mud of the street. Then groaningly, inch by inch, he drew himself erect.

"I am a playwright," he wept. "I belong to the *Académie!* My works are produced at the *Comédie Française*. I am a writer and an artist and a genius. A genius, I tell you, a genius!" He stood there swaying in the flickering light of the lanterns. Before him, the soft clop of the horse's hooves died away into the silence. And there was no other sound in the street but the rasping of his breath, the beating of his heart, and the racking sound of his sobs.

XXII

LATE in August of 1853, Stephen Fox, Etienne, and Paul Dumaine rode into New Orleans. It was raining, a hard, steady downpour, unbroken by any wind. The black clouds massed low over the bayou country and the lances of the rain slanted down at a sharp angle. Yet even this deluge, which had lasted now for more than a month, did not bring coolness. The heat was sticky and stifling.

"*Ma foi*," Paul murmured. "What a climate!"

Etienne looked at his father. Stephen was clad in old, shabby clothing, but little better than the garments of a slave. The dress of the two young men was no better.

"Father," Etienne complained. "You should put your foot down! This is a great foolishness! What's more, it is a dangerous foolishness. Have you no authority in your own house? This charity might cost mother her life."

"Aye," Stephen said grimly. "So I've told her, but she would go. The people need her, she says. I fear I've grown soft of heart in my old age."

From the direction of the city came a low, thunderous noise; a slow, deep-bellied booming, and clouds of inky smoke, blacker even than the rain clouds, billowed upward into the air.

356

"What on earth—" Paul began.

"Cannon," Stephen told him. "And the clouds are smoke from barrels of burning pitch. They tried the same remedies twenty-one years ago—when ye nearly died of the plague, 'Tienne. And in all that time, they've learned nothing. There is no more and no better sewage now than then, and the doctors are as abysmally ignorant! Why, Aurore and old Caleen are saving more people than any twenty of them. I hope ye have a strong stomach, Paul."

"Why?"

"The sights ye will see would sicken a he-goat! The people are dying faster now than they did even in 'thirty-two. They've stopped trying to bury them. They simply dump them on the ground of the cemeteries and leave them there to rot. Every house has its dead and dying. Ye can't even burn the bodies because of this accursed rain."

"How many have died, father?"

"Twelve thousand. Aurore tells me that the rate is two thousand a day. And everyone who has not left the city has the fever in some measure. Aurore recovered from a childhood siege so she fancies herself immune. Here, give me your handkerchiefs."

The two youths passed them over, and Stephen drenched them in a rich perfume he had brought in a large vial.

"Bind them over your mouths and nostrils," he commanded. "Even from this distance the stench is formidable."

They rode into the twisted, deserted streets of the dying city. Paul's horse shied with a mincing, dancing step. The young Frenchman brought the animal under instant control, leaning down at the same time to see what had frightened his mount. There in the street lay the naked body of a young woman. Even in death she was lovely. From her crumpled, twisted posture, it was evident she had been thrown from the window of an upper story.

"The death cart will pick her up," Stephen said. "In two or three days perhaps."

Paul got down from his horse, tugging at the cords that bound his cloak.

"No, no," Etienne said harshly. "Save your cloak, Paul. She has no need of it now, and you would need a thousand cloaks to perform such missions of charity."

Sighing, Paul remounted.

"She was beautiful," he said. "What a pity—what a great pity."

Down by the levee a gigantic warehouse had been converted into a hospital and in this Aurore and old Caleen labored together with a dozen nuns and two or three other public-spirited women. Most of the regular hospitals of the city had been abandoned. A week before, Doctor MacFarlane had entered the largest of the infirmaries only to find it occupied solely by the dead: doctors, nurses, and patients alike had perished in a single night. Now all the churches, warehouses, and other public buildings had been pressed into service, and the priests paused in their labors among the sick to administer extreme unction to the dying and chant short masses for the dead who lay upon the straw between the pews, side by side with those in whom the tide of life was slowly ebbing out.

Stephen and Etienne and Paul dismounted before the warehouse. Stephen unslung the saddle bags in which he had brought wine and a few dainties to tempt Aurore's fading appetite, although he knew well that the entire store would find its way to some one or another of the dying. In addition, he had brought a change of linen for his wife and a bag of tobacco for old Caleen.

Aurore's lovely matronly face was pale and thin, and the circles that ringed her hazel eyes were purple, but she smiled bravely at her visitors.

"I'm so glad you came," she said brightly. "Here, Stephen, help me turn this man over. He's been lying on this side for four days now, and I'm afraid he's getting bed sores."

Stephen looked at her wordlessly. Then firmly he caught the bloated limbs of the fat old Irishman and heaved him up and half over. Instantly Paul Dumaine was at his side tugging away with him, but Etienne stood back, his pale eyes colder than ice. Aurore was right. The man did have sores. And not even the perfumed handkerchiefs could keep down that stench. Paul reeled dizzily to the door and was sick upon the ground. Aurore looked after him anxiously.

"He'll be all right," Stephen told her. "But ye—ye're coming home with me!"

"No, Stephen," she said gently. "That I cannot do—my place is here. But I wish you'd take Caleen back. She's too old—and this is much too much for her strength."

"Aye," Stephen said grimly. "But I wish ye'd reconsider. I am not well fitted for the rôle of widower!"

Aurore laughed.

"Don't worry, darling. I shan't die. Life with you has been too good—I'm not anxious to take my leave of it. But there are things that must be done by somebody and this is one of them."

"Where is Caleen?" Etienne asked.

"Probably out in the sheds with the Negroes. She performs daily miracles, 'Tienne; but I fear for her life if she stays on. She has been attending blacks and whites alike and every patient in this place swears by her. Still . . ."

"I'll talk to Caleen," Stephen said. "But ye know well, Aurore, that neither I nor anyone else has ever been able to make the old devil do aught that she didn't wish to. I'll make the attempt, but I'll wager she won't leave ye."

Stephen was right. Caleen flatly refused to budge. And in the end they had to ride back to Harrow without either Caleen or Aurore. The trip back was a long one. At one intersection they were detained for a full half hour by an unbroken procession of carts, stacked railing high with bodies.

"Those ships that were in the harbor when we came," Paul said suddenly. "They brought it in. You remember what the man said, 'Tienne?"

"Yes. It has been definitely proven that those ships were the carriers that brought in the disease. But as father says it is the fault of the city authorities that it was allowed to spread. That stupid ass, MacFarlane! Why he even published a statement that our miserably primitive sanitation was a preventative against the fever! He should be hanged!"

"Aye," Stephen said. "He and all his fellows!"

Upon reaching Harrow their first act was to strip off the sodden clothes they had been wearing. Stephen rang for Georges.

"Take these rags," he said, "and burn them. If they won't burn, bury them. But on no account are they to be given to any of the people. Ye understand me, Georges?"

"Yas, maître," Georges said doubtfully. "But these good clothes, them—why maître want em burnt up?"

"They're diseased," Stephen explained patiently. "Ye don't want all of Harrow dead of the fever do ye!"

"No, maître!" Georges quavered, taking the clothes gingerly by the fingertips; "I sho don't, me!" Then he went scurrying off down the long hall.

"Wash your hands afterwards!" Etienne called out after him.

It was a miserable summer at Harrow. There was little that Etienne could do to entertain Paul. Visiting, one of the chief pleasures of plantation life in the deep South, was actually dangerous. One never knew in what house one might run into a case of the fever in its most virulent form. The tracks were closed, and all assemblies were forbidden. This of course put an end to cock-fighting, animal-baiting, the theater, the opera and even gambling. In that summer of 1853 there was exceedingly little for two healthy young men to do.

Paul, however, was quite happy. He entered into the life at Harrow as though he had been born there. He painted portraits of everybody—Julie, Etienne, Stephen, and even some of the Negroes. He wandered all over Harrow, even in the driving rains, making sodden little sketches from which he painted huge landscapes.

Julie dogged his footsteps from morning till night. Cheerfully Paul took over many of the duties of Miss Hartly, a vinegary Boston spinster who had been Julie's tutor and governess.

"What happened to her?" Paul asked Etienne.

Etienne laid a cautioning hand on his friend's arm, nodding significantly toward Julie who was listening quite brazenly to the conversation. Then he jerked his head toward the door. Paul followed him outside, his eyebrows arching upward at all this mystery.

"What's this all about, 'Tienne?"

"Julie—I didn't want her to hear. What happened was that the old fool suddenly decided that she could no longer remain in the employ of a family that kept slaves—or as she put it, that practiced domestic servitude!"

"Well—why can't Julie hear that?"

"Paul, you just won't understand! This is a very ticklish business nowadays, and the quarrels over it grow very bitter. Julie is still a child, we don't want her mind upset by these things. Why, the Le Blancs stopped speaking to father for almost a year because he proposed a system of gradual emancipation."

"And you, 'Tienne—what are your views?"

"I agree with the Le Blancs. Father is a sentimental old fool!"

"'Tienne!"

"Sorry, Paul. He is, though, however much you may admire him. But let's talk no more of this."

So throughout that terrible summer, of whose toll no accurate count has ever been made, life went on much the same at Harrow. Julie rose at seven, had her pre-breakfast snack of *café au lait* and a roll, then sat down at the piano to practice her music for an hour. For another hour she would read, all the time glancing wistfully at the clock whose hands crawled so slowly toward nine when Paul usually awakened.

After breakfast, Paul spent most of the morning until lunch instructing her in French and drawing with a patience that Etienne found amazing. Then at noon, they were served lunch in the study. The lunch consisted of sliced bread and butter covered with marmalade or guava jelly, accompanied by a slab of jujube paste and washed down with lemonade or orange-flower syrup or tamarind juice.

From lunch until dinner, Paul painted while Julie sat by his side, scarcely daring to breathe, and watched his deft brush moving over the canvas. But the other usual activities that kept her long summer days sc full and happy were sadly curtailed. Of course she could study after dinner, with the help of her father or Paul, but because of the eternal rains she could no longer ride the fat Shetland pony over the place, or play in

361

the yard, or swing, jump rope, or risk her neck on the joggling board. And no longer did the music teacher ride up to Harrow twice a week to hear her lessons on piano. Nor could she attend her weekly dancing class.

Most of all, she missed her mother. Stephen rode daily into the plague-stricken city, but nothing could induce Aurore to leave as long as she was needed. Harrow suffered from her absence; but there were always the sick to be aided, comforted, saved when she could save them, and sent to their God in peace when she could not. And at her side there was always Caleen, moving like a gaunt black shadow, working with matchless skill over blacks and whites alike. More than one young progressive doctor listened carefully to Caleen when she explained her methods. Afterwards they applied Caucasian method and science to what was to Caleen magic and ritual. The number of cures in the warehouse increased steadily.

Finally in the late Fall the rains abated, and the fever left New Orleans. But because it would be weeks before the city could be cleaned up even to its normally filthy state, most of the wealthy Creole and American families lingered at their summer cottages on the shores of Lake Pontchartrain and the social season opened at last with a nervous, hectic brilliance. There were parties and entertainments without number, and at last Etienne was able to do justice to his obligations as host. Paul was wined and dined and fêted to the hilt. Many a dainty fan fluttered invitingly in his direction; and many a fond papa suddenly found himself faced with the necessity of digging deep in his purse for the necessary commission in order that his fair, or not so fair, daughter might have her portrait painted by the celebrated Paul Dumaine, fils, of Paris.

Only one thing marred the joyousness of life at Harrow. Two weeks after the epidemic had officially been declared over, a wagon rode slowly up the alley of oaks before Harrow. In it were Aurore, a manservant and all that was mortal of old Caleen.

Stephen looked down at the lean, covered figure.

"How long?" he asked.

"This morning, Stephen," Aurore whispered. "'Twas not the fever. She died of old age and weakness and fatigue."

Stephen's face was stern and set. He turned to Georges.

"Summon Inch," he said, "and have Jean-Jacques and Raoul help ye carry her into the hall. She will lie in state at Harrow—not in a slave cabin. God knows 'twas as much her home as mine. She did as much and more to make it what it was."

A few hours later, bathed, clothed, and her limbs decently composed, Caleen lay in state in the great hall at Harrow. Stephen commanded the funeral invitations to be sent out just as if she had been of his own blood. But actually there was no need of them. The word spread through the Negroes from plantation to plantation and from them to the city. In the end, Stephen was forced to keep Caleen above ground for three days, while more than three thousand people, Negroes and whites alike, came to pay their last respects to the indomitable old matriarch.

Most of these were people whom she had saved from the fever, their relatives and friends. Some few came out of curiosity; but for the most part many a Creole lady or American woman of gentle birth wept openly beside the elaborate coffin. And the priests gave their consent to bless the earth wherein she lay, holding that she had gained absolution from her voudou practices through the strength of her good works.

Inch stood tirelessly beside the bier, his black face unmoving. It was not until, at the final rites, he saw Aurore, overcome with grief bury her head against Stephen's shoulder and weep aloud, that he permitted the tears to slip silently down his smooth cheeks.

"She gave her life for you," he muttered. "She—a thing that you owned like the mules that draw the cane wagons. This is a thing that must end—it must!" He felt a soft hand on his arm. Turning, he looked into Julie's tear-wet face.

"Don't cry, Inch," she said. "Caleen's in heaven now. The good God knows how good she was."

Inch looked at the lovely, golden haired girl.

"I wonder," he said harshly, "if there too she is a slave!"

Then he turned again to the grave where old Father DuGois

was chanting the final mass. Julie's black eyes widened staring at him standing there stiff as a rod of iron.

A month later, Etienne and Paul were riding upon the levee near the city. It was a bright November day, and the air was as warm as Spring.

"You've cut quite a swath, Paul," Etienne laughed. "Every girl in three parishes is in love with you—including Julie!"

"She is sweet, your little sister, 'Tienne. I sometimes wish she were older. As for the others—no thank you!"

"Not up to your Parisian standards, Paul? I think you wrong the Louisiana belles."

"In beauty they match and top anything France has to offer. But frankly, 'Tienne, they have no brains. Never have I met such insipid conversationalists!"

Etienne's heavy black brow sank wickedly over his left eye.

"The women of Louisiana," he said, "are designed for other purposes beside conversation."

"So I have discovered," Paul laughed. "But afterwards it is so difficult to get free of them. 'Tienne . . ."

"Yes, Paul?"

"What on earth is that?"

Etienne half rose in his saddle. A hundred yards down the levee a crowd was surging around a figure on horseback. As they drew closer, they could see that it was a girl.

"I wonder what . . ." Etienne began.

"*Mon Dieu!*" Paul gasped; "'Tienne look! She's riding astride like a man!"

Etienne touched his spurs to the palamino's side and the two of them cantered up to the group. As they neared, the pedestrians made a lane for them. The girl sat very straight in the saddle. Her riding dress had been slashed to the waist, and under it she wore a pair of masculine riding breeches, which fitted snugly into the tops of slim riding boots. Her little hat was of the latest fashion, and her whole attire was indisputably expensive.

Paul was looking at the clubbed masses of black hair, drawn softly down upon her neck in a huge ball, and the deep brown eyes that were alight with an unholy glee. The lips were full and very red, and the smile was mocking to the point of insolence.

But Etienne was talking to the short, ugly man in the battered stovepipe hat who was leading the girl's horse.

"What's the trouble here, officer?" he asked.

"This 'ere girl," the policeman said, "were making a scandal. I'm booking her fur indecent display in public."

Etienne looked at the girl, then back at the policeman.

"The lady," he said smoothly, "is—ah—a distant relative of mine." His hand went into his pocket and came out with a well-filled purse. "Perhaps your honor might be prevailed upon to release her—to our custody?"

The policeman pushed back his tall hat, and his eyes bulged at the sight of so much money. Etienne pulled out a ten-dollar bill.

"Well—uh—that is—" the policeman floundered.

Etienne drew out another.

"Right you are, sir!" the policeman grinned. "These things ought by rights to be handled within the family." He passed the reins over to Etienne. Etienne gave him the money.

"And now, cousin . . ."

"Ceclie," the girl said; her voice was soft, and very pleasant.

"Cousin Ceclie—if you will ride with us, we'll try to devise a suitable punishment for your high crimes and misdemeanors!"

The three of them broke away from the crowd in a spanking trot, and all the people laughed and cheered.

"*Ma foi,*" Paul said. "*Ma foi,* but you're beautiful!"

"Perhaps Mademoiselle would be so good as to tell us her name," Etienne suggested.

"It's Cloutier," the girl said, "Ceclie Cloutier."

"But I know the Cloutiers," Etienne said, speaking very rapidly in French, "and they are none of them like you!"

The girl's face darkened into a frown.

"Speak English," she said sharply. "I don't savvy Frog!"

365

"You're a Cloutier," Etienne said in English. "And yet you don't speak French, how can that be?"

"My father speaks it. He tried to teach me, but I wouldn't learn. I don't like it. 'Tis a womanish language!"

"*Ma foi!*" Paul Dumaine said.

"Who is your father?" Etienne demanded.

"Phillippe Cloutier. We came here from Texas. I wish I were back!"

"Perhaps," Etienne said with a slow smile. "Perhaps I can change your mind."

"Never," Ceclie declared. "Silly, simpering women, and lisping affected men, ready with a '*La!*' at every breath. There's not a one of you that can ride a really spirited horse or hit the side of a barn at above ten yards."

"Perhaps," Etienne said, "but there are other things—that we do quite well."

"Such as?"

Etienne reined in his horse so that the animal sidestepped quickly. A half second later his flank was rubbing against Ceclie's booted leg.

"Such as this," Etienne said, and swept her up into his arms. She rested very quietly, gazing up into his face, her hands still against his chest.

"If you kiss me," she said, "my father will kill you."

Etienne looked down at the young face, white beneath the inky masses of hair. The lips were full and carmine, and the thin nostrils flared. A spirited filly, aren't you? he thought; but I'll break you if it takes all winter.

"'Twill be a sweet death," he said, and kissed her hard upon the mouth, tightening his arms about her waist.

"Cry, damn you!" he muttered, his lips moving on hers. "Cry —beg me to release you! We'll see who's master here!"

But she made no sound. Etienne loosed his grip and sat back looking at her, his pale blue eyes blazing.

"My God!" Paul said. "What savagery!"

"You hurt me," Ceclie said very quietly. Then her full lips widened into a smile. "Were you ever in Texas?" she whispered.

"No," Etienne said harshly. "Why?"

"You're like a Texan—yes, very like!"

"I take it you mean that as a compliment?"

"Yes."

"You're not angry that I kissed you? You don't want to slap my face?"

"I'm not one of your soft Louisiana women. I don't say what I don't mean or act as I don't feel. Besides, I liked it."

Again Etienne hauled at the reins.

"No," Ceclie said clearly. "Not here—again. Later when we have more time—and," looking at Paul, "no audience. Goodbye Mister—"

"Fox—Etienne Fox. Wait, I'll—we'll see you home."

"No, thank you. My father would not like it. And he is a man for all his Louisiana upbringing."

"Then when shall I see you again? How?"

"I'll arrange it. You live at Harrow, don't you?"

"Yes. How did you know?"

"My father speaks of yours with great admiration—almost with envy. Goodbye, Etienne Fox—'til we meet again!" She brought her riding crop down sharply against the mustang's flank. The tough little prairie horse stretched out his long, ugly head and broke into a headlong gallop. The girl leaned forward over his neck like a jockey.

"Venerable saints!" Paul said. "The girl can ride!"

Etienne sat very still on the palamino, looking after her.

"I think," he said, "that this will be more than I bargained for ·—yes, much more."

XXIII

Lᴀᴛᴇ in December, Stephen Fox stood with Aurore just inside the great doors of Harrow and looked out over the desolate landscape. It was raining—the usual cold winter rain of the bayou country that had a way of penetrating down to the very marrow of one's bones. Despite the warmth of the hall, Stephen shivered.

"Why do you tremble?" Aurore asked. "'Tis not cold here."

"I know it. But just looking at that rain makes me think it is. 'Tienne must have taken leave of his senses to ride abroad in such foul weather."

"He seems troubled lately. I wonder if there's anything wrong . . ."

"Some young filly, I'll wager ye. After all, the lad is very young."

"Stephen, look!" Aurore said, taking his arm. "That's not 'Tienne is it?"

"No. 'Tis no horse of ours. None here has such a racking gait."

"The horseman seems small. Perhaps it's the distance. . . ."

Stephen leaned forward, peering through the glass.

"The horsewoman ye mean," he said.

"Stephen, you're wrong. That rider sits astride."

"Nevertheless, 'tis a woman. See, she is closer now."

"Oh, Stephen, how shameless!"

"Softly, Aurore. This is a new day, ye ken, and there'll be many new things in it."

"But, Stephen, to expose oneself like that . . ."

The horsewoman had reached the foot of the great stairs and, dismounting, threw the reins to the shivering Negro who had come out at the sound of the hooves.

"Well," Stephen said, smiling, "'tis a good exposure, I must admit."

"Stephen!" Aurore said, "you're a devil!"

"If I hadn't been, ye wouldn't have married me. But come, we must greet our guest."

They stepped out upon the broad upper gallery, just as the girl reached the top stair.

"Good day, Mademoiselle," Stephen said, his white brows settling quizzically over his eyes.

"Good day, sir—and Madame," the girl said politely. "Is Mister Fox in?"

"I am Mister Fox," Stephen told her. "Won't you come in?"

"I mean Mister Etienne Fox," the girl said; "I'd like to speak to him for a moment."

Aurore's eyes went to the riding dress that was split from waist to hem, and the close-fitting riding breeches that followed every line of the slim young body beneath.

"No," she said sharply. "He isn't in. Whom shall we tell him called?"

"My name is Ceclie Cloutier."

"Phillippe's daughter!" Aurore said. "But, my dear, you talk like an American!"

"I am an American," Ceclie said tartly. "Please tell Etienne I'm sorry I missed him."

"Oh, come in and wait a bit," Stephen said. "'Tienne should be along any minute now."

Ceclie looked at Aurore, and a little mocking half smile played about her mouth.

369

"I don't think I'd better," she said. "I've been gone overlong now, and father will be furious."

Stephen opened his mouth to protest, but Aurore shot him a fierce warning glance. He subsided muttering. Ceclie turned and bounded down the stairs with a laughing goodbye.

"Such effrontery," Aurore began, "of all the brazen, shameless . . ."

Stephen looked at his wife with a frown.

"Best of all in ye," he said slowly, "I liked your unwillingness to censor. Please don't change now, Aurore."

"I'm sorry, Stephen. The girl upset me. It's just that I want so much for 'Tienne . . . "

"The lad can take care of himself," Stephen said.

Not five minutes later, Etienne came up the stairs, his face as black as a thundercloud.

"Why so glum, lad?" Stephen laughed. "So fine a lad as ye— one who has the girls pursuing him to his very door!"

"Girls?" Etienne growled, "what girls, father? What do you mean?"

"Well, one at least. A little black-haired creature with a bewitching Western drawl . . ."

"Ceclie!"

"Then you know this girl, 'Tienne?" Aurore asked.

"Of course! Where is she? How long ago was it?"

"Not yet five minutes. You should have seen her as you came in. But, 'Tienne . . ."

"I didn't come by the road. See you later, Mother and Father, I'm off!"

" 'Tienne wait!" Aurore cried.

Etienne turned frowning.

"Yes," he said. "Yes, Mother?"

"I'm not sure I like this. The sort of girl who would come— alone and uninvited to a young man's house . . ."

Etienne's eyes were blue ice.

"And you, my good aunt-mother," he said, "on the many visits you made to Harrow before you married my father, was it always my poor dead mother you came to see?"

"'Tienne!" Stephen roared, "ye'll apologize for that!"

"No," Aurore said, "you need not apologize, 'Tienne. It was your father that I came to see. But not in such a manner as this. You see, your father did not know, and I had no hope. Now ride quickly after this girl of yours, or you will never overtake her."

Etienne turned, and went bounding down the stairs, but, before he went, he glanced quickly at his stepmother. The look was puzzled, but there was no longer any surliness in it. A moment later, Stephen and Aurore saw the palamino swinging around the curved drive in a full gallop, with Etienne almost standing in the stirrups, making full use of his crop.

"Still he has it," Stephen murmured, "that streak of cruelty in him. Come, my dearest, don't let a wild lad trouble ye too much."

Ahead of him on the bayou road, Etienne could see the miniature figure of Ceclie moving away from him, far in the distance. He slashed down savagely with the whip, until the palamino was heaving and throwing flecks of foam backward into the driving wind. He gained steadily. At last, when he was only a quarter of a mile behind her, Ceclie reined in, and sat very quietly in the icy rain until he came up to her.

"Ceclie!" he called, sawing at the bit until the great gobs of foam about the horse's mouth were streaked with crimson. The palamino rolled his eyes and threshed about with all four feet. Gradually he quieted.

"Poor fellow," Ceclie said gently. "You ride like a greaser, Etienne!"

Etienne made a gesture of impatience.

"You wanted to see me," he said. "What was it, Ceclie?"

"I don't know. I'm not sure I want to anymore. Any man who would abuse a horse . . ."

"Sacred name of a camel!" Etienne exploded.

"Now I wish I'd learned that effeminate language. What was that you said, Etienne?"

"Nothing," Etienne said shortly. "You ride from Rosemont to Harrow in a pouring rain, and when I do catch up with you, you talk about horses!"

"You want to know why I came?"

"Yes!"

"Father won't permit me to have callers at Rosemont, and I had to see you—that's all."

"And now that you have seen me . . . ?"

Ceclie gazed steadily up at him.

"You're strange, you know: black as a nigger—and with eyes that you stole from somebody else. They don't fit you, 'Tienne. They can be almost kind when you aren't thinking. But you try to be as mean as the devil. Why?"

"Is this why you rode all that way . . . ?"

"No. I wanted to find out whether I still liked kissing you."

Etienne bent down to her. Her hands moved caressingly over the back of his neck, the fingers working through the rainwet curls for a long, long time.

"And do you?"

"Yes. Very much. I never kissed anyone before. I didn't think I'd like it. I didn't think I'd like a man like you. You're deceiving. You look all soft and refined and polished, and you aren't. You're like steel. It's nice being in love with you, 'Tienne."

"Oh, my God!"

"You're sorry I love you, 'Tienne?"

"No—only what on earth are we going to do about it?"

"What do people in love usually do about it?"

"They marry. Only you're not old enough. Your father won't permit you to have callers, and certainly . . ."

"Certainly what, 'Tienne?"

"Certainly you cannot continue to visit me at Harrow. 'Twould make a hideous scandal."

"I see. You care about that very much, don't you? The formalities and outward show. I'd ride across hell to be with you, 'Tienne. But perhaps I'm making a mistake. Perhaps you don't care very much about me after all."

Etienne's face darkened. He reined in beside her and swung down from the horse. Then he lifted her down, holding her high in the air, then letting her slide down slowly against him. He drew her closer, tilting her chin with his free hand. Then he kissed her, so hard that her lips bruised against her teeth, and

372

his slim fingers, hardened by years of riding and fencing, bit into her flesh. At last he released her and stepped back, but her arms were locked about his neck and her whole weight swung against him loosely.

"See what you do to me?" she whispered. "I—I cannot stand . . ."

Etienne stood there very stiffly, but suddenly a great trembling swept through him and he quivered all over like a man half frozen.

"Convinced?" he growled.

"Yes. But don't kiss me again, 'Tienne. I'm afraid I couldn't bear it."

Etienne looked down into her face across which the rain had plastered wisps of hair.

"This doesn't alter the problem," he said. "It only makes it worse."

"I know. In two years when I'm eighteen, you can ask father for my hand. If he refuses, I'll marry you anyway."

"Two years! Name of the name of God!"

Ceclie looked up at him, frowning a little.

"We don't have to wait," she whispered. "Words said before a priest and a record in the Cathedral won't make me any more yours than I am right now."

"Ceclie!"

"I shocked you? I'm sorry. I don't know how to say things nicely or how to hide my feelings. I haven't had much of an education except the things my father taught me. And the things we prize in Texas—the ability to ride like the devil and shoot the ears off a coyote at a full gallop—don't mean much here. Perhaps you wouldn't want me as a wife anyway. I'd only disgrace you before your friends."

"Then to hell with my friends," Etienne said. "Two weeks ago I didn't even know you. Now I can't contemplate life without you. But I'm sure of one thing—I shan't make a mistress of you."

"Why not? I should like being your mistress very much."

"Ceclie, you're impossible! I can't explain it. Only—only I want to be able to look at you like father looks at my stepmother. I

373

don't want to have shamed you. I want to worship you, and the world to honor you . . ."

"Well—if that's the way you want it, 'Tienne . . ."

"That's the way I want it."

"And in the meantime?"

"In the meantime, I suffer."

"*We* suffer," Ceclie corrected. "But I'm glad, 'Tienne. I do so want to be a lady. Father's tried so hard to make me one."

"You are a lady," Etienne said, "a great lady. The mistress of Harrow can be no less. It's like being a queen, Ceclie."

Ceclie looked back down the bayou road toward the alley of oaks. The rain drove down through the air and made a sea of mud. It was impossible to see a hundred yards, and Harrow was miles behind them.

"I know," she said. "It frightens me—that house. It seems to dwarf the people in it—all except your father—and somehow, it has a life of its own. I'm not sure it wants me, 'Tienne."

"That is a mad idea, my darling. Have you it shall, and that's all there is to it. Now you must go back before you catch your death of cold. I'll ride with you to the gates."

"Will you, 'Tienne? You shouldn't—and I shouldn't let you. You're soaked to the skin already. But every minute from now that I shan't see you will be a minute out of my life. So ride with me, my 'Tienne, and please don't make me ride fast—I have so little time left with you."

Etienne helped her up and swung into the saddle. They moved off together, slowly, through the driving rain.

Through the rest of the Winter they met almost daily. The weather continued to be almost unbelievably foul. Etienne grew thin and drawn. He spoke little and his words had always an edge. Riding out from Harrow in the eternal rains day after day, never daring to be with Ceclie where it was warm and dry, knowing he could not be alone with her not even for an instant, having to fight the battle for them both was enough to break a much stronger man than Etienne. And Stephen watched his struggle and pitied him, but fifty-four years had at last taught him when to hold his counsel. So he offered Etienne no advice.

374

Aurore had suggested that they call on Phillippe, but Stephen knew too well the quality of Phillippe's pride and the depth of his bitterness. So all of Harrow sat brooding, waiting upon time.

"When you go," Ceclie told Etienne, "I shall run up three flights of stairs to my room and throw myself across the bed and cry all night. I often do that now—like one of your soft Louisiana belles. I never cried before. Oh, 'Tienne, 'Tienne . . ."

"No," Etienne growled. "No."

"I hate you!" she stormed. "You're meaner than a sidewinder! No, I don't. I love you. I love you so much that all inside I hurt. And only you can make me well. Kiss me, 'Tienne, please, please kiss me until I go entirely out of my mind. Even that would be better than being half mad!"

She threw her arms about his neck and clung to him, her eyes closed, and her breath sobbing up from her lungs. Etienne's hand swept up and broke her grip, then he was flinging himself into the saddle and thundering away down the muddy road.

When he reached Harrow, he strode through the hall and up the stairs to Paul's studio, leaving an inch-thick trail of mud behind him. Paul looked up from the picture he was painting, and his lips curled into a slow smile.

"So," he said kindly, "it grows worse, my old one?"

"Much worse," Etienne groaned. "There is the necessity of doing something about Ceclie and that with the utmost quickness or else I die!"

"So? The answer is simple—sleep with her."

"I'm not a Parisian, Paul!"

"Then what you need is a safety valve—you know, like a steamboat. And I think I have one for you. Come around here."

Wearily Etienne crossed the room until he could see the painting. He stopped short before it, as though arrested by an invisible wall.

"Name of the name of sacred God!" he whispered softly like a prayer.

"You like her?"

"But of a certainty! Only she does not exist. A woman so beautiful is but a figment of your disordered intelligence."

Paul shrugged.

"She exists all right. And the only thing wrong with this painting is that it does not even approach her loveliness."

"Then who is she? What is she? She looks oddly foreign—I don't place the type."

"She's a quadroon, 'Tienne. She says she has thirty-one years, yet she looks like a girl. She allows me to paint her in the nude—as you see—yet she will not permit me to lay a finger upon her."

"That's not an especially good recommendation for a safety valve, Paul!"

"You're your father's son, 'Tienne. You have a way with women. You'll ride in with me tomorrow?"

Etienne was studying the picture.

"Yes," he said slowly, "yes!"

Early in the afternoon, Etienne and Paul turned their horses into Dauphine Street. Etienne's heavy black eyebrows rose.

"She lives here?" he asked. "I thought you said she was a quadroon."

"She is. And she doesn't live here. She has a house on Rampart Street. You know, 'Tienne, it's marvelous what that little touch of dark blood can do to their coloring. Makes it richer, somehow, and vastly more interesting . . ."

"But where are we going?"

"To my place. I have a studio between Dumaine and St. Phillips. Your Louisiana belles have been wonderfully kind. I've decided to stay here, 'Tienne. 'Tis so much more artistically stimulating than France."

"Good. I'm very glad of that, Paul. But I thought you were going to let me see your quadroon."

"Not my quadroon, 'Tienne. She is very much her own mistress. You'll see her, all right. She comes to the studio to pose. She permits no whites to visit her house. Of course I pay her well."

"She permits! *Mon Dieu*, Paul, it seems that she is uncommonly high flown for a Negress."

Paul looked at Etienne steadily.

"One word of caution, 'Tienne. This most prized model of

376

mine has no need for humility. She is the loveliest woman I've ever seen. She is financially secure—having some sort of trust fund set up for her by a former protector. In addition, she manages a boarding house for wealthy bachelors that is a model of taste and propriety. She feels no inferiority, so if you attempt to put her in her place . . ." He shrugged expressively.

"I see. If she has all this, why then does she pose for you?"

"She has a son who is now being educated in New England. The money I pay her helps."

"Then this protector of hers made no provisions for his offspring?"

"I asked her about that. She said that the break between them came while she was carrying the child, and that she never told him. Pride and pique, 'Tienne. Women are queer creatures."

"In that you have much right," Etienne sighed.

They dismounted in front of a typical house of the old quarter. While Paul searched through his pockets for the key, Etienne stood by, watching him with somber eyes.

"It's not locked, monsieur." The voice floated down from the gallery. "You're very forgetful."

Etienne backed out into the muddy street and gazed upward. The woman was leaning over the wrought-iron balustrade. She wore no hat, despite the steady drizzle, and her hair was clubbed into a soft knot on the back of her neck. It was a tawny chestnut, her hair, and despite the thick overcast Etienne could catch the gleam of golden highlights in it.

"*Ma foi!*" he whispered, "you didn't lie—did you, Paul!"

"I never lie," Paul said, putting his weight against the door. It groaned open and the two of them went into the gloom of the hallway. Then they were mounting the stairs that led to Paul's studio. As they reached the landing, the voice came out again to greet them.

"Come in, messieurs." It had a haunting, lingering quality, so that Etienne was sure that still he heard it after it was gone, a rich contralto that caressed the ears like the notes of a soft, golden gong. He looked at Paul, his pale blue eyes luminous in the semi-

377

darkness. Paul smiled and the two of them went in together through the door.

She was standing in the middle of the room. In her maroon velvet riding dress, she had the figure of a girl. She looked at Etienne and her fine brows rose, then the sooty lashes swept down over her great eyes. Green, Etienne decided, but of a coloring I've never before seen.

"Desiree," Paul Dumaine was saying, "may I present my friend, Monsieur Etienne Fox?"

"Fox?" she said, and her voice sank deeper in her throat than before. "Fox? But yes, of course, Fox—those eyes . . ."

"What about my eyes?" Etienne demanded.

"They are very blue," Desiree murmured. "There are not many men with such eyes. Yet otherwise you are not very like—the coloring is different—but still there is the carriage and the tilt of the head and something of the same arrogance . . ."

Etienne turned helplessly to Paul.

"You talk riddles, Desiree," Paul said; "'Tienne is like whom, or not like whom, or—what on earth are you talking about?"

"He reminds me of someone whom I knew once—long ago. But since you have company, I had best be going back."

"Going back! Aren't you going to pose today as we agreed?"

"In the presence of Monsieur Fox? That makes a great deal of difference."

"I don't agree—what matters one more pair of eyes?"

"Monsieur is an artist. His gaze is impersonal. While Monsieur Fox is . . ."

"Is what?" Etienne growled.

"A Fox, perhaps. Goodday, messieurs!"

"No," Etienne said. "Stay and sup with us. This affair of the picture we will forget for the evening, but the pleasure of your company is quite another matter."

Desiree looked at him, and the little flakes of seagold caught the light of the candles and sparkled in her green eyes.

"Very well," she said softly. "I will stay."

"You see?" Paul hissed. "I told you!"

Desiree sank down upon the divan and watched Etienne. He

378

pulled up a chair and sat facing her, looking gravely into her eyes.

"You are very beautiful," he said. "But already you must have tired of hearing that."

Desiree smiled slowly; the wine-red lips curving upwards at the corners for a brief moment.

"And you're like someone else, too," Etienne declared; "someone I knew—but who? For the life of me I cannot recall . . ."

"Monsieur was in Paris—recently from the accent. Perhaps you knew my brother."

"Your brother?"

"Aupre Hippolyte."

Etienne's black brows almost met over the bridge of his nose.

"Yes," he said, "I knew him—well. Where is he now?"

"Gone back to France. The—the climate here didn't agree with him."

"The climate?"

"Well—there were other complications . . ."

"Such as?"

"Truthfully, monsieur, he was set upon by footpads and beaten so badly that he almost died of it. It was his spirit, perhaps more than his body, that was broken. I nursed him back to health and then I sent him away. I hope that he is happy there."

"But these—assailants of his?"

Desiree shrugged.

"God will punish them," she said.

"But didn't he—recognize any of them?"

"He couldn't bear to talk about it, monsieur. I didn't urge him."

"Good," Etienne said. "You were very wise."

Desiree sat very still looking at Etienne. From time to time the amazingly long lashes would sweep down and hide her eyes. When they moved, Etienne caught the gleam of dull gold at their roots. But most of the time she looked at him very candidly without any attempt at concealment.

Paul busied himself with the preparation of supper, for he lived very simply without a servant of any kind. At once Desiree sprang to her feet and ran to help him.

"No, no," he said. "Today you are my guest."

"And a very lovely one," Etienne declared. "I don't think I've ever seen anyone else quite so beautiful."

"Thank you, monsieur," she said. But she continued to help Paul and in a few minutes the little table was spread with cheese and *brioche* and steaming *café au lait*. Etienne watched the way her hands moved, pouring the coffee. There was something regal in their grace. With a sudden sense of guilt he forced himself to remember Ceclie. Dear little Ceclie—as untamed as a prairie filly, and as strenuous almost. The way these hands moved was restful. On a fevered brow they might be cool. And that voice, so slow, and soft and deep, the vowel sounds singing. Never would it grate upon one's ears, hoarse and beside itself with passion and anger. Yet there was fire here—a smouldering flame that would never burn out. Dimly he sensed how it could steal deep into a man's veins and slowly, persistently, sear away his senses. This is a danger, he thought; the cure could be worse than the disease . . .

"Desiree," he said.

"Yes?"

"I should like to see you home. And afterwards I want to visit you there."

The dark lashes swept down over the great green eyes.

"I'm sorry, monsieur," she murmured, "but that is quite impossible."

"Why?" Etienne demanded.

"You are white. There are oceans of blood between us."

"That has not always been considered a difficulty in Louisiana."

"I know. But the days of the Quadroon Balls are over. There hasn't been one in half a dozen years now. 'Tis better so."

"I don't agree. There was dignity and beauty in those arrangements. Now, life has become needlessly sordid."

"Perhaps. But for me the time has passed for arrangements of any sort. Since the days of the *Cordon Bleu*, I have known much loneliness, but also I have known much peace." She stood up. "*Adieu*, messieurs," she murmured.

Etienne frowned. Then, very slowly, he got to his feet.

"You're right," he said deliberately, "I am white. But there is one thing you've forgotten, Desiree. I am a Louisiana white—born on this soil and of it. I have never permitted my wishes to be gainsaid by one of your race—even one who holds so slight a membership in it as yourself. And I don't propose to begin now. This is your cloak?"

Desiree looked at him and her eyes opened wide so that her lashes caught the light of the candles fully and for once were all burnished gold with no shadowy darkness anywhere. The little golden flakes in her green eyes swam together and made a ring around the lightless, widening pupils. When she spoke her voice was rich and deep, with a huskiness in it, just a trace, so that Paul and Etienne, listening, were unsure that they had heard it.

"Yes," she said. "Yes—that is my cloak."

Etienne held it out to her, and she slipped it around her shoulders. Then he took her arm, and the two of them went out the door together.

XXIV

STEPHEN FOX broke the seals on the letter that the post rider had brought him from New Orleans. His blue eyes danced over the page, pale in his lean, lined face.

"Saints and devils," he said, "what an abomination Mike makes of the English language!"

Aurore looked up from her sewing.

"What is it, Stephen?" Her voice saying his name made of it a caress.

"A letter from Mike Farrel. As nearly as I can make out from the spelling, he is going to race the *Creole Belle* against the *Thomas Moore*—downriver from St. Louis to New Orleans."

"At his age! I thought you told me he had retired."

"So he had. But ye know how Mike is. Never would he refuse a challenge. And the stakes are already a hundred thousand dollars. The results will be cabled to Europe and the wagers are enormous. 'Twill be his last voyage, he swears."

"When is this race to be, Stephen?"

Again Stephen scanned the letter.

"The twenty-seventh, he says. Why that was yesterday! If he makes any speed at all he should pass Harrow tomorrow morning early. Julie!"

The clear, tinkling notes of the piano stopped abruptly.

"Yes, Papa?"

"The *Creole Belle* will pass the landing in a race early tomorrow morning. See that ye are up or else ye'll miss it. 'Twill be a sight to see, I tell ye!"

Julie burst into the room, her black eyes sparkling.

"We can watch it from the belvédère, can't we, Papa? And Mike will win, I just know he will!"

"Aye," Stephen laughed, "the *Belle* can show a clean pair of heels to any packet on the river. Why didn't the old pirate let me know earlier! Why, I could have gotten in a tidy wager . . ."

"Stephen, Stephen!" Aurore said. "Will you never get that gambling fever out of your system?"

"No. All of life is a gamble, my dearest, and so far I've won the highest of stakes: this house, the land, you . . ."

A soft flush stole upward over Aurore's face.

"You must marry an Irishman, Julie," she said. "They always manage to say the nicest things—even when they're wrong. 'Tis that stone with the unpronounceable name that they kiss."

"If I can find one like Papa. He's the sweetest old thing, isn't he, Mother?"

"Thank ye, my dears. Now must I call the servants to remove all the bouquets ye've tossed?"

"Oh, Papa!" Julie laughed.

Stephen ran a lean hand through his daughter's golden curls.

"Back to your piano, me lass!" he laughed. " 'Tis thinking I am that I heard a false note."

"Oh, I can't play now!" Julie protested. "I'm too excited!"

"Let her stay, Stephen," Aurore said.

"Ye see?" Stephen growled playfully. "In my own house I have no authority."

The heavy figure of old Jean-Jacques, the butler, hovered in the doorway. He coughed respectfully to gain their attention.

"Yes?" Aurore said. "What is it, Jean?"

" 'Tis a young lady. She wants to see you, her."

"Show her in here. Do I know her, Jean?"

"I think so, yes, maîtresse. But, maîtresse—"

"Show her in, Jean."

383

The butler spread wide his hands in an expressive gallic gesture, and his eyes rolled in his black face.

"All right, all right," he said, "but she half wild, her! Can't nobody tell nobody nothing in this house, nohow, no!" He turned angrily and ambled out into the hall.

Aurore turned to Stephen, her eyebrows rising. There was the clatter of booted feet in the hall, and Ceclie Cloutier was leaning against the doorframe, her young face completely devoid of color.

"Where is he?" she said, the great tears making streaks down her pale cheeks.

"Where is who?" Stephen demanded.

Ceclie looked past him as though he were not there, her brown eyes fixed upon Aurore.

"You're keeping him from me!" she stormed. "You are! I know you are!"

Aurore turned to Julie, whose eyes were big as full moons.

"Leave us," she said crisply. "Go upstairs to your room, Julie!"

"Oh, Mother . . ."

"Do as your mother tells ye!" Stephen said quietly. Julie turned and ran from the room. Stephen waited until the clatter of her footsteps was gone from the great stairs, then he turned to Ceclie.

"And now, young lady," he said. "Would you please explain the meaning of this?"

"'Tienne," Ceclie whispered. "I haven't seen him in three weeks. At first, I thought he was sick, but then he stayed and stayed away from me."

Aurore studied the girl's pale face then she said gently:

"Won't you sit down, my dear?"

Stephen rose and pushed forward a big chair. Ceclie dropped into it, looking very small and lost within its depths.

"Now," Stephen said kindly. "Begin at the beginning, little Ceclie."

"I was raised in Texas," Ceclie said. Aurore looked at Stephen seeing him wince at the 'raised.' "I don't know how to do things right. I wanted to see 'Tienne, and father said I was too young

384

to receive company, so I came here to see him. Afterwards I found out that that was wrong. Even 'Tienne scolded me about it. Then I started meeting him anywhere, anytime I could. Mostly we sat on horseback in the rain and talked and talked . . ."

Aurore looked at her sharply.

"Yes, I kissed him!" the girl said defiantly. "Anybody would want to kiss 'Tienne—anybody at all!"

"I don't doubt that," and Aurore smiled.

Ceclie sank back against the chair. Then she straightened and looked Stephen full in the face.

"But that was all, sir. 'Tienne is a gentleman—a real gentleman."

"I should hope so," Stephen said.

"I never kissed anyone before I never wanted to. But if I don't see him soon I'm going to die. I hurt all inside from wanting him so . . ." She buried her face in her hands and shook with sobs.

Aurore got up and crossed to where she sat. Gently she put her arms around the girl's shaking shoulders.

"Ceclie," she said softly. "Never by word or gesture did I forbid Etienne your company. You must believe me. And today my husband will ride out to Rosemont to ask your father to permit Etienne to call upon you properly."

Ceclie's eyes shone with joy. "Oh, Madame!" she wept. "Madame!"

" 'Tis nothing, my dear. Love can be a great burden. Now as to Etienne's whereabouts—that I cannot tell you, because truthfully, I don't know. He stays away from Harrow for days at a time. This I do know: he usually stops at Paul Dumaine's studio on Dauphine Street. We see Paul often—oftener in fact than our own son."

Ceclie got to her feet at once.

"I shouldn't seek him there if I were you," Aurore said gently. "That, too, would be improper. Be patient. We shall have him out to Rosemont within the week."

"Thank you," Ceclie whispered. "Thank you, so very much!"

She took a step forward, and then, before either of them could reach her, pitched forward full length upon the floor.

Aurore sank down beside her.

"Get water, Stephen," she said. "The poor child has fainted."

Stephen strode through the doorway and was back in a moment with a glass. He raised her head while Aurore got a little of the water down Ceclie's throat. Slowly the brown eyes came open.

"I'm sorry," the girl whispered. "I'm so terribly sorry!"

Aurore looked at Stephen, but he was gazing into Ceclie's face, snowy white beneath the black hair.

"How long," he said, "has it been since ye've eaten, child?"

"Four days," Ceclie whispered. "How did you know?"

"I know the symptoms of starvation. I suffered from it enough in my youth." He turned to Aurore. "Have the servants put her to bed. Give her brandy and milk and afterwards a little soup. But no solids. I'm riding out to Rosemont at once. Phillippe and I will have to have this out—and at once!"

It was very still at Harrow after he had gone. Ceclie lay abed sipping her hot, spiced brandy and milk. Her brown eyes rested upon Aurore with something very near to devotion shining out of them.

"I wish I could be like you," she said. "Father tried to teach me to be a lady, but I wouldn't learn. I never wanted to—before. Now I do. 'Tienne is ashamed of me, that's why he doesn't visit me anymore. And father is too. He says I talk like a nigger. Tienne talks French so that it sounds like singing. It's beautiful, but I can't understand a word he says. I'm so wild and ignorant. I know I'm not good enough for 'Tienne, but I love him so . . ."

Aurore thought rapidly.

"How would you like to come over here every morning and have lessons with Julie?" she said, "I could teach you French and English grammar and needlework, and Julie could teach you what she knows about the piano—though the good God knows that's little enough . . ."

"Oh, Madame, could I?" Then Ceclie's face fell, and all the

eagerness went out of her voice. "But father would never permit it," she said.

"That remains to be seen. Now try to sleep until your father comes for you. It won't be long if I know Phillippe."

Four hours later, when Phillippe Cloutier reached Harrow, Ceclie was sleeping soundly. The tall Creole stood beside the bed and looked down at the slight figure of his daughter. The lines in his hard face softened.

"Perhaps I have been harsh," he said, "but 'twas for her own good, I thought. She is very young, Stephen."

"Aye, and in your concern with rebuilding Rosemont, ye've neglected her sadly. Ye should have married, Phillippe. A girl should not be without a mother."

Phillippe smiled wryly.

"How could I? I am a man of taste. You would have me follow in your footsteps like a jackal and take what was left after you had taken the best?"

"There were many lovely girls in Louisiana in your day, Phillippe," Aurore said.

"Yes, but none like the sisters Arceneaux. 'Twas grossly unfair of Stephen to marry both of them!"

"Thank you, Phillippe, for the pleasantry. But I have a request to make of you . . ."

"Anything that you ask, Aurore. . . ."

"No, wait. I want you to let Ceclie come here daily, accompanied by her woman, and study with Julie. You're not much of a teacher, Phillippe."

"Ceclie will not learn! I've tried and tried . . ."

"To cram it down her throat. Now she wants to learn. I'll see that she's properly chaperoned. Etienne will see her only at your house, and with your permission."

Phillippe frowned.

"Very well," he said at last. "'Tis not that I distrust the boy —anymore than I distrust any boy. I remember well how I was at that age. And you cut quite a swath yourself, Stephen."

"Softly, Phillippe," Stephen smiled. "My wife knows already too much of my past. Don't remind her, please!"

387

Aurore looked down at Ceclie who was sleeping like a small child in the huge canopied bed.

"Don't awaken her, Phillippe," she said. "The poor little thing is all worn out. Let her rest the night. We'll send her back to you in the morning."

"No—I'll come back after her, though 'tis a hellish long ride."

"Then stay yourself," Stephen said. "The *Creole Belle* will pass here in the morning in a race with the *Tom Moore*. 'Twill be a sight worth seeing."

Phillippe grinned wickedly.

"For that I'd stay in Hades itself," he said. "A thousand on the *Thomas Moore*—even odds, Stephen?"

"Done! In fact I'll give ye two to your one. There is no packet on the river that can catch the *Belle*."

"Now look what I've done!" Aurore wailed. "I asked Stephen to bring you over here, and you start him gambling again!"

"Forgive me, Aurore. But a chance to shake down Stephen Fox is too good to miss. Now if you'll show me where I am to sleep . . ."

"Come with me," Stephen said, "but have your purse handy!"

First in the morning, before it was light, Julie and Ceclie climbed the stairway to the belvédère atop the roof of Harrow. Far below, they could see the river gleaming even in the darkness. It was quite empty—not even a *bateau* marred its even surface.

"Shouldn't be long now," Julie whispered. "They're still sleeping, the lazy things! Maybe we'll see it first."

"I hope so," Ceclie said. "Harrow is nice, Julie. You're a lucky girl."

"But you're going to live here too—when you and 'Tienne are married. I'm going to be so happy, having a sister. I never had anyone but 'Tienne and he's away most of the time."

Ceclie's lovely young face clouded.

"Perhaps that won't ever happen," she said. "Perhaps he doesn't love me any more."

"Oh, but he does! How could he help it, as pretty as you are?"

"Thank you, Julie—still I haven't seen him in so long. But don't let's talk about that now. I hope the *Creole Belle* wins, even if father is betting against it—just because it belongs to you—and 'Tienne."

They waited very quietly in the darkness, staring upriver until their eyes were blurred with the strain.

"Oh, dear!" Julie wailed. "Won't it ever come?"

As if in answer a slow belly-deep booming rolled downstream, and the fields threw back the echoes.

"What was that?" Ceclie demanded.

"A cannon! That was the signal, Ceclie! Papa! Mother!" Already she was bounding down the stairs. Before she had gone down half a flight, she met her parents and Phillippe Cloutier coming up toward the belvédère. She locked arms with her parents, and turned back again, half dragging them along.

"Hurry up, you slowpokes!" she said. "It'll pass before you get there!"

"Softly, Julie," Stephen laughed. "That gun is a good five-miles upstream. We have plenty of time."

"To see the *Belle*, perhaps," Phillippe said, "but if you don't hurry, you'll miss the *Tom Moore*."

"Another thousand!" Stephen roared.

"Done!" Phillippe declared.

"Stephen!" Aurore wailed, "you'll impoverish us!"

As they reached the belvédère, there came a louder, nearer booming.

Phillippe Cloutier's lean, sardonic face twisted into a half smile.

"The second signal," he said. "The *Moore's* ahead, Stephen."

"Aye, but the *Belle* will pass her before she rounds the bend. Ye watch, Phillippe."

The morning sky was beginning to lighten a little now, but, as they watched, a tongue of flame rose up suddenly straight and

389

tall, from beyond the curve in the river, and above it, the sooty smoke clouds billowed.

"What's that?" Ceclie asked, turning to her father. Phillippe half turned toward Stephen.

"A bonfire," Stephen said, "at the headwaters of my land. They are very near, Phillippe."

The little group settled into silence, waiting.

Upriver, just around the bend above Harrow, the *Creole Belle* was laboring in the yellow white swell boiling back from the *Thomas Moore's* paddle wheels. High in the glass enclosed pilot house, Mike Farrel peered through his lone squinting eye at the river.

"Damn it!" he bellowed, "what the hell's the matter below! Are all them Nigras asleep or dead? And still, be Jesus, she pulls away from us! Here, yez," he said to his pilot, "ride her in! I'm gonna squeeze her guts! I'll git up speed, I will. Afore I'll have Stevie watch me beaten I'll bust her boilers!"

Then he was stamping down the stairs, as spry as a youth for all his seventy-odd years.

"Daft!" the pilot muttered, "completely daft! When they gits that old . . ." He leaned forward, watching anxiously for the sand bars.

"Juniper!" Mike roared. "What the hell ails yez, yez black bastard! Can't yez git up so much as wan thin ounce o' steam?"

The black fireman pointed a trembling finger at the pressure gauge. The needle was quivering nervously just on the brink of the red danger line.

"To hell with that! Git them Bumboes going!"

Juniper raised his voice above the whistling, thumping, pounding noise of the engines.

"Mo' steam!" he bellowed. "Mas' Mike want mo' steam!"

The black gang turned frightened eyes toward the old captain. Then they started to heave the logs in, but at a snail-like pace.

390

Instantly, Mike descended upon them, roaring. A few well-placed kicks, and a half dozen swings of Mike's hamlike fists to the sides of black heads brought a noticeable acceleration.

"Yez burr-headed sonsofbitches!" Mike panted; "git yez all a move on and fast or 'tis thinking I am of heavin' wan of yez in to make grease!"

The whites of the Negroes' eyes rolled fearfully in the semi-darkness. Streamers of orange red flame escaped the edges of the firebox door. Mike stood there, watching the gauge. Slowly the needle climbed upward toward the red line.

Mike pointed a hairy finger toward the safety valve.

"Tie it," he said, "tie it down, Juniper!"

"But Mas' Mike!" Juniper wailed.

"Tie it, I sez, or—be Jesus—I'll flay yez inch by inch 'til yez look like a skinned ape! Get going, now!"

Juniper approached the safety valve. But as he attempted to tie the release down, his hands trembled so that the length of stout cord fell to the floor. A moment later Juniper joined it, skidding forward on his face from the force of an expertly aimed kick from Mike's hobnailed boots. Then calmly, Mike tied down the valve himself.

"Now, Gawdamnit," he said, "break out them bunches of fat lightwood, an them six hogshead of tallow!"

"Please, Mas' Mike!" Juniper quavered, "you kills us sho'. You blows us all to hell an' back! Mas' Mike, fo' Gawd's sake!"

"Then," Mike said quietly, " 'twill be the fastest ride to hell that ever the devil seen! Git moving, yez!"

Juniper moved off, driving the blacks before him, his heavy, African lips working in a silent prayer. A moment later they were back, rolling the hogsheads of tallow, and carrying the fat, resinous lightwood that would burn like tinder.

"In with it!" Mike said, "all of it!"

"All?" Juniper whispered.

"All!"

The firedoors came open and the yellow flame stood out through them for a full two yards. Then the sweating Negroes were hurling the hogsheads of tallow in, and the bunches of lightwood. Mike stood back, quietly watching the pressure gauge. Steadily it crawled up past the red mark, up, up, up. Satisfied, Mike turned again toward the stairs.

Up in the pilot house, the pilot was clinging to the wheel and alternately cursing and praying. From the great paddle wheels the water boiled into instant spray, and towering waves rode backward over the river. The *Creole Belle* rocked and quivered like a wild thing, and inch by slow inch she overtook the *Thomas Moore*.

On the levee of Stephen's plantation, the Negroes were screaming at the top of their lungs. Shotguns crashed into the air. Great oil- and grease-soaked bonfires flamed all along the mound of earth.

On the belvédère, Ceclie and Julie were hugging each other, thrilled into speechlessness. Stephen leaned forward, peering at the bend, his white brows bristling over his pale eyes, and the scar upon his temple glowing like a brand. Phillippe leaned back, his long, crooked segar smouldering.

Then the two boats were rounding the bend, blasting the towering plumes of thick black smoke up into the air, exactly abreast. At the same instant, they loosed their whistles, and the river was split with the deep, slow, lostlonesome bellows.

"Holy Mother of God!" Stephen whispered.

Even as they watched, the *Creole Belle* drew ahead—white water showed between the packets and widened steadily. Stephen turned triumphantly to Phillippe.

"Ye see!" he crowed.

But Phillippe was leaning forward, his fingers bands of iron closing vise-like upon Stephen's arm. His lips moved, but no sound came out of them, no sound at all. Frowning, Stephen turned again toward the river.

A long tongue of flame shot out of the bowels of the *Creole Belle* and rolled majestically across the face of the river. Then afterwards came the ear-shattering roar of the explosion. The flames mounted up into the morning air, roaring straight up for two hundred feet, carrying bits of hulkwood, and fittings of metal with them. They turned over slowly in the glare of the fire, then almost weightlessly they dropped toward the surface of the river. Up in the pilot house, wrapped in the flames, Stephen's keen eyes could see even from that distance, the pilot, dead, hanging half out of one of the smashed windows; and the gigantic figure of old Mike hauling upon the wheel, swinging the *Belle's* bow inward, angling for the landing.

"Oh, my God!" Aurore wept, "Oh, my God!"

Now the *Belle* was a sheet of living flame, blazing from stem to stem, but slowly, persistently, old Mike fought her in toward the landing. Up ahead, the *Thomas Moore* was reversing her engines, trying vainly to stop her headlong momentum in time to be of aid to her stricken rival.

And Stephen Fox was sprinting down the stairs calling as he ran:

"Georges! Inch! Jean-Jacques! Jean! Raoul! Henri! Pierre! Peter!"

The Negroes came racing toward the landing.

"Flour!" Stephen roared. "Every sack that ye can find!"

Phillippe and the girls were at his heels, and behind them came Aurore.

When they reached the landing, Mike had driven the *Creole Belle's* bow into the soft mud, and was holding her there with all his remaining power. And now, the passengers, they that remained alive, were running over the bow onto the the wooden pier, which was itself already smouldering. Like living torches they ran, hair and clothing aflame, to fall upon the muddy earth, and roll there, twisting and screaming.

Already the Negroes were busy, beating out the flaming garments, stripping them from men and women alike, and rolling the naked, pitifully burned scarecrows that had once been human beings in the flour that the racing wagons brought up. Some too far astern to reach the landing, plunged blazing over the side, to sizzle out in the boiling water at the *Belle's* side and sink in the treacherous shoal currents.

Stephen and Phillippe worked like demons, burning their hands raw beating and tearing at the blazing clothing. Aurore and the two girls poured sips of water through the cracked and black-

393

ened lips of the dying. And up in the pilot house, Mike Farrel perished, as he had lived . . . grandly!

Of those who got ashore, only five were living at the end of an hour. These were borne up to Harrow and laid tenderly in the great beds. Julie walked along beside Inch and Jean-Jacques as they bore between them the slim figure of a lad of some seventeen years. By some odd chance, his face and hair were untouched, though the rest of his body was horribly burned. And the face was as handsome as a young god's, with a fair almost girlish beauty. Heavy locks of blond hair curled damply over his forehead, and the ribbons of sweat ran down into his eyes. He made no sound, but bore his anguish silently, his great blue eyes fixed upon Julie.

A few yards away, Ceclie was lifting the feet of a young woman, while a slave girl struggled at her head. The black girl was sobbing aloud.

"Hush, nigger!" Ceclie snapped. "Crying won't help now!"

Julie turned to Inch.

"Take him to my room," she whispered. "I will care for him there."

Inch nodded, and he and the fat old butler started up the stairs.

They laid him upon the bed, and Julie motioned for them to leave. Then slowly, carefully, she cleansed away the flour and dirt from his blistered, blackened body. Then she washed him all over with sweet oil. As tenderly as she worked, from time to time the boy jerked violently, and a faint ghost of a moan escaped his lips.

Still Julie worked on, her young cheeks tear-wet, and her lips trembling. When she had finished, she stood up and, blushing furiously, drew up the sheet to cover his nakedness. Beneath the cloth, the boy writhed.

"No!" he whispered, "no covers! I can't bear it!"

Julie drew the covers down from over his body and sat down beside him.

"You—you're an angel," he got out. "I'm not dead yet—am I?"

"No," Julie wept, "and you won't die! You can't die! I won't let you!"

The boy's fair face twisted into a grimace oddly resembling a smile.

"You—live—here? This—is—your—home?"

"Yes," Julie whispered. "Yes."

The boy's face was frowning.

"You're so good," he muttered. "I don't understand—I don't understand . . ."

"What is it you don't understand?" Julie prompted.

"How—someone so beautiful—can live—upon wealth gained from the sweat of other men's faces." He drew himself half up, his voice growing stronger. "My father says . . ."

"Your father?"

"Thomas Meredith—the abolitionist—we're from Boston. He says that nothing more wicked exists under the skies of heaven than a system that uses—" He sank back, his breath gone.

"Please be quiet," Julie begged. "You mustn't exert yourself, really you mustn't!"

"Men like brutish beasts," young Meredith went on as though he had not heard. He looked at her, his blue eyes peering owlishly under the lids from which all lashes had been singed away.

"What—is—your name?"

"Julie," the girl sobbed.

"You—are—so lovely," he whispered; "like an angel—Julie. I like—that—name—Julie. I want to—die—saying it. Tell my father —and my brother Tom that Dan said . . ." He fell back, unconscious upon the bed.

All through the day, Julie watched beside him. He talked frequently, wildly—often to people who were not there. At times he seemed to be making a speech.

"I tell you," he said strongly, "they are children of God, no less than we! And the blackness of their skins can not hide His image. They are our brothers whom we permit to be sold like cattle, driven to labor in the fields under the cruel lash, torn from the bosoms of their loved ones and carried miles away . . ."

Towards night he awoke again, but this time his eyes were clear.

"Light the candles, Julie," he whispered; "it grows dark—very dark . . ."

"But they are lit, Dan—that's your name, isn't it? 'Tis very bright in here."

He looked at her, smiling.

"Yes, yes—'tis bright. Where you are 'twill be always bright. But bring the—candles closer, Julie—I want to see—your face."

Julie turned and ran across the room. A moment later she was back, holding the silver candelabra close to her cheek.

"See, Dan—see!" But there was no answer. Julie looked down at the boy. Then slowly, she bent down, placing the candelabra upon the floor and, pillowing her face upon her arms, she wept.

An hour later, her face still and composed, she went in search of her father. She found him in his study, his thin face lined and drawn, staring out upon vacancy.

"They all died," he said; "and this lad of yours?"

Julie nodded dumbly.

"A pity—" Stephen muttered. "He was too young to die."

"Father . . ."

"Yes, Julie?"

"I want to go North to school."

Stephen looked at her, his white brows climbing upward until one of them touched the scar.

"Why, my little Julie? We have good schools and good tutors . . ."

"May I, father?"

Stephen frowned a little. Then his face cleared.

"Yes, Julie," he said. "Ye may go when ye're sixteen." He stood up, looking down upon his daughter.

"Come," he said. "I think your mother needs us." Then he opened the door and they went out together into the great hall.

XXV

First in the morning, after the Cloutiers had gone, Etienne Fox rode up to Harrow. He sat bent over his horse, his face morose and sullen.

Plague take that quadroon wench! Not even the finished sophisticates of Old France had so devilish many ways of eluding a man. A look—a gesture—a laugh cutting through a serious moment like the blade of a knife—all these and more she used with casual ease while he fretted and fumed and got exactly nowhere—the worst was her constantly varied harping upon the difference in their ages: "You see, monsieur . . . I used to go there . . . do this . . . see that . . . but that was years ago before you were born . . ."

"Damnation!" he would roar. "You know well that there is but eight years between our ages!"

"So little?" she would murmur. "It seems more . . ."

There must be a way—some way—of bringing her to heel. He paused suddenly, sniffing at the air. That smell! Had something been burning here? Harrow? His heart contracted at the thought, and he dug his spurs cruelly into the palamino's sides. But when the horse rounded the curve into the alley of oaks,

397

the house was still there, gleaming in all its snowy beauty among the trees.

Yet the smell persisted. He turned toward the steamboat landing, his pale eyes dilating as he looked. It was a smouldering ruin. Beyond it, in the river, lay the blackened hulk of what had once been a fast river packet. He rode toward it and sat there very still looking at the wreck. Something about its lines seemed familiar to him, but it was too far demolished for him to be sure of its identity. Then he was leaning forward, peering at an object in the water. It was a long section of plank, painted green, bearing the letters *Creole Be*—the rest was missing, the ornate gold letters ending abruptly in splintered, charred wood.

"The *Belle!*" he whispered. "Sacred Mother of God!"

As he rode up the alley of oaks, he saw a large group of Negroes busy in the bare plot of ground next to the family burial grounds of Harrow. They were working with picks and spades, digging a huge trench more than six feet deep that curved away from the river for fifty feet or more. Beside them, laid out in orderly rows, were a line of oddly grotesque bundles, completely wrapped in cloths. Etienne studied the bundles for a long time before he realized what they were. Then, slowly, he began to count them. When he had counted more than a hundred, he stopped.

"*Mon Dieu!*" he whispered. "Did none of them escape?"

He turned his eyes toward the spot where his mother lay. There, not very far off, a cross of wood marked a fresh grave. Etienne caught his breath. Someone of the family! Had father attempted . . . ? He swung down from the horse and ran across the muddy earth. The words carved into the rude cross stopped him.

"Michael Farrel," they read. "Born—" then a blank space, "Died: June 3rd, 1854. Rest in peace."

"Old Mike," Etienne murmured. "What a man he was! So he died with his ship. He would have wanted that . . . still to die thus . . . By the good God, how they must have suffered!"

He walked slowly back to where the horse stood. Slowly he remounted and rode silently up to the house.

In the hallway, Stephen met him. Father looks tired, Etienne thought. His years begin to tell . . .

" 'Tienne," Stephen began.

"Yes, Father?"

"Is it asking too much to request that ye favor us with your presence once in a while? Yesterday we had great need of ye. The *Creole Belle* . . ."

"I saw," Etienne said harshly.

"And the Cloutiers were here. Phillippe granted ye his permission to call upon his daughter."

"He did!"

"Yes, but I don't see . . ."

"That's grand, Father! No more conversations on horseback to the accompaniment of icy trickles pouring down my back. I'll see her at once!"

" 'Tis time, I should think."

Etienne turned to his father, his black brows forming thunderheads that half hid his pale eyes.

"What do you mean by that, Father?"

"Ye're so devoted to your little prairie flower, and yet ye let three weeks elapse before ye see her at all. 'Twas not so with the youth of my day. We were more persistent wooers."

"My absence was my own affair, Father. I'm twenty-four. I don't have to explain my coming and going to a girl, and by heaven—"

"Softly, 'Tienne. Ye need explain nothing. What's between ye and Ceclie is of concern only to the two of ye. But 'tis thinking I am that when a lad stays away from his own home for days and nights upon end, common decency demands that he say a word to his parents! Twenty-four or an hundred, ye have no right to cause your mother anxiety."

Etienne looked at Stephen, and one corner of his mouth crawled upward into a wicked smile.

"Please tender my dear Aunt-Mother my humblest apologies," he murmured, "and say to her that I was kept from home by the so far unsuccessful pursuit of a quadroon wench called Desiree who is more beautiful than any Negress has any right to be."

" 'Tienne!" Stephen roared.

"You would have me lie, Father?"

"No. But this is a thing not to be tolerated! Ye must cease this folly at once!"

"Folly? Perhaps—but such an enchanting folly, Father. Surely I'm permitted to sow a few tares to the wind."

"Etienne Fox!"

"Now really, Father, I'm disappointed in you. After all, I am your son. You can't expect me not to have inherited some of your . . . more interesting characteristics?"

Stephen's snowy brows eased away from the bridge of his thin nose, and his blue eyes took on an icy calm.

"All right, 'Tienne," he said. "Ye learned your lessons well in Paris, I see. I'm too old to quarrel with ye. But this I must say: this dalliance with a Negress must stop or else ye must seek a home elsewhere and that is final."

He turned on his heel and strode toward the great curving stairs.

Etienne studied his back as he went. Then something like a light gleamed in the youth's eyes; on his face was an expression of sudden realization.

"Father!"

Stephen turned.

"Yes, 'Tienne?" he said softly.

Etienne spoke slowly, watching his father's face.

"This Desiree is no child. She is now thirty-two years old."

"So?"

"Sixteen years ago, when I was eight, she was already sixteen years of age. She was very beautiful then, wasn't she, Father?"

"What do you mean, 'Tienne?"

"So beautiful, in fact, that you wrecked Harrow and broke my mother's heart because of her! Of course it is the same! Desiree Hippolyte. Desiree of the tawny hair and haunting voice. Desiree of the seagreen eyes with the gold of an enchantress in them! You recognize the portrait, Father?"

"Yes," Stephen said harshly, "I recognize it."

400

Etienne threw back his head and hurled his laughter upward toward the high, vaulted ceiling.

"Oh, what a piece of work is man!" he said. "And almost I was beginning to think that you had developed a moral sense in your old age! What is it, Father? The dog in the manger attitude—or have you really broken with her over all these years? Answer me! No—don't answer. 'Tis no longer important what you would say. You know, Father, you looked most important standing there cloaked in righteous indignation. But pretense is such a shabby garment and reality can be so damnably hideous—" His laughter broke upon a high, edged note, strangely like a sob.

Stephen's pale eyes were looking past Etienne out over the oak grove which stretched down the gentle slope to the river.

"There are many kinds of hell," he said, half to himself. "I have created mine in mine own image. I had hoped that ye would be wiser than your father, 'Tienne—that ye would avoid his mistakes. 'Twas too much to be hoped or expected. Go as ye will, lad, and shape your own perdition."

He turned with great dignity and went up the stairs. He went very slowly, like a man very tired, and very old.

Etienne watched him, frowning. Then he ran to his room, calling out to Inch to bring fresh linen, and draw water for his bath. There was no answer.

"Inch!" Etienne roared, "Inch!"

But it was old Jean-Jacques who came at last, trembling before Etienne's fury.

"Inch ain't here, him," he quavered. "He tell me to give you this, yes!"

Etienne took the letter and broke open the seals. His eyes danced over the elegant, flowing script; then his face was purpling with rage.

"My good master," he read aloud, "when you receive this I shall be already many, many miles away—on the road to freedom. I shall never be brought back alive, so if you cherish, as I do, any pleasant memories of our childhood, do not send pursuers after me. To explain why I have done this thing is difficult, especially since I know how and what you will think. You will

401

say that you have treated me kindly: and so you have, apart from a few cuffs and kicks, which were more the results of over-indulgence in wine than any real cruelty on your part, and a fairly frequent use of invective in speaking to me, arising, no doubt, from my insistence upon deserting the station in life to which, in your opinion, I was born.

"The trouble is, I think, that I have not the mentality or character of a servant, and certainly not of a slave. I don't want to be treated kindly like a valuable animal: I want to be treated like a man. Almighty God when he granted me the boon of life gave unto me something which he did not bestow upon the palamino which you ride, namely, a soul. It is therefore something of an affront to Him that you attempt to *own* me in precisely the same sense that you own your horse. God gave me Freedom of Will. You, my dear master, are for all your wealth and power, a mere man. You cannot take away what God has already given me. Since, in the sight of the Eternal, I must bear the final responsibility for what I do and say and think, it follows that I can no longer permit my thoughts, words, and deeds to be shaped by the whims of another.

"Forgive me this letter and my flight. But it was becoming impossible for me to breathe at Harrow. Remembering my mother, who died rather than submit to servitude, and my grandmother, who longed all her life for freedom, I can do no more than to take the risks. For man does not live by bread alone, nor is he clothed by the castoff garments which a master gives him. There is a world of the spirit in which such a man as I can eat out his heart in longing, enwrapped in the terrible cloak of his wounded dignity. I do not want your protection, nor the easy life at Harrow; I want nothing done *for* me, but many things done *by* me. In short, I want freedom, and i shall achieve it, with the help of God."

It was signed, very simply: "Inch."

Etienne's eyes danced like arctic fire; but his voice was perfectly controlled when he turned to Jean-Jacques.

"Draw water for my bath." he said, "and bring pen and paper. You write, don't you?"

Dumbly the old butler nodded.

"My father was a fool to allow his blacks to learn so much. Hurry now!"

Twenty minutes later, Etienne sat comfortably in his bath.

"Write thus," he said to Jean-Jacques. " 'An advertisement: Run away from me at my plantation, Harrow, my manservant, Inch. He is coal black in color, dresses extremely well after the fashion of a white. Possibly traveling under forged credentials, as he can read and writes an excellent hand. Will probably attempt to pass himself off as a freeman. Speaks English with a slight accent, and French with great fluency. Anyone notifying me of his whereabouts, or capturing and returning him to me at my plantation near New Orleans, will receive a liberal reward. Signed, Etienne Fox.' "

Jean-Jacques' pen scratched busily over the paper.

"Put it there on the table when you have finished," Etienne said. "I'll have the *Picayune* run it with the note that other papers please copy. Now bring me my clothes and some coffee. I have much to do. And have a fresh horse saddled for me; I must ride back to the city within the hour."

Three quarters of an hour later, Etienne swung around the sweeping curves of the drive leading to the oak alley. He was mounted upon another of the justly celebrated palamino horses that were known throughout the bayou country as the hallmark of Harrow. Many another planter looked upon the sleek, beautiful animals with envy but, despite many requests, Stephen Fox never sold one of them, nor put any stallion out to stud upon his neighbors' lands. So it was that at Harrow alone of all the state of Louisiana were the rich silver-buff horses with the snowy manes and tails to be found.

Etienne's mind was busy with diverse thoughts as he rode. First, he decided, the newspaper office, then a brief call at Paul's studio. After that—once more, the last time, perhaps— the little white house upon Rampart Street where he had been tormented past human bearing. This time he would win the hand. He held all the cards; and, by Heaven, that lovely yellow wench must be humbled! Thinking upon the precise method of

403

this chastisement made him reel in the saddle, so quickly he forced his thoughts into other channels.

Ceclie . . . dear little Ceclie. A prairie flower, Stephen had called her. Father was often wonderfully apt with words. Once she had been tamed—not too much—and taught civilized manners and a little grammar . . . what a wife she'd make a man! No need for Desiree then; no need for anyone; Ceclie would combine in herself the best features of wife and mistress. Of a straightlaced convent-trained Creole wife, one expected submissiveness, but no ardor . . . but Ceclie . . . Ceclie . . .

His eyes turned to the burial plot which he was even at that moment passing. Julie was kneeling upon a fresh-made grave a little apart from the common grave where nearly all of the victims of the disaster lay. Odd that this one should be honored by separate burial; odder that Julie should single him out for her prayers. On the other side of the road, Stephen stood with bowed head beside the grave of Mike Farrel. Poor father, Etienne thought briefly . . . he has had his share of grief. 'Twas beastly unkind of me to taunt him so. Oh, well, there is time and to spare to make amends . . .

In his studio on Dauphine Street, Paul Dumaine was putting the finishing touches upon the painting for which Desiree had posed. He labored under the handicap of having to paint from pencil sketches and memory, for Desiree was not present.

Plague take 'Tienne, anyhow! Paul thought. She was most punctual until he came. Sighing, he laid aside his brush, and walking a few feet away, studied the painting. Desiree had posed upon a low couch covered with a panther's skin, and the effect of the painting was splendidly barbaric. Yet Paul was vaguely dissatisfied with it. He studied it patiently, trying to discover his errors. The long, clean body upon the canvas glowed softly, the curve of waist and thigh and breast so perfectly reproduced that Paul was conscious of slow, voluptuous tingles at the base of his spine. That was it! He had made her appear

sensual. Desiree was sensuous, to be sure, but not sensual
Always he had the impression of fire under perfect control, of
dark, smouldering passions held in check, so that only in the
green eyes did now and then a flicker appear. Well . . . he'd
have to have her in for one more sitting, and that would be the
end.

He walked closer to the painting and picked up his brush.
But before he could touch it to the canvas, he was interrupted
by a firm knock upon the door.

"Come in!" he called, but did not leave his place. I'll have to
get that lock fixed someday soon, he thought, though there
seems to be no risk. They aren't enough interested in paintings
in New Orleans to steal one.

Then the inner door creaked open. Paul turned. Ceclie Cloutier stood in the doorway, smiling a little breathlessly.

"Come in, come in!" Paul said; "I'm more than honored!"

"Thank you," the girl said. "I want you to do me a favor,
Mister Dumaine . . ."

"Anything within my power . . ."

"I want you to paint a miniature of me . . . for Etienne. I'll
buy a case to fit it so that he can carry it with him always. Will
you do it?"

"Well," Paul began doubtfully, "I've never painted in miniature
. . . but for you . . . and 'Tienne . . ."

"Thank you, sir. I knew you'd do it. You always seemed so
kind . . ."

Paul smiled.

"If Mademoiselle will sit over there . . ."

Ceclie started across the room.

"I haven't much money," she began.

"Mademoiselle wishes to offend me? From so dear a friend of
'Tienne's the price is not one cent. Besides, I shall thoroughly
enjoy this. 'Tis always the keenest sort of pleasure to paint such
a rarely lovely girl."

"You say nice things . . . nicer than 'Tienne does. He barks
at me something awful!" She walked over to the easel, at which
she had been throwing quick glances since she had entered the

room. Now she studied the painting at length. She whirled on her heel, facing Paul.

"You didn't make that up!" she accused.

"Of course not," the artist laughed, "I had a very beautiful model."

"You mean a woman sat here naked . . . and let you look at her all that time?"

"But yes! Of a certainty. You see, Mademoiselle, that which I find beautiful—I paint: a sunset—or a woman. And I look upon one as impersonally as the other."

Ceclie looked at the painting again.

"No man," she said finally, "could be impersonal around a woman who looks like that. I wish I were so beautiful. But then I couldn't bear you looking at me so; I'd be too embarrassed." She looked at Paul and a mischievous little smile played around the corners of her mouth.

"All the same," she said, "I wish I had a picture of me like that. I'd give it to 'Tienne!"

"And have him shoot me? No thank you, Mademoiselle! Now if you'll turn your face a little more to the right . . ."

His fingers flew over the paper, making his first rough pencil sketch.

" 'Twill not be easy," he sighed. "Your beauty is as much of the spirit as of the flesh."

He worked diligently for a half hour.

"Mademoiselle is tired?" he asked.

"A little. 'Tis the smell of the paint, mostly. I think I'll go out upon the veranda and catch a breath."

She got up and Paul walked with her out upon the gallery. They looked up and down the narrow street. Suddenly Ceclie took hold of Paul's arm.

"Look!" she said breathlessly, "isn't that 'Tienne?"

Paul turned his head in the direction that she pointed. A ray of sun fell between the houses and gleamed upon the palamino's satiny coat.

"Yes," he said. "Yes it is."

They stood there waiting for Etienne to ride closer. As he

neared, Paul leaned over the wrought-iron balustrade. But Ceclie caught at his sleeve.

"No, no!" she whispered. "Don't call! I want to surprise him."

Etienne did not look up. His eyes were clouded with thought, so that what he saw made no image upon his brain. Then, at last, his vision cleared.

"Ceclie's horse!" he whispered, gazing at the short, ugly animal. "Oh, my God! I don't want to see her now—tonight will be soon enough. Well, I'll have to forgo talking this over with Paul. Later perhaps . . ." He pulled his horse up sharply and cantered away down the street.

Up on the gallery, Ceclie turned her great brown eyes upon Paul.

"He didn't stop!" she whispered. "Why, Paul—why?"

"I don't know," Paul began, but Ceclie was already gone, flying through the little studio, dipping gracefully to pick up her hat without even slackening her speed.

"Ceclie!" Paul cried. "Mademoiselle! Wait! Don't follow him! Please, Mademoiselle!"

But Ceclie's booted feet were already clattering upon the stairs going down.

"Name of a name of a diseased pig!" Paul said. "No good can come of this! No good at all!"

Ceclie flung herself into the saddle and thundered down the muddy street behind Etienne, but at the corner she pulled the mustang up abruptly.

"No," she whispered, "I musn't overtake him. I'll let him go wherever it is that he's going . . . and then I'll know why he stays away from me so long . . ."

She started out again, holding the vicious tough-mouthed little beast to a walk. Etienne rode on ahead, without even turning his head.

Then Etienne was turning the horse into Dumaine Street. Quietly Ceclie followed him as he crossed Burgundy. A block further on, at Rampart Street, he pulled the palomino up for a moment. Ceclie reined in instantly. But Etienne sat for a moment without moving, then he rounded the corner into Rampart. Ceclie waited a long time before she followed him.

As she cautiously turned the little mustang around the corner, she drew in her breath and held it. Then it all came out in an explosive rush, for Etienne had already dismounted. He walked firmly to the door of the little house that sat flush with the street and knocked. Ceclie was so close she could hear the knocking.

Then the door was opened, and a woman stood there, smiling a little at Etienne. Ceclie's brown eyes widened.

That woman! The woman of Paul's painting! She who had sat all day unclothed before a man's eyes . . . "No, 'Tienne," the girl whispered. "No!"

But Etienne had stretched out his arms and drawn the woman to him, his face alight.

"Here in the street?" the woman said clearly. "Monsieur is impetuous!"

Ceclie yanked the mustang around in a tight semicircle. Then she was slashing at his shaggy hide with all her force, hurling him through the cool, sunny streets back in the direction that she had come.

It took only a few minutes for her to cover the few blocks back to the studio. She leaped from the saddle and, pushing open the door with the broken lock, she ran up the stairs. Paul was not in the studio. He had stepped for the moment into his pantry to get a tall bottle of wine. It was better to get drunk, he had decided, than to sit and brood over the inevitable catastrophe.

Ceclie stood in the middle of the studio staring at the painting of Desiree. Her breath came out from her nostrils, loud in the silent room, and she trembled all over like a tormented animal. Then her eyes fell upon the short flat-bladed knife that painters use to scrape off excess paint. Quietly she bent and picked it up. She stood looking at the picture for a long, long time before she pushed it slowly through the painted figure at the exact spot that the heart would have been had it been alive. She drew it up and down then across, and again across at a diagonal.

When she had finished, the painting was a mass of tattered shreds hanging from the frame.

"Mademoiselle," Paul said softly.

She whirled, facing him.

"You realize," he said sadly, "that you have destroyed what to me was priceless? A thing I can never replace?"

He walked over and fingered a shred of canvas, stiff and heavy with paint. Tears sparkled in his eyes.

Ceclie looked at him.

"Yes," she said fiercely, "yes, I've ruined it! But I'll give you another. Set up another canvas, Mister Dumaine!" And already her fingers were busy with the buttons of her riding habit.

"No!" Paul said. "For God's sake, no!"

But the jacket fell softly to the floor. Ceclie sat down, tugging at her boots.

"Ceclie!" Paul said, "you don't know what you're doing!"

A long moment later, Ceclie stood up, making no effort to cover herself.

"Now," she said, "I'm as beautiful as she! Aren't I, Paul? Aren't I?"

Paul bent swiftly and lifted one of the largest of the prepared canvases that stood in a row against the wall.

"Yes," he whispered. "Yes. Oh, yes!"

In the little house on Rampart Street, Desiree stood very quietly facing Etienne.

"I shan't come again," Etienne said harshly. "This is the last time I'll trouble you."

Desiree smiled, the little golden flakes swimming in the deep green of her eyes.

"I'm sorry," she said. "I've enjoyed your company."

"So much that you've driven me half mad!"

"About that, I am more than sorry; but monsieur asks the impossible."

"Why?" Etienne demanded.

409

Desiree looked at him and her eyes were wide and grave.

"Because I don't love you, monsieur. I am not innocent, as monsieur knows; but my body is not a thing to be given lightly, lovelessly because monsieur wills it so. And then I cannot help but make comparisons . . ."

"Between me and my father?" Etienne demanded.

"Yes."

"And in this comparison, I suffer?"

"Yes."

Etienne's blue eyes blazed in his dark face.

"Yet I shall have you," he said. "Now!"

He caught her by both her arms and jerked her to him, tightening his hands around her waist until the slim body ground against his. Desiree stood very quietly looking up at him, and her face was still and unfrightened.

Etienne kissed her, driving one hand in at the small of her back, bending her over backward until her lips broke against her teeth. She made no struggle. Her body was like an inanimate thing: utterly without response.

Suddenly he pushed her away from him, holding her at arm's length.

"Well," he growled, "aren't you going to beg for mercy!"

Desiree shrugged.

"No," she said. "If you have so little shame . . ."

"Shame!" Etienne said. "Shame!" Then he lifted her as lightly as if she were a leaf and strode through the door into the bedroom. He tossed her upon her high, canopied bed. She lay there looking up at him, her green eyes very clear. Then as he bent to her she closed them as if shutting out his face, and her right hand swept up under the great silken pillow.

Etienne caught her by her shoulders and shook her.

"Damn you!" he said. "Damn you!"

But she did not even open her eyes.

It was over in an incredibly brief time. Etienne sat up, his pale eyes somber. He felt weak and sick, his victory ashes and dust in his mouth.

"Desiree," he whispered.

Slowly the green eyes opened. Her hands came out from under the huge pillow—holding a knife with an eight-inch blade that gleamed bluely in the dusk.

"Desiree!"

She sat up, holding the knife and looking at him. Then ever so slowly her fingers loosened until the knife fell to the floor. It landed point down, and stood and quivered in the planking.

"Go," she said, and her voice was throat deep and husky.

"My God!" Etienne whispered.

"I've had that a long time," she said. "You see, monsieur, my brother never reached France. He died aboard ship from the internal injuries your Negroes gave him."

"Then why . . . why?"

"Because I couldn't. You were Stephen Fox all over again . . . in walk and tone of voice and small arrogant gesture. So many times I planned it . . . if ever you touched me . . . if ever you mentioned my brother's name . . ."

"I see," Etienne said. Then very quietly he walked toward the door. In the doorway he turned and looked back at her. She was still sitting there in the same position. Not even her eyes had moved.

Etienne turned then and went out into the street. He moved very slowly, like a man already old.

XXVI

THE packet *Thomas Moore* pushed her way upstream against a four-mile current. The smoke stood up from her high twin stack in stiff, hard pants and her engines labored. Here, where she rode, the river was so broad that the opposite bank was but a dark smudge upon the horizon. The nearer bank slipped steadily backward, levee and quays and rude river towns dotting the shore at intervals interspersed by mile after mile of cotton lands. Only now and then could the passengers see a cane field; Louisiana had made her choice: Cotton was King.

Down upon the lowest deck where the bales were piled high and the hogsheads of sorghum and molasses crowded every available foot of space, Inch stood gazing back down river. He was quietly dressed, after the fashion of a white, complete to stovepipe hat, black broadcloth coat, white shirt and waistcoat, huge flowing black bow tie, and black boots that had been polished till they shone. He was smoking a cigar as he gazed, and the fragrant blue smoke wreathed his face in a cloud. His eyes were narrowed into a squint by the glare of the sun on the water.

Behind him at some distance two white men were standing, studying his back.

412

"So that's the nigger you're talking about," one of them said.

"Yes, Cap'n. An' he jes don't look right to me. I seed his papers when he come aboard, still . . ."

The captain frowned. Then deliberately he walked over to where Inch stood, turning sidewise to get his great bulk through the narrow lane between the bales of cotton. When he was close, he touched Inch with a horny finger.

Inch turned, his black face expressionless.

"Yes, sir?" he said.

"Lemme see your papers," the captain growled.

Without any hesitation Inch drew them out and passed them over. The captain studied them briefly and passed them over to his first officer.

" 'This—is—to certify,' " the officer read aloud, " 'thet Pierre, my Negro manservant, is granted his freedom upon my death. Provided he emigrates to some free state within three months of my demise . . .' "

"My master died two months ago," Inch put in smoothly. "Now, under the terms of his will, I must go."

"Your master was of the plantation Stillwater near Baton Rouge, wasn't he?" the captain demanded.

"Yes," Inch said, "sir . . ."

"But you come aboard in Nawleans. Why?"

"I was visiting relatives. And I had to buy some new clothes—" again the barely perceptible pause—"sir."

"That was where you was wrong, nigger," the captain said heavily. "You hadn't oughta bought them duds. Nobody woulda noticed you then." He turned to the first officer.

"Why didn't you check up on him when we stopped in Baton Rouge?" he demanded.

"To tell the truth, Cap'n," the first officer said, "I didn't think about it."

"You never think," the captain growled.

"Lock him up?" the first officer said hopefully.

"Naw. Ain't nowheres he kin go. Besides, he just might be tellin' the truth." He turned to Inch. "Look, boy," he said, "you

413

stay in plain sight. I wanta be able to lay hands on you if I find out you're lying about being free."

"Yes, sir," Inch said. The captain turned and went forward. The first officer followed him at some little distance, looking back over his shoulder at Inch.

Inch's heart beat a snare roll under his ribs. What was to be done? It was just now the beginning of the Spring of 1854 and the water was still icy. He looked toward the nearer bank, slipping backward slowly as the *Thomas Moore's* powerful engines drove her upstream. Ashore, he had a chance. There were people—white people—who would help. Grandmère Caleen had known about them, and even the passwords. Thank God now for that knowledge. Still the Underground Railroad was but a poor substitute for his bolder plan of traveling upriver in style. It would have been something if he could have done it, but now . . . now . . .

The fields a little way ahead were green with the first small shoots of cotton. In them, as far as Inch could see, a few Negroes worked. They were widely scattered and almost out of earshot of one another. Now it must be done, while there was yet a chance.

"I'll have to wait till we're a quarter mile upstream," he mused, "maybe a half. Then the current'll land me just about here. I'll swap clothes with one of the field hands. He'll be glad to get these things, even if they are wet." He looked around. No one was in sight. He took the stub of cigar out of his mouth and flicked it into the water. The current caught it and whirled it away down stream. Slowly he loosed his cloak and laid it gently upon the deck; then he took off his hat. The boots cost him a keener pang—they were soft calfskin, made by the best bootmaker of Paris; but what must be, must be.

Now it was time. He stood on the rail, staring down at the water. A wordless prayer trembled upon his lips. Then he was gone over the side. As the icy water closed over him, he remembered to seek depth, because near the surface the great paddle wheels created a murderous suction. Down, he went, down— swimming downward, forcing himself toward the muddy bottom. The great shadow of the *Tom Moore* was above him; then he

414

was shooting upward like a meteor, his lungs bursting, his head pounding with the pressure of the water.

He broke water some yards behind the packet, and the great tidal waves from her sternwheel broke over him, hurling him downstream like a chip. When he had recovered his breath, he struck out strongly for the shore, turning his eyes backward at every stroke toward the steamboat.

Half a mile downstream, his feet touched bottom. Slowly he crept ashore, trembling from head to heel from the cold. There, not twenty yards away from him, an old Negro worked, singing softly to himself. Inch lay on his belly amid the low cotton stalks and studied the man. If only I could see his face, he thought, then I'd be able to tell whether or not to ask him to change clothes with me. For a long time he waited, then, at last, the old man turned. Inch shook his head regretfully.

No, he decided, the risk was too great. The old man's face was serene with contentment. Ten minutes after the exchange was made, Inch knew, such a one would be on his way up to the big house to report the matter. It was such blacks as this that had brought down failure on nearly every insurrection that had been attempted in the South. One day, a way must be devised to handle these traitors, but now—how on earth was he to move on? He'd be spotted in a minute in these clothes.

Despairingly, he stretched out his hand. Then he was very still, and his eyes glowed in his black face. There at his fingertips was a stone—a large stone. Quietly he grasped it, and started crawling forward on his hands and knees, toward the old man.

A scant five minutes later, he was moving forward through the fields, barefooted, the hoe slung over one shoulder, and the battered hat drawn far down over his face. As he went, he was singing, softly, in tune to the rustle of his ragged osnaburg jacket and linsey trousers.

On the bayou road, Etienne rode toward New Orleans at a fast trot. Again Ceclie had refused to see him! The first time he had put it down to pride and feminine pique; but this made six times in a row. No, there was something definitely wrong here. Well, damn it all, he wouldn't try again! She'd come to him on her hands and knees—or would she? He groaned dismally, kicking the palamino forward.

He stopped first at the sheriff's office, to inquire whether or not any word had been received about Inch. As he expected, there was no news. The black appeared to have made good his escape. This was a great vexation. There were so many things upon which he had come to depend implicitly on Inch.

He rode aimlessly through the streets of the old quarter. Ahead of him, the doors of the Saint Louis Hotel—which had been rebuilt from the original City Exchange after that structure had burned in 1841—opened and a group of young men spilled out into the street, all talking and laughing at once. Etienne recognized them: there were Pierre Aucoin, Henri Lascals, Jean Sompayrac, but there were also Bob Norton, James Duckett, and Walter McGarth. When Stephen Fox had come to New Orleans, such a combination would have been rare; but today one thought little about whether a person were of American or Creole origin. The Creole belles were going out of their way to marry "uptown" as the expression was; the Americans had all the money, and were in full control of the political life of New Orleans. In fact, there were a surprisingly large number of Creole youths who could not speak one word of French!

Young Norton ran out into the street and grasped the bridle. "Down with you, 'Tienne," he roared, "and join a bunch of good fellows!"

Smiling, Etienne dismounted.

"And what," he asked, "shall I do with my horse?"

Henri Lascals laid a finger along his slim, aristocratic nose.

"Well," he said, "I don't think there's a glue factory handy . . ."

"That *cayeuse* won't even make decent glue," Duckett drawled in his deep Texas accent. "Jus' shoot him an' leave the carcass lay."

"A horse," Etienne observed, "is a man's best friend. He doesn't

416

drink up my liquor or purloin my women. He goes where I want him to, and . . . "

"Oh, my God," young Sompayrac groaned. "He's sober! He's coldly, obscenely, disgustingly sober."

"We'll fix that," Aucoin grinned. "Walter, go get a nigger from the hotel to take care of that off-color nag, while we take 'Tienne in to catch up on his drinking."

Norton and Lascals locked arms with Etienne, and all of them, except Walter McGarth, who had gone in search of the hotel's groom, went back into the bar.

Lascals pounded the bar.

"Waiter!" he roared. The waiter came, frowning severely at the noisy young men. "For me, a *crusta*—and a *pousse-café* for Pierre and one for Henri. You, Bob— What'll you have?"

"The same," Norton declared.

"Jim?"

"Whiskey and water—Rye," the Texan drawled; "and order Scotch for Mac."

Lascals looked at Etienne.

"For this lackadaisical, erstwhile drunkard," he said, "*four* Sazeracs."

"Four!" Etienne said. "My God, Henri, two would kill a man!"

"You'll make a cheerful corpse. Yes, waiter, I said four Sazeracs."

A half hour later, they were all talking and singing at the top of their lungs. Henri Lascals was admiring his own image in the mirror.

"You know, 'Tienne," he declared. "I am a very handsome lad. Yes, very. I should have my portrait painted. By the way, where is Paul? We haven't seen him in more than three weeks."

"Nor have I." Etienne said.

"Let's go up there," Bob Norton suggested. "They tell me he has gorgeous paintings . . . such women!"

"And all in complete *déshabillé*," Henri gloated.

A slow grin spread itself across Jim Duckett's lean, tanned face.

"Well," he drawled, "what are we waiting for?"

417

Out on the *banquette*, they broke into twos and marched along, swaying grandly.

"Don't know how Paul does it," McGarth groaned. "Judy-Ann caught me taking a peek at her ankle—just a peek—and I had to go down on my knees—and at that it was two weeks before she'd have me back."

"You're not a Parisian, Mac," Etienne pointed out. "The French have a way about them."

"But you're French," Bob Norton put in, "or at least half . . . and I don't see you cutting much of a swath. That Ceclie Cloutier's had you dangling all Winter."

"Too true," Etienne moaned; "but look at Pierre, here, and Henri, and Jean. They're as pure Gallic types as Paul himself, and they're in the same boat with the rest of us. It isn't the blood, Bob, it's the training. Why, in France, the proud papas take them on their knees at the age of two and say: 'But of a certainty, *mon fils,* when one goes to the woman, one kisses her thus!'"

The whole group rocked with laughter. Suddenly Etienne felt Henri's hand upon his arm.

"Look, 'Tienne," he said, "isn't that Paul riding away from us? Yes it is! Of all the miserable luck! We'll never see those paintings now!"

"Who's that with him?" Walter McGarth demanded. "I'd swear it was a woman, but women don't ride cross saddle . . ."

Bob Norton shot a wicked glance at Etienne, seeing his face darken even in the rapidly fading light.

"I know one who does!" he chuckled. "No wonder you never got anywhere with Ceclie, 'Tienne; you've got too much expert competition."

Etienne turned and faced him, his heavy black brows meeting over his nose.

"You're mistaken, Bob," he said evenly. "That's a man with Paul."

"Like hell it is! A man with long black hair spilling down over his shoulders?"

"I said you're mistaken, Bob," Etienne said quietly.

418

"Now look, 'Tienne," Bob said, his voice rising. "You want me to deny the evidence of my own eyes? Who do you think you are?"

"You're drunk, both of you," Jim Duckett declared. "And I'll be damned if I'll see a couple of good friends shoot each other up in a tomfool duel. If it is Ceclie, Bob, which you don't positively know, it's still a matter between her and 'Tienne. So shut your trap and let's go back to the hotel since we can't see the paintings anyway."

"Wait," Etienne said, "maybe we can see them."

"How?" Jean Sompayrac demanded. "There's no doubt that that was Paul who rode away just now."

"The lock on that door doesn't work. Paul's been planning to have it fixed for the last seven months, but when it comes to anything else besides painting and women, my good Parisian friend isn't all there."

"Think he'll mind?" Lascals asked.

"What if he does? Who's going to tell him? We aren't going to steal any of his pictures are we?"

"Well," McGarth grinned, "I wouldn't swear that I mightn't lift one if they're as interesting as you fellows say."

Etienne turned in toward the door of the studio. He put his weight against it and pushed. Slowly it groaned open. Then they were all going up the stairs, laughing throatily in the darkness.

Inside the studio, it was black as pitch.

"Make a light somebody," Pierre Aucoin said, "I want to see if I'm here or if you left me back at the hotel."

Etienne, who had often visited the studio, walked straight to the candlelabra before he struck a match. The soft glow stole through the room and all the young men turned. Here were the landscapes: the river and the oaks of Harrow; the house itself, portraits of prominent people in various stages of completion; studies of Negroes; and three nudes—all of Desiree, and all painted from memory in vain attempts to recapture the picture that Ceclie had destroyed.

The seven youths bunched around them.

419

"Name of a name of a name!" Henri said. "How did he ever get around to *painting* her?"

"Simple," Aucoin said. "First one exhausts oneself, then the rest of the evening may be devoted to painting."

"No," Jean declared, "after three brush strokes there would be the necessity of exhausting one's self all over again!"

"You Creoles!" Jim drawled. "Still . . . the wench has her points. Taming such a filly wouldn't be a half bad way to spend an evening . . ."

"Or a month," Walter grinned.

Bob Norton had wandered away from the group and was diligently searching for other nudes. In the middle of the studio he stopped before a huge canvas, draped with cloth. He lifted one corner of the cloth and a slim white leg glowed softly before his eyes. He raised the cloth higher.

"Here's the best one!" he roared. "'Tienne, come help me get this damned cloth off!"

In the next instant half a dozen hands were tugging at the cover. It came free, rocking the easel so violently that Etienne was forced to steady it with his hand. Then the veins at his temple were standing out and throbbing visibly. Behind him Bob Norton's voice came out in a softly whispered: "My God!" Etienne whirled.

"Yes," he said harshly, "yes, it's Ceclie! But you've seen nothing—do you hear? Nothing—all of you!"

Jim Duckett frowned.

"Easy, 'Tienne," he said. "You're a bit too ready with your threats for my liking. I've seen that painting, by God! But if you want my word as a gentleman never again to mention I've seen it, you have it. And that goes for the rest of the boys. But don't threaten me. I should regret having to kill you."

Etienne swayed a little on his feet, his dark face drained of all color.

"You know, Jim," he said slowly, "at the moment that would be almost a kindness."

He turned again to the painting smouldering upon the canvas. The figure was reclining, and there was provocation, and slow,

420

spine-tingling invitation painted into every line of it. He had not realized that Ceclie was so beautiful; every curve of that perfect body sang from the canvas, and the song was the one Ulysses heard, straining against the cords that bound him to the mast. Here was consummate artistry; but, Etienne realized, Paul had merely done her justice.

Behind him, someone stirred. Etienne started at the sound. He had forgotten the others existed. His hand went into his pocket and came out with a jackknife. Slowly, carefully, he cut the painting from its frame and rolled it into a huge roll. Then he turned to the silent group.

"Let's go," he said. His voice had a rasp in it.

The others looked at one another. Then one by one they followed him down the creaking stairs and into the street.

It was well after midnight when Etienne reached the gates of Rosemont. He dismounted and opened them, then he climbed back upon his horse and rode on again toward the house. At this hour, no groom could be expected to take care of the horse, so he left the reins trailing over the horse's neck and started up the steps.

Twenty minutes of thunderous knocking at last brought out the butler. He stood there blinking like a fat, black owl, rubbing his eyes with the back of his hands and saying:

"Suh? Suh?"

"I want to see Miss Ceclie," Etienne snapped.

"She sleep, her," the butler got out. "It ver' late now, monsieur, yes."

"Awaken her!" Etienne said.

"But, suh, the ole maître, he don't 'low . . ."

"I said awaken her!"

"Awright," the butler said, "I go tell her, me. But Maître Phillippe gonna be powerful mad . . . yes!"

He shuffled away, head bent toward the stairs.

"Tell her it's about the painting," Etienne called after him.

The old Negro nodded and crawled snail-like up the stairs. Etienne started pacing up and down the hallway, holding the painting tightly in his hand. Then, after a few minutes, there

421

was the swift whisper of footsteps on the stair. Etienne looked up. Ceclie was in nightdress, and her robe fell loosely from her shoulders.

So it's true, Etienne thought, you are like the painting. What a pity that such an artist as Paul has to die . . .

"Well?" Ceclie said, "well—what is it, 'Tienne?"

Wordlessly, Etienne unrolled the painting.

Ceclie looked at it, then her brown eyes raised to Etienne's face.

"Yes, I posed for it. Beautiful, isn't it, 'Tienne?"

"You sat there like that and let a man look at you? You did that, Ceclie?"

"Yes."

Etienne's eyes were colorless beneath his black brows, and his voice terribly quiet.

"What else, Ceclie?"

The girl smiled at him.

"What concern is it of yours, 'Tienne?"

"You were going to marry me, remember. Everything you do is my concern!"

"So?"

"I asked you a question, Ceclie!"

"Do you really want me to answer it, 'Tienne?"

"Yes."

"Your friend is a very great artist . . . in all things."

"Ceclie!"

"He is very gentle and tender. Yet he's strong—so strong that he makes even pain—exquisite."

Etienne's pale eyes caught the candle flame like twin mirrors. His lips moved slowly, shaping the words, and his voice was very quiet.

"You whore!"

Ceclie took a step backwards as though she had been struck. Then she came forward again, walking deliberately up to him until her mouth was inches from his face.

"Yes, yes!" she said, "there is such a word for a woman. But what is there for a man? Tell me, 'Tienne! Give me a word vile enough to describe you! I could not ride up to Harrow to see you, because that was wrong and people would talk. I couldn't kiss you and be with you always as I wanted. But you could leave me day after day to go and wallow with a Negress! At least Paul is clean and sweet and gentle; at least I don't have to scrub off my skin with lye soap to get rid of niggerstench! Go on, 'Tienne, tell me the word! What is it?"

Etienne's eyes narrowed to slits in his dark face.

"Don't talk like that, Ceclie," he said, "I'm warning you!"

"I will talk! I'll talk all I please. You had all my love. You know that. Oh, my God, how I loved you! But you must go to your Negress, and I must sit patiently and wait for you to come back when you'd had your fill . . . like one of your pale Louisiana women. You forgot I was one quarter savage, didn't you, 'Tienne? It never occurred to you that I could match and top anything that you did! How was she—your Negress? No, don't tell me! Just remember—and when you see Paul, compare notes!"

Etienne stepped back away from her. Then he slapped her, hard across the face. She stood there, facing him, and a little trembling started in her limbs, and grew and grew until she quivered all over like a willow sapling in a high wind. Where his fingers had struck, her face was very white, then the red was coming in until the shape of his fingers was printed angry and crimson across her face.

"You have a weapon, monsieur?"

Etienne whirled.

Phillippe Cloutier was standing there in the doorway, clad in a dressing gown. His eyes searched the youth briefly.

"I see that you have not," he said quietly. "Then we'd best postpone this until tomorrow morning. Is the oaks agreeable to you?"

Etienne licked his dry lips.

"Yes," he got out, "yes—quite."

"My seconds will wait upon you at eight o'clock. You'll be so good as to indicate your choice of weapons then. I'll meet you at—say—eleven. I dislike rising too early. But perhaps you have a counter-suggestion, Monsieur Fox?"

Etienne shook his head.

"No," he said, "none."

"Very well. Come, Ceclie. Good night to you, monsieur."

Ceclie did not move. She was staring at her father.

"No, Father," she said. "No!"

Phillippe turned to his daughter.

"I gave you an order, Ceclie!"

"But you can't! You mustn't, Father! You can't kill 'Tienne! You can't, I won't let you!"

Phillippe looked at his daughter.

"You're a fool," he said coldly.

"I don't care what he did to me. I don't care and it doesn't matter. Look there upon the table. Look and see how well I deserved that slap. Go on, Father. Look!"

Phillippe hesitated. Then he crossed to the table and stared at the painting spread out across the table. He looked at it a long time, staring at the corner where the painter's signature was lettered in. When he spoke his voice was weary.

"I see," he said. "You'll accept my apology, monsieur?"

"I—I forgot myself, sir," Etienne said. "I ask your forgiveness and mademoiselle's. That was a hard thing to take."

"You know where this Dumaine lives?"

"Yes."

"Then you'll guide me there. Jules!"

The old Negro appeared at once through the doorway behind which he had been listening.

"Yes, maître," he quavered. "Yes?"

"Have horses saddled for Monsieur Fox and myself. And, Jules . . ."

"Yes, maître?"

"Bring coffee. It's beastly cold at this hour."

"Father," Ceclie whispered, "Father . . ."

"Go to your room, Ceclie. I'll attend to you later."

"You . . . you're going to beat me?"

Phillippe's voice was cold.

"No," he said. "There are more fitting methods. You'll excuse me, Monsieur, while I dress?"

The sky was lightening a little when they reached New Orleans. But the sunglow was weak, and the air had a bite to it. They rode silently until they reached the studio. Then they dismounted. They walked very slowly to the door and knocked.

Paul's voice floated down the stairway. It sounded almost relieved.

"Come in, messieurs," he said. "I've been expecting you."

Etienne and Phillippe stood in the doorway staring at the young painter. He was haggard, and his hair and clothing were in wild disarray. But his voice was calm.

"Well," he said. "I take it that you have something to say to me."

Phillippe looked around the studio.

"You've done well, monsieur," he said. "Louisiana has been kind to you. I'm afraid we pay too much attention to this democratic rot to have so enriched and honored the son of a penniless, worthless dauber!"

"My father was France's greatest painter in his day," Paul said. "I cannot permit you to insult his memory."

"And your mother? A barmaid? Or a can-can dancer? Or simply a daughter of joy?"

Paul shrugged wearily.

"I had expected a challenge," he said. "But since it pleases monsieur to provoke me into challenging him— Very well. I'll meet you at any time and place you set." He smiled a little. "About weapons—you had no need to go to so much trouble; I would have granted you your choice anyway."

"The east bank of the river—ten miles below the city for the place—"

Paul nodded in agreement.

"This afternoon—about five—"

"Very well—and the weapons?"

Phillippe smiled thinly, and his face was no longer that of a Parisian gentleman. It had the lean, controlled hardness of the Texan frontier.

"Bowie knives," he said flatly, "across a handkerchief, at three paces."

Paul's face paled. For a long moment, he said nothing. Then he inclined his head toward Phillippe.

"Very well," he said hoarsely, "I'll meet you."

"You'll provide me with seconds, 'Tienne?" he said. "I really don't know anyone well enough . . ."

Etienne nodded. He did not trust his voice. It might have a quaver in it, if he spoke; it might reveal something of the sickness spreading in cold waves through his middle. Damn Ceclie anyway! Yes, damn her and Desiree and all manner and condition of women!

Riding away from the city with Phillippe, he was silent. From time to time he glanced at the older man. Phillippe's face was bland, as though he were returning from a business trip. Paul was my friend, Etienne thought; and, whatever happened, Ceclie started it. A duel with the clochemardes or rapiers could be a beautiful thing—all grace and skill. Even with the pistols there was a certain *éclat* to it. Besides, duels between Creoles seldom terminated fatally. That was an American idea, this cold, deadly insistence upon killing one's opponent. But Phillippe had been too long in Texas. Knives—good God!

Phillippe half turned in the saddle.

"You seem troubled," he said gravely.

Etienne cleared his throat.

"I am," he said. "This that Paul did was a great wickedness, but, sir—knives! Indians or Mexicans might fight thus, but you are a gentleman, and so is Paul . . . I can't see . . ."

Phillippe laughed drily.

"Oh, I shan't kill the boy," he said. "I'll just notch his nostrils and his ears like a sow. Then we'll see how he'll fare as a seducer!"

Etienne said nothing. The sickness in his middle was a physical thing. He had a horrible fear that in another moment he was going to vomit there before Phillippe's eyes. But at last there was the fork where their roads separated. He half rose in the saddle.

"*Au revoir*, monsieur," he murmured.

"*Au revoir*, Etienne," Phillippe Cloutier said, " 'til five!"

" 'Til five," Etienne echoed. Then he touched spurs to his borrowed horse, and galloped off in the direction of Harrow. For the first time in his adult life, he felt the need for council. He had a strong desire to lay the whole thing before his father. But what could he say to Stephen?

As he rounded the drive into the courtyard of the house, he saw Stephen's big palamino coming toward him. He pulled up abruptly, licking his dry lips.

"So early, lad?" Stephen smiled, "and that horse—where did ye get so ugly a beast?"

"At the Cloutiers. My own was spent. Father . . ."

"Yes, 'Tienne?"

"Father . . . Today there's going to be a duel . . ."

Stephen's white brows bristled.

"Ye young fool!" he said. "The day for that sort of folly is gone forever. Who is it that ye're to fight? I'll go to him and convey your apologies."

"Even if he were wrong?"

"Aye. There are few quarrels worthy of so high a price as a man's life. Who is he, 'Tienne?"

"You didn't always think so, Father. I understand that you made damned sure of Hugo Waguespack!"

"I always thought so. And if that fat fool hadn't thrown himself into the path of my ball, he'd be alive today. But I've explained my past to ye far too often now. Tell me the name of this man!"

"Easy, father . . . I'm not to fight. The quarrel is between Phillippe Cloutier and Paul."

"Phillippe would go so far as to fight a boy?"

"Yes, Father. The provocation is great, though. Paul . . . dishonored Ceclie . . ."

Stephen looked at his son.

"While ye were running pell mell after Desiree, your Ceclie turned to other consolations. How little ye know of women, lad! Was that quadroon witch, beautiful as she is, worth this?"

"No. But what should I do now? Monsieur Cloutier has his choice of weapons . . . and he chose bowie knives, Father, across a handkerchief at three paces!"

427

"Holy Mother of God! When is this butchery to take place?"

"This afternoon . . . at five."

"Good. 'Tis thinking I am that I had better deal myself in. Paul is a fine lad. I won't have him slaughtered because ye were a fool and your Ceclie a spiteful minx. Go up to the house and try to rest. Any word yet of Inch?"

"No—the ungrateful scoundrel seems to have gotten away clean. But I'll have his hide if ever I do catch him!"

"About that, too, ye'll have to think twice. I'll join ye at two. Tell Georges to have fresh horses ready." He turned the big palamino's head toward the fields.

At half past four in the afternoon, Stephen and Etienne were already at the appointed place. Etienne dismounted and walked back and forth through the muddy bank.

"What are you going to do, Father?" he demanded. "And how?"

"I don't know. 'Twill depend upon the circumstances. But I won't see the lad hurt. Now will ye stop that damnable pacing?"

At a quarter of five, Paul Dumaine arrived with his seconds. They were Henri Lascals and Pierre Aucoin. Paul was perfectly composed, but his face was very white. Stephen went to him at once.

"Ye'll apologize," he said. "This is nothing to die over!"

"I'm afraid Monsieur Cloutier won't accept an apology," Paul murmured. "I'll do my best. 'Tis all I can do now." Stephen took his arm and the two of them walked a little apart from the others. Etienne could see his father talking earnestly.

At precisely two minutes of five, Phillippe arrived with his seconds and the surgeon. Under his arm he carried a case. Dismounting, he opened it and walked over to Paul. The great blades of the knives gleamed like silver in the sunlight.

"Your choice, sir," he said.

"Wait," Stephen said. "The lad has a statement to make."

"This is none of your affair, Stephen Fox!" Phillippe declared.

"Aye. But I'm making it my affair. In this business of the knives the lad has no skill, and, damn it, Phillippe, I'll not see him murdered!"

"You want to take his place?"

"If necessary. But hear him out, Phillippe."

The little group of men gathered closer around Paul.

Paul looked at Stephen, then at Etienne. He cleared his throat.

"Gentlemen," he said. "This duel was occasioned by the accidental discovery of a painting which I made of Mademoiselle Cloutier. The painting was of such a nature as to place grave implications upon Mademoiselle's reputation. I want only to say that Mademoiselle is entirely blameless. I painted the picture as a jest to plague my good friend Etienne Fox. It was done without Mademoiselle's knowledge or consent. She posed only for the head, thinking that I intended it for a miniature which she had promised Etienne as a gift. The figure was posed by an octoroon. I say this to clear Mademoiselle Cloutier's reputation of any hint of stain. As for myself, I do not attempt to justify my gross error. I place myself at monsieur's pleasure."

"You lie!" Phillippe spat out.

"Softly, Phillippe," Stephen said. "If ye say that the lad lies, ye yourself impugn your daughter's honor. 'Tis most ungentlemanly of ye!" He turned to Paul. "Now, lad," he said sternly, "ye'll apologize for this folly or, by heavens, I'll have your hide as though ye were my own son!"

Paul smiled slowly.

"I do apologize," he said. "I freely and humbly apologize to Monsieur Cloutier and to all the other gentlemen present for my misconduct."

"Do ye accept it, Phillippe? Or do ye wish us all to take the contrary view that ye have no faith in your own?"

Phillippe's face was mottled with rage.

"You're a clever bastard, Fox!" he got out. "What else can I do now?" He whirled on his heel and strode back to his waiting horse. Paul turned to Stephen.

"Thank you, sir," he said.

"Think nothing of it, lad. Life seems to be made up largely of hellish scrapes. But if ye'll take my advice, I'd suggest that ye leave the state—for a while at least—until this blows over.

Go North; there are many people of wealth and distinction who would delight in being portrayed by so skillful a hand."

Paul half turned in the direction that Cloutier and his party were riding.

"I should hate having anyone think I ran away," he said slowly.

"To hell with what people think," Stephen told him. "I've lived all my life without bending an inch to public censure. Your pride is one thing, but to intensify such a bitterness is quite another."

Etienne was staring at the retreating back of Phillippe Cloutier.

"He'll hate you forever, Father," he declared.

"So? There's never been much love lost between us. Come, lads, we'd best be getting back."

Paul Dumaine turned to Etienne.

" 'Tienne," he began, and half extended his hand.

Etienne's black brows bristled, and his eyes were as pale as water.

"There is nothing to be said between us, Paul," he growled. "Ever!"

Stephen looked at the two of them standing there facing each other, drawn up very stiff and proud.

"Young fools!" he snorted, and threw a lean leg across the palamino. Etienne mounted in his turn, but Paul stood very still, watching his friend. Stephen turned in the saddle and saluted the young painter gravely. Paul returned the gesture, his eyes fixed upon Etienne, who sat like a statue in the saddle, staring out over the river. Stephen looked from one to the other of them; then he shrugged.

"Come, lad," he said, and the two of them turned their horses' heads northward, toward New Orleans.

XXVII

SPRING came late that year in the upper reaches of the Ohio Valley. The river itself was still half choked with ice, and a thin miserable drizzle whined earthward toward the snow-covered ground. It was composed about equally of sleet and rain, with a few feathery flakes of snow drifting down at long intervals. On the South bank of the Ohio, not three hundred yards from the river, the farmhouse stood, so shrouded in Winter white that from the packets, butting their way westward through the floes toward the Mississippi, it was all but invisible.

Inside the house, the logs blazed on the hearth. Beside it, the farmer dozed in a big rocker. His grey beard, cut square at the bottom, rose and fell gently on his ample bosom. His wife sat in the other chair, her knitting needles clicking busily. Her steel-rimmed spectacles were pushed far up on her thin forehead, but the keen old eyes with the thin humorous lines at the corners followed easily the rapidly moving points of the needles. Suddenly the needles were still, and the old woman leaned forward, her thin, pinched nostrils flaring. The logs crackled upon the hearth. But outside, the silence was frightening. The rain and sleet drifted down past the window with a faint whispered whining. The farm woman sighed. Her hands took up their busy movement.

Then again she stopped. The whole world crashed into stillness. But this time she did not hesitate. She stretched out her hand and shook her husband firmly.

"Silas!" she whispered.

He came awake at once without even blinking. It was a faculty born of long practice, this ability to pass from deep sleep to the most acute awareness. Many times in the past it had saved their lives.

"Yes," he grunted. "Yes, Hope?"

"There's somebody outside . . . in the snow. I can't even swear I heard him, but I know he's there!"

Silas got up and crossed the room, as silent as a cat for all his great bulk. He drew on his sheepskin-lined jacket and a coonskin cap. Then he took the ancient flintlock rifle down from above the mantle. He stopped for a moment to change the priming. Stepping to the door, he drew it open cautiously, standing well to one side of the opening. Many were dead or imprisoned who had forgotten to be careful. The wind came in the doorway crying. Silas stood there waiting. Then at last he pulled his cap down over his ears and strode out into the storm. The moment the door closed behind him, the world disappeared. He took a cautious step forward, then another. Fifty yards forward he went. There was nothing. He retraced his steps and started out again at an oblique angle to his first path. Still nothing. The third time he set out again, on the other side of his first path. At the end of his counted steps, he stood for a moment in the empty waste; then shrugging, he turned back toward the house.

"Hope must be daft," he muttered. But before he had gone three yards, he stopped. Something *had* moved. Out there in the drifted snow, a few feet to his left, something was moving in the snow. He must have passed it by scant inches on his first trip. He turned and floundered toward the moving object. When he was close, he bent down.

It was a Negro clad only in a rude shirt and trousers, shivering in the snow. His feet were bare, and where they had rested, the snow bore a dark stain. Silas shook him, bending down his ear.

The black lifted his trembling, cold-greyed face, and his lips moved briefly.

"Liberty!" he whispered.

Silas smiled.

"Lies northward!" he said, completing the password. Then he bent and picked the Negro up, holding him like a babe in his giant arms. He strode forward, step by measured step toward the house.

Hope opened the door to his muffled knock. She looked down at the frozen black face.

"Dead?" she asked.

"Not yet . . . see what you can do."

Instantly the old woman was busy; her lean fingers flew, loosening the Negro's clothes.

"Got any tea?" Silas demanded.

"Yes—there." Silas put the tea leaves in an earthen pot, and set a small saucepan of water on the hearth to boil. Then he went to work chafing the thin wrists and arms that were a purplish grey from the cold, with handfuls of snow. A few minutes later, the water in the saucepan was bubbling merrily. Hope took it up and poured it into the earthenware teapot. She looked at Silas.

"Yes," he said. "Lace it with the rum."

" 'Tis the last," she told him.

"Use it!" Then tenderly as a woman, the big man lifted the black's head. Hope poured a few drops of the fiery liquid between his clenched teeth. The adam's apple moved in the thin throat, then the teeth parted. Instantly the old woman poured a huge draught of the tea down the Negro's throat. Almost at once they could see life flowing back into the cold limbs. The grey left his cheeks and the rich black shone like velvet. Silas took cold water and began to bathe the frozen feet and hands. His wife poured drink after drink of the rum-tea down the Negro's throat.

433

Then the eyelids were flickering open, and the great brown eyes, surprisingly light for one so black, rested on their faces.

"Thank you," he whispered. "Never before I started did I believe that there were white people who . . ."

"Don't talk," Silas growled. "Save your strength."

"You'll rest here 'til you're better," the woman said kindly. "Some night—when the weather moderates. It really should be warm now, but the winter lingers."

"No," the Negro said sharply. "No! They're after me! You'll get in trouble."

"Nonsense, boy. We've been through all that before. You can't go now. Why, you wouldn't even reach the river alive. What is your name?"

"Inch," the Negro whispered. "I am called Inch."

Two nights later, a dinghy slipped between the lessening ice floes and pushed its way to the other side of the Ohio. Inch stepped ashore. He was warmly clad, and on his feet were good, stout boots, many sizes too large for him. He sank down upon the frozen ground and kissed it.

"Free soil!" he murmured. "Free!" He turned to Silas, who was sitting quietly in the boat. "Thank you," he said. "The saints will bless you for your help."

"'Tis little enough," Silas said. "I could not live with myself if I didn't strike a blow against this damnable traffic in human flesh. But you're far from free, Inch. You've still got to be cautious. You remember the name of your next contact?"

"Yes—William Walker in Cincinnati. I should reach him by tomorrow."

"'Twould be wiser far to push on to Canada; but, since you insist, Boston will be safe enough. Milliken will put you in touch with a law office where you can get work. But I meant to ask you—why law?"

"I read for the bar when I was in Paris with my master. If I can pass the Massachusetts bar I could be of great service to my people."

"Good! The best of luck to you, young Inch!"

"Thank you. And to you and Madame, the blessings of God!"

A month later, Inch climbed down from a railway car in the bleak and ancient city of Boston. As he edged his way through the great crowds in the station, he was conscious of an aloneness so vast that all of life seemed swallowed in it. He started walking. He had not the faintest notion of where he was going; but he did not ask directions. Later, when he had seen it all, and dragged in many more lungfuls of free air, he would ask; but not now. He had a strange desire to listen to the secret heart of this his chosen city. Here, men were free, black men as well as white. It was a thought to be savored long and quietly.

At Harrow, on the next day after the duel which Stephen had ended before it began, Etienne Fox was feverishly packing his valise. This was no easy task, for he was oversupplied with clothing, and to make the right choice was difficult. He must be richly dressed, but not too much so, for extravagant display would be fatal to his plan. As he pondered, he heard a muffled cough from the doorway. Turning, he saw his father's lean frame draped against the doorframe.

"So, lad, ye're planning to leave us?"

Etienne frowned angrily.

"Why aren't you in the fields, Father?" he demanded. "You always go at this hour."

Stephen shrugged.

"Perhaps I'm clairvoyant," he said; "but somehow I knew ye had mischief afoot. Well, out with it, lad. Where are you going?"

Etienne smiled, a slow, mocking smile.

"To the river—to follow in the footsteps of my esteemed father," he said. "I already have a place engaged on a packet. The captain is willing to have me permanently aboard—for a cut of my winnings."

"Ye're a fool," Stephen said without heat. "'Tis no life for the likes of ye."

"You can't stop me, Father!"

"Aye—that I know. But a packet gambler must be a successful one. Are ye sure ye can manage it, 'Tienne?"

"I play as well as you do!"

"Ye should, for I taught ye all I know. But that remains to be seen. Suppose I make ye a sporting proposition?"

Etienne's black brows met over his nose.

"What sort of proposition, Father?"

"Oh—just a friendly game of poker."

"And the stakes?"

"One half of the land now—against your giving up this tomfool idea."

Etienne gazed at Stephen and the matching sets of eyes held and locked.

"Done!" he said. "I was never one to turn down a game."

Stephen smiled.

"Come into the study, lad," he said softly.

Inside the study, Stephen busied himself clearing a small table. When he had finished, he set out a cut-glass decanter of brandy, his own white clay pipe and a box of cigars.

"Cut for the deal, 'Tienne?"

"Yes."

Stephen ruffled the cards and set them upon the table. Etienne passed his hand over them, then abruptly he cut the deck half way to the bottom. He held up the bottom card. It was the king of diamonds. Stephen smiled. Then his hand moved. The deck was cut to within three cards of the bottom. Without changing his expression he exhibited the card. It was the ace of spades.

"All right," Etienne growled. "You deal."

"Draw or Stud?"

"Draw!" Etienne declared.

The play went on throughout the entire night, first one winning, then the other. As the first grey streaks of morning stole into the window, Stephen looked at his disheveled red-eyed son.

"Now to make an end," he said. "We're even, aren't we?"

Etienne put down the smouldering stub of his cigar.

"Yes," he said. He had the oddest feeling that Stephen had

436

been toying with him all night, that even when he won it had been by his father's contrivance.

"Ye're agreed to stand by this hand?"

"Yes." Etienne's voice was muffled.

"My deal," Stephen said blandly. His hands, moving, made a whitish blur.

Etienne picked up the cards and looked at them. Then he took up one from the deck, discarding another. Stephen did the same. Again Etienne drew and discarded. But after the third draw, Stephen rested. Etienne looked at his father. This would have to do. He had three of a kind: the queens of diamonds, hearts, and clubs. The other two cards he held were unimpressive: a deuce of hearts and a trey of spades. Still, such a hand was hard to beat. He spread it fanwise upon the table.

Stephen glanced down, and the white brow over his left eye crawled upward toward the scar. His smile was full of bland mockery.

Slowly he revealed his hand. He held the ace, king, queen, jack, and ten of spades.

"A Royal Flush!" Etienne said. "Such a hand wouldn't happen once in ten million years! You cheated, Father!"

Stephen continued to smile.

"Perhaps," he said. "And perhaps this is the ten millionth year. But if I cheated ye and ye didn't detect it, how on earth could ye ever match such sure-thing players as Canada Bill, or George Devol? 'Tis thinking I am that ye should choose another profession. But ye lost, and I expect ye to abide by your wager like a gentleman."

"I won't!" Etienne stormed. "I won't!"

Stephen opened his mouth to say something, but old Jean-Jacques was standing in the doorway.

"A lady to see the young maître," he said, then leaning close to Etienne, his black face beaming: "It's Mamzelle Ceclie!" he whispered loudly.

Etienne glared at him.

"Tell her I won't see her!" he said. "Tell her to go away!'

437

"Don't be a fool, lad," Stephen said. "At least ye could hear her out."

Etienne stood up.

"All right," he said. "Show her in, Jean-Jacques."

Ceclie came into the big hall and stood looking small and lost in the vast expanse. Etienne hesitated a moment, then walked firmly toward her. He saw the black hair clubbed under her little hat, and the trim green riding suit clinging to the slim young body. When he was close she turned a face devoid of any color up to him and put out one hand.

"I've come to say goodbye, 'Tienne," she said clearly.

"So?" he grunted.

"We're going back to Texas. Father's selling the place—at a terrific loss. You know why, 'Tienne?"

"No, why?"

"Because I disgraced him so. He swears he's going to put me in a convent in Texas."

Etienne looked at her wordlessly. She came up very close to him and her brown eyes were tear bright.

"You—you're glad I'm going, 'Tienne?"

"It seems to me," Etienne said drily, "you should ask Paul."

Ceclie took a step backward.

"I should have expected that," she whispered; "but I didn't somehow. I guess it's because I love you so that I forget everyone else exists."

"You love me!" Etienne mocked, "so much that you become Paul Dumaine's mistress! So much that you pose for obscene portraits. . . ."

"My picture was beautiful!" Ceclie declared. "I wanted to give it to you . . . so that you'd hurt inside just a little the way you made me hurt! But it wasn't any good, was it, 'Tienne? I ended up by ruining everything for everybody."

She stopped and looked up at him.

"Maybe one day you'll understand," she said. "Maybe you'll know how it feels to be dying inside your body by slow inches. When you get like that, when you can't even breathe, and your middle's so empty you can feel the echoes, and your eyes are

438

blinded, and your ears stand up like a burro's listening, listening
. . . Oh, for God sake, 'Tienne, kiss me so I can go!"

Etienne stood looking at her, then he caught her up in his
arms. He tightened his grip about her waist until she moaned a
little, but her mouth clung to his, hot and sweet, the lips parted.
Her fingers were moving among the soft curls on the back of his
neck, working gently. Then, fingers were digging into his flesh,
feline and fierce, and her mouth was caressing his, hot, demanding. He tightened his grip once more, pressing her backwards
until her lips broke against her teeth.

Then he released her, and she hung against his arms, her face
very white and her mouth poppy-red and swollen.

"Never let me go, 'Tienne," she whispered. "Never!"

Etienne drew her gently to him.

"Say it wasn't true about you and Paul," he said harshly. "Say
it, Ceclie! Even if you lie!"

She smiled at him, her eyes soft with tenderness.

"All right," she whispered, "I'll say it, but what good is it?
Now you'll never know. If you love me, it won't matter. I'm
yours, I've always been yours, since the day I was born. But if
you doubt me, let me go quickly while I can still bear it."

Etienne looked at her.

"We'll be married today," he said. "Then we'll both leave this
accursed place. We'll go somewhere new—like Kansas. But by
heavens, Ceclie, if ever in your sleep you call me 'Paul' I'll
strangle you!"

He turned and looked back toward the study where Stephen
sat, drawing in long puffs of fragrant blue pipe smoke.

"I'd better tell father," he said. "Come, Ceclie." He put his
arm about her waist and the two of them walked through the
open door into the study.

"Father . . ." Etienne began.

Stephen put the little clay pipe down slowly.

"So," he said, "ye've made it up, have ye? Are you both sure
ye aren't making a mistake?"

Ceclie's face flamed scarlet.

"I . . . I know what you think of me," she said. "But is this one thing going to be held against me forever?"

Stephen smiled.

"By me—no," he said. "There was much that was wrong on both sides. The point that worries me is—can either of ye grow big enough to forget? 'Twill be a hellish marriage if both of ye are forever digging up the past to throw it in the other's face. For there will be quarrels, ye know. No man ever lived with a wife year in year out without a sharp word or two passing between them."

"There is no past, Father," Etienne growled. "It died five minutes ago. I'll never resurrect it."

Ceclie said nothing, but her great brown eyes turned upward to her lover's face and rested there, glowing.

"Good," Stephen said, rising. "Now we'd all better ride out to Rosemont and see Phillippe."

At once all the color disappeared from Ceclie's face.

"No!" she said. "He'll never consent!"

" 'Never' is a big word, little Ceclie," Stephen said. " 'Tienne, go and tell your mother. Ask her to join me as soon as I am dressed for riding."

When Stephen came down the stairs, he found Aurore already waiting. She was dressed in her riding habit and held a crop loosely in her hand.

"I'm going with you, Stephen," she said clearly; "I could always handle Phillippe better than anyone else. There have been too many challenges already."

"Then ye approve?" Stephen asked. "About that I had some doubt."

"No, Stephen," Aurore said slowly, "I don't approve. A marriage should be based upon perfect trust. And neither Etienne nor Ceclie has demonstrated enough stability to suit me. But who am I to say? I married a man who didn't even love me and whose reputation was anything but savory . . . and it worked. A new start in a different part of the country where no one has heard the whispers . . . Besides how long would my disapproval deter them . . . or yours, Stephen?"

"Not five minutes," Stephen grinned. "The lad is of my blood. Well, if Phillippe will hold his fire until we get a chance to talk to him we might persuade him. Anyhow, 'tis worth a try."

They found Phillippe having a frugal breakfast alone in the great dining hall of Rosemont. When the butler announced them, he came out, his face frozen. Grimly he saluted Aurore. Then he turned to Stephen.

"So, Fox," he said icily, "you find it necessary to bring your wife when you have difficult business."

Stephen's white brows flew together.

"Softly, Phillippe," he began, but Aurore was raising her hand.

"I came of my own free will, Phillippe," she said, "because I know what bad-tempered wretches both of you are. Now, you listen to me. These wild, headstrong children of ours have decided to get married. So we came to ask your consent. It seems to me to be the best thing. Nothing else will so effectively silence wagging tongues!"

Phillippe turned to Etienne.

"So, lad," he growled, "you want this girl of mine in spite of all she's done?"

"If she'll have me," Etienne said, "in spite of all I've done."

Phillippe looked from one to the other of them. He smiled mockingly.

"Birds of a feather," he said. "The good God in his wrath could have devised no more fitting punishment than to force you two to spend a lifetime together. You have my blessing. In fact, I'll come along to see the knot well tied."

"Oh, Father!" Ceclie said breathlessly. Phillippe glared at her.

"Don't thank me!" he said; "I'm heartily glad to be rid of you!"

Etienne's face darkened.

"You're a beast!" he said.

"So? That I don't doubt. And so must your father be also, for the two of us to have had such children. Come in, all of you, I shan't detain you long."

It took all of Stephen's powers of persuasion to talk old Father DuGois into performing the ceremony, but at last it was done, and on the next afternoon at five o'clock, when the great parade

441

of boats moved majestically away from the quays, Etienne and Ceclie were aboard one of them, bound upriver for Kansas. Etienne's pockets were well-lined with money with which to purchase his new lands and, in addition, he had a blank draft, signed by Stephen against the latter's Philadelphia banking account.

In another of the packets, Paul Dumaine was sailing away from New Orleans forever.

XXVIII

B<small>Y EARLY</small> November of 1854, the cane crop was all in. The weather continued warm and Spring-like, and the crushers in the sugar house were rolling and thumping. The Negroes went about their work with grins upon their faces, for the time for the harvest and celebration was almost at hand. Julie rode everywhere over the great plantation with her father, and met every post in vain expectation of a letter from Etienne.

On the morning of the last day of the harvest, she was already mounted on the fat Shetland awaiting her father when he came down the steps. Stephen smiled at the round, eager face.

"Don't ye ever sleep?" he asked with mock gruffness. "I wouldn't have gone without ye."

"You're so slow, Father!" Julie complained. "You're getting almost as lazy as that fat old Monsieur Le Blanc."

"Heaven forbid!" Stephen grinned as he swung into the saddle. "Well—where'll we go first this morning?"

"To the low fields—down by the river. We can see the road from there and—"

"And the postrider comes that way. Don't worry, Julie, that scoundrel of a brother of yours will write us soon. Well, the low fields it is. See if ye can get some speed out of that fat beast. We're late as it is."

"It's all your fault, Papa," Julie pouted. "You just wouldn't get up!"

"One grows old, daughter o' mine. Ye must have patience." They set out at a swinging trot down the alley of oaks toward the levee. But, before they had gone half way, a hired carriage turned in from the bayou road and came toward them. Julie's face shone with joy.

"Maybe it's 'Tienne," she breathed. "Perhaps he's decided to come back!"

"That I doubt," Stephen said. "But we'll soon see who it is."

As they came abreast of the carriage, the driver pulled it up, and Stephen's palamino danced alongside of the door. Stephen lifted his hat courteously.

Then Julie's face fell. The man who was leaning out of the small half window bore not the slightest resemblance to Etienne. He was very lean of face with a big, thin-lipped mouth that looked as though it was made for smiling. His voice, when he spoke, was very deep.

"Is this the plantation of Mister Stephen Fox?" he asked.

"Aye," Stephen said, "and I am Stephen Fox. Whom do I have the honor of addressing?"

The wide mouth widened still further into a smile and the dark grey eyes had a sparkle in them.

"Southern courtesy," he said. "I'd almost forgotten how it was." He half turned to someone hidden in the shadow inside the carriage. "You see, Tom," he chuckled; "I told you."

"Yes, Dad." The boy's voice came out clear and strong.

"My name is Thomas Meredith," the man said, looking at Stephen. "And this is my son and namesake. Tom, say hello to the gentleman and the young lady."

The boy's head appeared through the window. His face was that of his father, but softened by youth. Seventeen or so, Stephen decided.

"Good morning, Mister Fox," he said, and his voice had a Yankee crispness to it that was totally absent from the speech of his father. He turned his enormous light grey eyes upon Julie, and his long, very dark lashes blinked rapidly. A heavy lock of dark brown hair escaped his hat and curled damply over his high, white forehead. The wide, extremely mobile mouth spread and trembled a bit at the corners. A mite too sensitive for a lad, Stephen thought.

Julie's cheeks reddened under the steady gaze, but she couldn't help smiling.

"My name is Julie," she said clearly.

"An enchanting name," the older man said, "for a lovely lady."

Stephen put his tall hat back upon his head.

"Ye're very welcome," he said. "Come up to the house."

"But you were about to leave . . . you had some business perhaps . . ." Thomas Meredith said.

"A routine inspection. It can wait. We don't have guests often, and 'tis always a pleasure, especially for Julie. She's a sociable soul—like her mother."

"'Twill be very pleasant meeting Madame Fox. It's been a long time since I've talked to a Southern lady. We're from Boston, you know."

"The lad, yes. But ye—I'd have guessed Georgia or Alabama from your accent."

"Correct! I was born on a plantation near Tuscaloosa. But it's been more than twenty years since I set foot on Southern soil."

Stephen turned the palamino in a mincing circle, and Julie rode the pony to the other side of the carriage. The driver flapped the reins and the little cavalcade moved slowly off in the direction of the house.

"You're wondering why we came?" Thomas Meredith asked.

"Frankly, yes."

"You have a son of mine buried upon your land. We came to view the grave and arrange for the removal of the body to Boston."

Julie's eyes opened wide.

"Oh, no!" she said.

"My sympathies, sir," Stephen said gravely, "but about that last intent, I hope ye'll change your mind. The grave has become

445

quite a shrine for Julie, here. She tended the lad in his last hours, and he seems to have made a lasting impression upon her."

"Dan was like that," Thomas Meredith murmured. "His mother has never quite recovered from his loss. But you've made me feel better already . . . just knowing that he received such tender care."

"We did all we could; but 'twas quite hopeless. I don't think the lad suffered too much."

They rode the rest of the way in silence. On the far side of the carriage, young Tom Meredith was casting sidelong glances at Julie. She sat very straight upon the fat pony, but her cheeks were hot and red.

When they reached the house, Aurore was already waiting upon the upper gallery. The sharp eyes of the Negroes had seen the carriage a long way off, so that she had had ample warning. Thomas Meredith and his son got down from the carriage, and went up the broad stairs with Stephen and Julie.

Aurore smiled and put out her hand.

"Welcome to Harrow," she said.

Thomas Meredith bowed over it.

"Thank you," he said. "We're doubly honored."

"Aurore," Stephen said, "may I present the Thomas Merediths —father and son—of Boston. Gentlemen, Madame Fox."

Aurore smiled.

"Come in," she said. "You're in time for late breakfast."

They went into the great hall. Young Tom Meredith stood opened-mouthed, just inside the door.

"Tom!" his father said sharply.

"It's—it's a palace," the boy whispered. "Like you read about in books."

"Certainly there's nothing like it in Boston," his father declared. "Now you begin to understand our Southern friends?"

"Yes, Dad!" the boy said. "No wonder they fight so hard for—" He stopped suddenly, his face covered with confusion. "Sorry, Dad," he said.

"It's all right, son," Thomas Meredith said. "But don't forget again."

Stephen's white brows rose quizzically.

"Ye're among friends, lad," he said kindly; "here ye may speak freely."

Aurore lifted a graceful hand.

"Come," she said. "Breakfast is waiting."

She ushered them into the dining salon. The moment they were seated, the Negroes appeared bearing the gleaming twin pitchers with the *café au lait*, and steaming mounds of *pain perdu*. Thomas Meredith tasted the strange food gingerly, but young Tom was staring curiously at the Negroes.

"Ye don't have many blacks in Boston," Stephen observed.

"Only a few," the boy said; "I can't get used to them."

Julie put down her cup.

"But your brother Dan said you were abolitionists," she blurted.

"Julie!" Aurore began, but Thomas Meredith was smiling.

"Dan was right," he said softly; "but you'll forgive us this time, won't you, little Julie?"

Aurore looked at the tall man, and her face was puzzled.

"But you're a Southerner," she said.

"Yes, Madame. I was born in Alabama. When I was twenty, my father died and left me Pine Hill and three hundred slaves."

"And ye freed them all and sold the place. I remember that well," Stephen said. "It created quite a furor."

"Yes," Thomas Meredith said, smiling; "so much so in fact that I found myself most unwelcome in Alabama. That was when I went to Boston."

"Why?" Aurore demanded. "Why did you do it, monsieur?"

"You ask me something very difficult to answer, Madame. It's a thing about which people often feel very keenly . . ."

"Ye'll find us strangely civilized," Stephen laughed. "Please say what ye want to. Then perhaps my good wife will cease to think me mad."

Thomas Meredith's eyebrows rose.

"My husband has often expressed a desire to do exactly what you did," Aurore explained. "But his friends and I have always held him back. Abolitionist sentiment has always seemed . . .

447

well . . . a little peculiar. It isn't too difficult to understand how a fanatical Northerner with no real knowledge of the Negro's characteristics and no financial stake in the matter could think as they do, but a Southerner . . . and a cultivated gentleman like yourself . . ."

"Thank you for the kind words, Madame Fox. Frankly, I don't like to talk about it. All the discussions seem to hinge on a sort of offensive assumption of moral superiority on the part of the anti-slave man. Some of my co-workers in the cause are indeed strange bedfellows for me. But let me put it this way: no matter how little grounds your Garrisons, Phillips, and Thompsons have for their bitter denunciations, the fact remains that from a moral standpoint slavery is wrong."

"I don't see it," Aurore said crisply. "We treat the Negroes kindly—much more so, in fact, than you treat your mechanics and hired laborers in the North."

Thomas Meredith smiled.

"Two and two do make four, don't they, Madame? Except when two are apples, and two figs. Two wrongs have never yet added up into a right. And wrong is forever on the same side of the scale so you can't make them balance out and cancel each other. Besides, there are abuses as Madame well knows."

"Only a few—a very few."

"More than I like to think about, Madame. The way that the blacks are brought in is unbelievably brutal. Oh, I know that the trade's been abolished; but it still flourishes illegally. Has Madame ever seen a slave ship—or smelled one?"

Aurore shook her head.

"Often as many as half the Negroes aboard," Thomas Meredith said, warming to his subject, "die during the voyage—from starvation, crowding, unsanitary conditions, and brutal treatment. Even in the interstate trade the mortality is high. Would Madame sit down to dinner with a slave trader?"

"Heaven forbid!" Aurore said.

"All over the South they are social pariahs. Why? They are coarse, cruel men. Again, why is the trade in the hands of men of that type? There is no moral stigma attached to buying a

448

slave from one of them, but to make a living by dealing in black flesh is held despicable by the very people who sanction it—good, kindly Christian people like Madame herself."

Aurore drew herself up very stiffly in her chair. Stephen looked at her out of the corner of his eye—a wicked grin upon his face.

"But most of all I'm opposed to it because of the way it demoralizes the Southern white and limits his chance of gaining a livelihood. More than three quarters—nay, eighty-five or ninety percent of the whites of our region don't own slaves. Slavery is profitable—for us. But it keeps millions of whites scratching for food out of the rocky earth of the mountains and existing listlessly in the fetid, fever-ridden swamp bottoms. I've seen the cabins with dirt floors, children as dirty as pigs, and the emaciated slatternly women old years before their time. . . . Forgive me, Madame. I didn't mean to offend you."

"And you haven't," Aurore said. "Please go on. This is a way of thought that is new to me."

"The point is—that as labor these whites can't compete with the Negroes. And no section ever grew to greatness on a system that benefited such a small part of the population. Then there are other things—not perhaps fit for the ears of ladies."

Stephen looked at Julie.

"Ye've finished? Well, suppose ye show young Tom about the place. Peter will saddle a horse for him."

Obediently Julie rose. Tom looked at his father, his thin face shining with eagerness. Thomas Meredith nodded. Julie put out her hand and young Tom took it. Together the two of them went out into the great hall.

"Before my wife," Stephen said, "ye can speak freely. Ye'll find her quite a feminist—much too enlightened for her own good!"

"What I meant—if Madame will forgive me—is the widespread practice of concubinage with slave women. Why, here in Louisiana I've seen Negroes as white as any Scandinavian. And these mulattos, quadroons, and octoroons constitute a real danger. They're sensitive as all get out, and much more inclined to revolt than the blacks. Besides this debauching of our best young men doesn't make for good physical health or mental stability."

Aurore looked at Stephen.

"In that I agree," she said. "Most heartily!"

Stephen's face was beet red, and the great scar glowed clearly.

"Ye're right, of course," he declared. "But the trouble is . . . I don't see a solution. 'Tis we who are enslaved no less than the blacks. Suppose I were to free my Negroes? What then? What would they do? Who would care for them? Ye've seen how freedmen fare. Your own Negroes for instance, how did they make out when they were set free?"

"Some—a few—splendidly. They emigrated to Boston and New York and started small businesses: laundries, carpenter shops, bootblack stands. Some of them became paid house servants for wealthy New Yorkers. The vast bulk of them got along—a sort of hand-to-mouth existence; but the rest . . ."

"Aye," Stephen said. "What about the rest?"

"They got into trouble. Petty thievery, mostly—and, asking your pardon again, Madame—prostitution. There was even a murder or two. The fact is, they weren't ready for freedom. But that's what we've got to do now—make them ready. For they're going to be freed—either soon and violently—or, God willing, in the future gradually of our own free wills. That's the way I'd like to see it. But we've talked enough about this, don't you think? I'd like to see the spot where Dannie lies if you'll be so good . . ."

Stephen rose.

"Come," he said, "I'll show ye."

Young Tom Meredith sat uneasily on the gentle old nag that had been saddled for him and looked around over the vast acres.

"It—it's so big!" he said.

Julie laughed.

"Come on," she said. "You haven't seen half of it yet!"

They rode away from the house past the *pigeonnieres* where

the doves circled and wheeled. On the other side was another small but richly ornamented building.

"What's that?" Tom demanded.

"That's where you're going to stay—you and your father. It's called a *garçonnière*. It was built for 'Tienne—he's my brother—and his guests."

"I'd like to see the slave quarters."

"Why?"

"No reason—I just wanted to see them, that's all."

"Well—all right. But they're nothing much to see. We go this way."

A few minutes later, young Tom sat upon the nag looking down the long rows of neat, whitewashed brick cabins. Negro children played on the steps, and here and there old grandmothers came out to wave at Julie, their black faces shining with pleasure.

The boy's thin, sensitive face was intent and frowning. He turned his great light grey eyes upon Julie.

"Where's the whipping post?" he demanded.

"The what?"

"The whipping post—where you beat the Negroes."

"You've been reading that horrible book!" Julie snapped. "I just wish I could get my hands on that old Mrs. Stowe! I'd show her, I'll bet you!"

"But you do have one—somewhere—don't you?" Tom asked almost hopefully.

"Of course not!" Julie said angrily. "We don't beat our Negroes. You Yankees are so silly!"

"I—I'm sorry," young Tom managed. "I didn't mean to make you mad."

Julie's anger vanished at once.

"It's all right," she said. "You know, my father's going to let me go North to school—when I'm sixteen."

"He is! Then please come to Boston. We have some dandy schools for girls . . . and then I could see you . . . everyday, maybe."

At thirteen, Julie was already a lady—and a Louisiana lady at that. Her eyelids fluttered slowly, and just a hint of warm huskiness crept into her voice.

"You—you'd like that—Tom?" she murmured.

"Would I," Tom began, "would I!" Then he stopped, his face covered with blushes and confusion.

"I'm glad," Julie said. "I was hoping you would. But come on, I've got a lot more to show you!"

Before he returned to the house, young Tom had seen the sugar house with its impressively massive machinery, the chapel, the infirmary which was mostly occupied by Negro babies busily sucking on bottles of herb tea or eating mush while their mothers worked in the fields, the steamboat landing, the still unremoved wreckage of the *Creole Belle*, and the grave of his brother.

He stood silently before the little mound of earth, gazing upon the great marble headstone that Stephen had caused to be erected. The corners of his wide mobile mouth trembled a little.

"He was a good boy, my brother," he whispered. "He loved everybody. I don't know a soul who disliked him either. I sometimes wonder why God lets things like that happen. If somebody had to die why did He have to take the smartest and the bravest and the best . . . me, now . . . nobody would have missed me."

"Oh, don't say that, Tom! I'd have missed you—very much."

Tom looked at her, his grey eyes very wide and grave. He put up his hand and pushed back the heavy lock of dark hair that persisted in falling across his forehead.

"But then you wouldn't even have known me," he said.

"That would have been worse," Julie murmured.

"Julie," Tom said, "Julie . . ."

"Yes, Tom?"

"I . . . I . . . we . . . I guess we'd better be getting back to the house."

Julie looked at him, the tiniest smile playing about the corners of her mouth.

"All right, Tom," she said. "And you'd better get some rest—we'll be up late tonight."

"Why?"

"Tonight's the harvest and celebration. You'll see some fun! Come on, now."

She dug her heels into the pony's fat sides, and started off at a brisk trot. Young Tom followed her more slowly on the ancient nag.

"Fool!" he whispered bitterly at himself as he rode. "Stupid fool!"

At eleven-thirty, all of Julie's guests were present at Harrow. There were Victor and Hebert Le Blanc and their sister Aurore, and James Drumond and his two sisters Helen and Martha. All these children were about Julie's own age. Young Stephen Le Blanc, although he complacently acquiesced in his father's plan to marry him off to Julie when she came of age, scorned the company of these infants as he called them from the lofty vantage point of his twenty-four years, and rode away to the city to join in more adult pleasures together with his friends Pierre Aucoin, Henri Lascals, Jean Sompayrac, Bob Norton, and James Duckett. Walter McGarth, who like the rest, belonged to the same group of youths that had also included Etienne, was away at Harvard, studying law.

Promptly at midnight, the whistle upon the sugar house split the night with its cry, and a slave put the torch to a huge pile of dried cane stalks. The flames ran up them to the very top and pushed the night back with its leaping, yellowed light.

Stephen, Aurore, Thomas Meredith, Andre Le Blanc, Amelia, and Mr. and Mrs. James Drumond stood in front of the sugar house before the bonfire. The Negroes came running up laughing and cheering. Stephen nodded to one of the field hands, and the Negro opened the doors of the warehouse. Instantly the blacks swarmed in, and began rolling out the hogsheads of *vin de canne*. Down near the slave cabins choice cuts of beef were already turning on the spits over beds of glowing coals. Truly the Negroes lived for this night.

"They'll get drunker than lords," Stephen told Thomas Meredith. "But they deserve it. They've worked well this season."

Meredith was looking at his son, running with the other children into the sugar house itself. His hands, like the others, were filled with almond sticks, called by the Creoles, *batons amandes*, and little *pain patates*, or potato cakes. Around his arms were strung long strings of pecan halves. These the children would dip into the boiling sugar to make a confection known as *chapelets de pecanes*.

"I'm awfully afraid, Mister Fox," he whispered, "that you're corrupting my son with so much magnificence. Before long you'll have him insisting that I buy him a few hundred acres and as many Negroes!"

"The lad has the breeding and carriage of a Southerner," Stephen declared aloud. "With so fine and sensitive a face, ye'll never make a merchant of him."

"You're right there, Stephen," Andre Le Blanc declared jestingly. "Why, that boy has the lines of a gentleman about him. 'Twould be a crime to turn him into a Damnyankee!"

"I see I'm outnumbered," Thomas Meredith laughed. "Well, I think I'll partake of a bit of that barbeque. It smells amazingly good."

"I see you've got it seasoned Texas style," Jim Drumond said. "We learned a lot of things there, didn't we, Stephen?"

"Aye. Chiefly, I think, how much misery, pain and discomfort a man can endure for a cause which he doesn't even understand. Wait, Andre, I'll help the ladies. I wouldn't want ye to split that elegant waistcoat."

"Isn't he a disgrace!" Amelia laughed. "Remember how slim and handsome he was on the night that you introduced him to me, Stephen?"

"I do—well," Stephen said; "but ye've forgiven me for that— I hope."

Amelia smiled gently.

"We've been very happy, Stephen. In fact, I'm very grateful to you—really, I am."

Stephen was bending over Aurore, placing the plate of steaming barbeque in her hands.

"So have I," he murmured, "divinely happy—much more than I ever deserved."

"It's just that I had to wait so long for him," Aurore said. "I'd

454

thought and thought about it, and studied him from every angle. So when he finally took pity upon me, I knew just how to please him—or, what's more important, I knew how to avoid displeasing him. He's so good, really, in spite of the fact that he gets an unholy delight out of trying to appear most wicked."

"Thank ye, my dear. But angels have always been notoriously fond of divils. Wine, Mrs. Drumond?"

Andre rubbed his pudgy hands over his ample waist.

"It's been a good life," he declared heavily.

"The best," Amelia echoed.

Young Tom Meredith broke away from the other children and came running toward the grown-ups.

"Dad!" he cried. "May I go abroad to school next year? To Paris, Dad?"

Thomas Meredith looked at his son, and his big mouth widened into a smile.

"A Grand Tour, eh? What on earth gave you such an idea?"

"They were talking French back there and it sounded so beautiful. Especially Julie. And I couldn't understand a word they were saying!"

Thomas Meredith put out his hand and pushed the wayward lock back from his son's forehead.

"We'll think about it, son," he said. "Especially Julie, eh? Yes, we must give the matter a thought."

XXIX

THE Merediths, father and son, lingered on at Harrow for more than two weeks. The day that they took their leave was one of those rare Winter days when the sun plays hide and seek with mountains of fleecy, purple and white clouds. The winter rains, for once, were late in appearing, so the long golden sunswaths slanted in over the burnished face of the river and softened the edges of the whole earth. Where Dan Meredith lay in his long sleep, the light was especially mellow; it seemed to lay like a glow over the grave and to paint soft haloes around the marble headstone.

Young Tom Meredith stood with his father beside it, the sunlight making golden fire in his bared brown hair. A little further off, Stephen and Julie watched them silently.

"Dad," young Tom whispered.

"Yes, son?"

"Let's leave him here. It—it's a kind of heaven in itself. I'd get the horrors thinking about Dan lying in that half-frozen ground by King's Chapel. But here in this sun and this air . . . Why, almost the whole year 'round he can have flowers. Julie will bring them; she promised me."

Thomas Meredith smiled gently at his son.

"Don't envy the dead, son," he said. "Who knows what life has in store for you?"

Tom looked up.

"You're a wise one, aren't you, Dad? But that's too much even to hope for. Well—what about it, shall we leave him here?"

"Yes. And now we'd better say our goodbyes. The Foxes are a grand family. Our abolitionist friends rather oversimplify things; you see that now, son."

He turned and walked toward Stephen and Julie. Young Tom followed, his grey eyes wide and grave.

Stephen put out his hand. Thomas Meredith took it firmly.

"This has meant more to us than ever I can tell you," he said. "We'll write—often. The country has need of men of good will in both sections. And if ever you visit Boston—"

"We'll call upon ye. That may be sooner than ye think."

Young Tom was holding Julie's plump white hand in his own slender fingers.

"Goodbye, Julie," he said simply.

The girl's black eyes were searching his face.

"No," she said. "Not goodbye—*Au revoir*, Tom."

The slow red climbed into the boy's thin cheeks.

"I—I don't know what that means," he said. "I don't know French."

Julie smiled.

"Someday you'll know, Tom," she whispered. Then: "You may kiss my hand, Tom; it's customary, you know."

The boy bent awkwardly over her hand, his face fiercely hot. Then he was gone, running toward the waiting carriage, without even a backward glance.

Thomas Meredith raised his hat toward the bélvèdere upon which Aurore stood, and made her a sweeping bow. From far off the little group could see the flutter of her white handkerchief. Then the two of them climbed into the carriage. The Negro clucked over the reins, and the horses moved off slowly.

"Dad," young Tom asked, "What does *au revoir* mean?"

"It means 'Until we meet again.' Why do you ask, son?"

"Oh . . . nothing . . . no reason, Dad." He put his head out of the window and looked back toward where Julie stood, just in time to see her raise the back of her right hand to her lips.

" 'Til we meet again," he whispered, " 'til we meet again!" And in his heart was a kind of glory.

Stephen turned to his daughter.

"Julie," he began, but the tears were there in her eyes, growing faster than she could wink them away.

"So," Stephen whispered; "already it begins. Never weep over a lad, Julie; there is none of them worth it."

"Oh, but he is, Father, he is!"

"Perhaps—that remains to be seen. He does seem a good lad —that I'll grant ye. Come on, we'd better rejoin your mother."

As he turned toward the house, Julie suddenly caught him by the arm.

"The postrider, Father! A letter from 'Tienne! It is—I know it is!"

Stephen took the bulky envelopes from the rider.

"Aye, ye're right," he said; "here's one from 'Tienne. But this one isn't from him—it's for him. We'll have to send it on. 'Tis from young McGarth, and 'tis postmarked Boston of all places."

Julie was dancing up and down like a plump pink kitten.

"Open them, Father," she said. "Both of them!"

"Why what a minx ye are! I'll do nothing of the kind. The one from Etienne we'll read, but the other we'll send on unopened. A man has a right to his private correspondence—even your brother, Julie."

He broke the seals on the letter.

" 'Dear Mother, Father, and Julie,' " he read. " 'We finally arrived at the town of Lawrence after a horrible journey. I must confess that Ceclie stood it much better than I. She is becoming a most enchanting wife—very steady and capable, yet very devoted withal. Kansas, and particularly Lawrence, has proved a great disappointment to me. The town is a hotbed of abolitionists, who openly boast of their intention to make the territory over into a free state—which God forbid. Yet, so great are their numbers that I have no doubt that they will be able to accomplish their evil ends; therefore I am removing immediately across the border into Missouri where I am confident of obtaining just the sort of lands suitable for my purposes. My mail will reach me at the general post office of Lawrence until I furnish you with a more exact address. Until such time, I remain, your devoted, obedient son and brother,

"'Etienne'"

"Oh, fudge!" Julie pouted. "He isn't coming home!"

"Of course not, Julie. Ye shouldn't have expected that. Come along now, we must let your mother see this letter."

A few weeks later, Etienne Fox rode into the offices of the sheriff at Lawrence, Kansas. The sheriff took his booted and spurred feet down from his desk and greeted him courteously. The sheriff was violently, aggressively proslave, and between these two who had nothing else in common, this fact had made a bond. The proslavers were too much outnumbered in Kansas. The sheriff had a feeling that this slim, icily controlled young fellow was an addition to their forces that was not to be sneezed at. Of course, he was much too polite, and his ways were foreign; but there was nothing soft about young Mister Fox—nothing at all.

"Mornin', Mister Fox," he drawled. "What kin I do fur yer, now?"

Without answering, Etienne laid down the letter that Stephen had forwarded him from Walter McGarth. The sheriff took it up, screwing his face into an ugly squint. Reading was not one of his best accomplishments. He had to spell out the words.

"I take it," he declared heavily, "that this heah nigger he's talkin' erbout run away from yer?"

"Right," Etienne declared.

"Hell of a thing. The gawddamned ungrateful bastid not only runs away but gits hisself mixed up with them thievin' abolishers!

459

Well, rest easy, Mister Fox; yer'll git yore nigger back. I'll send a deputy after him this very day."

"Thank you," Etienne said.

"Good thing, too. Throw the fear of Gawd into some of these sonsofbitches right here in Lawrence." He got up and walked to the door with Etienne. "How's yore place acomin'?" he asked.

"Great. I've got most of it cleared already—and I'm expecting two dozen more prime niggers tomorrow."

"Thet's good. I'll be aridin' past thar some of these fine days."

"You do that," Etienne murmured politely, but with a complete lack of enthusiasm. "You'll be most welcome."

"A cold fish," the sheriff muttered to himself as Etienne went out the door. "But he's a real gentleman—no mistake about thet!"

Inch walked rapidly along the snow-covered sidewalk of State Street in Boston. With him was the venerable Frederick Douglass, striding with as firm a step as his youthful companion. Inch looked at the white-bearded old man in awe. That there was anywhere a black man like this one was something he had dreamed but never quite believed. But now he had heard the old man's ringing oratory thundering out even in Faneuil Hall itself. That was a thing to be proud of no more than of the fact that Frederick Douglass was the living proof that a Negro could be a scholar, a statesman, a valiant champion of his oppressed people—and a gentleman. And he, Little Inch—a black slave lacking even a last name, unless he chose to call himself Fox, which, indeed, he'd never do, had been elevated to the company of such a giant. The thought made him glow, despite the cold.

It had all come about when the Millikens discovered how well-educated Inch was. They had introduced their black helper, who swept and cleaned their law offices and read Blackstone at night, to Wendell Phillips, Theodore Parker and Thomas Wentworth Higginson. These men had instantly seen in Inch a perfect medium of propaganda. Here, they could tell their audiences, is

460

an example of the intellectual heights to which a black man can rise. Here is proof positive that Doctor Douglass is not an exception—that other Negroes can, if given the opportunity, attain as high a knowledge. Much was made of Inch's perfect command of the French language—and the few Bostonians who could speak and understand that tongue were constantly tossing phrases at him. In short, Inch was being lionized by the abolitionists. It was a heady feeling, but his native caution bade him go slowly.

"When we are all free," he said to Douglass—the phrase was a constant one now—"we'll elect our own representatives to the Congress, and then . . ."

He never finished the sentence. For the long, lean white man who had been following him with the deadly deliberation of the South written into his every movement stretched out his hand and touched him on the shoulder.

"Yore name is Inch, nigger?" he drawled quietly. It was much more of a statement than a question.

"Yes," Inch said, "what do you want . . ."

"You're under arrest. You better come along quiet."

"Now, see here," Inch began.

"Go along with him, young Inch," Fred Douglass said. "You'll be taken care of—depend upon that."

Inch looked at the white-bearded chocolate face, then slowly he bowed his head. The street was very cold, suddenly.

He was not, he discovered, to be kept like a common felon in the city jail. Instead, he was confined, under very heavy guard, in the courthouse. Inch wondered at the numbers and the heavy armament of his guard. Certainly it did not take fifteen-odd policemen to keep one slim black in custody.

What he did not know was that at that very moment Faneuil Hall was packed to the rafters with an excited, seething crowd of anti-slavery men and women. Wendell Phillips was pouring forth his most impassioned oratory, deliberately inciting the crowd to riot. But it was a curiously Boston style of rioting that finally ensued: coolly, carefully planned, with lieutenants to direct it.

461

Mr. Higginson and a few others were to proceed directly to the courthouse and wait there until Phillips arrived with the crowd from Faneuil Hall. Then, with an elaborate show of seeming spontaneity, an outbreak was to occur. During the confusion, Inch was to be rescued and spirited away to Canada.

Inch walked back and forth in the little anteroom that served him as a cell. Outside the sleet whispered against the window-panes and the already fallen snow became crusted and hard. Listening to it, Inch shivered.

The Reverend Mr. Higginson drew his cloak up around his neck, and squinted into the driving sleet. Why the deuce didn't Phillips come? It was confoundedly cold out here, and at any moment some policeman might emerge from the building and discover the plotters. The sleet thickened. Here and there a snowflake swirled through it.

Two short blocks away Wendell Phillips and Theodore Parker were standing on the glazed ice of the street looking at the wreckage of their carriage. The horse was threshing about between the splintered shafts, unable to rise. His left hindleg was broken in two places. Theodore Parker looked at Phillips. Mutely the abolitionist nodded. Parker walked around to the horse's head, and began to stroke it gently. The animal quieted. Then holding his hand over the horse's eyes, Parker shot the beast very cleanly between the eyes. The dark blood rushed out from the wound and covered Parker's hand. When the icy air struck it, it steamed.

The two men set out on foot for the courthouse. But, long before they reached it, the mob had gathered, and the attack was under way. Confused, leaderless, the men hurled themselves through the drifts at the side entrance in Court Square, but one of the policemen had already locked the door.

At once a small detachment of the anti-slave forces streamed away from Court Square to return a few moments later with a joist. Twelve of the strongest men lifted it, and pointing it at the side door, started forward at a dead run.

Down below, Inch could hear the jolting, shuddering blows of this improvised battering ram. He stood there, frozen, listening. Stout as it was, the door could stand only so many of these terrific blows. It gave way at last with a splintered crash, and with a howl the mob poured through the doorway.

But the police were ready. Arranging themselves on either side of the door, they lifted their clubs and waited. Then, as the mob poured in, they brought the clubs down with all their force upon the heads of the abolitionists. It was all over within a few short minutes. Inch stood there weeping, watching the men hurled back, seeing them driven ahead of a solid wedge of blue-coated policemen out into the blinding sleet. Outside, the mob broke before the attack of the police, and started running away from Court Square, diving into every available street.

Afterwards, it was very quiet. The policemen returned, panting from their work, and led Inch away to another room with a stouter door.

The trial, which took place upon the following Monday, was a foregone conclusion. In its entirety, it lasted less than half an hour. Richard Henry Dana pleaded for Inch with all the skill and brilliance at his command, but there was no denying the fact that Inch was the person described in the articles presented.

At last, Commissioner Loring made an end. Looking down from the bench, he bade Inch stand forth. Adjusting his glasses, he read aloud:

"'The prisoner, one Inch, a black of twenty-four years, is said to have escaped from the plantation Harrow, near New Orleans, Louisiana.'" He put down the paper and glared at Inch.

"Are you the person so described?" he thundered.

Inch nodded dumbly.

"And did you make such an escape?"

"Yes, sir." Inch's voice was barely audible.

"Then, gentlemen," the commissioner declared, "I have no alternative but to return this man to his lawful owners. I am cognizant of your sympathies, which, to a degree, I share. But the law is the law! I hereby sentence this man to be returned to his master, one Etienne Fox, now residing in the state of Missouri, in proximity to that section of the Kansas border occupied by the town of Lawrence. Bailiff, dismiss the court."

A policeman took Inch's arm. As he was being led away, a young woman broke through the crowd and ran up to the bench. Wordlessly she slapped her hand down upon the bench, and a handful of tiny silver three-cent pieces clattered over it and fell to the floor. There were thirty of them. Two huge patrolmen led her away while the crowd rocked the courtroom with their outcries.

The following day, at high noon, Inch was led from his cell into the full light of day. It was a bright sunshiny day, very clear and very cold, yet both sides of State Street were lined with men and women. Inch looked about him in awe. Every four feet along the entire length of the street a soldier stood with fixed bayonet to keep the crowd back. Three huge, ugly cannon commanded the sidewalks, loaded with grapeshot, their fuses cut and ready. The Suffolk County Militia was present too, holding their nondescript weapons awkwardly, and casting sheepish glances at their disapproving neighbors.

Inch walked slowly at first with his head sunk upon his chest. But out of the corner of his eye he saw shop after shop closed and draped in black. Even the flags were at half mast, and reversed, so that the blue field with the stars hung down while the striped end was attached to the poles. As the little procession passed the Old State House, Inch could see a huge coffin swinging in the air, bearing the inscription:

"The Funeral of Liberty!"

On the sidewalks the women wept and the men hissed and booed the soldiers. Slowly Inch straightened. By the time he reached Long Wharf where the revenue cutter was waiting to bear him away, he was walking fully erect, his slim back very stiff and proud.

XXX

Sᴛᴇᴘʜᴇɴ Fox sat looking out of the window of his study. It was a warm day, and before him on the table the great ledger books and dozens of old letters lay scattered in careless profusion. Under his hand lay a blank sheet of paper on which he had written the date: "June 17, 1858," and the words: "My dear Julie." But the pen was held loosely between his thumb and forefinger; he had written nothing more.

The letters which lay open and spread out before him were nearly all from Etienne; only one or two showed the neat, daintily feminine softness of Julie's small hand. His eyes strayed over Etienne's letters, and here and there a phrase leaped up to command his attention:

"The town of Lawrence was sacked last night—God be praised! Eight hundred men under the direction of my old friend the sheriff, and the United States Marshal performed this necessary task of extermination with neatness, efficiency and dispatch. They smashed the presses of that filthy abolitionist rag [Etienne's language was often unfortunately intemperate, Stephen reflected] and burned that pest hole that the New England Emigrant Aid Society calls a hotel . . ."

465

Curiously, Stephen looked for the letter's date. The ink had faded somewhat in the two years, and Etienne's handwriting was none too clear, but he was able to make it out: "May, 1856." Stephen frowned. The words in that angular, bewildering script kept tugging at him, demanding his attention.

"John Brown . . . a grim, and terrible man . . . you'll hear more of him, mark me, Father . . . Pottowatomie Creek . . . five men murdered . . . cold blood . . . all proslavery.

"Osawatomie . . . Frederick Brown, son of this monster, was killed last night, and his demonic father forced to flee the country. Justice and right have prevailed." This and the cryptic announcements of the births of Stephen's grandchildren: Victor, 1856, Stephen II, 1857, Gail, the only granddaughter, 1858. A mention or two about the sad state of the new plantation, a word about Ceclie; but always again and again the bitter smoke and bloodshed of the flaming Kansas border. Here slavery was being fought over and men were dying.

Stephen frowned, picking up his short clay pipe.

The letter from Julie . . . It still must be answered. Walking over to the desk he picked it up and read it again:

"Dear Papa:

"I am at last becoming accustomed to this accursed school. Miss Shephard is really very kind, and Boston is a wonderful city. But I'm so homesick I could just die! How is Mother? Does 'Tienne write often?

"I still haven't seen Tom Meredith. I made inquiries, discreetly of course, and it seems that he and his father are abroad, but that they will return soon. I am very anxious to see Tom. I wonder if he has changed. Does all this sound silly—for a young lady of seventeen? Please write me and tell me about everything and I do mean everything!

Lovingly,

Julie

"Miss Angelina Shephard's Female Academy
  #30 Shirley Street, Boston
    April 30, 1858"

466

He looked up, still holding the letter in his hand as old Jean-Jacques appeared in the doorway.

"Monsieur Andre, maître," the old black murmured.

Andre was only a step behind him.

"Well," he said, without any preliminaries; "they've done it!"

Stephen lay the letter back upon the desk and his brows rose.

"Who?" he asked. "Who has done what? Ye aren't very clear, Andre."

"Sorry. Nobody or nothing is very clear any more. The country is hellbent for perdition! I tell you, Stephen, it means war. . . ."

Stephen lifted his hand in a futile effort to check the outburst. But Andre was already beyond the stopping point.

"A house divided against itself cannot stand! What does he mean by this nonsense, Stephen? War? Will he send an army down here to liberate the niggers? Oh, if he only would! We'd show him then how a Southern aristocrat fights. Why, we'd push his filthy mercantilists back into Canada within a month! And this is the man this gang of cutthroats intended to nominate for the presidency! This long, gangling, uncouth son of an ape! Have you seen his pictures, Stephen? *Foi* what an ugliness!"

"Drawings, Andre. Pen and ink sketches by caricaturists who think as ye do. They're no authority. I think Mister Lincoln is quite a man . . ."

"My God!"

"And I also think he hasn't a ghost of a chance. 'Tis still almost two years 'til election time, and long before then Douglas will have slipped a halter around Abe Lincoln's neck. There's your man to watch, Andre—little Stephen Douglas. But enough of politics—what say ye to a drink?"

"Time you offered me one," Andre grumbled. "It's hot enough to melt the hinges of hades! You've been to the city, Stephen?"

"No. How goes it there? Is the insurrection over?"

"Virtually. The Know Nothings are still beating up a few Vigilantes—when they catch them. But for the most part the city is quiet."

Stephen took the long, cool drink from the tray which Jean-

Jacques had brought. He sat holding it untasted, staring past Andre out the window.

"Eleven dead," he muttered. "Armed men taking over the city by force. Marches and counter-marches. Fraud, bribery, violence. And every election is the same. I tell ye, Andre, I sometimes think 'twould be better for the black Republicans to take over. Perhaps they would clean house for us. God knows we won't do it for ourselves."

Andre snorted. Then, lifting his glass to his lips, he downed it in one long pull. A trickle of moisture dripped down over his pudgy chin onto his waistcoat. He stood up.

"I won't quarrel with you," he said. "In time you'll see I was right about these things. Give my Stephen's regards to Julie when you write—and mine."

Stephen made no attempt to stop his abrupt departure. Andre, with his growing political sensitivity, was becoming a ticklish guest. And there was still this accursed letter to be written. He sighed and picked up his pen.

June melted into July in a blaze of heat. All over the land men waited. They read Hinton Helper's *Impending Crisis* and George Fitzhugh's *Cannibals All* or *Slaves Without Masters* and the arguments grew hot and fierce. Only two hundred and twenty-five thousand men actually held slaves ran the theme of Helper, while in the pine barrens and the clay hills and the swamp bottom white men rotted in idleness. Look at your Northern wage slave, shouted Fitzhugh. Ill-paid, overworked, abused, turned out in his old age to die— All over the land men waited, and tempers grew hourly shorter.

In the middle of July Julie came back to Harrow after a month's visit with the Thorn family of New York. But she was a changed girl. No longer did she ride to the bottom lands with her beloved papa or meet the postrider to take the increasingly bulky letters from Etienne. Instead, she sat in the salon, playing pensive airs upon the grand piano, and answering her mother absently or not at all. At seventeen Julie was a true Arceneaux beauty with the lightest touch of the diablerie of the Foxes thrown in. The plumpness that had marked her girlhood had given way to a soft slimness that now, under her haphazard methods of eating, was becoming actual thinness.

"What ails ye, girl?" Stephen demanded. "Ye eat less than a bird, and one has to bellow in your ear to gain your attention. Are ye daft—or is there some lad?"

"No, Papa," Julie said lifelessly. "There's nobody. Only sometimes, life seems so useless . . ."

Stephen smiled.

"I'll wager that in another year ye'll find that it can be most interesting. Come, now—what say ye to some breast of chicken under glass and some Haute Sauterne?"

"Oh, no, Papa—I couldn't eat a thing!"

"Ye know, Julie—I don't think I'll send ye back to that school. Boston doesn't seem to have agreed with ye."

"Papa! You wouldn't do that! No, Papa! I've got to go back— don't you understand? I've got to!"

"So—the wind still lies in that quarter, eh? I hope ye won't be too disappointed when ye see your Yankee lad again."

"If I see him again—Papa, why doesn't he write?"

"I don't know, light o' my heart. But if ye want that pale ice-water stripling I'll dust off the family shotgun . . ."

"Now you're teasing me again! I think you're being horrid!"

Then she was gone dashing up the stairs to her room.

"Poor little thing," Stephen murmured. "Well, she's a Fox, all right. What she wants, she wants with all her heart. I'll have to do something about this . . ."

Going into his study he picked up his pen and drew a sheet of paper toward him.

"Thomas Meredith, Esquire," he wrote, "Meredith & Son, Merchandizers, State Street, Boston . . . My dear sir . . ."

It was late September before a reply came. There were two letters, one of them addressed to Julie. She took it in her hand, holding it as though it were something fragile and precious, and walked up the stairs like a sleepwalker. It was, like the one addressed to Stephen, postmarked from Paris, France. Her fingers trembled as she broke the seals, and it was a long time before the letters stopped dancing.

" 'Dear Julie,' " she read, saying the words aloud, repeating them like a caress, " 'Dear Julie—I've wanted so long to write to you, but I dared not. You were something I dreamed about—like one dreams of angels. I couldn't find the words to say, to tell you— I fear that I go too fast. Then your father's frank and friendly letter was forwarded to us here, saying that you spoke of me often, that you asked about me—Julie, Julie, that brought a kind of happiness that a man shouldn't be asked to endure too often. I thought I'd die of it.

" 'And you go to Miss Shephard's school! I know it well. Then I shall see you, and soon! 'Tis Harvard for me, instead of the University of Paris as I'd planned. Father was amenable to suggestion—for, in his own quiet way, he likes you as much almost as I. My pen falters. Au revoir, Julie—and now, at long last, I know exactly what that means!

" 'Ever
" 'Tom' "

XXXI

Wʜᴇɴ Stephen and Aurore pushed open the door after long
unanswered knocking, they found Julie face down upon her bed
sobbing into her pillow.

"Julie!" Stephen barked. "What ails ye, child? Did that young
Yankee pup . . ."

But Aurore was looking at her daughter with a gentle half
smile upon her face.

"Men are forever fools," she said. "Don't you remember how
I cried, Stephen, upon the day we were married?"

"Holy Mother of God! But Julie is so young. I had no idea
that this thing—this childish attachment could cut so deep."

"She's your daughter, Stephen—and mine. Come, leave her
alone for a while."

Going down the stairs, Stephen was frowning.

"I think ye'd better go with Julie this year to Boston. After all
Julie is of my blood, and we Foxes are notoriously impulsive.
A mother's care . . ."

"Listen to the *pater familias*! Don't be so pompous, Stephen.
I shan't do anything of the kind. Julie has goodness bred into
her bones, and this boy didn't seem the type to . . ."

"Aye, but that was years ago. Since then he may have changed. He's lived in Paris, remember."

"You should know about Paris! But I doubt that the boy has developed into so accomplished a rake as the man I married. He's had his father with him all the time, and I think he lacked the inclination."

"No man lacks the inclination," Stephen growled. "What most of them lack is opportunity!"

"Stephen, Stephen," Aurore moaned. "What a thing for you to say!"

Afterwards, the whole of Harrow was changed. Music soared up from the grand piano, but it was joyous music. Julie's eyes were bright. She ate well, and rode with Stephen again over the vast plantation. And between her and Aurore there were hours of whispered conversation, which broke off abruptly whenever Stephen entered the room.

What concerned Stephen most in his somewhat straitened circumstances since his bankers Hammerschlag & Brothers of Philadelphia had gone under in the speculative avalanche of 'fifty-seven, was the sudden increase in bills. Most of these came from Olympe, the milliner; but their number was almost equalled by those from Pluche and Ferret, importers of Parisian fashions. Several times he was on the point of calling a halt, only to be met by a protesting:

"But, Papa, you wouldn't want the Yankees to think me dowdy?"

Stephen groaned. Never had he been able to deny Julie anything.

Finally, upon the last day of the month, he and Aurore stood upon the wharf at New Orleans and watched the boat bearing Julie northward for her second term find its place in the five o'clock parade of upriver packets. It was an impressive sight, that parade: boat after boat slipped away from its moorings and headed upstream, the black clouds of wood smoke from their high twin stacks mingling in a pall of blackness that shut out the afternoon sun.

Winter came early in Boston that year. And Winter has never in any year been a time for lovers; but for Julie and Tom, it had to do. Tom came back from France early in the term and wasted a full month in vain attempts to see Julie. Miss Shephard would brook no contact between the young ladies of her school and members of the opposite sex. But no one in history has ever successfully devised a method short of murder that could keep apart a young couple determined to be together, and Miss Shephard succeeded no better than the rest.

Julie saw Tom. On Sundays on her way to early Mass, which she and the other two Catholic girls in the school were permitted to attend unchaperoned; at night from her window while he stood shivering in the snow-blanketed street below; and upon the long afternoon constitutional walks that Miss Shephard insisted that they take—she would meet him—accidentally of course, but the accidents occurred with amazing frequency.

For them both this was a kind of torture. The words whispered hurriedly, the brief hot pressure of hands, the awkward, hasty kisses were building up slowly into a situation that had to end somehow, and showed more signs of ending disastrously than any other way. But, in the end, Miss Shephard herself brought matters to a happy conclusion. She did so by the simple expedient of walking into Julie's room at two o'clock in the morning, just as Tom was walking away from a spot below Julie's window after exchanging a few chattering words and many shivering sighs. Then she stunned Julie into speechlessness by making the accusation that Tom had been in Julie's room and confined her to quarters until Stephen could be notified to come and get her.

There was only one answer to this. By eight o'clock of the same morning Julie's note was already in Tom's hands. Julie ate nothing, but spent the entire day in alternating storms of weeping and furious activity, hurling all her belongings into her traveling bags.

Promptly at midnight, Julie heard the gravel smacking against her window pane. Quietly she opened the window. There was a low, bumping sound as the ladder, its ends muffled with rags, came to rest against her casement. A moment later, Tom's face appeared. He was shaking with nervousness, but a broad grin split his face.

"Julie," he croaked.

Julie scurried across the room and came back with her bags. Tom took them and started down the ladder. A moment later Julie followed him. At the bottom, Tom took up the bags again. Julie looked up at the ladder.

"Leave it," Tom grinned, "so old Shep can have apoplexy!"

They dashed off then down the darkened street. At the end of it a carriage waited. Tom dropped both the bags and took Julie in his arms. He kissed her very long, and very hard. From inside the carriage there came a smothered giggle.

"Witnesses," Tom said. "I've thought of everything."

They were married by a Justice of the Peace, who lost his glasses and mumbled through the ceremony from memory, forgetting half of it. Then they took a train, an hour later, for New York. They went to the best of hotels, for Tom was well supplied with money for the honeymoon since the elder Meredith was in on the secret; but Julie lay in her new husband's arms and cried and cried, thinking about Harrow.

Tom held her close to him, and brushed the long golden hair with his big hand.

XXXII

AURORE stood on the gallery and watched Stephen pounding up the alley of oaks at a hard gallop. He was standing in the stirrups waving something in his hand.

He shouldn't ride like that, she thought, not at his age. But then Stephen never remembers that he's nearly sixty. *Ma foi*, how fast the years have gone! Here I am three times a grandmother, and 'twas only yesterday that I used to ride that same road just to see him—"Stephen! Be careful for God's sake!"

But Stephen was down from the still-plunging horse and running up the great stairs.

"They're coming!" he cried. "They're coming!"

Aurore smiled a puzzled smile.

"Would you please calm yourself, my husband, and tell me just who is coming?"

"Julie! Day after tomorrow! Call the servants, Aurore—the place must be cleaned inside and out!"

"Softly, Stephen. I take it that her impetuous Yankee is with her?"

"Aye," Stephen growled. " 'Twill be a bitter pill, but I suppose we haven't much choice in the matter."

475

"No, Stephen. He seemed a good boy the little time we saw him before. But what's done is done . . . and we really shouldn't have expected cool heads of our children."

"Ye're right there. But this accusation that Miss Shephard makes against him and Julie . . ."

"She's a vicious old witch—that woman! I don't believe a word of it!"

"Nor I. Still I'd like to hear from Julie's lips what really happened."

Aurore walked over to her husband and took hold of the lapels of his coat.

"Stephen," she said gently. "Don't ask for an explanation. If Julie doesn't volunteer to tell us, don't assume that her silence is a confession of guilt. There are some things in the heart of a woman—and our little Julie is a woman grown, Stephen— that are not to be shared—not even with parents as tolerant as we try to be. Promise me, Stephen."

Stephen looked at his wife and the white brows smoothed.

"All right," he said, "I promise, but just the same I hope Julie will tell us the whole story."

"I'm certain she will," Aurore said.

As Stephen went into his study, he could hear her summoning the Negroes. The house would be set in order—there was no doubt of that. Seating himself at his desk, Stephen opened his other letters. One of them, as he expected, was from Etienne. His son had proved a steady correspondent. This fact pleased Stephen as much as it surprised him. His relations with his son had been anything but smooth, yet, time and again, unwittingly by some odd turn of phrase, Stephen had discovered how much the younger man admired and respected him. His advice was asked on all sorts of matters: running the plantation, dealing with the Negroes, even, to his puzzled amazement, the management of a much-too-spirited wife.

"It goes well with us here," the letter read, "after a fashion. That is, we manage to eke out a living. Ceclie currently suspects me—not without some justification, I must admit—of carrying on an affair with one of the ladies of the town . . . Her tantrums

476

of jealousy are something to behold! Inch continues surly and unreliable. I have a feeling that he is preaching emancipation to my Negroes. I made the surprising discovery that an astonishingly large number of them could read simple sentences and even write their names. When I confronted Inch with this fact he made no attempt to deny that it was he who had been teaching them . . . so I had him whipped . . .

"I have grown a beard. It adds enormously to my dignity and even to my control over my household. . . ."

Stephen sat holding the letter in his hand and gazing out over the landscape. At fifty-nine, he was thinner, and the red had all but disappeared from his hair. The lines about the corners of his eyes, and the two that descended from the thin, flaring nostrils to the edges of his mouth had deepened. His face, even in repose, was as keen as the blade of an ax. The eyes, bluer and paler than ever, had taken on a look of constant reflection, so that they seemed to be always fixed on far distances. "He looks *through* you," his friends said.

The streamers of moss in the oak trees caught the afternoon sun rays and blazed. Under the levee, the river went quietly. The Negroes sang as they worked under the bright October skies, but word and note and cadence were drowned in the vast distances. On the chocolate-colored waters a steamboat whistled, pounding upstream toward Natchez. It's all so peaceful, Stephen thought, how long . . . ?

Early the next morning, Stephen and Aurore met Julie and her husband at the wharf in New Orleans. They had come down from New York by coastal streamer, around the tip of Florida and upriver from the gulf. The trip had taken more than a month. As they stepped ashore, Aurore burst into sudden, unexplainable tears. Julie stood looking at her mother, her black eyes very wide and bright.

"Mother," she began, "what on earth . . . ?"

Stephen smiled at her gently, his blue eyes alight.

" 'Tis the shock of seeing that ye're no longer a child," he said. "Ye've changed, Julie. In carriage and air and everything." He put out his hand to his new son-in-law.

477

"Welcome home, Tom," he said.

Tom gulped two or three times before answering. Then he took Stephen's hand in an iron grip and got out:

"Thank you, sir. I'm awfully glad . . . I hadn't expected . . ."

"What's done is done," Stephen said. "Though I think that Julie rather cheated her mother. Aurore had entertained the idea of a wedding in the Cathedral—with white wedding gowns and oceans of flowers, but then young folk are so headstrong!"

"I'm sorry, mother," Julie said, keeping her arms around Aurore's waist, "but then, you see, we had to get married rather suddenly."

Stephen's brows made white thundercaps.

"Papa!" Julie said, stamping her small foot. "If you think what I think you're thinking, I'll never speak to you again!"

"Wait, Julie," Tom said. "Your father knows you too well for that. And I hope that I can prove to him that Northerners can be gentlemen."

"That ye've done already. Come children, 'tis no short ride to Harrow."

As soon as they reached the plantation, Aurore sent Negroes with invitations to the Damerons, the Nortons, the McGarths, the Le Blancs, the Lascals and the Sompayracs to dine with them that night. Julie would have preferred dining alone in the company of her family, but Aurore loved to entertain, and this was the best excuse she had had in years.

Promptly at six the guests began to arrive. By seven they were all there, and the great salon rang with laughter and toasts. The ladies of course made veiled hints for information about the affluence and social position of young Tom, which the lad answered with a simple directness that was more than a little disconcerting.

"My father is a very wealthy man," he said. "He owns one of the largest mercantile establishments in Boston. I hope that you folk will forgive me for that, but really neither cane nor cotton will grow in Massachusetts!"

"What does grow there?" Amelia asked after the laughter had subsided.

478

Julie made a face.

"Beans!" she said in a tone of extreme dislike.

"Beans?" Amelia asked. "You mean red beans like the Negroes eat?"

"Something like that—only they're smaller and lighter in color. And the Bostonians cook them in little earthen pots with molasses and strips of bacon. And then instead of feeding them to the pigs as they should, they eat them themselves!"

"You know, young man," Andre Le Blanc said with heavy joviality. "You robbed me of a daughter-in-law. I had been confidently planning on having Julie for my son's wife."

"I'm sorry, sir. I didn't know about that."

"Would it have made any difference if you had?"

"Truthfully, no, sir. I would have fought every Creole in Louisiana for Julie."

"I don't blame you. Julie is a rarely lovely creature—like her mother before her. May I propose a toast, gentlemen?"

The men all nodded. Andre got to his feet, lifting his glass. The clear wine caught the light of the immense crystal chandelier and sparkled. The light fell softly upon the bare shoulders of the women and the dark evening attire of the men. The white tablecloth and napkins threw it back, the silver glistened with subdued fire, and the jewels at neck and earlobe and cuff and shirtfront blazed. Stephen had a feeling that time was arrested for the moment, that the dark, tumultuous torrent of events was held for a little while in check. Andre stood there, holding his glass.

"To Madame and Monsieur Meredith," he said. "May their union prosper—and may their felicity herald a renewal of cordial relationships between the two great sections of our homeland that they represent." He made a short flourish with his glass and lifted it to his lips.

"Papa!" the voice was young and masculine, growling from the doorway. "Don't drink that toast!"

They all turned at once. Young Victor Le Blanc, the blond twin, was standing there in the doorway. His clothing was dusty, and his young face was red and streaked.

Slowly Andre lowered the glass.

"You had better explain that," he said. "And fast."

"I come from the *Picayune's* offices," the boy said flatly. "While you sit here eating with a damned Yankee, Southern soil is being outraged! Not four hours ago a Yankee abolitionist named John Brown attacked Harper's Ferry in Virginia. The fighting is still going on."

Stephen looked at Aurore.

"Holy Mother of God!" she whispered.

"He's freeing the slaves and arming them for insurrection!" the boy went on, his voice hoarse with passion. "At this very hour daughters of the South go in peril of more than their lives!"

"Silence!" Andre thundered. "I won't have such intemperate speech from a son of mine!"

"Intemperate, Papa? Intemperate! While he holds the Federal Arsenal! While he seizes the railroad and sends his followers foraging over the country! Is war intemperate, Papa? Is rapine and sudden death?"

Stephen stood up.

"Ye're mistaken, lad," he said quietly.

"I only wish I were, sir," Victor said, almost weeping with rage; "but I'm not. I've been working at the newspaper offices all Summer. I was there when the first wire came in. And they're still coming in—every hour brings worse news." He turned to his father. "So, Papa, if you drink that toast, I say before this whole company—including the ladies—God damn your soul to hell!"

Andre put the glass down untasted upon the table.

"I have not drunk it, son," he said quietly.

Stephen looked around the table. Every glass stood full and untouched upon it—every glass except one. Julie held her glass in her hand; then with every eye upon her she stood up and very slowly drained it, tilting back her head until the last drop was gone. Instantly Tom Meredith was upon his feet, his face very white. In one gulp he too drained his glass and stood beside his wife.

The chairs scraped back from the table. Stephen nodded to

480

the servants. In a brief moment they were back with the hats and cloaks.

"I am very sorry," Stephen said. "Perhaps after we've all had time to think . . ."

"Think!" Andre snorted. "What is there now to think about, Stephen?"

XXXIII

Waking sometime in the vast night of January 1861 (the year the world ended, afterwards to be born again—but not the same thing; no, never again the same) Stephen Fox was unsure what night it was or even that it was night, or what year. He lay very quietly by the slim form of his wife, an old woman now late in her fifties and thrice a grandmother, in a state of half awareness. It is such times as these, he reflected, that the borders of time and space melt, blend and disappear, so that what was, is; and also what will be. He stood again by the Mississippi awaiting Mike Farrel's flatboat, watching at the same time with no sense of confusion old Mike (the same but different in age) dying in flames in the *Creole Belle*. He stood at the side of young Andre Le Blanc, slim, elegant, and almost too handsome, in the Place D'Armes looking into the lovely white face of Odalie, and knelt weeping with no transition in time or space beside her bed as she lay ravished in the arms of death (the final lover, and the greatest one).

In Ireland he had hungered. In Ireland he had begged, lied, schemed, and stolen. But the mists were swirling thick and black about that part and the night descending. In America the jeweled skies were high and clear and the rains lashed the earth and the prairie winds bellowed and the sun smashed down with hammer-blows, It was one thing, this Nation, something new under heaven, one Nation indivisible . . . the palmetto fronds before Harrow, the oak trees trailing streamers of Spanish moss, the river, the river. . . .

The river and also the mountains and the prairie lands and the swamps. The plains of Kansas . . . poor, bleeding Kansas. New England, blizzard-whipped, but with flowers blooming in its heart. The sun on the mesa in Texas. Adobe huts, Navahoes, Greasers . . . dead Greasers, lying bloated in the roasting sun, and exuding that smell that you never could remember because there was never again anything to call it to your mind, never again the sick sweet smell of putrefaction, of blood, bone and sinew rotting in the sun. These and the faces of the dead (again living—remembered): Odalie, Pierre Arceneaux, Old Caleen, Achille, La Belle Sauvage, Hugo Waguespack, falling like a pole-axed bull, my bullet in his heart, making the same sound a log would, striking the earth. They were all there, black and white alike, and the mind made no distinction. Was it because in the final democracy of death all men were truly equal?

These and the tenuous fine-spun memories of his youth; faint and vivid at the same time, the women he had loved and lusted after, the ones whom he had merely lusted after—a fine distinction, that—nicely drawn. Lying there open-eyed staring at the ceiling, high and cool in the darkness, it was the everscent, the unrelated, the small peculiarities that came back with sharp distinctness. (Desiree's body had been long and cool, just off-white in the darkness, in the daylight pale golden. Odalie was cool glacier-ice, snowy-skinned, with volcanoes of frozen-over passion imprisoned beneath—and Aurore was like her. True ladies of the old South. Ladies. Reserve, dignity, dutiful submission to a repugnant obligation . . . Well, they had learned, both of them, that cologne and cleanness and the twice daily bathings could not hold back the animal sweat, the panting, scalding-hot female-smell of giving and taking and wanting to be hurt, to die into ecstasy and to come alive again . . . with the blood running

483

slow and warm, the body sweat-dewed of the she-thing mastered, conquered and subdued.) But I am sixty-one years old and the young flame is an ember, glowing amid the ashes and the dust.

The place, the river, the city (New Orleans) and the land . . . all of it North, South and West. California and Texas, South Carolina and Massachusetts. The cities: New York, Boston, Philadelphia (city of brotherly love), Memphis, Vicksburg, Corinth, Natchez, Baton Rouge, New Orleans. The land all of it . . . his land, America. Young giant of the West. The New Idea . . . "That all men are created equal . . . that they are endowed by their Creator . . . by their Creator . . . by their Creator . . ." His land, America . . . all of it.

A house divided against itself cannot stand. The last, best hope of earth . . . that as long as it exists their empires of exploitation, degradation and misery totter . . . and men everywhere have hope. My son growing upon the soil, and young Inch, black, speaking cleanly and purely the language of Racine. Young Inch. Black, black, black . . . three million blacks sweating in the sun . . . and John Brown out of his grave and marching the earth through the whirlwind and the fire. They hanged him in Virginia but he is not dead . . . no, not dead, not ever dead; you cannot kill an idea. And because of that idea Harrow must perish, its Negroes gone, the slave cabins tenantless, the fields parched and weed-ruined, the house itself burnt.

Burnt? How did he know that? That was not a memory . . . that had never happened. "I don't know!" he said aloud, crying the words at the darkness, "I don't know! I don't . . ."

"Stephen!"

"Sorry, my dear; I must have been dreaming."

Getting out of bed after she had turned over and gone back to sleep, he crossed to the window. Now it was raining, a hard, pitiless downpour, unstirred by any wind. On the horizon there was the sound of distant thunder. Like guns, he thought. Like the guns that a few days ago had fired upon the *Star of the West* as she came to relieve the garrison at Fort Sumter in the harbor at Charleston.

484

"Oh, my God!" he groaned. This was the end. The end of the young idea, the giant of the West, the brave new world of which men everywhere had hope. Abe Lincoln striding out of Illinois like a prairie wind. Abe Lincoln not yet in the White House, Abe Lincoln who might never have been there had not his enemies split and quarreled among themselves so that although he got a minority of the popular vote cast he had won a majority in the electoral college. If Lincoln is elected, we will secede. Well, Lincoln had been elected and they had seceded: first South Carolina, then Mississippi, then Alabama and Florida, then Georgia and now in Louisiana time was running out. (Thus a condemmed man must feel as the gallows hour approaches.) This and Julie . . . dear little Julie in bleak Boston and Etienne in Missouri with the grandchildren he had never seen . . . this and the signs and portents in the sky and time running out for the brave new world and the young idea dying. How would it be to kill men like the Merediths, linked to him now by indissoluble ties, sighting over the heavy revolver barrel, pulling the trigger, feeling the grip smack against his palm . . . how would it be . . . how?

Now the rain was slowing and there was a faint lessening in the darkness so that the river showed beyond the levee. Still, there was no real light yet. Stephen wondered if there ever would be any light again in this world. Sighing, he turned to go back to bed. But now at last he heard it, the thunderous knocking at the door, far below on the gallery. He drew on his robe and started down the long curving stairs. Where the deuce were the Negroes? Surely one of them should have heard such a clatter. He went swiftly through the hall and threw back the bolts on the great doors. A tall man was standing there in the darkness, rain dripping from his hat—a huge slouch affair in the Western style—and from his cloak, so that he stood in a little pool. His great black beaver of a beard was rainwet too; the candle-flame picked up the droplets glistening in the softly curling hair.

"Well, Father," he said. "Don't you recognize me?"

" 'Tienne! Holy Mother of God! How on earth . . . why . . . Come in, come in, lad—ye're drenched!"

Etienne came into the long hall, trailing little trickles of water upon the magnificent rugs. He looked about him like a stranger, half amazed at the vastness and the grandeur of Harrow.

"Father," he said, "Father . . ."

"Yes, lad?" Stephen was pulling the bell cord, arousing the servants.

"It's different somehow. 'Tis just as I remembered it, yet it seems changed . . . larger . . . I don't know why. I guess I've become too accustomed to squalor. A log house in a Missouri prairie where the wind never stops howling . . . how's Mother?"

"Very well—I'll have her called. But first some dry clothing for ye . . ."

Old Jean-Jacques was creeping through the hall, so old now that he could scarcely move.

"Awaken Georges," Stephen told him, "and have him bring dry clothing. Tell Suzette to make coffee. Have ye eaten, 'Tienne?"

"No, Father."

"Tell her then to prepare a breakfast, Jean-Jacques." He turned to Etienne. "And now, lad, where are the children? And Ceclie? Ye haven't left them in Missouri, have ye?"

"No, Father. They're resting at the Saint Louis. But I couldn't wait until morning. I had to see the old place and you and Mother."

"Thank ye, lad, for that. But what about your own place? Ye're not in any trouble are ye, 'Tienne? If it's money that ye need . . ."

"No, thank you, Father. I don't need anything. This last year the place showed a profit. So I cleared off all my debts, sold my Negroes—all but Inch, he's with Ceclie and the children in New Orleans—and brought them back to Harrow. They'll be safer here, Father . . . if you don't mind having them."

"Mind? Are ye daft, lad? 'Twill be the greatest pleasure of my life. But ye said something about their safety. Were they in any danger?"

"Yes. This secession business . . . it means war, Father. And

486

already in Missouri there have been barns burnt and a few houses. Your free-soilers aren't a squeamish people."

"And your proslavers? They draw very nice distinctions, I suppose?"

"We've had to fight fire with fire. 'Tis a bloody business. I wanted Ceclie and the children out of it."

Georges was coming through the hall with the dry clothing. Georges' woolly thatch was white, and he had children grown, offsprings of his marriage with the long-reluctant Suzette, who were now house servants at Harrow.

"Monsieur 'Tienne," he chuckled. "You a man now, yes! What a fine beard! People call you Judge Fox, now, sho—yes?"

"Light a fire in the study, Georges," Stephen said; "then go up and call Madame. Come, 'Tienne, 'tis best that ye change."

Afterwards, in the study, the three of them sat beside the fireplace, talking over their coffee.

"I had a letter from Julie," Etienne said. "That husband of hers has enlisted in the Federal Navy. I wrote her back immediately and suggested that she join us all here—I don't like the idea of her being way up there among those Yankees alone."

"Nor I," Aurore said. "The Yankees will never reach us here— if something should happen . . ."

"Something will happen," Stephen declared. "Ye may depend upon that, Aurore."

" 'Twill be soon over," Etienne said. "Why, we'd be in Washington within three weeks after it started—but I'm not sure those Yankees have any stomach for a fight."

Stephen snorted.

"They fought ye well enough in Kansas, didn't they? Seems to me they won that one. Kansas came in free. And what do ye propose that we use for ammunition? Cotton bales? Where are our foundries to cast cannon? Think ye that they will sell us the arms with which to fight them?"

"Well, from the arsenals we've taken—"

"About one hundred thousand pieces of arms—only about ten thousand of which are modern. Most of the rest are smooth-bores, and flintlocks to boot—vintage of 1812! And we'll need half a million—mark ye that, 'Tienne."

"But we're better fighters . . . and we're more accustomed to the open, more responsive to command."

"Ye speak as though the Yankees are a different breed of dog. We're all Americans, remember. Think ye that your Ohio, Iowa and Illinois farm boys are not as at home in the field as we? 'Twill be a bloody business, 'Tienne, which we cannot hope to win. They can lose man for man with us and still come up with thousands in the field after we're bled white. How many railroads run out of New Orleans? Two! How many factories do we have for uniforms, boots, saddles, spurs, equipment of all sorts? I'll tell ye, 'Tienne, none! 'Twill be a long and frightful war if it comes to war and we will lose. That's why I'm going to do my utmost to keep Louisiana out of it. Perhaps then the others will think twice."

"You paint a dismal picture, Father."

"But a true one. Still, that's not my only reason for the stand I take—nor even the chief one. Ye see, I was a man grown when I came to this country. I made comparisons and soon I knew that there was nothing like this land in all the earth. The thing ye would destroy is infinitely precious to me. I don't believe any longer in aristocracy—even self-made aristocracy such as the South has. Ye can't have a land like America unless the people —all the people—have a hand in its shaping. And the South has never dealt fairly with the people. Why, we've treated the Negroes better than we have our own. What of your landless white? Your mountaineer—your swampfolk? Must they go on eating the clay of the earth to keep from starving?"

"The people," Etienne sneered, "that rabble!"

"Rabble? They used that word in France, 'Tienne, and heads rolled into the basket. Either ye give the people their freedom— or they will take it, and ye and yours will perish in the whirlwind."

"Even the blacks?"

"Aye. Remember Nat Turner? Remember Haiti? Remember Saint Domingue?"

488

"Yes," Etienne said. "But that will never happen here!"

"No? Perhaps not—but freeing the blacks would not destroy our economy. Slave labor is about the most inefficient there is. There is only so much work ye can get out of an owned thing, no matter how much ye beat him. 'Twould be cheaper in the long run to pay them a wage."

"They'd only squander it," Etienne declared; "and the next day you'd have to feed them."

"Would Inch squander a wage? We have two hundred sixty thousand freedmen now—and they all seem to get along. But enough of this—ye must be dead for sleep. I'll ride into New Orleans and bring in Ceclie and the children while ye rest."

Etienne smiled, stroking his enormous beard with his hand.

"Yes, Father," he said. "Anyway, 'tis certain that we can't solve the problem—or anything like it. You have my old room ready?"

"Yes," Aurore said, slipping her arms around her stepson's waist. "And I'll have Georges up as soon as you're awake—to shave off those horrible whiskers!"

"You'll have to indulge me in that," Etienne laughed; "I've grown quite attached to them."

When Stephen came back from New Orleans, riding in the yellow coach, holding his two-year-old granddaughter, Gail, in his arms, while the two boys, Victor, named after Andre's son, and little Stephen crawled all over him, peering out the windows, anxious to be home, he found a delegation waiting upon him. He excused himself and conducted Ceclie and the children upstairs, then returned to the grand salon to talk with his guests. They were all working men, sitting ill at ease among the magnificence of Harrow, rubbing their big-knuckled, horny hands together.

Stephen called a slave and ordered wine and cigars for the whole delegation. Then he faced them, smiling.

"Well, gentlemen," he said, "What can I do for ye?"

Hearing the faint touch of brogue still present in his speech, the big-muscled man sitting near the front smiled and got to his feet.

" 'Tis Irish ye be, Mister Fox? I'd heard sich, but ye seemed too foine a gintilman—too much a lord. Well, so be we, and 'tis that in part that brung us here."

Stephen waited patiently.

"We be the representatives of all the trade guilds and unions in the city, and 'tis thinking we was that we'd need a spokesman whin this business of secession come up for the voting. They wouldn't listen to us—these quality folks—but ye be wan of thim. Yit we've heard tell that ye've been on our side many a toime. That's true, ain't it?"

"Yes, I see among ye men who've attended fêtes here at Harrow. Ye know, gentlemen, I was once a typesetter and a printer's divil. But first, I'd better find out how ye want your votes cast. I can't agree to vote for something in which I don't believe."

"And sure 'tis that that we wouldn't ask of ye," the spokesman said. "We be ag'in' it—this secession business. And ye?"

"I'm your man," Stephen said. "To secede from the Union is a folly—nay more, 'tis a wicked folly. Ye men who come here from other lands know well what this country means. If slavery becomes too powerful, what chance has a free working man?"

"None. But this be queer coming from ye, Mister Fox—seeing as how ye hold as many niggers as any man in the state."

"Aye. But 'tis written in my will that upon my death they're to be freed—not sold, but freed. When I came to this land, 'twas in my mind to rise in life and everybody else could go hang. But 'tis an old man, I am now, by all the saints, and I know that we've all got to rise together or else we fall separately. I want to see this the best land in all the world for the common man, and if we have to rid ourselves of the aristocracy to do it, then we're best rid of them and quickly say I. At any rate, gentlemen, 'twill be a pleasure to serve ye."

Shortly thereafter the workers took their leave, having consumed an enormous quantity of wine and cigars. Two days later he was notified in writing that he had been elected union delegate-at-large to the special secession convention. The family watched him leave in complete and utter silence, for there was not one of them who approved of his views in the matter. Stephen wished that he had Julie there to say an encouraging word; but although she had written that she was coming home to stay during Tom's absence, she had not yet arrived. So it was that Stephen had to ride away from Harrow with the faintest kind of goodbyes, and no good wishes.

He made the journey upriver to Baton Rouge by packet, and took his seat with the other delegates. He listened quietly to the debates on the subject, and when his turn came, he rose and began to give figures covering the extent of Louisiana's trade with the North as compared with its foreign trade, the amount of Louisiana capital held and working through Northern banks, the almost total absence of ownership of any seagoing bottoms by any firm of Louisianians, the lack of any kind of gun works, or large-scale manufacturing establishments of any sort within the state, the lack of the facilities or the raw materials to manufacture gun powder, and a detailed analysis, based upon his personal knowledge of the two countries, of why any belief that England and France would do much more than talk in behalf of the Confederacy was doomed to disappointment. In closing, he pointed out that the idea that the North and the rest of the world were economically dependent upon the South whereas she herself was self-sufficient and self-contained was a suicidal fallacy. That the upper Mississippi valley could not live if it were cut off from the gulf, as had been asserted in ringing oratorical tones by a previous delegate, he contradicted by reading figure after figure of trade increases in commodities in cities along the route of the Erie Barge Canal, and comparing them with the decreases and often complete disappearances of such commodities from the New Orleans market.

"The fact is, gentlemen," he concluded, "the upper Mississippi valley has been getting along without us for years, but we never bestirred ourselves to notice it. I ask ye therefore before ye take this fatal step to name me one type of weapon or one military

491

article of any sort that is manufactured South of the Mason and Dixon line. With what will you fight them? Your bare hands?"

In the end he was howled down. These were facts. The South has always preferred oratory.

When the vote was counted, it was one hundred three in favor of secession to seventeen against. Stephen Fox and several other of the minority delegates got to their feet to protest: they well knew that the division between Union and secession delegates as they had been informed was almost equal. There were turncoats in the hall that night. Finally a recount was made of the popular vote and the chairman read:

"For Union delegates: 17, 296; for secession delegates: 20, 448."

A difference, Stephen calculated, of merely three thousand, one hundred and fifty-two votes in a by-no-means-unquestionable tally. Less than one eighteenth of the voting population of the state, an amazingly small fraction of one percent of the total population. Louisiana was out of the Union. May God and the Virgin have mercy upon her soul.

The next day, back in New Orleans, Stephen Fox offered his services to the Confederate Army of America.

XXXIV

Early in February, 1861, when Julie finally reached Harrow, she found that Etienne was already gone, swallowed up in the vast wilderness that lay to the northward. Her father, his offer to serve finally accepted by the army after the personal intercession of Colonel Andre Le Blanc and Brigadier General Duncan, was in command of a regiment of cavalry under General Mansfield Lovell, whose troops were assigned to the defense of New Orleans.

Nothing had changed—except that there were no men at Harrow other than the Negroes. Ceclie, her temper growing daily more waspish as no word came from Etienne, required delicate handling. But the children were a delight. Someday, when this silly, all but bloodless war was over, Julie decided, there must be other children . . . with unruly dark hair and wide grey eyes.

She saw Stephen often, for there was nothing in the military situation that prevented him from visiting Harrow. The tall, rapier-lean figure of her father was exceedingly handsome in the fine, tailored grey uniform of a Confederate major; but he spoke little, and his eyes were troubled. Julie alone knew how much his decision had cost him, so with him her manner was one of perfect understanding tempered by a little sadness.

The weeks drifted on and nothing happened. Colonel Walton took Baton Rouge without fighting, taking his Washington Artillery upriver on the *Natchez* along with the Chasseurs à Pied, the Crescent Rifles, and the Orleans Cadets. Major Paul E. Theard with his Bataillon d'Artillerie on the *Yanic* took Forts Jackson and St. Phillips some ninety miles below the city at Plaquemine Bend. Fort Pike at Rigolet, and Fort McComb on the Bayou Chef Mentur were also in Confederate hands—all this without the firing of a shot.

It was a curious comic-opera sort of war, complete with splendid uniforms, flags and martial music. Life had never been so gay in New Orleans. There were parties and dances without number, the colorful uniforms adding glamour to the occasions. For a long while mail still came through from the North, so that Julie knew of the progress that Tom was making in his training and even a little of the confusion and blundering that were to mark the first year of Federal operations.

Then in April the picture changed: Major Anderson (Bob Anderson, my beau, Bob!) marched out of Sumter to the salute of fifty guns, bearing with him the shot-torn burned flag which at the last was to be wrapped around his body when they lowered him into the grave, and took ship aboard the relief vessels that President Lincoln had sent, sailing away to New York and glory even in defeat. And Pierre Gustave Toutant Beauregard, late of New Orleans, whose guns ringing Charleston harbor had smashed the wooden structures on the island into flaming splinters, sent in a grey-clad garrison.

Now, indeed, it was war; but in New Orleans, few cared. The young men of the city strutted in their fine uniforms and battalion after battalion marched away to the North. A few women, like Julie and Ceclie, wept, their tears falling against the wall of silence separating them from their men. But most of them waved their silken banners from the galleries and cheered their men onward with blissful ignorance of stench and mud, lice, dysen-

494

tery, bullet-spattered brains and the dreadful grating of the surgeon's bone saw.

Near Washington, on Sunday, July 21, 1861, a picnic was held. A stream of spectators in buggies, carrying their lunch baskets, rode out to Bull Run Creek at Manassas, Virginia to watch "Northern Shovelry make Southern Chivalry" bite the dust. It had all been announced beforehand—the time, the place, the opponents. But on Sunday, the Union troops were pouring back into Washington, saved only by Colonel Sherman's hollow square whose murderous fire cut down the Confederate cavalry. There were guns, hats, blankets, haversacks strewn every foot of the way for twenty miles, and every lawn in the Capital was filled with whipped, dog-tired, hopeless men lying in the drizzling rain of Monday morning.

This was war—the face of it—and civilian spectators had seen what it was like. The dust of the dry Sunday came up from the ground and choked the nostrils but that wasn't enough. Hot bloodstench is a strong scent, horseguts dripping through the shellslashed bellies and tangling in the feet of the pain-maddened animals until they fell screaming to the earth are not calculated to help a picnicker's appetite. They puked up their lunches, these watchers, and rode deathpale and sickened back to Washington. The wounded men were quieter than the horses. They lay in the mud that hot young blood had made of the bone-dry earth and they did not cry. They died holding the pictures of sweetheart, mother, and wife in their hands and left bloodfroth on the photographs where they had kissed them.

This was war . . . the face of it. And in New Orleans, they danced. . . .

The entire Missouri border, where Etienne Fox rode with the proslave irregulars, was flaming. Monday's Hollow, Underwood's Farm, Big River Bridge, Springfield. Minor skirmishes, these, but the dead, crow-tormented in the Missouri cornfields, were no less butchered, limb-smashed, minie-pierced than those at Bull Run. And up at Harrow, Julie Fox Meredith thanked the saints that her Tom was in the navy where he could never meet her menfolk. But Ceclie wept and stormed and slapped the children and cursed and prayed for Etienne at one and the same time.

Stephen rode up to see the women at Harrow, saying gloomily: "Yes, it goes well now, but tomorrow . . ."

Tomorrow was the Fall of 'sixty-one and the Winter of 'sixty-two. Tomorrow was Ulysses S. Grant at Donelson, the men marching in an almost Summer sun, throwing away their overcoats and blankets, betrayed by the weather dropping to ten above, the bloody earth stone-hard. Tomorrow was February 16, 1862—"No terms except an unconditional and immediate surrender can be accepted. I propose to move immediately upon your works." The North had found its man.

In New Orleans, at the St. Louis and the St. Charles, they danced. In Royal and Conti they gambled. The whores did a landoffice business. Life was never so gay.

Lincoln's do-nothing Napoleon, McClellan, idled, whining for men and more men, begging for material. ("Sending men to that Army," Abe groaned, "is like shoveling fleas in a barnyard.") Then McClellan moved at last upon Manassas, but Johnny Reb had upped stakes in the night and was gone, so McClellan marched back upon Washington. Reinforced, he marched south again, fell upon Yorktown, finding it empty, guarded by wooden log cannon as was Manassas, and took it thus, wiring heroic Napoleonic phrases to Washington.

And blackbearded Etienne Fox lived in the saddle, riding out of Missouri into Arkansas, fighting at Pea Ridge, then sweeping back into Missouri, hearing the whine of the minie balls at Sugar Creek, Leesville, Elkhorn Tavern . . . seeing it all end at the last in disaster for Confederate hopes. Missouri stayed in the Union.

Young Lieutenant Thomas Meredith, Junior, United States Navy, standing aboard the gunboat watching the mortar shells loop into Fort Pulaski, off the coast of Georgia . . . this too was tomorrow, the fort taken, and three hundred sixty prisoners with it. This and Island Number Ten in the Mississippi, taken by Commodore Foote and General John Pope.

"Yes, it goes well now, but tomorrow . . ."

Now, again, it was April in the land. The lavender, pink and white crepe myrtle were ablaze with blossoms. There were the white oleander, the yellowish pink mimosa, and the feathery green and gold acacia. The magnolias drooped heavy and waxen, and above the cruel spines of the yucca the great blossoms made Spring snow.

At the Lascal plantation, below New Orleans, the flowers were as bright as at Harrow, and the air as perfume-laden. Here, in the morning, the sun riding in over the river, Camile Lascal stopped halfway down the page of the letter she was writing to her brother Henri, and walked out into the garden. The river showed golden through the magnolia trees and on its surface nothing moved. Camile walked over to the trellis where the red ramblers were. She'd cut one, and press it to send to Henri. Henri loved flowers, and God knows he had scant chance to enjoy them away in the North fighting with the Louisiana Grays for her and for all fair women.

She took out her scissors and snipped at the stem. The scissors were dull and the rose held. She caught the stem in her hand and twisted. The rose gave but she got a thorn into her finger. She pulled it out, sticking the injured finger into her mouth, raising her head as she did so. Then her brown eyes widened for the river was no longer empty. A low schooner was butting its way upstream.

Camile turned and ran back to the house. A few moments later she was back with the pearl opera glasses. She leveled them at the schooner, rapidly twirling the adjustable knob. She could see it clearly now—even the name: S-a-c-h-e-m, she spelled out; then she swept her glasses upward. Then she was running back to the house, calling the Negroes as she neared it. There was no further doubt about it—that was a Yankee flag. Ten minutes later, not even having stopped to don her fetching riding habit, she was pounding northward, toward New Orleans. . . .

General Mansfield Lovell received her cordially and thanked her for her information. Afterwards he called out a guard of honor and had the lovely Creole lady inspect the troops. And

497

Camile rode homeward, escorted by six handsome cavalrymen, feeling quite the heroine.

But when Major Stephen Fox, who was present at Headquarters when Camile brought in her message, suggested that one of his companies be sent to reconnoiter the general said:

"Humph! Arrant nonsense, Major Fox! I can't have my cavalry worn out because a silly girl thinks she's seen a Union sloop!"

But the *New Orleans Picayune* found it necessary to reassure the citizenry. It marshaled up a most militant air and described in detail the dam a quarter of a mile below the forts which would hold any flotilla on earth for at least two hours during which time it would be under heavy crossfire from both the forts, mounting one hundred seventy guns of the heaviest caliber, many of which would be served with red-hot shot.

Stephen paused as he read this. If such a dam existed then General Duncan's engineers were the marvels of the earth, for a week ago when he had visited the forts he had seen no sign of any such dam. As for the guns, he himself had counted only one hundred twenty-eight, of which at least an hundred were hopelessly antiquated. But, possibly the *Picayune's* reporter had better information than he. He read further.

"Between New Orleans and the forts there is a constant succession of earthworks. At the plain of Chalmette, near Janin's property, there are redoubts armed with rifled cannon which have been found to be effective at five miles range."

Now by the saints, somebody must be crazy! There were batteries at Chalmette, true enough, but they were ancient smooth-bore cannon which couldn't carry half a mile. And between Chalmette and New Orleans there wasn't even a drainage ditch! Any really good gunners could knock out Chalmette in half an hour. He picked up the paper, frowning.

"At Forts St. Phillip and Jackson, there are three thousand men, of whom a goodly portion are experienced artillerymen, and gunners who have served in the navy." Well that much was true, he'd have to grant the *Picayune* that.

"In New Orleans itself, we have 32,000 infantry, and as many more quartered in the immediate neighborhood. In discipline

498

and drill they are far superior to the Yankees. We have two very able and active generals, who possess our entire confidence, General Mansfield Lovell and Brigadier General Ruggles."

Stephen let out a long, slow whistle. There were, to his certain knowledge, only three thousand troops quartered in New Orleans and perhaps seven thousand more in the vicinity. As for their superiority in discipline and drill, that remained to be seen. These accounts might have been printed to fool the enemy, Stephen thought. He got up at once and, mounting his palamino, rode out of New Orleans toward Harrow. Aurore and the children, by which term he meant both Julie and Ceclie as well as his grandchildren, must be warned. With such idiotic bombast in the saddle, New Orleans was certainly in danger.

Twenty miles below the forts, Admiral Farragut had called a conference of his officers to hear the report of Captain Gerdes of the *Sachem*. By reason of the fact that he was second in command of the gunboat *Itasca*, Captain Caldwell, commanding, Lieutenant Thomas Meredith was present at the meeting. Captain Gerdes had done well. The artillery ranges had been calculated to the yard, and flags placed along the banks marked exactly the position that each vessel was to occupy. Admiral Farragut gave strict orders that once in position, the vessels were not to be moved a foot. They were to be ranged in two lines on either side of the river.

Listening to the orders, Tom could feel the hammer pulse at the base of his throat pounding away. It was for this he had schemed, begged, pleaded, employed cajolery, bribed—so that he might be transferred to Farragut's command. Even if the objective had been Mobile, as he had thought, still it would have been worth the effort. But New Orleans itself—that had been beyond his wildest dreams. Soon they would break through,— just beyond New Orleans Julie waited, not knowing that she waited, and no city on earth must stand between them! If he had to smash New Orleans into ashes he'd get through. Within the week he'd be at Harrow. Beyond that, his mind stopped, unable to contemplate the bliss awaiting him.

He returned to the heavy oaken deck of the *Itasca* and made

499

a thorough examination. The guns were polished and ready, the fuses already cut, the shot piled up beside them and the canvas powder bags. All around the deck bales of cotton were lashed to the cabins and wrapped in heavy iron chains. This would provide armor of a sort; but, damn it, if anything happened to the *Itasca* he'd swim upriver to Harrow!

Now the nineteen mortar schooners under Commander Porter were moving upstream, pushing ahead against a four-knot current. And the *Itasca* too was slipping into line, taking its place among the convoying gunboats—six in all, two of them double-ended ferry boats from New York City. The shores slipped backward with agonizing slowness. It would take them all day and half the night to reach the forts.

Just before morning, the mortar schooners anchored around a bend in the river just out of sight of the forts. Parties of men went ashore into the thick woods that crowned the bend and, lying off shore, Tom could hear the sound of their axes. When the sun came up, the masts of every vessel had been disguised with leafy boughs, so that from a distance, it was impossible to say where the forest left off and the schooners began.

As the darkness left the face of the Mississippi, Tom could see feverish activity taking place aboard the nearest mortar schooner. The short, fat gun, as broad across almost as it was long, and anchored to the heavy timbers, was being elevated until its ugly muzzle pointed skyward. Now the gunners were ramming home the charge, and groaning under the weight of the thirteen-inch diameter, two-hundred-fifty-pound mortar shell. Then the gun was ready. Tom saw the gunner jerk the lanyard but, brace himself as he would, he was still shaken by the explosion. It rolled out over the river, awaking echoes, and young Meredith could see the black ball arching against the sky, then dropping lazily in a perfect parabola. But before it dropped into the fort, another mortar spoke, then another, and another until the face of the river reverberated to the belly-deep booming of the cannon. The smoke drifted up from the muzzles, and already the nearer gunners were as black as Negroes. Then, some time later, the guns in the forts began to reply. Tom saw a geyser of dirty,

500

yellow-white water rise thirty feet high in midchannel. Then another was pointing skyward as the shells in the forts probed closer and closer to the hidden flotilla. At last it had begun.

On April 25, 1862, it rained. The day came drumming up in rain and the face of the river was rain-stippled. Standing upon the belvédère, Aurore looked downriver toward New Orleans. The rain lanced down into her face. Her cloak and the shawl which she had tied over her head were already soaked, and wisps of white hair were plastered tight against her forehead. She bent forward, taut with listening. But no sound came from the city. Of course, she didn't really expect to hear the guns. They were at the forts ninety-odd miles below New Orleans . . . more than an hundred from here. And as long as the great chains stretched between Forts Jackson and St. Phillips held, no Yankee would be able to steam upriver. Pray God they held! But she shouldn't worry. To do so was something like sacrilege. The good God would protect that chain . . . yes, the chain, and the forts, and her Stephen standing now just back of his gunners on the ramparts of Fort St. Phillip, and squinting into the teeth of the Yankee guns. Still it wouldn't be amiss to beseech a special benediction of the Blessed Virgin. Her lips moved swiftly in the dim rain-wet air.

The sound of hoofbeats on the alley of oaks caused her to open her eyes quickly. Leaning over the balustrade, she could see Ceclie pounding up the drive, her horse's hooves clopping dismally in the sea of mud. Cross saddle as usual, Aurore murmured, and in spite of herself, she could not repress a tiny feeling of disgust. But she turned and went down the narrow stairway, closing the trapdoor behind her. Her garments trailed wetly on the stairs as she went down, but she did not stop to change them. Ceclie might have news. Panting a little from the exertion, she rounded the last great sweep of the gigantic spiral of stairs, and paused half way from the bottom.

Ceclie was standing facing Julie. Her face was grave, almost hard. She had thrown her riding hat into one of the big chairs. Where it had struck the cushions were stained with water. Aurore looked from her to Julie. The girl was swaying on her feet, her young face a chalky mask. She turned toward where Aurore stood and her voice was high and edged.

"Oh, Mother," she wept, "Mother!"

Slowly Aurore came down the steps and slipped her arms around her daughter. But her eyes were fixed on Ceclie's face.

"They broke the chain," Ceclie said harshly. "Like a piece of string. Then they ran the forts. Every ship we had on the river is either sunk or ablaze. They knocked out the guns at the Chalmette in twenty minutes without even stopping. New Orleans is burning. Warehouses, sugar, cotton, wharves, steamboats —everything. The people are in a perfect frenzy."

Aurore opened her mouth but no sound came out. She wet her dry lips and her voice was a husky dry whisper.

"The men in the forts," she got out; "Stephen . . . ?"

Ceclie looked her straight in the face, and her brown eyes were very hard.

"Dead or captured," she said and strode past them up the curving stairs.

XXXV

From the decks of the gunboat Pinola to which he had been transferred when the *Itasca* had been wrecked by a round shot through her boilers, Lieutenant Meredith looked out over the city. A black pall of smoke hung over the entire waterfront, and the great flames of blazing cotton which the mobs had dragged from the warehouses and set afire to prevent its falling into Union hands bloodied the sky. Molasses and wine ran down the gutters, and the crash of breaking glass could be heard even where he stood. The levee was black with howling humanity hurling curses at the Yankees, shaking their fists and even brandishing weapons. New Orleans was running true to form. That city could make even a civil war baroque.

But now the small boats were putting two men ashore. They were both officers, and Tom recognized them at once. Captain Theodorus Bailey and Lieutenant G. H. Perkins stepped ashore alone. Tom gasped. Was there to be no escort? Why, that howling mob would tear the officers to pieces. Had the old man gone daft?

But the old man, Admiral Farragut, knew exactly what he was doing. He had lived in the city in his youth, and gauged the tem-

503

per of its inhabitants exactly. The Orleanians would shout and swear, but they wouldn't lay a finger on the men. Watching them disappear from sight, Tom thought about Julie. How much longer would he have to wait before he saw her? Had she changed? Perhaps now, after so much blood had stained the Southern earth, she no longer wanted to see him. He felt sick and miserable and completely empty of triumph.

For the Johnny Rebs were beaten, there was no doubt about that. Their last hope, the gigantic ironclad *Louisiana* had been slipped from its moorings near St. Phillip early this morning, and had drifted downstream, blazing from stem to stern, her mighty guns bellowing. She had swerved in upon the *Harriet Lane*, where Admiral Farragut had been talking over the terms of surrender with Lieutenant Colonel Higgins, commander of Fort Jackson, and had blown up so close to the schooner that the *Lane* had almost capsized. There was nothing that the Confederates could do now, even if they wanted to. He frowned looking at the densely packed crowds. There must be some way of getting upriver to Julie!

At eleven, while he was listening—or rather, not listening—to the Chaplain deliver the usual Sunday morning sermon, the air was suddenly heavy with cannon fire. At once every man jumped to the alert. Tom ordered his men to issue small arms and stand by to repel boarders. But after maintaining a vigil of more than an hour, they were put at ease by the Captain's orders and the explanation given.

It seemed that the *Pensacola*, anchored off Esplanade Avenue, had sent ashore a party to raise the United States flag over the recaptured Mint. The men had done so, but no sooner had they returned to the *Pensacola* than the flag had been torn down and dragged through the streets by a party of four men. The maintop howitzer had opened fire, but apparently it hadn't hit anything.

This opera bouffe was growing tiresome, Tom decided; why the devil didn't Butler come?

But he had to endure five more days of waiting before General Butler's troops appeared in the city. The Negroes were out in droves, laughing, singing and cheering the Union troops as they marched down the levee to Poydras, on Poydras to St. Charles, down St. Charles to Canal, and on Canal to Custom House. The whites muttered curses and threw overripe fruit. It was still comic opera, but New Orleans had met Benjamin F. Butler, the best and most capable administrator it had ever had, and certainly the most hated. Later they were to become better acquainted.

The next day, while Butler's men were arresting W. B. Mumford (a man in his forties, a husband and the father of three children, but forever thereafter to be spoken of in New Orleans as a rash, impetuous lad for his outrage against the flag), the *Cayuga* was ordered upstream to investigate the report that irregulars were operating in the bayou country to the north of the city.

Watching the *Cayuga* standing out from the wharf, Tom's mind was busy with a thousand schemes. He had tried vainly to transfer to the *Cayuga* for this upriver trip, but without success. He considered taking French leave, renting a horse, making his way up the levee to the river road. But who would let him have a horse? Certainly not Ben Butler's cavalry. And to approach the citizens of New Orleans in his blue uniform would get him exactly nowhere. Besides, even if he secured the animal, how would he get through the sentries? Nothing to do now but wait.

Up at Harrow, Julie, too, was waiting. The plantation was an island, shut off from all contact with the outside world. No word from Tom. No word from Stephen. And Etienne, too, lost to them, his fate unknown. All of them dead perhaps. Or maimed. Or blinded. Or taken prisoner. Pray God, it was the last! No matter how bad the food at Rock Island or Fort Jackson or Camp Douglass, no matter how brutal the guards, still they would then be alive. Still they could come back to her, these men of hers. Please God, let them be captured and out of it!

It was a bright day, and the sun rode high over the river. Julie sat with her mother upon the upper gallery and gazed at the river. Aurore's face was drawn and working. Julie stretched out her hand to pat her mother reassuringly, but her fingers stopped inches from Aurore's shoulder. Her whole body froze. Aurore,

505

too, leaned forward, listening. A thin cloud of blue-grey smoke swirled upward from the cypress grove and afterwards came the ragged crash of musketry. The two women stood up. Then the sky was split with the deep-toned boom of a cannon, and even from where they stood they could see the great white splinters hurling upward from the trees.

An instant later they saw the troop of horsemen burst from the shelter of the trees, the riders crouched low over the horses' necks, and come racing up the drive straight toward Harrow. Julie looked at her mother. Then, without a word, the two women went down the stairway.

The men were hurling themselves from their mounts and running up the stairs into the house. They were all thin, bearded, unkempt. Julie walked out upon the lower gallery and lifted her hand.

"Gentlemen," she called, "I must ask you to explain . . ."

A tall man stopped before her. His black beard was matted with dirt and twigs. His pale eyes gleamed queerly out of the heavily begrimed face. He put out a horny paw and caught her under her chin, and his big, looselipped mouth split into a grin. Julie could see that his teeth were broken, blackened, and largely missing. His breath was fetid.

"Likely filly, ain't you?" he said. "'Tend to you later when I ain't so busy with the damyankees. Now git!" He whirled her around and slapped her smartly across the behind. Julie was speechless.

"Why, you . . ." she gasped, but the tall man was already past her and running up the stairs.

Julie turned toward the river. There, just opposite the landing, a gunboat drifted lazily. From its masthead the stars and stripes flapped listlessly. Julie could see the crew working feverishly, elevating the muzzle of the squat black mortar. She turned wide-eyed to Aurore, but at that instant the whole North Wing of Harrow blazed with musketfire. They could hear the shrill whistle of the minie balls whining toward the gunboat.

Then the mortar aboard the *Cayuga* spoke bass thunder, shaking the sky and the river. The two women stood there frozen, and

506

watched the great black ball climb swiftly to the top of its arc, hang there lazily for agonizing seconds, then hurl down to smash into the central floor of the North Wing. The walls of the second floor bulged out slowly, then with terrifying deliberation they crumbled and the flames leaped skyward, past the roof. Afterwards all the guns were silent.

"Oh, my God!" Julie whispered, "Oh, my God!"

But now the *Cayuga* was butting in to the landing, and a detachment of marines were springing ashore, coming forward on the double. The young lieutenant at their head came to a stop before Julie and Aurore and saluted smartly.

"Buckets," he said. "Where've you got them!"

"The Nigras will show you," Aurore said with great dignity. Then she disappeared into the smoke-filled interior. The marines raced around to the stables. In ten minutes a long line of marines and Negroes were passing buckets hand over hand and the fire was being checked at a dozen points. It took them four hours to put it entirely out, during which the water and the bayonets, which the marines used to rip down curtains and draperies in the path of the flames, ruined almost half of Harrow. Julie stood at her mother's side all the time, her face tear-wet. And Ceclie held her two youngest children under her arms, and stared at the fire with an expression of rage on her face that was terrible to see.

When at last it was out, the young lieutenant turned to the women, his smoke-blackened face lined and grave. He drew out a small notebook and a pencil.

"I'm afraid I'll have to place you all under arrest," he said. "Your names, please?"

"Madame Stephen Fox," Aurore said, "and this is my daughter, Madame Thomas Meredith."

"Meredith?" the lieutenant said. "That's odd. We've got a Lieutenant Tom Meredith aboard the *Pinola*—no relation, of course?"

Julie was clinging to Aurore, her face ablaze with joy.

"Oh, Mother!" she wept. "Mother!"

The young lieutenant's eyebrows rose.

"Her husband," Aurore said drily. "You'll let him know?"

"But of course! No wonder Tom was moving earth and heaven to go on this trip! Married to a Reb!"

"Thank you," Aurore said. "Now, if you'll excuse us. . . ."

"You're not to leave the grounds," the lieutenant said. "I'll station a couple of sentries—as much for your protection as for any other reason. And if Madam will permit me, I'd like to say that Lieutenant Meredith is a very lucky man."

He saluted them and took his leave. They stood on the gallery and watched the marines moving off, bearing on improvised stretchers the blanket-wrapped bundles that had been men and fighters. Julie and Aurore wept, but Ceclie's face was clear and still.

"God damn them," she said; "God damn them to hell!"

The next day young Tom Meredith rode up to Harrow. He dismounted at the foot of the stairs and flew up them three steps at the time calling, "Julie! Julie!"

But when the great doors swung open, it was Ceclie who stood there, staring at him, not a muscle in her face moving.

"Please," he began, "is Julie . . ."

And Ceclie went up on tiptoe and spat full into his face. Then she turned and marched back into the house. He stood there, blinking foolishly, wiping his cheek, when Aurore crossed the vast hall and came up to him.

"I'll send Julie to you," she said calmly; "if she wishes to come. But I cannot invite you in—not in that uniform. Now, if you'll wait outside. . . ."

Slowly Tom turned and went back through the door. He started down the stairs, his head sunk upon his chest. Then behind him was the clatter of small slippers and Julie's voice came down to him breathlessly:

"Tom! Oh, Tom!"

He turned and stretched out his arms.

In the Summer the sky above the prisoner-of-war camp at Fort Jackson was naked and cloudless. The river was bronze. Inside

the fort the heat simmered and danced. Bending over the sand-
piles, shoveling the sand into the canvas bags to be used as
bulwarks if ever the Confederate forces swept southward was
killing work, even for a young man. And Stephen Fox was sixty-
two years old. The goatee was a shaggy red beard now, silver-
streaked and unkempt. And the muscles of his arms and back
were trained down to corded sinew, every fiber of which ached.
The sweat dripped down from his beard. Where it struck the sand
it sizzled. Sweat-stink caught in the nostrils and lodged there
until it was so usual a thing that the senses no longer registered
it. And the belly caved in against the ribs with the eternal hunger.

Step by step the gigantic Negro guards marched the sentry
tours, blacksweat glistening on their foreheads and bared arms.
Now and again some young blade of the city, gazing ruefully
at cracked and blistered palms which had once been as white
and soft as a woman's, would inch over to one of the guards
(braving the blacksmell and niggerstench) and whisper: "I say,
Uncle, how about letting up a bit?" The answer was almost
always the same—the rich, midnight Negro-bass rumbling:

"Who's brother is Ah? Yo maw's or your paw's?" Or:

"You ain't no kin of mines! Git your lazy ass on back to wuk!"

Now and again Aurore would come out to the fort bearing a
pass wangled from General Butler. But they talked little. Steel
herself as she would, the sight of her Stephen, dirty, half-starved,
the raw sunsores visible under his long hair (white now, with only
a scarlet thread or two running through it), scratching absently
at his armpits where the vermin feasted was too much. And,
indeed, there was nothing to be said.

No, we haven't heard from 'Tienne. Yes, the children are well.
Julie—as well as could be expected under the circumstances.
The heat is terrible for her in her condition. And the diet isn't
any too good. Ceclie—nothing about her—no, never tell him
about Ceclie! (Ceclie riding into town in a new riding dress—
new when all the other women were in rags. Ceclie leaving the
children entirely in the care of Julie and herself and disappearing for days. Silk stockings, too—silk! And the officers riding up
to Harrow—Yankee officers! She who had spat into Tom's face,

509

and who had sworn venomously to her hatred of them. And
'Tienne dead perhaps or maimed or blind . . . or mad. . . .)

There were other things she did not tell him either as the days
dragged into years. (We'll be in Washington in three weeks—
remember.) How it was at Harrow, she and Julie, with the help
of the few Negroes who had not fled to the riotous camps below
the city, digging up the floors of the smokehouses and washing
the dirt to obtain the precious salt. Burning corn cobs, putting
the ashes in a jar, covering them with water, allowing the water
to stand until it is clear. This, Stephen, makes an acceptable
cooking soda when used one part to two parts sour milk. And the
coffee that you drink here, my darling, bad as it is, is at least
coffee, not sweet potato squares, dried in the sun and after-
ward parched, ground up and boiled. And tea of sassafras leaves,
or blackberry leaves, or cassena or youpon. But of milk we have
plenty—even at four Yankee dollars a quart—thanks to Ceclie.
Julie weeps when she has to drink it, knowing its source. But
Ceclie doesn't care, Stephen . . . she, I fear, hasn't any heart.

But I cannot tell you these things, my poor old darling. Not
these nor how it feels to watch you dying by inches and jesting
about your rags and your vermin. When this cruel war is over
. . . if you survive, you'll know nothing but happiness then,
Stephen . . . I'll make it up to you then, Stephen . . . then. . . .

Riding back to Harrow to find Julie in tears (she was often
in tears now) over the loss of a needle, which, truly, in view of
the fact that they were now quite impossible to replace, was a
catastrophe. Going into the kitchen to cook the evening meal
(the cook had long since fled in the company of a handsome
black lad from a colored Yankee regiment) and finding that
the only available skillet on three plantations was now out at La
Place in the hands of Amelia Le Blanc. Looking up at the smoke-
ruined walls and ceilings of Harrow, streaked by the oily smoke
from the rags set as wicks in pans of grease. At first she had
had candles, made of sweet myrtle berries, boiled and refined into
a translucent, aromatic wax. But after the Negroes had fled,
there was no one to gather the berries. Julie could not—she, herself, had no time, and Ceclie . . . Even pineknots could no

510

longer be obtained; so grease tapers provided the only illumination at night.

This was her day: First in the morning she made breakfast, cornbread and clabber for the children, the meal for the bread being ground by her own hands. She and Julie had some of the imitation sweet potato coffee, and the thick hunks of cornbread —nothing more. (Ceclie took no breakfast, preferring to sleep 'til past noon, after which she dressed and went out.) Then she trimmed the dried thorns which she used as pins and pinned the ragged clothing together while she mended and altered them. Buttons made of persimmon seeds were sewn on or, if she wished to be especially elegant, she made them of gourd, cut into moulds and covered with gaily colored cloth. After that she and Julie wove bonnets of corn shucks, palmetto or even of grass. Then the re-dying of dresses as the colors never held after a washing. Then carding, spinning, knitting, tearing up old linen sheets and underwear for bandages and lint. The floors of Harrow were quite bare now—the magnificent Persian carpets having gone into the mills and looms of the starving Confederacy.

And at last supper—of any green and growing thing they could find, and then bed and fitful, exhausted sleep that was the only release from the torments of existence, from the gutdeep, gnawing hunger pangs and the endless, eternal worry.

By the time that Julie's son was born, a thin, listless infant of less than six pounds, New Orleans had won its battle with General Butler. Apart from his famous—or infamous, depending upon the point of view taken—Women's Order (". . . hereafter, when any female shall, by word, or gesture, or movement, insult or show contempt for any officer or soldier of the United States, she shall be regarded and held liable to be treated as a woman of the town plying her vocation") and the hanging of Mumford before the Mint whose flag he had destroyed, General Butler was the best administrator that New Orleans ever had. During his rule, there was no yellow fever, for he had had the streets cleaned and the gutters flushed, instead of talking about it as New Orleans had done for so many years; and the quarantine laws were rigidly enforced. The poor of the city were fed, for the first time

511

and almost for the last time, in the city's history—though his method of raising funds for this purpose brought anguished howls. And under him, the city prospered. Though the people upon the great plantations like Harrow suffered, the city dwellers were almost unaware there was a war. It is certain Butler prospered, and his brother even more so; but it is equally certain that his prosperity hurt New Orleans not one iota. At Fort Jackson, Stephen, listening to the reports, developed a wholehearted admiration for the hornyhanded old Massachusetts pirate.

"New Orleans is a filly," Stephen grinned. "A touch of the whip and the spurs won't hurt her any!"

In the end, the North, bowing to the furor that the Woman's Order, Number 28, had caused even in the capitals of Europe, recalled him.

At Harrow, things grew steadily worse. Julie, due to her diet, had no milk in her breasts, and the baby was dying slowly of starvation. Then, one day, Ceclie strode into the room with a Yankee haversack slung across her shoulders. In it were jugs of milk and rich foodstuffs that Harrow had not seen in years. Mutely, Julie shook her head.

"You're a fool," Ceclie said calmly. "You'll let your baby die because of your silly pride? Here, take these things. There are more where they came from." Then she was gone, her new, expensive boots making a rich clatter on the stair.

And Aurore came into Julie's bedchamber to find her daughter feeding the infant rich whole milk, which the little fellow was sucking lustily through a clean rag stuffed into the neck of a bottle. But Julie was crying like a whipped child, her whole body shaken with sobs.

"I can't let him die, Mother," she sobbed. "Tom hasn't even seen him! But you know how Ceclie gets these things . . . and 'Tienne away at the front . . . Oh, Mother, Mother! I could just die!"

"Hush, child," Aurore whispered; then, her hazel eyes very cold and clear, she stood up. "It's time I had a talk with Ceclie," she said. "This can't be permitted any longer. . . ."

She opened the door to Ceclie's room without even knocking. Ceclie was seated before the mirror, combing out her long black hair. Even in the dim light, Aurore could see the lip salve, scarlet upon her mouth and the blaze of rouge showing through the rice powder. She looks hard, Aurore thought, hard. . . .

"Well?" Ceclie said harshly.

"Ceclie," Aurore said firmly. "You can say that what you do is none of my business . . . but it is. Everything that happens at Harrow is my business now that Stephen and Etienne are gone. These men . . . officers . . . Yankee officers. . . ."

Without answering her, Ceclie got up and opened a drawer in her bureau. She drew from it a letter whose creases were worn deep in the thick, yellowish paper from much opening and refolding. As she took it, Aurore could see that it was tearspotted, the ink lines blotted and fading. It was dated Pittsburg Landing, April 9, 1862.

" 'Dear Madame Fox,' " she read. " 'It is with a heavy heart that I communicate the following melancholy intelligence to you. Your husband, Lieutenant Colonel Etienne Fox, is missing in the action at Shiloh Church and must be presumed dead. He was last seen leading his cavalrymen in a charge upon the Union lines in a pouring rain on the seventh instant. I have been informed that the entire group was cut down by a concentration of musketfire and grapeshot. Colonel Fox was one of my bravest and most able officers, and I bitterly regret his loss, which shall be avenged. With deepest sympathy for you and yours in your hour of sorrow, I remain, your most obedient servant, Brigadier General N. Bedford Forrest, Commanding.' "

Aurore raised her eyes to her daughter-in-law.

"And you kept this from me all these months?"

"Yes. You and Julie had enough to bear. So what does it matter what I do?"

"You dishonor his memory," Aurore said. "You shame his children. Consorting with Yankee officers. . . ."

"Yankee *medical* officers, my dear mother-in-law. Don't tell me you hadn't noticed that?"

"No. And I don't see what difference . . ."

513

Again Ceclie turned to the bureau. From the bottom drawer she dragged forth a wooden box. The muscles of her forearms strained, lifting it. She put it upon her bed and unlocked it, throwing back the lid. It was filled to the brim with little white vials, dozens of them, all packed with a white, saltlike powder.

Aurore looked at her wonderingly.

"Quinine," Ceclie said. "I was hoping to get more of it . . . much more. But now there is no time. I am going across Lake Pontchartrain with it tonight. I've got a boat . . . old and leaky as the devil. So . . . if I don't come back. . . ."

Aurore's eyes softened. She looked at the girl, a long slow look.

"Yes, yes I did everything you think to get them. But there are boys in the hospitals dying of the fever for lack of medicines. Boys Julie played with. Friends of 'Tienne. You'll take care of the children for me? Teach them what a man their father was. Say nothing of me . . . they'll forget quickly enough."

Aurore stretched out her hand and put it upon Ceclie's shoulder.

"I'm going with you," she said.

"No. I can't let you. What would Julie and the children do if . . ."

"They'll have to take the chance. I'm going, and we're both coming back. I can't judge your actions any longer. I'm not wise enough. But this thing must be done. I'll be ready in ten minutes."

She went back into Julie's room. The girl was sleeping, the baby held gently in her arms. Aurore bent and kissed them both. Then she went into the room where the children were. They were sleeping like cherubs. She kissed them all, then, straightening, she went down the stairs where Ceclie waited.

It was pitchblack and the rains cried against the earth. They saddled their own horses and rode out, Ceclie riding cross saddle like a man. When they reached the lake, hours later, the wind had freshened the water into white caps. Ceclie uncovered the boat from among the reeds near the shore. She picked up a tin pail and handed it to Aurore.

"Get in," she snapped, "and start bailing."

It was morning before they reached the other side of the lake.

514

During the night the gale had died, and the water was calm. But they were skinsoaked and bruised and aching in every muscle. When at last the prow of the *piroque* crunched into the weeds Aurore was so weak she could hardly stand. Ceclie took the heavy chest under one arm and slipped the other around her mother-in-law's waist. Then, half dragging, half supporting her, she stumbled up the sandy beach.

The surgeon general of the Confederate Armies himself welcomed them when the sentries brought them in. He snatched at the chest as though it were gold-filled, and when he saw the contents, the tears ran down into his beard.

"God bless you, ladies," he croaked. "God in His mercy bless you!"

Afterwards they walked down the long rows of the bare frame hospital. The stench of gangrene was everywhere, thick and heavy on the air. As they turned to enter one room, the surgeon general stopped them, but not before they had heard the last grating scrape of the bonesaw. They stood there, frozen for an instant, then they heard the sizzle of the hot iron searing the torn flesh. The smell of the burning came through the door, and with it the last mortal shriek of the poor wretch within.

The doctor came out. His white gown was dirty and blood-stained, so that he looked like nothing on earth so much as a butcher from the slaughter pens. But neither of them fainted. The women of the South were past the fainting stage in the Spring of 'sixty-three.

When they got ready to go back, they found that their boat had been caulked so that it no longer leaked. And as they reached the southern shore of Lake Pontchartrain, by nightfall of the next day, they found the Yankee sentries waiting for them.

"My son was in that hospital . . . dying," Aurore lied with great dignity. "I had to go to him . . . pass or no pass."

The young Yankee officer sighed, looking at her white hair. His mother was like this . . . only not half so beautiful.

"You may go, ladies," he said wearily; "but please don't try a trick like that again."

XXXVI

It was lost finally. And no man could say exactly the day or the hour, for there were dozens of days, thousands of hours. Of course there was Palm Sunday, April 9, 1865 at the McLean house on the edge of Appomattox village, ninety-five miles west of Richmond in Virginia. But that was merely the formal conclusion, the ceremonial burial of what had been a long time a-dying. It had been lost years ago at Shiloh Church and Donelson, at the Seven Days and Second Bull Run, at bloody Antietam, Fredericksburg, Chancellorsville, Vicksburg, Gettysburg, Chickamauga, Missionary Ridge, in the March across Georgia, at Nashville, in South Carolina, and finally at Appomattox. It was lost, perhaps, when old Edmund Ruffin yanked the lanyard of the first gun at Charleston Harbor sending the roundshot screaming upon Sumter.

It was lost, too, in far and in obscure places: at Manchester and Leeds in England, when thousands of textile workers calmly accepted starvation as the alternative to supporting the naked hideousness of slavery; in Tennessee, forty miles above Memphis, on April 12, 1864, at tiny Fort Pillow at Washington, where Abe Lincoln sadly walked the night streets in a shawl. . . .

Lieutenant Colonel Etienne Fox, of the CSA, sat on the deck of a steamboat late in April of 'sixty-five looking out over the Mississippi. In a little while now, he would pass the once-great plantation of Harrow, but he did not intend to stop. First, New Orleans, and a night of rest and thinking. Then in the morning he would go back to Harrow to face whatever he would find there.

Already the cane was high in the fields, and the cotton was up and greening. Nothing had changed—everything had changed. He had the curious feeling that he was an intruder-ghost here in the land of the living. A strange bewhiskered ghost with guts rotted by dysentery, a minie ball aching dully in his shoulder, another in his thigh, three fingers of his right hand left behind him at Chickamauga . . . all his life, in fact, left behind at various places, and at various times: Shiloh Church, Murfrees-boro, Chickamauga, Nashville, and in nameless towns and villages. Because never again would there be any forward looking; nothing in the future could conceivably stand against the blood and flame of the past.

Now, until he was dead finally (not at Shiloh—where a ball had merely creased his tough skull and left him covered with the maimed and dying wounded), he would awaken in the night remembering. How it was at Murfreesboro—sleeping in the icy mudpools while the rain whipped down all night and his horse's black coat steamed . . . the wheels of the cannon digging in, and the whipcrack above the straining horses that could not budge them . . . The men in ragged grey and butternut brown standing in the cottonfield and stuffing the bolls into their ears against the drumshattering thunder of the artillery; the riderless horses flying in every direction (a gutshot horse screams like a woman in childbirth, but wounded men don't cry); the curious silence in the midst of battle that comes when the uproar has lasted long enough so that the brain in self-defense seals off the passage from the ears . . . and the retreat . . . picking his way between the bodies, resting at last by the smoking mound of raw horse flesh that had been three horses and was now less than one, their riders too indistinguishably co-mingled (man-blood and beastblood are the same color upon the earth and just as thick and steaming), then riding off again only to stop beside the bodies of two young lads, one of them fair and blond, the other dark, yet each of them with the other's features mirror-imaged, and recognizing with no sense of shock, or regret, or any sort of feeling that these were the Le Blanc twins, Victor and Armand, lying there in each other's arms, tenderly . . . He had turned to go then, but at the last Armand had moved, so he bent and disengaged the boy's arms from around the frozen corpse of his brother, and tried to lift the lad. But he could not, for the bloodpool was now ice, and the frozen rags one with the stone-hard mud. He remembered that he had straightened up and that he had not said anything but stood there looking at the boy frozen to the ground, seeing his blue lips moving and his finger purplish black and trembling pointing to Etienne's heavy Colt. He took it out, and passed it over, unable to do the job himself, watching as Armand got the icy muzzle into his mouth, but too far forward, so that the stiff thumb slipping from the hammer jerked the pistol, and when the smoke had cleared the boy no longer had a face. . . .

At Shiloh it had rained. He remembered with painful distinctness how his guts had knotted with fear as he had ridden forward into the place where the whole ridge exploded into flame and the earth had risen up and smote him. Then, later, waking under the hot steaming mound of dead and near-dead, smelling the blood-stench and burnt cloth and urine and feces and powder and cold deathsweat, he had lain quietly and waited for death that did not come. The Yankees had dug him out at last and herded him aboard the steamboat and taken him to Camp Douglass in Chicago.

If he could have read that letter, regretting his supposed heroic death, he would have smiled wryly through his black beard. He would have known as Ceclie could not that it was the work of a division clerk, and that old Nat had merely scrawled his name to the bottom of it. Never on earth would that old war horse have been capable of such clean phrasing. But he did not know it as he came awake aboard the Union steamboat butting up-river toward Chicago and the prisoner-of-war camp. He did not learn of it until long after Forrest had exchanged a Union Brigadier for him ("Git me that Gawdamned Cun'l Fox back. He's a uppity Frenchified sonofabitch but, Gawddamnit all, he fights!")

He had despised General Nathan Bedford Forrest at first, with that cold and deadly loathing that Southern aristocracy has always reserved for the slave trader; but you just couldn't hate old Nat long. The old war horse was completely honest and Etienne personally had seen fifteen horses shot from under him—at Shiloh, at Murfreesboro, at Chickamauga, at Nashville and in the campaign in Tennessee.

Now the packet was rounding the bend above Harrow. Etienne stood up painfully as the great white house came in sight. Then his pale blue eyes were widening, seeing the ruined and smoke-blackened North Wing. On the gallery three women stood and waved at the steamboat, and Etienne's breath came out in a great sigh. They at least were all right. He would not alter his plans.

As the house drifted back out of sight, a Negro, clad in Union blue, shouldered past Etienne and went forward. And Etienne shuddered, remembering Fort Pillow.

That was a minor action, one of the least that he had been in, but he remembered it like a Brady photograph and he would remember it every time he saw a black—so that ever afterwards he would have to steel himself to endure the presence of Negroes. He remembered the day—April 12, 1864. He had moved up with General Forrest from Mississippi into Tennessee. They had caught General William Sooy Smith flatfooted and sent him reeling back upon Memphis. Then they had ridden like a prairie fire across Kentucky to the banks of the Ohio and had held Paducah for nine hours while Forrest mounted a command of raw Kentucky recruits with 'borrowed' horses.

Riding back into Tennessee, he remembered being puzzled at the tone of Ceclie's letters which had at last caught up with him. She seems almost sorry I'm alive, he thought bitterly. The letters were stunned and mute. The children are well. Julie has a son. They are both doing as well as could be expected under the

519

circumstances. Your mother, too, is getting along splendidly. Never a note of gladness. (The breathgone "I love you, love you, love you, oh, my darling!" hot-whispered into his ear, of many nights, lost, lost, the fierce nails pressing into his bare back, piercing the flesh, bringing the blood as they had ground out their tiny share of ecstasy—of this, nothing, as though it had never been.)

Then Fort Pillow had come in sight, and he had forgotten. It was fatal to think of anything but the business at hand. It had been very easy—that fight. There were only six hundred men in the outworks and old Nat had driven them back into the fort within an hour. Then seeing that it was hopeless, the Union commander had hoisted the white flag. Etienne remembered it flying cleanly against the blue April sky. Beside it flew the Stars and Stripes.

Then the men were swarming forward over the works, the Columbiads in the woods thumped and thundered, the small branches splintering down before them and the whole place stinking of burnt powder. Then the Union soldiers were marching out in good order, their arms raised above their heads in surrender. Etienne heard the sharp intake of breath from the Georgian at his side.

"Gawdamighty! They's niggers!"

Looking back again, Etienne saw that perhaps two hundred of the men in blue were blacks. At his side the Georgian was crying like a child.

"I hopes to die!" he wept, "if paw ever finds out I fit agin niggers! Why you Gawddamned black bastids—a-fittin' ag'in' white men! Take that!"

His rifle roared and a black boy crumpled grotesquely. Then another soldier shot and another until they were all firing into the close packed mass of black humanity.

Etienne jerked out his sword and began to lay among the men with the flat side. Blows that would have knocked a man unconscious under ordinary circumstances went unnoticed. Here and there in the ranks a man cried out against the slaughter.

520

"Hold it, fellows—this ain't right. Them niggers done surrendered. . . ."

But his voice was lost in the crackle of musketry sweeping through the ranks of the Negroes like flames through a cane field. Etienne remembered that the sweatsmell was different, an acid lungstinging stench like a dogfox in rut. Then the men were surging forward and he was being swept along with them. They were stabbing with their bayonets and clubbing with their musket butts. A tall lanky mountain youth had knocked down a big brute of a black and was carefully, systematically, beating out his brains with his gun butt. Etienne remembered that he kept at it long after the Negro's head was an unrecognizable bloody pulp. There was another boy, with the face of a girl and long lashes that swept his cheeks when his lids drooped. He was using his bayonet with the precision of a surgeon, his footwork as graceful as a ballet dancer. Step, side step, sweet curving arch of back and houndtooth-lean belly, the gutspike going in just above the navel ripping sidewise, so that the Negro's guts tumbled out in pinkgray sausage rolls, then the withdrawal a full step backward, and the half whirl in search of another victim. He was very good and very precise. He was almost dainty. Etienne found himself swept along with the tide, hearing his voice yelling like the rest and his sabreblade crunch through black bone and sinew. Then, at the last, a little, emaciated yellowish Negro started to run away from the screaming, dying, unarmed mass. The girlish youth lifted his rifle like a javelin and hurled it through the air. It caught the little mulatto in the back and hurled him forward on his face. The bayonet went through his thin body and sank eight inches into the soft ground. Etienne stood and watched him struggling to get up, pressing down with his hands in a macabre sort of calisthenics, raising his body up, up . . . but the bayonet was fast in the earth, and all he could do was to slide his body up and down the blade, the blood bubbling up at the top, the whole blade reddened. Etienne felt very cold suddenly. He sat down upon the damp earth and threw up on the ground. For days thereafter he couldn't get the smell of vomit out of his black beard.

There were some two hundred-odd Negro soldiers in Fort Pillow. Of these, six or eight escaped. All the rest were put to the sword and their white officers with them.

Life now would have to be lived out in memory. In dreams in the night, nightmare screaming. In forever backward-looking. In never forgetting. And not for him alone but for the whole South . . . all of it.

The first person Etienne saw when he stepped off the boat in New Orleans was Walter McGarth. He came rushing forward, putting out the one hand he had left and crying:

"'Tienne! So I'm not the only one! Thank God for that!"

"The only one?" Etienne demanded.

"That came back. All the old crowd, Pierre Aucoin, Henri Lascals, Jean Sompayrac, Bob Norton, Jim Duckett . . . they all got it, 'Tienne. I hear some of the Le Blancs survived—but then, there were so damned many of them. . . ."

Etienne's face was lined and grave.

"What's next, Walter? What do we do now?"

"Pick up the pieces, I reckon. You've come to get your father, 'Tienne?"

"My father?" Etienne said harshly. "Where is he? I didn't know. . . ."

"He's in the hospital. That's right, you couldn't have known what with mail like it is. They moved him and some of the other sick prisoners up from Fort Jackson. They're being released to relatives when they're well enough to go home. You go to the Provost Marshal—no, I'm wrong. Now you go to the Commissioner of Police. His office is at the St. Louis. . . ."

Etienne was off at once, tossing a muttered thanks back over his shoulder. Everywhere in the streets of New Orleans were Union soldiers, swaggering, laughing, drunken. Many of them were Negroes. Etienne saw a black ride past in a fine carriage, at his side a pretty mulatto girl with diamonds gleaming at her ears and throat. The time is out of joint, or, cursed spite . . . He walked on very rapidly. Rounding a corner he ran head-on into a gigantic Negro in the uniform of a policeman.

"Gawddamnit, white man," the black growled. "Why the hell don't you look whar you's gwine?"

Etienne's eyes shot lightenings, but now was no time for delay. He stepped off quickly into the gutter and hurried on. Finally he was going up the steps of the Saint Louis and into the lobby.

Inside he was stopped by another Negro policeman who demanded his business. When Etienne told him, he disappeared behind the doors of an office. Etienne looked at the legend on the door. "Cyrus R. Inchcliff," it read, "Commissioner of Police." In an incredibly short time, he was back, holding a folded paper.

"Heah yo pass," he grinned. "The Commissioner say you's a ole fren of hissen. He tol' me to tell you to come back by heah when you gits yo daddy. He wanta see you bof. An' you better do hit, too, or else he jes mought change his mind 'bout sottin' yo daddy free."

Etienne had gone before he had finished speaking, striding as fast as his stiff leg would let him. The pass, apparently was quite in order. For a few minutes after reaching the hospital he was conducted to a broad inner gallery on which many patients sat enjoying the sun. He edged his way between them, until at last on the end of the gallery he came to the tall man with white hair and snowy, neatly trimmed mustache and goatee, sitting very quietly in a chair.

"Father," Etienne ventured, "Father . . ." But it was not until the man turned that he was sure. The great scar was there, and the fierce old falcon eyes.

" 'Tienne!" Stephen whispered, " 'Tienne!"

Etienne took a step forward, then with a strangled cry he swept the thin, frail old man into his arms.

Stephen pushed him back and looked at him, seeing the unabashed tears standing in his son's eyes.

"Easy, lad," he grinned, "I'm all right. The girls would have taken me home last week, but I wouldn't go. I wanted to wait until ye came. The damyankees have been good to me here. All the women nurses are in love with me."

"I don't doubt it, Father," Etienne said, relief flooding his voice. "But come on, let's get out of here . . . I haven't even been home yet. . . ."

"Ye have my release? Everything is in order?"

"Yes, Father. We'll go up to the superintendent now."

"How are we going to get home? Ye haven't any money have ye? If ye have . . . ye're the first Confederate soldier I've seen with any."

Etienne's black brows flew together.

"I haven't a cent," he growled. He stood there a moment, frowning. "There's one thing we might do," he said thoughtfully. "This police commissioner claims to be an old friend of ours . . . and he practically ordered us to return to his office. . . ."

"Then we'd better go. Things have changed, 'Tienne."

"So I see. Well, let's get the formalities over with."

Half an hour later, they emerged into the brilliant Spring sunlight. They walked very slowly, for Etienne soon saw that his father was incapable of a faster pace. On the *banquette* outside the St. Louis, they paused until Stephen had got his breath back. Then they climbed the steps into the lobby.

Without hesitation, although there were half a dozen other people waiting, the black policeman ushered them into the office. Then both of them were standing there frozen, their eyes wide in their faces, for the man who was striding forward to greet them was coal black, and very familiar.

"Inch!" they both said at the same time, upon the same breath.

" 'Tienne!" Inch said, "and Monsieur Stephen! How glad I am to see you!"

Etienne's glance slashed over him briefly. The mustache was new, black even against that coal-black face. That and the dressing gown of finest silk and the faintest suggestion of heaviness about the man.

"You'll have coffee, of course?" Inch said, pulling upon a bellcord.

"I never . . ." Etienne began, but Stephen was chuckling deep in his throat.

"Of course," he grinned. " 'Twill be a pleasure to sup with the Commissioner of Police of the city of New Orleans!"

524

Etienne paused. Father was right. Instinctively he had taken the correct line. Treat this black ape with amused toleration. He looked at Inch to calculate his reaction, but he was smiling blandly. No, Etienne decided, there was nothing of humility about his former servant. Inch seemed perfectly at ease, enjoying perhaps this reversal of fortunes.

"Come into my study, gentlemen," he said politely.

They followed him, Stephen's eyes gleaming with amusement, but Etienne walking very stiffly, with his head erect upon his shoulders. At the door the policeman lingered a moment until Inch dismissed him with a short wave of his hand.

"And now, 'Tienne," Inch began.

"You've forgotten your manners," Etienne said harshly. "I taught you better, Inch!"

"There have been changes," Inch murmured smoothly.

"None that I recognize!"

"Too bad," Inch said. "But let's not quarrel. Politics is no subject to discuss on an empty stomach. You'll have supper with your father and me, won't you?"

Etienne nodded grimly.

"Good," Inch said, and Etienne knew that the Negro was refusing to address him at all in order to avoid giving him his title. He felt the short hairs on the back of his neck rising in fury, but he controlled himself and ate the excellent supper that a servant brought in answer to Inch's ring.

"Brandy?" Inch said when they had finished, pushing forward the decanter.

Etienne poured a glass for Stephen and one for himself. He sipped it slowly, savoring the flavor with his tongue. Suddenly he put down the glass with a crash.

"Yes," Inch said. "It's from Harrow. I have many treasures from our former home."

"Our!" Etienne choked. "Our! Damn it, Inch!"

"I am sorry," Inch said softly. "I didn't mean to offend you. These things are not mine now . . . nor yours. I hold them in trust for the future."

The long black fingers went into a drawer and came out with a deck of cards.

"*Vingt-et-un?*" he suggested.

"And the stakes?" Stephen asked.

"None . . . except your good will. Your liberty I've given you already."

"That you will never have," Etienne growled. "I'm out to smash you, Inch . . . I'm warning you. This . . . this impossible situation . . . black men ruling white . . . has to go! It's unnatural, Inch. Nature herself is against it. I'll see it stopped if it costs me my immortal soul!"

"He is very like you were in your younger days, sir," Inch smiled to Stephen; "all Irish. Cut for the deal?"

"No, you deal," Stephen said.

The game went on silently, with furious concentration. The sun came in the windows with the morning haze. Etienne stood up.

"We'll be going now, Inch," he said.

"So early? Wait a bit . . . I want you to meet my son. He'll be up within the hour."

Etienne sank back in his chair. He looked across at his father. Stephen was smiling to himself, his pale eyes illuminated as by an inner light.

"Ye've done well, Inch," he said gravely. "But I'm afraid it won't last."

"It must last," Inch said. "It must."

He stopped suddenly—for there were the sound of footsteps upon the stair.

"One word of caution, gentlemen," he whispered. "The lad was with Colonel Shaw at Fort Wagner. Sometimes he is . . . well . . . odd . . . the terrific artillery fire, you understand. . . ."

"Perfectly," Stephen said, "I've seen many such cases. But with rest and quiet. . . ."

The boy was hesitating outside the door.

"Come in, my son," Inch called.

The door crashed open abruptly and instead of the child they

526

had expected, a young man of perhaps twenty-five years stood in the doorway . . . a young man with white skin and red hair and freckles that dusted his high forehead. The little hairs that were on the backs of his hands were golden and his eyes were a hard, pale blue, the brows above them whitegold, almost invisible against his fair skin.

"Good morning, Father," he said simply, like a small boy. "Good morning, gentlemen."

Etienne stood there staring at the young man. It's father all over again, he thought; so he must have looked when he first came to New Orleans.

"How do you like young Cyrus?" Inch asked. "Cyrus, this is Monsieur Stephen Fox and Monsieur Etienne, his son."

"Fox?" Cyrus echoed blankly. "Fox?"

Etienne was studying the young man.

"Cyrus, hell," he declared; "that's . . . "

"Softly, 'Tienne," Stephen warned.

Inch smiled broadly.

"You're mistaken, 'Tienne, in what you think," he said. "It was perhaps the virus of Harrow in my veins that gave him that shape and color. Or perhaps some prenatal influence upon his mother . . . still he is very like a Fox, is he not? I'm extremely proud of him. Few black men have such sons."

"Fox?" young Cyrus whispered. "Fox?"

"So you were ten years old when you got him," Etienne declared. "That boy's at least twenty-five and you're my age. Inch, you're an insolent bastard. Why I don't strangle you . . . "

"It would be most unwise. White men are hanged in the South now for killing blacks. Besides, you haven't met his mother yet. . . ."

"Nor do I care to!"

"Oh, come, 'Tienne, you could indulge an old man his vanity." He walked to the doorway and called:

"My dear!"

"Coming, Cyrus!"

Stephen stiffened. The voice floated down the stairway like the lower notes of a soft, golden gong. Stephen's face was bleak.

First the boy . . . so like, so like . . . and now this! Etienne's naturally dark face darkened (The light was bluish along the edge of that blade . . . when she dropped it, it stood and quivered in the planking. "Because you are Stephen Fox all over again, in walk, and look, and small arrogant gesture," she had said. . . .)

"Fox?" Young Cyrus puzzled. "Fox?"

Then the footsteps were coming down the stairs quickly.

She was almost the same despite her forty-three years. She had grown heavier, perhaps a trifle matronly; but the tawny skin was the same and the hair with golden fires flickering in the highlights and the lips which alternately petals of rose and wine flames to sear away the senses. She looked from one to the other of them, and all the golden flakes in her sea-green eyes swam into a circle about her widening pupils.

"Good morning, gentlemen," she murmured. " 'Tis good to see you again. . . ."

"Fox!" Young Cyrus said triumphantly. "Now I've got it! Madame Ceclie Fox the great beauty that Colonel Shane of the Medical Corps was always raving about. She used to come to the hospital when I was there . . . everybody was in love with her, she was so beautiful. Do you come from Harrow, gentlemen?"

Grimly Etienne nodded.

"Then you know her? Oh, but she was beautiful! She was Doctor Shane's mistress. . . ."

"Cyrus!" Inch roared.

"Let him go on," Etienne murmured. "You wasted your time at that law school, Inch. You should have studied at the *Comedié Française*. This is beautifully staged." He turned to the young man who was standing there with a look of blank amazement on his face.

"Please tell me more about Madame Fox, lad, I'm most interested."

The dazed look left the eyes.

"I used to worship her from afar off," he said. "But she wouldn't let anybody near her except Colonel Shane and maybe

528

that artist feller--Dumaine, his name was—that used to draw battle pictures for the newspapers."

"Not Paul Dumaine?"

"Yes, yes—that's it! He and Colonel Shane quarreled over her . . . and some say there was a duel, but I don't know about that . . . Do you like butterflies, sir?"

"Butterflies?"

"Yes. I have a wonderful collection of them, if you'd like to see it."

"No!" Etienne roared. "Come, Father. We're going—now!"

Inch made a gesture, touching his forehead with his finger.

"Don't regard the boy's words too seriously, 'Tienne," he whispered. "Gunshock victims have strange fantasies at times. I don't know that he ever really saw Madame Fox. . . ."

"Inch," Etienne said very quietly. "Don't come too close to me. Killing you would be a pleasure."

Stephen Fox got to his feet slowly. When he spoke, his voice was very deep.

"I don't know whether or not this is your way of taking vengeance for your years of bondage, Inch," he said. "If it is, ye're being unwise. 'Tis a delicate course ye must steer. For when the headship passes back into the hands of the race for whom God intended it, 'twill go hard with ye if ye've made enemies. Ye can't win, ye know that."

"Yes," Inch said, a little sadly. "I know it. This came too soon. We weren't ready. White men will rule the South again . . . perhaps for always." He paused, his eyes resting blankly upon Desiree as though she were not there, then he spoke again, more than half to himself.

"The beast of prey runs alone, gentlemen. Man is a herd animal . . . like cattle."

"Ye mean?" Stephen said softly.

"That the spotted Brahmin claims no lordship over the red Jersey. They all browse peacefully in the meadow . . . together."

"Never!" Etienne said.

"Never is a long time," Inch said quietly. "You'll find a carriage outside waiting to take you to Harrow. And if there is ever anything that I can do . . ."

"Thank ye," Stephen said. "Goodday to ye . . . and Madame." Then the two of them were gone, out into the bright sunlight of the new morning.

Riding out to Harrow, Etienne was silent. The carriage swayed up the Bayou Road and the river was golden in the sunlight.

"'Tienne," Stephen began.

"Yes, Father?"

"I think the lad lied. Inch has a dangerously subtle mind."

Etienne looked at his father, his black beard bristling.

"No, Father," he said quietly. "The boy didn't lie."

"Ye have no proof."

"No. Only a feeling . . . something about the tone of Ceclie's letters after she had discovered I was alive."

Stephen turned his pale eyes upon his son's face.

"Ye'll do her no violence," he said. "Send her away if ye must, but ye are not to lay hands upon her. Promise me that, 'Tienne."

Etienne looked past his father out over the face of the river. Nothing moved over its surface, no proud packet running downstream with the current, its whistle shaking the banks.

"I shan't touch her, Father," he said.

The silence between them was thick and heavy. It had a texture to it, surcharged with tides and currents of thought.

Now I must begin again, Stephen thought, and I am old. It must be left to the young men—'Tienne and the rest. And I fear that they will look forever backward to what was. Ye can't turn the world back again, ye must go forward. If they try to shape the world again in the image of the past, they'll waste generations and mountains of blood and treasure in something that cannot succeed because of its very nature. If there is any one thing upon the face of the earth that is unconquerable 'tis human freedom. And if they try to take it away again from the blacks they will end by losing it themselves.

He looked out over the cypress grove, and the oak alley which had now come into sight. Beyond them, through the trailing streamers of Spanish moss, the house gleamed whitely—all except the blackened ruin of the North Wing.

"We must rebuild it," he said.

"No, Father," Etienne said. "We must never rebuild it. Leave it as it is so that never in any generation will any man of our blood forget. We'll build a new house—out on the old Waguespack place—but let Harrow stand as a reminder of what we suffered and what we will never—forget or forgive!"

They got down from the carriage and started up the alley of oaks. Half way to the house, Stephen stopped and mopped his forehead with his handkerchief.

"For a little while," he said, "we lived like gods. I'm not sure that it was good for us."

Etienne shrugged.

"Come, Father," he said, "the women will be waiting."

Before they reached the stair, Julie came flying down to them and behind her Aurore, her white hair gleaming in the sunlight. Ceclie came more slowly, the children clustered fearfully about her skirts.

"Oh, Papa," Julie wept. "'Tienne! I'm so glad . . . so glad!"

Stephen kissed them and, after him, Etienne embraced the two women; then he strode up the stairway to where Ceclie stood. But he did not kiss her or the children. He stood very quietly looking at her, and his eyes were bleak and fierce.

"So," she whispered, "you've been told . . . you know . . ."

"Yes," he said.

"'Tienne, 'Tienne," she whispered, "I thought you were dead . . . I didn't know . . ."

"No explanations, Ceclie!"

He turned and rejoined the others. In the salon, the talk was loose and disjointed. So many years were lost and never could the threads be rewoven or the pieces put back together again. While they talked, at a nod from Etienne, Ceclie got up and went up the stairs.

A few minutes later, Etienne stood up.

"You'll excuse me," he murmured. "There's something I must say to Ceclie." He left the salon and went into the study. From his holster he took the heavy Colt Navy six and spun the barrel. No, he decided. It wouldn't do. It was far too heavy. He opened his father's drawer and took out the little double-barrelled derringer that is still called among the Foxes the "Waguespack pistol"—erroneously, of course, since it was a standard dueling pistol that Stephen used against Hugo; but legend is no respecter of fact. Carefully he cleaned and oiled the richly ornamented weapon. Then he loaded it, breaking it across the breech, slipping the shells in both barrels. Putting it into his pocket, he went up the stairs.

Ceclie was waiting for him, her eyes very wide and dark.

Without saying anything, he took out the pistol, balancing it loosely in the palm of his hand. Ceclie's pupils dilated like the eyes of a cat in a darkened room, the pupils so wide and black that the brown of the irises was a thin golden ring around them. She inclined her head briefly toward the derringer.

"For me?" she said.

"Yes," Etienne said. The word moved over his lips drily, escaping into sound on a husk of a breath.

She looked at him, a smile of pure amusement lighting her eyes, so that they flamed suddenly, feline and joyous. Then she put one white arm upon the mantle and let her small body relax. The motion was effortless, fluid. Her eyes caught and held his as she came erect slowly, her young breasts outthrusting, conical and high.

She never would suckle the children, Etienne thought bitterly. Her body has no further use beyond this—beyond provocation and madness. Such a little thing to end it, one small muscle tightening, and that red mouth will burn no more against mine or any man's, whispering lies. A pennyweight of powder and a ball not even full thirty calibre. . . .

"Well," she said, "what are you waiting for?"

It will make a hole, he thought, a small, but dreadful hole, black-ringed against her white flesh, halfway between those strawberry rosettes, proud now, and puckering. And her life will pump through. He looked down suddenly at her hands. Slim. Cool and sweet-moving in the darkness against his hard-muscled flanks. Fierce-tender and feline. Dagger-nailed, ecstatic. Moving no more, sweet-whispering through his hair, never again the sweet, hot, fierce, desire-taloned ferocity. . . . A gasp caught in his throat and became a burn.

She took a step forward, and her hand came out and closed over the barrels of the derringer. Then gently she pulled it away from him, ever so slowly, his cold, nerveless fingers slipping down over the rich silver-mounted butt. She stood there, holding the pistol, then, suddenly, she began to laugh. She laughed all over in great windy gusts of sound, metal-hard and ringing.

"So, 'Tienne," she said, "you don't like playing the cuckold? Why? The rôle fits you so well. You were designed by nature to wear horns."

"Ceclie!"

"You coward! Your honor must be avenged—and with ceremony, too! I must die for doing exactly what I wanted to, when I wanted to, and with whom. No, 'Tienne. I'm afraid I must decline the honor of dying. You just aren't worth it. Once I had gone so far that I hated you. Now I don't. I don't even pity you."

She walked around him, still holding the pistol. In the doorway, she turned.

"I'm leaving you, 'Tienne," she said. "I'm going back to Texas." She looked at the richly ornamented weapon, then, abruptly, she broke it open, and stared at the chambers. Her eyes widened enormously, dark in her white face.

"Two bullets," she whispered, "one for me, and one for—"

"Yes," he said, "yes!"

She looked at the pistol again, then she tossed it lightly upon the bed. She started back toward Etienne, walking slowly, her brown eyes burning like great dark coals, never leaving his face. Then she was close to him, and he could feel the warmth of her, hear the rustle of her breathing.

"I'm flattered," she said, and there was no laughter in her voice. "But don't you see—it's no good? This thing between us

533

is a kind of poison. It's a sickness in the blood. All I do is torment you, and make you wretched and love you and hate you at the same time . . . Oh, 'Tienne, let me go! Keep me now and I'll leave you tomorrow or betray you. . . . There's nothing. . . ."

But Etienne's big hands came down upon her shoulders and the fingers dug in until the flesh purpled beneath them. Then he held her against him hard and found her mouth.

She tore free at last, her lips poppy-red and swollen.

"I'll leave you," she warned. "I'll betray you! And there is still nothing. . . ."

But he held her to him, breath-stopped, saying: "There is now, Ceclie. There is now!"

"Yes," she said, and her eyes were enormous, eclipsing her face, diamond-bright, tear-jeweled. "Yes, 'Tienne! That's all there is. Now." Her lips, moving, made small flames inches from his bearded mouth. "Ah, yes—now. Now! Now, 'Tienne! Now."